After...Happily Ever After

Nature of Desire — Vampire Queen — Knights of the Board Room — Daughters of Arianne

To fans of Joey W. Hill's work, these series have special significance, because they contain many of her readers' favorite characters. Because they are her favorites too, Joey doesn't like saying good-bye at "The End" any more than her readers do. So here for your reading pleasure, at last available in compilation form, are novellas and shorts revisiting these characters. Poignant romantic moments, erotic encounters, holiday celebrations...wherever daily life might take them.

These stories have become a way for Joey to take a breather and simply immerse herself in the pleasure of spending leisure time with past characters. We hope you will enjoy the same experience when reading them!

Cantrips: Volume #2

SWP Digital & Print Edition publication November 2016

Digital ISBN: 978-1-942122-53-1

Print ISBN: 978-1-942122-54-8

Cantrips: Volume #2

Minor Magics Crafted to Amuse and Entertain

A Collection of Vignettes by

Joey W. Hill

Table of Contents

Foreword

"Cantrip" has several meanings. What amused me initially, due to my "storywitch" moniker, was that the first one I read was the Scottish source, "A witch's trick." But the definition that applies the most to these volumes is "minor magics meant to amuse and entertain."

My first vignette, a short story written around 2008 revisiting Mac and Violet of *Natural Law*, was offered to readers who wanted more about these two. I didn't have an idea for another full-length book for them, but the idea of revisiting them in a short story format was a lot of fun for me, and the readers received it enthusiastically. I enjoyed the breather from deadline pressure and a full-length storyline arc to instead do a slice-of-life moment with favorite characters. So the definition of Cantrips above resonated on multiple levels.

Since we have been repeatedly asked about offering the vignettes in print and ebook compilation volumes, your wish is our command, and these volumes are our answer. Going forward, as long as there is a demand for them, we will release a new volume of vignettes when we have enough to make a book. Volumes 1 & 2 of *Cantrips* are only the first two of what we hope will be more "vignette volumes." Currently they represent all vignettes written through 2016.

Now, these vignettes come with several caveats, as follows:

1. **The individual, digital download versions of these stories have always been—and will**

continue to be—offered for free. Right now they reside at the JWH Connection, a wonderful fan forum run by a handful of very enthusiastic ladies who independently promote and support my work. To find the forum and the vignettes, visit storywitch.com/community for more information.

2. My readers have told me all of the stories can be enjoyed even if you haven't read the books, but you may get plot spoilers or miss some emotional nuances between the characters that were developed in their specific book(s). However, when needed, each vignette is prefaced by a short explanation to help you figure out what the vignette is about, and to identify the series/books from which it originated. This will help you seek out these titles if you decide you'd like to read some of them first.

3. Many of the vignettes were written as serials (a different segment every couple of weeks), and then compiled into one download at the fan forum upon completion. As such, you may notice a little redundancy in these segments as certain concepts are "recapped." We could have edited that out, but we wanted to keep them essentially as they were written.

They say the best gifts are handmade. As the number of my loyal readers have grown—an amazing and humbling thing—writing these vignettes has turned out to be the best way to say a heartfelt thank you for the insights and wisdom, laughter and smiles, you all have offered to me. You enrich my life greatly, and I thank you for that.

I appreciate all you have done, do, or will do, to support my work! And I hope you enjoy your Cantrips.

The Proper Punishment

A vignette featuring Peter, Dana and Ben from the Knights of the Board Room Series.

Originally posted in serial format, 6/29/2012

Peter and Ben originally appear in the first book of the series, Board Resolution, *and reappear throughout the series. Peter and Dana's full story is told in Book III of the series,* Honor Bound. *Ben's full story is told in Book V of the series,* Hostile Takeover.

Background: *In* Afterlife, *Book IV of the* Knights of the Board Room Series, *Dana mentioned a night that Peter and Ben shared her. This is the vignette about that night.*

§

"Are you scared, Sergeant?"

Dana knew the proper way to respond to that, especially when he spoke to her as a subordinate. "Sir, no *sir*."

It didn't matter that her hands were cold and there was a little quivery thing happening in her stomach. She'd felt the same way on the first day of basic training. Apprehensive, anticipating, telling herself and the drill sergeant she was ready to kick ass, but still freaked out by the unknown. Of course, things had been a little different then. For one thing, she'd had her sight. But Peter knew she wanted this. He knew her.

"You're lying. I want you scared. So you tell me the truth."

3

"Terrified, Captain."

"Not all terrified." He cupped her bare ass, fingers slipping between the cheeks and lower to find the slippery heat. "Bad, bad girl. That's what got you here. Pushing the boundaries, disobeying a direct order. Down on your hands and knees."

If he'd ordered her just to her knees, she could anticipate having her mouth stretched by his cock, a punishment she never stopped craving, but all fours said he was going for another approach. She was naked, still damp and flushed from her bath. She didn't blush easily, but she'd been cleaned inside and out, Peter as thorough in his methods as a prison cavity search. He was getting her ready, getting her mind in the right state for tonight. Though she didn't know the exact game plan, she could already sense it was going to be further than they'd ever gone together.

The thought brought more terror, more anticipation. But she was his. His fiancée, his toy. His slave. She trusted in that, in him, like she trusted nothing and no one else.

She went down on hands and knees, following the solid length of his leg. He'd put his foot where he wanted her, her waist pressed below his knee. It was the body language they'd worked out that told her what ground was safe. When they took walks along the gravel road winding through the bayou that surrounded his Baton Rouge home, she didn't have to take her cane. She could feel the uneven ground on the edge of the road, the gravel under her other foot, his heat close enough to steady her path, keep her straight.

When she'd been recuperating from her injuries, the hospital staff had tried to make her walk outside. She'd been paralyzed by fear, sightless, most of her hearing gone, no anchor to her world. She'd refused, just flat sat down on the ground until they brought a wheelchair and took her back inside. Thinking back on that time, she was ashamed of herself, her weakness. But then Peter brought her here, and he'd made her go out for a walk on his property. Though the panic had closed in, his stable presence, his lightest touch on her shoulder, telling her he was there, helped her beat it down. Her captain held her world stable. He was Atlas. Emotionally and physically, the big bruiser. The thought gave her a soft smile, even with the nervous coil in her belly. As she reached the floor, she realized his foot was on a metal bar, lying flat on the floor. She felt the length and diameter of it as he adjusted her, so her knees were planted on either side of the bar. They were in the workout room, but this wasn't a piece of equipment that was usually there. He'd brought in something new, likely hidden it from her until now. Her palms got a little clammier, heart thumping faster.

"There's a chin rest six inches in front of you. Put that defiant chin of yours there."

She shuddered when he slapped her ass with an impatient hand. He knew she embraced his hardcore Dominant side, but there was a different air tonight. Something was up. This new piece of equipment, the thorough bath. Before she'd even gotten out of bed this morning, he'd put her service collar on her, a wide strap with a decorative waterfall of chains and a D-ring for tethering. While his St. Christopher medal hung from that D-ring, that was the only sentimental piece. The design couldn't be interpreted as anything other than what it was—a slave's collar.

He'd had her sit up on her heels on the bed, her fingers laced behind her head, arms already trembling as he locked the collar in place. When she wore it, she was expected to be in full submissive mode. Following his orders, speaking only when spoken to or if she was given permission to speak. Then he'd pushed her face to the mattress, angling her hind end in the air, and strapped a butt plug into her rear entry. He'd been inserting progressively larger sizes for the past couple weeks, no explanation. Her ass wasn't his favorite orifice for fucking, but he'd done it several times lately, with a fierce enthusiasm that suggested he was not only preparing that area...but reminding her that every penetration point belonged to him.

It made a girl think...wonder...

He'd fed her breakfast from his hand, ordering her to sit quietly by his foot as he watched football. When he wanted beer, snacks, lunch, he sent her to the kitchen to get them for him. At half time, he'd put a nipple chain on her, one that connected to the collar, and then held her in his lap to toy with the chain, run his cold beer over her nipples. Occasionally he pressed the glass bottle against her hot cunt, making her writhe and gasp, beg for a release he didn't grant her. Instead, he put her on her knees and had her suck him off, pushing her down hard on him until he came, jetting into the back of her throat.

Then he'd wiped her mouth with a bar napkin, given her buttock another firm slap, and put her at his knee again. After the game, he'd snapped a leash on her and led her into their home office. Placing her in a chair across from him, her legs spread wide and ankles strapped to the frame so he could see her pussy, he worked on some plant reports for the Costa Rica operations. After awhile, saying he was concerned she might be getting bored—totally unconcerned that she was so aroused and sexually frustrated she might internally combust—he rolled a lap desk up to her and made her work on her required lesson plan report for the youth group. He'd tucked her ear phones on her head so she could hear what she was typing on the Braille keyboard, ensure she hadn't committed any typos.

The man was evil. She was going to need a lot of prayer to banish this from her mind before standing before her group of rambunctious teens.

Okay, he could be ruthless and twisted, but even for him, this was a lot. Something was going to happen tonight. She thought of the things they'd talked about in the past. Over time, he'd really plumbed her mind, made her tell him the deepest, most shameful fantasies she'd ever had, even the one she'd been most hesitant about, not sure how he'd take it. The Knights shared their women in limited, foreplay kind of ways, but not the actual biblical definition of *sharing*. Not two of them fucking one of their women at the same time. She not only had that fantasy, but she had a definite face for the third member of the party. When she'd finally had the courage to admit it, Peter had merely grunted in a thoughtful kind of way, then asked her more questions. A lot more, so in-depth they caused her to squirm, and that took some doing.

She'd been a sub since she was a teenager, but some things were hard to admit to oneself. The extreme level she craved in her fantasies, her fear that the reality, at best, wouldn't be anywhere near as good. And even worse, that it could destroy the good she already had.

But Peter had taught her to trust him on certain things. Her captain didn't merely live up to fantasies—he blew them out of the water. Which was why the prospect of what might happen tonight both thrilled her into near climax and scared her shitless, all at the same time. Of course, not to be crude, but with the thorough bath and careful diet he'd kept her on today, he'd taken care of the latter. An herbal enema, probably provided by Rachel and Jon, had also flushed her out good, because apparently that part of her was going to be drilled in a way it had never been before.

Would Peter be doing those honors...or had he done what she didn't dare to imagine?

"Focus, Sergeant." She drew in a sharp breath as a switch landed across her hindquarters, enough to elicit a yelp. If he'd pulled out the switch, he was amping things up. He'd caught that little smile, and he was sending a message. It was time to get down to business—and remind her again of why this was all going down.

"Don't you forget for a minute this is a punishment. You disobeyed orders, and your gorgeous tits won't get you out of discipline for that."

She scowled, even though she kept her expression toward the floor. Yes, she'd disobeyed a direct order, but every once in awhile she had to do that, or the man got way too overbearing. She wasn't porcelain. But in his mind, she'd really crossed the line this time, which meant he was going to make the punishment fit the crime. She craved punishment, in that love/hate way a sub like her did, but that didn't mean she wouldn't push out a stubborn bottom lip about it.

The church where she worked was in a rough neighborhood, but she'd grown up in a rough neighborhood. She knew the boys of her teen youth group were being actively courted by the local gangs. So Monday, instead of waiting for Max, the K&A limo driver, to pick her up in the church alcove where she usually met him, she'd left a message with the church secretary that she'd headed down to the corner market and that he should meet her there.

She intended to pick up some fresh tomatoes from the Korean grocer, as well as do some reconnaissance with him about the things he saw on his street. She hadn't anticipated making contact with the gang members who hung out there. She might have left it alone, been on her way, but she recognized the voices and knew two of her boys were with them. It didn't take long to figure out she was overhearing a recruitment meeting. And yes, she'd damn well interrupted it. Threatened to shove her cane up the ass of someone that, according to Max, looked like he did body disposal, but big had never scared her. The idea of her boys, young men whose hardworking single mothers had no time to keep them out of the clutches of those parasites, falling into that life just like her brothers had... hell no. Not while she was breathing.

According to Peter's interpretation of Max's report, the thugs were eyeing her like candy thrown in the street when he arrived with the car. Huge exaggeration, she was sure. For fifteen minutes of the day, he hadn't known exactly where she was and what she was doing, and it had freaked him out. That's all. She'd told him as much, tartly mentioning there was a fine line between obsessive stalker and protective lover. She wasn't helpless. There had been yelling, and she'd gotten into it with him, toe to toe, though that had necessitated keeping her chin *way* up. She couldn't see him, but that didn't mean she didn't know how to meet the blast of heat coming from those storm gray eyes.

When they fought about things like that, they were Peter and Dana, soon-to-be husband and wife, and they got it ironed out in an equable fashion. But later, when the intimate undercurrent of their relationship, Master and sub, raised its head, there was a different kind of accounting involved. Him emphasizing that he was bound and determined to protect and care for her, and her understanding that was something he needed, as much as she needed the reassurance of it.

It was their little ritual, though maybe this one had earned her a punishment more daunting than usual. Or more thrilling.

She knew the type of equipment that had a stabilizer bar on the floor, a chin rest. A fucking machine, though sometimes that part could be removed so it was simply a restraint system. She couldn't tell if or how it had been modified, but she was sure she'd soon find out. He was tethering her service collar to the bar underneath the chin rest now, keeping her there. He took the chin rest up another couple inches, forcing her to lift her upper body, thrust out her naked chest.

It was impossible not to quiver about it. When he took her into uncharted waters, which he continuously, miraculously did, she would shake like a newbie sub, and it would only get worse—or better, depending on the perspective—as he continued. Now what felt like netting was being pressed against her breasts. He wrapped them twice, binding them tightly together, then crossed the tail ends between, rolling the excess netting to form a shoulder harness that attached to the wrap in back and held her upper body in an even more rigid upward angle.

He rubbed her nipples, the rough friction of the netting making her draw in a breath. Then he went to those torturous light brushes that sent spasms through her pussy. Back to harder rubbing, which caused her to pull involuntarily against the chin rest, only to discover the tether was so short it kept her in place.

"Be still for your Master." He ran his hands over her compressed bosom. "That's awfully pretty, girl, seeing your tits like that. Now...just to keep you focused."

Focus? He was insane, right? Oh hell, the clover nipple clamps. He clipped them on her around the netting's hold. They hurt, and of course his pull on the connecting chain only tightened them. When he tugged upward, apparently looping the chain over the frame holding the chin rest, she had to bite back a pitiful whimper. "To make sure you keep that upper body lifted."

But though he was willing to torment her like this, there were other things he found unacceptable. Leaving her to breathe through the pain of those clamps, he attached a vertical bar beneath her that had a padded platform and foam wedge insert. The wedge followed her body from just beneath her breasts to the crease between hip and thigh, giving her support. Even with her upper body lifted, the wedge was doing the work. Peter had taken into account the limitations of her joints and spine, though it also suggested how long he intended for her to be in this position.

He could be a ruthless Master when he was a bit pissed with her, which she knew he was, but no matter how vulnerable and exposed he made her feel, he never forgot to take care of her.

"Coming off now." A short cry tore from her lips as the clovers were removed, that brief but intense pinch. He massaged her with his fingers. "There we are. Stiff and big, like cherries. That's the way they'll stay or you'll get these clamps again."

She missed his touch immediately when he withdrew, but then he was stroking her thighs, cuffing them to the pole holding the padded platform. "I'm going to get you warmed up now, but if you come, you're going to be in big trouble. Worse trouble than you're already in, and you're in deep shit."

She bit her lip as the dildo slid into her pussy, confirming she was strapped to a fucking machine. As he explored with his fingers, making sure it was going in at the right angle, she tried to lift her hips further to press into that welcome contact. Then she made an incoherent noise as he shifted, probed her ass. The machine had dual attachments. The lubricated plug that he guided into her opening wasn't as thick as the plug she'd been wearing up until dinner time. However, as it went in, what seemed narrow became far thicker at the base, stretching her rim.

Nothing was predictable about the toys Peter might use. With Jon, the engineering genius of the K&A men, helping with design, the only thing certain was it wouldn't be the usual assembly line sex toy equipment.

The one in her pussy was thick and long, with a clit stimulator that would hit her each time the dildo thrust home. She knew the shape and feel of that phallus, because it was an exact model of Peter's cock. Given that she was a little more hardcore and...well, graphic in her desires, than Cass or Savannah, Lucas and Matt's wives, Jon had given her the phallus as a Christmas gift. She'd tried to extract the story of how he'd obtained the mold from her husband, but Peter had nixed that.

If you ever tell her, he'd advised Jon, *I'll use every bit of training I have to kill you and make your body disappear. I'll miss you, but it will have to be done.*

The motor engaged. Held rigid, she moaned as the two pieces began to do their job, sliding in, pulling out. A little breathy squeal emitted from her throat as she realized why the anal plug was different. The narrow end was like a tongue. A flexible tongue that lapped along her channel inside and licked around her rim, several rotations, as it came out. When it plunged back in, all the way to that thick base that stretched her anus to the point of burning, it paused a few seconds, then the tongue piece started up again, working its way back out once more. Both pieces were well lubed, and the heated tingling said one of Jon's mysterious oils was at work on them.

Peter was in front of her again, cupping her breasts. "I should jack myself off over these lovely tits," he growled. "Let you smell me dripping off your nipples. Mark you as mine before he gets here. Let him see you looking all used and bound up, ready for our pleasure, the way a good slave should be."

He. Her fantasy was about to become a reality, she knew it. It set off an explosion of reaction that took her so perilously close to climax she had to lock every muscle against it, breath rasping desperately through her nose. Peter's visual of jacking off over her breasts, something that never failed to excite her, wasn't helping.

"Yeah, I thought that would turn you on. Your pussy's dripping at the idea of serving your Master and his friend. But you're going to have to do your penance first. Prove to me you can be good enough to deserve that."

"I can be bad enough to deserve that," she gasped, showing teeth. She cried out as he compressed her nipple in two fingers, held it in a patient, steady strong grip like the pincers of a crab. Even as the pain built, shooting out from the contact, her pussy spasmed further at the rough treatment, at his unspoken demand.

"I'll be good...I...promise. Please."

He let her go, gently massaging the nipple, working that netting over it.

"We'll see. Right now, you're going to hold one image in that stubborn rock head of yours. Me ripping a hole in that netting, working my lubed dick in between your breasts until I come. You keep that picture in the forefront of your mind, like I'm doing it, but you hold back that orgasm. You let go before I give you permission, your ass is going to be on fire, and those clover clamps you hate are going back on until you're screaming for mercy. Understand?"

"Yes, Master."

"So docile now. Such a pain in my ass the rest of the time."

"You like me that way." Dana yelped as he pinched the other nipple, a quick twist that had a curse whistling out between her lips. "Fuck. I didn't mean it, Master."

"Yeah, you did. Insubordination is your thing, Sergeant. You're a discipline junkie. What are you supposed to be thinking of?"

"Your cock...jacking off between my...tits."

"That's it. Feel those plugs fucking you, think about if you can be good enough to deserve the real thing. No coming."

"Yes, Master. Please..." *Oh fuck.* He adjusted the machine, and it moved at a faster pace, hitting her clit more regularly. *Oh God.* He intended her to fail. He wanted to inflict maximum punishment tonight, and if "he" was who she thought it was, he'd brought the right man to help him.

"He's pulling in now. I'm going out on the deck to join him for a drink. While we're out there, we're going to watch you through the glass doors. I want to give him time to enjoy the view and think about how he's going to fuck that sweet ass of yours."

He gave her one more stinging slap on the buttock. As the sliding door opened, then closed, it left her alone with her rasping breath and the whir of that machine turned up to a higher setting. Desperation closed in fast, because there was no way she couldn't come.

Which meant she'd be entirely at his mercy, his and Ben O'Callahan's, if she'd guessed right. She hoped—and feared—she had.

§

It was a good thing he and Ben had done sessions together before, because otherwise Peter might have experienced some good-natured self-consciousness as he closed the glass door behind him. Out of consideration for Ben, he'd untucked his T-shirt, but he was sure Ben could tell from his gait that he had a hard-on as substantial as a brick. The guy didn't miss much.

The door had double glass and an air seal, which meant Dana couldn't hear them through it. Her cochlear implants had improved her hearing considerably, but that was outside their range. He'd put the radio on his belt, however, so he could hear her. The gasps, every sexy little moan as that machine pumped into her pussy the way he was on fire to do himself. Listening to those sounds was going to give his dick a permanent zipper tattoo, but having the radio was a safety precaution, to make sure her breathing was doing okay, that she wasn't in any distress that wouldn't be immediately obvious from the incredible view.

As he gave her an appraising glance, watching her beautiful body twitching, fighting the climax, her lean muscles taut and brown skin still a little dewy from the bath, he thought of the windows in Amsterdam where women titillated through glass, encouraging a man to come inside and pay for their services. Unlike there, where he couldn't be sure their services were willing or clean, he could work up a pretty good fantasy about it with Dana. She loved to role play. A glass box would be a nice weekend construction project. Jon would have a great design twist for it, he was sure.

Positioning himself on the deck so he could keep one eye on her, he watched Ben get out of the Roadster in the front drive. They'd planned this for a while, but events earlier in the week had told him it was time. It fit with an extreme punishment, but he also knew his girl would love it. He loved to see her surrender to pleasure, as much as she seemed to love giving him minor heart attacks.

The grim smile that twisted his lips helped ease the abrupt, exceptionally strong wave of possessiveness he felt, seeing Ben here, her fantasy about to become reality. The possessiveness was on the safe side of mild homicidal tendencies, but still...

Ben was looking as polished as always. He'd obviously come from the office. Though he often had paperwork to do on the weekends, today he must have had a meeting, because he was dressed to the nines in one of his custom-tailored Italian suits.

On the other hand, Ben could have incorporated it as part of tonight's plan, because a submissive reacted differently to a man in a suit, particularly when she was completely naked and vulnerable. Dana was blind, but she could tell by smell or touch what Ben was wearing. A power suit, underscoring business dominance, was equally capable of emphasizing the titillating difference between Master—completely in command, and sub—completely at his mercy.

His hair was rakishly feathered over his forehead, and his afternoon shadow gave him a dangerous look Peter knew wasn't contrived. He had a bottle of whiskey dangling loosely from his fingers, seal unbroken. A sub-warming gift, perhaps? It would be just like Ben to do such a thing. In the other hand he carried a case of Peter's favorite beer.

"I was going to offer you one of those," Peter said. "I also have some of your preferred Scotch."

Ben shrugged. "Seems to me I'm the one getting the favor, so I wanted to bring a gift."

As he reached the deck, he stopped a couple steps short of the top, propping his foot in that casually virile pose that inspired Captain Morgan commercials. Except on Ben it looked natural, not pretentious. Peter made himself shift to the right so Ben could see through the glass doors. Interestingly, Ben held his gaze another key moment. Though Ben was wearing dark sunglasses, it was clear to Peter that Ben was taking stock of his frame of mind. Fucking intuitive lawyer.

When his gaze did shift, it went to the radio on Peter's belt, registering the soft moans and little gasps stimulating Peter's cock like electrode stimulation.

Only then did Ben's attention move to the glass doors. Pulling off the sunglasses, he hooked them in the open collar of his shirt. He'd apparently removed the tie in the car. His green eyes coursed over Dana, clearly visible at this angle. On all fours, body bound to the fucking machine, neck collared and tethered to the chin support, her body undulating with the stimulation, as much as her restraints allowed her.

Ben's gaze flickered back to Peter. "Can she hear us?"

"No. Not yet." Peter gestured to the radio. "I can make this two-way when we're ready for it. She can't hear through the glass."

Ben nodded. "Damn, Peter. That's the finest thing I've seen in a while. You are a fucking lucky bastard."

"Yeah." As Ben continued to study the tableau, Peter took a seat on the bench that ran the inside perimeter of this outside deck. He'd relieved Ben of the beer and wine, put both in the outdoor mini-fridge and cracked a cold one for himself. Though this was a hell of a lot different, he'd shared subs with Ben before, and knew his cues, same as Ben knew his. As such, he locked himself into the familiar mode of giving the other man time to study, evaluate.

"You put the clovers on her, worked up her nipples like that?"

"Yeah. She won't need them again. I've got her trained so they pretty much get swollen up like that if I barely touch them. The clovers just added a bit of pain to the equation. They can calm her down if she gets too close to the edge, too fast. Or be used as a punishment."

"Then we'll need them again soon. She's going to go

over. You told her she couldn't?"

"Absolutely. I expect she's fighting it with everything she's got at this point. If she doesn't lose control before we go in there, I want you to push her over, do the honors."

Ben flashed a smile, a baring of fangs. "To make it that much worse of an offense."

Peter nodded, took a swallow of the beer. "She's guessed what's going to happen tonight, but I've refused to tell her outright. I told her I called in reinforcements, since my discipline hasn't drilled the lesson into her head about her personal safety."

"Yeah. You far enough away from it not to lead with temper?"

"I never use my temper on a sub. And never on my fiancée. Not on my life. You know that."

"I know. You took it out on us. Matt almost put you in timeout. She scared the crap out of you, buddy." Leaving the stairs, Ben took a relaxed seat next to him, stretching out his legs and putting an arm on the rail. "Thank God you're mild-mannered Dr. Banner 99% of the time. Else we'd have to have Jon build a cage for your Hulk side. You wanted to single-handedly start a gang war."

"Max tried to downplay it." Peter shook his head, a muscle flexing in his jaw as he remembered. "But when he got there, five of those street shit losers were standing in front of her, flashing their 9mms like bling. If it hadn't been for the grocer and the teenagers..." That smile twisted his lips again despite himself. "The whole neighborhood is scared of them, but when they started getting hostile toward Dana, the grocer came out with his broom and that knot of scrawny teenagers had formed a wall. Max said they looked like they were going to pile on top of her to take a bullet if needed. No one was going to hurt Reverend Dana. She doesn't even have the certification yet and they already call her that. Fuck, she never knows her limitations."

"Because she doesn't have any." Ben arched a brow. "When people stood up for her that never even stand up for themselves, those gang members knew they had to step back. That's why it never went beyond threats and posturing. On the street, you know when something's the real thing. There's something about her. When she talks a certain way..." He shrugged. "She even makes *me* believe God gives a shit. Sometimes."

"Glad to hear you believe in Him."

"Oh, I've never doubted God's existence." Ben glanced back toward the glass doors. "All I have to do is see a sweet ass like that. She was definitely one of His better days, as the song goes."

"Cretin." Peter took a swallow of the beer. Dana was moaning again, pleas that became more prominent to the men's sharp ears. "Please...Master..."

"Damn, Peter. She's struggling like hell in there." Borrowing the beer, Ben took a swallow, handed it back. "You ready to do this? Cause I'm a go when you are."

Though he said it in a steady, casual tone, not like a quarterback gung-ho to charge the field, Peter knew Ben was as much a Master as he was. He'd probably started getting hard the moment he'd seen her. Since Ben didn't have the benefit of a shirt tail to pull out, Peter kept his gaze on Ben's face. He didn't really look at other guys' equipment, but seeing it tonight would have a particular significance. One that had him momentarily stalled.

"Yeah. Fine. But first...I know we've talked game plan, but there are a few things I want to hit again before we get started. She's hardcore, can take a pretty high level of pain, probably a seven or eight for a certain length of time, but she's not a pain junkie, Ben. Her thing is extreme domination. She craves to be broken psychologically and overwhelmed with pleasure. She can't...there are certain things her body can't handle. The one side is weaker. Watch her left arm. It will start to shake..."

"Peter." Ben turned fully away from Dana, showing Peter had his full attention. "You're her Master. You're going to be there every inch of the way, and I always watch your tells. Tonight especially, I'll be following them. On everything. Dana belongs to you, and I won't do a single thing to her you don't want. Are you sure *you* want this?"

"She wants it. She's always fantasized about it."

"Not what I asked." Ben held his gaze. "No way I move

another step in that room if I think you aren't fully invested. You're too important, bro. I know she feels exactly the same way. As much time as you spend protecting her, you sometimes miss that goes both ways. A fantasy can't even hold a candle to the way she watches over you, wants you to be happy."

"I know." Something loosened in Peter's chest. "Yeah, I want this and I don't want it, if you get that. I know she'll love this, that she'll get off on it so hard, and I want to see that happen. I know it won't change a thing between us, unless it's for the better..."

"Yeah, she'll be grateful to you forever for giving her a taste of a real cock."

"Asshole." But the smile felt real this time, not so forced. "I love her, Ben," he said quietly. "I want this for her. I trust you to give her the fantasy in spades. I'm also worried something will go wrong and it won't be everything she wants it to be. I don't want to disappoint her. I want to protect her."

"She'll be as safe with me as she is with you. You know that. Her wellbeing comes before everything else."

Peter inclined his head and sighed, giving Ben a wry smile. "And then there's the caveman part."

"Oh, that." Ben snorted. "The part of you that wants to throw me out on my ass and then pee a ten-acre-wide circle around the house to scare off any male dumb enough to think he can cross that line." He nodded toward the fridge. "That's why I brought the beer. You'll have enough piss to do that when this is all over."

"Asshole," Peter repeated, but his gaze went back to his slave. He studied her with Ben, both men registering every gasp, how her entreaties were becoming more insistent. Her body was a restrained sinuous line, rolling and rippling with the motion of the dildos, a light sheen of sweat on her. She was biting her lip in concentration, her eyes squeezed shut, not to block visuals she couldn't see, but to add to her resistance as she tried her best to obey her Master. She would deliberately cross him on certain things, just to prove how strong she was, and yet, on things like this, she surrendered to him 100 percent. Peter loved her so much everything ached. His cock was the least of it, and it was throbbing.

"So we going to do this?" Ben asked at last.

"You bet your ass."

"No, you bet hers. It's prettier. I'd much rather fuck it than yours."

"Thank God. It's hell, trying to remember not to bend over around you."

"You're begging for it, you know you are." Ben flashed that smile again. "Want to turn on that two-way function, see if we can work your girl up some more? She was Army, after all. I think she can be stretched further."

"You got it."

§

Every minute seemed like ten minutes. In, out. Swirl, lick, lap, tease from the plug. Then the clit stimulator hit when the vaginal dildo went into deep plunge mode. Slow, slow, rotating withdrawal. The lubrication was steady, constant, so they both apparently released a certain amount at intervals. For her pussy, it wasn't as important, since arousal was trickling down her legs like a running brook. She'd followed orders, was still imagining Peter's come dripping down her breasts, over that netting. She imagined it in detail, his hand fisting his cock, the seed spurting from it, hitting her heated flesh, because he'd ask for those particulars. He'd know if she made it up off the top of her head, last minute. He was way too smart like that.

The sweat rolling over her nipples and curves was too much like she imagined his come would be. She wanted his scent, though. She loved the smell of it on her skin, on her lips, her tongue.

"Oh, God...please..."

"I love hearing a slave beg. Bet her cunt is sopping wet by now. Like sticking your cock in a vat of warm pie filling. Nothing sweeter."

Ben's voice. She knew Peter would have the radio to listen to her outside, to make sure she was okay. As a result, it only took a second to realize he'd turned on the two-way so she could hear their conversation. Which meant they were sitting out there, probably drinking and listening to her moan, gasp, pant. Bastards. Bastards she wanted with her, touching her, fucking her...making her beg for everything.

"Nice. I'm partial to blackberry."

"Course you are. We know how you are about black girls. Well, this black girl. Blackberry's a tart fruit, got a little bite to it. Just like her. Warm it up in the microwave, stuff her cunt full of it and then have Lucas eat her out. That's a dessert he'd never pass up."

Was Lucas there as well? No, Peter had implied only one other man. They were just giving her more provocative images to drive her crazy, and of course it was working hellishly well. She bit down on her tongue and tried to stop her contracting pussy from losing it. Hard to do when that plug kept shoving in, licking at her, and the other dildo kept hitting her clit, over and over...

"Fuck..."

A clicking tongue. "Language, girl," Peter admonished. "We have guests."

"Verb. Not...expletive," she gasped.

"Got to give her kudos for a three-syllable word at this point," Ben observed. "But if that was a verb...there was no 'please' with it, baby girl." His voice got deeper, sending chills to the base of her spine at the sudden sensual menace. "You were issuing a command to two Masters. A slave who does that deserves what she's going to get."

She swallowed a cry as the threat made her arousal impossibly higher. "Please...Master...going to..."

"You having trouble following a direct order, Sergeant?" Peter barked through the radio. The commanding admonishment made her stiffen, hold herself even more rigid. Her muscles were starting to cramp.

"Help...no, sir. Fuck...help..."

The solid thump of the sliding glass door vibrated through her knees. She nearly came right then, just from inhaling the wash of male heat. She knew the scent of every K&A man, as well as their unique way of touching a woman, though none of them except Peter had fucked her. At least until tonight. Ben had an intriguing blend of smells. A light aftershave, the clean scent his dry cleaner used, which told her he was wearing one of his suits with the perfect cut over his shoulders and his ass. She'd gotten that descriptive tidbit from Cassandra. He used a body wash that had a touch of aloe as well as a linen-like fragrance, suggesting he had skin that was sensitive to more abrasive soaps. An ironic factoid about a man who Peter had told her was truly the most dangerous of the group, for a variety of reasons.

Oh God...she couldn't...

The machine stopped, the plugs withdrawing, but she was spasming, vibrating, on that near cusp of climax that was pretty much a climax all of its own, if they were measuring intensity. But then she yelped, that intensity stopped short as something ice cold pressed against her exposed pussy, her vibrating clit.

"Nice to know this swill Peter drinks is useful for something. Easy there. Easy." Ben touched her face, fingers whispering over her cheekbone, along her throat. He had to be squatting right next to her, because coated the left side of her body. The touch familiarized her anew with him. They always did that, like wolves reintroducing their scent, a reminder of their bond as a pack, and that she belonged to them as much as to Peter, an idea that never failed to stimulate. "Going to be a long, hard night, baby girl. Want to be sure you aren't worried about who's making it long and hard..."

She managed to pull it together, nip at his fingers. "You're the only one who gets away with calling me baby girl."

"Because you know I can rock you on my cock all night and make you coo for more..."

"Or because I'm fully restrained."

He chuckled. She wanted to smile, but even though she had zero percent vision and less than a hundred percent hearing, she was always able to detect something in Ben's tone in moments like these. He could use the sensual teasing, the purring tone, so easily, but there was a knife edge beneath it. He not only knew how to intertwine cruelty and kindness, he was an expert at compelling a woman to crave it. As a lifetime sub, she'd figured that out the first time he'd taken her hand, even before Peter had given her that harrowing insight.

Ben could tease, be a charmer, but he reminded her of what Gran used to say about Gran-da, the kind of parent he was.

He loved his babies more than life itself, but he never left no doubt he would take one out of this world if they sassed him.

So though he was teasing her now, things were too full inside her, realizing the significance of him being here, of what Peter was giving her, of where they were going to take her tonight. Way past the point she thought she could go. "Ben..."

"That's 'sir' for now." His tone sharpened, bringing her attention back to pinpoint focus. Her body almost tried to snap into an attention stance. "Going to get harsh with you tonight, girl. You've been scaring my boy here, and I don't tolerate that. Got to knock you back in line, and I won't make it easy. You going to fight me, make it worth my while?"

She swallowed. "Yes, sir."

He rose then, still trailing his fingers along her body, seducing her with that mesmerizing touch. The touch of an intimate stranger, here by Peter's decree. "You behave, or Peter's going to let me shove this beer bottle up your cute ass. I won't stop at the neck. Got to make sure you can take something at least half my size."

She'd have made some sardonic comment except she knew he wasn't kidding. She'd felt his substantial attributes against her ass in past encounters. Through his clothes only, but it was intimidating. And she didn't intimidate. Not anymore.

"You've been mouthing off a lot lately. Forgetting your place when it comes to your Master."

"I'm not breakable," she retorted. "He needs to be reminded of that sometimes."

"Oh, honey." Ben let out that warm, scary chuckle again.

"You're breakable. When we're done with you tonight, you'll know it." He rolled that bottle across her labia, sliding it up the channel between her buttocks so ice cold glass was pressed against her rim and her cunt. She couldn't help it; she was wiggling, trying to move away from it.

Then Peter's earthy scent, like marsh and live oak, things immutable and strong, was in front of her. He captured her breasts once again, thumbs and forefingers holding the nipples, bearing down in that slow, gradual build-up of excruciating pain that made things clench in her lower extremities.

"You keep still while our guest is examining you, Sergeant. Still as a statue."

She gasped at the pressure of those fingers, then the slow roll as he eased up enough and twisted, such that spirals of sensation went through the curves, sending hard shudders through her. Then those incredibly gentle palms with their rough skin were kneading the tautly held curves through the netting. The lines dug into her flesh, he had her wrapped so tight. When he took the webbing off, she'd be marked with those crisscrosses, able to run her fingers over her breasts and feel the marks.

"Tell me how your Master prepared you for me," Ben said conversationally, continuing to insinuate that bottle against her flesh. She wanted to squeal from the need to move. She was actually whimpering in her throat. Before she could answer, Ben's fingers were probing her well-lubed ass, and the whimper escaped. "I'm waiting for an answer," he ordered.

"Plugs of different...sizes." She drew in a breath as two of his fingers eased into her, through the sphincter muscles. But he was moving them, doing something that felt like a butterfly teasing those sensitive tissues, making it hard for her to think.

"More details. When did he have you wear them? How long? What did they feel like going in? Did he put them in or make you do it while he watched?"

"The first time, while he watched. He had me bend over the bed, push it in from the back while he stood over me, watching. It was...it felt not so bad. And when it was strapped in, it made it hard to think. I was surprised how...arousing it was, with no clit stimulation."

"Why? Honest and straight out, no thinking."

"There were just nerves there...I didn't expect. It also made me feel...used, subjugated. He'd made me stick something up my ass, made me walk around with it that way."

"There's the soldier. Did he fuck your pussy with the plugs inside you?"

"Yes." She swallowed. Peter hadn't said if she could answer these questions, but he was right here, so she assumed brutal honesty was required.

"Tell me how he fucked you. Where he did it." A yearning noise caught in her throat as Ben pushed with those fingers, stretched.

"He...had me kneel outside on the docks, and took me from behind, his cock in my pussy. It was...so full. When he was down over me, he told me one day he'd share me. He wanted another man, one he trusted, to know how sweet it was to fuck his beautiful slave. And he would do it so I'd know I was all his, to do with as he pleased. Share me if that was what he wanted."

The words had been the final straw, pushing her into a hard orgasm. Her cunt spasmed even now over the memory, the fantasy Peter was making come true. It was surreal and scary and... She was tough, she knew she was, but an odd emotion hit her. She wasn't sure how to deal with it.

"Master? May I ask a question?"

"*Now* you're all sweet and docile. Ben, you're already a good influence. Yes, you can ask."

"Am I...is it okay to tell him these things? I'm sorry, I should have asked first."

"Yes, you should have." Peter's voice was stern, but the hands on her breasts gentled further, stroking. "How do you think I should punish you for that?"

Oh, she hated those clovers, but she knew that was the answer. "The clamps," she whispered.

He idly toyed with one of the nipples, an easy tweak that

still rocketed straight through her core like a much harder pinch, telling her how wound up they were making her. "No, I don't think so. That last smartass remark probably deserves the switch. I'm going to let our guest decide degree and quantity."

Oh, hell. She loved and hated that switch, he knew that. "Yes, Master."

"I don't want him to feel neglected while you're taking your punishment. Ask him nicely for his cock."

She couldn't breathe. "I...sir, please. May I suck your cock for you?"

"In a moment." She let out a strangled cry as Ben pushed those fingers in deep, so deep she could feel the pressure of his knuckles digging against her rim. It burned, but his thumb dipped into her cunt, playing in that slick area. "You've stretched her out good, but not too much. It's no fun unless I get a few tears out of it, a little begging for mercy." He paused. "I'm thinking ten strikes. Start at a medium degree, but work her up to screaming by the end of it."

As his fingers withdrew, she shuddered. It had been a while since she'd shook this hard during a session. It was overwhelming. With Peter, there was always that...connection. It was still there, but with this element involved, with Ben, someone she knew, someone who was part of their intimate family, and yet not so familiar when it came to this, it took it to an entirely different level. It made her less Peter's submissive, and even more truly a slave, here to be used for the pleasure of the males in the room, regardless of her own desires.

Which Peter of course knew terrified her and yet turned her on big time, the fantasy dipping its toe in reality in a way that was too mesmerizing to refuse. While a part of her was shrieking *no, no, no, no,* an even bigger part wanted to make her Master proud. Which meant she had to say something. Peter liked her sassy side, to a point.

"I'm not a girl," she said. "I don't scream from a little bitty stick."

The breath from Peter's amused snort caressed her face. "Sounds like a challenge to me, Ben."

Ben grunted, then pinched her ass, hard. "You're going to be so hoarse, Reverend Dana, your congregation will think you have laryngitis. I might have to attend Sunday school that day, just to listen to you and think about you strapped down and naked like this."

"If you're going to grace the inside of a church," she gasped, "I'll have to make sure the lightning rod on the steeple is in good working order."

He gave her another pinch, one that made her squeak. She was pretty sure he'd just bruised the muscle with his powerful fingers. "Your concerned parishioners will be asking how you lost your voice," he continued mildly, "and you'll be lying, sinning with those fuckable lips, telling them you have some kind of bug. Because I don't think those good church ladies will appreciate hearing about having your ass whipped and fucked so hard, you came a dozen times and wore out your lungs. Keep mouthing off, you'll be having to explain why you can't sit down, either. Want to talk back to me again?"

As he waited, a significant pause, she set her lips in a stubborn line. She didn't let herself back down from a challenge. When she'd gone down to the market, it had been like that. She'd been a little afraid, going into an environment where she couldn't see, knowing there was danger there. But the biggest fear she had in life was that she'd let Peter protect her from too much, too often and, as a result, she'd slide back into being that cowering person again. The one who'd been afraid of everything, even living, after she woke up blind and deaf. She wasn't going to do that to Peter. She wasn't going to be less of a partner to him than he was to her. And that, as much as anything, was why she'd taken the risk of going down to the market. And why she did something probably just as foolish now.

"I can take anything you've got," she said, before she could lose her nerve.

"Whether you can or can't doesn't make a shitload of difference to me, baby girl. Because you will."

They never cursed in front of women, not like that. Ben sounded a little mean. She was goading the sadist to the top, on purpose. What the hell was she doing? She was starting to feel out of control, that was what. With Peter, though he held all the reins, they were familiar reins. She hadn't acted out like this, actively bratted, in a while. She wanted to fight Ben. Wanted to prove she wasn't weak. If he let her out of this thing, she could kick his ass. Didn't matter how unlikely that sounded, it was what it was. Fight or flight was kicking in, and fight was winning.

"You're misbehaving, girl," Peter said reprovingly. He'd moved during the exchange, was now behind her, and Ben's scent had shifted into his place. A second later, fire sliced across her hindquarters, the damned switch Peter wielded with expert skill. Though in all fairness, she gave him lots of opportunity for practice.

She bit down on her reaction, but she knew she wasn't going to have the additional reinforcement of locking her jaw, because there were other plans for her mouth. Ben's fingers were there now, thumbs inserting themselves in the hinges of her jaw. Though she tried to draw back, the tether brought her up short.

"Wider," Ben ordered, and she obeyed on instinct, though she protested as a ring gag was maneuvered behind her teeth. A big-ass ring gag, one that made her jaw ache to hold it, and rendered her tongue useless, at least for speaking, because she had no ability to move her mouth or lips at all. The ring gag was strapped in place just as Peter landed strikes two and three. Her breath rasped out like a steam engine. Fuck, it always felt like it was cutting through skin, even though her captain knew exactly how to do it without leaving anything more than short-term welts. That top layer of nerves was just that damn responsive.

In between punishments, he massaged healing balms into her ass that kept it soft as a baby's bottom, and as sensitive. No leather-butt for her, not with the kind of aftercare the K&A men wielded as effectively as every other weapon in their arsenal.

"Going to be drooling a bit with this," Ben observed. "I've put a towel between your palms. Don't want that mess on my expensive shoes. But I think...yeah, hand those to me, Peter. I know what a tit guy you are. You always have the right thing to keep the headlights nice and perky."

Another set of clamps, but not the clovers, thank God. These screwed on, but maintained a steady pressure. It was uncomfortable, but not screech-level painful. Plus, it was an unsettling distraction, Ben handling her there so personally, his fingers pinching and adjusting her nipples, knuckles sliding along the curves of her breasts. She was so used to Peter's touch there, because he was a true breast guy, such that it wasn't unusual to wake with his palm curved possessively over one. Or he'd suckle her awake, or come up behind her to cup and squeeze, rub his cock against her ass, kiss her neck while he indulged his need to fondle her tits about a hundred times a day.

It meant they were incredibly easy to stimulate, to arouse, so she was panting when Ben ran the connecting chain up to the ring gag, hooking it there with no slack, the two strands of chain pressing against her wet bottom lip.

"Yeah, he's got you trained to come just from breast play. That's hot, baby girl. Makes me want to get even rougher with you." Ben's voice held a low growl of approval. "Every time I push in, you're going to feel the tug on those pretty nips. You better hope I don't start pounding in there and forget myself, or you'll feel like you're being suckled by barracuda."

What came out of her mouth then was unprecedented, but it was pretty much unmistakable, even with the gag. The next switch strike fell in the high degree mark, and she cried out, she couldn't help it, not with her mouth wide open. The sound was muffled, though, because Ben rubbed his groin across her mouth. He was still wearing the slacks, hadn't opened them yet, but she felt the weight and shape of him, hard against the fabric. When he pushed against her lips, she moaned. Peter squeezed her ass with his big hand, a caress, warming the striped areas, and the noise became a plea.

Ben stayed against her stretched-open mouth as the next three strikes came. She did cry out again, tears beginning to fall despite herself, damn it. It was breaking open, that thing inside of her that Peter always found, but she hadn't expected it this fast.

Ben backed off. Her nostrils flared, smelling the heated

length of him, the scent of pre-come as he opened the slacks. Putting his hand on her head, he guided himself into her forced-open lips. Damn if he barely pushed through that big-ass ring, shoving the meat of himself into the hot wet cavern of her mouth, all the way to the back. She'd only taken part of him, and probably not the largest part.

"Work that tongue against him, girl," Peter said. "Show him it can do something other than mouth off."

She lashed at the base of Ben's cock, wishing she could suck, but her smart mouth had deprived her of that pleasure, hadn't it? Maybe if she focused on being a good girl, a *really* good girl, they might take out the ring gag. Ben worked himself past her gag reflex. From what she'd learned from Savannah and Cass, and the men themselves, none of the Knights were small in the cock department, so it was a survival skill to deep-throat without choking. She'd been good at it before, but Peter had helped her hone the skill. She'd been an eager pupil, wanting to give her captain head that would send him out of control and spewing down her throat as often as possible.

Those skills stood her well now, because she had to force the throat muscles to relax, even while her jaw was held rigid by that ring gag. She lashed at Ben with her tongue like a cat's tail, trying to curl and stroke, flail and flick, stimulate him. He had a rich cologne smell down here, telling her he put it on his balls, something that turned her on to no end, a man making sure his stuff smelled good to a woman.

"I'm wondering if she needs another ten," Peter commented. "What do you think, Ben?"

She made a small noise of complaint before she could bite it back. Ben tightened his fingers on her scalp, pushing himself in deeper. The nipple chain pulled just as he promised. She choked against him.

"Do you have any say in this, Dana?" Ben asked.

She couldn't shake her head much, but she managed. Even mouthed a desperate, garbled "No sir," against him.

When the switch strike came again, she sobbed against his cock. But Peter only gave her three more before replacing the sting with his mouth. As his lips and tongue cruised over her abused flesh, his fingers slid down her wet labia, soothing, stroking. He was dialing it back a little, giving her a little breathing room, so to speak. It was a relief, since her ass felt like it was on fire.

"Time to switch places," he said, when she was shuddering from the overload of sensation. "I want to see you fuck my slave, Ben. Teach her some manners."

"This one wouldn't have manners if you kept her this way 24/7. Course..." Ben paused, apparently considering as he continued to slowly work himself in and out of her frantic mouth, his fingers tight on her scalp. "She's an ask-for-forgiveness, not ask-for-permission slave. A prevention program would cure that. Put her in this kind of set up a couple hours each day, switch her ass every other day, no matter how good she's been. Keep her mind on her Master's will."

"It's a good thought." Peter slid his fingers in her cunt, scissoring, and she made another strangled, pleading noise. Lash, flick, tease that heated, thick cock. *Please...help. Fuck.* "Especially seeing how responsive she's being tonight. I've never seen her so wet."

"You have the cam running? The others will want to see this."

The idea had her clenching against Peter's hand. She swallowed hard, and was rewarded with more of Ben's salty, slick taste. Just imagining Matt, Jon and Lucas in the darkness of the board room, the five men watching a replay, overwhelmed her mind. Watching the close up of her body being used by two of the five Masters, all of them evaluating technique and her responses... When she was around them, she'd feel the knowledge of it in their touch, their voices, how they'd seen her naked and exposed.

Another of those pleading, moaning noises escaped her.

"Audio and video, so she can listen to it later as well. Might even convert those sexy begging and crying sounds she's making into my new ring tone, when she calls me."

She pulled herself away from that precipitous, mindless edge, enough to give him a creative, garbled response. Both men chuckled. It also earned her a swat from Peter's big hand on her tender ass.

"See?" Ben sighed. "She's a hopeless brat. All right, clear out. Much as I love her sweet mouth, you're hogging my preferred end."

Peter squeezed her ass, fingers running lightly down her thighs in contrast, and then he was gone. For just a moment, Ben was as well, and the lack of stimulation, after such an overload of it, was almost destabilizing. Then Ben's hand replaced her captain's on her ass. He rubbed briskly over the switch marks, then gripped a cheek hard, fingers bruising, almost lifting her up off the frame with that single hold point. Just when she thought she couldn't take the compression a moment longer, he released her and smacked. Hard, with a sweeping motion that came up from below, rocketing through her muscles. It hurt, but with her legs spread, the vibration that resounded through her pussy balanced it. When he did it to the other buttock, she made an animal noise, rocking forward in the frame from the strength of impact. He gripped both cheeks in powerful hands, squeezing roughly even as he brushed his thumbs over her labia, a light patter of movement that had her writhing again.

Peter had moved in front of her; she could tell by scent and shadow. However, he stayed out of reach, such that her entire focus had to be on what Ben was doing to her. She kept on with those guttural moans as the lawyer subjected her to more stinging blows, bruising grips. It was as if she was being tenderized for his fucking. The second the remarkable thought hit her mind, she knew she was right.

"I know you can do this to her tits, but you can do it to her ass as well. Make her come just by stroking it, spanking, licking, rubbing it." Ben spoke matter-of-factly over her head to Peter. "Women love it. Once you teach them to surrender to it, the ass is as sensitive as the cunt. Put her over your knee when you're doing it, you add the psychology to it. She'll be biting down on your pants' leg, screaming as she comes."

Her heart ramped up as Peter touched her face at last. He traced the big ring gag on the inside, his finger stroking her tongue briefly, the silky wet insides of her mouth. Then she heard the buckle of his belt being unfastened, the more decided zip of jeans being opened, versus the less detectable slide of the zipper on what had been Ben's suit slacks. If she hadn't had the ring gag in, she would have parted her lips, showing her eagerness to service her Master. Taking his cock in her mouth never failed to steady her, and she sure as hell needed steadying at the moment.

A wave of Peter-scented air, and she knew he'd pulled his T-shirt over his head. She offered a soft sound of pleasure when he squatted in front of her, rubbed the balled-up handful of heavy cotton against the side of her face, over her lips, not just to take away the saliva there, but to give her that reassurance, that intimate touch of his clothes, his scent.

"You're making me proud, girl," Peter told her, and she knew she'd jump off a cliff for the man.

However, the two Masters had other plans for her. As Peter took the T-shirt away, Ben brought her back out of that comforting haze. When he probed the switch marks, she jumped. He was scraping something sharp over them. It was a single steel point, one that dug into one of the more sore spots, making her moan against Peter's cock as it slid into that ring. "Damn, I like the ring gag," her Master noted. "You can really slide back deep."

"It keeps them from talking, keeps their mind on their proper business," Ben noted. "Consider it my gift to you. You need it with this one. Tsk, tsk." The chiding rebuke came as she did her best to try and kick him like a mule, despite the fact her thigh was strapped to the fucking machine frame. She strangled on a curse, her voice vibrating against Peter's cock, as Ben pricked her with that talon again. It had to be part of some kind of bear claw glove, or an attachment for one finger that simulated it.

"If we ever get another bad girl in the group like this one, we can tie them ass to ass when they misbehave," Ben said. "Use a double-headed dildo and make them slap against each other, fuck each other's asses as we play carousel, have them give head to the whole group. That would be a pretty picture. Even more so if we can talk Matt and Lucas into letting them eat Savannah and Cass's pussies while we watch."

"Damn, Ben. Fuck. Don't make me harder. I'll choke her."

Ben's words made her even hotter as well, which she was sure he intended. Though she'd come just a little while ago, her body was humming like it had never happened. She was on the edge, immersed in what they were doing to her, keyed up, wound up, scared and hyper stimulated. No wonder her trembling was shaking the frame. She visualized the scenario, her and this imaginary woman, the next that would come into the group, which meant Jon or Ben's fated mate. She, Savannah and Cass had talked about it. Just as it had happened for the other three, it would be the same for Ben and Jon. They would each find that one woman, that one submissive who was it for them, their soulmate. And the possibilities for more mind-blowing sessions like this would grow.

Peter knew she wasn't averse to playing with girls. Now she imagined the privilege of Savannah standing before her. Matt would unzip his wife's fashionable tailored skirt, push it down to pool around her ankles. He'd make his lovely ice princess put her cuffed arms above her head, loop the connecting ring over one of the suspension hooks disguised as plant hangers in the board room. He'd then slide that hook along its track, bringing Savannah closer to Dana, waiting on all fours, her head yoked up like it was here. She'd smell Savannah's fragrant pussy, the cool perfume smell of the woman's soft, silken skin. Matt would spread her legs with gentle but relentless hands, holding her steady, positioning her before Dana's mouth. She'd be wearing one of those dainty, beautiful slips of lacy underwear, and Dana would be so eager to tongue her through it, she could already taste the splotches of arousal on the crotch panel. She'd make the princess of the Knights moan, Matt holding her tight against his big, powerful body as he teased his wife's throat with his mouth.

"She's in the zone now, big time." Peter knew her too well. "Time to flip her."

"Absolutely. Let's take her to the weight bench."

She was released from the frame, from the chin rest.

Peter even removed the ring gag with strong, tender fingers, but when he had withdrawn, possibly to put it aside, she gasped as Ben's grip landed on her nape, a hard hold that pushed her cheek down to the flat top of his shoe, because he was squatting next to her. As he massaged the tendons of her fragile neck, his voice was terrifyingly mild.

"You start talking back again, you'll have that gag back in there, you mind me?"

"Yes, sir."

Then Ben was gone and Peter took over. He ran his hand over her scalp, stroking, bringing her back up onto her heels. His thumbs massaged her sore jaw as he put his lips on her cheek, over the tracks of tears. "Easy, girl," he murmured. "My good slave. My beautiful, perfect wife."

It squeezed her heart. They weren't married yet, but sometimes he said things like that, because for both of them, it was already the truth. Peter was the one to lift her, to carry her to the weight bench, and she was glad of it. When it came to being carried, moved into unknown territory, she was still tentative about that because of her blindness. But she trusted Peter to carry her through hell. He'd done it before.

She was laid out on her back on a short padded bench that was segmented. The head rest was dropped so it was at forty-five degrees, the perfect angle for taking a man's cock down her throat. Her hips were positioned on the opposite edge of the bench. Peter guided her hands to her sides, curling her fingers around the sides of the bench at her hips.

"Ankles on my shoulders." Ben slid his hands down under her knees to her calves, lifting her legs so her feet were on his broad shoulders, against his suit. It was so soft, there must be silk in the wool. Since her toes were now on either side of his head, of course she couldn't resist curling them in his hair, catching the thick strands.

"Smartass. Peter, she needs something to occupy her."

A noise of pleasure hummed in her throat as Peter guided his cock back into her mouth, that padded head rest giving her the stability so he could thrust in hard and long, his hands on her shoulders to hold her body steady. Most days she dreaded the workout room, because her body would never again have the flexibility and strength to achieve the endorphin rush a good, hard workout could bring. However, she had nothing but enthusiasm for this kind of workout. She flat-out loved giving him head.

It's a win-win, girl. It was what he'd said, the first time he realized it. She'd had her fingers on his mouth when he made the comment, felt that wry, sexy smile.

Giving her that distraction was calculated, because Ben was occupied with something a little more unsettling. He'd switched both her feet to one shoulder, and was holding her ankles together as he wrapped them in tight webbing, just like what was around her breasts. He put padding between the key joint areas before he passed it several times around her soles and ankles, restricting even the movement of her feet, and worked his way up her calves. He tied it off above her knees. Just like across her nipples, she felt the cut of the thin lines against her flesh as Ben ensured the webbing was snug. But he wasn't done.

"Palms flat against your thighs, arms straight. We won't let you roll off."

That was the least of her worries. When she obeyed, he began wrapping her again, overlapping where he'd just finished off. As he kept going, around her hips, over her mound, putting delicious, tantalizing pressure on her clit, Peter tightened his hand on the side of her head, reminding her to keep her mind on the business of servicing his cock. She needed the reminder, because it was disconcerting, being immobilized, her arms up to her elbows now included in the wrap around her lower torso.

Ben stopped beneath her breasts, tying off there. She was now mummified from breasts to feet, a few strategic rips in the netting capable of giving them access to every part of her, while the netting itself gave them full view of what her body could offer them.

"Look at the mermaid we've caught," Peter murmured. "What do you think she'd be willing to do to get free?"

"Not really relevant, since we're not going to let her go." Ben shifted her legs to his other shoulder. The fact she had to rely on him to move her suggested she had a mermaid's tail in truth, her feet and ankles bound so she couldn't flex them, her legs held together such that she didn't have an inch of space between them. His fingers found their way into the netting over the seam of her tightly compressed buttocks. Her drawn-in breath became a shudder when those strong fingers flexed and she felt the netting rip. Just as she'd predicted, he'd created enough of a hole she could easily guess his intent.

She'd envisioned him taking her rear entry while she was on all fours, sucking Peter's cock, or while she straddled her Master, but this...she felt truly helpless. She hadn't imagined having her ass fucked while on her back.

"Not paying me enough attention, Sergeant." Peter made her choke on the size of him in her throat. She renewed her efforts on him, suckling, licking. Her focus increased threefold, partly because it would help her manage the anxiety, and partly because of the fervent pleasure she felt when she inspired her captain to come like this.

It will be all right. You want this. They'll take care of you.

As Peter's hand flexed on her shoulder, his breath becoming a harsh rasp, she lost herself in the thought, the trust, even more. She usually swallowed his seed, but even before he spoke, she sensed he wanted to do it another way. Because he was sharing her with another.

"Move back a minute, Ben," Peter grunted, the strain in his voice. Though she'd only seen it once, she remembered what he looked like at that precipice point, all those fine, fine muscles taut on his chest and shoulders, biceps bunched and rippling the *Don't Tread on Me* snake tattoo. There'd be a fine sheen across his firm tanned flesh. If her hands were free now, she'd reach up, slide her nails over that slickness. His hands would close over hers, holding her wrists pinioned against his thundering heart as he came.

"Beg him for it, Dana," Ben commanded.

"Please, Master," she gasped. "Please come... Mark me."

Peter gave her the first swallow as he started to come, but then he pulled out, pressed forward so her forehead was against his thighs as he jacked off on her breasts. She could feel the vibration of his severe, shuddering breaths, the masculine groans of repletion. Warm, salty come splashed against her nipples, making her cry out her own pleasure. It trickled down her sternum, against her throat. She licked her lips, craving any stray spatter. He must have seen it, for he caught her jaw, letting her suck down the last stream as he thrust back in rough, making her work to stay in rhythm with him.

When he finally slowed, he gave her the reward of letting her clean him, which she did with desperate sucking noises. Her pussy was hot, wet and needy, such that she was undulating like a mermaid in water, seducing the fishermen who'd caught her in their net, begging them for what she wanted.

As Peter stroked her throat, smoothing his slick come over the vital pathways there, she realized Ben had been busy during her distracted haze. A cool metal hook was slipped in the netting between her ankles. Her fingers tightened instinctively against her sides, though they were ineffectual at stopping anything as her hips were cranked a few inches off the bench, her legs now held in the air by some form of suspension system. Peter passed his hands over her shoulders, below her body, her back and hips, gauging the strain.

"All right, Sergeant? Don't you think of lying to me."

"Yes..." Becoming so sexually helpless apparently came with breathlessness, so it was practically a whisper.

"Neck is comfortable?"

"Yes, sir."

Ben slid down her legs, hooking his fingers in the net over her thighs, caressing her torturously close to her mound, her needy pussy. "Too bad I bound her hands. I could have had her lube me up real good with those clever fingers of hers. That's where having another slave around is useful. She could lick all your come off of Dana's nipples, then get down on her knees and work this oil over me."

"Well, don't look at me to oblige." Peter's dry humor registered vaguely. She was far more focused on his hands, pausing over her breasts to give her a rough squeeze, then moving to her ribs, fingers sliding under her to caress her back, her hips. She could feel his heat leaning over her, wanted his mouth on hers, but she had a feeling he'd hold that gift away from her for now. Unless she proved she could be the best slave ever.

"Please..." She licked her lips. "Master, I could make him slippery with my mouth."

"Appreciate that, baby girl," Ben chuckled, a husky sound of male pleasure. "But as hot and wet as your tongue is, we're going to need some really slick oil. You've got a tight little ass. I don't mind dipping into the well for a mix, though."

She gasped as he popped another couple strings in the netting, so now his fingers could sink into her pussy. He dipped in to the last knuckle and swirled around. Without any clit stimulation, she groaned, unable to do anything more than take it since they had her so bound up.

"Ben." A pause, and a silent exchange between the men, the reason for it immediately obvious when Peter put an additional foam wedge beneath her lower back and lifted hips, Ben making an adjustment to the suspension so she now had full support below the waist. She hadn't even noticed the building ache in her hips and back until now, but that was why Peter had been caressing her so thoroughly. In time—probably the worst possible time—it would have been a distraction.

Was it possible to love the overprotective giant any more than she already did?

"Don't want our mermaid on the hook to get distracted by the wrong kind of pain," Peter murmured, brushing his lips along her cheek, her ear. She wanted his lips desperately, and was rewarded when he brought them down to hers. However, he channeled her hunger by holding pressure on her forehead, her throat.

"Unh-unh," he muttered against her mouth. "You stay still and let me sample that mouth of yours, taste myself on you."

Peter was a master at restraint and deprivation. The kiss took it one notch below screaming need, the way he nibbled, plunged his tongue into her mouth, swirling it around as he covered her lips. His fingers locked on her

38

throat, over the collar he'd given her. Ben's fingers continued to work in and out of her cunt... Now there was a shuddering pause where she assumed he was adding her lubrication to whatever he was putting on his cock. She imagined him standing there, looking at her body in an almost meditative way, all helpless and bound for him and Peter as he fisted himself, got that big cock nice and glistening, to put it up her ass.

"Master..." She breathed against Peter's mouth. Not a request, just a need to say it...to be sure. "Master."

"Yes." That one word acknowledged what she was trying to convey. There was a visceral satisfaction in his voice, her primal territorial male. "You belong to me first, but you also belong to him, because that's the way we work. If I wanted all four of them to fuck you—Matt, Jon, Lucas, Ben—you'd do it, because you love being my slave. Our slave. I want to see Ben fuck you."

"Yes, Master. I want to please you more than anything. I want to please them, because I'm theirs, too."

The desire to brat or sass was being blasted away by something far stronger, this mindless desire. Peter knew how to get her there, and he and Ben had managed, with overwhelming sexual dominance, to push her into the depths of that ocean. Her body was amped up to a thousand revs, vibrating with the need to come, to give, to surrender. It was crazy, but she loved, craved and feared it, all at once. It was all out of her control.

Before her injuries in Iraq, she'd been a hardcore sub, one who needed a firm hand to keep her from taking over the session. Peter had picked up on that right away. But as serious as that had seemed, Iraq had taught her what losing control truly was. It had terrified her to the bone, and she'd tried to hide, to stop living. Peter had collared her, made her his and brought her back to life, not taking no for an answer.

Like tonight, he still took her places that terrified her, but only to give her gifts beyond her imagining. The night they'd met, he'd broken into her soul and compelled her to accept him there. The fully functioning, sighted person she'd been then hadn't been brave enough to let anyone do that. But Peter had been her Master, able to override her will, even before she ever called him that.

Over and over again, he'd proven he knew what she craved and needed before she did. Thinking back to the corner incident with the gangbangers, she knew it was the faith in herself he'd given her that overrode every weakness or perceived handicap. She would always defy him when necessary to remind him she wasn't fragile, because he made her want to be strong.

So in essence, the bratting was his fault. However, since she did have *some* sense of self-preservation, she'd save that observation for another time.

Ben's fingers were back in her ass, beginning to work the oil in there. The determined thrust of those digits, the way the movement sent anticipation and anxiety spiraling through her stomach, told her the point of no-return was fast approaching. But before she could tense up about it, an involuntary reaction, Peter's rumbling voice cut into her apprehension.

"Who do you see licking my come off my slave's beautiful tits? Savannah? Cass?"

"Oh, fuck. Savannah." Ben's primal noise was pure lust. "With Cass straddling Dana's hips like her Harley. She could rub their gorgeous cunts together, tease their clits while Savannah licked your spunk off her throat and nipples."

"Damn, Ben, you're doing it again."

"You're going to have to perform again pretty damn soon, soldier-boy. Don't want to tell Lucas you went all limp-dicked on me."

"Bite me." When Dana made a similar noise of animal desire, caught up in their fantasizing, Peter nipped her ear, nuzzled. Ben worked another finger in, stretching her, making her burn and whimper. He had so much lube in her, she could feel the warm oil sliding down her spine from the crease between her buttocks.

It drove her even crazier, the way they were talking over her, so deceptively indifferent, crude and male. The fact she knew they were hyperaware of every response they were pulling from her, only intensified it. Peter's fingers tightened on her throat, teasing her under the collar.

"So who would you want it to be, Dana, hmm? Savannah? Cass? Or someone else?"

He knew, the cunning bastard, because his favorite bedtime stories were her girl-on-girl fantasies. Which usually pushed bedtime back by at least fifteen sweaty, quick-and-hard-fuck moments.

"Rachel...my physical therapist. When she bends over me...she has beautiful lips...I want to kiss them. Touch her...breasts. They're big and full. Just the way you like 'em, Captain. I bet she has large, pink white girl nipples."

"Yours are my favorites." She groaned, a noise of primitive pleasure, as he put those powerful hands over the netting and tore it just as he'd promised at the beginning, releasing the blood flow where the lines had pressed down. "They don't need to be big. They just need to be yours."

"They're yours," she whispered. "Not mine."

"Damn right. It's all mine. Your pussy, your tits, your ass, everything from head to toe. Heart, mind and soul."

"Yes, Master." She cried out as he leaned over her, put his mouth on one nipple and began to suck, taking her in. She knew he had to be tasting himself as well, how he'd marked her. He was so good at gripping both breasts when he did this, kneading and squeezing just the right way, so it intensified the pull on her nipple, making her cunt ripple, her clit harden. It took her a moment to realize from the pressure against her rectum that Ben was stretching her out with at least four fingers, two from each hand, making her feel fuller.

"There we are, nice and dripping, just the way I want her." He removed the digits slow, teasing the sensitive ring of nerves. "Isn't that PT the one Jon has a thing for?"

"Mmm." When Peter spoke against her flesh, he flicked her nipple with a deft tongue. While she gasped and made more whimpering appeals in the back of her throat, they conversed as if simply enjoying a shared meal. She was in danger of permanently losing her mind. "Cagey bastard won't say, but you can tell he's got his eye on her. She's married, though. Fuck it all. Wears a ring."

"Damn. He won't touch her then."

Dana wailed and strained her neck, pressing her face hard into Peter's bare chest as Ben's mouth invaded her rim, tongue darting out to lick her thoroughly. When he blew on her, it activated a tingling heat reaction in the oil. Her anus contracted like her cunt, eager, hungry for cock. He pulled his mouth back enough to slide a finger around the rim, teasing her with light touches, little strokes, short penetrations. She writhed, groaned. Her wide range of chirps and notes were like an alarmed, captured bird.

"In the real world, she may be married, but in this room, Rachel can be whatever we want her to be," Ben said softly, but not so softly she couldn't hear him. "Tell me what she'd be doing to you, Dana, if we had her here."

"She'd...do what you and my Master commanded," she said breathlessly. "Lick his come off of me. Get on her knees and suck your cock...put oil on it, the way I wanted to do it. Maybe...lick my pussy to make that wetter for Peter."

"And wetter for you, too. You like girls, Reverend Dana. We all know it." He gave her ass a little smack through the netting that had her flexing against it, increasing the rough friction of it pressing on her flesh. "Who's that controller from Weston Textiles, Peter? You can tell the way she looks at Savannah she likes the girls. And she goes to Surreal. Voyeur stuff, but I bet Jon could charm her into spreading her legs. You could order Dana to go down on her while we watch."

It was fantasy, she knew it was, but as fantasies went, it was a good one. It never failed to arouse her, scenarios where she was directed by their desires, their lusts, all their cocks getting hard watching her. While she expected the controller was sexy as hell, she liked Rachel better. It might not make sense, given the therapist's marital status, but it felt like Rachel should be in their circle. The controller, whoever she was...wasn't. It made a difference.

In the beginning, it had surprised Dana, how intuitively she comprehended the code that bound the Knights, but given the amazing connection she'd felt instantly with Peter, she supposed it shouldn't have. The first time she'd been shared by the Knights, the first time she'd felt the press of Cass's hand on her fingers and Savannah's cool lips brush her cheek in welcome, it had been there. No matter how much they talked up the fantasies to make this kind of moment more incredible, the Knights would never initiate another into the full circle who wasn't destined to be a permanent part of it. Peter had let her touch another woman the first night he'd shared her with them, in a club environment, but it had been brief, more titillation than anything.

These boys did *not* share their toys. Except with each other.

Ben went to work on her rim again, teasing her with that tongue. Oh, God, that made her crazy. She was squealing, convulsing from head to toe as he held her fast, plunged his tongue into her, worked it there, traced the rim and then sank his teeth into the meat of her buttock, a hard bite that caused her to cry out again as he did it twice more, a hard, prolonged clamp that told her she'd have teethmarks in her ass for a couple days.

While he did that, Peter kept suckling and nipping at her breasts, thumbs under her collar, pulling on it, reminding her of his claim on her. If she could see, she was pretty sure she'd have black spots in her vision. All other thoughts were disappearing, everything about the sensations now... She'd never been so aroused without coming, but they were making her utterly insane without pushing her over. They'd created heaven and hell together. She was begging, nearly wailing.

"Please...please, God...fuck. Please..."

"Ssshhh." Peter nipped her breast, a sharp admonishment. She knew he didn't mind hearing her cry out, so it had to be because he wanted her to turn that outburst inward, make the energy-build even more extreme. She shook like she had a fever, trying to obey.

"You're ready, baby girl." Ben's large hands were on her buttocks, pulling them open, the very air against the lubed opening enough to make her quiver. "You push out against me, the minute you feel pressure. Peter, keep working her."

She thought she heard that smooth zipper sound again, telling her Ben had remained fully clothed throughout this. It put a provocative picture in her mind. Peter had stripped off his shirt, so he'd be wearing just his jeans and boots. Her captain's upper body would be flexing and curved over her as his clever mouth worked her nipples and breasts, his large hands cradling her face. A contrast to Ben, in his expensive suit and shiny shoes, his green eyes intent as he opened his slacks, pulled down the briefs to stretch that thick, monstrous cock out in his grip, guiding it toward her ass...

She yelped as Peter bit her nipple, just as Ben set the head to her opening, started easing inward. She knew from the ring gag how thick he'd be, but holy God, feeling it was a different matter. And she did mean that as a religious plea, the Lord forgive her.

"Flex against him, girl," Peter said in a growl. "Open up for him. Let him in. Do it."

Her Master was ordering it, so she bore down, tried to will all her muscles to relax in a way they never had before. He was in maybe an inch or two, and it was stretching and burning like holy hell. She gasped, tears leaking out of her eyes.

Ben came to a halt. When he put a hand on her thighs, she realized he intended to do more with that hand than just steady her. His fingers found her clit, started to stroke in small circles. It was already swollen to the size of a ripe fruit. As she squirmed and gasped, Peter went back to the suckling pull on her nipples, squeezing her breasts in his big, heated hands, the combination that could shoot her right into orgasm.

Ben adjusted her, the angle and the pressure of her body holding her ass flush to his pelvis. The fabric of his open slacks were against her lower back, then she was catapulted to another realm of pleasure as Peter's hands slid away from her breasts and Ben's took their place. Holding and squeezing them as Peter suckled them. Oh God...the idea of it, the two of them working together, was amazing. Then she cried out as the head of Ben's cock broke through that tight inner ring of muscles.

"There you are," Ben muttered. She cried out again as Peter's hand covered her mound completely, two fingers sinking into her cunt as his thumb began to massage the clit on the outside.

"No...no..." It was that odd denial that came with overwhelming stimulation, because they were relentless, ruthless. For her every squirm against the flicking, rubbing, teasing of her clit, Ben was moving forward, making headway, in the literal sense. And taking full pleasure in squeezing her breasts, while Peter continued to suckle the nipples that were large and stiff as a result of all the stimulation. She was being split in half, her ass on fire, but that oil in there was still warm and tingling, trying to work with it.

"Help..." She didn't know what kind of help she needed, and she didn't want anything to stop, and of course her Master and Ben just made her hotter, wetter.

"No help for you here, baby girl," Ben growled. "You broke the rules, disobeyed your Master. Now you're going to pay the price. You take my cock, every inch of it, and you beg for forgiveness."

"I'm sorry...I'm sorry...oh, God...no...it hurts...don't stop, please don't stop..."

"Not planning to," Peter said, giving her another nip. "Not until you're the most well-fucked slave a Master could ever want."

"Oh God..." She was doing the mantra now. She had utterly no control, with Ben holding her legs and pushing inward and down. She'd never felt so full, and she was sure they planned to eventually have Peter fuck her at the same time. Oh, God, she'd be split in half. But it was all right. She was all theirs, that was all that mattered, that she served their lust, their will. She had no mind, no desires that weren't theirs. She wanted them to split her in half.

Peter came back to her mouth, his hands once again taking possession of her breasts while Ben's slid down her belly, teasing her navel before he banded his arms against her thighs and calves again, holding her suspended legs tighter against his body, for a deeper penetration she was sure.

This time she couldn't help it. She sank her teeth into Peter's lower lip, needing to consume him. He shifted, held her head, met the passionate kiss with an overwhelming one of his own, taking control of it, dominating her just with his mouth, the grip of his hands, the heat of him vibrating against her. And then she let out a guttural moan as Ben sank all the way home. His balls pressed against her ass cheeks. It hurt like hell, but God, it felt...unbelievable. She wanted him to pull out, she wanted him to never pull out.

"There you are. Fuck, tight as they come. Just the way I like it." He moved incrementally and she whimpered again. Good, agonizing, incredible. "Tell me you like it."

"I love it. Love it..." she whispered. "Please, Master. I want you both."

"You'll get us both. But you'll do Ben first. He's our guest, after all."

"Ohhh..." She screamed as Ben pulled out a few inches, slid back in while his thumb passed over her clit, down between her labia, tickled the flesh there. Peter swallowed the sound, keeping his hands on her jaw, holding her steady as Ben did it again. And again.

She was rasping into Peter's mouth. "I can't...I might come. It feels...different." Like she was coming, but not. Like she wanted it to continue forever, even as she was pretty sure her rectum had been torn open.

"You don't come until your Master orders it." That from Ben, in a stern, no-nonsense voice that snapped her mind right back into lock, particularly when he gave her clit a sharp pinch and she jumped. His cock shifted inside of her in a way that had her groaning.

"The idea's tempting, though. We could spend the rest of the night punishing her, every time she comes without our permission." Peter's chuckle was this side of lust-saturated evil. The two of them could teach Satan a thing or two about tempting the purest soul to sin.

When he shifted, she realized he'd stood up. A moment later, those hard, denim-clad thighs were on either side of her head, pressing into her shoulders. He was leaning forward...

"Nooooo...oh God oh God..." His mouth replaced Ben's fingers on her clit, and then Peter's tongue was dipping into her cunt, sucking her juices, licking her labia.

She fucking came apart, just as Ben took advantage of the inevitable climax to ramp things up on his end. He started to thrust in earnest, making her feel the slide of him in and out of her impossibly stretched rim. He was pumping her good, even though she realized—with dread and amazement—he was still restraining himself. Right now it felt like she was being jack hammered. She'd lost her grip on the cliff, on anything. Turning her head toward Peter's leg, she bit his inner thigh so hard she was pretty sure she would have struck blood if he didn't have the jeans. Her climax roared over her, shuddered through her entire body, seizing her heart, lungs, mind, taking her up so high she couldn't even imagine where the earth might be.

She was screaming, spiraling, coming so hard her juices flooded Peter's mouth as Ben kept fucking her ass and Peter sucked on her clit, tongue fucking her pussy. Ben's arm muscles were steel around her legs, holding her steady against his body as he worked himself into her. She wanted to feel him come, wanted to feel that cock jet inside her, but she was losing focus, things getting gray.

"Help... Master..." *Peter.*

Everything went dark, inside and out.

§

"There she is. She's coming back to us. Blacked out on us, soldier."

Peter was cradling her against his chest. She was lying...where was she? Out on the screened porch, where she could hear the marsh birds talking in the night, the frogs warbling, the cool touch of the fresh air, flowing in and out of her lungs with each breath. The netting was gone, leaving her fully naked. She also registered that Peter was lying beneath her, the heated skin of his upper body pressed to hers, his cock beneath his jeans a fairly erect bar against her inner thigh where it lay between his. He was stroking her temple, her short-cropped hair. She was a noodle, too limp to move.

"Not over yet, Sergeant. Your punishment isn't done."

If she'd had the energy, she would have quaked at that.

How much more could she handle? Of course, as punishments went, it was already the most incredible punishment ever. They were going to kill her, but she was already resigned to that. What a story she'd have when she reached the Pearly Gates. They might lock her out from pure envy.

That aside, the hardness of her Master's cock told her the most important thing about why she had to accept more punishment. She wasn't done until her Master's lust had been sated, until he was satisfied. That was a slave's top priority, right?

His hand glided down her back. She felt another set of hands, Ben's, slide over her rump. Her other foot was in the lawyer's lap, and he was massaging her toes, teasing the sole a little bit with occasional brushes of a glass that likely held his preferred whiskey. But now he set it aside, leaned down and kissed her there, making her smile tiredly.

"Ready to give out yet, baby girl?"

"I serve my Master," she whispered. "And you."

"That's the right answer. Because you're going to give us each one more go, and you're going to come again yourself before you're done. Dinner always comes with dessert. It might be quite a bit shorter, but it will be a sweet finish to the evening."

She had no idea what they had in mind, but she was simply drifting, loose, willing to do whatever. A wave of pleasure swept her, a residual of her climax, as Ben lifted her, his arm sliding under her waist, the other across her chest, just over her breasts to support her as Peter adjusted beneath her, opening his jeans. Ben nuzzled her hair, her ear, gave it a nip. "Made me harder than I've ever been, baby girl, hearing you beg for mercy and more pain, all at once. He kissed away your every tear."

"You savored every one of them."

"I haven't done it right if I don't make them cry...and come. And why are we doing it?"

She closed her eyes. She didn't know why she did, except it was a different kind of darkness, the kind that matched what was in his voice. Sinful temptation.

"Because I'm being punished. For disobeying my

Master."

"For endangering his property. For being careless with it. That's not going to happen again. Ever. Or I'll come back and you'll learn what a real switching and hard fuck is all about, not this little tickle we're giving you tonight."

She swallowed, barely breathing. "Yes sir."

"Now you go down on him and suck him good, until he decides he's hard enough to fuck you. No hands. You rely on us."

She wasn't sure what he meant until he moved her back on the bench, so her head would be more in line with her Master's cock. Sitting her back on her heels on the boards, Ben guided her hands behind her and latched them together with a pair of padded cuffs. Despite the harshness of his words, he steadied her hips, Peter's hands closing on her shoulders to control her descent as they folded her forward. The benches were wide, intended for a man Peter's size to nap the afternoon away, so there was plenty of room for her to be between his knees. Peter levered his cock up to her mouth, his hand moving to her nape as Ben's hand curved over her shoulder.

When they pushed her down on Peter's cock, she discovered immediately they had no intention of letting her control anything. The men worked in tandem with those hands on the nape and shoulder, pushing her down, drawing her back. It took any strain off her back or leg muscles, them controlling her descent and rise. It also brought her lethargic libido back to life, her being treated as an object to serve their lust. She showed her eagerness to be a good slave by finding the energy to suck Peter hard, doing all the things her Master liked. Tracing the head, sucking the tip, licking all along his length. Peter was getting thicker and tighter, hips lifting to drive himself in her mouth.

She was on auto pilot, too exhausted to think, but she was aware, amazingly, of the tight coil happening between her legs, a neediness for her Master to fill her there. She moaned, part protest, part pleasure, as Ben took advantage of her position, haunches in the air, to start giving her ass random smacks. Smack, knead, squeeze, then teasing her rim, thrusting his fingers in, showing her she was still well-lubed. *Smack, smack...* When she whimpered against Peter, a miraculous trickle of new arousal headed down her thigh. *Oh God.* She really was going to be able to do this.

Peter pushed her to exercise, to do her physical therapy, but she hadn't realized she could go to this level, mentally or physically, where it truly was only about being a mindless slave, serving their desires. In some far distant place, she realized she genuinely didn't have any will of her own at the moment. She was loving it, amazed by it, a little scared. But she never wanted it to end, even as she was afraid her body was going to give out. They kept pushing her so close, as if they knew the very edge of her limits.

But they did, didn't they? She knew Peter did. Knew to the nth degree how much she could take, how to take her just past that edge to give her the sense of accomplishment, that she'd exceeded her own expectations. This was no different, even as it was also a whole new universe.

"Fuck, that's good. Let's bring her up." She was lifted, brought up Peter's body, her fingers briefly gripping a combination of denim and flesh as she straddled him with Ben's help. Peter banded his arm across her shoulder blades, bringing her back down to his chest and keeping her cheek pressed to his shoulder. Ben's hands were firm on her hips, working her down onto her Master's cock, one beautiful inch at a time. Moaning, she sighed her pleasure as Peter filled her. Home. It was the one key thing that had been missing before, as much as she loved her captain's mouth on her pussy. He ground into her, a few hip circles that had her groaning with need. He knew the inside of a woman better than any man she'd ever known.

"All right, girl. Time to go. You aren't going to last much longer, and you have a to-do list." Now he sat up and rose with that awe-inspiring strength he had, as if she weighed no more than a toddler to him. As he made her wrap her shaking legs around his hips, he was moving, taking her inside. She tried to focus, figure out their destination, despite the incredible ripples of pleasure that came as his cock moved inside her with his body's movements. From the direction and the cool wood smell, they were approaching the guest bedroom.

Ben was still with him; she detected his unique scent, the brush of his hand across her bare back. Peter paused in the doorway, pressing her against the frame to kiss her, to pump his hips for a couple hard thrusts. Her breathy, pleading sigh in his mouth spoke of her love and need as he held her there. She wished she could put her arms around him. As if they'd pulled it right from her mind, Ben was unlatching the cuffs, his fingers brushing hers before she slid her hands over Peter's broad shoulders, dug her fingers into that PEACE tattoo that arced across his back. Her shoulders were so weak, it was an effort, but she was determined. She wanted to hold him.

"Into the bedroom now." Peter murmured it against her mouth, hiking her back up his body. It smelled like sea marsh, because he'd opened the screened windows at some point earlier in the day. She could hear the calls of the night creatures. Pausing a moment, just holding her there, he stroked her neck, pushing her head down on his shoulder. He was obviously waiting, which meant Ben was preparing something. Her vague worry about that turned into trepidation at his next words.

"We may be headed toward the finish line, but I think your slave needs one last reminder, Peter. Consider this a gift for that preventive maintenance program we discussed." Something like a pair of slim straps brushed against her haunches. "Jon wishes he'd invented this one himself, but it's a nice little piece I picked up from the Stockroom. It's called a Quirt Viper, because it's a quirt with fangs. At least that's the way it feels when used right."

The snap and smack sound came with a sting on her rump. She arched with a gasp, fingernails digging into Peter's back before she could stop herself. Holy ouch, but fuck. After that initial zing of pain, her still wet pussy – despite how exhausted those internal muscles were – clenched against the head of Peter's cock, still lodged halfway inside of her.

"She had a nice reaction to that," Peter observed, a touch of hoarseness in his voice that told her she'd squeezed down on him damn good. "Arch against me, baby," he demanded. "I want to suck on your tits while he punishes you. You keep milking my cock like that while he's doing it. Fuck, I might come while he's whipping you."

He put in an additional cautionary, one that had her choking between laughter and despair. "Watch my balls, Ben. You hit me with that thing and I'll tie your dick in a knot around your throat."

"Any excuse to get your hand on my dick..."

Peter's mouth descended on her breasts, leisurely suckling and nipping as Ben resumed with the quirt. She flinched and cried out at each hit, Peter kept a firm grip on her nape, holding her upper body in that arched back position so he could have his pleasure with her nipple and breast. Tears began to run down her face, even as his suckling was making her squeeze on him in rhythmic need, obeying his directive.

"Please...it hurts...please!"

They had a way of detecting when the desperation, the breaking point had come. It had come far quicker this time, but she expected they were ready for that. Every nerve and muscle was stretched thin. She couldn't hold onto anything in her whirling universe except Peter's shoulders, and her fingers were trembling on his slick flesh. Ben paused.

"Please what? You know what we want to hear, Dana. You know what your Master wants to hear."

"I'm sorry," she sobbed. "I'm sorry for endangering your property, Master. For disobeying you."

"And you'll never do it again?" Ben's voice was merciless.

She shook her head, even though everything else shook worse as she imagined what they might do to her. What Ben might do to her. "Have to..." she gasped. "Have to know...that I'm strong. Can take care of him, too. Not always about me. I can't...promise not to do that."

"An honest sub, even if she's crazy foolish brave." When that quirt made a slapping noise, she flinched, anticipating the blow, but Ben had tossed it aside. He dropped to a knee behind her and his mouth became busy on her ass again, teasing and nipping the curves, the way Peter was nipping at her breasts. It was like they were slowly devouring her, tongues moving over her flesh, over her nipples, over the curves of her buttocks, then in between. Peter was working his mouth in between her squeezed-together breasts while Ben tongue-fucked her ass again. She gasped, a low moan, as he replaced his mouth with oiled-up fingers to re-lubricate her.

"Help...no...I can't take anymore..." She was bobbing between them, instinctively humping against Peter's tantalizing half-embedded cock, lifting her ass for more of Ben's penetration. She screamed when he withdrew his fingers and gave her an entirely unexpected and sharp pop with the quirt that stung her nerve endings and completely shattered her mind.

"Sorry...please...no...anything, Master..."

Peter covered her mouth with his, swallowed her pleas, kissing away her tears, moving back to her frantic mouth. Her fingers were kneading his back. She wanted him deep inside of her, but instead he shifted her, withdrew. She barely managed to bite back the wail of frustration, liberally laced with curses. But that last quirt strike was going to leave a mark, and she knew Ben would love a reason to give her another. Peter had his threshold, and it was pretty extreme, at least between the two of them, but after tonight, she knew Ben was downright scary. It wasn't just that she didn't know where he would stop. It was the realization there was something about him that would keep her from asking him to stop, no matter what. At least not while she was safely in her Master's arms, such that anything Ben did was Peter's will as well.

Their hands on her were implacable, terrifyingly confident and smooth, no hesitation, no way to let her back out. It was still like being pushed toward a plane's open door. The chute was on her back, and she was going, but in the end, it was still a leap out into the sky, away from the safety of the plane.

"I love you, Sergeant," Peter murmured against her ear.

Everything came to a halt, everything getting still as he paused for that long moment, holding her head against his shoulder, letting her feel the pounding of their hearts together, chest to chest. "You scared the shit out of me. I'm never going to stop protecting you. Taking care of you. Loving you."

Tears squeezed out her eyes as she heard the rough truth of it in his voice. "I know. I don't want you to. Knowing that is what makes me so brave. So really...it's all your fault."

Ben's low chuckle vibrated against her rim. "She's incorrigible. I guess the only thing that's going to make her an obedient slave is fucking her brainless."

Please God, yes. And please let me survive until the end. Even though I don't think I ever want it to end.

As Ben withdrew, she thought she detected clothes falling to the floor, the creak of the mattress. When Peter moved forward, put his knee on the bed, her foot brushed a bare thigh that wasn't his. That, and the audible clues, the movement of air in the bedroom, gave her a delectable visual of the fate that awaited her. Ben was lying on the bed now, his knees off the end of it, feet on the floor. His thighs would be spread, his feet planted wide so Peter had room to stand inside their span.

Now her husband lowered her, tender as laying a baby down in her crib, only he was easing her into Ben's embrace. And the man was at last fully naked, God bless America.

Peter was heavy muscle, a soldier through and through. In contrast, Ben had his own muscular hardness, the kind she expected those cable channel street fighters had. But that hardness was a momentary distraction from a far more invasive hardness. As Peter held her upper body still suspended, encouraging her to keep clinging to his shoulders, Ben clasped her hips and guided himself back into her ass. "Push out, baby girl." He muttered the reminder. "You're still hot, slick and tight as heaven. Fuck. There you are."

She pushed for all she was worth, ready for the agonizing, burning discomfort this time, embracing it, breathing through it, pressing her face into Peter's neck, feeling the tautness of his shoulders under her hands. She sighed against him, long and deep, as he pushed his cock into her pussy, only part way again. Her pussy sucked on him like a vacuum, wanting him deeper. Two powerful males taking her like this... When her buttocks pressed against Ben's hard body, the nerve endings registered how her ass was still throbbing from the quirt. It merely turned her on more.

Peter cupped her head protectively, his other hand supporting her back to hold her at the right angle. "Squeeze down on me, girl. Give me that tight glove I love so much."

She did, and drew in a breath as Ben began to go deeper. "He's..."

"Yeah, he's a horse. You can take him again. I know you can. The pain's part of it for you."

Ben did it easy and gradual, even more so than last time, coming into her on a slow tide of movement. Peter lifted and lowered her body with firm hands, moving her up and down on his own cock in slow, slick glides. Ben came in a little further on each downward stroke, the men moving together like a well-oiled machine. All of Peter's wonderful muscles flexed against her body, while Ben's hands were firm and strong on her hips, his thighs pressing the backs of hers.

Fuck. She was a small woman. Tough, yes, but certain parts of her weren't as tough as others. She wasn't sure if she was going to be able to do it this time, take all of him. Then Ben's lips nuzzled between her shoulder blades, teasing the tattoo that was there. Athena. The warrior goddess. Nothing they did was random, and his touch on the ink centered her, helped her bear down, mindful of her service to her Master, to both Masters. Peter's fingers were there, stroking over the same area. Ben stilled as Peter pushed in all the way to the balls, and her ass contracted in reaction. She cried out in animal pain and pleasure as he slid down even further. Oh, God, it wasn't possible that she could be this full of cock and not die.

"There we go. Fuck, she's a pleasure all the way to the root. Twice in one night. Most women couldn't do that."

Ben squeezed and kneaded, lifting her buttocks, massaging her around his cock in a way that sent pleasurable sensation rocketing through her lower body, like a powerful climax, only different. Peter withdrew an inch and drove in, the impact of his cock teasing her clit. She hitched over a sob. "Master..."

"Absolutely. You're heaven, sweetheart. How does it feel, having us both all the way in like this?"

"He's all the way in?" Hope and panic warred in her voice.

Ben gave a laugh, a sound she was pleased was a little strained. "Damn well near, girl. Not many can take all of me. Not the first evening like this. You ready to surrender it all to us?"

"I want to feel you both come inside of me. Please."

"You going to hold out, let us take you for a rough ride first?"

"Anything you want. Whatever my Master and you want." She practically begged for it.

"All right, then." She could sense the silent communication between the men. It was like battle, that synergy, everyone so in sync that it created a volatile type of sorcerer's spell, full of darkness and fire, a sense of another dimension or plane of existence, where horrible and wonderful things could happen.

They both pushed in deep, two sets of male hands gripping her. She cried out, long and desperate, and kept making sounds of lust and pain. It felt like Ben was ramming into her, working her on his cock with a Master's pure dark pleasure, as Peter did the same with her cunt, thrusting deep, pulling out long. It was as if she was the anchor point of a glorious machine sparking with energy on every rotation of the pistons. In, out, in, out, deep thrust, long pullout, her ass on fire, stretched so wide, drilled so deep, her pussy full of her Master as he rotated those fine hips of his and speared her with his cock, making her feel every movement of it inside her, against her slick tissues.

She was calling on God again, mouth open wide and screaming. She'd gripped Peter's shoulders once more, and her teeth snapped down on the right one, the reaction of a seizure victim when it became too much. Because of her exhaustion, or their damnable skill as master torturers, they were holding the climax beyond her reach. With this much sensation, she should have been crashing over, but instead she was wavering on that pinnacle like a buoy on a stormy sea, them holding her there like two fierce weather gods, dueling to see who could keep her rocking the longest before they tipped her over, tore her from her anchor line.

"Beg, baby girl. Beg your Master." Ben's voice had that fierce, implacable sound, and she was helpless to do anything but obey.

"Please, Master....please come for me. Both of you...want to please you...want to be yours in all ways...want you to own me, fuck me...fucking own me...my cunt, my climax...all of it..."

"I do, girl. I do." Peter's hoarse voice nearly undid her, and the tears came anew. It was too intense, too crazy. "Please..."

They started to come and, as they did, they changed angle, or thrust, or some other devil-be-damned thing, because suddenly that climax wasn't out of reach. It was here, and it came down on her like a freaking building implosion.

It started in her ass of all things, and deep in her cunt, swirling out in the tingle behind her nipples, that feeling that Peter had left there. All the sensations spread out and, when they touched, it was like three different sets of live electrical wire. It set her on fire. She was screeching like she was being killed, but it was the best kind of dying ever. She was bucking on them, against them, and they were ramming into her, talking rough and dirty to her, telling her she was their slave, their slave to fuck however, whenever. She was loving it, dying from it, screaming from it...

It was the most amazing orgasm she'd ever experienced, that anyone had ever lived to tell about... At least she hoped she'd live through it, because she was headed for that dark vortex again at full speed. Though she tried her best to hold on with her fingernails, scarring Peter's strong shoulders, she lost the fight.

But that was the point wasn't it? She fully surrendered to them both, and was lost in the blissful death they'd given her.

§

She woke to find she was still clinging to Peter's strong shoulders, but they'd changed position. He was lying fully on the bed, her sprawled halfway across him, her thigh over his. Ben was massaging oil into her shoulders, moving down her back, over her buttocks. When he slipped between them, putting something cool and soothing on all the abraded tissues, she whimpered and trembled, but it was okay. He was as gentle now as he'd been brutal before. Peter stroked his fingers through the oil, teasing her nape, the sensitive area between her shoulder blades.

"I love you," she whispered.

"Sssh," Ben admonished her quietly. "I told you not to tell me that where Peter can hear you. It makes him insecure."

She wanted to smile, but even her face was exhausted. "Ass," she mumbled.

"You have a very fine one, girl. Don't tempt me to give it another workout." Ben worked his fingers in her cunt and ass, and she let out a little mewl. "There you go. Let that stay in for a little while. It will make everything feel better, so your Master can take you again tonight. He's already hard for you, the fucking beast."

Holy Mother of God, he was. When she shifted her thigh, bringing her knee up higher, Peter's cock was stiff against his belly. He made a quelling noise, though. "Be still. It'll wait. I just keep thinking about the way you looked, and felt, and all I want is to fuck you again. You're a treasure, girl."

"Yours. All yours."

"You bet that sweet ass." As his large hand passed gently over it, Ben withdrew, because she heard him cross the room, go into the bathroom.

"Thank you, Captain." She closed her eyes but, daring another punishment, she found enough energy to shift her body further on top of him. She knew his body well enough she was able to lodge that broad head in the opening of her pussy, and sighed in pleasure. His fingers tightened on her.

"I said no, sweetheart. I'm not going to hurt you."

"You won't. I need you. I know... I know you need to be there, so you know you're the one, the only."

His touch on her back stilled. His palm was flat on Athena, fingertips brushing the other tattoo, the one of the Lord's Hands in prayer, wrapped in dog tags. "I'm that transparent, am I?"

"You're a big male animal. It's what you all do." She smiled against his chest, emitting a soft noise as he slowly eased her down with minimal discomfort, so he was all the way back in. However, when he pulled the light sheet up over them both, she knew he was going to be content to lie there like that, no actual fucking, just cunt and cock joined, heart to heart, soul to soul.

She might have dozed a little, because when she became aware again, she had a sense they were alone. "Did Ben go?"

"Yeah, he headed out. Left a kiss on your ass, over the sheet."

"I wanted...I should thank him."

"You did. Trust me." Peter's arm tightened on her. She heard that growl in his voice that she loved, reasserting his claim.

"Thank you, then. For the best punishment ever." She smiled against his chest as he groaned.

"I guess that means I'll have to come up with something even more severe next time."

"My heart won't take it."

"Neither will mine." He squeezed her. "Sleep for now, Sergeant. You can turn my hair gray another day. For now, just be my sweet slave and hold me while you dream."

"Forever and always, Captain."

You're All Invited...

A vignette featuring Lyssa and Jacob and friends, characters from the Vampire Queen Series.

Originally posted 12/22/2012

This vignette featured Jacob and Lyssa, who kicked off the series in Book I, Vampire Queen's Servant, *and many of their friends, who have appeared in subsequent books of the series. There was also a special guest appearance by Dante and Alexis, characters from the* Daughters of Arianne Series. A Mermaid's Ransom *is their book (Book III of the Daughters of Arianne Series).*

Background: *in 2011, I did a brief vignette about Jacob and Lyssa going to the mall at Christmastime. It was so well received, I decided to return to Lyssa's Atlanta home the following year and bring you all with me, to share their very special Christmas party with family and friends...*

§

Gideon studied the eight-foot fir tree that towered up to the vaulted ceiling of the sunken living room. Besides being wrapped in what he was sure was well over a thousand lights, it had been decorated with ribbon, popcorn strings, and numerous ornaments that had been collected by Lyssa over the past several hundred years. The older and more delicate ones were toward the top, whereas the lower branches had disproportionately thick clusters of more expendable wooden ornaments and balls, suggesting that was where Kane had focused his decorating efforts. Whiskers was in the process of batting at one of the balls, studying her reflection in the glossy crimson surface. A few moments ago, Bran had slunk off, threatened by Ingram with bodily harm if he or any of his canine siblings tried to eat the popcorn strands—again.

The mantel glowed with candlelight set amid fresh garlands. All three of the entranceways to the room were likewise framed with lit greenery. The back wall displayed a cloth mural, reindeer bounding in a snowy field, snowflakes dancing across the dark blue sky above them. The air smelled of forest, cinnamon and sugar cookies, compliments of the fir tree, the red candles and Ingram's efforts in the kitchen, respectively. Piano instrumentals of Christmas carol favorites filtered from the discreetly disguised speaker system.

In short, the room was a holiday paradise. The outside of the house was festooned with a million more lights, and there was a life-sized nativity scene planted in the front yard. A full complement of glowing wire angels were hark-the-heralding in the air above them. Luminaries lined the quarter mile driveway. He'd helped Jacob and Ingram light all 526 of them just before nightfall. That would teach him to get here a day early.

When Jacob appeared at his elbow, Gideon glanced at him wryly. "Don't take this the wrong way, because you obviously worked your ass off on all this, but it's like I'm in the Twilight Zone." He dropped his tone, offering a decent Rod Serling imitation. "We find ourselves in the midst of a peculiar amalgamation, where poignant Hallmark movie meets the Addams Family Christmas special. Very special guest stars Hannibal Lectre and Jeffrey Dahmer will demonstrate the proper way to marinate a turkey."

"It could be worse. It could be the Manson Family Christmas."

"Oh, you mean the Council Christmas party you had here last week? I was so disappointed to miss that one. *Not.*"

Jacob grinned. "Tim Burton and Stephen King could

have written the screenplay together. Lady Helga insisted all the servants band together and sing Christmas carols for the Council's entertainment. Naked. Lord Stewart's servant plays the piano, so there we were in the atrium, doing rounds of 'We Wish You a Merry Christmas' and 'Jingle Bells.' Belizar was acting like the grumpy uncle who's always invited to the holiday festivities, though he's a killjoy. But he cracked a smile a time or two."

"Isn't it enough they demand unnatural sex acts with their meals? Singing Christmas carols is cruel and unusual punishment."

"Lady Carola's servant has an excellent baritone. Mariela, Lord Uthe's servant, is completely tone deaf, but she goes at it with charming enthusiasm."

"She's a hot blond Amazon with a face like Grace Kelly." Gideon snorted. "She could bray like a mule and no one with testicles would complain. Except maybe Lyssa."

"Careful." Jacob shot him a warning look. "After that, they rated the best kiss under the mistletoe. Servants-only participating, of course."

Gideon turned a narrow eye on him. "If you tell me you got to kiss Mariela, I'll have to regret not being invited." When he winced, Jacob gave him a sympathetic look.

"How long is it going to take you to remember Anwyn can hear all your thoughts?"

"Apparently a little longer." But a smile curved Gideon's lips as he glanced across the room at his vampire mistress. Sitting on the staircase that led into the living area, she wore a gold dress of some glittery, clingy fabric. The gathered neckline showed a generous curve of breast, along with a gold pendant shaped like a delicate dragon, set with a dark green stone. With her sable hair down and curling around her face, she was breathtaking. Daegan was sitting a step above her, his bent thigh providing her a place to lean as he had his back against the wall. A drink dangled from his hand, the other on her shoulder as they studied the tree.

The number of packages under the fir suggested Santa's sleigh had tipped over there. Gideon could see Anwyn was still worrying about that, thinking they hadn't brought enough gifts for Jacob, Lyssa and Kane, but both he and Daegan had assured her they had.

She's a thousand years old and wealthier than most Middle Eastern oil countries, Gideon reminded his mistress now. *You bought her some hair combs she liked when you two were shopping together. She won't expect that, and she'll find the fact you remembered charming. For Lyssa, it's not just a bullshit saying – to her, the thought is what counts most.*

Fussing over these types of things must be a woman thing. Gideon was happy to get a new package of Hanes T-shirts and a six pack of beer for his Christmas gifts and didn't give it much thought beyond that.

Now you tell me. Daegan sent him an indifferent look over Anwyn's head. *I bought you Fruit of the Loom.*

Let me guess. The ones in girly pastel colors that the boy bands like to wear?

You've spoiled the surprise.

Gideon's vampire master was as dark and debonair as usual, in a gray suit with black shirt open at the throat. His hair was long enough it teased the collar, strands of it scattered over his forehead, accentuating the glitter of his dark eyes. Looking at the two of them, Gideon couldn't tear his gaze away. Sometimes he had a hard time believing that he belonged to them both.

We'll be happy to remind you as often as needed, Gideon. Anwyn's brown eyes had a touch of gold in them, picked up by her dress, and her moist lips curved, showing the tip of a fang. *Maybe more than that. So you're not thinking of tall blonde women.*

"I really am going to pay for that one." Gideon shook his head, then looked at his brother. When he shot a punch at Jacob's abdomen, his brother fended him off, but Gideon still managed to knock him back a step. "Stop grinning like that. You never answered the question. *Who* did you get to kiss?"

"They put all the names in a hat and drew two at a time." Jacob turned toward the tree, studying it with excessive interest. Gideon lifted a brow.

"If you tell me you had to kiss Torrence, I swear I will

puke all over your shiny black shoes."

"Well, we did win the prize. The female Council members were quite taken by the way he groped my ass."

"Oh, fucking hell."

Jacob chuckled and gripped his shoulder. "I need to go check in with Lyssa. Keep an eye on things down here?"

"Always. Do you want to take Kane with you?"

Gideon nodded toward his nephew. Dev currently had the vampire child engaged with a toy the bushman had made for him. It was some kind of carved three-dimensional puzzle, an elephant whose trunk, legs and ears came apart from the torso. The joints had been brightly colored to match their corresponding pieces on the body, to help the child know what went where. As Dev comfortably squatted next to the boy, he guided Kane with a finger tap here and there. A light smile was on his lips, his serious sea-green eyes watching the boy figure it out.

Danny sat nearby, talking to Anwyn. As usual, the blond-haired, blue-eyed vampire looked like something right out of a Disney tale, only tonight she'd gone more hot Barbie than innocent Sleeping Beauty with her wardrobe. The snug wraparound green velvet dress with a blue satin bow edging the low back and trailing down her hip emphasized every curve. She wore a topaz anklet with her black stilettos that drew the eye to her fuck-a-man-into-the-ground legs. Of course, next to Gideon's Mistress, she might as well be one of Cinderella's ugly stepsisters.

Nice try. Anwyn sent him an unimpressed look, but he gave her back an image that softened it. Last night, while she and Lyssa had been talking, he'd dozed off on the floor next to where his Mistress had been sitting. When he woke later, Lyssa and Jacob had gone. Anwyn was lying next to Gideon on the floor, the two of them there by the Christmas tree. He'd put his hand on her hair, looked down at her gazing dreamily up at the tree, and seen real contentment and ease on her beautiful features. Glancing up, he'd seen Daegan stretched out on the couch, reading, watching over them both. In that moment, he knew he'd never want—or need—more than this.

No matter how many hot blondes I see.

Anwyn pressed her lips together, tossing her hair over her shoulder, but he saw the sparkle in her eyes and the approval in Daegan's gaze. Gideon lifted a shoulder. It was only the truth.

"He seems pretty occupied now," Jacob said, drawing Gideon's attention back to Kane.

"Yeah, right now." Gideon snorted. "He'll be trying to snack on the breasts of any available female the moment he gets bored."

"I wonder where he picked up that genetic trait?"

Gideon blinked at Jacob. "You really want to start throwing that rock, brother?"

Jacob held up his hands in surrender. "He's been better about it of late. Ever since Lyssa told him the next time he did it, she'd harpoon him like a baby seal."

"Her soft maternal side is really getting out of control. In case she meant it, you better take him with you. Mason and Jessica should be here soon, and you know my nephew thinks Jessica is his personal hot fudge sundae with a cherry on top."

"God help us when he's a teenager."

"Don't worry. If Kane holds onto his fixation on Jessica past puberty, Mason won't let him live to see eighteen."

"Comforting." This time, Jacob's quick punch went under Gideon's guard, making good contact with his kidney. He was gone before Gideon could retaliate. That was all right. Gideon knew how to bide his time, lay an ambush. He'd start by taking off all the tags on Jacob's presents and putting his own name on them instead.

"Ingram." He caught the majordomo's attention as the man brought in another tray of appetizers. "Do you have a Sharpie?"

§

Lyssa finished adjusting the strand of rubies at her throat, smoothing the dark green velvet dress over her bosom and hips. Her shoes were a matching velvet green, sprinkled with diamond rhinestones. Perhaps the green and red combination was a little over the top, but she was feeling unusually...festive. Turning, she saw the two main reasons for her mood. Standing in the doorway were her boys. Kane was at Jacob's knee, one hand hooked onto his father's jeans pocket, the other clasped around a poinsettia corsage.

"Tell Mama your new word." Jacob nudged him forward and Kane smiled at her, showing the tips of his fangs.

"Bee...boo...Byeeootiful. Bootful. Mama."

"Yes, she is." Jacob's blue eyes glowed warmly at her. She smiled and shook her head at him. Despite her age and having seen the things she'd seen, that particular look of his could weaken her knees and speed up her heart rate. She considered it her own closely guarded secret, but like most of her secrets, she suspected Jacob already knew it. He certainly used the look to good effect, with excellent timing.

Your reaction never fails to amaze me, my lady. A simple drifter, lucky enough to fall into your good graces.

"If you're trying to soften me up, you are centuries too late." But when Kane came to her, she knelt to take the corsage. It was affixed to a barrette, so once she thanked her son for it, putting an affectionate hand on his tousled hair, Jacob came to slip it into her tresses. After he did so, he caressed her face, dropping his hands to her hips to draw her close for a kiss. Then he stepped back, his gaze sweeping her.

He straightened the necklace, adjusted the velvet scoop of the neckline, and turned her to retie the back laces of the dress more smoothly. Being mirror and helpmeet became second nature to any servant. With amusement, she remembered their family dinner last night. On the way to have coffee in the library, she'd seen Gideon stop Daegan. The cynical former vampire hunter had brushed a glittering cluster of sugar granules off his Master's jaw. It had ended up there when the vampire assassin indulged Kane's desire to offer him a bite of a cookie.

Such moments were one of the few times a servant's familiarity didn't require permission. Not that she really held Jacob to that standard anyway, unless they were in formal circumstances...or she was trying to make a point with her stubborn, handsome servant.

Kane had wandered to the window to look at the Christmas decorations they'd placed in the side courtyard, specifically for his benefit. Accordingly, they were mostly blow up caricatures of Santa, penguins, polar bears, elves and other common Christmas motifs. The train set, whose cars were big enough to allow a child his size to ride, wound in and out among them, since they'd bought more track to allow the train a greater range.

"I still cannot believe I let the two of you talk me into all those tacky blow-up things."

"Yes, you can. Admit it, you love the one of Santa on a John Deere tractor with Rudolph."

"I didn't even know what a John Deere tractor was."

"And now you do. The person that learns something new every day never grows old."

Seeing his son was distracted, Jacob bent to kiss her shoulder, fingers caressing her left breast, eyes lingering on the low scoop neckline the rubies only enhanced. "The most dangerous vampires in the world are assembling in your living room," he said against her throat, "while my brother is probably shaking packages, trying to figure out what's in them."

"There goes that crystal set for Danny." She sighed. "But since it will give me the opportunity to beat him, I will consider it worth the money."

"Play nice. It's Christmas."

"I prefer being naughty." She turned in his arms, dusting some powdered sugar off his chest. "You've been in the gingerbread."

"Ingram took that cooking class with his new lady friend. He gets the whole puppy dog eyes thing going on if you don't sample everything he makes."

"A poor excuse. If you get fat, I will get another servant."

He arched a brow and kissed her even more intently, hands dropping lower on her hips. She framed his face in her hands, long nails sliding into his hair as she leaned into him. She didn't often do that, simply melt into his arms, but there was something about tonight that made her feel...soft. It had been a challenging year, but tonight felt like a small, precious reward for all of it.

"It's one you deserve, my lady," he said against her lips. "When are our two special guests expected?"

"They'll be a little late, but I think it's best that way. Once they arrive, they can meet everyone all at the same time."

"Like tossing a kid into cold water, rather than making him go in an inch at a time, having to readjust every few moments?"

"Exactly." Her gaze became somewhat unfocused. "Mason and Jessica have arrived."

A moment later they heard the dogs joyously barking. Kane ran over to the west window, where he had a better view of the front drive, and Jacob stepped up behind him. As Jacob put his hand on his son's head, he was unaware of how Lyssa studied them both. Her handsome knight in profile, wearing a V-necked sweater over jeans. The sweater showed off the broad shoulders and well-developed biceps, and his copper-streaked hair was brushed to gleaming waves, his blue eyes intent on what he was seeing outside. Her gaze slid down over the curve of buttock, the length of thigh. She had a sudden desire to be close to him again, run her hands over the body that was all hers.

When he chuckled, she saw what he was seeing through his mind, but she came to his side anyway. They'd put velvet collars with jingle bells on all the Irish wolfhounds tonight. Since they were bounding around and just ahead of Mason's red Jaguar XJS, they only needed antlers to look like reindeer pulling a sleigh.

"Jesca, Jesca, Jesca." Kane flew out of the room, while Jacob cast Lyssa an amused look.

"He's not even four, and he knows their car. You know a boy's first love is the hardest to get over."

"Hmm. I'm more worried about his reaction to little Farida. He may see her as competition and dump her in the potato bin."

Jacob shook his head. "Not a chance. He'll take one look at those pretty amber eyes and be lost."

"That rule only applies when his genitalia gets bigger

than his brain. I expect Kane will be as well-endowed as his father, but he has a few years to go before that balance shifts. Thank God."

"Your inflated opinion of my gender never fails to overwhelm me." He pinched her and earned a feline smile, a flash of her eyes that said she'd take her revenge for it later. But when he offered her his arm, requesting the honor of escorting her, her lips softened along with her eyes.

When you look at me like that, my lady, it never fails to make my knees weak.

Charmer. Let's go be with our guests.

They traversed the staircase to the wide main hall. As they moved along it toward the wing of the house where the festivities were happening, she took her time. Jacob, Ingram, John and Kane had put a lit Christmas tree in between every suit of armor that lined the corridor, with bunches of mistletoe hanging from the light fixtures. Jacob had kissed her beneath every one of them, and then Kane had wanted his mother to kiss him as well. John had merely made a face, but of course he was at the age he was supposed to think kissing girls was gross.

Ingram had watched them with that bemused look she sometimes caught on Gideon's face. She'd heard his Twilight Zone comment to Jacob and, though his sardonic wit amused her as always, she understood the faint unease behind it. As Jacob had said, her house was filled with dangerous vampires. But even dangerous vampires could love Christmas.

She strolled along the passageway, enjoying the Christmas decorations around her and Jacob's strong biceps beneath her hand. The delightful anticipation she was feeling was something she'd experienced for the first time last year, when they'd managed a smaller version of this gathering with Gideon, Anwyn and Daegan, but things had been a little different then. Now, matters were more settled. For the first time in many years, she hoped to establish traditions. Not just in terms of Council rituals, but her own personal rituals.

She and Rex had captured it briefly, in their early years

together, but it was a shadow of what she was experiencing with Jacob, with Kane, with those now in her large living room. These were people she considered her extended family, in every sense of the word. The other Christmas festivities she'd offered these past couple weeks, to the Council, to the overlords in her Region, those had been more formal affairs, though enjoyable in their own way. Tonight was different. No politics, no games. Simple fellowship, friendship and family ties. These vampires knew more about her true self, the meshing of Fae and vampire blood, as well as her feelings for Jacob, and accepted all of it.

Ingram hadn't been sure about John being here when other vampires were. For the formal vampire events, she'd agreed, making sure he had his grandson at sleepovers during those times. But Kane and John were almost inseparable now, and Ingram had met most of those who'd be here tonight, so he'd tentatively relented to his grandson's plea to be his "assistant," a job John took very seriously. He'd made lists to help his grandfather with the catering arrangements, carted clean linens to the guestrooms and done a variety of tasks. She'd been amused to see Kane doggedly following John around earlier in the week while the older boy informed him of all the things that had to be done, all while emulating his grandfather's grave mannerisms.

She'd given Ingram her personal pledge that John would come to no harm. It was evidence of how far their relationship had come that Ingram had believed her, for once without looking toward Jacob for reinforcement.

As they reached the end of the hall, the subject of her thoughts came through, rolling what she assumed was Mason and Jessica's luggage. "They're freshening up in the blue bedroom, my lady," John assured Lyssa. "Lord Mason said they'd be down directly. I'm taking their luggage up to them now. Granddad's keeping Kane occupied in the kitchen until they get back."

John was a handsome boy, going through a growth spurt that made him tall and thin, even though he hadn't hit double digits in age yet. The smooth brown skin and long lashed dark eyes reminded her of a young African prince she'd once known, back in the sixteen hundreds. Or was it fifteen hundreds?

As he continued up the corridor, intent on his mission, Lyssa glanced after him. "What is it he wants to be now?"

"Last week it was a wizard like Dumbledore," Jacob said. "This week I think he's investigating nuclear physics."

"Closely related professions."

Jacob smiled, squeezing her hand. As they emerged into the living area, Daegan and Anwyn were already rising from their spot on the stairs, moving back to give way to her. Jacob noted the cordial bows in her direction from the two of them, as well as Danny, across the room. This was an informal event, so such courtesies weren't necessary. That made them a deliberate decision to demonstrate to his lady their earned loyalty and respect. It increased Jacob's already substantial regard for all of them. Lyssa noted the gesture as well, her jaw tightening a fraction, showing she was moved by it. She rewarded their unexpected formality by touching Daegan's face and giving Anwyn a warm smile. Well, warm for her.

Jacob's fingertips slid along her lower back. *Well done, my lady. I'm sure Anwyn is now a bit less certain you'll eviscerate her after wine is served.*

Smart ass. But she stepped up to Anwyn, brushing her cheek in a light kiss. His lady gave Gideon her usual censorious glance, conveying her expectation that he would misbehave. He responded with a glint in his eye that said whatever she had in mind in retaliation, she could bring it. Then he winked at her.

He will not make it to a hundred years old.

He will, with Daegan and Anwyn to protect him.

They are the ones most likely to dispatch him for his constant impertinence.

Jacob hid his grin at that. He knew—as well as his lady did—how Daegan and Anwyn felt about Gideon. He personally still found it somewhat surreal, seeing his brother, a former hardcore vampire hunter, so firmly bound to both a male and female vampire. But in their company, his brother looked the most at peace Jacob had seen him in over a decade.

Hearing Jacob's thoughts, Lyssa agreed. Despite her stern attitude toward Gideon, she cared a great deal about the surly vampire hunter. It was probably best not to let him know that, however.

Dev and Danny were her next stop. When they'd visited Danny in Australia back in the summer, Dev had looked sexy as sin in his regular sheep station garb of trousers and sweat-dampened cotton shirts that clung to his powerful upper body. However, she found him quite arresting in slacks and a dinner jacket, polished boots. The strands of silver threaded through his russet hair were highlighted by the Christmas lights. The rugged lines of his face creased at the sight of her and Jacob.

"G'day, Dev," she said, letting him take her hand and bend over it. He didn't brush his lips over her knuckles, but she felt the warmth of his breath across her skin, a pleasant sensation, along with the strength of his fingers, the gentle way he held her.

As he straightened, he offered a deferential nod. "My lady. Delighted to be here. I guess you saw Mason and Jessica rocked up. Or felt them, rather."

She nodded. He squeezed her hand, a familiarity he wouldn't normally take at a more formal affair. "This is a bonza thing here, tonight. A gift to all of us. Thank you, my lady."

"I've never seen you quite so polished, Dev. Not getting too fancy, are you?"

He flashed his cheeky grin. "Danny just likes to dress me up a bit, make me smell less like sheep on occasion."

"Well she did a very good job." Her gaze swept him. "You look very appetizing."

Regretting your decision already, not to go the usual route tonight, my lady? Jacob's fingers whispered lower on the back of her dress, over the upper rise of her buttock, a blatantly possessive touch he knew he could push in this company. Not that she thought he'd rein himself in too much regardless.

I enjoyed my night with you and Gideon enormously. I haven't had that distinct pleasure with you and Devlin. I might have to give it some thought. Perhaps after Christmas, you, me, Dev and Danny will curl up in that very large bed together. There are endless ways for four to pleasure one another. She gave him an image of her and Danny twined in an embrace, Jacob behind her, Dev behind his lady, teasing female flesh with mouth and fingers, cocks thrusting into the women they loved as those women added to the pleasure with one another.

Santa is definitely putting you on the naughty list. His reaction told her the idea had engaged his interest though, on several levels. She slid her hand back to tangle with his and then applied enough pressure, at the right angle, to have him stifling an oath at the wrench to his wrist.

Only if you behave, Sir Vagabond.

His sensuous chuckle in her mind was enough to slide a secret tingle up her spine, the same path his fingers had followed.

She knew what Dev had been implying. It *was* a different environment tonight. For one thing, the children—Kane, Farida and yes, John—were a big part of the evening, because Christmas, like a trip to Disney, required their special energy to make it that much more magical.

That last part was according to Jacob. Lyssa had of course never been to Disney, but if she capitulated to one of her servant's entirely insane ideas, that would be rectified in January. He'd proposed they take a short flight down and go to the park during the nighttime hours. Given that it would get dark after five-thirty at that time of year, and Kane was able to go outside within an hour after dark now, they could go for several hours before the park closed. That was likely the maximum amount of time her senses—or Kane's—could handle such close proximity to large groups of people. But Jacob said when she saw Kane staring in dazzled disbelief at the sight of Mickey fighting a dragon in an epic light show over the water, or viewing the fireworks over the castle, it would all be worth it. Jacob also wanted to get her on a couple roller coasters—something called Space Mountain—which meant she was intending to take Danny and Dev with them, so the two couples could switch off Kane when needed.

Danny pressed a kiss to Lyssa's cheek. Her blue eyes were dancing, and her next words picked up on Lyssa's line of thinking. "I can't tell you how...intrigued I am by our New Year's trip with you. It was so difficult *not* to tell Lord Belizar our plans. I would have loved to see his eyes pop out of his head."

Jacob grinned at her. "If we put you in the right dress, think how many people will be asking how you felt when the prince put the glass slipper on your foot."

"Or kissed you awake," Dev put in. "They'll also be wondering where all the little bluebirds are that are supposed to be flittering around your head."

Danny smiled sweetly, showing her fangs. "I'm not sure tonight was such a good idea, Lyssa," she remarked. "Servants do tend to forget their place when they're encouraged to be too familiar with their Mistresses."

"Think of the pleasure you'll have, reminding him of his place later," Lyssa said. "Let me know if you need help with that." Her jade gaze skimmed over Dev, no hint of a smile on her face, though her eyes glittered dangerously.

Danny nodded, linking arms with her. "Count on it. But first, let me give you a quick peek at the shoes I bought Anwyn in LA. You can tell me if you think she'll like them."

As they moved off to the tree and its stack of gifts, Dev glanced at Jacob. "You know they mean every word of that. Shows how wobbly we are, stirring them up, knowing there'll be hell to pay later."

"No. The wobbly part is that we've started looking forward to whatever they devise." Jacob chuckled. "Gideon used to call me brain-damaged. I told him now that he's become a member of the club, he gets to be the lead poster child for us. He'd argue the point, but..."

"Be a bit difficult, wouldn't it?" Dev glanced at Jacob's brother, currently using his height advantage to stretch up and take an ornament off the tree, so Anwyn could take a closer look at it. As she bent her head over the item, Daegan was behind her, studying the detail on the blown glass star. Gideon had his hand on Anwyn's hip, and Daegan's overlapped it, an entirely unconscious affection between the three of them. "If ever there was such a thing as a Christmas miracle, that one might be it," the bushman added.

"Yeah." Jacob sobered, thinking of where Gideon had been, how close he'd come to not being part of Jacob's future, or of any future at all. The hatred and violence had nearly eaten his brother's soul. "Truer words."

Dev squeezed his shoulder. "I think every pairing in this room is a bloody miracle." His gaze moved to Danny's trim form, the golden waves of her hair falling over her pale shoulders, her china blue eyes that focused on him as she saw his attention. Her lips curved softly, then she turned her attention to Lyssa again. Jacob knew she might put Dev under the lash of a single tail later for teasing her, but she'd soothe every hurt with her lips, her hands. Female vampires had that particular propensity. They were like terrible, beautiful goddesses who gave pain and pleasure. The man who worshipped and cared for one came to crave both as symbols of their bond. It all worked out the same to a vampire's servant. It might be crazy, but it was also happiness...and love.

§

Lyssa heard his thoughts, which returned her thoughts to the other reasons tonight would be different. Not just because of the children's presence. Every vampire here had a different relationship with their servant, closer, more intimate, and in this company they could feel at ease showing it. Politicized sexual games wouldn't dominate this evening's entertainment. For one thing, Gideon and Jacob were brothers. Second, since in this environment there was no stigma attached to it, Mason had made it clear he had no desire to share Jessica with anyone. The two surprise guests she was expecting would make that a full circle, because they were definitely not yet in a position to understand that aspect of vampire society.

As much as she enjoyed the carnal nature of her kind, she had to admit it was nice to have a night that was simply about this. It was going to be an evening of Christmas carols, opening gifts, maybe even a game of the Minister's Cat. Nothing flustered vampires like quick thinking games outside their usual milieu. She was interested to see if she could stump Daegan. In short, tonight was a family gathering.

You're dedicated to a common theme tonight, my lady. I like it.

She let Jacob into her mind so easily now, there were times she didn't even make a conscious choice about it. Their minds were just...together.

Danny had returned to Dev after their little tete-a-tete. Lyssa had assured Danny the shoes she'd picked out for Anwyn, a pair of black and white stilettos with six inches of ankle straps and intricate beadwork on every other strap, were erotic works of art. The young female vampire, a Mistress who ran her own BDSM club, would love them. And if not, Lyssa would take them away from her in a heartbeat.

Jacob came to her now with an amused twinkle in his eye. *A potential cat fight. The night gets better and better.*

She rolled her eyes. *Sure you won't miss the possibility of getting to share Jessica with Dev and Gideon for our viewing pleasure?*

He snorted. *I prefer this not to be my last Christmas. Plus, I have no desires for anything but you, my lady. You and your happiness.*

Jingle bells and toenails clattering down the hallway from the kitchen heralded Bran trotting into the main room with Fionn. They went right to Dev, recognizing the top dog person in the room. Dev obliged them both with a hearty tousling of ears and remarking on their Christmas finery. Then the bushman was straightening, turning with the rest of the room to greet Mason and Jessica, coming down from the upper guestrooms.

Mason looked as devastating as always. Like Daegan, he tended to go with more formal wear choices for such events, so he wore dark slacks and a shirt tailored of silk and linen which lay soft and inviting against his powerful upper body. His copper-colored hair was queued back to emphasize the aristocratic planes of his face, the thick tail of it falling down between his shoulder blades. Jessica's party outfit was a shining concoction of silver and white, the glitter sparkling over the form-fitting dress that matched her stockings and heels. Her hair was artfully arranged around her face, Amara's doing no doubt. She and her husband, Enrique, Mason's other two servants, had flown with him and Jessica as far as Atlanta, but would now be going on to the Bahamas, Mason's Christmas gift to them both. Amara and Enrique still served him in a variety of ways, including some sensual diversions with Jessica, but there was now only one servant that filled him, body, heart and soul.

Each time Lyssa saw Mason, the bond between him and his servant became even more obvious. It was good Mason was as intimidating as he was, because whereas Lyssa had flatly declared her love for Jacob before Council, she had a certain public reserve to her manner with Jacob. It helped the Council be more comfortable with the scenario. Mason's feelings for Jessica emanated off of him without word or thought. Jessica glowed in the bonds of that love like an eternal flame, becoming brighter and more confident by day. Though that confidence had not required it, the bearing of his child had certainly underlined it.

As the vampires in the room pressed forward, Lyssa could see the humor in Mason's eyes. It was an acknowledgement that, as welcome as he and Jessica were in this company, the vampires were most interested in the newest arrival. A vampire child's birth was such a rare occasion, it was as much a cause for celebration as Christmas itself.

"Mama." Kane was at her knee. He wanted a closer look at what Jessica was holding. Obliging him, Jacob picked up their son.

Kane stared at the baby in Jessica's arms. Farida stared back at him with calm amber eyes. When she reached out, waved a tiny fist at him, he touched it with a finger. She cooed in approval. "She's not a toy," Jacob mentioned helpfully to his son. "Very fragile, like your mother's porcelain rose collection. What did I tell you about that?"

"Look. Don't pick up," Kane remembered dutifully. "One

finger touch."

"Exactly." Jacob bit back a smile when Kane pushed a finger against the baby's forehead. Farida tried her best to look at it, eyes crossing.

Farida was a beautiful vampire child, her delicate features reflecting Jessica's beauty. She had her human mother's chestnut brown hair but a vampire's stillness to her steady gaze. There were the usual cuts on her lips from scores by the tiny fangs. They learned to retract them as they grew older, but in the beginning they needed them to feed, so their biology kept them at a constant length.

The baby was dressed in her Christmas finery, a miniature dress with a velvet red bodice, the skirt a fluffy white net over satin. The net had a mistletoe pattern embroidered across it. She wore red socks with white pompoms securely sewn to them.

"She's a little human kitten," Danny marveled, touching the pink fist. "Yes, you are, you beautiful thing."

"Kitten," Kane said, brow creasing. "Whiskers." He touched his own ears, obviously trying to understand how Farida compared to the furred and pointy-eared cat who'd disappeared at the arrival of too many new people.

"He's talking," Mason marveled. He touched Kane's head, a quick, affectionate stroke that made the little boy smile, even though his gaze was still fastened on Farida in puzzled wonder.

He's trying to determine if she's friend or foe. Typical vampire. Jacob winked at her, then responded to Mason. "He started, the way they do, out of the blue."

"She is utterly lovely, Mason," Lyssa said softly. She put her hand over his, large enough that it rested partly on Farida's small feet and Jessica's arm. As she did, Jessica looked up into her Master's face. The reassuring gaze Mason gave her told Lyssa all she needed to know. Though she'd seen it growing there ever since he'd taken Jessica as his servant, Lyssa knew she'd never seen the emotions so full blown in Mason's expression as they were tonight. Happiness. Contentment.

Dev was right. Tonight was a gift for all of them. There needed to be times and places they could celebrate things like this with other like-minded vampires. She would make it an annual tradition, even if she had to kill every bigoted, narrow-minded vampire to make it happen.

Good strategy, my lady. I'm not sure you want to share that plan with Gideon, however. He might take it as your personal Christmas gift to him.

"I heard a rumor that you have a special gift for us tonight." Mason gave Lyssa a warm look. "As if sharing your home with us on Christmas wasn't enough. So what is it?"

"You were always impatient to unwrap your gifts early. You'll just have to wait."

Jessica didn't succeed in keeping her expression neutral at that, and Lyssa gave her a quizzical look. Mason closed a hand on his servant's hair, about to give her a warning tug, but Lyssa slapped his hand away. The gesture almost startled a giggle out of the normally reserved Jessica. "You were about to say?" Lyssa said pleasantly.

Jessica cleared her throat, her lips quivering against the smile. "I had to sing *Falalalala* nonstop in my head to keep him from trying to guess what I got him. You're absolutely right, my lady. He's as bad as a child."

"What did you get him?" Jacob asked.

At Jessica's flush, her glance at Kane, Lyssa quickly guessed it wasn't suitable for sharing, but Mason showed her a glimpse into Jessica's mind, courtesy of his and Lyssa's blood link. Jessica had learned a new dance from Amara, something involving a pole, candlelight... A provocative image came through, of Jessica spilling candlewax on Mason's bare chest, his muscular arms loosely tied above his head with a pair of scarves from her dance. Then the image was abruptly cut off. Mason shot his servant a mock severe look.

"I was letting you share an *edited* version with her, *habiba*. Not the whole thing."

"It's all right." Lyssa sent Jessica a rare conspiratorial look that seemed to both terrify and bolster the young woman. "Later, you can tell me all of it. In detail."

Before Mason could threaten or object, she turned to all of them. "I have arranged a very special surprise for you tonight," she said. "Something even little Farida might appreciate." She bestowed her godchild with a warm look. She began to say more, but paused at the frisson along her nerves. Since she'd taken the blood of the vampire she was expecting, she had a few moments' lead time on the other vampires in sensing his arrival, with the possible exception of Daegan. Glancing at him, she saw he'd just gone on alert, shifting his dark gaze to her in question.

"It's fine," she reassured him. She nodded to Mason and Danny. "In a moment or two, you're going to sense another vampire. He's somewhat unusual, and new to our kind."

"He's a made vampire?" Danny asked.

"No. Born. But new to our world. He's partly from another race and, as such, he has been staying...below ground, for most of the past year. In a few months, he'll be coming to stay with me for a while, to learn more of our world. Your child is in no danger from him," she added, giving Mason a mildly reproving look at the concern she felt radiating from him. If he'd been Bran, he'd have been bristling and showing his teeth. "You think I would invite anyone to my home who would pose a risk to your child or mine?"

At her cool tone, his expression eased. Mason had never backed down from her, but he also trusted her. Except when he became over-testosteroned.

"That's not even a word," he told her, since she'd let him hear the thought.

"It is if it applies to the situation." Since Ingram was secondmarked now, she'd telegraphed to him they had guests coming to the front door, so the bell never rang, but it didn't matter. Bran and Fionn wheeled at the sound of new voices and bolted out of the room, barking as if they fully intended to eat whoever was entering the house. She heard Ingram issuing his usual dire threats to them, calming them down.

Dante, do not decapitate my dogs. It would start the evening off badly, and I will take back your gifts.

She sent the thought with a sharp push to it, to be sure it got through, and received a ripple of crimson heat in return. Reassuring enough, even though there was no form to it. He still wasn't quite accepting of her ability to speak in his head.

She wasn't concerned about this going badly, and not just because she had firm control over her household. It was because of what she expected from the servant who accompanied Dante. She could feel her as they approached from the front foyer, but it was a unique experience to watch it affect the others in the room like a calming mist. Mason's brow raised, his gaze sliding to her. "What..."

Lyssa smiled faintly, shook her head. The feeling of well-being expanded, though, making Farida pump her fists and small feet in a sudden explosion of baby laughter. Kane asked to be put down and moved toward the doorway, his eyes bright with curiosity.

Jacob shifted, but Lyssa put out her hand, giving him a reassuring glance. *He's fine, Sir Vagabond. I promise. Our son is safe with him. You've been around him before.*

Yes. Which is why he still concerns me. I don't doubt your intuition, my lady, but there's never any harm in being prepared, no matter how absent a threat seems to be.

She couldn't argue with that, but she gave him a push of emotion that told Jacob she wanted him to keep his watchfulness lowkey. *Let Dante have a sense of what a gathering like this can be.*

Understood, my lady. I'm simply prepared to help him understand how to behave at such a gathering so he can get the full benefit of it.

"Hmm." She shook her head at the glint in his blue eyes, then turned as Dante and Alexis entered the main room.

Fortunately, her other guests were wise enough to let her take the lead, not descending on the two new arrivals like they had upon Mason and Jessica with their new baby. She approached Dante and Alexis, studying their appearance. Dante wore a charcoal suit with a white shirt, his long black hair pulled back from his sculpted, Native American features and held at his nape. His eyes had large black pupils, surrounded by irises of an unworldly flame color, evidence of his half-Dark One parentage. They swept the room, his lips firm and unsmiling. He had a remarkably constant dispassionate expression, a charismatic statue that emanated an overwhelming dark magical energy and more than his fair share of aggressive testosterone, which was why she'd issued the warning to her guests.

His servant and guide in this world was a yin to his yang. Alexis's brown hair swirled around her gentle, beautiful features, her blue eyes filled with open warmth. Lyssa had purposefully instructed her to amp up the effect she emanated. The vampire queen knew it would help Dante with this transition, keeping the dangerous predators in her living room calm as well. That wave of good feeling was something that projected unconsciously from Alexis all the time. Even at low volume, it made people gravitate toward her, lose aggression and embrace the better sides of themselves.

It was a talent all those who carried angel blood possessed. And what better place for an angel than a Christmas party of vampires?

§

"Have you ever seen so many alpha males with their hackles raised?" Danny murmured to Lyssa. Kane was standing before the Christmas tree, explaining the variety of ornaments to Dante in his limited but enthusiastic vocabulary. Dante's attention upon the child seemed absolute, though Lyssa had no doubt the Dark Spawn vampire was completely aware of the keen regard of the referenced alpha males. Though they were arranged in casual stances around the room, every one of them had their gazes trained on him, and were staying close to those they felt were their personal charge to protect. Dev leaning on the doorway behind Danny, Jacob holding a position between Lyssa and Kane, Mason sitting on the arm of the wing-backed chair where Jessica held Farida. Daegan and Gideon lounged at strategic points that would make it impossible to approach Anwyn without being intercepted by one of them.

"He has a very odd effect on children," Alexis said, appearing at Lyssa's side with a heaping plate of treats from the bounty spread over the dining room table. The visible pleasure she took in all the Christmas decorations shone like the lights on the tree. "It's funny that children immediately sense from Dante what it's so hard for adults to see. But I think that's why the young connect to him. He still understands things much like they do. And the direct honest way they communicate is easier for Dante to understand. Or rather..."

"He trusts what they say. There's no duplicity to it. Not like adults."

"Yes." Alexis lifted the plate. "The cookies are excellent, Lady Lyssa. I don't think I'll be able to stop eating them all night. Your majordomo is an excellent cook."

"Actually, his grandson John made those, under his instruction. He has the makings of a great chef."

"I met him. He's a wonderful child. Actually, he's quite the young man already. Very mature for his age. And the aura between him and Kane when they're close to one another is spectacular. That friendship will be very important to them as they grow up. I'd like to have Dante try one of these cookies. With your permission...?"

Lyssa gave her a nod and the young woman wandered off toward the Christmas tree.

"She has a point," Danny observed. "I've never seen such a strong friendship develop so young between a vampire and a human child. Of course, most of the time such bonds are discouraged."

"Children need other children. They're part of growing up, and there are too few vampire children to help with that. But John has been fond of Kane since they met. In some ways, John is the older mentor, teaching Kane certain things. In others, it's as if Kane understands his strength and other qualities will surpass John's in time, so on his side of things, there's a certain..."

"Imperious quality," Jacob put in, with a wink. He'd shifted to a closer chair now. "The bond between the two of them often reminds me of you and Thomas, my lady."

She hadn't thought of that, and pursed her lips now, considering it. Her gaze returned to Alexis. The subtle shift of the people in the room as she passed them was an intriguing contrast to their reaction to her vampire master. Broad shoulders eased, and she received warm glances and nods in response to her own. She stopped and spoke to Anwyn a moment, bending down to where the vampire sat on the steps. Alexis was obviously complimenting Anwyn on her shoes, since they'd agreed everyone could open one gift tonight, and Anwyn had picked Danny's shoes off the top of the pile.

Gideon had put them on her feet, buckling each strap, his hands caressing her calves. Both he and Daegan had been intrigued by the provocative effect the stilettos created on Anwyn's attractive legs. Like the image of Jessica's gift to Mason, Lyssa expected the thoughts that had passed between the three of them were not meant for young ears. It was a good thing that vampires could do that in their heads, since John regularly circled through to check drinks and appetizers, as well as to eavesdrop and participate in the way a child gravitated toward glittering adult gatherings. Though he was a mature boy, there were some things John didn't yet need to hear. Lyssa remembered Ingram commenting once that *he* was too young to hear some of the things he'd overheard at vampire gatherings.

Dante's attention immediately locked onto Alexis as she came to him. She started telling him about the cookies in animated fashion, gesturing widely, probably an indication of how loaded down the dining room table was, and then a kneading motion with her fingers, explaining John's cooking skills. Dante watched her with that expressionless face, but Alexis had a gift for empathy. Lyssa was sure the girl knew everything the half breed vampire was feeling, and her emotions were responding to that with warmth and encouragement. He'd learned to show nothing on his face and, though Lyssa knew he was making progress, unbending a little bit in Alexis's company and a few others, he didn't know most of this group. As such, he would revert to his careful wariness.

Alexis didn't show any concern about that, though, offering him a bite of the cookie from her fingers. Lyssa heard her tell him what it was, watched his brows lift as he repeated the word. *Snickerdoodle.*

John sidled up to Alexis, staying there as she engaged him in conversation, laying a hand lightly on this thin shoulder. Apparently she'd made a good impression on him in the dining room.

Kane waved at Dante impatiently, then tattooed his thigh with a cloth angel Whiskers had probably knocked off the lower branches. Kane, however, wanted it out of danger. "Lift," he ordered. "Put him on tree."

"Lift" was one of the earliest words he'd learned to say, with haughty distinction. Lyssa saw Jacob's ironic glance toward her at the thought. She crossed her eyes at him, making him chuckle.

Without fanfare, Dante lifted Kane so he could place the angel on the tree. Lyssa saw Jacob shift closer in a subtle way, the flicker of Dante's lashes registering it. Alexis laid her hand on his arm, likely reassuring him of Jacob's intent. Dante held Kane until he was done, then lowered him back to his feet. He turned then, glancing at Jacob. Her servant met the crimson gaze. When Dante inclined his head, Jacob returned the wary gesture. Progress, on both sides.

"It's a girl angel," John informed Kane. "Angels are all girls, because they all wear dresses."

"Actually, it's just the opposite. All full-blooded angels are male." Alexis gave John a beatific smile and the boy fell in love in a heartbeat, swaying toward her.

What were you saying about that ratio of brain to...other male parts, my lady?

Well, we did say John was mature for his age.

Alexis put her hand on his shoulder and John blinked, somewhat recovering his wits. "So guy angels wear *dresses*?" he asked dubiously. It was a measure of his dazed state that he didn't question how Alexis knew such a thing.

"Not exactly. Many of them wear a half-tunic. Very masculine, like a Roman soldier."

"It's still a skirt," Gideon said. He'd shifted to the ottoman near them to examine packages more closely. He had a marker in one hand, causing Lyssa's eyes to narrow suspiciously. "But more like a mini-skirt."

"Do you really think it's a good idea to piss off angels?" Jacob asked his brother. "I'm sure more than one guardian angel has saved your ass."

"No doubt. But still in a mini-skirt," Gideon said. Anwyn was standing behind him, sipping wine and talking to Danny. At that comment, however, she reached down to swat at him. Gideon ducked under the blow and turned to catch her wrist before she made contact. Rising from the footrest, he smoothly swirled her into a turn, doing a passable waltz step. "She's been teaching me," he informed his astounded brother.

Alexis put her hand to her mouth, smiling as Anwyn gave her an upside down wink. Gideon had eased his Mistress into a dip, her sable hair brushing the carpet. Sitting on the steps, Daegan caught Anwyn's outstretched ankle, giving it a lingering kiss before Gideon brought her back up, holding onto her thigh so the leg bent around his hip. He swirled her around in another turn, throwing his brother a triumphant look. "See, an old dog can learn new tricks."

"Ass." Jacob offered the insult with affection, but pointed to the box on the steps with Daegan.

"Stop switching tags and open your gift from us."

"Typical brother. Interrupts me when I'm trying to make time with my girl." Gideon gave Anwyn a wink, dropped a quick kiss on her throat, and turned to take the box. When he opened it up, he blinked. "Wow. Hey, this is nice."

It was a bomber style jacket, but one that fell to thigh length, with a multitude of pockets and inserts inside, as well as a warm liner so it could convert to various weather types. He shrugged into it. "Hell, it's like it was made for me."

"That's because it was," Daegan said. Lyssa nodded, examining Gideon with full female approval, appreciating the line across his broad shoulders. The coat fit close to his body, not obscuring his lean, powerful form.

"We thought we'd remind you that you don't have to dress like you're living out of a lost-and-found box anymore," Jacob said. Gideon shot him a rude gesture, and Anwyn smacked him in the back of his head, right after

Daegan did. His brother gave them both a threatening look. "You've done that twice each, tonight."

"You've deserved it far more often," Anwyn said.

His midnight blue eyes flashed. "Even so, next one of you that does it, I'm going to smack back, and I'm going to choose the preferred body part."

At Lyssa's side now, Danny let out a whispered half-laugh, nodding discreetly toward Daegan. "If he tries to smack *him* in any choice places, I want a front row seat for that."

Ignoring Gideon's comment, Daegan had risen, shifting behind his servant to smooth his hands over his shoulders. "Perfect."

"How did you have it made without having me measured?" Gideon asked Jacob.

"Daegan and Anwyn provided the measurements."

At Gideon's curious look, Daegan lifted a brow. Anwyn stroked a hand down Gideon's arm. "We'd know every inch of your body in our sleep, Gideon. Perhaps particularly in our sleep."

"Well." Gideon cleared his throat at that, a faint flush in his cheeks that Lyssa found charming enough to shoot Jacob a warning not to tease his brother. Jacob abstained but the effort obviously cost him. He tucked his tongue in his cheek, his eyes dancing. Anwyn gestured to Gideon to turn, wanting to see him from all sides.

"Not half bad," Jacob wolf-whistled. Gideon curled his lip at him in a snarl, but seemed pleased.

Daegan straightened the lapels. "They did a fine job, vampire hunter. There are places inside to put your weapons."

As he proceeded to show him that, Jacob and Dev's amusement turned to male interest. As they came closer to see, Alexis returned to Lyssa's side. Her plate was empty. For such a small thing, she had a healthy appetite. "I'm ready any time you wish, my lady," she murmured.

"Now would be good," Lyssa said. When she'd had the idea for the gift, Kane had been the main reason for it, and she wanted him to enjoy it while he was still fresh and awake, not cranky. "I'll bring everyone out in about ten minutes."

Alexis smiled. "I'm so pleased to help you give your son his Christmas gift. I'll meet you in the pool house."

As she moved away, Danny gave her a curious look. "What is she giving him?"

"It's a surprise for all of you, not just Kane," Lyssa said.

Danny nodded, accepting that, but studied Alexis. John met her at the doorway, and she took his hand, asking him to guide her to the pool house. "I think she's the sweetest, most innocent thing here. And I'm including Farida in that count. What is she? She's not human. It's hard to classify, but she feels like sugar cookies, warm blankets and sunshine, all rolled into one."

"That's close enough to the truth of it." Lyssa turned her attention to Dev. He'd set his one gift aside while everyone else was opening theirs, but had now returned to his spot to slit open the wrapping with his knife. He folded it, prudently putting it back in his pocket before he worked the top off the box. Seeing the cable-knit fisherman's sweater, he made a pleased exclamation. The yarn was a sea-green color. Lyssa anticipated Danny would enjoy the way it enhanced that vibrant color in her bushman's eyes.

Dev fingered the heavy cotton. "This will be fine on cold nights. This is aces, my lady." He adjusted the collar, and his gaze fell on the label. Pure shock crossed his features. "Er...I didn't know you'd taken up knitting, my lady."

"I've known how to knit for quite a few centuries," Lyssa said, unruffled when Danny turned a surprised look upon her. "A lady knows her needle craft. I can sew, knit, and embroider. For a time, I enjoyed weaving tapestries. The one hanging in the main hall leading to the rest of the house—the one depicting my first wolfhounds, Bran's ancestors—is my work. I did it around the fourteen hundreds originally, though I've had to remake it. The fibers didn't hold up well through my travels, but the pattern is the same as the original."

"Of course." Dev exchanged an amused look with Jacob and Gideon, then tilted the box to show Danny the label. The embroidered cloth tab showed a single rose intertwined with an *L*. "I'm beyond humbled, my lady," he said seriously, standing to execute a formal bow to her. "You taking time to do such a thing for a daft old bushman means more than I can express."

"A daft old bushman who has cared well for my son, and who brings happiness to a lady I consider a dear friend."

Danny flushed at that. She'd gone to sit on the ottoman Dev had occupied and was running her hand over the sweater. Dev nodded to Lyssa. "I'll endeavor to keep doing so," he promised.

"I hope so," Lyssa observed. "Else I'll take the sweater off your corpse."

"And there she is," Jacob murmured, with a wink at Dev that he returned with a grin.

"Lady Lyssa?" Dante approached her now. As he did, he glanced left at Mason, sitting on the arm of the nearby wing-backed chair, and right, toward Jacob. Both men turned their attention immediately upon him when he moved her way, but the sparks in Dante's eyes showed no fear, just a simple expectation of countering violence.

If either of you so much as twitches, I shall castrate you. Lyssa sent the fierce thought to both males, even as she gave Dante a neutral nod. "You've not yet opened your one gift," the Dark Spawn vampire said. "Lucifer sent this to you. Should I put it under the tree, or would you like to open it now?"

Gideon met Jacob's gaze behind Dante. *Lucifer? The Lucifer?* He mouthed. At Jacob's nod, Gideon rolled his eyes. "Of course he did," he muttered to Daegan. "It's a shame the Lord of the Underworld couldn't make the party."

"Do you think it's a good idea for him to get acquainted with you any sooner than necessary?" Daegan asked.

Gideon bared his teeth at the vampire, but then shrugged, acknowledging the point.

Dante had turned slightly at Gideon's comment, his hearing obviously able to pick up every conversation in the room. The banter between the men was useful though. Lyssa could chastise the males in the room for being overprotective, but every one of them was exceptionally intelligent, even Gideon with his rough manners, and they were watching Dante follow their conversation like a Ping-Pong match. As such, they were starting to pick up what Alexis had noted. They could see he was making an effort to understand, that there was a...youthfulness to Dante that belied his power and actual age. Of course, in vampire terms, he was still very young, not much more than sixty by their estimate.

Lucifer's gift was in a small wooden black box, shiny and faintly smoke-scented. When Lyssa opened the catch at the top, it was her turn to look surprised—and enchanted. It was a multi-hued crystal, shaped like a rose. The crystal was touched with colors of pink, crimson and every shade in between, such that it looked like a glowing flame in her hand.

"Just what did you do to garner the good graces of the Lord of the Underworld, my lady?" Mason asked, his brow raised. Jessica was pointing to the gift, drawing Farida's bright eyes to it. Lyssa raised the crystal, making it sparkle. Farida's smile inspired the queen to give the baby the same in return. Then she responded to Mason's question.

"I visited with him several months ago to discuss Dante's transition to our world. Perhaps he merely wished to thank me for my cooperation."

"Or like every bloke she meets, she scared the piss out of him, and he wants to stay in *her* good graces," Dev muttered to Jacob. He hid his smile as Lyssa gave them both an arch look, that sensual promise of retribution again. Yet she didn't disagree with the assessment.

"Thank you for bringing the gift, Dante. Please convey my pleasure with it to Lord Lucifer." Stepping forward, she laid her hand on the young vampire's arm as she commanded the attention of the rest of the room. "I'd like to invite you all to the pool house now. The gift we have planned is ready."

As the vampires and servants prepared to head in the direction of the pool house, Lyssa glanced at Jacob. *I've told Mr. Ingram to join us.*

A good decision, my lady. He will love it. Everyone will. And this was a good decision, despite my misgivings. His gaze strayed to Dante. *Your heart and intelligence never outdistance one another, and both are far greater than most realize.*

I believe my heart has grown quite a bit, thanks to some very special influences in my life. One of which I won't name, because he tends to get a little too full of himself.

With a smile, Jacob offered her his other arm, magnanimously cooperating with her plan to allow both Dante and him to provide her escort to the pool house.

§

As they assembled in the spacious indoor pool area, exotic plants lit with Christmas lights gave a dim glow to the room, a flicker of diamonds across the water. Jacob looked around the perimeter of the pool house, taking in the various expressions of those anticipating the surprise.

Lyssa knelt at Kane's side. "Do you remember a few weeks ago, when we were decorating the tree and you said you wanted to meet an angel?"

Her son nodded, his blue eyes lighting up with anticipation. Lyssa put a hand on his shoulder and pointed toward the pool. "Then watch very closely."

Across the pool from all of them, Alexis presented her back to Dante. He slid the zipper down on her dress and untied her sash, holding the cloth in place an extra moment to dip his head and kiss her throat before he let it whisper off her naked body. While nudity was not an issue for vampires or angels, there was a pristine beauty to her, to the moment, that made it more like unveiling a breathtaking creation than a sexual experience. Still, Jacob saw Ingram holding his hands over John's eyes until she entered the water. But he took them away as he realized John might miss her startling transformation.

As she stepped gracefully into the water, golden patterns began to appear on her skin, an intricate tattoo scrolling over the flesh of her upper arms and back, her breasts and abdomen. They gleamed, reflecting the Christmas lights.

Her body shifted, shimmered. Kane drew in a breath—

actually most of the adults did as well— as her wings emerged from her back. The feathers were a pale gold color, ruffling a little from the transition. As the wings arched over her shoulders, she extended them fully. She was still moving into the water, had reached the bottom of the steps. When she made a lithe, twisting movement, it was obvious she was no longer being supported by her legs. A moment later, there were gasps as her tail, the red and gold scales gleaming, undulated in a graceful arc.

"She's a merangel," Lyssa said to her son. With their enhanced hearing and the echoing acoustics, every vampire and servant heard her. "Half mermaid and half angel. She can soar in the sky or swim in the deepest part of the ocean."

Kane was mesmerized, but again, Jacob couldn't say the adults were much different. Alexis used the propulsion of her tail and the extension of her wings to lift her body out of the water, drops sluicing off her skin and scales in a glittering display. Kane clung to Jacob's hand and Lyssa's skirt.

As amazing a display as it was, it was Gideon who caught Jacob's eye. Perhaps because of his earlier thoughts, his worries of what might have happened to Gideon, how close he'd come to losing him, seeing him this year had special meaning to Jacob. Sharing this made him want to look toward his brother and see how he was reacting to it. He wasn't disappointed.

Due to the possibility of Anwyn having violent seizures in moments of uncertainty, emotional excitement or transition, Daegan and Gideon would often flank her in obvious reassurance. Jacob had noted it in the way Daegan had stood behind her chair in the living room as they opened gifts, Gideon lounging against the side of her chair on the floor, his hand on her knee. But other times, like with the jacket, there was a different dynamic. Jacob saw that adjustment now.

Christmas held a lot of not-so-pleasant memories for Gideon. He'd spent plenty of them, in places far from the Christmas spirit. As his brother watched the merangel swim, Jacob saw quiet pain war with amazement on his face. Perhaps how wonderful this moment was contrasted too sharply with the desolate past. But Daegan stood at his back, hand on his shoulder, body pressed up against Gideon's, while Anwyn stood in front, her hands clasped over Gideon's on her waist, her head back against his shoulder. As Jacob watched, she turned her lips to his throat. Comforting him, reminding him he was here with them now, belonging to them. Daegan's head bent, lips nuzzling the other side of Gideon's neck while Anwyn reached up to caress their servant's jaw, linking them.

Looking over, Jacob saw Mason had Farida in one arm, Jessica inside the circle of his other one as she pressed against his side. Her lovely gray eyes were delighted and awestruck, an almost matching expression on their daughter's face. Even Mason looked more relaxed than Jacob had seen him since Dante had arrived, but perhaps it was because Dante was in their field of vision as much as Alexis. From the expression on his face, the unpredictable Dark Spawn vampire was absorbed in Alexis in a way every male in the room understood. She was everything to him, and he was enthralled, possessive and possessed, all at once. The same way Mason, Dev, Jacob, Gideon and Daegan felt about their females.

Your female, Jacob?

He gazed down into his lady's beloved face with warmth. *I could lie and pretend I didn't feel such a sense of possession toward you, my lady, but it's too blatantly written all over me. Possess, cherish, worship, adore...love. He loves her. He may not even understand fully what that is yet, but it's clear to all of us that's what he feels. The right woman tends to bring that out in us.*

"So does Christmas," she whispered.

Kane moved toward the pool now, though he brought his parents with him, as if they were his security blanket before this exotic creature. "Lift," he told Alexis. The word was a timid request this time, not an imperious order.

When Alexis moved toward the pool edge, reaching for him, her smile dispelled any trepidation he might have. It spread an angel's warmth and magic to every corner of the room, her special gift of empathy easing every heart.

Ingram crossed himself, a look of reverence on his face. Kane stepped forward, letting go of his parents. Lyssa let her hand linger on his head before Alexis lifted him, settled him on her hip.

It was a warmish night in Atlanta, so the roof of the pool house had been opened. It would allow Alexis to float into the sky above the building. But Kane wanted something else. As she began to ascend, he pointed at Farida, who'd become very animated, waving her arms fiercely.

"Lift her," he instructed.

As Alexis moved to comply, her golden wings lifting her above the waterline, Mason met the merangel's gaze. Jessica put her hand protectively on the baby. Lyssa spoke in his mind.

No harm will come to her Mason. Farida is safer with her than the most powerful vampire in the room. I promise.

Mason must have given the thought to Jessica, because he brushed a kiss over her brown hair before lifting the baby toward Alexis, using his greater height so the merangel didn't have to let her curved tail touch the concrete. Despite his reassurance, Jessica held onto the little booted feet an extra moment, a touch much like Lyssa's lingering hold on Kane, before she let her go. Alexis gave the concerned parents a smile, an extra push of that warmth to ease their worries, before she straightened.

Her wings rippled, flexing as she rose, taking the children up above the roof line. From that vantage point, Kane would see the Christmas decorations illuminating the yard all around the house. Farida didn't cry or fuss, but cooed in delight. Kane's hand latched onto Alexis's long hair with one hand, Farida's fingers in the others.

Lyssa reached into the bodice of her green dress, pulling out a small vial of silver liquid she'd stored there. Her half-sister's gift, a wary token of affection and Christmas wishes from the Fae Queen. Now Lyssa opened the vial, pouring the precious several silver drops in her hand. As they fused to her palm, she lifted it to the sky, calling up her own Fae blood to merge with her sister's magic to achieve the results she desired.

The assembled had their eyes on the merangel and the children, so what happened next was a complete surprise. They let out a collective sound of delight as snow began to fall from the sky above Alexis. The snowflakes glittered like diamonds, the blue and silver arcs around the large flakes making them look like thousands of tiny ice fairies.

John, standing next to Ingram, had eyes the size of saucers. Alexis would undoubtedly take him up next, for Kane would command it so. He included the other boy in everything.

The exercise of the Fae magic took very little effort on Lyssa's part, enough that she heard Jacob's response to her thought. *That might be so, but tonight Kane offered the gift to Farida first, my lady. Your son already recognizes the benefits of impressing a female.*

So it would seem. We will have to remind Kane to be understanding about that when John gets his first girlfriend.

At length, before Mason and Jessica could get too anxious, Alexis slowly floated back down. She immersed her tail in the pool up to where her upper thighs would be, so she was high enough to keep the children from getting wet. As she brought them to the edge, Kane wouldn't let go. He was stating his second favorite word in his repertoire.

"Keep." He was still holding fast to Alexis's hair and Farida's hand, and showed no inclination to release them.

Usually Jacob handled any pending tantrums, but this time Lyssa moved forward. Kneeling at the pool edge, she took her son's hands away from both females, squeezing them gently. "No," she said, meeting his stubborn gaze. "That's what's so special about Christmas. We have to let it go. So it can come back again."

Kane considered this. Full understanding wasn't there, but he rarely disobeyed either his mother or father when he recognized the tone that said he needed to comply. He let his mother lift him out of Alexis's arms and then, with a quiet noise, he switched his grip to Lyssa's dark tresses, burying his face in her neck. Lyssa tightened her grip on him, holding him close as Mason came forward to take Farida. Alexis caressed both children, nodding to Mason and Lyssa. "Blessings on them, now and always," she said. "And on all those who care for and protect them."

She took John next, just as Lyssa had anticipated, yet before Kane had to tell the merangel to do so. When Alexis brought the older boy back down, dazzled and blushing, she kissed him on the forehead, gave him a blessing as well. She included his grandfather in that, reaching out to grip Ingram's hand. The majordomo held it briefly in both of his, dipping his head to her.

Nodding to Lyssa, confirming she'd fulfilled the queen's wish, Alexis turned. She slowly descended into the water until it was obvious her tail had vanished and she was walking on human legs. As she moved across the pool, Dante was ready with a towel for her. When she came back up the steps to him, her wings vanished, leaving a brief scattering of feathers that disappeared in a sparkle of dust. Dante wrapped the towel around her. Lyssa saw that dispassionate expression slip as Alexis put a hand on his face and lifted up onto her toes to kiss him. Her soft, "I love you," only enhanced the warm energy encompassing all of them.

At Lyssa's gentle prodding, Ingram recovered enough to go to the wet bar, break out the champagne she'd directed him to have there. As he and John distributed the glasses, Lyssa made sure he took one for himself. The majordomo looked surprised, but she reinforced it in his mind.

You are a valued part of this family too, Mr. Ingram. Please join us in this.

The man nodded, putting his hand on John's shoulder as they all turned attentively to her.

Lyssa raised her glass, still holding Kane on her hip. Jacob saw the boy was starting to look sleepy, so many things happening in one night. Sliding his arm around Lyssa's waist, he bent over her to kiss his son. As he did, he felt Lyssa's fingers stroke through his hair. Then he straightened at her side.

"I told Kane we always have to let go of Christmas, so it will come again," she addressed the group. "But what we never have to relinquish is the love we feel for one another. The bonds of our family, which Christmas highlights for us and yet exists year round, a fixed star in the sky."

Jacob saw his lady's gaze touch every face present before she spoke again. "Thank you for sharing this night with us, and for giving me the gift of your presence here. Merry Christmas to you all, and may the blessings of this year follow us throughout the new year."

Here, here. Jacob's thought was echoed by the spoken responses of those present. Even Dante lifted his glass, emulating the others and Alexis, but it was to his merangel he turned when Lyssa spoke of blessings.

Jacob knew how the Dark Spawn felt. He bent his head again, meeting Lyssa's lips with his own. Their son's scent and heat pressed against them both, and he knew he could ask for no more than this moment. Love and family, however and wherever those bonds were formed.

It was the true magic of Christmas, and of every day he spent in the company of his vampire queen.

The Bet

A *vignette featuring Daegan, Anwyn and Gideon of* Vampire Mistress *and* Vampire Trinity.

Originally posted in serial format, 7/23/2013

Background: *In* Bound by the Vampire Queen, *it was mentioned that Gideon and Daegan had a friendly bet in play. When Lyssa asked Anwyn to give her the details, Anwyn replied: "Gideon thinks you'll have to beat Lord Belizar to a bloody pulp to get him to listen to reason. Daegan thinks you'll have to stake him and start from scratch. If Gideon wins"—she glanced at Daegan, confirming he was fine revealing the nature of the agreement—"he wants Daegan to set aside his Master role for one night. Gideon wants to . . . take Daegan."*

Long and short, Gideon won the bet (small spoiler for those who haven't read BbtVQ, yes, but nothing big – you know we couldn't kill off grumpy Lord Belizar), so this vignette is the long awaited fulfillment of those terms.

Part 1

"Son of a *bitch*, that hurt. Last time I take a vacation with fucking vampires."

Gideon grimaced as Daegan eased him down onto the amber-swirled Mexican tile in the kitchen. Anwyn dropped her purse on the counter and came around it to kneel next to him, leveling a severe glance at them both. "What the hell happened? I go into a shoe store for twenty minutes, and you're picking a fight with vampire hunters. Why are you putting him down here, instead of on a bed?"

"It was more like an hour. And you've been freaking out about using Lyssa's summer house for our vacation ever since we got here." Gideon grunted. "If I bled on the sheets, I figured you'd have kittens."

"It's not her summer house," Daegan corrected. "Summer homes are usually in cooler climates than the Florida Keys."

"Summer house, Easter house, Kwanzaa house...whatever chip it is in the potato bag, you know she's got plenty more."

"So says the man who's never had a mortgage payment in his life." Anwyn shifted her gaze to Daegan. "I saw part of it in his mind, but it was cloudy." It had scared her half to death, feeling the punch just beneath her rib cage. She forced her voice to remain even, though she was sure both men could feel her churning reaction. *I will not have a seizure right now. I will not.*

She knew that was why Daegan and Gideon had both insisted on driving the thirty minutes back to the secluded cottage before dealing with any of this, or even answering her basic questions. Daegan had driven, and she'd sat in the back with Gideon, holding pressure on the wound until the blood finally stopped and the skin started to knit. While dealing with the pain, Gideon hadn't been in a position to talk, and Daegan's attention was split between them and monitoring whether or not they were being tracked. He'd taken a circuitous route back to Lyssa's place, making sure.

So all that was handled, and she was done being patient. She set her jaw and put her hand on Daegan's arm as he sat back on his heels. Despite his warning glance, her nails dug in enough to convey her irritation. Yes, he was pissed off, but so was she. "What happened?"

"We ran into a vampire hunter Gideon knew," Daegan responded. "And a handful of his companions."

"Sure. Make it all about the kind of friends I have, rather than the fact you're a bloodsucker," Gideon mumbled.

"Please shut up, before I decide to finish the job," Daegan said mildly. "Five men were sitting in the alley outside the back door of a Chinese restaurant. They were dressed like restaurant employees and apparently taking a smoking break. Gideon and I were about fifteen feet inside the alley entranceway, waiting for you. When one approached to talk to us, we assumed it wasn't anything untoward."

"Until he pulled the stake and lunged for you," Gideon pointed out.

"Which you intercepted. With your chest." Daegan's dark eyes glinted dangerously. "You acted on instinct. Foolish instinct, I might add. I could have pulled my blade and severed his head if you weren't in the way."

"Yeah, because that's subtle, chopping off heads in a shopping district at ten o'clock at night. Besides which, *that* was the instinct I was preventing." Gideon met his gaze. "I didn't know him well, which was why I didn't recognize him right off, but Patrick isn't a bad guy. Most hunters might be adrenaline junkies wanting to be the hero of a Lost Boys sequel, but once they're in the trenches and see what's happening, something different takes hold. Vampires have a right to live, I get it, but you can't blame a guy for acting against what hurts him or his. If I ever get jumped by a cow wanting to beat on my ass for all the burgers I've eaten, I'm not going to be casting stones."

Daegan bit back a sigh, but returned his attention to Anwyn. "The force of the blow knocked Gideon against me and we went down like bowling pins."

"You could make it sound a whole lot cooler than that."

"She'd see it in your mind regardless."

"Even so..."

Anwyn slid to her hip, putting her hand over where the blow had been struck. The residual blood had made the torn T-shirt damp. The stake had gone in beneath the rib cage and pierced major organs. A mortal wound--if he'd been mortal.

"It's the splinters that piss you off." Gideon's lopsided smile, the close way he watched her, told her that she had her mind open to him, which still happened when she was agitated and forgot to shield herself. It was always a conscious effort for her, unlike other vampires for which a shut mind was the automatic default. "The skin heals up and sucks them in. It takes a couple weeks for them to work their way out, and they'll itch like crap until then."

"Watch over him." Daegan touched the top of her hand. *I'm going outside to get a better sense of whether or not we need to relocate.*

"They won't be coming after us," Gideon said, proving he could sometimes read the male vampire, even when Daegan was closed off to him. But then they were both hunters, weren't they? Their minds often followed the same track. Even now, both of them were focused on protecting her, not themselves, despite how much she wanted to personally rip apart who'd ever done this to her servant.

"Daegan had a hard-on to grab that prize for himself."

"Stop doing that," she snapped. "I mean it."

Gideon's attention shifted to her immediately, as did Daegan's, and she fought the desire to scream. "I am not about to have an attack. Unless the overwhelming urge to murder both of you counts. Just...I went to look at shoes. It's..."

She still wasn't used to it. Yet it was second nature to them, this constant vigilance against the possibility of assault, death. How many decades would it take her to figure out how to enjoy something as mindless as shoe shopping *and* remain hypervigilant, *and* still consider it a fun time?

Daegan's hands settled on her shoulders. As she shrugged him off irritably, she could sense him and Gideon exchanging a look. When she was in this mood, often Daegan would step back and let Gideon take the lead, since Gideon had the more empathetic perspective. But this situation wasn't supposed to be about her. She hated that it always came back to her, her state of mind, her reactions.

Daegan squatted behind her, slid an arm across her chest so his forearm rested over her breasts as he gripped her upper arm. His heat and overwhelming power cloaked her as Gideon's hand moved to rest on her knee, fingers gripping her thigh.

We're all right, cher. All of us. You are always our focus, because you are our center. Our goddess, our female.

She closed her eyes, feeling the flood of their emotions. They meant it. They weren't trying to reassure her, and that helped. It was all about that synergy they had as a triangle, the thing that could bring balance, no matter how fucked up all the rest of it was. She'd learned to take her mind out of the equation in moments like that and let that connection bring things back in order. The insidious whispers in the corners of her mind died back like the wind, leaving only the hum of her connection with them.

"If you say I complete you, I will skewer you both with kitchen knives," she said.

Gideon's fingers tightened on her leg and she opened her eyes. "I wouldn't have said 'our female,'" he said helpfully. "I'm much more progressive than that. I would have said 'our independent and self-sufficient member of the opposite but entirely equal sex.'"

"I really will stab you," she said darkly. "And I won't be sorry. We need to get that shirt off of you. Get you cleaned up."

"Give me a little time, and I can do that for myself. I don't need you to baby me, Mistress."

"If I want to baby you, you'll lie there and take it." She looked up at Daegan as he rose. "Do you think they'll come here to finish the job?"

"No. Going out to check is merely a precaution. I left them feeling sufficiently grateful to have their lives." Daegan's gaze shifted to Gideon. "I wouldn't have killed him, Gideon. I saw all of what you felt about Patrick and the others in your mind."

"You say that *now*. I felt your reaction when that stake went in. You were going to go all *Kill Bill Volume 2* on them, right there. Wrath of God stuff. He left them basically pissing themselves from the look on his face alone."

"I would not have killed them. If time had allowed it, I would have hurt them severely, merely for hurting you. You might consider that next time you step in front of an attack meant for me."

Nothing shut Gideon down like that kind of declaration. Noting their servant's flustered look softened her considerably, in a way his teasing and even Daegan's reassurances had not.

Daegan touched her cheek and rose. "I'll be back shortly."

She expected his desire to step outside was as much about a need to take a mental breath himself as it was to extend the reach of his senses even further without distraction. After all, he'd been standing within a stride of Gideon when the stake went in. For all the progress Gideon had made, there were times he still didn't realize his value to them. Or perhaps he did. There was something odd in his gaze as he watched Daegan take his leave of them. The other vampire noted it too, because the two males' eyes held an extra beat before Daegan pivoted and left the kitchen.

Gideon began to sit up, but she put a hand on his chest, holding him in place. "Stay there. I'm going to get you a fresh shirt, then I'll clean you up."

"Anwyn, the wound's already closed. I'm sure I can get up and handle it at the kitchen sink."

"If you get up while I'm gone, I'll put you back down on the ground. And you know you hate it when a girl does that."

His midnight blue gaze narrowed on her. "Think you're a badass, do you?"

"You know I am." She let her lips quirk, inciting a faint smile from him as he settled himself back on his elbows. He did reach up and slide his knuckles along her jaw, though. She sighed. "Sometimes I really do have the urge to stake both of you."

"Good thing we rock your world daily with awesome sex. Else you might not resist the homicidal urge."

"Hmm. You'd both best keep that in mind."

She rose with another warning look—*stay*—that caused him to "woof" and give her a look more in keeping with his usual smartass demeanor. But she could feel everything he felt and knew he was still in pain, that the wound had taken a great deal out of him. She didn't waste time finding him a clean shirt and a pair of jeans worn down to a soft fade. When she returned, she saw he'd lain back down fully on the tile. He might claim it was in deference to her desires, but she knew it was more than that. Out of their sight, he'd let himself give into it. The strain of the injury showed in his tense countenance. As she returned, he masked it and pushed himself back up onto his elbows again.

She put an arm around his back to help him sit up, and then nudged him to lift his arms so she could pull off the T-shirt. The stretch hurt him, and she bit back her reaction, keeping her face carefully expressionless, giving him his pride. But the towel had been soaked by the time the bleeding stopped in the car. The gouged wound was knitting too slowly. That, as well as his paleness under a day's worth of stubble, told her the truth of it. Their servant needed blood.

She wet a cloth from the kitchen sink and cleaned him up, pushing away his hands and protest about her tending to him. She wanted to get him onto the sofa as soon as possible. He'd be more comfortable there. She wiped away the blood on his firm flesh, her thumb following the track of the terry cloth over muscle and skin, feeling his quiver as she hit both tender and ticklish spots. It didn't matter how tough he was—as a vampire, she had an enhanced understanding of the uncertainty of life, and knew just how fragile even the most invincible male was.

She changed her mind about having him don the fresh T-shirt. The wound needed the air, and she wanted the direct contact with his skin, to feel the blood coursing under her fingertips. She moved onto her heels and slid her arm around his waist. "Let's get you on your feet and take those jeans off. You have blood on them, too."

"I can take off my own pants."

"Shut up," she said. "Listen to your Mistress."

She tweaked that taut wire between them whenever needed, that tether of connection he no longer denied, though it didn't always rest comfortably with his image of himself. He relented, at least enough to lean against the counter once he was standing. He did slip the button and tug down the zipper himself, pushing the jeans off his hips. With the slimmest of openings, she knew he'd ignore her order and bend to take them off, but she'd already anticipated that. Stepping in close, she put her fingers on the hard ridges of his lower abdomen, holding him there with a severe look as she squatted. Yes, he could deny that aspect of their relationship when he wasn't comfortable with it, but his discomfort now was from his intuitive sense that it was improper for his Mistress to be kneeling before him. His reaction only increased her own sense of possessiveness toward him, tightening the connection further.

After she removed the jeans, she indulged herself with a brief appraisal. She liked him covered only by the snug boxers that etched out the taut line of his buttocks, the curve of cock and testicles. Even at rest, his genitals presented an intriguing-sized package, nested under stretched cotton. When she'd first met him, he'd often worn saggy and loose cotton boxer shorts. She'd quickly compelled him to wear this style, which was far more pleasing—and revealing—to her gaze. He'd sworn if she ever made him wear a Speedo at a public pool, he'd leave her in an instant.

When push came to shove, she knew he wouldn't deny her, even if he turned twelve shades of rosy at being so exposed. However, she wouldn't be testing that challenge anytime soon. She wasn't always willing to have other women get such an intimate glimpse at what was hers. Not too long ago, she'd had to quell a killing urge when Lady Lyssa had taken his blood, though it had been a vital necessity for the queen's own health. Only Daegan's proximity had kept her from committing suicide-by-attack-of-the-queen.

Straightening so she stood in front of him, she slid a hand beneath her hair at the nape. She gathered the thick strands and slid them over her right shoulder, baring the left side of her throat. She could have given him her wrist, but she wanted his mouth in a more intimate place, a place that would allow her to put her arms around him and feel his heart beating against her chest.

His midnight blue gaze tracked the movement. Now he lifted his own hand, threading his fingers through her long tresses on the right side as she came closer. When he bent his head, she tilted her chin, closing her eyes as he teased her throat with his lips. He had the faint aroma of hops on his breath from his after dinner beer. She inhaled the soap he used and the overlay of sweat from the fight. As well as blood from his injury.

She could never get enough of what that mouth could do. As he traced her carotid with his tongue, she put her hand against his neck, sketching the brand she and Daegan had put there, a permanent collar in his flesh, matched by the same type of banding on his wrists. The branded cuffs bore the initials of the two vampires who owned him, the brand around his throat displaying a replica of the three teardrop third mark on his chest. She never tired of touching any of them, proof that he belonged to them entirely.

He gave her the edge of his teeth but not the bite, that piercing of her flesh that was as pleasurable as the coiling anticipation of an orgasm. Instead, he pressed his mouth to the delicate architecture of her throat. She felt like he was aware of every vein coursing with blood, every tingle in her skin, how to accelerate the former and intensify the latter. When he drew back, his hand on her waist, thumb idly caressing her hip bone, his dark blue eyes weren't so idle.

"Not tonight," he said. "Tonight I take from him."

He had taken blood from Daegan before, but the pointed emphasis of the words told her their servant meant something entirely different. "I want to take his blood the way he takes it from me," he added.

Though Gideon wasn't an articulate speaker, his mind could be a poet laureate, the way the thoughts and feelings meshed. She saw that he wanted to experience that sense of surrender...from Daegan. Gideon already understood it was a far more conscious and unnatural choice for his Master, but that would make the power of that surrender even sweeter, wouldn't it?

"I'm taking blood from him. And not just blood. It's time, Anwyn."

"Gideon." In their unique triad, they both knew Daegan was the alpha leader, but that didn't mean that Gideon ever stayed to heel for long. For that matter, neither did she.

When the men in her life went into testosterone overload, she didn't hesitate to exercise her own alpha tendencies and bite back. They really were a rather unique triangle, though it seemed to work for them. Mostly.

"I know what that tone means." Gideon tilted his head. "But I won the bet, quite a while ago. I'm not the patient one of this group, you know."

On the contrary, he was very patient. It was what had made him a deadly vampire hunter--one of the most successful in the history of such employment. Against opponents that outmatched him significantly in strength and speed, he watched and waited, and determined the key time to strike...and win. This wasn't a randomly chosen moment, though the precipitating event might have been.

Their vacation had been on the calendar for a while. A planned two weeks away from Club Atlantis for her, two weeks during which Daegan had made it clear he wouldn't be available for any Council assignments, even if the survival of vampire kind hung in the balance. Translation: he would not be available to Council's capricious wishes.

Lyssa had offered Daegan the use of her secluded cottage in the Keys. Surrounded by lush maritime forest, the cottage had an open air design reminiscent of Hawaiian retreats. Guests could walk out of the spacious living area with its big flat screen TV and fully equipped kitchen onto a screened porch almost as big as the whole interior. The porch included a hot tub, small indoor pool and comfortable sitting area. But in the back wing of the cottage was another attractive amenity, tailored specifically to the recreational interests of Lyssa and her guests. A "play room" for visiting vampires and their servants.

The whole set up was perfect. Away from friends or interruptions, the three of them could immerse themselves in each other. With hours of blissful solitude stretching before them every night, they could explore one another to their hearts' content, the peaks of pleasure as well as soul deep wells of need. They'd done a little bit of that since they'd arrived a few days ago, but not enough. It would never be enough.

Yes, their hunter had chosen his moment. He'd probably

been planning it for some time, concealing the bulk of the strategy in his mind that way that many servants learned, carefully keeping such thoughts out of the forefront of his mind when he was with the two of them. Now Patrick had given him leverage. That dangerous look on Daegan's face, how he'd gone out to take a breath as much as to check their security, underscored it. A wooden stake couldn't kill their third mark servant, but Daegan knew as well as she did that it wouldn't have mattered to Gideon if it could.

All three of them were protective, territorial, and nothing roused those instincts, and all the emotions attached to them, like an attack on one of them. Her own bloodlust was still too close to the surface, such that with very little thought she'd be back in the car, going to seek out Patrick and his ilk to make them suffer for raising a hand against her boys. No matter how amused the two males would be at being characterized that way, it was how she thought about it.

So the pot was stirred and, typical for Gideon, rather than letting it settle and simmer, he wanted to take it to a full boil. When she tuned back into him, she found he was regarding her steadily. "You have my back?" he asked.

She blinked and stroked a finger over the rough stubble along his jaw. "You need a shave," she said softly. "Yes, Gideon. I have your back. Always. In this, and everything else."

His reaction was gratifying to female senses. Despite the recent injury, the hunter in him came to the forefront, shifting his expression, his body language. It caused a similar shift in her own. The Mistress in her pushed away the rest. "Tread carefully, love," she murmured. "You're not cornering a housecat."

"Why do you think I asked you for backup?" He gave her his trademark cocky grin and they held that amused, conspiratorial look as they heard Daegan re-enter the house.

"Nothing," the vampire confirmed, coming into the kitchen. "We'll feel it if anyone approaches, but I think it highly unlikely our location has been compromised."

"Yep," Gideon agreed. "Means we can get on with our

night." He pulled on the jeans she'd brought him. That exercise, as well as shifting away from the counter, standing on his own, took an effort. Anwyn had to quell the impulse to move to his side and support him.

From the concern that creased Daegan's brow, it was apparent the male vampire hadn't been tuning into their conversation. "Why haven't you given him blood?" he asked Anwyn, an edge to his voice.

"Because he insists on taking it from you." She met his gaze. "Among other things."

That changed Daegan's focus. Anwyn was sure he was dipping into their minds, trying to figure out what was going on. It only took him a blink, and she saw myriad expressions cross his face, most of them hard to fathom. It would rouse his warrior's instinct, but there were other considerations here. Ones that would have him holding his tongue, waiting to see how Gideon would play this.

Their servant turned away from them to slide open the drawer under the sink, a place neither of them would have been likely to look since Gideon usually handled dishes. A clank of metal, and he removed a pair of beaten steel cuffs from it, the cuffs connected by three chain links.

He let the cuffs dangle from one finger draped by the links. "Something Lyssa had in her private stock. They can stand up to some resistance. Like if you get hot and bothered and start pulling against them without thinking about it. A normal vampire can break them, but not as easily as the run-of-the-mill ones."

Anwyn imagined it, those cuffs holding Daegan as he became intensely aroused. The flutter in her belly was acknowledged by the surge of anticipation in Gideon's mind. He knew how to get her fully on board with this, teasing the Mistress in her with the possibilities.

His focus remained on Daegan, however. "It's time, vampire. I won the bet. You going to be a pussy and renege?"

Daegan had become far more still. "You have to get the cuffs on me."

"No, I don't." Gideon tilted his head toward Anwyn. "She'll be doing it. You can stop her, but she'll fight you, which means you'll have to get a little rough, throw a few punches. A good right hook would probably take her down."

Daegan's eyes narrowed. "You know I would never strike Anwyn."

"An issue he doesn't have with me *at all*," Gideon noted wryly, shooting a glance at Anwyn. "Hence why she's handling the cuffs."

She couldn't help the twitch of her lips, but things were coiling up inside of her, watching, waiting. Gauging the tension in the room.

"Those won't hold me."

"No. Nothing short of a fucking Fort Knox vault would. They're just a reminder. To help you honor the terms of the bet." Gideon cocked his head, his midnight blue eyes showing fire. "Plus, having them on you so I can do what I want gets *me* hot and bothered."

The tips of Daegan's fangs showed. "How much harder will you be if you put them on me yourself, vampire hunter?"

"You're in my head. You already know the answer to that."

Daegan's eyes had gone darker, the whites disappearing. Following instinct, Anwyn shifted so she was behind Gideon. As she pressed against his bare back, her hands whispered over his chest and caressed the triple teardrop third mark, drawing Daegan's gaze to it while Gideon stood still under her touch. Her fingers dropped, sliding over the impressive musculature that layered Gideon's upper torso and the harrowing reminder of his mortality, the still healing wound. But she kept going, teasing the ridges of his abdomen.

Daegan's attention burned her knuckles when she molded her palm over Gideon's hip bone, her thumb briefly hooking in his jeans pocket while her other fingers traced the denim crease between thigh and groin. Letting go of the pocket, she followed the curve of a testicle and etched out his hardening length for the vampire's glittering gaze.

She slipped the button of his jeans, pushing beneath the hold of the denim to straighten his stiffening cock. Her body remained flush against his back, her mound rubbing against his ass.

When I asked if you'd have my back, I wasn't meaning it quite so literally.

She let her lips curve against his shoulder blade, but she rose onto her toes enough to look over his shoulder and meet Daegan's gaze. "He's already like iron, thinking about having you at his mercy."

Gideon lifted her questing hand and kissed it. It was different right now for the two of them as well. She was still his Mistress, but she was honoring the bet, not taking the lead, not making this any less than what it was supposed to be.

Daegan studied them. As Anwyn held her position against Gideon, she thought they both held their breath, two creatures bound as one as he deliberated.

With it being November, Daegan had been able to wear a light coat to cover his weaponry. He'd apparently removed those blades and firearms before he returned to Gideon and Anwyn in the kitchen, so that when he set aside the coat now they saw only the lean, muscled upper body in a fitted cotton shirt, tucked into belted jeans. With a long look at both of them, he pivoted. The move reminded her of when he practiced with his katana, the graceful flow of motion that was purposed for dispensing terminal justice in the Council's name. Now he made the move for an entirely different reason, though the impact might be no less life changing for those within range of it.

When he had his back to them, he lifted his arms.

Anwyn could feel Gideon's gaze tracking that arc of movement. His held breath, the sudden tension as Daegan laced his fingers...and put them behind his neck.

"Fuck," Gideon muttered. His shock mirrored her own. She was sure Gideon had anticipated Daegan honoring the terms of the bet, because when it came down to it, he knew what kind of male the vampire was. And he'd even done some extensive planning for this, if the cuffs were a hint of what was to come. However, like her, he hadn't given thought to the impact when they reached this vital fork in the road.

The moment when their alpha dog would permit himself to be leashed.

Part 2

Proving Anwyn's warning, that every step of this would be a delicate balance, Daegan tilted his head so Gideon saw a hint of his devastating profile. "Put the cuffs on me yourself, vampire hunter. It's your right."

The reality of it was...well, Gideon had to take a calming breath. Ball was in his court, right? As he stood there looking at Daegan, he was aware of Anwyn's quiet, thoughtful presence. She understood, didn't she? What it felt like, knowing this gift was all his to unwrap, to taste, to torment. Yeah, he'd planned and plotted, worked at keeping his mind blank on it when Daegan was paying attention, but until this second, he hadn't revealed the keenness of his hunger, even to himself.

How many times had he come into Daegan's room to shoot the shit, talk cable programming, or analyze strategies against whoever Daegan's upcoming target was? Even if Gideon wasn't going along with him, they'd talk it out together. At first Gideon thought Daegan was just humoring him, but that was fine. He wouldn't let pride stand in the way of making sure the vampire had all the benefit of his experience in creeping up on bad guys and taking them out.

Over time, from the give and take of their conversations, he'd realized that Daegan *was* listening, sometimes even altering his plans based on Gideon's input. And didn't that make him feel like a fucking grade school kid handed an A, for Christ's sake?

But there were other things that happened in Daegan's room that didn't make him feel like a kid at all. When Daegan turned away to pick up a brush or slap on aftershave, Gideon's gaze would linger on the broad shoulders—well, broader than one would expect, given his lean frame—and drift down to study how his ass was defined by the shift of his body as Daegan tucked in a shirt, fastened his jeans. As provocative as that was, even the tilt of Daegan's head as he listened to Gideon, often with that light smile playing around his serious mouth, was enough to make Gideon want to crowd him up against the wall, start a fight that would become physical fast in a far different way.

Christ, he loved the guy like he was a girl doing the he-loves-me, he-loves-me-not thing with the flower, only there was nothing girly about this hunger. It was raw, the whole-wolf-pack-waiting-to-tear-into-a-fresh-kill, taste-the-heart-while-still-beating, kind of appetite. Though his feelings toward Anwyn were no less intense, there was a wholly different feel to it. Maybe because he and Daegan were both far more protective of her, their sexual instincts never brushed as close toward violence as they did when nothing stood between the two males. Anwyn acknowledged it at times like this, in the way she stood behind Gideon, leaving the field of battle clear.

Gideon wasn't sure if he'd ever wanted something so much that had been held out of reach, but within touching distance, for so long. As the power of that thought filled him, Anwyn's hand settled between his shoulder blades, her wicked long nails scraping his bare back.

He's yours, Gideon. For tonight, he's yours. Care for him as he cares for you. She slid her fingers over to Gideon's arm, followed it down, and pressed the cuffs into his hand, the cold metal.

They weren't something he'd used very often. When he hunted, capture wasn't his first intent. As he clasped the bracelets, his glance strayed down to the branded cuff on his own wrist. It was the one that had the "D" initial on it.

Anwyn wasn't done with him yet. Her other hand had slipped to his waist, over his hip bone, and her fingers slid into his jeans watch pocket, leaving the key to the cuffs there, but taking full advantage of the act to push deeper into the main pocket and tease his inner thigh, the crease against his testicles, before she withdrew, stepping back from him again.

He gave her a half-amused, half-aroused look she returned with a heated look of her own. Yeah, she was getting into this. It only added to the tension.

Moving away from her one step, two steps, he took up position directly behind Daegan. He was one of only two people Daegan trusted behind him. The first time he'd realized that, it had meant more to Gideon than he'd expected. Even if he had to take it with a grain of salt, since Daegan didn't need his eyes to be fully cognizant of his surroundings. Hell, Daegan could fight blind and take out Obi-Wan and Yoda in one stroke.

You have yet to show me Star Wars.

You're too much like Darth Vader. Don't want you getting ideas about having your own theme music and a black cape. You already dress in black more often than Johnny Cash.

"I did agree to a blue shirt," the vampire said. "The one Anwyn bought for me. As well as this charcoal gray one."

"You're a regular fashion rainbow. And I have news for you. Charcoal gray is just another version of black."

"This from the male who shivers in T-shirts in the middle of winter because he refuses to wear anything else."

It was peculiar to have an exchange this way, Daegan facing forward, hands still clasped at the base of his skull, Gideon right behind him, the cool cuffs biting into his hand because he was holding them way too tight.

He'd tell the vampire to shut up, but even in this scenario, there were things he didn't push at Daegan about. Well, not as much. Whether he admitted it or not, there was a certain level of deference and respect he gave him. His Master.

Instead, he closed his hand over Daegan's right wrist and locked the bracelet around it. The click was loud in the silence. He brought the one arm down, then the other to secure the left so Daegan's knuckles rested against his superior ass. Gideon closed his hand over the chain connecting the cuffs, fingertips brushing the outside of Daegan's thumbs. And damn if the vampire didn't move one of them so it briefly curled over Gideon's knuckles. Daegan might be the cuffed one, but Gideon knew the male's touch could make him helpless. If Daegan commanded him to stay in place until he reversed their positions, Gideon the cuffed one, Daegan the one fully in

control...he would do it. Christ, who was he kidding here?
Now who's the pussy thinking about reneging? Daegan
thought at him.

Gideon's head came up sharply. "Too bad there's no way
to gag your mind," he retorted. But it helped him pull it
together. Putting his hand on the vampire's back, he gave
him a nudge. "I want you in the back room."

The cottage's back room was like one of Club Atlantis's
well-equipped public playrooms, only the craftsmanship of
Lyssa's equipment reflected private ownership use. It was
custom work and designed to accommodate the strength of
third mark servants. As they moved into the chamber,
Gideon inhaled the scent of a lot of glossy wood and well-
oiled devices. All the metal pieces put off a soft gleam, like
prepared blades. Being that it was a vampire's playroom,
there were actually a few of those mounted on a board
flanked by velvet curtains that could be dropped to conceal
them for aesthetic effect. Or drawn back, as now, for
titillating response.

The ceiling had spaced horizontal beams sturdy enough
to grace the belly of a galleon. Even if a coastal hurricane
took down the rest of the house, this room would still
stand. Wouldn't that be great footage for a catastrophe-
loving film crew? He had a flash from the movie *Twister*,
the two main characters running from a tornado and taking
temporary refuge in a barn which they discovered had all
sorts of scythes and wicked, sharp-bladed farm
implements. Bill Paxton declaring "I don't think so" and
Helen Hunt wailing "Who *are* these people?!"

He heard the chuckle in his mind from Anwyn, and
imagined innocent civilians stumbling on Lyssa's torture
chamber. They'd probably have a similar reaction, tornado
or no tornado. But it was all in the eye of the beholder. The
three of them looked at a room like this and saw something
most people didn't. And tonight, Gideon saw it from the
other side of the coin, the Dom's view.

The beams were polished, the multiple embedded eye
bolts and hooks providing a wealth of possibilities to
anyone with the desire to suspend someone like a fly in a
web. It wasn't his intent tonight, but the set up suited his

purposes. He stopped Daegan beneath one such beam.

Gideon knew where he wanted to go, what he wanted to do, what he planned to do, but he kept his mind away from all of that with the discipline that came from diligent practice. Daegan and Anwyn had both taught him certain types of anxiety, caused by the unknown, could make the experience even more intense.

You want me out of your mind, vampire hunter?

His kneejerk reaction to the question was such a strong negative, it translated to a tightened fist over his hold on the chain between the cuffs, as well as another wave of that lightheadedness. Fuck, he still hadn't fed. Why was it so hard to say exactly what he wanted with Daegan? Or Anwyn.

You are a creature of feeling, love. Not words. You feel so much, words are a foreign language to you. Anwyn had taken a position leaning against the wall, hands folded behind her hips as she watched them, blue-green eyes glittering in the dim light thrown by the wall sconces. *You want him out of your mind for the next little while. Not out of your heart and soul.*

He'd have no luck getting me out of there anyway.

Hearing that touch of arrogance in Daegan's response helped. Gideon ignored the fact he might have done it deliberately. Best not to dwell on how well they both knew him. At one time he would have called it manipulation and thought of it in a negative way. But now he knew it wasn't like that. Any more than a parent telling a kid he'd always be there for him, even if in reality it didn't always work out that way.

He made himself let Daegan go, shifting in front of him so he could meet him eye to eye. "Yeah. What she said. Get out of my head. Don't want you spoiling the surprise."

"I'm not overly fond of surprises," Daegan said.

"I'll file that under who gives a shit." Gideon glanced over his shoulder at Anwyn. "I'd like you to do the same. You'll get more out of it if there's a surprise factor as well."

At her arched brow, he shrugged. *I know you've looked forward to this, Mistress. You're already wet. We can both smell it.*

Her eyes became darker, like a deeper level of the ocean, reflecting all the depths within her. She inclined her head, but Gideon noted the way her gaze strayed past him to hold Daegan's. Then she broke that contact. Reaching up, she let down her thick waves of sable-colored hair, tossing it back on her shoulders as she slid out of her little short coat-wrap thing. It left her in her spaghetti strap halter and her snug, stressed jeans. Hot as hell as always, particularly since that thin tank didn't do anything to disguise the points of her nipples, pressed to the fabric.

He didn't know what that look between the vampires was about, but he was distracted by Daegan's withdrawal from his mind. Daegan could come and go there unnoticed, but he made a point of letting Gideon feel it now. Like someone leaving the room, but staying available on the other side of the door. Gideon figured that proximity must be the *in your heart and soul* part Anwyn had mentioned. Gideon couldn't deny he wanted Daegan there, always, and fortunately no one was asking him to acknowledge or deny it. Anwyn's withdrawal was more noticeable, though she'd gotten better at the stealth mode when she really focused.

Satisfied they weren't tracking his thoughts, Gideon moved behind Daegan, unlocked the cuffs. "Stay where you are."

Going to the supply cabinet, he withdrew a couple coils of half-inch nylon line. The rope was rough enough to hold a knot, but still silky enough to feel good against the skin. That had mattered. It was hard to explain why, but he'd noticed his vampires had the same compulsion. They weren't above using considerable levels of pain to tear away his control and leave only sensation, pleasure far above what he thought it possible for him to experience. But though they might be beating the hell out of him, they made sure the ways they bound him weren't pressing into bone or stressing his joints, despite the formidable tolerance he had as a third mark. They gave him only the right kinds of agony.

He wasn't sure he had any desire to hurt Daegan tonight, but they'd taught him lines could get blurred, lust crossing into bloodlust as easy as following the laws of gravity.

"Hands in front of you. Hold them together like a prayer fold, fingers pointed level toward me."

Those dark eyes watching him, made his flesh warm across his cheeks, but Daegan did it. With enough of a weighted pause that, when he finally complied, Gideon's dick hardened further. He ignored the cramping in his jeans, instead focusing on how those long fingers aligned, hands palm to palm. He looped the nylon around the vampire's wrists, a triple wrap, then knotted the line between them. He hooked Daegan's thumbs into the binding, another wrap, which immobilized the fingers that did most of the work when it came to getting free of restraints. Again, he had no doubt Daegan could still do it. The point was what being restrained like this could do to a guy's psyche.

Gideon tossed the two rope ends up over the beam. He caught Daegan's shoulder, a convenient prop to give himself an extra couple inches to snag the dangling lines as they came down on the other side. It underscored how casual a thing it had become to touch him. Tonight, when they'd wandered through a few stores with Anwyn, Gideon had noticed the two of them touched each other almost as much as they touched her. Daegan's body would brush his hip, his hand lingering on Gideon's back, a thumb resting on the skin side of Gideon's belt as the two men studied amusing T-shirt logos up on the wall.

They had taken him to a burger diner for dinner, Anwyn in the booth at his side, Daegan across from them both, but when Gideon stretched out his booted feet, he didn't question how comfortably his calf rested against Daegan's beneath the table. Anwyn slipped her feet out of her shoes and put a bare foot over Gideon's, so that he could feel the pressure of that light feminine weight through the leather. In her mind, he'd seen that she was teasing Daegan's ankle under the cuff of his jeans with the toes of her other foot. Their three-way connection made everything else in the world feel right, and knowing he wasn't alone in that feeling made it all the better.

Gideon brought himself back to the present as he pulled

the lines down, so that the two ends brushed the floor behind Daegan. "Raise your hands over your head," he instructed the vampire.

"You chose rope, not chain."

"Yeah. No need for overkill." But that wasn't why he'd chosen rope. He'd seen Daegan in chains. He never wanted to see that reality again, since it haunted his memories often enough.

Daegan might not be in his head, but for certain things, it wasn't needed. When he lifted his hands to comply with Gideon's directive, Daegan briefly hooked his fingers in Gideon's belt, a tacit acknowledgment. One that connected them to that memory, that understanding. "You worry too much about me, vampire hunter."

Gideon shrugged. "Rope is way more versatile than chain. Which makes it twice as effective, if you know what you're doing. There's a reason a spider web can hold something way bigger and stronger than it seems like it should be able to do."

Daegan gave him a look, but lifted his arms. The movement arched his upper body in an altogether distracting way. The vampire was sex in motion pretty much 24/7, clothed or unclothed. Gideon tried to conceal his reaction to it, then stopped himself, snagged by an intriguing realization. He didn't have to, did he?

He's yours tonight, Gideon. That's what Anwyn had said. They made no bones about ogling him like a hot rod pin up whenever they wanted. They considered him theirs to enjoy, however, whenever, they wanted. Which in turn made him hot as hell and kept his cock in a practically constant erect state. Would it have the same effect on Daegan, even if his makeup was a bit different than Gideon's in that regard? He was about to find out, because just that one motion, lifting his arms above his head, was revving Gideon's engines. Full horsepower. He was ready to slam down on the gas pedal, not hide a single damn thing about how he felt. He was the one in control.

But he'd use that control to both their advantage. Reining himself back with effort, he shifted behind Daegan. Gideon had studied Anwyn's rope tying books as well as reflecting on the techniques she'd used on him, diabolical twists and modifications that his being a more resilient third mark had allowed. He'd learned the knots in his spare time. When Daegan was off on his solo hunts, he'd tie up the practice dummy in the weapons room, learning how to do it smooth and fast, without hesitation.

Anwyn had also let him practice on Ella in the club public play room. Since she was a lush little thing, Gideon hadn't objected to having a live subject, despite Anwyn's amusement with, and planned retaliation for, the thoughts he couldn't control as he worked on aligning the ropes around her submissive staff member's very generous breasts. The petite submissive had enjoyed it all immensely, especially when James, Anwyn's head of security, lingered to watch after his shift was over.

When this day finally came, Gideon had wanted to be ready, so he'd even bitten the bullet and practiced on one of the male subs who had a similar build to Daegan. Though the man had been as aroused as Ella, Gideon had ignored that with stolid courtesy. He had no interest in getting it on with another guy except Daegan. While he still didn't understand that side of himself, he'd stopped questioning it.

He wouldn't say he'd remained completely detached, however. Thanks to Anwyn, he received more than additional rope tying skills from the session. She'd been very intrigued, watching male hands touching male flesh, and he'd reaped the benefits of that later in their private apartments.

Sometimes, he worked on the knots right in front of Daegan. When they were idle, watching sports or hanging out at night in one of the city spots, he'd have a bit of the rope in his pocket and he'd pull it out, work on the knots, counting out the fall measurements in his head, reminding himself of how much he'd need for what he wanted to do. When he felt Daegan's attention on him, he'd focus all his interest on the technique, not the application, but Daegan knew why he was doing it. Truth be told, it had been a sweet kind of foreplay. A couple times it had resulted in Daegan initiating some pretty rough sex, the vampire reinforcing who was in charge. They both knew that wasn't really what it was all about, though. Even if Gideon himself couldn't say why the terms of the bet had become so important to him.

He brought over a step ladder so he could pull the rope through the eyebolts, making the line taut enough that Daegan was a millimeter away from having to rise on the balls of his feet, his arms stretched even higher over his head. When Gideon dropped the tails of the rope, they brushed Daegan's shoulders. His still clad shoulders. Nope. That had to change.

Gideon came back to the floor and pulled out his knife. "Good thing it's not the blue shirt," he noted. Daegan had pulled the fitted charcoal gray shirt loose from his belt when he'd gone to check the perimeter. It was a very GQ look, and very irritating to someone wanting to eye his package, since the tails of the shirt hid it. Gideon wasn't in the mood to be imaginative about that. He was getting in the mood for one single thing at this point. Whatever he wanted.

"Do not—"

Gideon hooked the blade under the top button and sliced it off. Daegan gave him an aggrieved look.

"You could have just unbuttoned it."

"Yeah, my bad. And I nicked you. Clumsy of me." Gideon rubbed a thumb over the small wound, capturing the blood and bringing it to his mouth to taste. The sweetness made the room spin some. "I guess I should feed, since I'm going to need my Wheaties to give you a proper workout, right?"

With a twist of his wrist, he cut another button, made another shallow cut. To the three sets of enhanced senses in the room, blood was like the smell of popcorn, cotton candy and fried turkey legs at the fair, all rolled together in that irresistible call that made saliva pool and lips get licked.

Daegan eyed him with pupils that were expanding, darkness taking over dark. That, and the expanse of skin the now half-open shirt revealed, made him look even more tempting. Anwyn's desire for the vampire to keep his hair a little longer, so it fell over his brow and teased his neck, was a good look for him, Gideon had to admit. And Daegan was already way above ten in that department.

"You owe me a shirt," the vampire said.

"I have a Team Edward one on order. Bright orange. Another color for your eclectic wardrobe."

Daegan showed his fangs, and Gideon made the final buttons a rush job, slicing right down to the tails and letting the buttons hit the floor, bouncing and rolling away from them. Using the blade to nudge the shirt fully open, he studied the terrain of hard, warrior-trained muscle, the smooth layers over ribs, pecs and abdomen. Supposedly, vampires didn't ever get fat or flabby, but so many of them stayed in fighting shape, a survival requirement in the volatile vampire world, it was hard to say what a vampire couch potato would really look like. Definitely not like this. Daegan wasn't just in fighting shape. His body was sculpted for what he deemed its primary purpose—assassin, hunter—but to Gideon's eyes it had another purpose, and tonight it would serve his desires. The very thought...

Normally he resisted handling himself in front of Daegan unless ordered, but then he thought of how often Daegan would take himself in hand, stroke his own cock while studying Gideon's bound and contorted body. Wanting to touch his Master would become a howling need in Gideon's gut, just watching him do that.

The top button of his own jeans was still open from when Anwyn had touched him. He pushed his fingers down below the denim. As Daegan's gaze latched onto the movement, Gideon gave himself a nice squeeze and stroke, the vampire's features tightening as he did it again. God, was this how it felt to them, to see that fleeting savage hunger cross his face as it did Daegan's now? Perhaps there was even a different, more intense benefit to Gideon, standing in their shoes tonight, because he knew Daegan could make him pay for this later. Like how he'd fucked him after watching Gideon play with the rope, as if he knew part of it was a taunt from his servant. This was the mother of all invitations to reassert his claim in wicked, overwhelming ways that could make Gideon sore for a month afterward.

He was ready to take this to the next level. He wanted the damn shirt gone, nothing but skin covering Daegan's upper body. Shifting behind the vampire, he grasped the bottom hem to hold the fabric taut and sliced up the back with his blade. Though he'd claimed clumsiness, he showed his skill now, bisecting the cloth with one smooth stroke, then ripping it all the way up with a satisfying tear of cloth. Another two cuts at the sleeves, and he pulled the thing completely free, letting it flutter away to the ground. Picking up another coil of rope, he moved back to Daegan's front.

The vampire had stopped breathing, that particular stillness he did so well when he was hunting. Gideon slid a fingertip down his sternum, over the cut he'd made. It was already healing, but he dug his nail into it a little bit, experiencing what Anwyn felt when she used her far longer and sharper nails on some of the wounds she inflicted upon him. Often she'd soothe them with her tongue. Daegan drew in a breath at the slight pain, eyes flickering up to meet Gideon's.

"Yeah, keep breathing. Don't want you to turn blue and pass out on me. Want you conscious for every minute of this."

Daegan's gaze sparked. Gideon looped the line around his throat, eye to eye with the vampire for a tense, provocative moment before he turned his attention to creating the harness. The knots and diamonds, down the breastbone and upper abdomen, the loops around the waist and shoulders, were all elements that forced straight posture in an arms-down position. When the arms were stretched above the head, the design only exaggerated the arch to his body.

Gideon sensed Anwyn's interested study when he integrated a double twist loop around Daegan's throat, an X pattern he knotted at the back. He took the remaining fall of rope down, tying it off at the rope around Daegan's waist. It pulled Daegan's head back some, kept his back in that crescent shape unless he wanted to choke himself. It was a tie Gideon couldn't have done to a human without serious danger if that human started straining against the rope, causing pressure against the windpipe. However, in Daegan's case, it would be a reminder to keep his head still unless he wanted the choking sensation that could be unpleasant but not fatal to a vampire.

The line inside himself was pulled to near-breaking. Gideon circled Daegan slowly, gaze coursing over the arms, stretched up over his head, the wraps of rope binding his wrists and thumbs, his fingers curled in the knot between them. From personal experience, Gideon knew such a stretched position would turn his back into one plane of muscle and make his ass muscles tight. Now he saw it in Daegan's elongated, powerful body. Fuck, he wanted to be two people. One devouring Daegan like a ravenous animal, one standing back like a sadistic inquisitor, drawing out every powerful minute.

His attention slid back down Daegan's upper torso again, to the taper of waist and hip. With the shirt gone, he could see Daegan's reaction beneath the jeans, delineated further by the belt holding the jeans at his waist. Gideon wasn't the only one getting stirred up. And he was no longer going to deny himself the pleasure of checking out that response up close and personal.

Gideon shifted closer, putting his hand on the vampire's stiffening cock. The warning sound that came from Daegan at the aggressive move was violent music to Gideon's ears. Leaning forward, he covered the healing cut at Daegan's breastbone with his mouth, his fingers tightening over the guy's dick, as much of it as he could hold with the denim in the way. Daegan's cock jerked beneath his heated palm when Gideon used the tip of his tongue to tease that little bit of blood away.

He heard Anwyn step from the wall. She was out of his mind, but he wasn't out of hers. It was a tacit agreement, where he didn't pry too deep, but stayed in the surface layers so he could feel if one of her seizures was sneaking up on her. He'd felt her own hunger mounting, so even as she stepped forward, he anticipated her. He saw himself through her eyes as he turned his upper body toward her, just enough to show her one glittering eye beneath the strands of hair across his brow.

"He's mine right now, Mistress. You said so."

Crimson light flared in the blue-green irises, telling him the Dominant and vampire in her would only be pushed so far. Daegan had an even shorter fuse in that regard, which was why the terms of tonight's bet were such a sweet victory. Gideon wondered how much farther the guy's overdeveloped sense of honor would let it go. He hoped quite far, since for his own part, he was getting into the flow of it, the art of seductive challenge. "You'll get your turn," he said, low. "But he's mine first."

That sinful mouth curved in feral response. Acknowledgement, not necessarily concession. He was moving into the territory of being the only human in a room full of tigers, but the hunter in him liked the danger. Craved it.

Daegan let out a low snarl, a reaction to his challenge to Anwyn. That was all it took for the starving side to break loose. Maybe it was the blood hunger Gideon had right now, the need to restore strength. Or maybe it was knowing he could have it all, do it all, not just once, but over and over. Tonight, only he or the dawn would call it to an end.

He slid around behind Daegan, though he kept his hand anchored on the other male's response, squeezing and stroking it exactly because he could do any damn thing he wanted to it. Once he had Daegan completely stripped, he might just tie it up, too. It took a lot of painstaking knot work to completely encase a cock in a sheath of thin rope, especially a nice-sized dick like that. He'd have to handle Daegan's cock for quite some time, adjusting and stroking...

To keep his grip on the subject of his imaginings, he had to stay pretty close, which was no hardship. He put himself full up against Daegan's back and pressed his own sizeable response against Daegan's ass. Pushed hard. The beam creaked alarmingly, but Gideon knew his Master would exercise control. Control was everything in his life. Gideon looked forward to putting a dent in that, whatever consequences he paid for it. If Daegan broke the beam,

Gideon would tell Lyssa it was all the vampire's fault. That he was out on the beach, completely not there when it happened.

Gripping Daegan's jaw with his free hand, Gideon turned his head away from him. He rubbed his nose against the warm flesh of his neck, inhaling him, felt the thrum of tension through Daegan's muscles, the quiver in that fine, fine ass. Dropping the choke hold he had on his own restraint, Gideon sank his teeth into the side of the vampire's throat, like a wolf jumping a stag to take him down.

No hesitation. He knew the force needed to break through skin, and he doubled it, not holding back. He wanted Daegan to feel it all the way to the balls Gideon had firmly in his hand.

Human food would restore him, but too slow. He needed his Master's blood. If Daegan had been in his head, Gideon could well imagine the silky flow of his thoughts. *It's yours for the taking, Gideon.*

Tonight, it was all his for the taking.

Part 3

That first gush of blood brought more than one sensation. He'd waited too long to feed. However, as Gideon swayed, unable to stave off the dizziness, Anwyn moved. Pressing against his back, she stroked his sides, his hips. Her body, soft yet so strong, provided him support. When her hand covered his over Daegan's cock, he fanned out his fingers, giving her the opportunity to stroke him between those openings. It earned a quiet noise from Daegan, a tilt of his head, so it pressed briefly against the side of Gideon's.

That type of gesture could mess with Gideon's head, derail him, but he wouldn't think about the possibility of fucking this up. He'd planned his strategy, yes, but at a certain point during a hunt, instinct had to take over. The hunter could no longer think about failing or winning; else the prize would disappear. He just followed the flow of energy to its final conclusion.

Gideon curled his fingers over Anwyn's and removed their touch from that volatile area. He put her hand back on his hip, leaving both of his free so that he could curve one arm around Daegan's chest, hook his fingers into the rope crossed over his sternum as he drank that rich blood. Heated, filled with potent life. Gideon was all too aware how few had ever had the privilege of the willing gift of Daegan's blood. The number of people Daegan had allowed to tie him up had an even smaller membership. A club of one.

Gideon.

As the blood helped his world steady, Anwyn withdrew. She didn't say anything to him, but he felt her slip from the room. She would have her reasons, beyond powdering her nose or flossing her fangs. With that connection between their minds that was second nature to him now, making him a constant silent guardian in her head against the gremlins, he would know if she needed anything from him.

He licked at Daegan's throat. Along with the scent of the blood, he inhaled the aftershave Daegan used, the scents of the restaurant they'd visited tonight, the humid sea air that clung to his skin. Being a third mark came with some major perks. He'd never realized how arousing smell could be.

He didn't have the blood clotting agents that Daegan did, but the vampire healed so quickly, all Gideon had to really do was leave off the feeding and tease the area around the bite marks to keep blood from dripping down his shoulder, his chest, until the flow stopped. No hardship, that, but on second thought...

He let one drop escape and make its crimson path down the vampire's chest as he shifted in front of him. The blood met the nylon rope at the lower curve of Daegan's pectoral and fattened out there. As it was absorbed into the braid, it turned it pink. Gideon had crossed the rope at the sternum and made two columns of diamond sections down the ridges of Daegan's abdomen. Since that rope cross at the sternum highlighted Daegan's superior pecs in a way too tempting to resist, Gideon decided he needed a little clean up.

To get to its present point, the blood had rolled over a

nipple. Gideon laid his fingers on the firm flesh beneath the binding, stroking it as he leaned forward and licked the trail upward from where the blood had met the rope. When he went over the nipple, he earned a flex of that powerful body. It inspired him to linger a good minute, teasing the tight nub with teeth and tongue.

Daegan was sensitive around his nipples, so it was a pure pleasure to feel that jerk and quiver through his muscles, to look down and see his jeans straining to contain the erection beneath the denim. When Gideon finally moved up, he nudged Daegan's head up. Feeling Daegan give way, drop his head back on his shoulders and offer his throat—a move Gideon had been savvy enough to be sure the ropes did allow—was an indescribable feeling.

Just to make sure Daegan kept his head there, Gideon slid his hand up to the vampire's nape and took a nice handhold on the thick strands. They were just long enough to get a good grip.

It was amazing to feel the changes in Daegan's body. It was as if Gideon was caressing a panther, all coiled muscle that could become deadly in an instant. When he constricted his hand in his hair and the vampire let out a hiss of breath, that sense became even more pronounced, such that the flexing of Daegan's fingers in his bonds put Gideon in mind of the cat's lethal talons.

Fuck, he wanted to take him right now. But he wouldn't rush it. This wasn't going to be over in a slam-bam-thank-you-ma'am way. All the hours Daegan and Anwyn put into restraining Gideon, drawing it out, making him come again and again, using him, driving him, cherishing him in that crazy-assed way that made him feel helpless and powerful at once, all of it had taught him the power of denial. With it, they could make him insane to serve them however they needed, his mind destroyed by everything they did to him, taking him deeper into his soul and making him more willing to be theirs, every time, in ways he couldn't articulate.

He backed off several steps, but not to retreat. He needed to take a breath, pull himself out of sappy mode. He fully intended to poke this particular cat with a stick, aggravate him a little. Yeah, it was his nature, Daegan wouldn't expect anything different, but it was more than that, too. This wasn't about payback, but about giving Daegan a taste of that indescribable feeling, as close as Gideon could bring him to it. To get there, he needed to knock the vampire more off balance. What was more fun than getting Daegan riled up? Almost nothing. It ranked right up there with whiskers on kittens and bright copper kettles.

Right on cue, Anwyn returned. Gideon didn't have to look to feel her come back into the room. But when he did, he saw she'd changed clothes and was leaning against the wall again. Had she anticipated him that well, even while restraining herself from dipping into his mind as he'd requested? He guessed the answer to that was under the thin silk robe she wore, so short the hem caressed her upper thighs.

He extended a hand. Meeting his gaze, she came to him like the mysterious, exotic creature she was, with sensuous sway of hip, elegant arm movements, a toss of her hair. When she put her hand in his, she moistened her lips in that way that made a man's mind go straight to a vision of smoky dark bedrooms and sweaty, to-die-for sex. But she wasn't a porn flick. She was a goddess, inviting a male into her bed to worship every inch of her, beg for the bite of her nails, the arch of her body, the exultation of going off that pinnacle with her.

Since her blue-green eyes glowed like luminescent topaz in response, he suspected she wasn't completely managing to stay out of his head, but he wouldn't be chastising her for it. She wasn't as adept at that as Daegan and, if she was catching a stray thought here or there, that one certainly wasn't a bad one for her to overhear. Especially since he needed her complete cooperation for this next part, and he expected she was going to have a WTF moment when she realized his full intent.

He hadn't really talked to her about how she could participate, but she had a scary grasp of things like this. She'd know how to enhance the experience for all of them, just as she'd know when to back off and give Gideon his full due. Despite his earlier words, she wouldn't do that because he'd ordered it—never that with her, though he was still at a loss at why she could make him hunger as much to serve her as to overwhelm and take. She'd do it because she knew being a Mistress to him, both of them belonging to Daegan, being linked the way they all were, was never a straight line, but a maze, like a wild mix of adult Candyland and Chutes-n-Ladders.

His lips twisted wryly. Yeah, that was him. Mental poetry one minute, preschool Dick and Jane the next. But that was all right.

He'd imagined doing all sorts of things to Anwyn while Daegan could only watch. Daegan had done that to Gideon plenty of times, had trussed him up like a calf while the vampire went down on Anwyn. He'd have her screaming and writhing while Gideon's cock ached in whatever steel-pronged contraption Daegan clamped on it, so he was unable to release the lava boiling in his balls. One time, Daegan had put his lips over Gideon's after. His mouth stretched by a ring gag, Gideon could do nothing but fucking whimper as Daegan licked his lips, teased his restrained tongue and brought him the scent of his Mistress's cunt, a single stingy taste. Afterwards, he'd thrust his cock into Gideon's mouth, made him suck him off. *Then* he'd let Gideon come.

So maybe this part *was* a little bit of payback.

Gideon eased her between the two of them, turning her so she was facing Daegan. Not close enough for Daegan to touch, perhaps a couple feet between them. Gideon gathered up that thick, lustrous hair, pulling it off the closer side of her throat so he could taste her there. She shivered in reaction. It was one of a vampire's most erogenous areas. For Anwyn, who'd known how to savor the erotic to its fullest measure even before she became a vampire, it might even rank at the top, depending on the circumstances and provocation.

Putting his hands at her waist, Gideon fingered the sash of the robe, his slight pause a weighted request. She tilted her head and met his gaze. He held that look as he slipped the sash, let it fall and the fabric part. Then he let his attention wander downward.

Anwyn had definitely gotten into the spirit of things. She wore something Gideon had never seen on her before, a black waist cincher and nothing else, so her generous breasts spilled over the top and her hips flared beneath. Her bare, neat pussy was visible, the clit already flushed and swollen. She wore thigh-high boots that fit her legs like a second skin.

"Holy God," he said reverently, and her lips curved. When he cupped those ripe, irresistible breasts, she melted against him, her thighs parting over his knee as he insinuated it between them, let her ride it as he caressed the pink tips and made her purr. As he put his hand over her throat to hold her still and bite her shoulder, he got the reaction he'd sought. A growl—unmistakably Daegan's.

Gideon lifted his gaze to meet the vampire's. The irises were gone and his fangs were showing.

"You can push this too far, vampire hunter, by taunting me with what I have first claim on."

Holding his Master's gaze, Gideon let his hand drop. Anwyn drew in a breath against him as he cupped her mound, thumb passing over her clit, the manipulation spreading the heady scent of her arousal in the air between them. "Just testing that wild animal instinct of yours."

Anwyn moaned as he skillfully teased her clit in the way he knew she liked. While Gideon felt her pleasure as a woman and admiration as a Mistress for the path he'd chosen, he also detected some tension, as she grasped the hazardous game Gideon was playing.

While only a complete fucking idiot pulled a pin from a grenade and then stood right on top of it to get an up close view of how it went boom, Gideon was willing to take the risk. He wanted to push Daegan until he would abandon his sense of honor, let go of control entirely and act. Anwyn knew him inside and out, and she was a Mistress through and through. He didn't have to explain it to her. She'd gone after Gideon in a similar way when she was human, after all.

He put aside the recollection that he'd practically put her through a stained glass window as a result, and Daegan was a lot stronger than a human woman. That feral light in Daegan's eyes was a territorial surge, a response to Gideon challenging his dominance over Anwyn, over them both. Gideon had deliberately set the torch alight. Let the games begin.

"When this is over, I will punish her for allowing you to taunt me this way. Is that what you wish?"

"That only made her wetter," Gideon remarked. He lifted his fingers. "Want to taste?"

Daegan's face became that still mask. Imagining the vampire's lips wrapping around his fingers made Gideon's own hard-on worse. He had a fleeting thought that the blood surge might split his cock open like a banana, but it might be worth it. However, he had another plan for Anwyn's honey. Under the laser intensity of Daegan's attention, he put his fingers in his own mouth.

Sliding his arm around his Mistress's waist, he moved her forward, putting her fully against Daegan. He saw that still mask flicker, a flash of lust-filled reaction as those gorgeous tits pressed against Daegan's bare chest. Anwyn torturously straddled Daegan's thigh the way she had Gideon's, rubbing her pussy against it as her arms circled the vampire, her fingers finding a hold in the rope at his back. Since she hadn't tied the harness, she didn't realize her first choice of anchor point was the one that put pressure on his throat. Gideon clasped her arm and gently directed her to a different point. Daegan held against the pressure on his windpipe as if it didn't exist, his burning gaze never leaving either of them.

Having hunted with Daegan, Gideon knew how silent and still the vampire grew the closer they came to their prey. It was like he turned inside himself, became more predator than man. He was seeing some elements of that now. Gideon decided he'd take that as a good sign.

Anwyn had apparently decided in for a penny, in for a pound. Putting her mouth on Daegan's chest, she teased the flesh between the openings of the rope as Gideon had, following that same track over the opposite nipple. As she did that, Gideon hooked the stool he'd left within reach, pulled it over and stepped onto it. With Daegan stretched upward like this, he needed a little more height for what he intended to do next. Plus he wanted to be a few inches taller than him.

The position let him reach down, dig his fingers into Daegan's hair, and kiss him the way he'd kiss a girl. With an alpha's pleasure, conveying the demand to surrender, to give him everything. As he leaned in to underscore the message, it sandwiched Anwyn between them even tighter, an altogether pleasant side effect, her ass pressed against him.

Daegan's eyes lifted to his, that fierce light reacting to the kiss, to the taste of Anwyn's cunt lingering in Gideon's mouth, to her proximity between them. Expecting the bite, Gideon didn't flinch as the fang scored him, but when Daegan bit, something coiled up and released at once inside him.

Clamping his other hand under Daegan's jaw, he crushed his lips against the vampire's, tasting his own blood and feeling the fangs slice more tender areas of his lips and mouth. He made no move to defend himself, instead offering one of the few weapons he'd learned was effective against his Master. His full, uninhibited passion, revealed through the ferocity of the kiss. He tightened his grip on Daegan's neck and dove deep. He didn't care that Daegan might be biting him with savage purpose or as incidental passion, because either way he was kissing Gideon back just as insistently.

He almost lost himself then and there. He'd forgotten how lethal a weapon Daegan's mouth could be. He wanted to end this, wanted to sink balls deep in him, take them both to that conclusion together.

Anwyn didn't help. Reaching back to grasp his thighs, she ground her backside against his legs. She couldn't rub her ass against his cock with the difference in their heights, but it didn't matter. The sensation strummed right up his thighs into his balls. He couldn't stifle the groan. His capricious Mistress would switch allegiances as the mood struck her, and he felt the balance of power starting to shift decidedly back toward the vampire side of the field.

That thought helped pull him back. He wasn't going to

lose his one chance at this. No matter how sweet losing would be, winning was going to be the memory of a lifetime.

As he eased back, panting, he gave Anwyn a narrow glance. Her own expression was full of erotic mirth. He wondered what she'd do if he gave that gorgeous ass a healthy slap of reproof. Tempting as that was, he gave it a pass, since he had all he could handle trying to top one Dom. One mega-uber-Dom.

He nudged her out of the way with a look that had her gorgeous lips quivering with amusement and dire promises to be fulfilled at a later time, but she slid away. Moving back to the sidelines, she perched demurely on a stool, an effect seriously undermined by her keeping the robe open, a pleasure and temptation to the two males.

Gideon stepped back to the floor, pushing the footstool out of the way. He forced himself to calm down and steady his breathing. Licked his own blood from his lips. Daegan watched him, missing nothing, saying nothing. The tips of the vampire's fangs were still showing. His desire to break free was a heated blast of air, but before Gideon's eyes, the vampire reined himself back with that insane level of control only Daegan had. Gideon could well imagine what he would do if he let go of it, though. Daegan would knock him to his knees, hold him there, stiff cock pressed against Gideon's ass as the vampire drank deep, made it clear who owned whom. And that would only be the beginning.

"You remember what I've told you," Gideon said, making sure his voice was steady. "The vampire who gets overconfident is the one who ends up getting staked. You're going to get staked either way, so to speak, but just saying."

Daegan blinked once. Slowly. "I never underestimate you, vampire hunter. I trust you not do the same with me."

Not a chance of that, but Gideon gave him a suitably dismissive sneer. Daegan's brow quirked in response, then the vampire lay his head back, rolling his shoulders as if releasing some tension there. It was an entirely uncalculated move, but one that was such pleasure to watch, he heard Anwyn hum in approval. It stretched Daegan's body even further out of the jeans, so they got an even lower glimpse of that triangle of muscle pointing from his hips to his groin, which inevitably led the eyes to the impossible-to-miss erection just below the button of his jeans.

Circling behind Daegan, Gideon went to the supply cabinet to retrieve more rope. This time he chose the thinner parachute cord he'd picked out specifically for this and loosed it from its figure eight coil. As he shook it out, he doubled it then came back to drape it around Daegan's shoulders, a good holding place. Reaching out, Gideon hooked his fingers into the waistband of those stretched jeans and slipped the button. As he worked the zipper down, he had the pleasure of brushing the glans with his knuckles, but he didn't allow himself more than that. He was going to keep his eye on the ball from here on out.

Daegan was wearing his usual dark designer underwear beneath. They were made out of the softest cotton Gideon had ever felt, but that didn't keep him from teasing Daegan about his skivvies costing as much as his overpriced shirts. Maybe when he'd lived centuries, wearing comfortable underwear would be important enough to pay as much for it as a good steak dinner. When his Master and Mistress chose to let him wear underwear, that is.

He bent to remove Daegan's shoes and the thin socks. As he did, he ran his thumbs over the arches. Even the guy's feet were absorbing, which just showed Gideon had lost his mind when it came to Daegan Rei. He remembered crystal clear the first time he'd willingly put his mouth to his Master's feet. He'd fought exhaustion to do it, at the time feeling like there was nothing more important in the world than doing that one thing.

That was when he'd resolved the ownership question in his own mind. He knew he belonged to them both. It was because of that this was being permitted to happen. He wondered if they knew he realized that. Probably. As usual, he would probably have an even deeper understanding of the nature of that ownership before it was over. Anytime he challenged them like this, it usually resulted in that, didn't it? Maybe that was why he enjoyed the challenge so much...and so did they. Sometimes he thought it did the same for them. He hoped it did. This time, he hoped he'd show Daegan something about their relationship even the all-powerful, all wise bastard didn't already know.

When all was said and done, it wasn't about Daegan losing a bet. It was about...a thank you. For what they did for him, for what Daegan had given him. This was an opportunity for Gideon—if he didn't fuck it up—to provide his Master something like an unconditional offering to a god, versus a constant petition for something.

Oh, Jesus. How did he keep getting back into this state of mind? Thank God Daegan wasn't in his head. If he ever knew Gideon had called him a god, he'd have to stake him, just on general principle. Which would be like a suicide bomber tactic, given their blood connection, but it would have to be done. Anwyn would understand.

Returning to the practicalities of the present, Gideon pulled the jeans and underwear free of those distracting feet. When he set those aside and straightened, he was looking at Daegan fully naked, except for Gideon's rope on his upper body and throat. Despite the impressive girth and weight of Daegan's cock, the organ was curved up high, and pearled with fluid at the tip. Gideon had been on his knees plenty of times, taking that seed down his throat, Daegan's hand fisted in his hair. Sometimes while Anwyn was ramming a strap-on in his ass, her sweet breath teasing his neck as he ached to come but they made him hold out forever, until he was about to burst.

Eventually tonight, he'd be the one ramming his dick right up that tight, irresistible ass. He could feel it in such a visceral male way, but he couldn't think that *at* his Master, let alone say it. How odd was that? Guess it went to show how far he'd moved into territory he used to sneer at. Hell, he'd set up house there, complete with picket fence and little flower boxes.

When he slid the parachute line off Daegan's neck, he noted the vampire's lips were still damp from that crazy kiss they'd shared. "Going to tie up your cock now," he said. "Touch you how I want, get you hurting for it."

He closed his hand over Daegan's testicles, cradling them. Smooth as a baby's ass, firm as grapefruit, and it was so rare that he had the chance to freely handle them, he indulged in a nice pool ball roll over his palm, watching Daegan's cock jerk, those ab muscles ripple and flanks flex. As Gideon saw Anwyn lick her lips in his peripheral vision, he smelled the increase in her arousal, and knew Daegan registered that irresistible signal. The whole evening was going to be an orgy before it was over, him fucking Daegan, them fucking Anwyn...the to-do list never ended, thank God.

Gideon turned his attention to his sensual threat. Several wraps of the cord around the base of the balls, cinching them up like the top of a purse, then a triple wrap around his turgid cock before he began sheathing it in fine knot work, deft as a lady knitting, though he wasn't going to think of it that way, thanks very much, because the picture of a spectacled grandma hunching over Daegan's cock, knitting one, purling two, wasn't right for the mood, for sure.

Now as before, all that idle practice time paid off, because this was even more intricate work than the rest, and would have taken half the night if he hadn't done it a million times on a beer bottle. And quite a few raw vegetables. Anwyn, the cook in the family, had enjoyed picking him out different vegetables to use when Daegan was away on assignments. She'd also suggested Gideon do it a couple times on himself, to know what it felt like. Staying hard hadn't been a problem during that, since she'd parked herself less than a foot away and watched with intense, openly lascivious interest.

Speaking of which, Daegan's shaft was getting harder and bigger under his touch. Talk about a distraction. But then he noticed a change to the quality of the vampire's stillness. Gideon stopped and looked up to see those dark eyes focused inward, Daegan's body barely swaying.

"What is it?"

Daegan gave a slight shake of his head, fingers twitching. "It's different, being bound this way."

Maybe because he understood all too well, Gideon knew the vampire didn't mean having his cock trussed up. "Being tied up, not by an enemy. For this."

Daegan's gaze met his. "Yes."

"So, is it making you think about switching sides? Because I'm all about fitting you with a pretty pink collar and leash and having you walk around with a dildo up your ass. I'll have to remove the stick you always carry there first, but even so..."

Daegan's expression was a nice fuck-you to that. It was an affable-looking retort, though, such that Gideon couldn't resist trailing his fingers down Daegan's chest, hooking them in that X against his sternum to tug before he returned to his neck and shoulders, squeezing the tension there, kneading.

"I'll let your arms down before much longer."

When he did that, it would be to put Daegan on the ground, on his hands and knees. Gideon stopped with that image, because his mind split into twelve different directions every time it went any farther.

He returned to the wrap. Because of the close contact required to do the fine knot work, he was essentially stroking Daegan's cock the whole time, and of course Gideon indulged in more than was required for the functionality of the rope tying. The more motionless Daegan got, the more rigid his muscles became. It made Gideon want to stroke and tease him all the more, and he wasn't resisting the impulse. Tie a knot, run his fingers along the shaft, let his nails scrape the velvet-over-steel skin. Tie another knot. Once or twice a quiver actually went through Daegan as a result. Each time, Gideon glanced up to make sure he was okay. Each time, Daegan had that internal focus thing going. One time he licked his lips, making Gideon want to follow the track of his tongue with his own.

The cock sheath finished with a secure wrap under the flare of the head, but he needed another accessory before he could complete the design. He left Daegan's side once more, but it was a brief trip. Like the cuffs in the kitchen, he'd already placed what he needed ready to hand. Going to the supply cabinet, he removed the vibrating bullet from the top drawer.

He'd watch Daegan use it on Anwyn, press it deep into

the folds of her labia, the nose up against the base of her clit, which sent her to the moon. One of the things Gideon had learned in his extensive education with two excessively carnal vampires was that a guy's cockhead was just a much bigger clit. Less pretty than Anwyn's, for certain, no matter that she'd tried to talk him into decorating his with a ring for her to flick and tug on with those wicked fingers of hers. If she really wanted him to do it, he would, but up until now she'd used it a playful threat, no different than her promise to flay the skin off his back, ram a bat up his ass... On those days, he called her Lyssa-in-training.

Coming back to Daegan's front, he wrapped the bullet snug against the underside of Daegan's cock, the nose pressed right up under the corona. He wrapped it tightly enough to put pressure against the throbbing vein beneath the bullet. Parachute cord was a little like nylon, needing some extra knots and wraps to keep it secure, but since the more he looked at Daegan's cock laced into such tight bondage, the more he wanted to do to it, he had no problem with the extra work. It made him realize why sometimes, before a session was all over, Daegan and Anwyn had him tied up ten different ways. Lifting his head to stare into Daegan's face, he turned on the bullet to a medium setting.

The reaction was gratifying. Daegan's hips jerked, his body tightening in that unbelievable display that Gideon thought could turn any straight man gay, even if for only one quick and disorienting, what-the-hell paradigm shift. He wasn't going to cast any stones.

"It won't be easy for you to come, tied up like that, but it's possible. When I push the setting up to max, you'll feel like a tea kettle with the lid clapped on pretty tight. Eventually, you'll explode. You won't be able to help yourself."

Hearing that beam creak again, Gideon glanced up to see the muscles in Daegan's arms knot, unknot. "It's good you're fighting it. Like you always tell me, it's better that way."

"Using my words against me...vampire hunter?"

Had Daegan just been...breathless? Gideon heard

Anwyn's own breath draw in, telling him she'd caught the same thing. Laying his hands on Daegan's extended rib cage, Gideon ran hot palms up his sides and met the dark gaze. "Maybe using them for you. I want to see you let go. I want you to give me that."

"Just like you, I will not give in without a fight. And we both know I'm the better fighter."

Tit for tat, on the word-giving-back department. In the gleam of Daegan's eyes, Gideon saw he'd intended that additional dirt kick.

He knew how Daegan usually responded to *him* when he got mouthy. Raising a brow, Gideon shifted behind Daegan. The position change meant instead of his rib cage he now gripped the male's hips, fingers caressing flesh. His attention shifted down over the flexing ass. Due to the hum of that bullet, Daegan was making slight, involuntary movements like he was fucking. Gideon had to suppress a hard groan as his own cock leaped at the sight.

He'd intended the bullet as a distraction, a way to keep Daegan from going postal on him while he moved to the next phase—lubing up the vampire's ass. Unfortunately, he hadn't thought about how it would distract *him*. Anwyn had shifted along the wall so she could get more of Daegan's profile. From the vibrant light in her eyes, her riveted attention, he could tell she was just as mesmerized.

"Something wrong, vampire hunter?"

Okay, that was a taunt, he knew it was. With a grim twist of his lips, Gideon slid his hand over Daegan's hip bone, short nails scraping the groin area before he found his cock. He clasped it hard enough he felt the cord bite into the vampire's flesh. Finding the bullet with his thumb, Gideon bumped up the setting as he pressed it harder against that sensitive point beneath the head, same as he'd practiced on himself to determine the most effective way to do it.

Daegan shuddered. He fucking shuddered. At the flood of exultation, Gideon stroked him through the rope, squeezed harder.

"Fuck..." The harsh expletive, the powerful body rocking against him, was capable of making Gideon come just from

140

that, especially with Daegan's body rubbing against him. His attention shifted to Anwyn and, holy fuck, if ever Gideon needed a partner-in-crime, she'd be his first choice. Her stool was close enough to the wall that she'd leaned back against it. Her robe was wide open and she was massaging herself, teasing her wet cunt right where Daegan could see her. She kept her eyes on the vampire, her lips parted and eyes greedy.

"You want to fight, we'll fight," Gideon said in Daegan's ear. "Look at her. I want to fuck her from behind, so we can both look at you while I'm doing her. Her pussy will be sucking on my cock while you lose it, come into open air, showing us how much you want to fuck both of us."

"I will break your neck," Daegan promised, the threat real in his voice. Gideon brushed his lips on his neck. He licked at the place where he'd bitten him earlier. As he did it, he worked the tip of the bullet against Daegan's sweet spot, holding his shaft even tighter than the cinched rope. When he let his fingers slip forward, the tip of Daegan's cock was smeared with pre-cum. The vampire was resisting so hard he was vibrating, channeling the shudders into something more intense and concentrated.

"This is where I intended to start oiling you up for me to fuck," Gideon growled, "but I'm starting to get the hang of this whole Dom thing. It's not about sticking to the playbook, but taking the ball anywhere on the field I damn well want it to go."

Gideon slid under the other male's arm and dropped to one knee. He caught the rope at Daegan's waist to add more of a pull on the ones holding his arms above his head. As he did that, he licked that viscous fluid from Daegan's cock slit, tasting for the pure pleasure of it. He also worked his tongue around the vibrating bullet, knowing it would increase the sensation. His intuition was confirmed as Daegan groaned, his body rolling forward with an upward kick of the hips. Except for that last, jerky, involuntary movement, it showcased the sinuous and deadly grace the male could demonstrate with any weapon. He was the greatest warrior Gideon had ever had the pleasure of watching.

Abruptly, he twisted on the balls of his feet, so he could look toward Anwyn. "You know why I wanted to do this to him tonight?"

He spoke as if Daegan wasn't struggling not to come, as if Anwyn didn't have her fingers on her wet pussy, as if the atmosphere wasn't saturated with erotic intent, bodies fast approaching a precipice. But maybe that was the best time to say something important.

Anwyn, caught by the unexpected interruption, paused in her self-pleasuring, her eyes resting on him. "Gideon..." Daegan's rasp was a pleasure to hear, but Gideon tightened his fingers on his cock to roll the bullet around a little more.

"Not your conversation this time, vampire. It's between me and her."

He got a response to that which he expected was a creative mix of three different languages, all of which threatened him with bodily harm. He ignored it, holding Anwyn's gaze.

"In that alley, before they attacked us, he'd fucking relaxed. We were picking at one another about some kind of bullshit, and he grinned at me. He let down his guard for one moment, wasn't doing his usual angel in the Garden of Eden, sword pointing in every direction thing, and then that happened. It pissed me off."

Her expression stilled further, eyes flickering to Daegan then back to Gideon. "You were worried about me moving too soon on this," Gideon said quietly. "But it was the absolutely right time."

He waited until she nodded, and then he rose, meeting Daegan eye to eye. His words had sunk in to his captive as well. Even though in terms of sexual stimulation Daegan was practically on the edge of a cliff, hanging by his fingernails, Gideon could tell he had his full attention, that inner warrior guru shit that never totally let go. "I want you to know that sometimes you can let your guard down. Here, with us, in the safety of a house where we can feel what's coming a mile away, you can do it. You can give me everything and trust me with it, same as you've taught me to trust the both of you."

It was a long pause, the two of them eye to eye, and a lot of things happening in Daegan's eyes that Gideon wasn't sure how to interpret, but at this point, that wasn't needed. He put his hand on Daegan's jaw, took another taste of his mouth and licked at one of his fangs before pulling away. Then he dropped to one knee once more.

This time he stopped the bullet. He got it out of his way, unwrapped the rope, pulled it all off. He was probably a little rougher than intended, because he felt Daegan flinch, but he had his own hunger to sate now. "Don't you hold back on me."

Electronics didn't suit his mood, or the friction of the rope. As often as he'd knelt to service Daegan with his mouth as his servant, his slave—call it what it was—Gideon hadn't thought about it as he did now, as a power Daegan gave to Gideon through his preference for his servant's mouth. A privilege. Right here, Gideon could indulge the desire freely, because he wanted Daegan to come in his mouth, to give the vampire no other choice, to know that Daegan's desire to release superseded his infamous control.

He went down on him with a vengeance, his hands sliding around to grip the muscular ass, fingers kneading, pushing him deeper into his mouth.

Come for me, you bastard. Give it all to me.

"Gideon..." Daegan let out a hard groan and his hips jerked against Gideon. The beam made an ominous noise, the closest to a cracking sound yet, but it held. Thank God for Lyssa's building contractors, because rather than the roof coming down on them, Gideon felt the male shudder, jerk, shudder once more. His cock convulsed in Gideon's mouth, the vein pumping hard, and then Daegan's seed was jetting into his throat. Gideon tightened his grip on the base, sucked and sucked, licked and teased, milking him down to the last drop, even as he savored every shudder and ripple of his body until it was all done and Daegan was twitching at the pull of Gideon's mouth.

It was the most satisfied Gideon had ever felt without coming himself. His own state of fierce arousal only enhanced it. Score one for the home team. But it wasn't dawn yet. Gideon planned to put at least a couple more touchdowns up on the board tonight.

Looking up, he saw Daegan had his eyes closed, his chest rising and falling fast. He'd seen Daegan post climax plenty of times, and there was a different nature to this one, such that Gideon rose and put his palm on his chest, his other hand at Daegan's waist, steadying him. Gideon didn't give a shit about how invincible everyone thought the vampire was, that he could destroy his enemies with barely a flick of his fingers. He was taking care of him tonight. Easing forward, he put his mouth on his jaw to give him a sharp nip. Spoke with a casualness he didn't feel.

"While you're so relaxed, I'm going to get to work on a lot of lubrication. Because you know what a big dick I have."

Daegan's lips curved, and those lashes parted, giving Gideon a glimpse of wholly dark orbs with a flicker of crimson. At first that effect had been more than a little disconcerting, but Gideon had learned to appreciate it, probably because he now knew it meant Daegan was either about to destroy everything in his path, or he was feeling a seriously over-the-top Hallmark moment.

He was going to bank on the latter. Particularly when Daegan pressed against the ropes on his throat, increasing the strain on his windpipe such that Gideon stopped him with a hand on his chest, leaning forward so the vampire could do what he wanted. Daegan brushed his lips against his temple.

"Do your worst, vampire hunter. This fight isn't over yet."

Part 4

Gideon went to the cabinet of supplies again, withdrawing the bottle he'd stored there. He'd spent as much time choosing the right lubricant as a first-time mother spent on lotions to protect her baby's skin. Daegan might not appreciate that comparison, but it was Anwyn's reaction that had surprised Gideon.

He'd expected her to tease him about it, watching him

browse the Club Atlantis toy shop. He'd done her a disservice, overlooking her innate sensitivity to the situation. It was Gideon's first time fucking a guy.

There'd been that Council meeting where some pretty fierce games had been played, but he hadn't actually shoved his dick into another guy's ass, and definitely not one that mattered as much as this one's. So Anwyn patiently answered all his questions and explained the different choices. There were warming oils and lubes with different spices added to give things a tingle. There was also a heavy duty, functional lubricant for that really tight orifice or the first timers, to make sure it was as pleasurable as possible. Embarrassingly direct, that brand was called Tight Virgin.

Anwyn's serious assistance had reminded him that, long before she'd been a vampire, she'd been a Mistress, and she approved of him demonstrating the responsibility that all good Doms were supposed to show about their role.

Ella had joined them in the shop during the selection process. Her bright, inquisitive expression said she didn't know why Gideon was shopping for anal lube and she'd be more than willing to be enlightened. However, true to the professionalism and discretion Anwyn had trained or beaten into her—Gideon wasn't sure which—Ella didn't ask, though she did offer some oh-so-helpful input of her own.

"That one is the absolute best." She tapped the Tight Virgin bottle. "The Dom who fucked my ass the first time used it and, though it was still a bit scary and uncomfortable, it didn't stay that way long." She gave Gideon a wicked grin. "And the adhesion factor is off the charts. It clings to all the important stuff way longer than the others, so you don't have to stop to apply more, which can be such a mood-killer. If you greased a pig at a fair with it in the morning, you'd still be trying to catch him at sundown. That bottle is worth its price. Though I assume Mistress Anwyn is giving you a discount."

She stole a look at her boss and, getting an inscrutable look in return, she smirked at Gideon. "I tried." Then she escaped with a wink, grabbing the feather dust she'd come to get for the client in Private Room 12.

Gideon met Anwyn's amused gaze. "She's like a Disney educational porn flick, complete with the twittering birds and scampering rabbits. You're going to have to forgive the Daisy Duke *Dukes of Hazzard* fantasy that flooded my mind. I plead the pig greasing thing."

"I forgive nothing. You know that." Anwyn gave him a considering look. "Though Ella's Alabama roots do add to her charm. You should see her in her cut-off shorts and nothing else."

"You said that just to keep me in trouble," he chided her. She smirked at him, unrepentant, but nodded to the shelf.

"So what do you think?"

Gideon picked up the Tight Virgin. "This is the one you suggested, so if two out of three sex club professionals recommend it, I can't go wrong. Right?"

His Mistress had offered a half smile and leaned into him to brush her lips against his shoulder. As she did, she slid her fingers over the curve of his ass, tugging a crease where the denim cupped his buttock. He took it as acquiescence, but he also stood still. Whenever either she or Daegan were touching him a certain way, he knew to wait for them to draw away first. They'd taught him that, reinforcing the lesson during his forty days of intense training. As a result, the second they touched him, his brain immediately shifted to the required response.

He didn't always obey that directive, particularly when it was Daegan, but that was part of his and Daegan's thing. With Anwyn, he was different. She'd observed more than once Gideon was a dangerous animal that only his Mistress could call to heel. *Mostly*. He'd added that qualification to her comment, even as she gave him that feline look that told him she was 99% right, the 1% usually related to a disagreement about her safety.

That weird brain click not only locked him in place when they touched him, but sent a surge to his cock, aroused by the idea he was theirs to be touched, whenever, however they wanted. It was like brainwashing, the whole Dom/sub thing, but in a good way, because of the things that got washed away, leaving just pleasure and need. Service.

He'd only ever wanted to serve a purpose, to reach that deep well of meaning in himself, find a target for it that wouldn't destroy his soul when the silences in between got to be too much. They'd helped him find the well, and when the silence was overwhelming, they'd touch him, turn silence into stillness, and change the track of his brain.

Am I crazy to be thinking it's his first time, too?

Her gaze had lifted to his. "No," Anwyn said out loud. "Because I think it is."

§

Gideon returned to the present, standing there with the lube in his hand, and his Master waiting behind him, bound as Gideon had left him. What would the vampire world think of their biggest and baddest being ass-fucked for the first time, by a human? By his servant?

Okay, the biggest and baddest might be overstating it, but Gideon would split his money evenly in a throw down between Daegan and Lyssa, with Mason as a serious contender for second. He pushed the other thought away. He didn't give a good goddamn what the vampire world thought. Whatever happened here was going to stay between them. He might risk appendages to exploit Daegan's vulnerabilities for his own personal jollies, but he'd die in agony before he'd expose any weakness the vampire had to others. And that was that.

He turned and laid his palm between Daegan's shoulder blades, his eyes coursing over all the bindings on his upper body before his attention dropped lower. The rope he'd removed from Daegan's waist and groin had left faint marks there, and he tracked where it had been cinched over his thighs, just below his ass. Then his gaze followed the crease dividing the buttocks, and he thought about the things he would be doing to the orifice those muscular flanks concealed. He knew firsthand what it felt like to have those rim nerve endings stimulated. The more they were aroused, the more welcome penetration became.

He put the bottle down on a small rolling table next to him. Whether or not Daegan was a virgin, Gideon had no doubt the vampire would be a narrow fit. Tight-assed described Daegan with a capital T. He might appear all cool and calm, but laid-back the guy was not. Gideon hadn't compared him to the Garden of Eden angel with his amped-up multi-tasking sword for nothing.

He shifted the table so the lube was in Daegan's peripheral, where he could see the bottle, the long applicator tip. Gideon wanted to play with his head in the right ways, keep him focused on what was going to go down, but Gideon kept the title turned away from him. Now wasn't the time to rag him about being tight as a virgin. He'd save that for another time. He had other priorities—like loosening up Daegan's ass in a pretty incendiary way.

Gideon returned to the peg board wall, knowing exactly what he wanted from the myriad tools there. He plucked the rubber paddle off the wall. The flexibility of it, the material and thickness, could deliver a sting and wallop both. Just what he wanted.

As he pivoted back toward his captive, he noticed Daegan adjusting his shoulders. Gideon put a hand on the connecting point of shoulder and neck and felt the tension there. Retrieving the stool, he stepped onto it to adjust the knots and give Daegan a couple extra inches to put him more solidly on his feet.

"I'm fine, Gideon."

Gideon wrapped an arm around the vampire's chest. The elevated position had the added benefit of letting him push the heavy erection he was sporting right up against Daegan's back. Brushing his mouth over the vampire's temple, he indulged a heated, wet nip at his ear, enjoying the silk of Daegan's hair feathering over his knuckles as he wrapped his fingers around the side of Daegan's throat, eliciting that warning rumble in the vampire's chest.

"At the risk of repeating your own mantra, word for word: it's *my* job to tell you you're fine. And while you are fucking fine on a whole lot of levels, I'm not going to let you hurt in a way I don't want you hurting. Tonight, you're mine to protect."

A weighted silence, and then Daegan flexed his arm,

giving Gideon a push. "You are letting all this go to your head."

But his voice wasn't entirely...Daegan. Maybe slightly less in control? Was he ceding some of it to Gideon? A miracle beyond price, if so. A terrifying one, which made Gideon glad he'd spent so much time researching all this, even down to the freaking lubricant.

The vampire had given him an opening way too obvious to waste. Gideon dropped off the stool, pushed it aside and gripped Daegan's hips, grinding his cock against that firm bare ass. "You bet it's all going to my head. Going to feel like I'm splitting you in two, vampire."

There was a snort in reply, but he also felt an awesome quiver beneath his palms. Anwyn saw it, but suddenly Gideon wanted her to do more than that. He wanted her to feel everything, because this was too precious for her not to be experiencing it as directly as possible.

She'd stopped stroking herself between her legs while Gideon was adjusting the ropes. Instead she was cupping a breast, thumb brushing her erect nipple like a girl absently twirling her hair while considering a math question. It was clear she wouldn't keep her hands from herself while watching them.

"You can come back in, Mistress," Gideon said, meeting her gaze. "I want you to feel everything I'm feeling."

He sensed Daegan's approval of the decision. They both knew how much Anwyn got off on the interplay between the two males and, even when they didn't agree about anything else, he and Daegan were always united in their desire to give her all the pleasure she could take.

The vampire twitched in his bonds and leveled a sidelong glance at Gideon. "You are not issuing me the same invitation?"

"Not exactly, no." Gideon pursed his lips and squared off with him. "Can you let me in your mind without rummaging around in mine? Can you reverse the one-way mirror?"

"That's a rather extraordinary request for a servant to make of his Master."

"Meaning you won't do it, or you can't?"

Gideon twirled the paddle in his hand, held low at his side, and Daegan tracked the movement before his attention flicked back up to his face. "Just because you succeed in unbalancing me, however temporarily, you think you can manipulate me into doing your will, Gideon?"

There was that tone of cool hauteur that Gideon knew and loved. It never failed to send a ripple of reaction across his skin and straight through his balls. It also usually gave him an overwhelming desire to pop the shit out of the vampire. But Daegan knew that, didn't he? Reverse psychology. He wasn't the only one doing some manipulating here.

Gideon sidled closer, letting the paddle bump Daegan's hip, his upper thigh. He even gave his buttock a tap, a warning of what was coming, and took ferocious delight in the spark that ignited in Daegan's expression.

"I think you need to answer the question, vampire. Or you're going to get spanked."

God, it was worth it, Anwyn's choked, startled laugh, the full crimson flare in Daegan's dark eyes. As well as the breathtaking ripple of muscle. Gideon would remember to cherish the memory when Daegan was making him pay for it, as he surely would. But that was in the future.

"Just as I thought," Gideon said carelessly. "You can't do it. We'll come back to the question." Lifting the paddle, he gave it another dexterous spin and moved behind Daegan once more. In his mind, he could almost hear Anwyn's entire respiratory system take in an anticipatory breath. The tight feeling in his lower belly, cranking his cock up further, was just as strong a reaction. He couldn't fucking believe he was about to do this and, even more, how much he wanted to do it.

He'd researched this as well. He knew vampires had incredible self-healing powers. Those faint marks on Daegan's skin from the rope had already vanished. However, though Gideon bore third marks, which meant he could heal from most anything with his vampires' blood, pain still hurt like a son of a bitch. He expected it was the same with vampires. There was good pain and bad pain.

As a result, he didn't start with a slam out of the ball park. He went with a healthy slap with his hand, just for the hell of it, and to piss Daegan off. It also gave him the opportunity, after that sharp smack, to grab a cheek and give him a nice bruising squeeze. Man, the guy had an ass. As he eased off, he stretched out his fingers and let them dip in between to tease. As he did, he watched the reaction to his playing with the vampire's rim course through Daegan's breathtaking back muscles. It was like watching wind ripple through wheat grass.

"'I have absolutely no problem spanking men,'" Gideon pronounced, making sure the wicked note was clear in his voice.

It was a quote from an *Angel* episode they'd recently caught together, and he couldn't resist using it. He thought he heard Daegan grind his teeth and suspected he'd speared himself with a fang.

Jesus, it was a hell of a lot more fun to do this to an adult. The meaning was way different, wasn't it? Though it definitely connected to those weird good things from childhood about spankings; structure, order, boundaries. It was a sign that someone gave enough of a damn about you to make you behave. That someone was watching over you, keeping you in line. Even all-powerful vampires needed the lines. Loved ones to answer to.

Gideon swung. With a healthy crack, the rubber connected with both buttocks at the meatiest part. As the sound echoed through the room, his gaze clung to the impact point, watching the skin pink up nicely. Shame it healed up so fast, else he could tease Daegan about rubbing some baby butt lotion on there later. If he spoke that thought aloud, he might get to see that beam crack after all.

He swung again, and then he got into a rhythm, his own reaction getting more intense, until he couldn't resist checking out Daegan's. After about a dozen hits, he pressed up against Daegan and that reddening ass, reaching around him to find his cock. He didn't need his eyes to do it; he knew every inch of the vampire's body.

Fuck, he was back to being thick and hard as a tree limb. Message received, loud and clear. As Gideon stroked him, his hips moved of their own accord against Daegan's ass, a slow push and retreat, moving their bodies together, a prequel of the act to come. He noticed the vampire's chest was rising and falling a little more erratically than usual. He wasn't doing the stillness thing now. He was letting more of his reactions show. The room was so silent, but his and Anwyn's anticipation, and Daegan's growing explosive intensity, were sounds of their own, clear as an impending earthquake to canine ears.

Backing off, Gideon set the paddle aside and picked up the lube. He didn't want the first thing Daegan to feel to be that hard plastic tip, so he squeezed some out on his own fingers. Putting a hand on the vampire's side, he used the grip to hold him steady as he eased the other hand between the clenched buttocks. Really clenched.

"Ease up for me," he murmured, moving the hand at his waist up to Daegan's shoulder, kneading. "Just ease up and relax. Let me in."

He met Anwyn's gaze under Daegan's lifted arm, and the mind-to-mind connection clicked.

You are taking his mind into a place it's likely not been before, Gideon. Remember how it was for you at first, except he is not service-oriented, not like a vassal. He serves as a king serves his people, at his own discretion.

He stroked Daegan's rim with his greased finger, easing off the pressure. Bringing the other hand down, he transferred some extra lube to it and then brought it around Daegan again to clasp his cock, slide up and down.

"Feel that? It's like being inside Anwyn's sweet cunt, isn't it? Or my ass. Which isn't near as sweet, I admit, but hot and slick, clenching around you when you shove in there, take over." He said it against the vampire's throat, pressing his body against him even as his other hand remained between them, working more intimately against his rim. "I'm here. I've got you. Do you think I'd ever do anything to hurt you? That's why I wanted to get into your head while doing this. I can't hurt you physically, I get that. It's the deeper areas that you're going to have to trust me with for this, those layers you've never given up to anyone."

Gideon paused, closing his eyes, pressing his face into

the vampire's neck. As he did, he moved both hands to neutral area, gripping his waist, holding him tight against him. He let the emotions flood him, let them into his voice so Daegan could hear, know what they meant. How important all this was, something so much more than a stupid bet.

"I told you I loved you, that one time. Show me you believe it. You know what love is, even better than the two of us."

Daegan had loved Anwyn, never faltered in it, even when she'd turned on him, dealing with her transition. He'd accepted Gideon into their circle. At first, Gideon had thought he did it for Anwyn's sake, only tolerating the other male, but over time, he understood it hadn't been like that. The guy had the patience of Job, the heart of an angel. Literally. He had explored all the dark and light corners of love, knew them. But perhaps he'd never allowed the gift of it as deep inside himself as love could go, which Gideon now knew was bottomless. A full surrender was the only way into that closed circle, for servant *or* Master. And didn't that give a whole new interpretation to finding Heaven through the eye of a needle?

"Let me in, Master," Gideon urged against his flesh. "Give me that gift."

It was a good thing he was holding tight to Daegan, because suddenly it felt like the floor disappeared beneath him.

Daegan had spoken in his mind plenty of times, allowing Gideon into the surface layers when they hunted together or sometimes in the throes of passion, but never as deep as Gideon accessed Anwyn's mind. She had serious seizure issues he helped manage, making such a connection necessary, and her fledgling status probably made that more tolerable to her than to an older vampire with such thick shielding as Daegan had.

Since he'd started spending time around vampires— without his primary focus being how to kill them— Gideon had realized how rare it was for any servant to be given soul-deep access to their Master or Mistress. He only knew of one who'd been given that gift—his brother, Jacob, from the formidable Lady Lyssa. When it came to servants, however, vampires routinely had such license. Daegan and Anwyn were both capable of shredding Gideon's soul at will, one of the worries they'd had in Anwyn's first days as a fledgling. Even without seizure issues, most fledglings didn't take full servants until they had a few decades under their belt as vampires, so they could learn the control that would keep them from frying a servant's circuits. Daegan's influence, and Anwyn's own formidable will and love for Gideon, had made the early connection possible between them.

Of course, if either vampire ever did try to shred his soul, such an exercise of vampire power wouldn't be necessary to destroy Gideon. The act of betrayal would be enough. He was in that deep with them at this point.

Maybe he should be letting Daegan into his head, after all. Maybe seeing such thoughts would help his Master trust him. Gideon had that thought right before the floor-dropping thing happened. In that instant, he found himself tumbled end over end into the ocean of the vampire's mind. He was treading water in all the turbulent, complex layers of what was happening in this moment, but beneath him, accessible, were even greater depths, an infinite abyss of who and what Daegan was. Gideon had a thrilling, startling realization that he could sink down into layer after layer, and perhaps never find his way out.

But it was all his Master, and Daegan and Anwyn had become his guiding light through everything, even their own personal mazes. With that thought, he released any worries about that, letting himself float and get a grasp on his surroundings. On what was happening in Daegan's head in the here and now.

Uncertainty and fear weren't terms one applied to Daegan, but they'd stepped into some uncharted territory with this whole scenario in general. The paddle, lube and restraints had called forth even more specific reactions, like spikes in an EKG. As he examined those reactions, Gideon returned to stroking Daegan's rim. He didn't work it like a steam engine, roaring toward a destination. He took his time with it, wanting to see if Daegan felt the pleasure building, those crazy feelings that happened when someone was playing with your ass.

Holy fuck, he did. Gideon hadn't been sure a vampire would have that same kind of reaction, and maybe a vampire who'd been fucked there wouldn't. However, Daegan was...bemused...feeling a little trepidation. He was always in control, but this required giving that away. And he never gave control away.

I've *so* got you," Gideon whispered again. A promise, his voice rough. No way he would hide his emotion now. "I got your back. You know I always do."

The vampire had closed his eyes, his hands clenched in his bonds. "It doesn't have to be about who's the strongest in the room," Gideon continued. His gaze met Anwyn's, though he could feel her right there in his head, experiencing the extraordinary things he was, things beyond words in Daegan's mind. "You remember what I said about the first time she took me over? Hell, all I could think was here was this woman, half my weight, whose bones I could break with barely any effort, and yet, something about her, something about her scent and touch, the way she stares straight into my soul, makes me want to be on my knees to her. Give her everything, trust her with everything I am. It scared the ever-living shit out of me, because everything I am is some pretty ugly shit, things I'd never want near something as perfect as her, but it was like I didn't have a choice. I put it all in her hands, and damn if she didn't make it all stop hurting."

Those blue-green eyes glowed, her pink mouth softening. If he'd told her he loved her a million times, he knew it wouldn't mean as much as those words just had. He turned his attention back to Daegan.

"I know you're not me. But when you realize there actually is a person out there who can hold onto you when you have to let it all go... I think all of us have to find at least one person like that in our lives to open up parts of ourselves we never knew existed. And you have the miracle of two of them, right here in this room.

"I got you." He'd say it over and over, often as needed to help balance what he was seeing in the vampire's mind, emotions whose shape Gideon knew, telling him the reassurance was needed. "As long as you let me stay in your mind like this, I'm going to make sure I get you all the way home. All right?"

A long silence, those colors in his mind shifting, a wealth of emotions and reactions as hard to describe as Heaven and Hell and what drove them. Then Daegan's head moved against his.

A nod.

Gideon felt the shudder through the damn-near-invincible body, the infinitesimal relaxing of all the muscles, one by one. When he applied a little pressure on his greased fingers, they slid into Daegan's rectum, into that heated channel. The muscles gripped him as he probed and stroked.

Glorious fucking heaven.

Anwyn showed him Daegan's reaction from a different angle. His cock had stiffened further, fluid leaking from the tip. It made Gideon salivate, seeing it through her eyes, feeling her body respond accordingly, that three-way spiral that would eventually become a no-coming-back-from-Oz tornado.

Now that Daegan's channel was oiled up with his fingers, Gideon reluctantly removed them to retrieve the lube. Putting that plastic tip at the opening, he sunk it in deep and gave the tube a healthy squeeze. He'd make sure the guy had a whole mess of the stuff in there, then he'd be greasing up his own cock just as heavy.

As he withdrew the applicator, he replaced it with his fingers again, working inside that tight passage with more sensual purpose. The short chain connecting the cuffs clinked against the hook as Daegan's hips moved with him, and Gideon couldn't contain his own reaction.

"Yeah, that's it. God, you're tight. I can't wait to get in there, feel you squeezing my dick with those muscles." All the strength he felt in Daegan when they sparred, the grip of his hands, his arms, his thighs—Gideon was pretty damn sure his ass was going to be just as impressive.

Another jump in Daegan's cock, more fluid oozing from the tip. That was the breaking news through Anwyn's mind, her eyes. She licked her lips, making Gideon bite back a groan.

Christ, at this rate he was going to explode the second he was in Daegan's ass. That was where that whole third mark recovery rate came in handy. He could get it up again and again until dawn's light. Still, he'd almost rather go ahead and jack off against him now, so he could make that first time a long, slow hard ride.

He imagined the ropes of his semen lashing Daegan's lower back and ass, running down the curves as he spurted. He'd collect that cream and then use it to lubricate Daegan and himself further. He'd put him on his hands and knees, stand over him... No, kneel behind him, close...

Shit. Again, his mind shied away from it. Even when he'd fantasized about it, there'd been a hitch at this part, a niggling "off" feeling he'd ignored. But here it was, confronting him up close and personal, no more evading it.

One thing at a time. However he eventually decided to do the grand finale, it was time to take the rope harness off of the vampire. He started at the waist and went in reverse, loosening the diamond pattern, untangling all of it. He removed the loop around Daegan's throat, so when he was done, the only thing holding him was the rope wrapped around his wrists, attached to the beam so his arms remained raised above his head.

Standing face to face with him now, Gideon traced the impressions the ropes had left between the vampire's pecs, following the lines along the rib cage and below. Since the vampire had left the mind gate open, Gideon experienced the vampire's physical and emotional reactions to the contact. It was kind of amazing to *feel* how your touch felt to someone else. Gideon caressed his chest, and Daegan's every nerve ending responded to the simple act.

When Daegan fucked him, Gideon didn't give it much thought. At some subconscious, vague level, he knew Daegan was turned on by contact with him, but he never took it further than that in his own mind. Now he saw Daegan welcomed it, desired it...craved it. Gideon also came mind-to-mind up close with the awe-inspiring discipline Daegan was imposing on himself, suppressing his Dominant instincts. His natural, screaming reaction to all of this stimulus was to pull free, take over. Seeing the strength of that internal battle warring around his single touch, Gideon felt a rather unmanly quiver go through his legs, his lower belly. He considered himself a pretty alpha guy, all said and told, but next to that...fuck.

As the vampire's gaze flicked up, meeting Gideon's, he felt like a lion meeting the gaze of a T-Rex. The impact hit him hard below the rib cage. Whatever compelled him to submit to Daegan on a normal day tried to sit up and beg for it like a Pavlovian dog. Gideon found himself in his own internal battle, having to hold fast against that tide. Like the idiot he was, he tested it, his hand sliding down to wrap his fingers around Daegan's cock once more, just to see the fireworks of thoughts, colors, and hard-metal fuck-the-shit-out-of-you rock music happen in the vampire's mind.

From his side of things, he felt more than a cock stiffening in his hand. He felt how Daegan's mind reacted to the strength of Gideon's grip on him. His eyes devoured every defined muscle of Gideon's upper body, drank in the cock straining beneath his jeans. He'd turn savage if Gideon didn't strip soon and let him see it.

Since Daegan was still holding his gaze, Gideon learned that the vampire loved the blue of his eyes, the dark mystery of them, all that conflicting blend of brutal loyalty, fierce compassion and a killer's violence. The way they would intensify with lust or rage, soften with other emotions. The many ways his mouth could distract when he was spewing his sardonic wit. Gideon would have called it being a wiseass, but hey, the vampire had all those centuries of higher education.

Daegan wanted to taste his mouth again, like when Gideon had kissed him before. *Now.*

Gideon had to draw back. It felt like moving against a planet's magnetic force. If he closed that distance again, he'd simply surrender to the overwhelming power the vampire had over him. The conqueror would become conquered so fast it would be like a teenager's first sex, hard, fast and not anywhere as far as he'd intended to take this.

Maybe he couldn't match Daegan in a lot of ways, but he would prove he was equal to the vampire's resolve. He had his pride, after all. He'd never backed away from a challenge from Daegan, and he'd meet this one in his own way.

Calmer—somewhat—he reached out and stroked Daegan's hair at his temple. It was a safer gesture, an almost gentle movement, but the vampire's eyes kindled as if he'd done something far more provocative. It only took a single spark to set off gunpowder, after all. Gideon leaned in, cognizant that the vampire's head was no longer restrained by a rope around his neck.

"You want my mouth, then you don't move yours. Not a twitch." Gideon forced his voice to harsh command, which made Daegan's eyes narrow. Yep, the T-Rex was going to munch on the lion like a handful of pretzel thins.

"The bet was for you to fuck me, vampire hunter. Not give me orders."

Gideon lifted a shoulder. "If you can't stay still, I get it. Servants get a lot more practice at that kind of thing, so we're way better at self-control."

What a joke, given how often Daegan and Anwyn turned him into a mindless, rutting beast that had to be chained because he passed the point of understanding commands, let alone responding to them. Even so, the truth had never stopped Gideon from yanking Daegan's chain before.

Daegan became as still as the waiting predator Gideon knew he was. He thought it pretty likely Daegan could rip out an assailant's throat with his fangs alone. He didn't fear that, but still he came in slow and careful, humming his pleasure as he traced the vampire's lips with his tongue, enjoying the slight quiver, the taste of them as he played with the seam.

Oh, man. Lust surged in Daegan's mind. Gideon was surprised that this tested his control even more than the handling of his cock. Who knew male vampires were more like women in that regard, where the slightest erotic touch could turn their crank? Making him hold still while Gideon did nothing but play with his food, so to speak.

He was close enough that Daegan's cock bumped his

hip, and Gideon put his hand over it, holding it firmly against him as if soothing the beast, his thumb sliding over the ridged head, fingers stroking as his other hand slid into Daegan's hair, holding on, teasing his nape.

"Open up," he muttered against his mouth. "But you keep staying this still. God, you're fucking too much."

He sensed Anwyn's utter mesmerized stillness behind them. There was some of the same going on in the very center of himself. He licked Daegan's fangs, and learned all the ways Daegan loved his mouth, even when it was spouting bullshit. Gideon stroked his tongue, explored the vampire's mouth with lazy thoroughness. As he shifted, he moved so Daegan's cock was no longer against his hip but solidly aligned with his, separated only by the straining fibers of his jeans. He pinned him harder with his hand, iron bar against iron bar, and Daegan rumbled a feral noise that vibrated against Gideon's lips. His shoulder muscles knotted.

"You like that, hmm?" Gideon spoke against his flesh with a casualness he didn't feel. "You don't know how often I think about this. Just pinning you to the bed and fucking kissing you until you come against me." He gave him a hard rub. "The bet wasn't just for me to fuck you, Master. It was to take you, and we both know that's a hell of a lot more than me sticking my dick in your ass. Else you wouldn't be holding back so much. Like I said earlier, I can always count on your sense of honor. It's your Achilles' heel."

No it's not.

He heard that thought loud and clear, even in the maelstrom of everything going on in Daegan's head. It wasn't coherent thought, just pure feeling, but he received the missive as if it was tattooed on Daegan's forehead. *Anwyn and Gideon.* They were his Achilles' heel. The vampire would sacrifice his honor, destroy the universe and everything in between for them. For each of them, separate as well as together.

Then the vampire underscored the power of that thought by putting simple words to it.

I honored the bet because there is very little I wouldn't do for you, Gideon.

Daegan had never said the girly thing he'd finally compelled Gideon to say that once. *I love you.* But he didn't need to do so, did he? Those words weren't what love was about.

And in that realization, Gideon resolved the problem that presented itself every time he imagined Daegan on hands and knees. It was as obvious as the bond between them. That honor, driven by love, drove everything else. And he would never want his Master on hands and knees before him.

Even though he still fully intended to have what he'd been promised.

Releasing Daegan, he dragged the stool over once more, stepped up on it and began to loosen the ropes holding the vampire's arms up. He pressed his chest right up against Daegan's face, his hips against his abdomen. His hand jerked on the knot as Daegan's mouth found his flesh, fang scoring a nipple.

"Hey. Behave," he grunted, but there was a laugh in his own breathless response as he reached down and tugged the vampire's hair, hard. Then he'd loosened the hold of the ropes from the beam, and stepped back to the ground, holding Daegan's bound wrists by that connecting knot in between.

Pulling his knife from his pocket again, he cut off most of the fall, leaving just a short tether attached to it, about four feet. Now all his Master bore were those ropes on his wrists, the rest of him gloriously naked, his hair falling over dangerously glinting eyes, cock at a full state of readiness again.

"We're going to our bedroom," Gideon said in a voice that sounded thick to his own ears. "That's where I want to do this."

Daegan's gaze slid down his body with the same possessive heat it always held. That hadn't changed, not once through this, Gideon realized. He'd had that fleeting thought at the beginning, hadn't he? All this was possible perversely because of Daegan and Anwyn's ownership of him, Daegan's ownership of them both, a double layer of security that had given Gideon's emotions the courage to reach for every level of his and Daegan's relationship. To take, not just to fuck.

There'd been times he'd wondered about his brother Jacob's odd give and take with his Mistress, Lady Lyssa. She so obviously always held the reins, and yet she didn't, too. Gideon had resigned himself to never figuring it out totally, because it wasn't a brain thing. It was something beyond rational thought. Just like this.

"Perhaps I could help you with that first." Daegan's attention was on Gideon's aching cock, in a state way past the doctor's warning about a sustained erection, but that, too, was different for third marked servants. Not dangerous, but no less painful.

The vampire's attention lifted to his face. "Do you not want my mouth there, vampire hunter? Let me take your seed down my throat, give you room to become hard again and enjoy the terms of our wager fully."

"You're in my head," Gideon accused. Daegan shook his head.

"It is what I would do. What I would want if I was that hard before I fucked you. Sliding into your ass is a pleasure of the gods, Gideon. It is something I never rush." His lips twisted. "You might goad me to the point I waste no time on entry, but once there, I stay a good long time."

Such memories were hazed in red velvet in Daegan's mind, an arena-sized screen that scrolled right into Gideon's head, the times Daegan had taken him rough and hard. But, as he said, once there, he could bang him into weak-kneed, barely-able-to-walk, full submission.

He thought of Daegan dropping to one knee, opening Gideon's jeans and taking him deep throat. Daegan had sucked Gideon off before, but always from a Dominant position. Gideon beneath him, or turned upside down on a frame of some kind. If he was straddling Daegan's face, it was because the vampire's hands were clasped like manacles on his thighs as Gideon knelt before his Mistress, serving her pussy with his lips and tongue.

This part didn't hit the same wall in his mind as the hands and knees thing did, particularly when he saw Daegan lick his lips, and he again felt the vampire's dark wish to see Gideon's cock, unencumbered by clothes. Daegan wanted to take hold of it and shove Gideon over into climax, bring forth that response with his mouth. Since Daegan had initiated it, Gideon was all too aware if he capitulated that he was handing the reins back. But only a bit. Daegan had recognized Gideon's dilemma and there was a searing sweet pleasure to this that had a different flavor and tone.

In answer, Gideon dropped the tether to the ground and stepped on it, a symbolic gesture that he was still holding the vampire's leash. Then he opened his jeans. His cock practically gave an audible sigh of relief. After another thought, Gideon backed off a step, removed his boots, shed the jeans and stood before Daegan in those tight brief shorts Anwyn had admired on him earlier. Daegan shared that pleasure, how the style put all the emphasis on the front, on the cock and balls, the shorts style keeping the garment from looking like panties in the way that traditional briefs did. However, the far shorter cut of the legs versus boxers offered a good view of his muscular legs. Daegan's thought, not his. Absurdly, Gideon flushed at the vampire's avid and graphic appreciation of his body in the brief style.

Daegan dropped to one knee before him. Gideon adjusted the cloth downward, releasing his cock fully, and then his eyes closed as Daegan's hands came up and gripped him, double fisted.

He hadn't given Daegan permission; Daegan hadn't asked. That was how the one knee thing worked now, where his intention to put Daegan on all fours hadn't. It was such an odd thing, the subtleties between vampire and servant.

Anwyn appeared in his field of vision. She'd shed the robe so she was only in the waist cincher, her breasts quivering as she stepped up behind Daegan and threaded her long-nailed fingers into his silken hair. Gideon let out a guttural sound of desperate pleasure as the vampire's mouth closed on him. Daegan sucked him right to the back of his throat, letting him feel the prick of his fangs, but adjusting so they were an enhancement to the pleasure, not a distraction. Mostly. Anwyn watched the point of contact avidly, as did Gideon, seeing his Master's mouth stretch over his cock, slide all the way down. The heel of Daegan's hands, his thumbs, caressed Gideon's balls.

Hunger had exploded in Daegan's mind during that first suck. Gideon imagined that had resulted in another spurt of semen from the slit of the vampire's cock, thick enough to drip on the floor. He moistened his own lips at the thought, rasping out an erratic breath, fists closing at his sides as Daegan slid down his length and back up again, pulling on Gideon. He brought that boiling climax in his balls to full tea pot kettle whistle level.

Reaching over Daegan, Gideon captured Anwyn's gorgeous tits in his hands, fondling the curves with pure male demand. It won a challenging glint from his Mistress's eyes, but she allowed it, dropping her head back with a lovely sigh of arousal, her gleaming brown hair brushing her ass. He gave her nipples a hard pinch as he shoved deeper into Daegan's mouth.

"Fuck..." he groaned. Anwyn gripped Daegan's hair, and he heard the male vampire make a savage noise against his cock, a response as intense as theirs. Gideon was so close, but he realized he'd gotten so used to asking permission to come that he was hesitating at the brink. He met Anwyn's eyes. But it wasn't her lips on him.

"Come for me," Daegan snarled against his cock. "Gideon. Do it now."

He spurted like a fountain, bucking his hips against Daegan's mouth, his cock emitting one pure, thick gush of come, everything that had built up since this had started. It felt like the pressure of a dam release, with all the disorienting rush and power of the flow that went along with it. Gideon shouted out his climax, dropping his grip on Anwyn's breasts to overlap her hand on Daegan's head, his other falling to the vampire's shoulder, fingers leaving pressure marks there.

"Yes...*God.*"

Gideon discovered that Daegan's mind went as blank as his own in such a moment. One goal, one purpose. It was all about taking his length fully, sucking him down, making sure he gave his servant a full measure of satisfaction. Functional, yes, but the fiery streak of satisfaction he felt from Daegan was enough to twine around his cock and start the blood pumping once again.

Daegan had made room for the back stretch, but it was Gideon who was going to take them all the way home.

Part 5 (Finale)

Gideon took some deep, shuddering breaths, still holding onto Daegan's shoulder. He realized Daegan had spread out his fingers, thumb in the crease between his thigh and ball sac. He was helping to steady Gideon, holding him up, the same way Gideon had done for him earlier, after he'd brought Daegan to climax in the same way. Glancing down at his cock, still in a semi-turgid state, Gideon saw some streaks of blood. Vaguely, he remembered the vampire had grazed him a couple times.

"Got a little enthusiastic there," he grumbled. "You have switch blades in your mouth, you know."

"You zigged when I zagged. Which is not a problem when I'm in your mind."

Thinking back, Gideon did admit the fangs had scraped him when he jerked in involuntary response. Daegan had never scored him by accident when he went down on Gideon from a Dominant position, even when he didn't have his servant tightly restrained.

"No shit. Never thought of it as planned."

Daegan's gaze lifted. "It's why you wanted in *my* mind, is it not? To monitor my wellbeing?"

"You laughing at me for that?" Wrapping the tether around his hand, Gideon tugged the vampire to his feet. Daegan rose, all deadly grace and balance.

"You're still in my mind, Gideon. You know the answer to that. A vampire, like any predator, expects no one but himself to safeguard his wellbeing. Learning there are times when you may relax that guard...it's not easy for us, but that doesn't make it any less precious of a gift."

He was right; Gideon *could* feel that reaction in the maze of the vampire's psyche. Daegan wasn't mocking or rejecting the idea of Gideon's care. He was approaching it the way a wild animal approached something unknown to it, all senses tuned to evaluating the size and shape of it, but he'd passed the point of considering it a threat. Now there was curiosity, a little bit of wonder. Giving a seven-hundred-year-old plus vampire a sense of wonder, however brief, was undeniably kind of cool.

"I want you back in my head. Two-way, though. I want to be in yours for this last part."

Daegan inclined his head, and there it was. Usually it was a subtle click that Gideon's precog senses helped him detect when the connection was active. He noticed it had more of a jolt to it this time. It reminded him of a dog brought back to his yard after a trip, charging back into the fence to run around and sniff every corner, see what had crossed his territory, if anything had changed. Hopefully Daegan wouldn't feel the need to mark him the same way.

Daegan's gaze met his, amused. "I am forever torn between the desire to laugh or put my foot up your ass, vampire hunter."

"Same goes. Right now, though, I only want to do one thing." Gideon stroked a knuckle down Daegan's throat, winning a surprised flicker in his dark gaze at the intimacy, but he wanted to feel the swallow when he spoke the next words.

"I want to fuck you."

The vampire did swallow, and that constriction in his throat was matched by a similar reaction in Gideon's gut. He backed up, tugging the rope, and the vampire followed him. It was a powerful fantasy come to life, Daegan naked, his hands bound, following him into the bedroom. Following his lead, trusting him because Gideon had asked him for that trust.

You did more than ask, Gideon. You have earned it. A far more important distinction.

"You're way too articulate," Gideon said, despite the swell of emotion the thought inspired. "I need to get you back to four-letter words and heavy mouth-breathing."

"So we can be on equal intellectual levels?"

"Nice." Gideon gave the tether a sharp tug. "Not a smart

move, when your ass is going to be at my mercy."

"I have no fear of you, vampire hunter."

Daegan often arrogantly assumed no human could cause him physical harm, but the look he gave Gideon now said he meant something quite different. Daegan cocked his head, eyes vivid. *You assured me I had nothing to fear from you.*

Gideon pressed his lips together, not sure how to respond to that. Instead, he turned his attention to their new setting.

As if Lyssa knew her vampire guests might have an orgy in it, the cottage's master bedroom had an enormous bed. A great size for two tall men and one female. Usually, Anwyn lay between Gideon and Daegan. Not tonight, though. At least not right now.

The screened windows were open, letting in the night marsh sounds, the futile patter of bugs trying to invade. The smell filtering through the mesh was humid salt water and green maritime forest. Gideon could easily imagine Lyssa flying in that mysterious jungle when she transformed to her sleek Fae form.

Anwyn slid into the room behind them. Unhooking the waist cincher, she dropped it over the arm of a chair, so all three of them were pretty much naked, except for Gideon's shorts and Daegan's restraints. Her pale skin gleamed, her hair brushing her buttocks.

Gideon took Daegan to the bed and nodded. "In the middle, on your side. Facing the window. Facing her."

Anwyn's mind touched his, understanding what he wanted. Gideon held the tether, paying out some slack as Daegan complied, sliding across the bed and settling on his side, showing the curve of shoulder and hip, lean thigh stretched out. Gideon was the one who swallowed now. He could see in darkness like a candlelit room, and the play of shadows and light his vision provided etched out the line of Daegan's back, the seam between his buttocks, every line of muscle. The way his hair lay on his neck. The shape of ear and jaw.

Putting his knee on the bed, Gideon leaned over Daegan's head, giving the rope a tug. "Grip the rails of the headboard."

He felt Daegan looking up at him as he tied the tether to the slats just above Daegan's grip. It left the vampire's elbows bent at the level of his face, his arms not as straight as he'd been when standing, but that was fine, as long as his hands were out of the way. The main point was emphasizing he still wasn't the one in charge. Technically.

The position pillowed Daegan's head on his biceps. Gideon traced his back once more, admittedly a little fascinated with the way his callused, rough fingers looked against the unmarked skin. He didn't often get the chance to touch Daegan like this, and he was finding it damn addictive. His mind went to the trinity of teardrops on his own chest, proof of Daegan and Anwyn's combined third mark on him, the choice of the Powers-That-Be. The branded collar on his throat and matching cuff brands on his wrists were the choice of his Master and Mistress, their imposed will.

He sensed Daegan's attention to the thoughts going through his mind. "You wish to mark me as I marked you, vampire hunter?"

Yes.

"There's a blade in the drawer." Daegan nodded toward the nightstand on the opposite side of the bed.

Anwyn regularly teased them about their penchant for having a weapon in every room. She'd declared they could pull an assault rifle from behind the commode, or a grenade out of a fruit bowl. Gideon had pointed out calmly that they weren't that excessive. Given their capable hand-to-hand skills, they were technically well-armed, even if there were no weapons available. However, the fruit bowl idea was a good one. And grenades were a plus in any situation.

Leaving the bed, he circled to the side where Anwyn sat, facing Daegan. Withdrawing the blade from the drawer, he saw it was his military grade pig sticker. An aspiring burglar would wet his shorts if faced with it. Yet if he broke into this cottage, it wouldn't be the knife he'd have to worry about. At least two of the occupants would view him like a Domino's delivery. With extra marinara sauce.

Daegan spoke again. "Not that one, Gideon."

Anwyn drew in a quiet breath. Gideon glanced back into the drawer. There was a wooden knife lying next to his nine-millimeter. It was excellent craftsmanship—solid blade, sharp edge, wicked point. Jacob had given it to Gideon as a gift, partially as a joke, but with serious intent. Vampires had enemies and, whether the vampires in question liked it or not, a servant felt just as responsible for protecting them. Especially a servant who had been a vampire hunter.

Gideon turned the wooden blade over in his hands. By directing his choice, Daegan was verifying his earlier thoughts, telling Gideon he was one of the few in the world Daegan trusted. Completely.

"When I mark you, it won't stay. Not like mine." Daegan healed from anything. His angel blood even overrode the vampire blood, such that he couldn't tattoo himself. His blood and Anwyn's combined had worked on Gideon, though.

"Not like yours," Daegan agreed. "But do you feel their weight most on your skin or on your heart?" He nodded to the marks on Gideon's chest. "What's on your skin is merely a symbol of where the real collar and cuffs lie. That is all." *Mark me as you desire, Gideon. I will absorb it into my soul, and it will be as real there as what you bear on your flesh.*

Anwyn had shifted over Daegan's legs and was now kneeling behind him, her hand resting on his hip as she regarded Gideon with quiet eyes, serious mouth. With her gaze trained on them, Gideon lifted the knife and brought the point to Daegan's chest. His hand trembled, then tightened with hard resolve on the hilt.

No. He pulled it away, flipped it so it was pointing backwards, blade clutched firmly in his hand. Not even for this, no. He couldn't handle seeing that lethal wooden point so close to his Master's heart. Because of his mixed blood, Daegan had said he wasn't sure if he could be killed in the regular vampire way, but Gideon wasn't taking any chances. He'd seen too much shit in his life. Fate was too capricious. For all he knew, a mighty gust of wind might come through the screen, or Gideon could have a violent muscle spasm, and then *bam*, that blade would be thrust between Daegan's ribs.

Yeah, it was a stupid, childish thought, but he'd lost his parents to such a crazy act of fate. Then he'd lost Laura. As much as he loved those three faces of his past, it was a star against a galaxy, in terms of how he felt about these two faces of his present. Fuck the automatic dying if his Master or Mistress were killed. Losing either of them would kill him, period.

What they meant to him was far too precious to Gideon to ever take such a risk. He set the wooden blade aside and retrieved the military knife. For all its threatening appearance, it was much less worrisome.

"Gideon." Daegan's hands flexed in the bonds as if he wished to touch him. Gideon saw it in that kaleidoscope of colors in the vampire's mind, and felt an answering resonance in Anwyn's.

"Just shut up. Pretend you're tied up and at my mercy."

I am.

Gideon closed his eyes, enveloped by those colors. He put the blade tip against Daegan's flesh without looking, because he didn't have to do so. He knew where his heart was. As he pressed into the firm meat of the left pectoral, he felt Daegan still, internalize the pain. Gideon carved the marks into his flesh, feeling as if his own nerve endings burned in response. When he opened his eyes, there it was. A bold *G*, with a clean, sharp *A* right next to it.

"The two people you belong to," he said. "Say it. Say you'll never forget it."

Anwyn's hand had settled over Gideon's, both of them gripping Daegan's shoulder, which shifted beneath their hold as he looked between them, meeting Anwyn's blue-green eyes before coming back to Gideon's.

"I belong to the both of you," the vampire said, that Old World cadence he had making it even more formal of an oath. "And I will not forget that. Not ever. My heart, soul and body are yours."

Gideon nodded. With a sense of the same ritual solemnity, he licked the residual blood off the blade, collected the rest off Daegan's chest with his fingers and offered it to Anwyn. She took it straight from his hand, Daegan's gaze locked on both of them. Every line of him tightened as, with a playful look toward Gideon to break the mood, she bent and used her delicate tongue to lick around the edges of the wound.

When she straightened, Gideon offered a hand to his Mistress. "Switch places with me? I'd like you to keep him occupied."

That sparkle stayed in her beautiful gaze as she took his hand, sliding over Daegan with an intimate wriggle of her body that captured his attention just as Gideon intended. She reclined facing the vampire, aligning herself with Daegan's body as Gideon moved behind him and stretched out on his hip.

Bless her heart, Anwyn had brought the lubricant with her. Getting rid of his shorts, he leaned back to snag it off the other nightstand. As he rolled onto his back behind Daegan to grease up his own cock, he had the pleasure of being connected to their minds, knowing Anwyn was taking full advantage of Daegan's bound state to trail her fingers over those healing initials, put her mouth on them and lick the blood more thoroughly as her other hand dropped. Caressing his cock elicited a strong response from the vampire. With feral amusement, Gideon realized the vampire had a seriously sexist double standard. He got way more growly and aggressive about Anwyn taking advantage of his bound state than he had about Gideon doing it.

When he latched onto her throat, a reproof complete with the prick of fangs, her throaty purr was preceded by the appearance of her fingers sliding up along his shoulder, into Daegan's dark hair as she pressed her body full against the vampire's, teasing his cock with her slick pussy, but keeping it out of penetration range.

I shall tie you both up for days and torture you at my leisure.

He meant that shit. But Gideon intended to distract him from such dire intentions. Glancing down, knowing they were both in his mind, he gave them a front row view of him stroking his cock, spreading that lube on good and thick over the head, up and down the shaft. It was like feeling two lasers turn in his direction. He intensified the heat by drawing it out on purpose, thumbing his slit to rub some of what was oozing out of it in with the lube. Having been their servant a while, chained to them in a variety of ways, he knew just how to tease the Dom in them.

Don't tempt your Master and Mistress at the same time, Gideon. Being female, Anwyn has a far less well-developed sense of fair play.

Daegan's chuckle was muffled and cut short by an oath as Anwyn bit his nipple with her sharp fangs. But point taken. Gideon had had a similar thought earlier, right? Women had honor – it was just quite a bit more flexible than a male's. That whole context-versus-logic aspect of their personalities.

All tangled in each other's minds, where there were so many possibilities, he didn't have a problem with taking some risks, however. Gideon shifted, his thighs pressing up against the back of Daegan's, nudging until Daegan bent his knees to match, for that nice-and-tight spooned position.

The vampire's mind became clear as a mirror lake then, a stillness settling on them all. Anwyn had adjusted back when he moved his knees at Gideon's direction, but Gideon saw her twine her fingers with Daegan's bound ones on the head board. She had her eyes fixed on the vampire's face, watching every expression as she provided a reassuring bulwark on that side. They'd hold him between them.

Gideon used his fingers first, making sure the lube was living up to its reputation. Yep, still as slippery and warm in that taut channel as it had been earlier. Even so, Gideon guided his cock between his buttocks, painted some more on the rim with his tip. The vampire made an inarticulate noise, back muscles quivering. Gideon pushed himself even closer, wrapping his arm around Daegan's chest and putting his mouth against the back of his neck.

"Just relax and push against me. Same way you told me to do it." Well, at first. Then he'd learned the way of it. Now Daegan could toss him onto a bed and slam into him like a railworker driving in a steel spike.

Daegan's hands curled in their bonds and tightened over Anwyn's, but Gideon felt what else the vampire wanted. Needed. He wanted Gideon's fingers there, holding tight. *Wow.* That was unexpected. The vampire's mind was cycling, disturbing that lake calm, becoming harder to follow. Gideon struggled to keep a focus inside as well as outside.

"In a minute," he said. "You take me deep first. Relax that tight ass of yours. Prove something bigger than a pencil dick can squeeze into that narrow space."

"As soon as you find one to do so," Daegan muttered, voice strained. Gideon bared his teeth in a grin and set them to his carotid, eliciting that always arousing I'm-so-going-to-kick-your-ass savage vampire hiss.

"How about...now?"

He didn't push, he knew enough for that, but he eased in with relentless pressure. When that first ring of muscles gave way, then the next, he slid into the hold of a fucking incredibly tight, slippery channel that held him like a glove, those well-developed muscles rippling inside and out to clamp down on his dick in a way that had him fighting for control.

He gave the feeling to Anwyn and Daegan both, so she'd know the astounding pleasure of it, and Daegan would know the pleasure he was giving. When Gideon got all the way to the hilt, his thighs cradling the vampire's ass, his balls pinned hard against it, his cock deep inside, he put the hand that had guided it there over Daegan's head and gripped his fingers and Anwyn's, a three-way link.

"Given that it's your first time, I wanted to go in easy-like. But since you heal up so fast, now I want to fuck the ever-living-shit out of you." Stroking Daegan's chest, Gideon adjusted himself a little deeper, earning a grunt...and then way more than that.

Fuck.

It wasn't Daegan's convulsing muscles that caused the expletive. He should have been warned by that confusing mixture of signals he was getting from the vampire's mind. Suddenly, it was like he'd dropped two floors, now as deep inside Daegan's head as he was in his ass. He saw the shift in the colors, the vibrant rainbow clouds sucked away by darker, deeper colors, blood and storms, volatile and decadent both.

It took a harrowing moment of re-orientation to figure it out. Fortunately, the times he'd had to battle Anwyn's gremlins made it a quick adjustment. The vampire male had turned that corner, was facing the oncoming cyclone, where it was clear control might be wrested from his grasp by the response of his own body and even deeper places. Gideon knew Daegan wouldn't fully lose control—he was too deadly a weapon to ever do that—but Gideon's penetration had made him lose his grip enough that it had startled him. That hadn't happened in a *really* long time. He hadn't been prepared for it.

The last time someone had subjugated Daegan, Gideon had had a front row seat. The vampire had chopped up a dozen vampires like a sous chef. Now his eyes were closed, his focus on trying to brace against a force of nature that very few could resist. Especially if the ones bringing the chaos were those he loved and trusted in ways he'd never allowed himself before.

His fingers had clenched over the rope and his body was doing that all-over-quiver thing. He was devolving, not sure what way to go. Not sure how to find a reaction to this. A control.

When the situations were reversed, Daegan would deny Gideon any control, knowing not only was it part of being a servant, but it was in Gideon's makeup to handle such unpredictability from his own psyche. But Gideon also understood a Dom's nature better now, especially one as deep as Daegan's ran.

Even Anwyn could handle this kind of thing better, because she'd once been human. And therein lay the solution. He sent it to her in the same blink of time, not sure if Daegan was even tuning in. The vampire was fighting his need to break free of the bindings, resist where Gideon was taking him. He wanted to dissipate that tornado of feeling with his own indomitable will.

No. This is for Gideon. Give Gideon this.

Hearing the self-admonition, knowing Daegan was

holding on against the unknown for his sake, made Gideon's eyes sting, his throat ache. But he wasn't going to get all sentimental, hell no. He was going to fuck Daegan with unrestrained power, a hundred percent unleashed testosterone, and sweep all three of them away on that ride together.

Anwyn curled her lovely leg up over both of theirs and clasped her free hand around the back of Daegan's neck. Her breasts pressed against Gideon's arm across Daegan's chest as she followed Gideon's direction. She sank fully, completely onto Daegan's cock, all the way to the hilt. At the same second, Gideon pulled back just enough and then slammed back in.

Daegan's whole body jerked. Gideon shot the warning to Anwyn's head fast enough she pulled her hand free from their link on the headboard, an instinct that changed to a mental noise of protest when Gideon slid his hand into its place.

That powerful grip constricted, sending blinding pain through his fingers. *Jesus.* Had he just heard a bone crack? Maybe two?

It didn't matter. Leaving his hand in that grip was a sheer act of will, as powerful as the one Daegan was imposing on himself to stay still. Gideon found the brain cells to make his next pump into his ass more of a teasing seduction than an invasion, reminding Daegan he wasn't in a fight.

"We have you, Master." If Daegan had the same degree of muscles in his ass as he had everywhere else—a very likely possibility—Gideon might end up pulling back a stump. That should be a hell of a bigger concern to him than his fingers. He wasn't sure if a servant's appendages regenerated like a lizard's. He probably should have asked about that. Daegan was always chastising him for leaping before he looked, after all.

"You protect us. You don't hurt us. Not that way." Though Gideon hated to admit to any pain, he knew it wasn't just for him now. *You're hurting the crap out of my hand. Ease up. You don't want to hurt Anwyn like that.*

Daegan's grip relaxed instantly. Gideon followed

instinct, letting go of his chest to twist his upper body around and retrieve the knife he'd left on the nightstand. With one dexterous snap of his wrist, he cut the rope holding Daegan, letting the knife drop behind the bed. He pulled the rest of the bindings away, so the vampire was completely free. Daegan continued to hold the bed rails, though, telling Gideon he still had enough of his head in place to try and follow the dictates of the wager. The thought made Gideon slide his abused hand under the vampire's arm to clasp his chest anew with it, dropping the other one to Daegan's hip.

"Now it's all about what I want," he said against the vampire's flesh, tasting a light dew on his skin. Perspiration. Well, didn't that just fucking make him harder? He started to piston his hips into that incredibly fuckable channel. Plunge and retreat, the slippery heat making him crazy. Even with the pain to his hand, holding onto control was a bitch. Fucking Daegan's ass was a zone of red lust, spew-like-a-teenager heaven.

Anwyn, bless her for the tease she was, let him feel how hard and thick Daegan was inside her. Gideon was just as hard and thick. The more it sunk into his mind, all they'd done leading up to this, all the nuances of meaning exchanged, the more territorial he felt. He would come inside Daegan to emphasize what those knife marks on his chest had meant. His Master. *His.*

Ours. He met Anwyn's gaze and saw her parted lips, the glaze that said Daegan was going to send her flying pretty soon. With every thrust from Gideon, Daegan was balancing it with a counter thrust into her sweet cunt. Her giving Daegan a target for his own cock hadn't completely called the savage predator to heel. Her neck was bleeding where Daegan had bitten her. But tied to both of their minds, Gideon could see it was okay.

That whirl of crimson and dark colors in Daegan's mind like a storm surge had become a little tighter coil. Controlled loss of control. It said the vampire had consciously let himself wade at least hip deep into the new experience and all the sensations it brought. He'd let himself move to the close side of danger, just as Gideon had intended.

The vampire snarled, his body tensing like a spring.

"You're going to come for me, now," Gideon rasped against him. "Her cunt is just as slippery, hot and tight as your ass is to me. Fuck, you feel good."

As he pushed in harder, he reached across Daegan and up, grasping the headboard slat right in front of the vampire's face so he could drive up higher, deeper. It put his wrist right where he wanted it. Daegan bit into him like a wolf tearing into the thigh of an ox, but it was all right. Gideon understood. He'd reached the eye of the tornado, staring up at all the things that made up Daegan's world. He understood this, the monster beneath the man, and embraced it. No matter all the things he abhorred about vampires, there was nothing about Daegan he would reject from this point forward. Nothing. Daegan had seen all of Gideon's darkness, after all. Now it was quid pro quo.

Even among the volatile mix of passion, Gideon felt the miracle of Daegan recognizing that. The storm enveloped them as Daegan became all need, desire and power. If he didn't come, he might tear them both apart. And they'd embrace the destruction.

"Do it," Gideon gasped, feeling his own response coming, a result of being clenched by that tight channel. "Come for us, Master."

Daegan released with a harsh groan, a series of animal grunts that Gideon relished, especially when they combined with Anwyn's cry of climax, her pussy spasming around Daegan's cock. Gideon let his own flood gates break. It pushed Daegan to another level, the vampire's hips jerking in response as Gideon's seed shot into him. It made Gideon want to do it all over again, over and over. Never mind that a couple of his fingers were probably broken and his arm needed a million stitches. He'd heal. It was all good.

He pressed his face against Daegan's nape as his cock drained to the last. He was breathing hard. Holding him. Just holding him. As Gideon felt Daegan struggling to get a handle on things and calm down, Gideon wanted to say all sorts of mushy, stupid things, but he didn't. He settled for holding him like he'd never let him go. And he never would. Anwyn's arms were wrapped over Daegan's shoulders, her fingertips brushing Gideon's face, his hair, stroking and soothing them both. Their goddess.

"My boys," she murmured, confirming it. "My wonderful boys."

Her body was still shuddering with those delicious female aftershocks. Daegan dropped a hand lower to palm her ass and hold her more firmly on him. Apparently, Gideon wasn't the only one who didn't want to break the joining of their bodies.

He closed his eyes as Daegan put his mouth on his arm, laved it with his tongue, cleaning him up, making sure the blood was coagulating. But it was not himself Gideon was concerned about. As the haze cleared, he realized somewhere during the aftermath, Daegan had closed that gateway between their minds. Fair enough, things being kind of done at this point. But the vampire's body was making odd little shivers.

"Hey." Gideon rose on an elbow, putting his arm back across the male's chest, brushing his jaw along Daegan's temple. "You okay?"

"Yes." Daegan had his eyes closed, but he put his hand up over Gideon's. A long moment passed.

I expected it to be...different. I expected your humor, your wiseass comments. I expected some of your emotions. I did not expect all of mine, or what it all became.

"Welcome to my world, every time the two of you take me over."

A smile touched Daegan's lips but he opened his eyes, turning a serious gaze up toward Gideon. "You have given me an unexpected gift. Thank you. But you took an unacceptable risk."

"No, I didn't. Because no matter where you go in your head, we're there. You might strike out, but you always hold back. I wanted you to do a little less holding back tonight and know that we could take it. And that we trust you."

Daegan frowned. "I could have hurt you both. Badly."

"But you didn't." Anwyn spoke now, touching his face. "Gideon's right. You couldn't."

Gideon tucked his hips in tighter against him. "I fucking never want to pull out. Though it may be a moot point, as tight as you are. We'll have to go to the ER to get my dick removed from your ass."

"I'll find a blade and cut it off at the root first. That would solve many problems."

Gideon snorted. Daegan put his hand up to Anwyn's face, his thumb sliding along her cheek, her jaw. "You, *cher*, I always expect to be a wonder. You never fail to persuade me to do your bidding."

"Remember that the next time I tell you it's your turn to take out the trash."

"That's why we have a servant." When Gideon took a shot at his head, Daegan caught his wrist, his quick reflexes back on point. But Gideon took advantage of the turn of Daegan's head in his direction to crush his mouth to his once more. This time, the tide shifted. Daegan leaned back in his twisted position to grip Gideon's head and take over the kiss. He made it slow, thorough, long. Somewhere in that, his arm circled Anwyn and brought her into it. She propped herself on Daegan's body so three mouths were teasing one another, lips and tongues spreading wet heat.

When they finally eased back, Daegan clasped Gideon's arm, now draped over Daegan's hips. As the vampire kept Anwyn close, he glanced over his shoulder at Gideon with an expression that made Gideon's heart literally somersault in his chest. Jesus, fucking the guy had only made his obsession with him worse.

"Have I fairly delivered on the terms of the wager?"

"Hell no. We're going to have to do it all over again."

Anwyn chuckled. Daegan curled a lip. "Dream on, vampire hunter."

Gideon's own lips twisted at that, but he slid his hand up to Daegan's chest. It was new, to just touch him casually like this in the aftermath. Maybe Daegan wouldn't allow it tomorrow, maybe Gideon wouldn't feel as comfortable about the intimacy, but for tonight...it felt right.

"Yeah," Gideon said at last. "You did." He hesitated,

then pressed his palm against Daegan's heart, where he'd put that mark. Daegan's hand met his, and Anwyn's joined them.

"Thanks. Thanks for all of it."

Daegan's fingers tightened over him. "You will take my blood to help your fingers heal."

"Already healing." Gideon wiggled them to prove it. "I think what I took from you earlier is still working."

"Which would not have been necessary, if you hadn't stuck your chest in the way. As I told you—"

"Yeah, yeah. You could have diced the stake into Lincoln Logs before it came within arms' reach. You and Edward Scissorhands." Gideon grunted. "Spare me."

His cock had softened enough that he put his hand back down on the vampire's hip and withdrew slowly. Daegan had already slid from Anwyn's body, so the vampire turned onto his back, considering them both. Gideon had his own question to ask, though.

"What was that look between you two, when I asked Daegan to leave my mind, at the beginning? And don't get all cagey now." He narrowed his gaze at Daegan's lifted brow. "Yeah, I used a word from your pretentious vocabulary. Try not to faint."

Anwyn reached across Daegan to stroke Gideon's jaw, capturing his attention. "A Master never abdicates his responsibility to care for his servant. Even when it's simply care for his state of mind. Daegan wanted me to stay in your head, at least on the surface. He knew you would assume it was because I simply didn't have enough control." Now she gave him one of those penetrating looks in return. "And yes, I will make you pay that wrong assumption."

"Promises, promises, Mistress." Grasping her wrist, Gideon put his mouth against her palm, enjoying her nails scraping over his cheek, none-too-gently.

Daegan yawned—the bastard actually yawned. It almost made Gideon grin. The vampire must have seen it, because he pulled Gideon down next to him. He brought Anwyn down into a mirror position on his other side, albeit more tenderly. Once there, it was easy for limbs to get tangled,

Anwyn's thigh sliding over Gideon's where their knees both rested between Daegan's sprawled legs.

"Enough, children," the vampire said, closing his eyes.

"You know, I do protect the both of you as much as you protect me," Gideon pointed out. "Like one of those Egyptian guards, watching over the pharaoh and...pharaoh-ess."

If you wish to don a loin cloth like an Egyptian slave and fan us while we sleep, Gideon, we won't object.

Sure, I fuck your brains out, do all the work, and now you want me to fan you. With you vampires it's all me, me, me.

Daegan's lips quirked as he gave Gideon's hair a sharp tug. But they all settled then, the night sounds of the marsh taking over. It wasn't too far from dawn, such that Anwyn dropped off fairly quickly. Gideon dozed himself for a bit, but he and Daegan were on the same time clock. When they hit that vital hour before sunrise, they both woke, because Gideon's fledging Mistress needed the subterranean bedroom for full daylight.

Daegan carried her, Gideon securing the house as they passed through it. Once downstairs, they took their accustomed spots on either side of her on the bed, flanking her. Daegan propped his head on his hand, though, and laid his hand on her hip. When the vampire nodded to it, Gideon wasn't entirely sure the vampire meant what he thought he meant, but as Daegan's eyes met his, he was sure. *Well, hell.*

Taking a breath, Gideon laid his hand over the vampire's. He felt Anwyn's smooth skin between his splayed fingers. Some of the remarkable feelings from the past few hours returned as Gideon stroked the male's knuckles. An odd lump grew in his throat before Daegan gently disengaged his hand, leaning forward to lay that hand on Gideon's face and force him to hold his gaze. His expression told Gideon he was fully his Master once more...not that he'd ever stopped.

Correct, vampire hunter. I am always that. But...

He drew back, tapping his chest where Gideon had cut him, where the letters were no longer visible. But, as

Daegan had said, it didn't matter. Especially when he spoke the words in Gideon's mind now.

Your name is in my heart, Gideon. Always. Now lie down and sleep, and know we belong to one another, all three of us. Nothing can change that. I will never allow it to be otherwise.

Gideon reached out and put two of his fingers on the same spot, feeling the steady beat. *Same goes, vampire. You're not alone in that, remember? Or do I have to fuck your ass all over again to remind you?*

Daegan's lips curved at the challenge, those dark eyes gleaming. *Do not push your luck, vampire hunter.*

At that, he slid down behind Anwyn, motivating Gideon to do the same on the other side. As Gideon put his arm over her waist, his palm settling on the curve of her hip, Daegan's arm overlapped his, the vampire's hand coming to rest on Gideon's side, a result of the male's longer arms. Gideon didn't mind. Anwyn shifted in her sleep, tucking her typically cold feet between Gideon's calves for warmth, her hands finding their way to rest on Daegan's chest.

If there was any moment more perfect in the universe, Gideon didn't want it. He fell asleep, holding the feeling inside of him, the connection to the two of them, and was content.

First Christmas

A vignette about Marcus and Thomas, characters from the
Nature of Desire Series.

Originally posted 12/22/2013

Marcus first appeared as a key secondary character in
Book I of the series, Holding the Cards. *His and Thomas's*
full story occurred in Rough Canvas, *and they have made*
subsequent appearances in other books in the series.

Background: *In this story, we revisit Marcus and*
Thomas during their first Christmas together as a
married couple.

§

Finally on the plane. Planning a nap so I'll have enough
energy to do what I want to do to you when I get there.
Fuck, that made me sound old...

Well, you are in your forties now. Some decay is
expected. Don't forget, before Christmas Eve dinner with
my mother, you have to practice not using the f-bomb in
every sentence.

Decay? Fuck fuck fuck fuck, fucking fucked, have fuck,
will fuck, should fuck...

Thomas snorted. Propping an elbow on the top of the
ladder, he leaned against its steps as he sent a response text:
She'll smack you with a wooden spoon where it will do the
most good. I still have the mark from the last time she
used it on me. I was nine. Get some sleep. I miss you.

Pocketing the phone in his jeans, he turned his attention to the task at hand, adjusting a strand of lights on the eight-foot Christmas tree in their living room. Yeah, maybe it was overkill, but it was his and Marcus's first Christmas together as a married couple. The twinkling white tree lights reflected off the wedding band on his left hand. Though it had been a few months, Thomas still found himself staring at it a couple times a day. It represented a treasure he'd never expected to have in his possession. A treasure he'd never expected to have complete possession of him, but Marcus was his Master, now and forever. The ring said so.

That didn't mean the road was always paved in gold, though. Thomas surveyed the tree, suppressing a sigh. He'd wanted to text Marcus something like "Tree and house look great. Can't wait to show you." But Marcus would have responded with something like, "If you meet me at the door with a bow around your dick, that's all I care about." Typical banter, but it would have fallen flat for Thomas right now, part of a string of disappointments he'd hidden inside since the Christmas season had started.

It had become more and more difficult to involve Marcus in the traditions Thomas had thought they might enjoy together. Shopping for family members, decorating, planning the Christmas Eve dinner they'd agreed to host for Thomas's family. Marcus had claimed work, gallery showings, a new artist to supervise, yada yada. He'd nod or point when Thomas asked his opinion on dinner, gifts, decorations, but as soon as he could manage it, Marcus's eyes would cut away and his body language would avert in the same manner, not-so-subtle signals that he wasn't interested in anything more than perfunctory responses.

He was ready to show up for sex and anything that didn't involve Christmas, but the closer they drew to the holiday, the more he seemed to be pulling away. Marcus had bailed three days before Christmas Eve, saying he had to head off to New York for a few last minute issues. Though Marcus promised to be back before that night, Thomas had half expected to receive a text at any time since then, saying something had come up and Marcus wouldn't be able to make it home until after the holiday. Apparently his Master had realized that would be the final straw, causing Thomas to break all this open, confront what the hell was going on.

Thomas had tried to be patient. He understood this was the first Christmas Marcus had spent in a family environment in a long time, and his memories of past Christmases couldn't have been good ones. When he'd been living on the street as a teenager in New York, God only knew what kinds of things he'd been doing to mark the Yuletide. Thomas had rationalized it was best to let Marcus stand on the outskirts if that was where he needed to be this first Christmas, easing his toe into these waters. But Thomas had nursed his own hopes of creating a wealth of first Christmas memories with Marcus, and it was hard to put that away.

He was being selfish. In every other way, their first few months of married life were nothing short of wedded bliss. Though Marcus winced at such sentiment, he hadn't denied it when Thomas teased him with the term. They'd worked together on renovating the old farmhouse for their unique needs and style while maintaining the homey spirit of the place. Marcus wasn't as intuitive when it came to "homey", but he'd gone along on that journey with no hesitation, bemused and pleased by the choices Thomas had suggested to transform a house into a home.

He'd even seemed quite touched by the house warming gift Elaine, Thomas's mother, had brought them. Practical as always and realizing they were having to furnish and outfit a second home, Elaine had purchased a blue and brown glaze vase from a local artisan and stocked it with kitchen utensils. While the quality of the vase was nothing close to the standards of the NY art world, Marcus had been very complimentary of it and it now had an honored spot on the sturdy oak table.

The remembrance warmed Thomas and increased his sense of shame. He firmed his jaw. If the first Christmas was a tough one for Marcus, there would be other Christmases. When Thomas had danced with his mother at their wedding, she'd given him a piece of advice that resonated clearly now.

"This is the least important day of your marriage, Thomas," she'd said. She'd seemed so small in his arms, and yet those eyes and mouth of hers always conveyed a larger-than-life will. Much like the one the man he was marrying had, God help him. *"A marriage is far more than one day,"* she said. *"It's years and years of loving, laughing, crying, fighting and learning hard lessons about making your lives fit together. You build it one brick at a time, and some days you'll want to take that brick and bash it against his head. Other days he'll feel the same about you. Love becomes strong because of the hard times, not the easy ones."*

He got it. He did. He was in for the long haul. But God, he wished Marcus wanted to share Christmas with him, rather than just endure it.

"It's a shame Marcus isn't here to help."

Daralyn was a quiet slip of a girl, a shadow always watching and listening, so Thomas wasn't at all surprised she'd picked up on his mood as if he'd been bitching non-stop for the past ten minutes. She spoke from the floor, where she sat cross-legged, untangling a string of lights for the live garland coiled around her like a fragrant, pine-scented boa. Marcus and Thomas paid her to clean the house once a week, extra income for her above what she earned working at the hardware store with Rory. She also now lived in their small guesthouse, an outbuilding that used to be the farm's second hay barn.

The idea had been his sister Celeste's, or "Les" as they

called her. She'd offered up the wisdom in a quick heart-to-heart with her oldest brother. *"We need to start treating Daralyn like a grown-up. Maybe she isn't ready to live on her own in an apartment somewhere in town, but she needs her own place. A place where she's not sharing the house with Rory like she's his sister."*

The significance of that pointed statement wasn't lost on Thomas and, with Elaine's help, who was on the same track, they'd eased the shy young woman toward the idea. Since then, she'd embraced it fully, delighting in having her first "home", especially after Marcus and Thomas made it clear it was her space to paint and decorate as she wished. When he had the upper doors open in the main barn that was now his studio, Thomas could hear the soothing chimes she'd hung by her front door. Their music was brought to life by the breezes that came across the open fields.

Thomas cleared his throat. "He'll be here in a few hours. He caught a ride with some clients who were flying a private charter to Florida. They said they didn't mind dropping him off on the way."

Given how surly Marcus had been before he left, Thomas hoped he was in a better mood with his fellow passengers. Else they might drop him off over the state without landing first. He glanced at Daralyn. The young woman wore modest, serviceable jeans and T-shirt, her smooth brown hair pulled back in a tidy braid down her back, her usual attire.

"You know, much as I love having your help, you spent all morning getting this place in shape," he said. "You really don't need to be doing this, too."

She shook her head, raising remarkably beautiful hazel eyes to his before returning her attention to twining the now unsnarled lights around the garland. "No one should decorate for Christmas alone. It makes you feel sad."

Since Daralyn had spent her childhood with an abusive uncle and father who could have cared less about whether or not Christmas was celebrated, Thomas was sure she'd experienced that firsthand. The miracle was that she'd tried to do it on her own, in a household with nothing resembling a family. As a teenager, before they'd found out the reality of her situation, he remembered visiting her one Christmas and seeing a small tree. She'd probably dug it out of the untended overgrowth behind the house that was one step up from a shack. She'd hung it with a few sparse ornaments, all made by an adolescent hand. The candles in the window were the kind for storm supplies, but she'd put greenery around them to make them more festive. He wondered if she'd known the seasonal mythology behind candle lighting, to represent the Bethlehem star, to guide Mary and Joseph... It didn't matter. It had all been about hope.

"Daralyn is special," his mother always said. *"She may seem like a skittering mouse, but there's something beneath as resilient as an angel's smile."*

Since she'd been living under his family's protection, Daralyn had grown more confident, meaning she would actually talk without being addressed first, mostly. And she'd learned to interact with customers at their hardware and farm supply store, offer help when needed. But with the exception of Thomas, whom she'd inexplicably trusted from the first, she was nervous as a cat around men. She'd grown more comfortable around Rory, though. They'd all noticed it, how she watched him when she thought no one was looking.

Considering that now, he added a few more ornaments to the tree. "I think you should corner Rory tomorrow night," he said casually. "Tell him to kiss you under the mistletoe. If you jam the brake of his wheelchair, he can't get away."

He saw her hide her serious smile behind her hand. "That's just mean."

"Big brothers are mean. It's our job. He watches you, you know." Thomas had a vision of Rory trying to run him over with his wheelchair for initiating this conversation, but even his mother had said if they waited on the two of them, she'd be long dead in the ground before they exchanged their first kiss.

"Oh…well." Daralyn flushed, which was a good sign. It was when color drained from her face that panic hit. "I could never…*tell* him to do something."

The last part was delivered in a very quiet voice, but Thomas not only caught it, he understood the significance in a way she likely didn't. At least not consciously. Which was interesting, because Marcus had picked up on it the first time he met her, but Marcus picked up on a true submissive orientation like a coon dog on the scent of bacon frying three counties over. Thomas could just imagine his Master's response to such a provincial comparison.

Thomas hadn't been as sure of her status, given her traumatic history, but the more time he spent around her, the more he was sure Marcus was right. Though whether it would help or hinder her in a relationship was hard to say.

Giving her a thoughtful look, Thomas came across the room to take the garland from her. The two of them moved to the doorway where he'd already placed the hooks. As he hung the garland over them, Daralyn fluffed the greenery, arranging it for its best look. "You have a knack for this stuff," he said sincerely. "Mom loves the Christmas displays at the store. And the flower arrangements you leave when you clean here work great. Which is once again, over and above what we pay you to do."

"Oh no." She shook her head vehemently. "You shouldn't be paying me at all. You let me stay in the guesthouse for almost nothing—"

"It's a one-room space with a kitchenette and bathroom. And we had to add that, as well as insulation and a proper floor, to make it habitable. Between the work at the store and keeping us straight here, you do plenty. Neither one of us likes cleaning, but neither one of us wants to live in a pigsty, either. Then there are the nights you fix us dinner because Marcus is a workaholic and I'm too up to my elbows in my projects to even think about cooking. Not up for discussion. You're worth every penny." He nudged her. "If I were you, I'd badger us for a raise or a Christmas bonus."

She worried her bottom lip with even teeth, changed the subject. "Do you want the small frosted gold balls on this? I think that would look really nice."

He nodded. "That'd be the perfect touch. See what I mean? And you know, if you don't feel comfortable telling Rory, maybe you should *ask* him to kiss you."

Daralyn's braid fell over her shoulder as she bent over the box, retrieving three of the gold balls. She had a good figure. Good enough to have Rory's eyes roving over her, despite his best attempts not to let the rest of the family see him doing it. She needed some serious feeding up, though. A good wind could blow her away.

"Maybe I should," she said, surprising him. "But maybe you should tell Marcus it hurts your feelings, the way he's been avoiding sharing Christmas with you."

Thomas could deny it, but again, she didn't miss much. He met her gaze as she straightened. He needed to paint her in a field, lying among flowers, with that wistful smile on her face he sometimes caught there. It contained all the sorrow and joy of a broken world. Though he did a lot of erotic material that appealed to gay men, he wasn't limited to that. He could easily imagine a whole series with her as subject matter, the colors starting to mix in his mind.

She was watching him with that very smile now. "Marcus told me you do that, but it's the first time I've seen it. You're thinking of a painting, aren't you?"

He chuckled, a little self-consciously. "You shouldn't believe everything he tells you, but yeah. As far as sharing with him...I think he's dealing with some past Christmas stuff. As long as he's here and we get through, that's what matters."

Thomas stepped back, sweeping a critical gaze over the living room and kitchen. With the tree, lit garlands and assorted decorations tastefully embellishing the farmhouse décor, it looked like a country Christmas postcard. It had to have some kind of positive impact on Marcus, no matter how he acted. The tree was decorated with a variety of ornaments from Thomas's past, as well as ones he'd bought to make it his and Marcus's tree. Things he'd hoped Marcus would like, since the day they'd planned to shop for them together, Marcus had begged off with another business interruption.

It was excuses. All excuses. Daralyn was right. It hurt, because even though rationally Thomas understood that it was about Marcus's past, it felt like he was making a statement about their future together. When he'd asked Marcus a few weeks ago what he thought of going with the eight-foot tree versus six-foot, Marcus hadn't looked up from his laptop as he answered.

"Doesn't matter to me, pet. This is more your thing."

He could have meant decorating, being artistic, but Marcus made all the design decisions on his gallery, from the color of the walls to the type of flowers at the entrance desk. Linda, his manager, wouldn't dare change anything like that without consulting him.

"So, I'm working at the store until noon closing tomorrow," Daralyn said. "Between that and tidying up, I can be here by two to help you get everything ready for Christmas Eve dinner."

He waved a dismissive hand. "We're good tomorrow. You know we don't do meat on Christmas Eve, and mom prefers to keep it pretty light since she'll go to Midnight Mass. You're going to be helping her with the ginormous feast on Christmas Day, anyhow, so I don't want to see you until four tomorrow. Take a nap after work and think about that dress you're going to wear. Les told me it's pretty amazing."

"She talked me into it. I'm not sure I'm brave enough to wear it." There went that fetching flush in her cheeks again. Thomas could just imagine Les gently bullying Daralyn into the purchase. They were all in on the conspiracy, if they could just get his dumbass brother to make a move. Rory was determined to treat Daralyn like fragile porcelain, even as she'd evolved into his right hand at the store. Les was away at college pretty much except breaks, Mom was getting older, and Thomas was pursuing his art career. As such, Daralyn had stepped into that essential role in her usual quiet way.

"You better wear it," he warned. "You know how Les can be if she doesn't get her way. Now get out of here. I have a surly Yankee arriving soon. The Grinch is like Mickey Mouse compared to him."

"He's not so scary." She dimpled.

"Yeah, yeah. You're just like all women are around him. God's gift, yet completely wasted on the fair sex." *Thank God.* But he knew it was more than that. Even in his worst mood, Marcus always spoke gently to Daralyn. Thomas wondered if she ever got tired of being treated as if she were so breakable, but when it came to her own feelings, Daralyn tended to keep her own counsel about pretty much everything. Which was why her next words surprised him.

"He loves you so much." Her hazel eyes grew serious. A brief hesitation, then she touched his forearm, simple kindness. "I'm sure he doesn't know how it's making you feel."

"Yeah, well. He's had some *really* rough Christmases. So I figure this first one may not be so much about my feelings as helping him figure the best way through it. A relationship is a give and take like that."

"Maybe the best way is letting him see it through your eyes. Christmas is special. Not even one of them should be wasted."

§

Christmas issues aside, as the time for Marcus's arrival drew closer, Thomas felt a sweet anticipation building. Three days shouldn't seem like so much, especially now that they were together permanently, but the wonder of it hadn't eased off a bit. If anything, an absence of any length could resurrect the hunger for one another and increase exponentially with every hour that passed. Marcus's texts, marking how much closer he was getting to home, only intensified it.

When the Maserati pulled into the drive, the tightness in Thomas's chest was enough to steal breath and word. He came out onto the porch, leaning in what he imagined was a casual pose against the porch post, one hand hooked in his jeans' pocket. But as Marcus got out of the car, the way his Master's vibrant green gaze covered Thomas made him feel hot, slick and naked.

Marcus didn't take out his laptop, overnight bag, anything. He never did. He always came to Thomas first, one of the many little things that Thomas noticed and treasured. He might be being an ass about Christmas, but everything else told Thomas he was loved. That was all that mattered.

As Marcus came up the four steps to the porch, Thomas was already stepping away from the post to meet him, but his Master was having none of that, pushing him back against the post and rail, holding him there as he clamped his lips over Thomas's. His body, always surprisingly strong, pinned Thomas in place, his thigh thrust between Thomas's so firm muscle pressed insistently against Thomas's cock, already stiff as a board for the past thirty minutes, *so* ready for Marcus to arrive.

Thomas made a noise between a growl and a plea, and Marcus answered it with that feral note that was pure dominant animal. His tongue tangled with Thomas's, heated and wet, and his other hand was cupped fully around his ass cheek, digging in hard enough he almost lifted Thomas up on the rail. Actually, fuck, he did, putting Thomas's butt up there and himself between his legs, holding him by the side of the neck with one strong hand and the other shoving into the waist band of the jeans in the back, to caress the dimple between his buttocks. Marcus's thumb caught the silver and gold waist chain Thomas always wore beneath his clothes, the one that had a loop that cinched around his cock, held there by a metal disk lock only Marcus could remove. Thomas strained forward, wanting to rub his arousal against Marcus, but he made an imperious noise, stilling him.

It was a good thing the farm sat way back from the road, because these kinds of greetings would have gotten the community talking for sure. Since their closest neighbor, Mrs. Dearman, salivated at just the sight of Marcus, Thomas wouldn't put it past her to close the half mile gap between their properties with her husband's hunting rifle scope. But if she was being a peeping Tom about his Master, she deserved what she got.

His Master. He loved the way that sounded. Almost as much as "husband".

"Why aren't you naked?" Marcus demanded, lifting his head. "I swear to God, one of these days I'm going to fuck you right here on this porch in broad daylight. In the house. Now."

He had to add the qualification of daylight, since he had already done it at night. Several times. One night in particular, he'd strapped Thomas to the back porch swing, tying his wrists to the wooden arms, running the ropes down to Thomas's ankles so his legs were spread and dangling. All after he'd seated a vibrating plug up his ass. Then Marcus forced orgasm after orgasm from him. Giving him a hand job, applying a wand to his glans, going down on him. Thomas had been sure there'd be reports of some guttural wild animal barking in the night, the way he'd come over and over again that night. Marcus got in those moods sometime, where he wasn't satisfied until Thomas was so weak, so deep in subspace, that it took quite awhile to return to earth, shuddering in Marcus's arms, taking sips of water from his hand, relying on him practically to breathe.

Easing him off the rail, Marcus directed him inside, the screen door closing with a thump behind them. Marcus kicked the wooden door closed, latching it. He'd already found out neighbors and family had a way of stopping by and popping their heads in the door with the call of "anybody there?", a far cry from the layers of security at his New York penthouse.

Following Marcus's orders, Thomas removed the shirt and then pushed down the jeans, barely getting them to his knees before he found himself spun and pushed down over the kitchen table. He wasn't wearing any underwear and he was already lubed up, the way Marcus required him to be when he arrived home. Which was good, because Marcus was in a seriously insistent mood. Maybe the kind of mood he'd been in that night when he had him tied to the swing. Thomas felt everything in his lower body clench in anticipation...and trepidation, because Marcus in this mood wasn't a gentle Master. Not in the least.

Whereas before he'd been moving at a rapid pace, now Marcus slowed down, filling the dense air with a dangerous charge as he slid his fingers down Thomas's bare back to the upper rise of his ass, giving him an idle but very sharp pinch with his strong fingers. Thomas suppressed the flinch, channeling it into the electric energy running through his body instead. He quivered, eager to serve Marcus on every level of his being. It was that way when there was nothing held back. Marcus had been to the deepest levels of Thomas's soul, and he'd been there with Marcus, though Marcus, typical Dominant, didn't open that door as often, while demanding it always be wide open inside Thomas. He'd just kick it down otherwise. But that was okay, because Thomas had finally figured out the opening of his own door was key to opening Marcus's.

Marcus ran a hand down Thomas's bare back again, this time following the lines of muscle framing his shoulder blades, over the lower back, down to the rise of his ass again. "Higher, pet," he ordered in a silky tone. "You know you're required to lift your tasty ass high enough I can see your balls hanging between your legs. Don't make your

Master search for that slick hole of yours."

"No, sir," Thomas responded. That was new for them, too. If it was possible, Marcus had become even stricter since they'd gotten married, making Thomas feel every inch the owned submissive by requiring that he address him formally when they were fully in session. And Thomas loved it, which was of course at least half of why Marcus did it. The other half would be because it got Marcus's dick hard, too, and Marcus made no bones about being a selfish man. He could be, but he was a lot of other things too, and there were parts of Marcus's selfishness that Thomas loved as much as his generosity.

He lifted his ass, feeling the cut of the thin chain around his balls and cock, as it was designed to get tighter when he was fully erect, like now.

"Your text gave me an excellent idea." Marcus braced himself on one ass cheek, leaning over to pluck a wooden spoon out of the pottery vase. "So this is how your mother used to discipline you?"

"Dad would follow it up with a belt strapping that night, to make sure we didn't forget the most important lesson—to obey and respect our mother." Thomas gripped a slat of the table as Marcus twirled the spoon in his strong and graceful hands, then straightened, disappearing from his field of vision. Thomas inhaled the scent of old wood and cleaners Daralyn had used to wipe down the table.

"I'll clean up my language for tomorrow night, but in exchange, I want to hear that word come out of your mouth now. Often. Every time I use this"—the spoon tapped his ass—"You put it in a sentence I'll like. Statements, requests and outright begging are fine. But use it as a demand even once..."

Thomas suppressed a hungry sound as Marcus pushed his face to the table with a firm hand on his nape and rammed the stiff cock under slacks right up against Thomas's ass, rubbing that promise against his bare balls. "You make any demands of me, and you'll have to explain to your mother why you have to eat standing up."

Marcus smelled of New York. Rich cologne, expensive clothes, airlines, travel. But what was beneath teased

Thomas's senses even more. He wanted to be pressed up against his Master's naked body, inhale the heat of his skin, hear his heart beat, feel the shift of every beautiful inch beneath Thomas's touch. He wanted to close his fingers around the steel of Marcus's thick cock. Wrap his mouth around it. But those privileges had to be earned.

Marcus didn't start the punishment right away. Caressing Thomas's neck, his shoulders, he moved down his back again and molded a palm over one bare buttock. He stroked Thomas several times, that same terrain, up and back. Up and back. Fingers stilling, then starting again. The tenor of the touch changed, became more meditative, intent. The deepening silence cued Thomas to his Master's mood shift. He knew the look that would be in Marcus's eyes and wanted to see it. But when he started to turn his head, to look, Marcus made a quelling noise, clamping down on Thomas's neck again, reminding him to stay in the position he'd put him. He murmured something Thomas had to strain to hear, much as he'd had to strain to hear what Daralyn had said earlier.

"Just enjoying what's mine. All mine."

The roughness of Marcus's tone pulled at Thomas's very soul, but as if his Master knew exactly when they reached the line past which Thomas had to follow his heart and turn to his Master's care, rather than obey him blindly, Marcus switched the mood. Fast and hard.

The spoon hit, and it was obviously not the first time Marcus had wielded one as a Dom. The strike drove the breath from Thomas, and he had to scramble for thought.

"Please fuck me, Master."

Marcus clucked. "Hardly original, but it works for me. I want you so mindless a preschool book would be a challenge.

Thwack.

"See Dick fuck..."

That won an appreciative chuckle. "Smartass. Higher." A sharper command this time, telling Thomas that Marcus wasn't messing around. Jesus, Thomas was almost already on his toes. He had to grip the table harder for balance, but the strain in the back of his thighs, the arch of his body as he lifted his ass, just made him hurt for it harder. His cock was already pulsing, leaking come on the floor between the chairs. He was going to have to clean that up. No way was he letting Daralyn see it.

Thwack. Thwack. Thwack.

"Fucking hell... Fuck, this hurts... Fuck, it feels good."

Now the spoon was sliding over one cheek, then the edge was pushing between his buttocks, teasing his rim. Marcus worked it against him, rocking that curve against the tight puckered entrance as Thomas groaned.

"Nice and slick, just the way I like you."

"Yes, Master. You said you'd fuck me when you walked through the door."

"Is that a complaint? Is my slave being impatient?"

"Only because I missed you like fuck. Fucking missed you."

"Three more 'fucks' on the front end," Marcus mused. "Sounds like my property wants more punishment. Your dick is making a mess. Thank God she hasn't put the chair pads on yet."

He leaned over Thomas again, pushing the spoon harder against his rim as he plucked a rubber spatula from the vase. It was the kind of utensil used to turn cake batter. "Bet your mother never knew this hurts more."

Thomas sucked in a new breath as Marcus proved it, letting the flexible rubber sting its way across both buttocks, his upper thighs. He even gave Thomas's balls a quick pop with it, a strike that had him cursing under his breath. "Fuck..." His testicles were throbbing, his cock at maximum blood capacity. He needed to come, needed his Master inside of him. But he wondered if Marcus needed...more. Thomas swallowed, decided he was a couple candy canes short of a dozen, and did exactly what Marcus had warned him not to do. He made it a demand.

"Fuck me, Master. Now."

Marcus paused. The clock ticked on the wall, Thomas's breath rasping in counter point with it. Marcus shifted then, and his Italian loafer slid underneath the raised heel of Thomas's right foot, the toe pressing against where the ball of his foot pushed hard against the wood floor. Closing his hand on Thomas's hip, Marcus eased him down so his weight rested on the top of Marcus's foot. Thomas felt Marcus's hand between them, heard the belt being unbuckled, the slacks being unzipped, and then groaned as the tip of Marcus's cock traced that sensitive spot at the top of his buttocks. Painting his precum along those two rises, Marcus then pressed into the lube-slick seam. Not to penetrate, only to tease Thomas past bearing before Marcus took hold of himself, and began to stroke.

"No, Master, please..."

For a response, Marcus put his hand on Thomas's shoulder, pushed him down so his upper body was flush against the table, ass in the air. He kept jacking himself off as he held Thomas in that position. He was going to come against Thomas's ass, his lower back. Thomas squeezed his eyes shut, his cock throbbing, balls aching, hands curling into the wood of the table.

"I think you need a reminder of who's in charge, don't you, pet?"

"Please let me use my mouth on you, Master."

"Not this first time. This is what I want. And what matters most?'

"What my Master wants."

"Fucking right."

Thomas's heart was pounding high in his chest, and he groaned again as Marcus crowded up against him, so close Thomas felt his goddamn knuckles rubbing against Thomas's ass with every stroke. His hips were twitching, unable to help it. His balls hung heavy and tight between his spread legs and, when Marcus's breath started to come quick and shallow, he lifted his ass higher, giving his Master the canvas he wanted to paint with his desire.

The first hot jet of come hit his balls, his crack, then splattered outward over his ass cheeks, his lower back. Though he wanted nothing more than to have his Master fuck him, Thomas felt a near orgasmic euphoria, serving his Master this way, being entirely at his mercy as he spent himself on the body of his sub, his slave. Marcus owned every inch of him. Nothing in Thomas denied it.

When Marcus slowed down, he cupped a palm over

Thomas's wet buttock, rubbed that thick fluid over it, dipping in between to tease his rim. Then he did it to the other cheek. "Master," Thomas breathed. "Please."

"I'm going to amuse myself until I'm hard again. You'll just have to have a longer punishment, I think. Do you accept that, Thomas?"

"Yes, Master. Anything...as long as you're touching me."

"Jesus, you're perfect." The spatula hit again, and the way Marcus had coated his buttock, made it wet, increased the sting. Thomas imagined what it looked like, his ass dripping with Marcus's come, the way it would dry on his flesh.

"You'll be scrubbing this floor, pet. I might enjoy watching you do that naked, with a vibrator up your ass and strapped to your cock, so you'd have to keep scrubbing, every time you come."

"Fuck," Thomas breathed, and the spatula hit again. Marcus stopped talking and devoted himself with single-minded pleasure to the punishment, until Thomas was grunting with every blow, his fingers digging harder into the wood and mind spinning with the thought that Marcus truly was going to make sure he couldn't sit comfortably for Christmas Eve dinner.

The spatula was thrown on the table next to him, Marcus drawing him off the table to push him down to his knees on the wood floor. Thomas's gaze rose to his face. Those green eyes were hot enough to burn, the sinfully beautiful mouth taut. Thomas had his lips parted and waiting as Marcus pushed his cock past them. The insatiable bastard was already half erect again, and Thomas was only too eager to prepare him to fuck his sub.

"Easy pet. Slow it down." Marcus tugged his hair, curling his fingers deep into Thomas's scalp. "There we go. Manage the lust, pleasure your Master."

It was his pleasure to obey such a directive. Focusing, he sucked on the ridge of the head, worked his way up and down the shaft with a careful pace but fierce purpose, lashing every erogenous point and savoring the way it felt to hold Marcus's cock in his mouth. The one and only person allowed to do it now. Marcus's fingers flexed on him.

"My sweet pet. That fucking gorgeous mouth. All I could think about on the plane was having you on your knees like this. I'd have had you do it in front of every man there and let them wish it was them. You're the only Christmas gift I want. Now or forever."

Thomas swallowed, his focus shifting at the vehemence in Marcus's voice. He changed his strategy, sliding slowly all the way up Marcus's shaft only to lay kisses all the way back down, nuzzle it with his cheek, nip at his thighs, his balls, sucking one in his mouth.

"Jesus." Marcus's fingers constricted in his hair. Yeah, his Master loved having his balls sucked like that. He'd also learned Marcus loved to have his rim tongued, but Thomas wasn't allowed to do that too often. Most mornings, Thomas woke to find Marcus curled up behind him, a strong arm over his hip, chest or waist. His Master held on tight to what was his when he slept. Though on rare occasions, Thomas, the early riser of the two of them, would wake and find Marcus had turned to his other side in his sleep, presenting Thomas an irresistible opportunity. Thomas could work his way down the line of his spine with his mouth, winding his arms around Marcus to grip his turgid morning erection. When he reached his buttocks, he'd snake a tongue between to play. The first time he'd done it, Marcus's grip on the railings of the head board had almost broken them, so violent was his reaction to the pleasuring.

"Same goes, Master," Thomas said. "You're the Christmas gift I always wanted."

"Come here." Marcus pulled him to his feet. "Get rid of the jeans and shoes. I want you in the bed."

Thomas kicked all of it free, and Marcus propelled him to their bedroom. He didn't wait, pushing Thomas onto the bed, on his back, making it clear how he wanted him. Thomas slid over, making room as Marcus finished undressing. Thomas's gaze slid over his husband's body as Marcus shrugged out of the tailored shirt and slacks, the snug dark shorts beneath. The man was a god in every way, not an inch of marble flesh flawed. It never failed to make

Thomas insane with lust and overwhelmed with emotion to know it was his, to have and to hold, now and forever.

"Stay just like that, pet," Marcus said, making it clear he'd been doing his own appraisal. He put a knee up on the bed and then he was over Thomas, stretching his body out fully on him.

At first, Thomas hadn't been entirely comfortable doing it this way, but Marcus wasn't interested in his comfort in such situations. Thomas had learned to appreciate his way of shoving past his inhibitions. It was unnerving, how it shattered him every time to have Marcus take him face to face. Marcus slid his arms under Thomas's legs, at the bend of Thomas's knees. He guided himself into Thomas's well lubed entry without the need of his hands, he knew his sub's body that well.

That thick cock slid inch by excruciating inch into Thomas's tight channel, eliciting a mutual grunt of deep satisfaction. Marcus braced himself against the backs of Thomas's thighs, staring down at him with that firm mouth and penetrating eyes that refused to let Thomas look away.

"I love you, Master." It rasped out of his throat, so obvious he couldn't not say it.

Those green eyes flickered and the mouth softened. "Same goes, pet. Fuck, I missed you. I almost...but I couldn't. I just couldn't."

Thomas's brow creased but Marcus was done talking. He started working harder in Thomas's ass, and Thomas was already so close, he was holding on by fingernails. "Master, I'm going to come...if you keep...doing that."

"Part of the plan. But hold out until I'm ready. Else I'll beat you with a few more of your mother's kitchen implements. Teach you to be a really...good...boy."

Thomas groaned at each thrust punctuating the sentence. God, he couldn't...yes, he would. He would. Oh no...fuck...he...

"Come for me, pet. Come now. Let me hear you."

That wasn't a problem, because the groan-shout that tore from Thomas's throat couldn't be withheld. The climax that seized him had him bucking up against Marcus, intensifying with every thrust. Marcus changed his angle so he had Thomas's knees bent up tight on either side of Marcus's body, pretty much lifting Thomas's body all the way to the shoulders off the bed, Marcus's thighs slapping against his ass as Thomas was penetrated over and over and over, those powerful lean muscles in Marcus's body holding Thomas's weight.

His cock jetted all over his stomach and chest. Damn, he'd probably gotten the pillows, wall and headboard. Daralyn really better not come until four tomorrow, because it was going to take him that long to restore all the good cleaning she'd done. But that was a vague thought, everything else spinning, wild color and gorgeous green eyes burning into his soul, the best kind of heat there was.

"There you are pet...easy now. There you are."

He was shaking, something that happened every time Marcus took him over like this. The response never failed to please his Master, even though Thomas always felt unraveled afterward. But it was okay, because Marcus had a way of winding the spool again, as gentle in the aftermath as he could be ruthless during. When he slowly withdrew, Thomas shuddered. Marcus shifted them, curling around Thomas and cuddling him up into the coil of his taut frame. He was stroking Thomas's hair, his shoulder, lips nuzzling his throat. Thomas groped behind him, found Marcus's bare hip, gripped. Gripped hard.

"I love you."

"So you said." But the press of Marcus's lips under Thomas's ear lingered, his fingers stroking Thomas's chest.

"I missed you," Thomas added.

"I got that. I might have given you a thought or two."

The tender jest made Thomas squeeze his eyes shut. *Don't talk about it. Let it go. This is enough. Don't do that dumbass thing, talking about stupid shit during a vulnerable moment. This is enough.*

"Thomas." Marcus tugged him over onto his back, made him look up into his face as he leaned over him. He traced Thomas's mouth with his thumb, his other fingers settling on his throat in that light collar that could liquefy Thomas's will into water. He imagined a painting where he'd pour it over Marcus's feet to wash them, just like a biblical act of obeisance. "Thomas," Marcus repeated, drawing his attention out of that part of his head. His firm lips quirked, because he always knew when Thomas was painting. "Do you think I can't read when you have something else on your mind?"

"You don't want to hear it. And I don't want...it's stupid. Let's just let it go."

Marcus studied him. If he'd figured out what Thomas was thinking and said fine, we'll let it go, rather than allowing Thomas to talk about it, Thomas knew that would hurt worse. Fuck, he was acting like a girl, wasn't he?

"No," Marcus said quietly at last. "We're not letting it go. Let's have it." He flicked Thomas's nipple, making Thomas jump. Thomas bit his lip, but when Marcus made something an order, he couldn't keep the words from spilling out.

"I know you've had a lot of rough Christmases. I guess I hoped if you did stuff with me at Christmas...decorating, shopping, having a nice Christmas, it would help ease that. But it feels like you're avoiding all that because instead it makes it worse. I know I'm being selfish, but I was really looking forward to sharing our first Christmas together, all of it. But if it's not your thing, then you know, you could go back to New York and I could join you after Christmas with my family. Maybe we could do a trip somewhere that's not about Christmas. Like the Bahamas or Josh's island, until all the Christmas stuff is gone and done."

"Would it be easier to spend Christmas without me?" Marcus asked, his voice neutral.

"In your current mood, yes. But no. Because easier doesn't mean better. I'm starting to get what the better or worse thing means. I'd rather spend my worse day in the world with you than the best day without you. Because it wouldn't be the best day if you weren't there. I just...I feel like we're making one another miserable, me wanting you to do Christmas shit, and you so not wanting to do it."

"So you're trying to figure out how to make it easier for me." Marcus studied him another moment and then sighed. Rolling away from Thomas, he shifted to a sitting position, facing away from Thomas to brace his hands on either side of himself. Though the silken feathering of Marcus's dark hair concealed his profile, Thomas could tell he was staring out the window at the back fields. "Thomas, there really isn't a way to do that."

"I know." Even though it hurt like hell to acknowledge it, to hear Marcus say it. "I just wish..."

He wanted to reach out, stroke the bare line of Marcus's back. And he wanted to be closer. So to hell with it. He sat up and traced Marcus's back to his hip, curled his fingers over it. All the while sliding closer, until he had his thighs parted so he could press himself right up against Marcus's back, replete cock and testicles mashed against Marcus's ass, Thomas's legs framing his hips and Marcus's thighs, the soles of Thomas's feet dangling just above the floor on either side. He threaded his arms under Marcus's so he could put one around his chest, the other around his waist. Marcus's breathing was evening out from their rough fucking, but there was a stillness to him as Thomas completed the full embrace, putting his chin on his Master's shoulder, using his jaw to hold back some of that gorgeous dark hair, see his face fully.

"You know, at first I wasn't comfortable with positions like this. You nurturing, surrounding me."

"I know."

"Then, one day, I wondered why I'd ever resisted it." Marcus lifted a hand, closed it over Thomas's on his chest, even as he continued to stare out the window. "I'm your Master, Thomas, but there's a comfort and safe feeling to your love that I never realized I needed so much, not until you started exercising it with such marvelous consistency."

Thomas lifted his face, startled, but Marcus wasn't done. He cocked his head, his gaze and tone sharpening. "I don't ever want you to dismiss your needs, do you understand? I'll do more than blister your ass if you do. This works because you don't retreat an inch from who you want to be with me. You've been down that road, remember?" He glanced down meaningfully. "That ulcer is now under control. You do shit like that which sets it off, you and I are going to have a real problem."

Thomas swallowed, nodded. "But I..."

Marcus tightened his fingers over Thomas's. "The Christmas thing is no different from holding me like this. You need to keep pushing what you want. Telling me what you want. Telling me when I'm hurting you. I knew I was hurting you, which makes me ashamed of it, but it's when you call me on it that I have to face it and deal with it. My outside may be perfect, but the inside is a troll. You know that."

Thomas's heart wrenched at the matter-of-fact comment. He shifted his other arm so they were both around Marcus's chest and gave him a hard, admonishing squeeze. "No. I don't. And I don't want you to do that, either. You're all perfect to me. Even when you're a horse's ass, you're a perfect horse's ass."

Marcus snorted, a half-chuckle. Another tender feeling speared Thomas's middle as Marcus sighed and relaxed, letting them stay in this position, bodies leaned into one another.

"I'm sorry. I should have been helping you more with Christmas. It didn't matter for so long, you know. Usually at Christmas I did the party rounds, business functions, friend stuff where nothing got too personal, and then I'd go home, go to sleep, get up to a new not-Christmas day and it didn't matter. It matters this year, which reminds me of the few Christmases where it did matter, but it didn't go so well."

"I know." Thomas brushed Marcus's throat with his mouth. Then his shoulder as Marcus's chest expanded under his grip in another sigh. With their bodies pressed together like this, it felt like more than their flesh was bare. "I've tried not to push. I want to know anything you want to tell me. Actually, I really want to know all of it, because that seems to help you."

"Yeah, I know. Doesn't mean it comes easy. Maybe later, pet. It's just..." Marcus blew out a breath and rose, pulling out of Thomas's hold. He found his shorts and slacks, pulled them on, hooked the slacks, zipped, though he stripped the belt so they stayed low on his hips, an irresistible look that usually caused Thomas's senses to glaze over. Marcus pushed his hand through his thick hair, the strands waterfalling over his bare shoulder. "Did you get me a Christmas present? We said no buying presents this first year."

"I did not buy you a Christmas present," Thomas said truthfully. Marcus shot him a narrow look, but there was something behind his expression, an almost desperate, hunted look that had Thomas wanting to rise and go to him, but Marcus changed the subject. He gestured out the bedroom door, in the direction of the living room. "It all looks great. You haven't hung the garland on the porch yet, though."

"No."

"Well, let's do that. Maybe you can tell me why you picked out some of the ornaments you did. I..." He cleared his throat. "I'll be right back. You can get dressed."

He strode from the room. Thomas retrieved his clothes. As he pulled them on, moved into the living room, he saw through the windows Marcus had headed out the door to his car. He pulled out his computer and overnight bag, a gift bag from Macy's, and came back onto the porch. Thomas listened to the comforting squeak of the screen, the sound of Marcus's feet in the entrance hallway, the thump as Marcus dropped his luggage there. They were Thomas's favorite combination of sounds when Marcus returned from a trip where Thomas couldn't accompany him. That thought filled his heart as Marcus stepped back into the living room, and Thomas had to quell an entirely sentimental desire to go embrace Marcus again.

Instead he watched Marcus gaze at the tree, absorbing the details for perhaps the very first time. He took his time with it, as Marcus did when examining any type of artistic arrangement. After a long moment, a light smile tugged his firm mouth, and that warm feeling grew. "It really is beautiful, Thomas. You did a great job with it. But there are a few branches bare."

Marcus pulled a box out of the Macy's bag, extended it. "I didn't know if they would go with what you'd done, but red goes with everything at Christmas, right? I liked them, and thought you would as well. It's one of their guest glass designers who does special holiday collections. Oh, and I picked up a few additional things for your family."

So though they hadn't bought gifts together, Marcus had still helped provide surprises for the family. "That's great," Thomas said. Despite his reaction to what was in the box, he kept his tone just as deliberately casual as Marcus was trying so hard to do. The box held four red glass ornaments, glass balls in various spherical and oblong shapes.

"These are really nice," Thomas said sincerely, his throat a little thick. Marcus had made an effort, even before anything was said about his heretofore lack of one. It could have been plastic balls from the Dollar Store for all Thomas cared. His Master was so rarely uncertain except in this area of their lives, so he had no idea how much Thomas treasured every step he made, trusting Thomas's approval and love to care for him in those unknown rooms.

Reaching out, he touched his Master's face, then let the hand trail to his bare chest, resting his palm on Marcus's chest. Thump. Thump. That steady beat that meant so much to him. "Hang them with me?"

Marcus nodded, his expression neutral, but Thomas thought he was pleased with Thomas's reaction to the ornaments. "Let me get some hooks for them," Thomas added.

As he went to fish them out of the storage box he hadn't yet put away, the mistletoe hanging over the door caught his eye, reminding him. "Oh, I planted the idea in Daralyn's head she should kiss Rory under the mistletoe."

"Did she faint?"

"Nope. She blushed." Thomas straightened, hooks in hand. "Based on the way the conversation went, it's pretty clear you're right about her. Not so much like me, though."

"No. And what she needs isn't like me, either." On more familiar ground now, Marcus slid his hands in the pockets of his slacks as he watched Thomas put the box down on a chair and thread the hooks into the ornament eyelets. "What she went through with her father and uncle, they pretty much trained her to be a sub from day one and, horrible as the circumstances were, that's what she knows, her comfort zone. She can turn a curse into a blessing, because I've seen subs find their own strength and identity under a Dom's command in a way they can't do it otherwise. Think Rory has some of me in him?"

Thomas chuckled. "*He'd* faint at the thought. For her, I think it's more homegrown, innate, if that makes sense. She's not the kind of submissive that's going to be going to a club. And definitely not the kind that likes...pain."

"Like you do and need at times," Marcus supplied, with an intent, heated look. "The fact it still embarrasses you makes me want to apply it all the more often. How is that fine ass that belongs to me, by the way? Sore?"

"You know it is," Thomas managed with dignity. Despite the gleam in Marcus's eye, he returned to the question at hand. "Before his accident, Rory was an alpha, no question. Captain of the varsity team in two sports, that kind of thing. His confidence in himself is growing to the point he could reclaim that part of who he is. But alpha isn't necessarily a Dom. I don't really get a Dom vibe off him, but that doesn't mean it isn't there. He's my brother. You tend to block any sexual vibes from a sibling."

"Even in North Carolina?"

Thomas bared his teeth at him and Marcus grinned. "Regardless, an alpha can enjoy exercising Dom tendencies under the right circumstances since there are a lot of overlapping traits," he said. "As you said, this is less about restraints and spanking and more about giving her the safety that being under someone's command can provide. Do you think he could do that?"

"If the proper suggestions were planted. Which would be your area of expertise."

"Excuse me?" Marcus's brows lifted.

"I'm sure as hell not having that discussion with him. But beyond that, no matter how he acts around you, I think he respects you and senses... Well, don't get all inflated beyond your usual enormous ego, but he responds to your natural authority on certain things."

"Enormous ego?"

"Just stating the obvious."

Thomas held out one of the ornaments. Marcus took it, nodding when Thomas gestured to an empty branch as a suggestion. But he didn't move. Glancing at his profile, Thomas noted his jaw had gotten a little tighter, and the look on his face said his focus had once again shifted to something deeper inside, some paralyzing memory. Thomas closed his fingers over Marcus's hand, pulling his attention from the past to the present. With his quiet encouragement, they hung the red ball on the tree together. The tree lights shone off the glass with pretty effect.

"These are really nice." Thomas offered another ornament to Marcus. Even pulled back to the present, Marcus looked like he usually did right before he'd excuse himself for a phone call or anything else. This time, though, Thomas could see Marcus's awareness of it, his struggle not to let it take over.

"What were you about to say, in the bedroom?" Thomas asked softly. "You said 'I almost...but I couldn't...'"

Marcus glanced his way, looked back at the tree. Leaning forward almost stiffly, he hung one of the oblong shaped ornaments. Then stepped back and drew a breath. Jesus, this *was* really hard for him. It almost made Thomas feel guilty for pushing it, but then he remembered what Marcus had said. Marcus didn't say what he didn't mean and, beyond that, Thomas knew he was right. Marcus had shied away from Thomas's nurturing at first, yet when push came to shove, in rare, key moments, he had an aching hunger for it. Like now maybe. So Thomas brushed a hand along Marcus's back, delighted he hadn't put on a shirt as he pressed against his side and offered the third ball. Hooking his finger in the waistband of his Master's slacks, he stroked firm skin above it as he pointed to a higher branch. "That would be a good place for one."

"Yeah." Marcus cleared his throat, stretched. When he did, Thomas dipped his head to put a kiss in the pocket of his throat. He slid his hand up high enough to tangle it in Marcus's hair, tug his head back so he could suck lightly on the Adam's apple, give it a nip. The clearly demanding gesture was a trigger that tripped an interested ripple through Marcus's body. His arm coiled around Thomas's back as he came down, his palm settling high on Thomas's gloriously abused ass.

"You looking for more attention, pet? Another reminder of who belongs to who?"

"I think we both know the answer to that." Thomas reached for the last ball, but he knew he wasn't going to get away with that one. Marcus pulled him back and put one of those hot, sucking kisses on his mouth that had his fingers digging into Marcus's bare shoulders, an oath slipping from his lips as Marcus nudged his head to the side impatiently, breaking the kiss to give Thomas's throat a much sharper bite in return. His Master loved marking his skin. Once, in the throes of passion, he'd told Thomas it was his own personal canvas to decorate as he wished.

Marcus drew back. That heavy-lidded look told Thomas he'd probably be on his hands and knees before long, but he glanced past Thomas at the box, took a breath. "One more."

"Yeah." Thomas cleared his throat, retrieved it, holding it by the hook. "How about there, right near the top?"

Marcus looked at the branch and nodded, but Thomas noticed his gaze continued to the summit of the tree and stopped there. They didn't have a tree topper, so Thomas had grouped several ornaments beneath that point to mask it. Though Thomas had picked out other ornaments, he'd been determined not to pick out the tree topper alone. Even if they had to wait twenty Christmases to be ready for it.

"Want me to hang this last one?" Thomas ventured, when Marcus didn't say anything.

"No. I can do it." Tearing his eyes from the top of the tree, Marcus took the ball, moving in closer to the tree to reach up and hang it. But Thomas caught the hard tremor in his arm, fortunately in time to catch the ball when Marcus fumbled it from nerveless fingers.

He stepped back from Thomas and the tree as if he'd been poleaxed, staring at the ornament in Thomas's hand. "Fuck. I just... I can't. Give me some space for a bit, all right?"

Marcus pivoted and left the room, his shoulders tight, back muscles knotted. When he closed the door of the bedroom firmly after him, it was a clear message he was taking a few minutes alone. Thomas stood there, holding the red ball and hurting for him, but they'd gotten three out of four on the tree. Marcus had brought them home, and they'd had that talk...Thomas would hold onto the hope those things brought.

They loved one another. That was all they needed to figure this out.

§

Thomas gave him about fifteen minutes, then brought his bags to the door. Knocking before he eased it open, he found Marcus sitting on the edge of the bed, scrolling through his texts and messages. "Julie's flight is running on time," he said, not looking up. "She says she'll be on it if she doesn't murder her family. If that happens, she's relying on us to get her to a country which has no extradition."

"Good to know." Thomas settled down next to him and proffered a straight candy cane he'd plucked from a jar on the kitchen counter. Marcus glanced at it. "What's that for?"

"I figured if you were going to have a stick up your ass, it might as well be festive."

Marcus's lips quirked. Thomas bumped his shoulder, giving him a warm look. "Wiseass," his Master muttered. But he took the candy, setting the phone aside. Reaching over him, Thomas snagged the device, feeling the weight of Marcus's regard as he pocketed it.

"I'll let you know if anything important comes through."

Marcus pushed Thomas to his back on the bed. Sliding his touch down Thomas's chest, over the fastener of his jeans, he curled his fingers up and used his knuckles to give Thomas's cock a firm stroke. Then those long fingers reached into his pocket, fishing out the phone and teasing his testicles before they retreated. Thomas tightened his lips, holding back a protest when Marcus rose. He was glad he did, because Marcus surprised him. As Thomas pushed up onto his elbows, his Master moved to his sock drawer and tucked the phone in between folded pairs of footwear.

"Text Julie and tell her to use your phone if she needs anything. Gallery's closed until New Year's. I'll check it once a day to make sure Mom or John hasn't called, but it can stay there for now."

"Okay," Thomas said. Marcus turned from the dresser. Unwrapping the candy cane, he gave it an experimental lick, then pointed it at Thomas.

"Don't look smug or I will put the pointy end up *your* ass and break it off. Unpack my stuff."

"Since when did I become your maid?" But it was cheerful complaining. Thomas was happy to comply.

§

By the time they retrieved Julie from the airport one hour away, things were on an even keel. Thomas drove his Nova, Marcus not in the mood to drive. Plus the Nova was more comfortable for three than the sporty Maserati. The front bench seat allowed all three of them to ride up front, Julie between them. Her cheerful cynicism only enhanced the festive mood. "Oh God, Marcus, I should have caught that flight with you. I swear, I do it to myself every year. It's the Stepford Family Christmas."

"Damn. I watched the Walton Christmas special instead of that one. My loss." Thomas dropped his hand from the wheel to squeeze her knee. "Are you saying all the Ramirezes aren't as warm and fuzzy as you?"

Julie snorted. "My mother was giving me dual-cheek air kisses when I was a toddler. Hugs are only appropriate when there's a death in the family, and there's a three-second hold rule on those. God, I know I was switched in the hospital. The Waltons brought home a prissy tight-ass demon baby and my parents got me. They're leaving with my brother tomorrow for Europe. Their annual high-brow, ten-city tour for the twelve days after Christmas. They consider that a holiday tradition. Whatever. Not for me."

She drew her knees up so she could hook her bare feet on the seat edge, since she'd already dumped her shoes in the back. "I'm going to eat your mother's awesome strawberry pie, go shopping with Les and Daralyn in the closest Podunk town that has a mall with tacky Christmas decorations, and have an absolutely awesome time. Sometimes New York can be just so...New York. Way too full of itself. I'll come back to do the Times Square thing like any proper New Yorker, but for this week, I'm going to tease up my hair, chew on a straw and wear short shorts while looking for big, strapping farm boys."

"Thanks for not stereotyping us Southerners," Thomas said dryly. "Bitch."

"Takes one to know one."

Thomas chuckled. "God help the high school guys working for Rory as seasonal help. Every one of them is big and strapping."

"Ooh, thanks for the tip. Reduces my search time."

"I'd pass on the shorts," Marcus advised. "It's not North cold, but your cute ass will turn blue."

"Fine. I'll settle for a snug Christmas sweater that shows my big breasts, which can be perky with the right bra. I can do the cougar thing and teach those boys how to make some teenage girls really happy."

Thomas rolled his eyes but he couldn't help but throw her a fond look. "We're really glad you joined us. You know, you don't have to go over to Mom's tomorrow night."

"Nope. I'm not horning in on your first Christmas morning waking up as a married couple. We'll see you later that day. Your mom said you're coming over to cook an enormous turkey while she, Les and Daralyn whip up an orgy of carbs."

"I'm pretty sure she didn't use those words."

"Something like that." Grabbing Thomas's hand and seizing one of Marcus's, Julie squeezed them on her lap. "You guys look so happy with one another. The way the universe should be. One look between you two is a whole conversation. If I wasn't so happy for you both, I'd cut you up with a chain saw."

"Based on that comment, our offer to let you sleep over *tonight* might be rescinded," Marcus said. "What happened to your promising date with the online guy? Sounded like you were really compatible."

"Yeah, we were both apples. Only his apple already had

worms. I really should know better. I'm just going to sign up for one of those Friends with Benefits sites so I can have the occasional dinner and sex night and throw myself into the theater the rest of the time. There's always man candy coming through there anyway. Unfortunately, they're so used to being ogled, they don't know what foreplay is. They think they can just flash their manly goodies to get a woman wet."

"Well," Marcus began. Julie flicked his ear.

"Except for you, that doesn't really happen. And that's just one of God's cruel tricks. 'Hey, look at the world's most gorgeous guy. He's hung like a horse and was built to fuck but, oh, sorry girls, he's gay!' Not even bi, not even bi-curious, not even able to close his eyes and pretend, just to give a girl a break."

"You really need to let that go."

"Nope. I hold a grudge." She scooted into his lap, winning a grumbling complaint from Marcus about not squashing the horse's tender equipment, but she ignored him and propped her feet on Thomas's thigh as she crooked her arm around Marcus's shoulder. "Okay, so tell me about this new show you and J. Martin are planning." She glanced at Marcus. "Did Thomas pee himself when you told him?"

Marcus laughed outright and Thomas sent them both a narrow look. "No, I did not," he said.

"He did squeal like a girl. A bit."

"It's a long walk to the house. Nobody will pick up two Yankee city slickers."

Julie chuckled. "Not true. I've heard all about Southern hospitality. They might make us ride in the back of the truck with the pigs, but they'll still give us a lift. Hey, is there going to be time for a nap before dinner? I'm a bit jet lagged and would love to recharge."

"Absolutely. Marcus should probably do the same. He's fading around the edges."

"How can you tell?" Julie stared into Marcus's face at three-inch range, earning a glinting gaze. "He always looks in mint condition to the rest of us."

"As it should be," Marcus said.

Marcus had his arm around Julie, holding her securely, but he extended his other hand, no matter that she could see the gesture. Thomas took it, squeezing and was then amazed when Marcus left their hands linked, resting on Julie's knee. Yeah, all was good for now. Things were out in the open and just needed time to balance.

Julie yawned and dropped her head on Marcus's shoulder. "You know, if you paid me a stipend, I'd leave New York behind and become your live-in service sub. You could both repay me with the occasional orgasm. Or maybe a daily orgasm. Fair's fair. I'd even iron Marcus's endless supply of shirts."

"Where did you learn that term?" Thomas shot her a glance. He saw Marcus's eyes sharpen, reflecting his own concern.

"Well, that night you guys...you know, the thing you did for my birthday. It's gotten me thinking a lot since then. I've visited some sites, talked to some Doms. I'm intrigued. Don't know if I roll that way, but you know, I'm flexible, and it seems some people do it to keep things lively, not necessarily because they're dyed in the wool like you two."

"If you explore deeper than that, you keep us in the loop." Marcus tugged her brown hair, pulling her head back to give her a look Thomas recognized well enough to make his toes curl in his thick tread work shoes. "You don't go investigating that world by yourself, Julie."

"I'm not going to be taking any weird risks..."

"Julie."

"Fine, fine." She blew out a breath, looked at Thomas. "Okay, so there *are* some guys who can give you the instant-panty-flood with just a look. Wow."

He knew just what she meant.

Once back at the house, he checked on the thawing Christmas Day turkey and took some time to lay out what he'd need to prepare the Christmas Eve dinner, adding some to-dos to his prep list. While he did that, Marcus took Julie for a sunset tour of their place, the back fields, Thomas's studio, Marcus's office. Though he had an office area in the house, Marcus had another one in the studio barn so wherever Thomas was, Marcus could be if he so desired. Marcus had insisted, and that insistence had pleased Thomas ridiculously. God, he was so over the moon over the bastard. He'd never thought of two guys having a honeymoon period, but he guessed that was exactly what they had going. Which probably justified Julie's reaction about the chainsaw. He grinned.

Marcus and Julie came back to the porch eventually. Despite the cool temperatures, Thomas had left the door open so he could hear the rise and fall of their voices through the screen door. He checked on them a couple times, bringing both a glass of shiraz and engaging in some relaxing conversation before returning to the inside to finish cleaning up the things that he'd had out to decorate. Marcus and Julie both offered to help, but he told them to take their ease, letting Marcus entertain their guest while he caught up with the things Marcus's arrival had pleasantly put off track.

By the time he finished, he realized it had gotten quiet. Thinking they might have left the porch once again, but not recalling the telltale creak of the boards, he moved to the screen door. A smile crossed his features.

They'd both dozed off. Julie was stretched out on the swing, her head on Marcus's thigh, his arm lying loosely over her waist. He had his other hand hooked in the swing's chain, his head resting against it. Even in a doze, Marcus kept them in motion, the unconscious movement of the ball of his foot against the board rocking the swing like a cradle.

Crossing his arms over his chest, Thomas leaned against the doorframe and indulged one of his private pleasures—watching Marcus sleep. The unguarded look of that princely face roused protective, loving feelings in Thomas. Before they'd committed to one another permanently, Marcus had often chosen to sleep alone, and Thomas had suspected it was because Marcus didn't sleep well. But since they'd married, Marcus's sleep had become deeper and more peaceful than Thomas had ever seen it. One precious night, their bare bodies twined together in a damp, intimate aftermath, Marcus had spoken in the darkness, his voice slurred as he tipped on the edge of dreamland. He'd told Thomas he slept better with him because, with Thomas, he felt like he was home.

Thomas held the words buried in his heart like the treasure he knew they were.

As if he felt his regard, Marcus's eyes opened then, mere slits. Thomas held his gaze, letting him see everything he felt. Marcus's expression flickered, then he lifted a finger from the grasp he had on the chain, the slight movement clear as if he issued the command aloud. *Come here.*

Thomas slid out the door and crossed the porch, avoiding the creaking boards. When he reached Marcus, his Master reached up, curled his fingers in the neck of Thomas's shirt. Slipped several buttons with deft efficiency and slid his fingers inside, stroking flesh. Thomas bit back a sound as those fingers moved over his left nipple, teased, pinched. Then Marcus had hold of the fabric and was pulling him down to meet his mouth in a heated, promising kiss. Tongue stroking Thomas's, fingers sliding up to the side of his throat, his jaw, caressing, while Julie slept below them. Marcus moved his lips across Thomas's cheekbone, taking a firmer hold on his nape as he spoke in his ear.

"If you stand there looking at me like that, pet, we're going to be sending Julie over to your mother's a lot earlier."

Thomas drew back enough to meet his gaze. "If we put Julie in the guest bedroom, you might have time to take care of some things before she wakes up. You're pretty efficient."

"And my sub is very obedient when properly motivated. Take her there and meet me in our room."

Thomas scooped Julie off the swing, Marcus sliding an arm up under her to help support the move. It woke her enough she made a pleased noise and nestled further against Thomas as he carried her through the door and to the guestroom. Despite his preferences, she was a pleasant, voluptuous armful of curves. The straight male population were a bunch of morons for not appreciating the gift she was. He slid off her shoes, unpinned her thick, curly hair from its barrette, sitting it beside the night table as she rooted down beneath the covers, disappearing like a caterpillar in a cocoon. He grinned when the jeans she was wearing emerged from beneath and fell to the floor, followed by the lacy red bra she'd been wearing under her designer T-shirt.

"Does it match the panties?" he asked. In response, he was flashed a quick view as she lifted the covers, showing the bright red color, complete with tiny reindeer patterned across the silk. Then the covers came back down like the thump of snow falling off the eaves.

"Christmasy," she muttered. "Sleepy. Go away. Unless you want to come under and give me good dreams. Marcus wouldn't mind. Doesn't really count, right?"

He snorted and pressed a kiss to the crown of her head just visible above the covers, giving the general vicinity of her hip a pat before he picked up the jeans and bra, folding them neatly and placing them on the rocker. When he straightened, he saw Marcus standing in the doorway, watching him. A meaningful tilt of his head, and he'd disappeared down the hallway.

Thomas followed, closing Julie's door behind him. Marcus had stopped at their bedroom door and was watching him come his way. Thomas wasn't above being a tease, so as he came down the hall, he finished the job Marcus had started, unbuttoning his shirt all the way, shrugging it off his shoulders, reveling in the way his Master's gaze intensified. When he was within arm's reach, he wasn't at all surprised to be pulled close with an impatient hand. Thomas bit down on a noise as Marcus palmed him through his jeans, massaging his erection. He clamped the other hand on Thomas's tender ass, holding him in place.

"You stand still as a statue, pet," Marcus said. "Does it count?"

Marcus could give a hand job over clothes better than a lot of men could flesh to flesh, and Thomas found himself struggling not to thrust into his hand. As well as to figure out what he was talking about, then he remembered Julie's comment. Marcus moved his other palm to Thomas's throat, wrapping his fingers around it to hold him still as he kept working his cock. He squeezed hard enough that

Thomas's breath caught beneath the grip. "You better answer me."

"Hell yes, it counts. I'm only yours, Master."

"That's right. I'd beat her backside black and blue, but I think that's what she's angling for."

They both knew Julie meant it as a joke, nothing serious, just the usual harmless flirting, but Thomas was more than willing to roll with Marcus's reaction.

Marcus stepped back abruptly and jerked his head, telling Thomas he wanted him in the bedroom. Obediently, he moved into their own haven from the whole world, a king-sized bed with a pile of pillows and linens in brown and cream tones, masculine and earthy at once, the mahogany frame and color schemes a mesh of who they both were.

"On your knees, there." Marcus pointed next to the bed. "All clothes off."

Thomas complied, the quiver back in the limbs. Would that feeling that swept him whenever Marcus took control ever fade? Each time it only got sharper, cut deeper, as if the exercise of it was a sensual whetting stone. Marcus unbuckled his slim belt, unfastened and unzipped the jeans he'd donned to go pick up Julie. Reaching into the straining hold of his dark boxers, he stretched out a fully erect cock, almost at Thomas's eye level. Thomas licked his lips. Reaching into the night table, Marcus handed him the lube.

"Get me ready to fuck you."

An order straight from heaven, God forgive him if it was blasphemy. Thomas rubbed the lubricant over Marcus's shaft, taking time to pump up and down slow. Marcus closed his eyes, dropping his head back to his shoulders, obviously taking full pleasure in Thomas's touch, but in a few moments, he touched his head, stopping him. "Bend over the bed. If you want to keep that comforter from the dry cleaner, you better put on a condom."

They kept a liberal handful of them in the night stand, just for that kind of reason. Thomas had no doubts of Marcus's faithfulness. Not anymore. And there'd never been a reason to doubt his own. What he'd said at the door, applied to man, woman—fuck, even to his own hand. His body and all its responses belonged to his Master. Even so, it still thrilled Thomas, these odd moments of fierce possessiveness that a comment like Julie's could unexpectedly provoke in his Master. With that intuition that had only seemed to grow as he spent more time with Marcus, he suspected there was a connection there with Marcus's earlier discomfiture, but now was not the time to explore that. God, no.

As soon as Thomas was sheathed and bent over the bed, Marcus's hand was on the back of his neck, pushing him down to his elbows, and he was guiding his cock into Thomas's ass. Marcus could be gentle, merciless, teasing, firm, and all the points in between. Now he slammed home, balls deep.

Thomas grunted, fingers clutching the covers. His balls drew up, cock stiffening at the demanding treatment, making it all the more exciting. He knew Marcus would ask, but he would say it first.

"I'm yours, Master."

"Yeah, you are. Every fucking inch." Another thrust, followed by a slick, incredibly erotic withdrawal that made all of Thomas's nerve endings cry for more. Then re-entry, that push of Marcus's broad head through the rings of muscle, teasing Thomas even further. "God..."

Marcus leaned over him then, pushing him flat, his body on top of his, and began to piston his hips, hard and fast, so deep it was like Marcus was plowing earth. Thomas braced his legs, his elbows, felt his Master's breath on his neck, then his teeth as Marcus bit. His neck, his shoulder... He wanted Thomas to see the teeth marks for the next few days. Thomas groaned. "Master, I need to come. Please come for me first."

Marcus didn't respond, at least not in words. Instead he coiled both arms around Thomas's chest, using the strength of his upper body and the brace of his feet between Thomas's spread ones to hold them as he kept fucking Thomas with deep, long strokes, pressing Thomas's knees even further into the side of the bed.

"Master."

"No. You'll come for me first. Let me hear you."

Marcus left him no other choice. Thomas gave him that guttural symphony of pleasure, groaning and snarling through the spurting of his cock, groaning anew as Marcus let go with a hot shot of seed into Thomas's ass. "God..." Thomas managed. "God...Master."

Sometimes he suspected he interchanged the two in his mind, though he'd never be sharing that shocking thought with his mother *or* Marcus. It made a faint smile curve his lips, but as he put both his hands over Marcus's on his chest, felt the quiver in his Master's fingers, he knew arrogance didn't make a man invincible. "Jesus, that felt good."

"Yeah, it did. Your ass is the place I always want to be."

They were both cognizant of their guest, and how it was past dinnertime for all of them, so Marcus didn't linger as long as either of them might wish. However, he straightened and pulled out with slow reluctance, dropping a kiss between Thomas's shoulder blades before giving his ass a smart swat. "Now tell me what the hell is under the tree with Julie's gifts."

Fuck. The man missed nothing. He was like an eagle. Even so, Thomas hedged for time with an innocent "What?"

But as he twisted to his hip, one foot still on the floor, the other knee pressed to the top edge of the mattress, he was treated to the heated trail of his Master's gaze over his bare flank and realized what an unconsciously provocative pose he'd made. He held it until Marcus had looked his fill, giving him an approving nod before gesturing him to his feet. "Fucking tease. You make me want to do that to you all over again."

Thomas would have been happy to accommodate that. He moved to strip off his condom, but Marcus moved in and did it, wrapping it up in tissue and tossing it in the trash. Then he fished the wipes they kept in the side drawer and cleaned Thomas, before doing the same to himself. Thomas watched, wanting to do it, but Marcus shook his head, leaning in to brush his lips over Thomas's as he tossed the wipes and tucked himself back into the boxers.

"Put on your clothes and go get it."

How he could keep so focused on one thing while he shattered Thomas's brain into fragments was both a curse and a blessing. "It's not Christmas yet," Thomas teased him, trying to delay the inevitable. He'd planned to give Marcus the gift after the family event tomorrow, when everyone, including Julie, went back to his mother's house. He never should have brought it out where Marcus could see it.

Marcus gave him a look. As his Master fastened his own jeans, Thomas eased right up against him before he could zip them up, closing his hand over that tab. He eased it with care up over the sizeable package beneath, molding his palm over Marcus and earning a dangerous look.

"Getting pushy, pet?"

"Just needed to touch you. God, I want to touch you all the time."

Marcus wasn't in the mood to change the subject. "We said no Christmas gifts."

"We said no bought Christmas gifts. I made it for you."

A shadow cut through Marcus's eyes, an echo of what Thomas had seen when they'd tried to hang the ornaments. But he merely inclined his head. "Bring it in here."

Stepping back, Marcus buckled his belt. A belt that had strapped Thomas's ass more than once in this very room. The reminder made him shudder, and of course Marcus saw it, his hand lingering on the silver buckle in pleasurable promise it wouldn't be the last time. Maybe right now if he didn't get moving.

Thomas's lips twisted wryly at that. Punishment was a pleasure-sex thing between them, not a motivating threat, but he wouldn't put it past Marcus to give it a try if pushed. He pulled himself back into his own clothes, shrugging back into his shirt as he left the room. His skin was still vibrating, his cock still half-mast. It never seemed to settle down around Marcus, and the more demanding he was, like this, the worse it got.

He was sure Marcus knew it, normally. But he wasn't sure of Marcus's mood. Another reason he wasn't certain it was a good idea to give him his gift right now. It meant too much and he didn't want to spoil the work that had gone into it, taint the significance.

No, he couldn't be that way about it. He had to forge ahead, no matter the mood. They'd both made that decision earlier and he'd honor that, stick with it.

He brought the wrapped rectangular package—obviously a painting—back into the room and shut the door. Of course it hadn't blended with Julie's cheerful red and green wrapped boxes. He'd wrapped it in a silver paper with a froth of snowflake-patterned silver curly ribbon on it. Marcus, sitting in a cushioned occasional chair, gave it a bemused look impossible to decipher.

Thomas bit back a hundred nervous comments. "Do you want to open it, or do you want me to do it?"

He wasn't sure what he'd do if Marcus didn't even want to touch it, but in answer, his Master reached out, took it from his hands. Thomas propped his butt on the edge of the bed, six feet separating them. As Marcus loosened the paper, pulled it away, his eyes trained on what he'd revealed, Thomas shifted.

Long ago, Thomas had created his one and only self-portrait, the result of a challenge between him and Marcus. *I see you standing against a fence, farm boy. Leaning there like you've just finished a day of plowing. You're sweaty, streaked with dirt and you've taken off your shirt...you're wearing those working jeans that have no style, but they're riding low on your hips. Because you're leaning against the fence, they're straining over that fine ass you've got...the sunlight is just barely touching you, outlining your body. I can see the hint of sweat on your shoulders... He's just a farm boy taking a break after a hard day, never realizing how breathtaking he is in that one perfect moment. Everything about him is in that picture.*

Kate, the cow he'd raised from a calf, was in the background of that painting, because that was part of the challenge, Marcus claiming he'd never be able to sell a picture with a cow in it. But when Thomas finished it, Marcus had put it up at auction as he'd promised. In the end, Marcus had entered into a bidding war to retain it for himself. He'd mounted it on the wall of his gallery, directly across from his desk. Which was where it had remained until one volatile day, when Marcus thought Thomas was leaving him forever. In a fit of rage and despair, Marcus had destroyed it.

What Marcus held in his hands was that painting, recreated with some important additions. Now Kate had company, a brindle, long-haired billy goat almost as tall as she was, the type of goat who had confronted Marcus in the Berkshires, a much more fond memory. Thomas was still leaning over the fence, only the right hand he had braced on the fence was covering the hand of someone standing just outside the picture, only the viewer could see enough of the elegant, long-fingered male hand to see the silver wedding band on it. A wedding band with a lightning bolt design that matched the gold one on Thomas's hand, gripping the railing on his other side.

He'd done it to further heal the wounds and underscore the bond between them, the potential loss of which had caused Marcus to destroy the first one. Thomas knew he shouldn't say anything. Marcus was very specific about how he preferred his first impressions. No input, no noise at all. Particularly no self-conscious verbal wrigglings from the artist—Marcus's exact words of course—but this wasn't really something for him to market in his gallery, was it?

"It's a little sentimental, I know, the changes I made, but I followed my heart on it."

Straightening, Thomas slid behind Marcus's chair. As he looked over his shoulder, he tried to figure out what was going through Marcus's mind. Did he love it? Hate it? Think it was way too schmaltzy? It had all the signature layering and erotic tone of most of Thomas's paintings, but the art world was anything but sentimental. He hadn't made it for sale, though. He'd made it for his Master. A Christmas gift for his husband.

Marcus set it aside, rose. As he turned toward the door, the look on his face was so stark and exposed, Thomas stepped into his path, intercepting him. "Marcus."

Marcus laid his hands on Thomas's shoulders, gripped hard. He nodded, his lips tight. "Thank you, pet. It's everything a Christmas present should be."

Then he left Thomas standing there, wondering what the hell that had meant.

He would have chased him down to pursue it, but Marcus in certain moods was best left alone. Especially when they had a visitor in the house. So though Thomas was aching to offer help, comfort, anything, he waited, listening to Marcus cross the boards, go out the front door. A few minutes later, through the bedroom window, Thomas saw him shrugging into his overcoat and heading out over the back fields, a flat expanse Marcus sometimes preferred to stroll alone when he was in one of his solitary moods. Which was obviously what he was in now, because he was shaking out a cigarette and lighting it, something he only did in a state of deep agitation.

"Damn it," Thomas muttered.

§

By the time Marcus returned, Julie was awake. Thomas studied him closely as Julie chatted with them both, unaware of the problem. Marcus put a hand low on his back, leaned forward to see what was cooking for dinner. It was some venison stew and mashed potatoes Thomas's mother had sent over. Julie had whipped up a salad and Thomas had a cobbler baking in the oven for dessert. Marcus gave Thomas a direct look, a nod. Then he pressed his lips to Thomas's, a quick brush, and withdrew to pull out some wine, asking Julie her preference.

"Where'd you go?" Julie asked.

"I was making sure Thomas wasn't hiding a goat on the property," Marcus replied. When he gave Thomas an arch look, Thomas shook his head.

"Now you've spoiled the surprise. Don't you know Les and Rory are hiding him for me?"

"If that's the case, goat stew is going to be a Christmas Day special."

"You really have to get over that phobia."

"Marcus is afraid of goats?" Julie jumped onto that with both feet, which of course set off a whole other wave of teasing. Smiling ruefully at both of them, Thomas decided Christmas was going to be a little bit like a boat ride—some waters more choppy than others.

However, at least for the rest of the night, they seemed to be hitting perfect seas, since dinner ended up being a relaxed, entertaining affair, after which Julie proposed a sappy Christmas movie marathon. When Thomas went to their room to change into pajama bottoms, he found the picture propped carefully up on the chair for display.

Would Marcus hang it at the gallery, as he had the last one? He already had a photo of Thomas on his entryway desk there, a shot taken at their wedding. The two of them were laughing at something, Marcus's head tilted toward Thomas, that light smile on his lips, the look in his eyes the one that always made Thomas's heart tip. Thomas had his hand on Marcus's arm, a casual but unmistakably intimate contact. It had meant a lot to Thomas to find out Marcus kept the picture at work, where anyone coming in saw it. Just as it would mean a lot, knowing he'd hang this picture there again.

It still felt like there were things not being said, but remembering that photo said time was on his side.

Watching Christmas movies well into the late hours, they all sacked out on the sectional sofa. When they woke the next morning, the day was too tightly scheduled to catch time alone. They ate breakfast and then Julie helped Thomas wrap some more gifts, Marcus and he taking turns on the cooking. A couple quick runs to the grocery store became necessary for ingredients Marcus insisted they were missing.

Then there were the spontaneous drop-ins by several of the neighbors, bringing Christmas cookies and good wishes, interspersed with at least three phone calls from Les, checking on the evening's arrangements. In short, the usual holiday chaos Thomas was accustomed to experiencing, and which seemed to alternatively bemuse and amuse Marcus. After Betsy Dorsey and her ancient mother brought by their famous seven-layer salad, Julie pronounced it was official; she'd stepped into the Walton family Christmas.

Splitting the difference between her preference and Thomas's, Daralyn came at three. Marcus and she worked together on the lighter fare yet appetizing dinner menu Marcus and Thomas had planned. Julie continuously replenished their wine glasses and provided the entertainment, keeping them laughing and engaged, so that even Daralyn was openly laughing after awhile.

As they closed in toward evening, Marcus and Julie disappeared to get dressed, then relieved Thomas and Daralyn so they could do the same. Marcus wore a green dress shirt open at the throat and loose over black jeans, his hair brushed and gleaming on his shoulders. Thomas did his best not to ogle, but it was hard. Julie made no pretense of it, teasing Marcus in her usual blatant way, whereas every time Daralyn looked at him, she forgot what she was doing.

"We'll take over here. Go get beautiful, pet." Marcus sidled over and nudged Daralyn with a smile that had her blushing four colors of rose. "And Thomas should go get ready, too."

Thomas rolled his eyes. "You just can't help yourself."

"No, he can't. He loves to fluster and frustrate us," Julie said. "It's his sadistic side. Be sure and spit in his food tonight." Their guest directed that toward Daralyn. Julie was decked out in a little black dress that highlighted her lush curves. She'd made it seasonal with a glittering gold, red and green poinsettia-design pin that matched her tiny stud emerald earrings. Her abundance of hair was piled on her head and pinned with a glittering red barrette. For all her bohemian ways, Julie kept her Upper East Side roots polished, since that was the source of many of her donors for her community theater. She had hung her strappy black heels on a chair tip, however, and was wandering the kitchen in bare feet.

"C'mon, Daralyn," the woman said cheerfully. "I'll help you get dressed since everyone knows I'm useless in the kitchen."

Thomas blessed Julie's kindness. During their movie marathon last night, they'd clued her in on Daralyn's nervousness about the party, and neither he nor Marcus could help the girl get dressed. It also gave Thomas a second alone with Marcus. Happily, his Master was already anticipating him. As soon as the two women left the kitchen, Marcus pulled him closer, making Thomas's pulse jump as he ran a proprietary hand down his back and over his ass to squeeze him through denim. Then Marcus planted a nice lingering kiss on his mouth. "Go get ready for your family, pet. That's an order."

Thomas normally would have teased Marcus about trying to be so high-handed and lord of the manor, but something held him back. As he moved to the door, he stopped and gave his spouse a considering look. Marcus glanced up at him.

Setting aside the spoon he'd been using to test the gravy, Marcus moved back to the doorway with that unconscious masculine grace that always put Thomas in the mood to paint. Marcus touched his mouth with his thumb, swept it over Thomas's chin.

Reaching out, Thomas ran his knuckles down the open neck of Marcus's shirt, hooking there. "You okay?" No bullshit, no coaxing, just eye-to-eye, here-I-am, the-guy-who-loves-you.

Marcus pressed his lips together, green eyes darkening like deep pond water. "Yeah, pet. We're good. Leave it for now." He put his hand over Thomas's where it was propped on the frame, and squeezed. "I'm where I want to be, with who I want to be with. And I'm glad he wants to put up with me."

"Who said that? You're a pain in the ass." But Thomas leaned forward, kissed him. "Okay."

However, as he turned away and headed for the bedroom, he wondered if he was going to have the opportunity to help the complex man he'd married have as good a Christmas as he deserved.

§

There was a flurry of hugs and removal of coats as Thomas's family arrived for dinner, an unloading of a vast amount of gifts large and small, in all types and colors of wrapping. Thomas watched, filled with quiet pleasure as Marcus took his mother's coat and Elaine pulled him down the distance needed to her far shorter form for a hug. She patted him on the back. "Did you call your mother today, Marcus?"

"I spoke to her and John earlier in the week, and I'll call to wish them a merry Christmas tomorrow. Thomas and I are likely going up there for New Year's."

"He told me." Her look was approving. "I'll be sure to send some of my canned potato soup along with you, because I promised Connie I'd share the recipe with her."

Which meant they'd have to figure out a way to get a half-dozen glass jars of potato soup safely from here to Iowa on a commercial plane. Thomas hid a smile at the subtle look Marcus shot him, registering the dilemma. Marcus and his mother were still quite capable of butting heads and had had the odd argument or two, but now it was mostly about politics or how they should decorate the living room, not whether or not Thomas and Marcus belonged together. Sometimes their ways of expressing their viewpoints were so similar, it couldn't help but make Thomas's siblings snicker behind their hands. Especially Rory, who still insisted Thomas had married his mother.

She and Les had brought desserts to supplement what they already had. As Thomas took those and ferried them into the kitchen, he realized Daralyn had not yet made an appearance. Putting them down on the stove, he went looking for her. He found her in the cellar pantry, organizing soup cans.

"Daralyn, what are you doing?" He stepped into the small space as she turned, taking the can away from her to put it on the shelf before he closed his hand over hers. Her fingers were trembling, cold. And sure enough, she was pale, not flushed. Eyes too wide and bright, like a trapped wild animal. "Hey, it's okay."

"I...this may have been a mistake. I don't like being the center of attention. This is so different." She looked down at herself, clad in a green dress of velvet and gauze with a gold waist sash that brought out the hazel in her eyes. Her hair was loose and waving on her shoulders, probably the first time he'd ever seen it unbound. Les had loaned her the gold necklace with a delicate small cross their father had given her on her sixteenth birthday, a perfect accent for Christmas Eve night. She didn't have pierced ears.

Les had helped Daralyn choose well. The dress highlighted her figure, showing Daralyn was a lovely young woman. The scoop neckline showed a hint of her pretty breasts and the hemline was right above her knees. The outfit was age appropriate, but not over-the-top sexy, something that would have really spooked her. Apparently, just dressing up was enough to do that.

There were times prison was not enough punishment. When he'd learned her history, Marcus had said he hoped her father and uncle went straight from prison into the bowels of hell and roasted their fucking nuts off for all eternity. Thomas agreed with him.

He pushed that back for now. As if he had all the time in the world—and for this he did—Thomas eased a hip onto the step ladder they kept in here, drew her in between his knees and chafed both her hands between his. "How do you think you'll feel if Rory sees you and his jaw drops to his knees?"

"He won't, but if he did...that might be nice."

"You're going to be fine. Everyone in that room loves you. We're your family, the real one, the one that treats you the way you should be treated. You understand that, right?"

Daralyn nodded. "I'm sorry. I'm so sorry. I know I'm being rude."

"You wouldn't know how to be rude if you tried. You also don't know how excited Les is to see you in that dress. You don't want to disappoint her, right?"

Daralyn shook her head. But she still wasn't budging.

"Daralyn."

Thomas lifted his head, saw Marcus in the doorway. Earlier, he'd flirted with Daralyn, made her smile and blush. Now he gave her an even look that, while kind, was firm and not flirtatious at all. "Our guests are waiting. Come out and see your family."

Marcus's expression was a different version of the look

Julie had claimed could make her instantly wet. Not sexual this time, not exactly, but a look that tested the waters that they had discussed earlier. To good effect. As Thomas watched Daralyn closely, he saw a tiny click happen inside her mind, almost as if a platform had been placed right before her, a small square of stability in a tumultuous storm of uncertainty. She straightened, her eyes darting around as she processed her unexpected reaction. Marcus extended his hand. Not another word, because he'd made his intentions clear. When he let his Dom side rise to the top, Marcus didn't repeat himself.

With barely another blink, Daralyn put her hand in his larger one. Marcus steadied her up the two steps out of the pantry, guiding her past him. "There you go," he said.

Thomas heard his mother and Les enter the kitchen. "Oh, Daralyn. How beautiful you look." His mother's exclamation was followed by Les's delighted reinforcement. Daralyn disappeared, Marcus's hand sliding away from her lower back as she was drawn into the kitchen. Thomas heard her tentative reply to the compliments, the shy pleasure in her voice.

He met Marcus's gaze. Marcus nodded, a confirmation. "I'll talk to Rory after Christmas," he said, low. "If it's clear that he feels for her the way we're all pretty sure he does."

"Yeah." Thomas swallowed and rose. Marcus started to move away, but when Thomas lifted his hand, he stopped, arched a brow. Waited.

Cognizant of his family on the other side of that wall, Thomas nevertheless came to the bottom step with the request clear in his expression, the sudden tautness of all his muscles. Reading his desire, Marcus moved down a step, but he still had a significant height advantage. Thomas didn't care. He reached up, gripping Marcus's shoulder, and drew him down, his lips already parted to coax the hot kiss out of Marcus he needed like blood running through his veins. His Master. His gorgeous, broken, amazing, indomitable Master, who could make him hungry for the touch of his hands, mouth and cock, with nothing more than a quiet exercise of that side of him that could drive Thomas to his knees in a heartbeat.

Marcus proved it now by banding an arm around Thomas's shoulders to hold him hard against his chest, deepen the kiss, make it sizzling, a demand for surrender. Thomas wanted to simply moan into his mouth, convey every bit of his desires, feelings and need, all of which were overflowing his heart, soul, mind and cock.

Marcus broke the kiss at last, lifting his head and staring down into Thomas's eyes. He let his thumb rub over Thomas's moist lips. "You're going to embarrass yourself, pet. At least I wore a shirt with the tails out. You better stay in here a moment or two."

Marcus left him there, but with a molten look that said there would be a follow-up to that kiss later.

As Julie said—he and Marcus could have whole conversations without words.

§

Dinner and gifts, laughter and love. As if the gods themselves were having as much fun, at one point, trying to clean up discarded wrapping paper, Daralyn tripped while backing up. Fortunately, the arm of Rory's wheelchair was there to tumble right over, into his lap. He caught her, giving her a secure landing pad. Though Rory's legs couldn't support him, he was strong as an ox from the waist up. Since he'd taken over more of the duties of managing the store, he'd increased the muscle definition he'd had even before the accident, and age was starting to broaden and thicken his shoulders.

As she started to scramble up, all flustered apologies, he put a finger to his lips, a mute suggestion to silence. It startled her enough that she went quiet. His lips curving faintly, Rory lifted that finger, pointed up. Following the direction, she saw the mistletoe ornament. Thomas had strategically hung it in the open section of the room he knew would be Rory's most likely spot to park himself.

Rory bent closer, murmured something in Daralyn's ear. Her quivering hand fell on his biceps, fingers curving into his twill shirt sleeve as his arm stayed quite naturally curved around her waist, palm against her back. When he lifted his head, his lips brushed a loose strand of hair curved around her heart-shaped face. Daralyn stared at him, then nodded. His brown eyes warmed and he closed the distance between them to put a kiss on her mouth that, while light, lingered, as she seemed to draw all her breath and his into a dense ball of energy deep inside of her.

They were so wrapped in the moment, neither was distracted by the silent high five Les and Julie exchanged. Elaine reached over the sofa arm to the occasional chair where Thomas was sitting and gripped his hand. Thomas smiled at her, nodding, and glanced at Marcus, who was studying the couple with that intent look he had when considering a problem no one else thought could be solved, but to which he clearly saw a solution. Then his gaze shifted to Thomas, his brow cocking, and Thomas's smile deepened into a grin. Actually, everyone was grinning like fools, particularly Rory when he finally drew back and he and Daralyn continued to look at each other as if there was nowhere else they intended to look until the end of days.

"Let's finish up the gifts and then we'll do pie and coffee," Elaine said, smoothly taking the focus off of them before Daralyn would realize it was there and freak out. "Thomas, that Yankee of yours has put his gifts for us toward the back of the tree, which tells me they better be the best ones."

Though the ornaments had discomfited him, Thomas could tell Marcus was more in his comfort zone when it came to picking out gifts for his family. Knowing his Master as he did, Thomas suspected it had been easier—because he'd been shopping by himself—to simply shift into the mode he'd have used in past years to pick out appropriate, expected gifts for business associates. Saying "it was easier when it wasn't personal" didn't fit, because Thomas's family did matter to him, but it was clear that getting them gifts didn't cut as close to home. Still, handing them out and watching them be opened was a different matter. Thomas maneuvered Marcus into the occasional chair, taking a seat next to him in a chair pulled in from the kitchen.

His mother received a beautiful cashmere robe that

matched her eyes. Marcus had bought Les an elegant charm bracelet, with a few pieces already added, thanks to his close attention to Thomas's stories about his sister. He'd also included a charm-a-month subscription for it. Elaine said he was spending too much money and Marcus reminded her he was filthy rich. He'd gotten Rory a vintage replica Henry rifle, something Thomas's brother had mentioned back at Thanksgiving he was planning to buy once he'd saved up enough spare funds. It told Thomas at least one of the gifts had not been bought in a marathon run through Macy's.

Knowing Julie's love of music boxes, Marcus had given her a carousel made up entirely of monkeys, a whimsical piece done by an obscure eighteenth century playwright and clockmaker that Julie knew about.

"Oh my God," Julie exclaimed, opening it. "It's the first time you've ever bought me a Christmas gift."

"What are you talking about?" Marcus looked offended. "I give you a Starbuck's gift card and a Christmas card every year. And I play Monopoly with you on New Year's Eve and drink that horrible egg nog you make. That's a present and a half."

Julie rolled her eyes, but bounded over to give him a hug. "You know it's different." Bending to kiss his cheek, on the side where Thomas could hear her, she whispered, "He is *so* good for you. Don't fuck it up."

"It's Christmas, don't use the word fuck," Marcus muttered, with an admonishing squeeze.

He'd given each of them something tailored to their interests, thoughtful gifts that earned him another hug from Les and an additional kiss on the cheek from Elaine. Even Rory offered a gruff thanks, his eyes bright as he handled the rifle.

Daralyn didn't seem concerned that there appeared to be no more gifts under the tree, but of course Les, Julie and Elaine all gave Marcus a narrow look. Typical Marcus, he feigned obliviousness until Julie fired a thick ball of wrapping paper at him, accurate and weighted enough it bounced off his chest.

"What?"

Julie tossed him a mock glare. "Don't even try, Marcus Stanton. I know you wouldn't forget something like that."

"Like what?" But he rose, going to the bookcase and drawing a decorative envelope out from between two of Thomas's art books. It had a red and green design on the edges, and a gold sticker showing a vintage Santa delivering gifts held it closed.

Daralyn had settled on a foot stool near Rory, near enough she could have reached out and laid a hand on his foot if she were brave enough to do so. She wasn't, but it didn't mean that the connection wasn't felt in the energy between them.

"Crip." Marcus slapped Rory's head as he went by. Rory provided the obligatory punch in Marcus's side and follow up retort.

"Fag."

"You're getting better at that," Marcus observed. "You hit like a *really* strong girl now."

"Boys," Elaine said severely, though it was for the inappropriateness of the language, not for their habitual way of expressing affection.

Marcus squatted down in front of Daralyn and presented the envelope, meeting her surprised gaze. "This is from Thomas and me. It has a bonus for cleaning up our messes, and you're getting a ten percent raise both from us and the hardware store at the turn of the year. It also includes a registration confirmation for the local community college for the next four years. You can choose whatever you want, but you'll choose a minimum of two courses a semester. Rory and Elaine are going to arrange your schedule at the store however is needed so you can attend. The college has a GED course as well, so you can get your high school diploma."

Daralyn hadn't finished high school. Her grades had been dismal for obvious reasons, not from lack of desire to learn. The girl stared down at the envelope, turning it over in her hands. She didn't open it, but she pressed it against her chest, head bowed over it a long moment before she lifted her face. Her chin was quivering and her eyes were bright with unshed tears. "Thank you," she said. "I...thank you."

She fled the room. Les rose and went after her, dropping a quick kiss on Marcus's head because he was still sitting on his heels, and squeezing Rory's shoulder in reassurance before hurrying off in Daralyn's wake.

"That's what Christmas is supposed to be about." Elaine dabbed at her eyes. "We could have all saved our money and given that one gift, and that would have been a perfect Christmas."

Thomas nodded, reaching over to touch her knee. Marcus came back and took his seat between them, though Elaine gestured him forward and gave his hair a motherly stroke. He took the hand with a smile and kissed it, making Thomas's unflappable mother color a little and smack his shoulder lightly.

That was Marcus. He knew the right things to say and do when it wasn't about him. Yet as Thomas rested his hand on Marcus's arm, his Master turned it over, nudged Thomas into linking fingers with him. When Les and Daralyn returned, Daralyn composed once again, the two girls made Thomas and Marcus stay in place while they brought coffee and dessert from the kitchen. The activity steadied Daralyn, so Thomas was content to stay in his chair, his hand joined with Marcus's as the family chatted and ate dessert. He noticed Marcus bypassed the coffee and pie too, and wondered if it was for the same reason he didn't partake. He didn't want to let go.

When coffee was consumed and conversation was winding down to the relaxed exchanges of family members comfortable with one another, Elaine checked her watch and said it was time to go home and get ready for midnight mass. Les, Julie and Daralyn were going with her, but Elaine shook her head when Thomas offered once more to accompany them.

"No, you stay here your first Christmas night together." She sent an amused glance toward Rory. "Rory will also be delighted to turn in early and let us pray for him. He was up at the crack of dawn taking care of Mr. Grenham's animals so he and his wife could go pick up their son Ford from the airport in Raleigh. He's flying in from Afghanistan for a two week leave." Her fond expression for her younger son became tender as she ruffled his hair.

"Well, make it a good prayer," Thomas said. "You know he needs it."

"I heard that," Rory said through his yawn. "Butthead."

"Penis breath."

Elaine shook her head, but she chuckled, touched Thomas's cheek, and swept her gaze over him, Marcus and Rory at once. "I'll pray for all of my boys."

That comment had Marcus blinking in surprise, but she left it at that. Thomas and Marcus saw the family out to the driveway, and exchanged one last set of hugs with everyone. Giving them a wink, Julie warned she'd be back in time for pancakes in the morning. She and Les were kidnapping Daralyn for the full night, planning an impromptu slumber party in Les's room after Mass.

As they piled in the car and exited the driveway, Thomas lifted his hand in a wave. A deep breath later, he absorbed the fact that he and Marcus were alone. Their first Christmas Eve together.

"Let's leave the dishes for tomorrow," Marcus said, putting his arms around Thomas from behind, pressing his body full against him. Thomas closed his eyes as Marcus's mouth found his throat, his rich scent surrounding him.

"You can't be awake enough for that. You nodded off twice in the last thirty minutes."

"I'm awake enough to get inside you. That's how I want to fall asleep." Marcus's hand dropped, thumb hooking inside Thomas's belt, his fingers curling over his groin on the outside, stroking. "And when I wake in the morning, that's where I'll put myself first thing. I want my first Christmas morning memory married to you to be all about tasting every inch of your skin, listening to you begging me to come. I want to see you gripping the sheets, all helpless and out of control, feel your ass squeezing my cock and know that what I want for Christmas is underneath me, all mine. My farm boy."

"You really are a greedy bastard." Thomas turned his head, suppressing a groan as Marcus bit his throat again. He'd been in a biting mood today, and Thomas anticipated he'd be putting those teeth in a lot of dark, delicious places.

"Do you want me any other way?" Marcus asked.

"No, Master. God, no. God bless us, everyone."

Marcus snorted a chuckle against his flesh, tightened his fingers over Thomas's hardening reaction. "Tiny Tim isn't what comes to mind right now. Let's go in. I want my dessert. Your dick covered with apple pie filling and a scoop of ice cream off your smooth balls will be just the thing."

"Christ," Thomas murmured.

§

Marcus had gotten a second wind, as he often did. As a result, Thomas would have expected them both to sleep like the dead until morning, but the early years of living on a working farm, followed by the subsequent demands of running the store, early truck arrivals and deliveries, had given him an intuition for when he needed to wake. As such, he came fully out of slumber at 3 a.m. He was alone. He'd cleaned all the sticky pie and ice cream off him before sleep, but Marcus had wanted them both to stay naked, so now Thomas pulled on his new flannel pajama bottoms, one of his mother's usual Christmas gifts, and went looking for his husband. Not in his home office, the first place he looked. He checked the kitchen, peering out the window to be sure there were no lights on in the barn, despite the fact Marcus had said he wouldn't do any work until Christmas was over.

Brow creasing, Thomas moved into the living room where the tree had remained lit, per his family's tradition, for the entirety of the Christmas Eve night. He found Marcus sitting in a wing-backed chair on the opposite side of the tree, out of direct view of the kitchen. He was so still, Thomas might have passed over him without registering his presence, except Marcus was his true north. Thomas's senses always pointed toward wherever he stood, breathed, existed.

His Master didn't break his fixation with the tree, the expression in his eyes keeping Thomas from saying anything right away. When he finally shifted his glance to it, he noticed there was a new present there, all by its lonesome. It was a carved white pine box with a simple silver bow tied around it. Obviously something that Marcus had brought with him but not put out until now.

"I didn't know what to get you," he said abruptly, telling Thomas he'd known he was standing there. It didn't surprise Thomas, because his Master always knew where he was, too. The same compass guided Marcus, after all. "That's what was tearing me up, Thomas. I expected to have problems with the decorating, the tree, all of that. I didn't expect to get completely and totally fucked up about what to get you for Christmas."

Thomas came to him. He slid down to the floor, sitting on his ass, pressing his side against his Master's leg. Letting him keep the dominant position, thinking it might help. He touched Marcus's knee and left his hand there. "You said we weren't supposed to get one another gifts."

"Buy one another gifts. I read legal contracts. I see loopholes same as you. Plus, you know I'm a liar when it's convenient."

"No, you're not. That's the one thing you've never been. Not with me."

"No. Not with you." Marcus's gaze slid across the room. Thomas noticed now the picture he'd made for Marcus was here as well, propped up on the occasional chair that had been put back in its normal place, caddy corner to the tree, across from where they were now. "I have the money to buy you anything, but I walked into a bunch of different stores, looked online and nothing...none of it matched what I felt inside. It felt like... It was our first Christmas, damn it. I was treating it like getting a gift for the damn baby Jesus, and I just shut down over it. That's when I realized how utterly fucked up I am about all this."

"Marcus." Thomas curled his hand around his calf, but then changed his mind and stood up on his knees to lean against Marcus. He put an arm around his back, pressing his forehead hard against Marcus's temple. "You're allowed. You don't have to be invincible around me. How many times do we have to go through that? I'm the person you get to break around. It's part of the whole marriage deal."

Marcus swallowed. Leaning forward, he propped his elbows on his knees, which let Thomas slide his arm even further around him. Thomas shifted so he was on one knee, his other thigh pressing against Marcus's knee to form a *T*. "Tell me," Thomas said quietly.

"Okay." Marcus stared at the tree. "I need a cigarette."

"No, you don't. You have me. And we agreed you don't smoke in the house. You're not supposed to smoke at all."

"Nagging asshole."

"Yeah. Tell me. How about you start with what you meant earlier? 'I almost...but I couldn't.'" Thomas shifted his touch under Marcus's thick mane, ran his fingertips over the taut neck beneath. "You almost didn't come home for Christmas. That's what you meant."

Marcus shot him a glance, his eyes flickering, lips pressing together. "Yeah. I figured you knew. Expected it. That's when I realized I couldn't do that to you. That I didn't want to do that to you."

"Thanks. It would have hurt me a lot if you'd done it. Which was why, deep inside, I knew you wouldn't."

Their gazes held, a muscle flexing in Marcus's jaw. Thomas gripped his shoulder, a quick, meaningful squeeze, before returning to that stroke. He took pleasure in the sloping lines from neck to shoulder, passing over shoulder blades, combing his fingers through Marcus's hair, then bringing his touch back under it, into that light hold at juncture of shoulder and neck. "Tell me the rest, Master. Please."

Marcus sighed, dropped his gaze to his hands. "It's crazy, how kids still celebrate Christmas, no matter what else is happening. We had a tree at Mike's, some scraggly thing we stole Christmas Eve when they weren't watching the lots too closely. Hell, they probably would have given us something free, but we were so used to stealing what we needed by that time, it never occurred to us to ask anymore. We decorated it with everything from cut tin cans to paper chains made out of magazines. We'd even found each other some gifts, maybe not all of them stolen, who knows? Mike cooked us a ham and a bunch of fixings. We sat around a couple of card tables. It was the first Christmas since everything changed with me for my family. I was accepted, and *they* were my family. And by next Christmas, they were all gone. How is it people who were with you such a short time can mean so much?"

He lifted his head, looking up at the tree, and Thomas's gut wrenched as the lights reflected off Marcus's eyes, glistening with emotions he couldn't hold back. "I miss them, Thomas. They were the family who knew me, loved me and, even though we were all fucked up in different ways, it still...the closer we got to Christmas this year, the more I remembered that night. Emile sitting in my lap on the floor. I'd hit my growth spurt and felt so manly, holding him like that. He was never big; skinny and average height, built like a scarecrow. He was throwing popcorn at Toby, Mike threatening to kick the shit out of us if we didn't clean all that up while he drank beer and grinned at us in a Santa hat... He had that look that said he'd probably want a nice blowjob from me before he passed out, but that was okay."

Thomas held him. Marcus was leaning against Thomas's knee, letting him. Even draped an arm over Thomas's bent knee as he regarded the lights. "I know it's fucked up, but I loved them, Thomas. They were my first real family. Before I found you and yours."

Thomas could feel the jagged lump he heard in Marcus's voice in his own throat. "I know. I'm so sorry, Marcus." He pressed a kiss to Marcus's forehead, rubbed his back. Just held him. They stayed that way for a good long time, Marcus's head pressed against his as they looked up at the tree. Thomas stayed quiet, understanding whereas another person might vent or weep, Marcus simply leaning on him, holding his arm tight around Thomas's knee braced in front of him, was what his Master needed.

"So that was when I figured out what to get you for Christmas," Marcus said at last. "Christ, you were worried yours was sentimental. I almost didn't bring mine with me. Hell, I almost threw it away a million times before I even met you, and I never could. I threw away everything else, except Toby's picture, that one fantastic picture." Marcus shook his head. "You're going to have to go open it, pet. I don't think I have the courage to hand it to you."

Thomas brushed a kiss over his mouth and touched his jaw. "You're afraid of nothing, Marcus Stanton."

"Except losing you."

"Well, since that's never going to happen, you're pretty much fearless. You're stuck with my unrefined farm boy self forever." Thomas wiggled his ring finger at him. "You made a vow and the only way out of it is death."

Marcus gave a half snort. "You're not that hard to live with."

"Well, you sometimes are, but fortunately I'm Catholic and suicide is a mortal sin."

"Not the only thing they consider a mortal sin."

"Eh." Thomas dismissed that with a shrug. He eased away from Marcus, appreciating how Marcus reached for him, squeezing his arm before he let him stretch out to the tree, snag the box and bring it back, resting it on his knees. "This is great carving work."

"Yeah. I've kept it in that for a long time. The box was done by one of my early finds. Ian Holmberg."

"Right. He does fantastic wood sculpture."

"This was when he was doing more crafty stuff, but you can see the artist starting to come out in the way he worked the lid."

Thomas nodded. A trio of stars was burned into the top. Stain had been worked into the grain, making it look like a stormy sky behind the stars. The middle star was the largest, the Star of Bethlehem. Aware of Marcus's close regard, Thomas lifted the lid. Looked for a long moment.

"Unlike yours, the hands that made it weren't the giver's," Marcus said quietly. "But it wasn't bought. At least not with money."

"No. but that doesn't matter." Thomas lifted his gaze to Marcus, but his Master had his attention locked on the contents inside that chest.

"Your mom planted the seed a few weeks ago, when we were first talking about Christmas. She said the tree topper should be picked out together, because it would have special meaning when we brought it out every year. Since you bought all sorts of ornaments, but nothing to cover the top, I guess you felt the same way. Apple doesn't fall far from that sturdy tree, after all." Marcus's lips quirked, but there was no humor in his eyes.

Thomas was hard put not to rush to assure him too quickly. Understanding his lover the way he did, he looked back down and lifted out the contents of the box. It was a star, created out of twigs and a thorny vine. It was simply made, but whoever had done it had put a great deal of effort into it. Not too much or too little embellishment. The bark of the twigs had been peeled away and a stain used to create a pattern of swirled pale yellow with smudges of gray, the vine a dark green contrast. The whole thing had been sprayed with something to preserve it, giving it a soft luster.

"I think he stole the sealer, but the rest was probably gathered out of back lots."

"Toby?" Thomas asked.

"No, and yes. He was the 'artistic advisor.' Emile. Emile made it for me. For all of us. For that one and only tree we shared."

The lights of the tree touched Marcus's heartrendingly beautiful features, the quiet green eyes, his face for once without a mask of any kind. Just a mix of the boy he'd been and the man he was, who, at his core, was all about loving Thomas. His gaze turned to him now, showing that clearly.

"He said the vine represented Jesus's crown of thorns. Said he punctured his fingers quite a few times creating it, but that sort of added to the symbolism, so he didn't do anything to protect himself from it. I suspect some of his blood is soaked into the wood. When we put the star on the tree, I remember Emile put his head on my shoulder, wrapped both arms around me and said the star wrapped in thorns was like love. 'It hurts, but it's beautiful, too. That's why I like it. It wouldn't work if it didn't have both, you know?'"

Marcus's voice broke a little at that part, but when Thomas moved to put the star aside, he shook his head. Getting his resolute look, he put his hand over Thomas's, squeezed. "Let's put it on our tree. If you're okay with it being our first tree topper."

"You bet your ass." Thomas gave him a fierce look, layered his free hand over Marcus's.

When Marcus nodded, withdrawing his hand, Thomas rose, pulling the stool Daralyn had used earlier over to the tree. As he stepped onto it, Marcus rose, laying a hand on his lower back to steady him, his warm palm on Thomas's flesh, bare above the loose hold of the pajama bottoms.

"Hand it to me, Master? Please?" Thomas asked softly.

Marcus picked it up, turned it over in his hands, held it a moment. Lifting it to his face, he pressed a kiss against one of the twigs in the middle. "To the family of my past," he said, then lifted his gaze to Thomas. "For the family of my present and future. Merry Christmas, Thomas."

Thomas leaned down, and Marcus was ready for him, their mouths meeting in a long moment of intent contact, a hundred emotions passing between them. Marcus's fingers tightened on Thomas's shoulder so when he lifted his head, he found himself held in place, his Master's green eyes boring into his. "I'll get better at this. My job is taking care of you, and that means being better at this."

"Well, I don't want to make you think you can get out of harder work, but you pretty much made up for the past few weeks in the past ten minutes. And I take care of you, too, when you need it," Thomas added, with a severe look. "That's the way this works. Just remember that."

"You really are getting bossy, pet. Last thing I need is a nagging wife."

Thomas grinned. "Sometimes it's the first thing you need." Then he sobered as Marcus handed him the star. Taking it in reverent hands, he fixed it to the top of the tree with the twist ties Marcus handed him.

When Thomas stepped down, they looked at it together, shoulder to shoulder. But then Thomas turned his head and looked at Marcus's profile, long enough that Marcus slanted him a glance. "Pet?"

"Beautiful, but it hurts," Thomas murmured. "I know just what he means."

"I know you do. Every true artist knows exactly what those words mean. And I thank God for it, and you, even if

I don't ever thank Him for too much else." Sliding a hand to his nape, Marcus turned Thomas toward him. At the look in his Master's eye, the powerful things twisting in Thomas's chest started to descend lower.

"I didn't decorate the tree with you," Marcus said. "But I can decorate you."

Stepping away, he tugged the box of extra lights, ornaments, hooks and various other decorations out from behind the sofa. A box Thomas distinctly remembered putting away before Julie's arrival. "Strip, pet. I plan to have you under the tree, after I tie you up in some lights. If you're lucky, I might just pour a little hot chocolate on those sensitive nipples of yours, lick it off your cock. I want you at my mercy the rest of the night."

"Are you sure—"

Thomas sucked in a gasp as Marcus moved fast, taking him down to the carpet, pressing his body full against him, those green eyes close again. "Have you ever known me not to be sure when it comes to fucking you, pet?"

"No, sir." Thomas was glad he'd gone with the address when those green eyes deepened to emerald, the distracting lips curving. He'd noticed Marcus was like that. After sharing deep memories, it was as if he had to take Thomas over, take him hard and overwhelm him, to reassure himself that he was still in control, that Thomas wasn't going to disappear when he let the demons loose. But Thomas had his own response to that. Lifting his hands to Marcus's face, Thomas framed it, fingers firm and conveying that he *was* here. Always.

Things got quiet and intense as Marcus put one hand over Thomas's, linked fingers and squeezed, message received. That eased the harder edge to his expression. But not too much, thank God. When Thomas brought those linked hands down, it was to kiss Marcus's. It was his left hand, so he put his lips over Marcus's wedding ring, kissing it reverently, but providing a tiny tease of the flesh with his tongue.

"I'm at your mercy every day, Master."

Marcus's eyes gleamed, a moment before he pinned Thomas's hands out to either side of him.

"Then as far as I'm concerned, every fucking day is Christmas, pet."

The Season of Giving

A vignette featuring Kane, Farida and John, characters from the Vampire Queen Series.

Originally posted 12/22/2014

Background: *When this vignette was written, Kane, Farida and John were all children in the series. Kane is Lyssa and Jacob's son, and John is the grandson of Lyssa's majordomo, Elijah Ingram. Farida is Mason and Jessica's daughter. When it came time to write the 2014 vignette, I thought it would be fun to jump a couple decades in the future and see what these three would be like as young adults—and provide some speculation about a future book for them.*

§

"The gift is a custom order. I didn't want to have a servant pick it up. I want to pick it up myself, to make sure it's what I ordered for my parents." Farida sighed. "What's so wrong with that? It's the Atlanta mall, not Afghanistan."

"Easy for you to say." Kane gave her a look. "If something happens to *me*, *my* father won't remove all *your* appendages in the most painful way imaginable."

"Everyone thinks my dad is so scary. He's not so bad."

Kane and John exchanged a rolled eye look before Kane turned his attention back to their female friend. "You've never seen that side of Lord Mason," he said with exaggerated patience. "He'd hide my detached arms behind his back and say, 'Oh, we're just chatting, pumpkin pie.

Run along and get a snack from your mother.'"

"He does not call me pumpkin pie," she retorted and swatted at him. He intercepted the hand and squeezed it, an automatic reproof, though he noticed the faint scrape of her nails on his palm before she drew back and sent him a haughty look.

"I'm more concerned about *your* mother, Kane," John interrupted dryly. "If something happens to you, Lady Lyssa will strangle me with my own intestines. One less human in the world. Big deal."

"Not a chance," Farida disagreed. "She's the smartest vampire alive. She knows it's Kane who instigates the trouble. You just go along to do damage control the best you can."

Kane scowled at her. "Yeah, because no one would suspect we ducked out to go to the mall because little Miss Perfect Princess insisted on doing her own shopping instead of having Amazon deliver." He shot a glance at John. "Plus, don't hand me that shit. You know you're safe, because my mother likes you better than she likes me. Remember the Christmas when you had more gifts under the tree than I did?"

"Are you ever going to let that go? It was almost fifteen years ago. I was turning eighteen and entering college in the spring semester. You were eleven. It wasn't a milestone year for you. Selfish prick."

Kane shrugged. Under normal circumstances, it would have been their usual banter, nothing more. But this time the jibe pricked a little sharper. Since John had returned home from college for the holidays, they hadn't really hit their usual stride with each other. John had been his second mark for such a long time, so they could talk in one another's minds even while he was off at college. They hadn't done as much of that lately, either. John had been busy and Kane... Well, he didn't want to talk.

"Boys." Always intuitive, Farida offered them both a radiant smile and linked her arms through the crook of their elbows. "Stop pretending you aren't having just as much fun as I am, getting out of the house for a few hours on our own. How long has it been since you were at this mall, Kane?"

"A while. Maybe twenty years. We moved to Savannah soon after the last time I was here. I think they've added a couple floors since then." Kane frowned, surveying the multi-level mall. Though he suspected it had all been renovated since his last visit, he vaguely remembered the nearby toy store. He remembered a train trundling through the store, big enough to carry passengers under the age of six. He moved forward, taking the other two with him, and a smile crossed his face as a train emerged at the front, made the turn on its track and then carried the children back into the bowels of the store. Its route probably took them past strategically arranged merchandise.

Since so many things seemed to be changing this year, it was reassuring to find something that hadn't, reminding him of the many pleasant memories he had of the Christmas season. This was the time of year when his mother and Jacob were able to put aside Council demands and vampire politics and enjoy time at home with their small group of trusted friends and family. Like tonight, when they were out at the symphony with Farida's parents, Lord Mason and his servant Jessica, who had joined them at Lyssa's Atlanta estate for the week.

Kane's glance strayed back to Farida, one of the exceptional pleasures of the last couple Christmases. They stayed in touch throughout the year, through emails, texts and even the occasional letter. Farida liked the old-fashioned art of calligraphy, since she said it made her imagine she was a Victorian heroine, sending him penned letters with the fine swirls and scrolls. But having her here, face to face, was best.

The minute they'd arrived from the airport, she'd emerged from the car, run to him and thrown herself into his arms to give him an exuberant hug. Usually she followed up the affection with a punch in his stomach or a slap upside his head that made his ears ring. Her eyes had widened, mouth pursing a little in surprise when he anticipated her this year, catching her hand and spinning her so her back was against him, arms crossed over her chest and wrists firmly locked by his. He'd been tempted to tease the shell of her delicate ear with his lips, his body tightening at the feel of her against him, but instead he'd stuck his tongue in her ear, and then let her give chase to him through the house, the pack of Irish wolfhounds that always traveled with them chasing them both joyously.

Hell, having her here pleased him. Having both of them here pleased him. Maybe he should just focus on that so he didn't ruin it for all of them.

When John met his gaze over Farida's head, Kane let his lips quirk in the fond, exasperated expression they'd often shared as children. The expression that said, *yeah, she's a brat, but she's our brat.*

John grinned, his expression easing, making Kane wonder if his second mark was battling some of the same thoughts. He didn't know for sure, because he and John had a pact. Either of them could initiate mental conversation, but Kane wasn't supposed to cruise around in John's head when John wasn't talking to him. Kane had gone along with that, mostly. But some nights, especially lately, he dipped in there, just to hear the comforting sound of John studying a few states away, putting together amazing equations and theories Kane understood as well as Swahili written in pig latin. But it helped him sleep.

Feeling Farida's eyes on him, he set that aside and closed his eyes, remembering more about that long ago childhood shopping trip. His father had lowered him into one of the train cars. He recalled the smell of his mother as she touched his face, the comforting soundtrack of his parents' conversation as he rode in a stroller through the stores, alive with the sights and sounds of Christmas.

Tonight the mall was decked out with huge displays of poinsettias and animatronic snow scenes with elves and reindeer. Big sparkling snowflakes hung from satin blue ribbons from the high ceilings. The skating rink, which could be viewed from the rails of any of the upper levels of the mall, had an imprint of a laughing Santa Claus under the ice.

"We should go ice skating," Farida said. "I mean, we're here anyway. And you left a note, so they'll know where we are. It wasn't technically forbidden to leave the house while they were gone...right?"

Kane knew why they were all uncomfortable, seeking reassurance from one another. Born vampires in their twenties didn't go out without the protection of their parents or an older vampire, but neither of them were little any more, where they might be snatched by a vampire wanting a precious born vampire baby. The bloodlust thing could be an issue if it was triggered, but he'd fed earlier in the evening. He'd taken it from one of the second marks in the house he now routinely used for his meals. It was the first time he hadn't sought it from John when he was home, and of course John had noticed. Kane had tried to be casual about it, saying that the servant had already set aside some blood for him in the fridge, but he'd seen John's speculative look.

He shifted, aware that he shouldn't be thinking about this so much. He'd been all for doing this when Farida suggested it, but now that they were here he was suddenly, keenly aware that he was responsible for their protection, Farida and John's both. On one hand, it felt good to have that responsibility, any kind of responsibility, rather than being someone else's responsibility. However, the reality was a little...new.

But seriously, as Farida herself had said, what could go wrong? Even though his mother could be in his mind and therefore indirectly his father could, when Kane turned twenty-five earlier in the year, Kane had won a promise from Lady Lyssa similar to his and John's agreement. She'd promised to keep her forays into his mind limited to the surface, just to be sure he was okay, not following his thoughts moment by moment. It had been an indirect vote of confidence from her.

So as long as everything stayed even keel, they should be fine. They hadn't been told they couldn't go out. Damn it, he was a man, and they were picking up a gift from the goddamned mall, no more than a thirty minute drive from home. His uncle would say sack up and stop being such a baby. Okay, maybe not about this situation, because Gideon could be just as protective as everyone else about Kane and Farida, but in Kane's mind the sneering admonition still applied.

He'd hesitated too long. Farida was looking a little uncertain, paler. That stiffened his spine like nothing else could. No one was going to hurt her with him around.

"No, you're probably right," he said casually. "We should go back to the house. You might need a diaper change."

The look from her glittering amber eyes could have shrunk a lesser man's testicles. She might deny knowing about Lord Mason's savage side, but she'd inherited that look from him for certain. Though Jessica could be pretty intimidating when the moment called for it. Intimidating for a human servant, that is.

Until recently, he'd always thought of his own parents as his mother and father, not Lady Lyssa, Council Head, and Jacob, her human servant, but he was getting more conscious of the distinctions between vampires and mortals. He wondered if it was part of what his mother had warned him about, that he'd start experiencing changes in his twenties, bloodlust impulses tangled with vacillating emotions similar to hormone surges in a human teenager.

You start feeling your strength, unwisely before you are ready to exercise it, so it's essential you watch your temperament and your choice of words during this time of your life.

Great. John was almost two decades past puberty and Kane was just entering it, vampire-style. He had to be so careful of a lot of things. It felt like he was in a schoolroom, learning his letters, while the rest of the world accelerated.

He shrugged irritably. He was wasting this moment thinking about all of that. They were here. They might as well enjoy it.

He wandered with them to the rail and leaned on it, him and John flanking Farida, her slim hands clasped on the top rung. She wore a silver and amber ring on her middle finger, and her nails, touched with a crystal polish, were slightly longer than her fingertips. They tightened on the metal as she watched the ice skaters circle. "Oh, look at her." Farida pointed at one girl in a blue skating costume as she did a leap and twirl in the air, and landed gracefully. "I'd like to learn how to do that. I'd be a famous skater who wins the Olympics three times before disappearing mysteriously to mask my lack of aging. Or we could be a team." She nudged Kane. "You'd look good in one of those tight, sparkly suits."

"Yeah, that's never going to happen. I wouldn't mind seeing you in one of those dresses though." Leaning down, he caught her earlobe in his teeth and brushed his lips along her sweet nape, eliciting a shiver and a look at him from behind her dark glasses. Like most vampire females, there was nothing subtle about her beauty, extraordinary enough to cause most mortal males to lose their train of thought and walk into walls. Her thick chestnut hair was normally loose, thick and waving around her delicate face. She had Jessica's slim build but generous breasts for her frame. She'd downplayed all of it, though, with a pair of jeans, a purple T-shirt and a ball cap. Pulling her hair into a pony tail and concealing her amber eyes behind the glasses helped, but she had an air about her that would still catch a man's eye. Hell, her scent alone was enough, and he had an exceptional sense of smell.

She held his gaze as if knowing the direction of his thoughts, and her small pink mouth pursed thoughtfully. They'd been doing this awhile, what for vampires was low key flirting. Because of their carnal natures, sex wasn't that big of a deal, most vampires already sexually active by the age of sixteen, but something had held him back with Farida, and not just because they were actually on the same continent only two or three times a year. The closest they'd gotten to sex with each other was last year, when his family had visited hers in South America. One night, he'd come looking for her and found her feeding in bed, twined around a young second mark female with long-lashed dark eyes, olive coloring and yards of thick black hair. When Farida had invited him to join them for the meal, seeing the two women twined together was something no male would resist.

The human, Sarita, worked with Mason's horses, her body lean and toned, skin smelling sweetly of soap. Then there'd been Farida's more exotic scent. She'd kept the girl in between them and had stayed clothed, whereas Sarita was blissfully naked and accessible. Even so, her aroused, slick cunt wasn't what Kane had wanted. He'd reached over her, dug his fingers into Farida's nape and caught her mouth with his own for a fang-clashing, tongue-stroking kiss as the servant nuzzled his throat, nipped and rubbed herself against his cock. When he'd thrust into Sarita, Farida's lips had parted as if he'd thrust into her.

But they'd known one another so long, it felt like the actual thing needed to be more special. So they kept it at this not-so-playful level. In a weak moment, he'd talked about it with Jacob.

"The one thing you have is time, Kane. Let her grow up, and you grow up, too. Hormones may say rush, but I think you know how to deal with those until the time is right."

Yeah, he had a way to deal with his hormones. All he had to do was think about how he had to be with his parents or one of his relatives or godparents, to go and do anything. The first time he took someone that mattered to his bed, it wasn't going to be when he was still under their roof and considered a damn baby, needing a sitter.

As Farida continued to point out things about the skaters, his gaze scanned the crowd. When he realized he was doing that on instinct, staying aware of his surroundings, it reassured him, reminding him he'd had rigorous training from his father, mother and Uncle Gideon. As well as Lord Daegan, the vampire to whom his uncle belonged and one of the scariest vampires he knew. Even more dangerous than his mother. Maybe.

He hadn't decided to go out on his own tonight to be petulant, to prove "nothing could happen." He knew it could. He wasn't some reckless kid. He would stay vigilant. They could let him out on occasion on his own. If an overzealous Christmas shopper could trigger his bloodlust, he'd turn in his car keys and not show his face outside of home until he turned fifty.

He stopped the internal monologue, attention sharpening as his senses got a whiff of something that hinted of violence, that seemed not quite right. Across the big open space between the railings, past those standing against the railing on the opposite side, his gaze alighted on a couple. They were standing in the shadowy opening of one of the maintenance hallways tucked between two stores. The woman, probably around John's age, wore thick makeup, a tight top and short skirt, platform heels. A lot of young women wore risqué clothing on Friday nights, but there was a different quality to her, to the look on her tired, guarded face. He was looking at a hooker.

The big guy holding her arm in a lobster pincer clamp had to be her pimp. He was getting up in her face, giving her hell while she did her best not to flinch or spit at him, though she looked torn between the two impulses, inciting Kane's curiosity. She was tired but not cowed. But the guy still outweighed her, and she looked like it wasn't so much that she thought she could keep him from hitting her, as much as she'd learned the price of showing him her fear of it.

"Let's go over there," he said, nodding in that direction. Farida followed his gaze. Thanks to her vampire senses being as enhanced as his, it didn't take her long to pick up on the situation.

"Kane," she warned. "We don't get involved in human issues."

"I'm not getting involved."

Yet he was already on the move. His speed picked up, smooth as a snake cutting through water, as the male pushed the woman against the wall to make their conversation both more private and more menacing. As they rounded the railing, he tuned in enough to make out some of the conversation through the white noise.

"I don't give you room and board to spend your time shopping at the mall, Jackie."

"I was just picking up a gift for Nancy, Earl. With my money."

"You don't got no money that's yours. Everything you've got is mine."

"That's not true." She tried to yank her arm free. "I get twenty percent of what I earn."

"Your time is mine, and when you're wasting it, I take more."

"Is there a problem?" Kane stepped up with a smile pasted on his face he was pretty sure wasn't pleasant in the least. "Jackie, you never came back."

Earl was a bulky man with questionable taste in aftershave. He also obviously thought an expensive brown suit with a red tie and a reindeer stick pin were all that was necessary to reflect good taste and the spirit of the season, respectively. He turned a narrowed gaze on Kane. His eyes were the gray of a cinder block, his face pitted like one. "Who the fuck are you?"

"I'm the person who paid Jackie for her time tonight. Her entire evening. I don't like to Christmas shop alone."

Earl scowled at Jackie. "You didn't say nothing about hanging around with some rich guy. You trying to take my money, bitch?"

"I told her one of my conditions was absolute discretion. You are not discreet." Kane slid a gaze over him. *A life-sized pus boil can't be discreet.* He pulled out his wallet. "I can pay her for the night thus far and call it done. However, if you're willing to get lost and stop making it obvious what kind of relationship you have, she'll get the balance of it and you'll receive a greater benefit."

Jackie's gaze was shifting between the two of them, but fortunately she held her tongue, not calling Kane out as a liar. Her pale green eyes were wary, though. She didn't look like the type who trusted sudden turns of good fortune. That made him feel even less charitable toward Earl, not that he had any to begin with. He wondered if the red hair was hers or a wig, and had a feeling it was a wig. She was blond, wasn't she? A dark blonde. He frowned, wondering where that thought had come from.

"I'm her business manager," Earl said, interrupting his thoughts. "Before you do anything else with her, we negotiate it out."

The man's gaze was roving over Kane, sizing him up as a mark. Like Farida, Kane had downplayed his appearance. Male vampires were no less distracting on mortal senses. Farida had chosen dark glasses because her amber eyes were an unusual color. Not impossible in a day of colored contacts, but they drew attention. Kane had gone with brown tinted shades that muted the blue of his eyes. He didn't care for hats, but he'd tied back the thick dark hair that fell to his shoulder blades in a glossy mane.

He wore jeans, too, but according to Uncle Gideon, he'd inherited Daegan's sense of style. Whatever that meant, Kane liked dressing well. The jeans were a designer brand, his tan belt revealed by the casual fall of a dark green turtleneck over them. He wore a cashmere top coat against Atlanta's mild winter chill. To someone like Earl, he looked like money. He did have money, but that didn't make Kane respond any better to the avaricious gaze. The man's very scent offended him.

He could handle all that. He was handling all this pretty well, despite Farida's concerns about getting involved. Then Jackie opened her mouth to speak. Earl's grip tightened and twisted, turning her elbow in toward her body as he stepped closer, screening the painful move. Her features whitened with pain.

Heat swept up through Kane's chest, a rumble like low level thunder happening in his mind. He made himself take a breath, center, but that filled his nose with that offending scent again. Scent could be a trigger.

John stepped to his side.

I'm fine, John.

Yeah. I know. John still moved closer.

Triggered bloodlust opened his mind to John, whether Kane wanted to do that or not. As irritating as that was, it was an obvious symptom, telling Kane he needed to focus, get his shit together.

"Let her go." Kane laid his hand on Earl's wrist. With a simple squeeze, he forced the issue, shifting between him and Jackie and pushing Earl back a step. The movement was smooth, easy enough for Kane to accomplish, but touching the male took his reaction up another notch. Unfortunately, it did the same to Earl.

"Just because you paid for pussy don't mean you own it," Earl said, showing teeth. "Get your fucking hands off me."

"Kane," Farida said. She moved to his other side.

"Step back, Farida," John said urgently. She gave him a

startled glance and then Earl's gaze was on her.

"Why you need to buy a used-up piece of ass when you got this top grade one? Or maybe she's too expensive? You like pinching pennies, rich boy?"

Earl was wheezing, Kane noted with interest. Maybe because his hand was wrapped around his throat and he had the man pinned against the wall. He leaned in, his fangs starting to extend. He could almost taste the blood pounding rapidly through Earl's heart.

"You don't look at her," he said. "You don't think about her."

That aftershave smells like he milked a skunk and spiced it up with citrus, John said calmly in his mind. *If you drain him, you'll probably have that coming out your pores for a week. Your mother will make you sleep outside. Even the dogs won't sleep with you.*

No matter the time lapse between visits, it was always that way with John. He just knew how to support Kane, how to anticipate his needs, an intuition that exceeded even the expectations of a second mark's abilities. He heard Farida's chuckle, slightly forced, but still it penetrated. It helped ease the roaring, enough Kane could do what he'd been taught to do to bring it all the way under control. Counting, focusing on an image that would help calm him.

He imagined Farida ice skating, her smile as she found her footing. Even with vampire grace, she'd probably fall down a couple times while she learned, but she'd dust off her jeans and do it again until she figured it out.

Kane's grip eased enough that Earl could speak. "You want to be with Jackie, it's five hundred for the night," he rasped. "A thousand if you want her to stay over with you."

He had enough confidence in his public surroundings to still sound belligerent, but his rolling eyes and white face said he was also picking up on how little concern Kane had about that. "Cash," he added hopefully.

With effort, Kane let Earl go and drew out his wallet again. He put four hundred in Earl's hand. The pimp looked at it. "Where's the other hundred?"

"Your split is 80-20. You probably didn't pay close attention in math class, but that means the other hundred belongs to her."

"I hold her money for her."

"Not tonight." Kane closed his hand over Earl's fist, tightly clenched on the money, and jerked him closer. "You don't have to live to see tomorrow. One more word, and I'll make sure of it."

The man wasn't smart enough to cast his gaze down, to submit, and nothing could get a vampire's blood up like a direct challenge. He felt John's tension flood back into him. But he sensed his own response affecting Farida. Shit. She was having to fight back her own bloodlust. The two of them could rip apart this piece of shit faster than the blink of Christmas lights. He had a flash of Farida's T-shirt stained with blood, those pretty fingernails. That wasn't what she'd wanted tonight. She just wanted to pick up her parents' gift. Probably wanted a chance, just like he did, to do something unsupervised and not have it go bad.

He grimly hung on to that, to her needs and desires, even as the other side of himself howled for blood. His grip tightened, and a bone broke. Earl let out a pained grunt, a strangled squeal of pain.

Kane. Think of Farida. You have to protect her. We have to protect her.

John closed his hand on his shoulder, not to restrain him, but to remind him he wasn't alone. He had his back.

"I have paid adequately for her time," Kane said at last. Though a hiss tagged his syllables and Earl was still looking at him like he'd grown horns, he managed to sound civilized. "Your dislike of me or my abuse of your pride and person will not come back on her. Because if it does, I will give you reason to highly dislike me. For the short period in which your heart will still be beating while you beg for death."

Jerking Earl around, Kane shoved him out of the hallway, forcefully enough that Earl stumbled about twenty feet into the crowd before he could regain his footing. The distance helped. Kane took a deep breath of clean air, took another one. Fortunately for all of them, Earl pocketed the money and kept moving, hurrying off into the crowd.

Kane? Are you all right?

He bit back a curse as his mother's voice filled his head. He caught the faint sound of music, the orchestra at the symphony. Apparently they were on an overture, which went great with the boiling of his blood. Since she'd agreed to limit her infiltration into his mind to picking up on excess emotion, not specific eavesdropping on his thoughts, she wouldn't know the situation he was facing. Unless his bloodlust escalated, and then he was sure she would toss any promises of respecting his privacy aside and scour his mind like a steel-toothed rake.

I'm fine, my lady. He was a man, not a skulking boy, so he did what he should have done before he left. *John and I are at the mall with Farida, picking up her parents' gift. Just ran into an unpleasant human, being aggressive toward a woman. The situation is under control.*

Silence. He could almost feel the weight of her jade stare. She used silences in the way intelligence agencies employed far more aggressive interrogation tactics. But he was his mother's son after all. He stubbornly stayed quiet himself until she spoke again.

All right. Don't linger long. We'll discuss this when we get home.

He bit back the retort that he didn't feel there was anything further to discuss. A moment later, he was glad he had when she added, on a kinder note, *Pick your father up some of those gingerbread Moravian cookies from the Christmas Mouse. I'll add them to his stocking.*

Yes, Mother. She might be the oldest vampire alive, but she did understand his frustration. Sometimes.

I also suggest you take some extra blood from John as soon as feasible to help calm you. It would probably do Farida good as well, because Jessica said she left half of her blood meal in the refrigerator.

Kane frowned. He'd assumed Farida had fed as well as he had before she left. However, he had more pressing matters to address right now. Jackie stood between John and Farida staring at him, a million thoughts obviously struggling in her mind.

"See?" He nodded to Farida. "I'm fine. Not a problem. We're all good here."

"You are so your mother's son." Farida sighed.

John snorted. "I was going to say his father's. Have you ever seen Jacob react when someone threatens Lyssa?"

The newest addition to their party shot Kane an impatient look. "Don't really need to be part of your little chitchat party. What do you and your fancy friends really want?" She flipped back a lock of the brassy red hair and eyed them with a blink of the lashes lacquered with mascara. "You want me and her to get it on while you two boys watch, and then I do both of you? You've paid enough to cover that."

Kane blinked as John coughed and Farida hid a smirk. "Uh, no." Closing his hand gently over her wrist, Kane turned Jackie's hand palm up and put the hundred dollar bill there. "We didn't want anything. You just looked like you could use a break. Merry Christmas. You can buy Nancy a good gift with that."

She rolled her eyes. "Rich people charity. Makes you feel better because you intervened, helped save the hooker at Christmas. When what you've really done is piss Earl off so he'll beat the shit out of me if I don't avoid him for the next several days. Merry fucking Christmas yourself." Giving him a disgusted look, she stuffed the hundred in her bra and started to slide around him.

Her derision took him aback, but as the light shifted over her face, Kane reached out without thinking, brought her to a halt with a hand resting on her shoulder.

"Hey, what're you doing?"

He studied her, his eyes narrowing. Whatever he thought he'd seen, it was gone again, but he couldn't let go of something...familiar. "Is your hair blonde under the wig?" he asked, wondering if he was losing his mind. "Dark blonde?"

She tossed him a bored look. "So you like blondes. Big surprise. Most like the red this time of year. More Christmas festive. But yeah, I can be a blonde if you like."

He shook his head, sharpened his tone. "Is your hair dark blonde?"

When he caught the amused expression on John's face, the slightly unsettled one on Farida's, he wasn't sure how to interpret either. *What?* he asked John.

You also sound *like your mother sometime. The whole dominant vampire thing.*

Shut up. We're freaking her out enough.

"Yeah. Make up your mind, pretty boy." Jackie stepped away from him, shaking him loose. "I'm bitchy, but I'm honest. You've paid. You want something for your money, you tell me and you'll get what you paid for."

Kane straightened, considered. "Okay. I'd like to sit and talk with you a few minutes. Is that all right? The money's yours even if you don't want to sit with me. But if you're okay with conversation, I can buy you a hot apple cider."

"A hot apple cider?"

"You look cold."

Farida and John exchanged a glance. "We'll just go over there and wait on you," John said. He motioned to a bench close to the toy store.

"Thanks."

Despite Farida's thoughtful expression, she went with John without comment. As they withdrew, Kane gestured politely toward the kiosk for the hot apple cider. "If you want something to eat, we can get it as well. There's a bench by the rail there. It has a nice view of the ice rink while you're eating."

"Your dime, hon. I'll look at whatever you want me to look at."

"It's not like that." He pointed at the oversized bag she clutched on her shoulder. "Are you carrying your regular clothes? Non-work clothes, I mean."

She cast a caustic look over herself. "What, you don't like the 'twenty bucks and I'll blow you in an alley' look? Too much slumming for someone of your refined tastes?"

"Since I hope I've covered the rest of your night, I thought you'd be more comfortable in your regular clothes," Kane said evenly. "If you'll tell me what you want food-wise, I'll get it while you change in the bathroom."

She pursed her painted lips, shifted to a cocked hip. "What's to stop me taking off with your money?"

"You said you're honest," he responded simply. "I won't keep you long. I just want to talk to you a bit. But..." He lifted a shoulder. "I'd like to see your real hair. That's my one requirement."

She executed that cynical shrug again, shouldered the bag more securely. "I want a hot apple cider and one of those big Asiago cheese stuffed pretzels when I get back."

"You got it."

§

Farida frowned as Kane moved to the wheeled cart to buy a hot cider and a large stuffed pretzel and the prostitute went down the hallway to the restroom. "What is he doing?"

"Being Kane. People interest him. They always have. He gets in their heads, figures them out. He doesn't like not knowing the answers."

"You know him so well." She stayed silent a moment. "You did good back there. Kept us both okay."

"It's not so hard. All I have to do is remind him he's supposed to protect you. That always brings him right back on point." John stretched an arm out behind her shoulders, an affectionate contact between friends. She drew her feet up on the bench, looped her arms around her knees and laid her head back on his arm. "Hey." She rolled her head back and forth, testing the terrain. "You have biceps now. You must be working out."

"Some. Strength training helps mental focus, stamina, for long hours in the lab."

She chuckled. "I should have known. It wouldn't simply be because you were trying to impress a girl. Nothing normal like that."

John snorted. "Like me impressing a girl has ever been possible when I'm with Kane."

"Well, you're not around Kane as much anymore, are you?"

As his expression shuttered, she gave him a shrewd look. He drew her attention to Jackie's return. "Look at that. He got her to change clothes. She's actually prettier that way, I think."

Jackie wore an old pair of jeans that fit her lower body

well, but the long sleeved thin T-shirt and patched quilted vest for outerwear emphasized how thin she was, making Farida's heart twist with pity despite her wariness of the woman. It wasn't like she could do anything to hurt Kane, but John was right. Sometimes Kane seemed inordinately interested in the goings-on between humans, even unsavory ones. Still, Farida saw something in her face, maybe what Kane had seen. There was more there than just a hardened streetwalker.

The woman had removed her makeup. Though Farida could sense the age of a human and knew Jackie was no older than John, those years had taken a far greater toll on her. Farida watched the two settle on a bench, Jackie a little distrustful when Kane gestured her to sit first. Then he bemused her further by sitting down and leaving an appropriate amount of space between them. She offered him a sip of her cider a few moments later, hesitant, and he took one brief swallow, smiled. Kane's smile could muck up a woman's radar, even a pro's. He knew it, but his use of it was never calculated, making it all the more appealing.

Glancing at John, Farida saw the brooding look in his eyes she'd seen on both his and Kane's faces far-too-frequently during this particular visit. Especially when one was looking at the other and thinking the other didn't notice. Girls didn't have near as much drama as two men on the outs with one another did, she reflected darkly. Probably because girls believed in talking to deal with it, whereas boys... Boys liked to brood.

"Okay, what's bugging you?" she demanded.

John glanced her way. "What do you mean?"

"Something's not right between you and Kane."

John curled a lip. "Talk to Kane about that. He's been blowing hot and cold since I've been home. I shouldn't let him get to me."

"It's probably just the age thing." Farida pointed out the obvious. "You've gone off to school three times, first for your undergraduate and twice for your masters. You've traveled overseas by yourself to all sorts of places with that international study scholarship you won when you were twenty. You could be married and have kids by now, whereas Kane, only a few years younger than you, is so closely supervised we felt like we had to sneak out tonight like stupid human teenagers. Lord Brian is the only born vampire who's ever been accelerated enough in impulse control to be on his own in his twenties and thirties, and he's like this science genius. Like you," she added with a half-smile.

"If I could be half as smart as him, that would be something." John had tremendous respect and not a little awe for the vampire scientist. He shifted on the bench. "Kane told his mom where we are, by the way. I caught that before he shut me out again. She's okay with it. Wants us to pick up cookies for his dad."

"Oh. Well that's good. Think she told my father?" At John's wry look she rolled her eyes. "Dumb question."

"I get what you mean about everyone being overprotective of him," John said. "But you both understand why. If his bloodlust had gone full blown and pulled you in with it, that guy would be nothing more than a greasy spot, and your parents would have a mess to explain to Council."

"Of course we get it," she said impatiently. "We're not idiots. It doesn't mean it's always easy to take." She sighed. "Kane told me once he understands why we're not supposed to have fully marked servants until we're past fifty and can go out more on our own. We'd off our servants out of pure resentment."

"He said that?"

"He wasn't talking about you. Well, yes, but not in that way. You're not his fully marked servant." She put her hand on his arm. "Don't worry about it. You know how we can be."

"Yeah." But in truth, John was a little hurt at how short Kane had been with him since he'd been home. He felt locked out. He'd never been jealous of Kane's bond with Farida before, but until this visit he'd also never felt that detachment from Kane that John had felt from other vampires. That *'Oh, a human. Just a human. Not really one of us'* bullshit. He'd spent his entire growing up years around vampires. He was used to the attitude, had thought he'd accepted it long ago, but maybe that was because he'd never gotten it from Kane.

"This year, he turned twenty-five," Farida said quietly, watching his face. "My mother told me that's a weird year for a vampire male. A lot of changes happen, emotionally, physically. I asked Lord Brian about it and he told me all this stuff you would understand more than I did, but it boils down to him being more unpredictable right now. He's even more reserved with me, in some ways."

"In some ways. Not in others." John's lips curved as her cheeks colored.

"Yes. There's that. That's different too. More intense or something. Not sure how to deal with it yet."

John lifted a shoulder. "Choices aren't always what they seem. Never as straightforward as you think they'll be."

"Stop hinting and just spit it out," she said, giving him a narrow look. "Else I'll pinch you like I did when I was little."

"When was that? A month ago?" He fended her off with a grin, then sobered. "Okay, fine. I've been offered a position at a research facility in Switzerland. It's one of the most important think tanks in the world right now in terms of disease research. I'd be working with top researchers in the field. I wouldn't be much more than a lab tech at first, but still..."

"Wow. John, that's amazing. Brilliant, in fact." She gripped his arm, and John realized how much he'd hoped for this approbation from Kane, the light that sparkled in her eyes, her genuine pleasure at his accomplishment. "You must be over the moon. You've worked so hard for that kind of recognition, but I mean, this is even beyond that, isn't it? This is like a step beyond what you even dreamed would happen."

"Yeah."

And leave it to Farida, so insightful, to understand the crux of it in almost the next breath. "What does Kane say?"

"He doesn't," John said darkly. "He said 'congratulations' in this absent way and went on talking about something else."

"Oh, Kane. You ass." Her voice softened over it, though,

which actually helped some. It was as she'd said. Understanding something didn't make it easier to take, necessarily, but if he stepped back from it, it did make sense. He had hoped to receive recognition from his closest friend, but he'd achieved an accomplishment he'd thought years away, while Kane... Kane was worried he'd get into trouble for going to the mall.

She put her hand over his. "Once he pulls his head out of his own ass, he'll tell you how very proud of you he is. As I am."

"Pull his head out of his ass? I think you've been spending more time around Gideon."

"No, that one comes from my mother. She's said it about my father plenty of times."

"A singular honor only she and Lady Lyssa are granted. Anyone else who's said it probably is no longer breathing."

She dimpled at him, but wouldn't let him off the hook yet. "Is all this why you haven't pursued marriage and children, John? Do you even date? Men? Women?"

"Some. Both. And I do well enough with either." John's brow furrowed. "I guess I don't really have to try to explain it to you, Rida. He and I, we're not a relationship like humans being in love. It's just I've always...belonged to him. So when I told him about the think tank, I was hoping for some indication from him, some signal."

"And he pretended you didn't say anything significant."

"It's more than that." He struggled to find the right words. "It felt like he was saying, 'Yeah, that's great, but we both know you'll be staying with me and becoming my full servant.' Unless I say otherwise. Which he assumes I won't, and I...don't know."

Her brows lifted. "I guess most of us did. But Kane always said it was your choice."

"That's what he's always said. But lately it's like he's patronizing me. Assuming it's idle talk, because it's a done deal, no further discussion. 'Shut up, human, and do what the vampire says.'"

"Do you feel like that's what you have to do?"

Removing his arm from the bench, John leaned forward to clasp his hands between his spread knees. "I don't know." His voice dropped several octaves, suddenly laden with misery.

Farida's gaze turned to Kane, still talking to Jackie. She seemed to be relaxing more, their conversation easier. She even smiled at something he said, looked down at her cider. As he reached out, touched her hair, her gaze lifted to his face, uncertain but no longer as wary. Kane was studying her so hard, as if trying to recall something.

"Do you have any clue what Lady Lyssa thinks about it?" she asked John, keeping her eyes on them.

"Well, that was the surprise." John straightened. "Lady Lyssa hasn't said it directly, but if I had to bet on it, I think she's with my granddad. She supports me having a normal life, a family."

"Really? I mean, that's good. If you want it to go that way, it's important that you have her support."

"Yeah. I've been around her all my life it seems. Though I know nobody except Jacob probably gets everything about her, Kane says I sometimes read his mom even better than he does." He uttered a half laugh. "Want to hear something weird? The other day she called me Thomas. I'm not even sure she realized she'd done it, but we were debating something I was researching. She likes to do that, challenge me on ideas, get me thinking about it in a new direction. When I came up with a point that surprised her, she smiled and said, 'Thomas, you're wise beyond your years.'"

John sighed. "She loved him, too. Just not the same way she does Jacob. And when we've skirted around the edges of it in conversation, it's like she knows whatever I'll be to Kane, it won't be like...what she has with Jacob. And I think she knows that's not going to be enough for Kane. Or me."

"Is she right?"

"I think it was enough for Thomas. Sometimes I'm pretty sure the same would be true for me. I don't know." John ran a hand over his face. "Damn it, Rida, Kane knows I'll deny him nothing. I've never resented that before, never been angry at him about it. I get that he's going through shit right now, but I'm still a little ticked. You know?"

She put her hand on his again. Turning his hand over, he linked fingers with her. "I can't imagine having any two friends closer to me than you both are," he said slowly. "But it feels like there's this crack that's opened up in the earth between us, and I see Kane moving in one direction, above me, and me somehow descending so I'm staring up at him. I was in the kitchen the other day with the Council servants, and I felt a kinship with them that Kane couldn't share when he came looking for me. I thought, 'Good. You know how it feels to stand on the outside for no other reason than what you are.'" The bitterness fell from his expression and he shook his head. "Is it just jealousy? And can you even answer it? You're standing on that side of the wall with him."

It took her aback, but she realized he said it without belligerence, an honest question. "There are always divisions, John," she said, considering it. "I'm a female vampire, and there are differences between us and the males that make the females have our own little club mentality as well. But look at Mason and Jessica, or Lyssa and Jacob. The way they feel for each other bridges every gap."

"Yeah. Maybe I thought Kane and I had that in our friendship. But though I love him more than I think I could possibly love anyone, I'm not in love with him. Does that make sense?"

"I think there are so many different types of love out there," she said. "We usually screw up when we try to define one as better or more than another."

"Maybe so." At a loss with what to do with the subject for now, he turned it back toward her. "You don't seem to get as antsy as Kane does about the restrictions."

"It's a little different for us female vampires, as sexist as it sounds. The protectiveness does get irritating, but it's like it makes more sense to us, or we handle it better. Males, once they reach a certain age...they're safer."

John looked at her quizzically and she offered a little smile. "It's not a talk you guys would have gotten from Lyssa and Jacob, because Kane's a male. There are other threats to a young female, especially a higher-ranking one.

We're still a prize to certain sorts."

"We shouldn't be here." John started to stand up, but she tightened her grip on his hand.

"Nothing has changed. We're still only a few minutes from home, we're at a mall, it's Christmas. And now Lady Lyssa knows we're here. Right?"

Somewhat mollified, John eased back down, but she suppressed her frustration as she saw him take an additional look around them, gauging risk. "Hey, look at me. You asked why we handle it better. That's part of it. The rest of it is just Kane himself. I mean, look at him. He has an energy swathe of fifty feet out on all sides, the charisma of his father and mother combined."

John shook his head. "Which comes right back to the problem. How does anything compare to him, Rida? Anyone? He fills up all the space around my life when I'm with him. Until these past few years, I always figured I *would* be his first third mark when he makes that decision. So why should I slap at him for the same assumption? Maybe the one I'm really struggling with is myself."

"We're young, John. No longer children, but still facing so many new choices. That's what my mother says." She looked toward the male in question, at his noble, perfect profile, the easy way his energy surrounded and controlled the air around a woman, making her feel safe, overwhelmed, anxious and pleased at once to be in that unnerving center.

"I see the way he looks at you," John said, low. "He's thought a lot about you, but I don't know his mind on it."

She shrugged, feeling that heat tinge her cheeks again as John chuckled. "See?" he said. "It's like we're planets orbiting a sun. We can talk about choice all we want, but in the end our existence depends on his warmth. His light."

"Doesn't mean I won't slap his ear through his head if he needs it," she said defensively, but she cocked her head, considering. "He is important to me. But I don't really know how it's going to go between us. Am I in love with him? Or in love with him in this moment of time? Sometimes I think we'll end up the way his mother and my father have. A relationship that evolves into this wonderful close bond, even as they give their souls fully to someone else entirely."

Smiling up at John, she laid her head on his shoulder and slid her arms around him. "Then again, maybe we're all just being too damn serious about it. What we should be doing is just enjoying whatever our relationship is right now, without trying to lay down the track and direction it will take in the future. For instance..." She scraped a fang along his neck, teasing the pulse there with soft lips. "I'd like to share you with Kane, for a meal. I'd love to do that while you're home. We've never done that. I think it would be wonderful. What do you think?"

§

A smile flirted around her sensuous lips. Even though he knew she was trying to ease the mood, he could tell she was actually serious. She slid a knuckle up his abdomen to his chest, played with his skin through the buttons of his shirt. John put his forehead against hers.

"See? Sex is like breathing to vampires. It doesn't mean the same thing to you two it would mean to me. It's easy for you and him to overwhelm and then move on to the next meal. The next human chattel," he muttered.

She drew back, stung. "That was unkind, John."

He realized it almost at the same moment and cursed himself for the cruelty. He'd wondered if he should have come home for Christmas at all. Then he thought of how Kane had hugged him when he arrived. A hard embrace that had been a little fiercer than John expected before the vampire had detached himself, emotionally and physically, as if he had revealed more than expected. He tuned back in to Rida, the hurt on her heartbreakingly beautiful face. He wasn't the only one trying to figure out what the hell they were right now.

"I'm sorry, Rida. So sorry." Taking her hand, he pressed his lips to it. "You're right. That was unforgivable. I'm just dealing with shit. You didn't deserve that."

"No, I didn't," she said. "How could you say something like that, John? Kane and I aren't like a lot of vampires. We know what a relationship between a vampire and human can be. I've grown up seeing how my father feels about my mother, and I know you know how Lyssa feels about Jacob. We would never see you as 'chattel.' What a horrible word."

"I know that. But, no offense, it is different for you. You don't feel for me the way your father and mother feel for each other." He touched her face. "We're a weird combination of friend, brother-sister, Master-Mistress-servant, and lingering childhood crush, because I'm the familiar and the unknown at once."

He dropped his gaze to her hand, opening it up in his to trace her palm with a finger, run his thumb over her pulse, a caress. "Sex is a choice for you, Rida. For a servant, it's different, and even us second marks know that. Hell, I probably knew it way earlier than most." He gave her a wry smile. "My granddad was so relieved that I could piggy back in on Kane's sex talk with Lady Lyssa when I was a kid. He didn't know I could have been dropped off in an Amsterdam sex district and not received as thorough an education on the birds and the bees as I did that evening."

At her quick grin, showing he was completely forgiven, he continued, a little more relaxed. "After her talk, there was a follow up with Jacob as well. It was about sex involving servants. Expectations, etiquette and all that, proper behavior for when Kane started having sexual designs on humans. Which, for male vampires, happens at about thirteen, whether or not he's ready to handle it. Since that was around the age I started to be interested in seeing girls naked, male vampires and humans are about the same on that. The only difference is that safe sex for vampires isn't condoms. It's 'don't drain your partner of so much blood they die'."

He sobered. "I'm not making light of your feelings, Rida. But how long did it take Kane's mother to find her soul mate? A thousand years? And your dad? Up until then, when vampires and humans get together... Vampires desire, they possess, they value, but they hold all the control. Am I ready for that? Do I want that? Can I go there with the two of you and come back from it?"

Laying his head against the cinderblock wall behind the

bench, he closed his eyes. "I'm giving myself a headache."

"Just because you're trying to sound older and wiser than us."

"I am," he said loftily, slanting her an amused look. "And I always will be older. Until I'm dead and you outlive me by about ten centuries, give or take one."

"You told me once a headache is a sign you're working a problem too hard and you need to give it a rest."

She adjusted, curling up in her lithe, kitten-like way next to him on the narrow bench to put her head in his lap. When he looked down, she blinked her long lashed eyes. "So fine. I get all your moral fiber and noble principles stuff. But I don't think we can return your Christmas gift. We planned to fuck your brains out, the two of us, and I'm not sure I kept the receipt."

Pretending she didn't affect him was pointless, since a vampire could sense arousal across a football field. Confirming it, her lips curved. "Cat got your tongue, *old guy?*"

John rolled his eyes and started tickling her. She giggled, squirmed off his lap and squealed when he kept after her. She pushed him away so enthusiastically his head rapped against the cinderblock wall. "Ow."

"Oh, oh, I'm sorry." She put her hand on the back of his head, stroking. "You okay?"

"Yeah." He put his own hand in the offended area to make sure there was no blood. "It won't be my first concussion. Actually, I think I may have hit the dozen mark a couple times. Puberty with Kane was a bitch."

She sat back. "Thank goodness for the second mark, right?" She didn't turn, but she tilted her head. "Bet you a dollar he's checking on you."

John glanced over her shoulder to find Kane had broken off his conversation and was looking over at them to make sure the sudden short explosion of pain in his friend's head hadn't required him to come right away. John pointed accusingly at Farida. Kane shot her a narrow warning look and returned to his conversation with Jackie. Farida stuck her tongue out at his back, but then she met John's gaze.

"Whenever he makes you forget everything else,

remember moments like this. Kane loves you and wants what's best for you, John. When it really matters, he'll come through. You know he will."

He went back to being pensive, but she was having no more of that. Hopping up, she tugged him off the bench with her. "Let's go get my parents' gift and then we'll go into the toy store. I want one of those plastic guns that fires foam pucks out of it. Bet we could freeze them and give Kane a concussion. Revenge is best served cold."

§

Jackie had looked surprised when Kane didn't sit closer to her on the bench. She pulled out a cigarette, obviously remembered she was in the mall, put it away again.

"Do you need to smoke?"

"Doesn't matter. Nothing attracts a mall guard like a lit cigarette. I just hold it. That seems to be enough." She raised a brow. "Do you smoke?"

"No. It's never occurred to me. Wouldn't hurt me any, I suppose, but I've never cared for the smell."

She gave him an odd look. "So let's cut to it. What is this? Some Richard Gere, Julia Roberts fantasy?"

"You've seen that?"

"Still a classic, after all these years."

"Do I look like I need to pay for company?"

"Everybody has something they need, and most of the time it costs money," she said bluntly. "A rich guy has an easier time getting his main squeeze to agree to whatever fetish he's got, because there's compensation for her trouble. Fancy trips, nice house, whatever. But some guys, even if they got money, are all private about that kind of thing. He doesn't want the trophy wife or show pony girlfriend to know he's got those dirty urges. A working girl isn't going to judge."

Kane watched the way she moved as she spoke, the practiced, precise gestures, the hard eyes, but asking her to change clothes, and her choice to remove the makeup, helped him see the difference between the mask and the woman beneath. But he could also tell her armor was

275

important to her, vital. He shouldn't screw with it just because he was curious about what lay beneath it. He had a feeling she'd be in the wind the second he tried it anyway.

"No, I guess not. Well, don't judge me, but I just want to talk. Ask some questions. Is that okay?"

"As I said, your dime, and I've made my money far worse ways than this." She started to pull out the cigarette, remembered again and shrugged, obviously irritable with herself for the vulnerable tell. To distract her, he gestured to her face.

"I like you without all the makeup."

"Well, you're in the minority. Shows my age, not wearing it. Most men like thinking they're with Trixie Cheerleader. Makes them feel younger. Unless it's a really young man. Then he likes the older woman thing."

"I'll bet." Kane was fascinated by the play of light on her face, the wealth of expression she revealed with the barest shift or spoken word. She was a whole storybook, a painful, tragic one, and he was trying to figure out why he was reading so intently, what he was seeking.

"How long have you been doing this?" he ventured.

"Longer than most. I've been cut a couple times, beaten up, but always seem to come back to it. Nothing else seems to stick."

He reached out, touching the light scar on her face. She started to draw back, but apparently reminding herself he'd paid for the privilege, she stayed still. Kane traced it with a gentle finger, then moved to her hair, stroking it back. It was reddish brown, not dark blonde, but looking at her eyebrows, the fine layer of hairs on her arms that blended with her pale skin, he realized it had likely been dyed different colors, cut different ways. Yet it seemed familiar, for all that. She seemed familiar.

"Hey." She shifted. "What are you doing?"

Simple intimacy, gentleness, weren't things she was comfortable with. It angered him that she'd been hurt enough, misled enough, that that would be the case. He reminded himself that he knew nothing about her, that he might be romanticizing her situation. She might have a drug habit or other character flaws, ones that had led to so many bad choices that this was the only one she had left. He wasn't getting that impression, though. It seemed more likely that she'd been beaten down for so long she thought she had no options worth pursuing any more. This was what she knew, and the devil she knew was likely better than any other.

"Sorry." He glanced around at the mall, decorated in cheerful lights, glittering beauty, reds and greens. "You must hate Christmas."

"No. Not really." Her gaze followed his. "The nicest thing I ever remember happening to me happened on Christmas. It was when I was a kid, but it stuck, so it's the one time a year I always kind of hope something better will happen. And often it does. The johns usually tip bigger, for one thing." She chuckled in a way that didn't sound entirely bitter. "One of them gave me a box of Christmas candy last year. Kind of like you give your postal worker or your garbage people...someone who makes your life easier. That made me feel good, weird as it sounds."

"Sounds like someone who treated you with respect. The way you deserve." He couldn't help stroking her hair again, though this time he stopped before he did it, hand poised by her temple. "Do you mind very much?"

"No. It's just weird, the way you do it. It's...nice."

He smiled, pleased to hear it, and stroked his fingers through her hair more deeply, giving it a little tug. It was soft. She took care of it. She bit her lip at the tug and he caught the hint of arousal, something she immediately shuttered, tensing.

"Is it against the rules to enjoy someone's touch?" he asked.

"In a way. You have to stay detached to stay in control."

"I'd think it would be easier if you could lose yourself in it."

His father had told him it was that way for servants. Not only was that the reason why they could do things for their vampires they didn't initially believe they were capable of doing, but they could even derive intense pleasure from it. Comparing servants to a prostitute was an uncomfortable reality, but he didn't turn away from it, thinking it through.

"If you could enjoy it, wouldn't it be better?" he asked.

"No," she said. "Because it doesn't mean anything to the client, nothing permanent, and that would leave you with a hollow feeling. It's better if you don't feel anything. I mean, I have some regulars that I'm fond of, but I never forget they're clients. It's a business relationship. I don't know why I'm telling you this stuff. Fuck it." Taking out the cigarette, she held it unlit, giving him that narrow eyed look again. "You're not a reporter, right?"

He shook his head. He thought about what it would be like to lean forward, taste her lips, her skin. Her reaction to his touch had sparked a response from him, but he ignored it. Arousal was easy for a vampire, and if he took this in that direction, she'd slip back behind that mask in a flash. "What was the good moment at Christmas? If you don't mind telling me."

She lifted a shoulder. "Me and my brother were here, years ago before they renovated it. In front of that toy store, in fact. We'd been dragged along as the poster kids for a nonprofit collecting money and donations for a homeless shelter. We were staying there with our mom. She was sick, and I already knew she was going to die. My brother, he was younger, didn't realize." She put the cigarette to her lips, took it out, tapped it on her knee. Watched the skaters. "I was sitting there, hating being there, hating being on display like that, and then this couple came by with a kid in a stroller. He had the most amazing eyes..."

He was still wearing the tinted glasses, but she glanced up into his eyes, obviously using them as a reference for her remembrance. Putting the cigarette away, she reached up, drew them off and gazed at him a long moment. "Whoever did those contacts for you did a bang up job. They're like movie special effects."

You should see the fangs, he thought.

"So what happened?"

"Oh. The parents...the mother was so beautiful, and the man with her was so strong and handsome. It was like they came right out of a fairy tale. The little boy had this brand new stuffed bear in his arms."

Kane stilled. Caught up in the story, she didn't notice the flash of memory it sparked in him.

"They were giving them away with makeup purchases over at one of the department stores. I'd touched it on the counter when we came through, just one fingertip on his soft little paw. The sales lady behind the counter had given me the look. You know, the one that said she was sure I'd steal it if she turned her back." She looked him up and down. "No, you wouldn't know about that look. But it made me feel grubby and even more out of place."

She took a breath. "Anyhow, the kid, he gave me the bear. Just handed it to me. He had a lisp or something, like it was hard for him to talk. Later that Christmas, one of those trains in the toy store and a bunch of other stuff came to us at the shelter, and I knew it was the beautiful lady, because of the way she looked at me. I heard the volunteers wonder if she and her husband were movie stars, but I didn't think that. I thought she was old as time, like some beautiful sorcerer or witch. Scary in some ways, yet she understood how I felt. I wanted to be as beautiful—and as scary—as her one day. Even thought it was possible when I looked at her."

She took the cigarette out again to twist it deftly over her fingers. "Dumb, right? But it was the way the kid gave me the bear. For one moment, I'd stepped out of my life and was part of something different and extraordinary. Look..."

Putting the cigarette in her mouth, she bent to rummage in her bag. "Fuck, this is crazy, me showing you this," she muttered, "But what the hell."

She pulled out the bear. It was old and threadbare, patches of it shiny. As Kane looked at it, he realized the starting point of those patches would likely line up with the placement of her fingers when she'd been younger. They'd expanded as her hand had grown but she'd still gripped the bear the same way. For comfort, maybe, after lonely nights, hard times.

She held it on those bare spots now as Kane touched it. He noticed her fingers tightened on the toy, almost as if she expected him to take it away simply because it meant something to her. His heart tightened in his chest.

Stroking it with one fingertip, he lifted his gaze to hers. "I thought I recognized you," he murmured.

When her brow creased, he gestured to his face. "My eyes were blue then," he said. "Sometimes they still are. They change. Sometimes green, sometimes blue. Sometimes one of each. Depends on the light, my mood. And scary and beautiful is a great way to describe my mother. It was a long time ago, wasn't it?"

She stared at him. In a blink, her face whitened in anger and she proved what he'd suspected about messing too much with her shields. "I didn't tell you that for you to mock me, asshole. Fuck yourself and your money."

Yanking the bear away, she stuffed it into the bag and started to rise. He expected in the next blink she'd stomp away and be gone. He understood her well enough already to know not to use a physical gesture to stop her, so he went with words instead.

"When I gave it to you, I said 'Yours.' To make sure you knew I was giving it to you."

She stopped, uncertain, her hands clenched, spots of color in her cheeks. A wry smile curled his lips. "Given how possessive I was of my toys then and now, my parents about died of shock."

She paled a little bit. Gently clasping her wrist, he tugged her back into a seated position. "Here. Eat more of your pretzel. Drink some cider."

She'd been about to leave it next to her, and she'd eaten less than a third of it. She wrapped it up and put it in the bag, then clasped it against her protectively, studying him. "You have to be fucking with me, but you aren't."

He shook his head. "I promise I'm not. I did have difficulty talking then, but I think you understood me. I remember your face."

He stroked it as she went still. "Like a toddler does, everything dreamlike and hazy, but when you turned your head toward me, back when we were talking to Earl, I knew you were familiar to me. That's why I asked you to spend some time with me. I wanted to figure it out." He paused. "What happened to your brother?"

Pain suffused her features. He was asking her to deal

with too much, open up far more than she could probably afford. Yet he was reeling from knowing that his one simple choice, to give a child a bear, had kept a prostitute liking Christmas. A small gesture that had had a critical impact. The imbalance he'd felt of late suddenly took a back seat, steadying him so he could focus on this one moment rather than a million other things he couldn't change or control.

"Mom died, and he was placed with a different home. He was younger, cuter. I've never seen him again."

"I'm so sorry."

She pressed her lips together, looked away. "I kept a picture of him, but I'm not going to show you that. You're too close already."

"Sometimes strangers can make it easier to deal with things than people who know us better. You just told me you're in a profession that knows that better than anyone." He touched her knee, a gentle tease. "Right?"

"Yeah." She brought her gaze back to him. "This is pretty unreal. You know that, right?"

"In my world, the unusual can be pretty usual. Can I see the bear again? Please?"

When she complied, he looked at it in her hands. "I remember it as way bigger than that." He spread out his hand, saw how it dwarfed the stuffed creature. "I guess I grew some since then."

"A bit." She surveyed his six foot form, the breadth of his shoulders. "Got your daddy's build."

"You remember that?"

"I was ten. Old enough to notice that," she said dryly. "And I noticed the way they were with each other."

"Yeah. They're still that way."

"How long have they been married?"

"They're not," Kane said. "It's not that kind of relationship. But he is bound to her for his entire life."

He should have simply said how many years they'd been together, but he could already perceive how rare honesty was in her world. He didn't want to lie to her about...anything.

"You're weird," she said, but she smiled. It was strained but real. "Thanks for the pretzel and the cider." She lifted the cup. "I was pretty hungry. Hadn't eaten since breakfast."

"You didn't finish it."

"No. I don't eat a lot at one sitting. I'll eat the rest of it later tonight." She shifted. "Okay, well, I should go get Nancy's gift now. I mean, you can go with me, you've paid for the time...or..." She took a breath. "We can do whatever else you'd like."

While he felt a vague disappointment she was cutting their conversation off so abruptly, he understood. She'd just said it. He was getting too close. Stranger or not, she couldn't afford not to think of him as a client. He'd gained a small window of her trust, but she had to shut it to protect herself. She was likely hoping he could get a hint and be from beginning to end what she needed him to be. Given she'd probably rarely or never had that, he could only oblige, much as he wanted to keep her right here for much longer.

"No, I want you to have time to shop for your friend. But just one thing..."

He sent John the thought and heard the response. Kane lifted his hand without turning as John came up behind him, put the pen and blank card into it. He nodded a vague thanks and put the card on his knee, began to write. He felt John retreating, but realized he had never made eye contact with him as Jackie leaned out and watched John disappear back in the toy store. "Okay, that was weird, too."

"We're a weird kind of group." A good kind. He'd felt John's touch in his mind and answered it with a reassurance of his own. No words, but still an instant understanding. There was a comfort to that he couldn't possibly describe to anyone. Except maybe John. Or Farida. He wished Jackie could experience such a connection. Maybe she'd had it with her brother, and then had it taken away.

Tucking the pen into his jacket, he handed her the card. "You have no reason to trust me. I get that. But the number on there, all you have do is call it, tell them I recommended you. Kane, Lady Lyssa's son. I wrote it down. They'll call me to check it out, and then they'll give you a place to stay, and tell you about several different options they have for lodging and board and job training. A way to get you away from your life. And, if you're interested, to help you find your brother."

"No offense, but that sounds too much like the foster care system." She eyed the card doubtfully. He thought about how pretty she'd be with good nutrition, more sleep and less uncertainty in her life. He'd like to visit her, see that happen. "My life sucks, but I control it."

He doubted that, but he understood what she was saying. Even when you had few perceived choices, you tended to be pretty protective of them. "No one would control you. It's a safe place, that's all. You'd never have to see Earl again. If your friend Nancy needs the same kind of safe haven, she could come, too."

She took the card, ran her thumb over the writing. "I've been lied to a lot. Don't really trust truth anymore."

He put his hand over hers. "But something good happened to you on Christmas once. I'm hoping you'll believe the same person can do it for you again."

"People change from the time they were babies."

"I'm just as trustworthy now as I was then."

She laughed, and it was a nice sound, closer to the way he suspected she'd sound if she was able to laugh more freely and more often. "No offense, but you didn't look too trustworthy then. You looked like you were pretty much a troublemaker."

"And now?"

Drawing back, she perused him in mock appraisal. "Yep, pretty much the same. You can talk a girl into anything."

"Well, except that one." He nodded in the general direction of Farida, in the toy store. "And my mother. They both know me too well."

"It's good to keep those kind of people close. Best to always know who you really are." A shadow crossed her face and her fingers tightened on the card. Since she looked on the verge of handing it back, to avoid the temptation of hope, he closed his hand over hers again, tightening her fingers over the card.

"I bet who you really are was the person you were with

your brother. Maybe he lucked out, found a really good family, and you could be part of that. Maybe he's married and has kids. You'd be an aunt. I'll bet he thinks of you and misses you, too. A lot."

"I've done a lot of things to survive. Makes me not really aunt material. He wouldn't want someone like me around his kids." Her brown eyes went soft though, a little tremor in her chapped lips.

"Sounds like you'd be the toughest aunt at the PTA. Totally kick the asses of any of those soccer moms who get out of line." He touched her face. "I think he'd understand that you did what you had to do to survive, and he would be pretty damn grateful that you came back to him when you could."

She dropped her gaze back to the card, to their clasped hands. "Okay, I'll think about it. I...I really need to go."

He rose as she did. After a moment's hesitation, she held out her hand, an oddly formal gesture. Rather than shaking it, he just closed his fingers over hers again, ran a thumb over her pulse. It was automatic for him, the sensual testing gesture when touching a woman, and he didn't think to restrain it until it was too late. Fortunately, she didn't react with offense. Instead he saw her lips part, and her eyes light with curiosity at her own conflicted response to him. How often did a prostitute let herself feel desire, let herself yearn for anything related to a man's touch?

He thought about drawing her into a quiet corner of the mall, sweeping her hair back from her throat, taking that draught from her that his mother had suggested, but then he dismissed the idea. He'd have to cloud her memory to do that, and it was important that she remember their discussion here. Important to him as well.

She smiled thinly, an apparent self-deprecation at her reaction to a handsome man, then she tucked the card and her hand back in the pocket of her quilted vest, holding the strap of her bag with the other one. For all that it was intended as outerwear, the vest didn't look like it provided much warmth over her jeans and T-shirt. While Atlanta wasn't Minnesota, it was December, and they were having a cold snap. He shrugged out of his cashmere overcoat and held it out to her. "Take this and put it over your clothes. It will work better than what you have."

She shook her head and took a step back. "No. It's not my size."

"It's warm." And if she didn't call that number, she could sell it and make rent for a couple months.

"I told you I didn't want your charity." Her chin set in that stubborn jut again.

"I get that, too." He closed that step, leaned in, met her gaze. "Put on the damn coat, so if this is the last time I ever see you, I don't remember you cold."

Despite John and Farida's teasing, he knew he *did* occasionally channel his mother, as well as his father's more authoritative side, but the tendency toward dominance, a compelling desire to overwhelm, to take over and claim surrender from a human, particularly one that attracted and intrigued him, was an unavoidable vampire trait. Even Farida had her fair share of it. Yet Kane had far more, and it seemed to grow stronger with every sunset.

In his flirtations with Rida, when he was hovering a breath from kissing her, he'd see her eyes soften and her lips part, telling them both which one held the upper hand. Registering that awareness in her eyes could raise his blood temperature exponentially. Still, for all that it was an expected vampire trait, and one he was starting to experience quite regularly, seeing that click happen in a woman's eyes was always like tasting blood for the first time, the rush of energy and wanting more.

The satisfaction he felt at the shift in Jackie's gaze, telling him she'd capitulate to his will, at least in this, turned to amusement as she slipped off the vest and extended it with a defiant look. "A trade, then."

He accepted it, noticing it had been sewn a couple times to keep the filler in the puffed square pattern. The zipper was broken. But she'd patched it with some pretty floral pieces and a couple glittery stars, which actually made it look pretty trendy, at least based on what he'd noticed other females in the mall wearing. "It's lovely. The color will match my eyes."

She snorted and pulled on the coat. Despite her best

efforts, her expression altered at the feel of the cashmere. "Oh...wow."

"Yeah, it's soft." Turning her toward him, he buttoned it up the front. "Better?"

She looked up at him. He saw it, a flicker of hope, the same look he remembered when she took the bear. His grip tightened on the lapels. He wanted to take her home. He wanted to make sure she would be safe. That she would find her brother. Giving her that bear and the remarkable coincidence that had brought their paths back together tonight made her his responsibility.

Yet the coat and the card would have to be enough. She put her hand over his, unlocked his fingers, that wary look back in her eyes, and he forced himself to let her go, let her step back.

"At least call them to talk," he said. "Promise me."

She pressed her lips together. "Maybe. Thanks, Kane. I hope...well, best to you. Thanks for this, no matter what."

She shouldered her purse once more. She hadn't noticed him slipping some more money in there. She'd be smart enough to hide it when she discovered it, though, because if Earl totaled up his take against hers, she was the one who'd gotten the eighty percent, which she deserved far more than that piece of shit did. A dollar was more than Earl deserved. As he envisioned what the man actually deserved, another little spike of bloodlust shot through his gut.

Kane made himself stay still and manage it as he watched Jackie move away into the crowd. He kept watching her, and she looked back several times to see him still doing so. Finally, she reached an intersection of hallways, lifted her hand and was gone, slipping through people like the shadow she was in their world, a creature that lived on the fringes. She was right. The coat was oversized, down nearly to her ankles, but that was okay. It would keep her warm.

He should have at least tried to get her address, find out more about her. But he could have pushed too hard and she would have disappeared before he gave her the card. He had to hope the choice she made was the best one for her. She wasn't part of his world. He couldn't make her choices for her. He didn't have that right, no matter that the vampire in him pretty much said he should because, well...he was a vampire and she was a human.

If he'd handled things better, maybe she would have let him call the number for her, stay with her until the contact from Mason's safe house came and took her under their protection. Then he'd know for sure she'd be fine, safe, and no one like Earl would be in her face again. He thought of her as a little girl, homeless. He thought of all the luxury in his life, the love of his parents, and he was angry, dissatisfied, with no particular target for it.

He was useless, had no power. It didn't matter if he could dominate a woman sexually. What did that mean? No better than kids playing king of the castle on a playground.

He moved toward the toy store as John and Farida were coming out. Farida had on a head band mounted with coiled springs tipped by colorful felt Santa Claus faces, a pair of festive antenna. She was trying to get John to wear one with reindeer and he was dodging her. When Farida turned her attention to Kane, she read his face and sobered. "Everything okay?"

"Yeah. Fine. I gave her the number of one of Mason's safe houses. She might call it."

"What? You didn't overwhelm her with your masculine charm and make it happen?" she teased.

When he curled a lip at her and turned away, Farida touched his arm. "I was only kidding. I'm sure it will turn out all right."

John was watching him, too closely. "Hey, you think it might be time for some blood? If you want, I can grab a cup of the cider and give you guys a shot the discreet way."

"I don't need anything right now. Particularly a human telling me when it's my feeding time."

"Kane." Farida looked at him sharply, but he made a dismissive gesture, thrust Jackie's vest at her and stalked away. Yeah, he was being a jerk. He'd seen the hurt look on John's face before he'd quickly masked it. Stick a pin in and pull it back out, then pretend because the wound closed it didn't matter.

He left them behind, striding through the mall until he reached an open area with a fountain. There was a statue of a frost fairy on top, surrounded by a mobile of hanging snowflakes that sparkled. The fountain was edged in rope lights in ice blue and white colors that sparkled like water bugs skittering across water. Teenagers were throwing coins into the pool and making wishes. He wondered what simple things they were wishing for. A car from their parents when they got their driver's license. A girlfriend or boyfriend. To be popular, to be pretty. To be older.

Yeah. He could get behind that one. Kane tossed a coin in, but he didn't wish for that. He wished for Jackie to call that number. Then he took out another coin and wished to be older. Sitting down on the wall, he trailed his finger in the water, swirling it so the water over the array of shiny coins at the bottom wavered. He made a figure eight. A circle. A heart. Closing his eyes, he took a breath, then another. He needed to center, to make it all make sense.

To keep from ripping out Earl's spine, he'd grounded himself in the ways he'd been taught. But there were other methods he used to calm himself, things he could do when it was just about the struggle between him and his wildly vacillating moods, his penchant for sticking his foot in his mouth or saying thoughtlessly cruel things just because he wanted to lash out. Maybe a twenty-five year old vampire should be stuck off in a cave somewhere for about a decade. He expected most parents had the same thoughts about their teenagers, but the constant comparisons to humans almost half his age, even from himself, really wasn't that fucking helpful. Especially not at this moment.

So he shut his eyes again, breathed, and decided to risk a method he hadn't shared with anyone. So far, he'd done it only by himself, but he wanted to do something, anything, that broke him out of this mode. He wanted to feel like a bird finally coming out of a cage, stretching his wings and proving that yes, he could fly without crashing.

Opening his eyes to mere slits, he watched the ripples he'd started with the movement of his fingers expand, creating more ripples. The figure eights became other figure eights, other circles. It was as if there were a drawing pen moving over the water, making swirls and shapes, zigzags, heart shapes, cutting back across itself. He had the pleasure of seeing the teenagers start to notice it. They pointed and grinned, began looking for whatever device or contraption was causing the effect. All he had to do was keep his hand in the water. Feeling the energy and movement of the water, it was so effortless to call to it. Like children on a playground in truth.

The water began to jump up in small plumes, picking up on the Christmas music beat filtering through the mall. "Joy to the World" couldn't be a more perfect choice. At the crescendo he took a breath, absurdly pleased by the wave of oohs and aahs from the gathering crowd as a wall of water lifted, like the legs of a chorus line. The jets of water crashed back in to the pool in a sparkling display.

He could make water change its nature, use its energy and power. He didn't understand how he did it, just that he did. The ability had started around his twenty-fifth birthday as well, and he hadn't really talked to his parents about it yet. Because he'd wanted it to be his for a while longer, something that didn't have to be discussed and regulated.

It felt good to see the faces of the kids. He looked up to the second level just in time to see Jackie leaning on the rail, watching with everyone else. Only instead of looking at the water or commenting to the people around her as others were doing, her attention rested on him, her gaze shifting to his dripping hand as he rose and turned to face her fully. He slid his hands into his jeans pockets but when he looked up again, she was gone.

§

"There he is," Farida murmured, unnecessarily. John could still track Kane anywhere because, well, Kane couldn't ever really lose him. It was one of the reasons second marks for young vampires had to be well-trusted members of the household, because the vampire didn't have the mind control to completely block his location from that second mark servant until the vampire reached his forties, generally. Something John wisely didn't point out to Kane too often, though he was sure his friend was well aware. And ignored it like everything else John could do.

Well, fuck him, damn it. John was getting a little sick of it, the walking-on-eggshells and worrying about the big bad vampire's feelings. So Kane couldn't get out in the world just yet and do everything he wanted to do. Boohoo. *Welcome to the human world, asshole. Only once you are able to get out, you'll be able to rule the damn world for a jillion years. I only have a certain amount of time to learn and grow and be out there. Or I can be your servant and it will be all about you for the rest of my three-hundred-year life.*

Showing that she'd probably picked up on his agitation, Farida touched his arm. "Let me go be with him on my own a second."

"Fine."

She gave him a glance but left his side to go to Kane. Kane had been standing at the fountain watching some kind of water show they must put on for the holiday season, but he'd now moved to one of the store display windows so he could study a selection of men's coats. Farida pressed up against him, slid her hands around his waist and under his shirt to caress him. Kane tilted his head, speaking to her, then he latched onto her wrist and brought her in front of him, leaning down to kiss her. It was a more thorough kiss than John had seen him give her before. Watching two exceptionally beautiful people get one another hot and bothered, while the display behind them twinkled and turned with festive Christmas lights, was like seeing a Hallmark Christmas movie marathon meet an erotica film fest.

Being in a semi-state of arousal around vampires was something every servant at any mark level had to manage. But these were his childhood friends, and he'd been away from home awhile, so it was still a bit shocking to feel his hormones react as strongly as they did to them. Farida had gotten it started with her little tease back there on the bench, but John reminded himself it just emphasized what he'd said to her. Sex with them would mean something far different to him. Or would it? Was it better for him to think they would be more detached, because if they weren't, if they felt the way he did, how could he ever walk away?

Sometimes it was all so much, he felt like he couldn't breathe. How could he want two different things so much and choose between them?

Kane lifted his head and pinned him with a look. This time, the look was what John often saw on Lyssa's face when she looked toward Jacob.

I think I'll take you up on that drink now. Only I don't want it in a cup of cider. I want to go somewhere private, here in the mall. Suggestions?

When in public, all servants scoped out places a vampire could seek out privacy for a variety of reasons. Whether or not they were on the outs with one another, Kane had relied on John to do that. Which, being an idiot, John had.

He pivoted and began to walk, aware of the two of them falling in behind him. They were probably casually ambling, Kane's arm slung around Farida's shoulders, hers around his waist. They looked like a young, extraordinarily beautiful couple shopping at the mall. While it appeared like they were aimlessly wandering, John could feel Kane's gaze on his back like a laser target.

He took them to a narrow hallway with no restrooms or other public facilities on it, just a passage leading to the mall offices that were closed this time of night. A maintenance closet was nestled back in an alcove about ten feet long, shadowed and removed from view.

Fine. He'd give Kane a drink. Farida, too, if she wanted or needed one. That would restore equilibrium. John stepped into the shadows, leaned against the wall and waited, not sure why his heart was pounding or his palms were damp. Farida slipped in ahead of Kane, giving John an unfathomable look, one that made her look far more exotic and mysterious. Then Kane was there and it was like the contrast between a dainty, sleek cougar and a saber tooth tiger. Putting his hands on the collar of John's sweater, he curled his fingers into it, his knuckles against John's collar bone as he leaned in. John tilted his head away, exposing the vein. He was hard and getting harder, and when Kane pressed his thigh against him, he bit back a groan.

"I didn't say I wanted a vein first, human."

John snapped startled eyes to Kane, saw the crimson licks of flame there. Kane grasped his jaw in a powerful hand and took his mouth, cupping the back of his head as he delved in, kissed John with heat, pinning his body against the wall, his arousal grinding against his own. Kane was an impressive thickness and length, almost driving thought from John's head.

Kane, fuck, what are you...

It was hot, overwhelming, and then Kane broke the kiss, cruised down John's throat. John drew a shaky breath. Okay, now on with the feeding. Sure, just a little different approach from the usual... John had thought about Kane's mouth on him, but to have it suddenly happening and all too real was unexpected. Unbalancing.

Slipping in under Kane's arm, Farida wedged herself into the space Kane left when he shifted. Now they were both pressed against him, her breasts rubbing against John's chest. Her slim hands slipped under John's shirt as they had Kane's, her palms likely still warm from Kane's flesh. Her mouth was on the other side of his neck, nibbling, tiny kisses. Then Kane gripped one of John's wrists, pulled it out to the side, holding it fast. Farida did the same to the other, the two of them pinning him, holding him helpless. She was feeding off Kane's mastery, John could sense it, and the two of them were pulling him under, a sensual assault where it was like he was drowning and never wanted to breathe.

Kane bit into his throat, and Farida went for his wrist. Kane's larger fangs were a deeper invasion, but the contrast of male conqueror versus female seduction was overwhelming. John's cock was iron against his jeans and, when Kane's hand covered it, started to rub, and Farida straddled John's thigh, he couldn't control himself.

Don't. Not here. Christ, Kane...

Pulling his touch back a second before it would have been over, Kane met John's gaze. "You don't tell me when I need blood, John."

John blinked. Swallowed. "Yeah. Got it."

Leaning down then, Kane kissed Farida with John's blood on his mouth. She put her fingers between them, stroking Kane's lips. When they drew back from one another, she licked her fingertips with feminine delicacy. Then she lifted on her toes and touched her mouth to John's, let him taste himself.

Her mouth was sweet, the tips of her fangs a prick against his lips, and he inhaled her scent, falling forever under her spell. No wonder Kane couldn't resist her. John didn't think anyone could, as much as he knew he and Kane would do anything to keep her safe.

Kane drew her back then, breaking the embrace. As John watched, Kane took the decorative scarf she'd draped over her T-shirt up around her throat, a double loop he tightened in both hands as he leaned against John, pressing the point of his shoulder into one side of his chest while Farida leaned against the other. John watched her lips part, the tilt of her chin, how Kane used that restrictive hold to bring her up to his mouth for another brief kiss before he loosened it.

Then he blinked, startled as Kane took it off of her and covered John's eyes with it, tying it behind his head. He spoke in John's ear, a sensual rasp. "You know I'm very particular about who looks at her, John. Usually it doesn't bother me if it's you, but I'm feeling particularly possessive."

Pulling John's arms up behind him, Kane boxed them and bound his wrists with the excess from the scarf. "Now she can do whatever she likes to you, and I don't have to break all your fingers for having them on her. A win-win."

Kane had definitely never moved into this territory before, but hell, being around vampires and their propensity for bondage games, it wasn't a total surprise. What was a surprise was the leap in his own arousal as Kane increased the sense of restraint by closing his hand over John's overlapped forearms and bit his neck again. He pressed against the vampire's hold, more aware of his second mark strength than he'd ever been. Kane gave a half chuckle and responded by shoving John harder against the wall, increasing that grip on his arms and increasing the penetration of the bite. John fought not to spew inside his pants like a kid, but he was fast losing the battle.

Especially since Farida had her lips on his neck, her thigh wrapped around his hip, rubbing her core against him. "I want one of his hands, Kane."

The vampire obliged her, freeing one from the scarf, and she captured it, bringing it back down and then between her thighs. The denim was thin, barely thick enough to be considered leggings. He could feel the satiny give of her panties beneath as she rubbed his fingertips over herself. Her breath came out in a short gasp that tightened his balls.

Bring her to climax, John, Kane ordered. *Satisfy her.*

He didn't have to do much of anything, the two of them pretty much in control of all of it, but he mustered enough brain cells to massage her, learning the shape of her beneath her clothes, sensing the damp heat there, for him and Kane. Or just for Kane. He was the intermediary.

No. She's wanted you to touch her too. It's both of us, John.

Yes and no. He knew how it was with vampires and servants. In Farida's mind, whether or not it was true, she saw John as Kane's servant, an extension of him. The obvious inevitability of his fate sent a shot of despair through him. He couldn't resist it, or them.

Her breath was on his neck as she drew closer. "You were wrong," she murmured in his other ear. "Sex isn't like breathing for us. It's like blood. It's drawing in life, and everything about it. It nourishes us, body, heart and soul."

The climax took her then, an orgasm much like Farida herself. Soft and feminine, overwhelming and intense. She caressed John's cock, which was as hard as what Kane had pressed against him. He wanted to come, Christ he did, but in some ways this stasis was even more pleasurably excruciating. It didn't matter, anyway. They were in control of all of it.

§

"Fuck this." Kane slid his hand around Farida's waist and clamped his other hand over John's nape. "I want you both. Now. Let's go home and whatever the hell happens tomorrow happens."

At least he'd have this done and over with, this confusion of want and need. He didn't think there was such a thing as erectile dysfunction for vampires, but he wasn't going to wait to see if the general impotence he was feeling in all other aspects of his life would infect his dick as well.

He saw that flash of shadows in John's eyes, but knew his second mark wouldn't deny him. John wouldn't ever deny him. The thought came with a hard twist of guilt, but before he could silence it with an inward snarl, something far more critical interrupted him.

His head snapped up and he pivoted, releasing his hold. In the time he'd assumed a protective stance before them, Farida had detected the same threat and moved shoulder to shoulder with him. When he opened his mouth to demand that she step back, she set her chin, her eyes shooting sparks that said she'd protect him just as readily as he would do the same for her and John.

He'd opened his mind to John automatically, so John already knew what they were facing. The human male vibrated with the desire to step into line with the two of them, like they were the Three Musketeers, but his second mark suppressed the urge. Unlike Kane, John always thought through his emotions before acting. From a lifetime in Lady Lyssa's household, the young man knew there was nothing a servant could do to endanger and undermine his vampire master worse than trying to appear as his equal. Especially in front of another vampire.

"What a delightful surprise."

The vampire's voice was faintly accented, but Kane couldn't place his origins. From the scent that had preceded him, Kane already knew he wasn't someone familiar. As the vampire came into view, Kane saw the male was wiry, knotted, giving the appearance of salted rope, unbreakable. He wore jeans and T-shirt, not much different from many of the other twenty-somethings in the mall, but Kane guessed he'd stuck to the shadows, because humans would have instinctively shied from him, or turned around and stared, as if he was a homeless person who'd wandered in. There was something off about him, different from other vampires he'd met.

A feral quality. Kane inhaled again and noticed his scent was wild like forest, pure nature, untouched by the world of humans. Kane had been around the Fae, and they could be like that, but this vampire was no Fae.

Could he be a Trad? One of those vampires who eschewed Vampire Council, human servants and the comforts of industrial society, living on the fringes of human and vampire existence? He'd never met one, but in the tales he had heard, they were always far more unkempt and unpleasantly pungent than this.

This male seemed clean, and his dark brown hair was in a smooth, thick braid to his waist. His face was unrelenting stone, his flat eyes chilling Kane. Then they sent his blood boiling, because they turned quite deliberately toward Farida, and coursed over her with obvious, covetous intent.

Kane shifted to block his view, bumping Farida back behind him with his shoulder. He'd usually act toward her with a sense of fairness, but not in a situation like this. He curled his lip back in a warning growl at the vampire. The male leveled that dead gaze back on him, and his lip peeled back as well, only in a smile as real as plastic flowers stuck into the mound of a fresh grave.

"A lovely girl-child. With the lineage of a born vampire, and a born vampire herself. Quite a prize. All alone."

"Not alone." Kane held his position, thankful that Farida didn't fight him on this, though her breath skittered along the outside of his arm, her fingers brushing his back, then curling into his shirt. She was scared. Fuck, so was he, but feeling her fear stomped his into dust, replacing it with other, far more aggressive feelings.

Kane, John warned. *He's trying to—*

"It takes so little to push a young vampire to mindless bloodlust. You can actually see it start to boil up, like blood out of a fresh kill. I like young males. It's a pleasure to see the savagery you should embrace as your birthright still so blatant in you. Unlike your older counterparts, who neuter themselves with the illusion of impulse control."

He cocked his head, studying Kane. "You're old enough to have taken an annual kill, youngling. You know what it's really supposed to be like. Not feeding yourself from nice, tidy little servants like this one." He nodded toward John. "We could kill him together and, while part of you would be horrified, another part of you would revel in it. Finally off the leash, the yoke forever gone. We could paint this pretty girl child in his blood, take her together, and she would let her own bloodlust take over. You would see me as no threat then, but as destiny."

Curling his lip back, he showed fully elongated fangs. Farida's hand spasmed on Kane's shirt as his own curled into fists. The Trad's attention never left Kane, measuring, waiting. Knowing. A smile played on his lips. He knew all he had to do was shift that avaricious gaze back to Farida, who was standing too far outside the shield of Kane's body...

His response to Earl hadn't been even close to this. John reached into him, lent him the energy he could, and Kane took it, no room for pride or argument. Christ, he wished John was his third mark, to give him even more stability. As it was, John's cool rational mind in his own, as well as his own logic, distant though it was behind that rising, roaring wall, told him the Trad could play him too easily. The only thing in their favor was the Trad's desire to toy with them.

I can control this. I can.

No, he couldn't. He needed to reach out to his mother, call for help.

Every ounce of pride rejected the idea, but Kane yanked his pride out of the way with the same violent force he'd pull out one of his own teeth with a pair of pliers. Fast, to get the agony of it out of the way.

My lady, I have a problem.

He felt her presence in his mind instantly, and didn't waste any time, showing her the situation. Her flood of annoyance—not at him—brought a surge of relief. It was what he expected of his mother when she had things well in hand. Though she might be covering her real feelings to help steady him, he'd take the mummery, because it infused his bloodlust with a shot of calm, temporary though it might be.

Help is on its way. Do not leave that spot, no matter what threat he issues. Do not let Farida leave your side. Hold onto her. Both of you.

Reaching back, he caught one of Farida's wrists as John closed ranks behind him and grasped her other one, both of them shielded by him. Yeah, he might lose control, but he would channel the bloodlust, use it to fight this bastard back with whatever he could. Like the sharp wit he'd inherited from his mother. No. On second thought, he'd channel his uncle.

"Kind of surprised you Trads are after some of us civilized vampires." He eyed the other male. "What? You need someone to teach you how to brush your teeth? Wipe your ass with something other than poison ivy leaves? Is that why you're skulking around a mall rather than coming out in the open where the Council can catch you?"

Kane was gratified to see a flash of surprise from the Trad before it was quickly masked. *I can think past my rage, asshole. Maybe not for long. Just long enough.*

Farida jumped in then, her expression cool. "Maybe instead of talking about blood and death like a cheesy horror movie, you could go get a frozen yogurt and chill out. Leave us the hell alone."

"Or what?" The vampire looked around himself, emphasizing the seclusion of their surroundings. "What would you do, cry rape? Attract police attention? Would you like to see what would happen if they tried to put cuffs on me? Or him?" The Trad nodded to Kane. "He would slaughter as many as I did. You don't restrain a young vampire, unless you know what you're doing. And the police won't." The vampire's eyes were mocking. "But I would. I could take him to the floor and stake him in an instant."

"Lady Lyssa's son?" Tossing her hair back, Farida leveled a contemptuous gaze on him. Suddenly she was every inch the aristocrat her father was. Kane could still feel her fear, held below the surface, but her amber eyes were filled with fire, her chin up as she didn't flinch from the vampire's gaze. While a part of him wanted to admonish her to stay quiet, not attract attention, another part of him was fiercely proud of her. She wouldn't cower. Not in this lifetime. "There'd be nowhere in our world you could hide," she added firmly.

"Your world, perhaps not. But we Trads inhabit a wholly different world from you 'civilized' vampire folk." His dark gaze glittered again. "We need females with pureblood breeding potential to increase our ranks. We will take you into shadows so deep, little girl, you will never be found. And if your parents ever catch up to you, by the time you're found, you will no longer embrace these ways." His attention shifted to Kane, pinned him. "She will carry my scent, not yours. I will make sure of it. Personally. Every night."

Kane, steady, steady.

John's thought was almost a shout in his mind. Kane felt his other hand latch into his shirt next to Farida's, forming a triangle of contact between them.

Though they were both behind him, he knew every detail of Farida's face without looking at it. Her scent was in his nose, her touch upon him. And John. He knew the sculpted lines of John's graceful body, the exceptional intellect, the smooth way he had of talking, the troubled look in his eyes as he fought with himself over where he and Kane were now. They were two friends at a cross roads. Yet he wanted him to have time to figure out things, both of them to figure out things. He wanted to go home with them tonight, be with both of them.

Yet ironically, the same thing that could steady him was starting to turn against him, because he couldn't stop himself from imagining this Trad harming either one of them.

"Yes. It's starting to boil up in you even now, isn't it?" The Trad's expression became colder. "It makes it so easy for a vampire my age to overpower you. Like taking candy from a baby."

"You never had to take candy from him as a baby," John muttered.

John, shut up. He thought if he drew the vampire's wrath, he might give Kane an opening. It might, but Kane didn't want him risking himself like that. "'*We* need females'?" Kane gritted, bringing the Trad's attention back to him. "What is that? Delusions of grandeur, the royal 'we' shit?"

"No." The Trad was done waiting. Kane could see him gathering himself, measuring the distance to Farida, and Kane tensed, getting ready. "I am not alone."

"Neither are they."

The Trad let out a startled half snarl and pivoted. In his frustrated expression, Kane saw a flash of the same violence that had been boiling up inside of him. That part the Trad had praised, even as he threatened to use it against Kane.

He wanted to leap forward onto the Trad's back, take advantage of the moment. Control was a thin thread, but the conflict had moved to a different playing field and he knew his best move was remaining motionless, fighting to maintain control. *You never attack when you are not in control of yourself.* His mother and Daegan had both taught him that. They'd hammered such lessons into him to the point he'd wondered a couple times if the two of them had thought he was mentally defective. But that repetition helped him hold his ground now, focus on finding that balance as the Trad faced the newest arrival.

They teased Farida about her father, but the truth of the matter was no joke. Lord Mason was the second oldest vampire in the world, a member of the Vampire Council and about as civilized as a bear coming out of hibernation on an empty stomach. And that was a normal day. When someone was threatening his daughter? The bear would seem like a fluffy bunny in comparison.

While Kane was staying at Farida's home, he'd heard a tale whispered among the staff. The infamous "Djinn" or "Demon of the Sahara", was the legend of a monster who'd cut a bloody swathe through the desert tribes several hundred years ago. Yet somehow that legend was connected to Farida's father. Looking at him now, Kane well believed it.

It wasn't the way he was dressed that gave it away. His copper-colored hair was pulled back from his sculpted aristocratic features, a sleek look for his formal dress for the symphony, black slacks and jacket, white shirt open at the throat. But the formal dress only framed what lay in his eyes, the set of the mouth. The amber eyes narrowed on the Trad were as primal as the Trad considered himself, though in truth, the Trad didn't know what savage was. The surge of petty satisfaction almost pushed Kane over that edge, but John's continued steady presence in his mind and through his touch helped. That, and the deflating relief, knowing he was no longer the only thing standing between Farida and this bastard.

"Die here," Mason said. "Or leave and I hunt you another day. Your choice."

The Trad was in profile to Kane, and he saw the smooth veneer disrupted by a frisson of uncertainty. Mason, on the other hand, didn't move. Not even a twitch of muscles in his face. Older vampires could do that, the "statue thing" John called it. It was almost like they were dead, but in a come-back-to-eat-your-heart-out way that scared anything with half a grain of sense boneless. If anything, it was as if where Mason stood was becoming a black hole, capable of sucking everything else in around it.

"I am not alone," the Trad repeated. "In case you didn't hear."

"My hearing is acute." Mason's gaze glittered. "Your two companions are dead."

The Trad stared at Mason. "You bluff."

Farida drew in a breath. Kane remained still. Mason wouldn't bluff. No matter that not a copper strand of hair was out of place or a smudge of blood marred his shirt, he'd dispatched the Trad's backup, and was fully prepared to do the same to the Trad. Likely the only thing holding him back was distaste about killing him in front of his daughter and the headache of concealing the body from their human surroundings. But it wouldn't stop him.

"I'm done speaking. Decide." Mason's gaze locked with the Trad's. Pending violence vibrated through the hallway like a tuning fork struck against a steel beam. For an instant, it was as if Kane's hearing was filled with that humming heat, a promise of blood and death.

Then, with a hiss, the Trad was gone, using vampire speed to vacate the hallway.

Mason turned back toward the main corridor, stayed that way. No one spoke, knowing he was tracking, making sure the Trad was not doubling back. When he at last glanced over his shoulder, Kane felt all three of them let out a sigh of relief, though he tried to mask his as much as he could. It didn't matter, though. Mason's attention wasn't on him, a cut as sharp as a knife. He extended his hand. "Farida."

Her fingers tightened on Kane, a brief reassurance, and then she obeyed, leaving Kane's side to place her hand in her father's. Her expression was neutral, but when he briefly touched her face, giving her a stern look, she offered an uncertain smile and put her hand on him, as if reassuring herself he was who she thought he was. When her fingers gripped his shirt, she briefly betrayed the fear Kane had sensed below the surface, but she straightened her shoulders and lifted the red bag in her other hand. "I have the Christmas gift I picked up for you and Mama."

Her eyes remained serious. She wasn't patronizing him, but Kane wondered what thoughts were passing between father and daughter. Mason cupped her face a little more firmly, then he shook his head and turned his attention back to Kane.

It took a huge effort, but Kane wouldn't look away from those cold eyes. He could still see the death that awaited the Trad there. If it had come to it, Lord Mason would have killed everything within the mall walls, including him and John, to keep his daughter safe. Kane couldn't argue with that. He felt the same about Farida. But he couldn't do the same for her. He wasn't old or strong enough.

"I have a car waiting," Mason said at last. "I am taking Farida home. You two may accompany us if you wish."

Kane cleared his throat. "We brought my car. We'll head that way."

Thank God. I'd rather ride home in a car full of angry snakes. That from John, and he couldn't argue that, either.

"As you like." Mason tucked Farida's hand in the crook of his elbow and turned to leave the hallway. He tossed one last terse comment over his shoulder. "Your mother wants you home now."

Great. Just cut off my balls and stuff them in your pocket, why don't you?

"Jesus, Kane," John muttered. "Don't tempt him."

§

When they arrived back at the Atlanta estate, Kane knew without being told his mother would wish to see him right away. Before John could ask the inevitable, Kane shook his head. "I'll take this one alone."

He spoke more brusquely than intended, but he'd had time to think. They hadn't spoken much in the car. John had driven because Kane was still wrestling with those unsettled emotions, sparks of bloodlust that might transform a simple traffic snarl into an incident of vampire road rage if Kane was at the wheel of the BMW. Even now, because he had no outlet, no way to calm it, too many things unresolved, he couldn't seem to settle. He picked up some second mark banked blood from the refrigerator and downed it like medicine. Unbidden, he thought of what the Trad had said about hot blood pumping from a heart. He forced that out of his mind, made himself finish the blood, did a few more centering exercises.

It didn't help. He should go to the workout room, try to burn it all off before he did something unforgivable. He wished the bloodlust had blocked his mind enough that he hadn't realized a couple things that just pissed him off worse. Which was why he'd been too short with John and John had left him in the foyer, his expression impassive. Things were just as fucked up between them as they'd been since John had come home. Damn it, fuck it all.

Kane, I am in my study. I am waiting.

With a sigh, he headed that way, though he wondered if they might all be better off if she let him blow off steam first.

It was no surprise to find his father there, sitting on the

step ladder used to draw books from the higher shelves. What his mother called her study was a library with walls and walls of books, well over ten thousand volumes. When Kane was a child, Jacob had held him on his hip and they'd pulled slim graphic novels out from between classic volumes and historical tomes. They'd stretched out on the rug together, reading about superheroes. Wrestling, talking about whatever came into Kane's head, all the questions he had about everything. It had been so easy to ask then, because he hadn't feared any of the answers.

His father was in his habitual jeans and a Henley pullover in a dark blue color that reflected his midnight blue eyes. Glancing up, he met Kane's gaze as he entered. Kane couldn't tell anything from his father's expression, but that wasn't unusual. The only one more circumspect about revealing emotions than a thousand-year-old vampire was her servant.

Lady Lyssa hadn't changed since she arrived home, still wearing a black velvet gown with a jade clasp at the one shoulder, the other shoulder bare, the whole thing following the lines of her slim figure as lovingly as his father's hands would, and did, quite often. She'd piled her hair up in some elaborate style before she left, but now it was loose, the shining straight wall of it down to her hips, strands caressing her arms. All vampires were beautiful, handsome, off the charts. But Lady Lyssa was something beyond that, too beautiful to ever be mistaken for human, her Fae and vampire blood mixing to scramble the brain of any male alive. Add the queen element to it, her natural air of authority and dangerous power and, if her beauty didn't scramble a man's brain, her ability to make his testicles shrivel up into his body, a pure survival instinct, would. But he was her son. It was different for him.

"You wanted to see me?"

She cocked her head. "I'm glad to see you are safe and home."

He wasn't in the mood to play games. "Mother, how was it Mason was already so close?"

"I could not stop him from coming to you, once he knew you were at the mall."

It was odd, to feel that residual tingle of bloodlust spurt at her words, like a lie detector. "When did you second mark John?" he asked.

At the flicker of her gaze, his mouth tightened, his fingers curling. "You promised you would never lie to me." He took a step forward. "I don't believe you'd break that promise, unless you perceived you were protecting my wellbeing, preserving my friendship with John. Do you think I value that friendship so cheaply I would turn on him for alerting my mother to a threat?"

"I don't know, Kane." Her expression cooled. "You are ignoring his heart of late. It would not be a far leap to think you might accuse him of betrayal. Even though he knew he was risking his friendship with you, the thing he values most in the world, to protect you and Farida."

Did everything come back to that? John's feelings, John's struggle. He remembered John's gaze when he kissed him, the surprise, the desire, the helpless pain as if he were being torn in two...

"Kane," Jacob began quietly. "You need to listen to your mother."

Kane turned away with a head shake, a sharp movement of his hand. A surge of anger, surprising in its force, made him want to snap at Jacob, tell him this was between vampires. *It doesn't concern a servant, damn it.*

The thought startled him as badly as an attack of bloodlust might have done, to the point it took him a heart-stopping moment to assure himself he hadn't said such a horrible thing aloud. He wondered if it was as good as said, though, because his mother had gone very still. He had a bellyful of resentment about a lot of things tonight, violence and anger roiling through him at what he'd fallen short of achieving, but nothing made him feel as much shame or piercing regret as those words did.

He expected he'd turned paler and so he set his jaw, trying to re-marshal his defenses. Lyssa spoke, her jade eyes on his face. "Jacob, I'd like a moment with Kane."

Jacob nodded, sending Kane a look that contained compassion as well as wisdom, the things he'd come to expect from his father. Everyone knew more than him about everything, it seemed.

When the door closed behind Jacob, Lyssa moved back to her desk. "So let us talk, 'vampire to vampire.'"

"My lady, I apologize. I—" He spread his hands out and shook his head. "Damn it all."

"It is not to me you owe an apology. But we'll deal with that later. I think you now understand why vampire parents are more protective of female children. That was my oversight. I thought only of you and your protection when teaching you. But Farida herself was well aware and took the risk."

"Didn't matter. I should have known." He wouldn't put that on Farida. He thought again of how the Trad's gaze had clung to her. What would he have done to her in the shadows to force her to embrace their ways? He thought of Jackie, the things she'd done simply to survive. Beautiful, strong, amazing, delicate, fragile Farida. He loved her, he knew he did, but their feelings for one another were so new in a sense. Whereas her father or mother's love had been a bond they'd shared with her since her birth. Very little was more precious in the vampire world than a born vampire's birth.

He was so tired of the guilt he felt for every action and misstep he took, but he knew no one was to blame for any of that but himself.

"It's simply growing up, son," his mother said, uncharacteristically gentle.

"You're not supposed to listen to my mind."

"Mother's prerogative." She came around the desk and put her hand on his shoulder as he stared out the window. The estate staff had put a long line of spiral Christmas trees along the drive, their light reflecting against the lawn.

"I'm proud of you for calling for my help," she said firmly. "It was the act of a man, not a child. Even Mason knows this. Bloodlust at your age is nothing you can help, Kane. Even for all that, you controlled it far better than most your age would have."

"I think Mason wanted to stake me, then and there. Still does, probably."

"No. Your godfather loves you, Kane. Almost as much as

he loves Farida." She touched his face, drew his gaze. When they stood together like this, it still sometimes surprised him, how petite she actually was. He was an inch taller than Jacob now, so his mother's head barely reached the top of his shoulder. And her face was as deceptively fragile as Farida's.

She sighed. "But Mason has known terrible loss in his life. I do not think he could bear losing his daughter or Jessica. Most times he's able to keep those feelings in perspective, but when either of them is threatened, he becomes a little less rational."

Which told Kane the Trad's days were numbered. He wouldn't mourn him.

Putting a hand on his shoulder, Lyssa eased Kane into the window seat and tucked herself into the space across from him. She left her high heels on the floor and propped stockinged feet on his thigh as he covered one with a hand. There was always a casual affection between them, another touchstone. She was helping to ground him. "It's more than the usual frustration tonight," she said. "Did something happen to make it worse?"

"No. It's not that. Yes and no. Do you remember years ago, me giving a bear to a homeless girl, at the mall?"

"Yes. I'm surprised you do."

"I didn't really. Until I met her tonight." He told her briefly of his interaction with Jackie. As he spoke, her jade gaze never left him. His mother never failed to listen. She listened so well it tended to be unsettling, because she heard things beyond the words that were said. At a time like this, though, it eased the turmoil in him to tell her about it, to see her faint smile of surprise at how they had connected, and the approval at how he'd given Jackie the opportunity to reach out to one of Mason's safe houses.

"It doesn't feel like enough, though." He spread his hands out. "I wanted to help her so much more."

"I knew I shouldn't have let your father read all those superhero comics to you."

And the surge of resentment was back. Rising, he moved away from her to stare out another window. Several of the Irish wolfhounds, descendants of Bran, Maggie and Fionn, the original pack members he remembered from childhood, were sniffing around the lit trees, deciding if they needed to be marked.

He remembered when Bran had died of a grand old age, at their Savannah estate. Kane had rarely seen his mother cry, but that had been one of those times. The landscapers had found the dog in the garden mid-afternoon. At Jacob's direction, Bran had been left "sleeping" there. John's grandfather had sat with the dog to be sure no scavengers or anyone else molested him until Lyssa woke. When she did, she immediately came out to the garden, taking only the necessary time to wrap a robe around herself. She'd knelt over the giant hound's body, laid her cheek on his great head and wept while Jacob knelt over her, held her.

Kane remembered it because it was the one time she hadn't seemed conscious of anything else. She didn't care that the other servants in the house or visitors there on Council business saw her grief. When he'd come and put his hand on the dog's side, unsure if he was welcome, worried by her tears, his mother had put her hand on him, drew him close to her side and let him help hold her while she cried, connecting the three of them, their family.

Loss bound as well as divided people, didn't it?

"Do you really think this is about some childish desire to change the world, Mother?" he asked quietly. "Do you view me as a child still? I don't think I could bear it if you did."

Lyssa's voice was neutral. "Perhaps I'm reminding you that selflessness starts with self. It's not what you can convince or coerce others to give up that matters, but what you yourself are willing to do to make the world a better place."

"Is this what you expect of me?" He waved to her desk where stacks of paperwork spoke of the Council matters pending. "To lead vampires as you have done, for whatever ultimate goal they have?"

"Our goal is no different from the human one, my son. To exist. And do more than exist. To live without fear, without threat of extinction, fully embracing who and what we are. And like the human species, our threat of extinction most often comes from our own actions. But to answer your question, no."

Humor flirted over her lips. That was the other thing about thousand year old vampires. Things amused them that didn't always make sense to those with far less years. He tried not to let himself be annoyed by it. "I have many expectations of you," she continued, "but serving on the Council is not one of them."

"You want me to be happy."

"If your actions deserve that, yes." Now she gave him an even look, a cool one. "Unhappiness often guides us to better decisions for ourselves than unearned bliss. I expect you to live up to your potential. To be a credit to your raising, to the things we have taught you, as a springboard to learn more, and take our knowledge to a higher level for yourself and others. But I have hopes for you. Hopes for love, for happiness. For joy in the simple things that we so often overlook."

Rising now, she came to him and took his hand. Without the shoes, she'd lost several inches, but it didn't diminish her. If anything, the energy pulsing around her surrounded him, held his attention. "Sometimes I think that is the greatest gift Christmas brings us, my son," she said. "A slowing of time, an awareness of the value of simple things. Like being able to touch my son's face, see his handsomeness, his determination and generous heart there. As well as the regret when he knows he's let his temper get the best of him. When he doesn't know how to fix things with his friends, his family, those he loves."

He bowed his head, pressing his face into her palm. "Any advice?" he said glumly. "I don't have much pride left tonight. Might as well give asking advice a try."

"A true last resort for a vampire," she said, with a half smile. "I think you already know the answer. It's easy to talk about how the world should change, but how can you change, Kane? How can you give and sacrifice to make the world a better place?"

"Vampires don't give and sacrifice. We demand and take."

Lyssa chuckled. "We are arrogant, selfish, powerful. But those are also strengths when it comes to making things better. We demand justice. We take away power from those who don't deserve it. And we are more than that, more than one thing. You can be selfless, kind. You wouldn't be angry tonight if that wasn't as much a part of you as all the rest."

Her gaze softened upon him. "Look into your heart. Change starts there, with your own actions."

He wanted to argue with her some more. It would be easier than taking the mirror she'd just handed him and looking at the image he knew she was referencing. "You're talking about John."

"Ignoring and pretending a choice isn't there can be just as bad as forbidding that course of action outright, especially when the heart you're ignoring belongs to someone who loves you. Do you think letting him go halfway across the world will be easy for his grandfather? Ingram is getting close to eighty now. John will come home periodically, but it is likely Elijah will pass from this world when John is far away."

"If he'd just let you mark him, he could prolong his life."

"Yes, he could. But that was not his choice. Elijah misses his wife too much. The last time I offered him the choice of third mark, he told me his wife would be expecting him in a certain amount of time, and he couldn't let her down. He wouldn't keep her waiting longer than that." She returned to the window seat, crossed her legs. "He also told me that John was on a good path, and his job there was done. He'd done what a grandfather, parent or guardian was supposed to do. Make sure John is a responsible, good man who can take care of himself and will have plenty of love and gifts to give to others. Wouldn't you agree?"

"Yes, I would. He's…" Kane grimaced, his chest tight all of a sudden. "He's a better man than I am."

"No." She shook her head, her jade eyes warm on him. "He's a very good man, but so is my son. John wouldn't be so devoted to you otherwise. Do you know what Elijah said about his wife? It touched me, so I remembered it exactly. 'I want my wife's arms around me once more. We had to walk our separate ways awhile, while I did the things I'm supposed to do. That's what life's about, doing what you need to do, so when you come together again, the time is right. No regrets and you've earned the rest."

She shifted, crossing her legs. "He said he had to be sure he'd earned having her arms around him. Anything else and he said she'd give him hell there at Heaven's gate. Probably send him right back down to finish things, even if he had to do it as a damn zombie."

Kane gave a half chuckle. "Sounds like him. Sounds a lot like his son, too."

She nodded. "But it's that way, with those we love. Do you understand?"

"Yes. But understanding and wanting to act on that understanding are two different things."

Her lips curved. "You are always honest, my son. But like Ingram, I know that your father and I have done what we are supposed to do. You are a good man."

"But not yet one who can take care of himself."

She shrugged. "There are times in our lives when none of us can care for ourselves alone. We need the guidance, love, support and yes, sometimes the rescue, of those who care about us. That is a gift, my son, not a burden. And yes, a young vampire has to endure that care for longer than a human male, but your compensation is a much longer life span. You understand that, but resist its yoke. Every born vampire has been where you are. You think I did not chafe at restrictions in my twenties?"

"Or Mason?"

Her gaze darkened. "Mason lost his parents young and fell into the wrong hands, my son. He understands firsthand what happens to a young male vampire without the proper guidance."

She beckoned him to her, more imperious now. Rising, she put her hand back on his face. "Patience is a great sacrifice to ask of a young vampire male, but it is patience I require of you. You have always understood that, but perhaps after tonight you understand better?"

"Yes." He nodded, and meant it. "I understand."

"I know you do."

As he kissed her hand, she touched his head, a mother's benediction, containing forgiveness and wisdom both. "How was the symphony?" he asked.

"Lovely. But not as good as the orchestra I heard play the same repertoire in the eighteen hundreds. Older is not always better."

He smiled. "But most the time it is."

She snorted at him, gave him a push. "Impatient boy. Begone. I want to replay a few of the pieces in my head."

She curled back up into the window seat, this time where she could gaze out the window, watching the dogs and the Christmas lights. It was a gentle dismissal, so he touched her shoulder and moved to the door. He didn't expect her to speak again, so was surprised when she did, just as he was reaching for the latch.

"Son?"

"Yes, mother?"

"I love you more than the sun and the moon. You know this?"

"Yes, I do." He knew it for a fact, was glad for it. She nodded, her gaze still trained on something outside, though her next words told him her attention was fully upon him. Like a spear through the heart.

"Do not ever let me see disrespect for your father in your thoughts again. If you'd spoken those words aloud, I would have put a stake up your backside and yanked it out. You could have spent the next few days trying to figure out how to remove the splinters."

Now she turned her head toward him, and he saw something different in her eyes. Her expression spawned more than a dozen memories of his father through his mind. The things Jacob had been and done for both of them. Kane realized he'd disappointed her and, even worse, he'd hurt her. Crossing the room to come back to her, he did something he'd never done before. He dropped to a knee, bent and lifted the hem of her skirt, pressing his lips to it. "My lady," he said, "I have done something unforgivable, to you both. How do I make it right?"

Her green gaze was timeless, and he saw a glimpse of many things. Fierce love, which he knew was for both him and his father, as well as the shadows of wisdom and pain. But her expression eased enough that the barbs coiled tight in his gut loosened. "Go to him and tell him you love him," she said quietly. "And that you're sorry. We know you, Kane. One thoughtless moment cannot erase all the good we know is in your heart. And your father has always been far more forgiving than I am."

"You're telling me." He let humor come back to the surface, holding his breath until she flicked his ear.

"Impudent rascal. Now I do want you to go. Send your father back to me when you're done."

Rising to his feet, he cleared his throat. "I feel I should also ask Lord Mason's pardon. Would now be a good time?"

"Hmm." She sobered. "He understands his daughter is an adult, Kane. She chose to go with you. She is likely even now berating him for being too heavy-handed toward you and John. But vampire males have their own code, as your desire to seek his absolution shows. He will appreciate it, but I believe he will appreciate it more tomorrow night."

"As always, I defer to your wisdom, my lady."

She snorted, flicked his ear again, and sent him on his way.

§

Farida had chided her father for his coolness toward Kane, but after the brush with the Trad, she couldn't push the suit too hard. Her mother's counsel, not so much spoken as indicated with a discreet nod toward the door, had said her father would need some time to settle from the events of the evening. Older vampires tended to need their long silences, their minds traveling places probably unfathomable to those who were centuries younger, but she and her mother both understood those silences. Many times growing up, Farida had curled up in his lap, reading or dozing, not needing him to say anything, just cognizant of his arm loosely around her, the strength of him surrounding her. She thought with particular fondness on the times he'd held both her and her mother in his lap, the two of them talking about anything...the horses, a pending trip, the color Farida was going to paint her nails. He listened, smiled occasionally, said little, but she never felt ignored. If anything, sitting in his lap, she'd always been certain she was the center of his universe, her and Jessica.

Sometimes, that could be a pain in the ass, but it was one she never took for granted. So, heeding her mother's advice, she'd given him a hug, told him she loved him and then slipped away.

She hadn't been sure of her destination until she found herself standing outside the door to Kane's suite of rooms. When she knocked and heard him grunt in acknowledgment, she smiled and slipped inside.

He was sprawled out in an occasional chair before a lit fire place, staring at the flames. Though he seemed to be brooding, his gaze cut to her immediately, making her heart trip. Yes, vampires were all dominant, but when she was with him, alone like this, it was always clear there were some more dominant than others. For all that she held her own with him, there were times that hold was merely fingertips on the edge of a cliff. The look in his eyes right now added to that trepidation, so she responded as she always did to uncertainty. Straightening her back, she lifted her chin and gave him a faintly amused, "what the hell do you think you're looking at?" expression.

He extended a hand, palm up, and she came to him. When she did, he closed his hand over hers, drew her forward until she realized his intent was to pull her into his lap. She would have tumbled over the chair arm, but he controlled the movement, turning her with a smooth flow like water. She curled up there, nestling her backside into the nice firmness of his groin, and braced her feet on the chair arm, putting her arms around his neck.

She wanted to ask if things had gone badly with his mother, but that sounded like a child's question to another child. *Did you get in trouble?* Something about his pensive expression, the way he looked at her, made her feel quiet, as if she were dealing with a different person than she had earlier in the night.

"I have to let him go. Don't I, Rida?"

She noticed his eyes had transformed to the one green, one blue. She'd noticed that early in their relationship, the way the hues would change. Sometimes all blue, sometimes all green, sometimes a wild mix. They had been like that at the mall, she remembered, when he'd been watching the water display.

"Yes." A simple answer seemed best. She knew he was talking about John.

He nodded. His gaze roved over her face in that way that made everything inside go still. Winding his fingers in her hair, he slowly pulled on it until she dropped her head back, shuddering as he brought his lips to her throat. He teased her with a puncture, a slow draw of her blood. Then his mouth found hers, her lips parting as he drew the kiss out, stroking her cheek with his long, clever fingers. She emitted a low growl-purr when his fingers closed over her throat.

"You've never had a man, have you, Rida?"

She raised a brow, trying to hide the tremor in her fingers. "You've never asked that before."

"I didn't want to know the answer."

"Kane." She touched his face. He turned it toward her palm, biting the heel of her hand, then those brilliant eyes were on her face.

"Want to see what I can do?"

She nodded. "Always."

He smiled and gestured toward the flames. When she looked over her shoulder at the fire, he started tapping a pattern on her thigh as if he were playing piano keys. The touch was distracting, but she caught the motion in the fire. A key pressed down, a flame leaped up. Then a hard tap, a higher leap. She narrowed her gaze. "Kane..."

She drew in a breath as the fire stretched up higher, spilled out of the grate and spread out over the floor in thin rivulets without burning it, leaping up like dancing snakes as he raised his hand. As he rotated his fingers, they twisted into one funnel, became a burning rope that reached for her. He clasped her wrist, extending her arm toward it. She watched in amazement and no fear as the rope twined around her wrist, replacing his hand. There was heat and weight, but no burn. Then it slipped away, melting back into the fireplace. And his hand gripped her wrist once more, tightening.

"I want to be the first inside of you, Rida."

She looked up to find his face very close. His other hand cupped her jaw. As her lips parted, now she let him feel the tremor that captured her. Bringing her closer, he spoke against her mouth. "I *will* be the first inside you. Say it."

She nipped at his lip, drawing some blood, and earned his growl as his hand tightened in her hair. Yes, bloodlust could be provoked, but it could also become something else.

"Yes. You will," she murmured. "But why now? I thought you always wanted to wait until..."

"Until I didn't feel like I had a babysitter. I realized tonight a lot of that is my own hang up. I don't want to wait anymore. Too much is changing. I look at John, and he's the other half of my brain, my courage, my sense of honor. I look at you and see the reasons I want to be smart, brave and honorable."

He took a breath, met her gaze. "Which means I have to let you both go for awhile, to figure out if I can stand without you. And to make sure I'm not standing in the way of who both of you want to be. How you want to love and live."

Feeling a frisson of panic, of worry, she tried to give him a haughty look. "You don't have to let me go to do that. Get over yourself."

"I think there's something in you that...waits for my permission." His hand tightened on her when she started to be affronted. "I don't mean that with any arrogance, Rida. I mean it. It's something inside us, between us. And when you do it, Christ..." His eyes held a flame that took her breath. "I never want to let you go. But tonight, I realized just how incredibly precious you are to me."

Her heart softened, lurched. "Kane..."

He shook his head. "If there comes a time you give me the precious gift of yourself, on every level, I want it to be because you know that's the decision you want to make, not because we were caught up in some transition, growing-up type of feelings. I'm not sure of anything else in the world, but I'm absolutely sure you're worth waiting for. You are, forever, my first love. You'll probably be my last, when we're coming down to the end of things, but we have a ways to go between then and now to figure everything out, right?"

"All right, what have you done with Kane? The insensitive jerk, my impatient best friend?" A bit overwhelmed despite her attempt at humor, she touched his face again. He recaptured her hand, held it between them.

"He's still here. I'm a vampire, after all. I'm not going to let you go without taking something for myself. Which is why I'm going to be the first."

That blue and green color deepened, his lips curving in a smile. She swallowed, lifted her chin again. She knew she couldn't mask her nervousness, and usually he'd look amused by it. She'd smack him for it, they'd wrestle, the moment would pass. But not this time. What was happening right now wasn't childhood play.

She wasn't a child. She wanted him to be first, the choice just as much hers as his. So she lifted her arms to him, her eyes luminous, her mouth soft. With a surge of strength, he rose from the seat, holding her in his arms, carrying her. He'd hauled her over his shoulder before, more childhood wrestling, but this was the first time she remembered him carrying her the way a lover would. He brought her in front of the fire, held her there, looking at her a long moment before he stretched her out on the rug, putting her beneath him. As he lowered himself onto her body, she shuddered at the new feeling. They were both still clothed, but it was also the first time she'd felt the full length of him like this.

She knew they were young for vampires, that they could live for centuries, but she wondered if anything could feel as amazing as this. If anything would ever immerse her the way his touch, the weight of him, the hunger in his eyes, did.

He'd just made clear that he understood all that they would be, where they might go, how their paths might split, but he'd finally – finally – decided to claim this marker, the one no other would possess, to connect them. Whatever had changed tonight, shifted in his mind, she thanked all the divine powers for it.

She was still wearing the T-shirt and jeans she'd worn to the mall, but she'd removed the cap and loosened her hair so it flowed over her shoulders. Lifting her up enough to remove the shirt and then lowering her back to the rug, he stared at her quivering breasts, cradled in black lace. Then his mouth was on them, his hands drifting through her hair, stroking it, bringing it tumbling back against her shoulders, her upper arms. As he kissed his way in a leisurely track over her breasts, she stretched out her arms, one hand moving toward the flames again.

"Do it again," she whispered.

He lifted his head a few inches, those eyes glowing. Clasping her hand, he tangled their fingers before he guided them into the dancing flames. She watched in fascination as they played over their flesh and slid up her forearm, an orange and red serpent. A different kind of heat spread over her flesh as Kane turned his attention back to her, to his exploration with his tongue and lips. She arched with a sigh as he pushed the lace away to find her nipple, tease and taste it, give it a gentle suckle, a less gentle score with his fangs.

"You did the water at the mall, didn't you? Splashed those people watching, made them wet."

"Mm-hmm." He opened her jeans, slid them off, leaving her only in a couple scraps of underwear. Then he slid down between her legs, his warm breath coming through her panties. "Now I'm going to make you wet."

She was already there. She shivered anew and then writhed under his touch as his mouth closed over her, teasing and stroking through silk. Kane might lack confidence in other areas, but not in what he wanted from her. A climax built quickly, brought to intense life from every tease and flirtation they'd shared since she'd gotten out of the car a few days ago. His strong hands held her as she bucked, a pale leaping flame herself.

He slid the panties down her legs, on his knees between them as he gazed down at her bare cunt, stroked it with his fingers. He eased a couple into her, testing. She wouldn't have a virginal barrier anymore, as much as she'd played with toys and female servants, but it still felt like an offering only to him.

She reached for his belt, fingers sliding along the head of his cock, pressing hard against the denim. She hadn't touched him so blatantly before. She took her time with it, learning the feel of him, sliding up and down, wanting more, wanting him hard in her hand, inside of her.

He obliged her on one count, standing to remove his clothes. He was as finely made as she expected. The last time she'd seen him fully naked was when he was eleven. They'd dared one another to wade in the pond on the property. He'd stepped in a nest of copperheads and they'd bitten one of his legs six times, potentially fatal to a human. Not to a vampire, but the pain, temporary though it was, had been brutal. When Kane had been rolling around on the bank, gnashing his teeth and cursing, she'd told him to hold still. Blown cool breaths on the angry flesh, then sung him a song to calm him down, help him until the pain faded away and the wounds healed. It was probably then that she'd fallen in love with him and he with her, his head in her bare lap, his fingers curled in her long hair as she leaned over him and softly hummed the words of the lullaby her mother still sometimes sang to her.

Pushing herself up on one hand, she ran her hand down his thigh, though her gaze couldn't help but go to his erect cock. It had grown quite a bit since he was eleven.

"I want you in my mind, Kane. I want us to mark one another."

His gaze flicked to her face, surprised. It was possible for vampires to do that. The second mark serum used on a servant would allow them to talk in one another's minds, though they retained the ability to block one another if they wished, as long as their strength remained on par. He would grow far stronger than her, she knew. He already was stronger, but she trusted him. That was the gift she was giving him. Her eternal trust, no matter where their paths forked or crossed.

Their parents, with centuries of friendships, betrayals, loss and gain behind them, would have likely forbidden it, warned them that it wasn't wise. But that was why she wanted to do it. Before life and experiences changed them.

Maybe the act itself would keep them from ever breaking each other's heart.

He understood the momentous nature of what she was asking, what she was giving him. He dropped to one knee, cradled her face in both hands. "Rida, are you sure?"

"I've never been so sure about anything."

She rolled to her knees, nudged him back into a standing position. Her on her knees added intriguing flame to his gaze. She was sure to keep her eyes on his, showing him she meant every moment as she put her mouth high on his thigh. His arousal was a strong scent. She laid her other hand on his opposite thigh, thumb caressing the base of his testicles. Then she bit, feeling the shudder that went through him, her eyes closing as his hand closed on her hair. She released the serum, and felt him twitch again, because it had a burn to it. But then it was done.

You have a far sweeter bite than the snakes did, Rida.

She smiled at the sound of his voice in her head and nuzzled his thigh. She wanted to turn her head, close her mouth on him, but she felt uncharacteristically shy about that. This moment was different between them. When she tried to make herself overcome the feeling, do it anyway, he stopped her, showing he understood.

"No," he said. "Not tonight. I like you on your knees, Rida, but not because...of that. It makes me feel overwhelmed. I want to protect you, hold you, and yet keep you there on your knees, your mouth..." He stopped, his eyes blue flame, her breath short.

"Dominant vampires," she murmured. "Maybe I'll have you on your knees one day."

"You already have had me there," he said with a serious smile. "Plenty of times."

Laying her back into the nest of the rug, he knelt between her legs again. He retained one of her hands, their gazes not breaking from one another as he guided himself between her legs. The contact between sexes was an excruciating pleasure, and she closed her eyes, savoring it, the way he fitted himself to her, figuring out her shape, the right angle to pleasure and care for her, the way he started to press inside her, stretch her with his size.

When he lowered himself onto her, she lifted her hips to meet him, her lips parting as he pressed inside one lovely inch after another, taking his time, letting her feel every explosion of sensation that each forward movement created. When he was seated, she was trembling again. She put her hands on his shoulders, dug in. Then tilted her head to the side. "Please," she whispered.

He thrust deeper and earned a moan from her, her nails biting into his flesh. His mouth was on her throat, nuzzling. His fangs slid over her flesh, teasing. She lifted up against him restlessly. "Kane."

"I like that begging note."

"Shut up and do it."

"Yes, Lady Farida." But a glimpse of his eyes belied the teasing note in his voice. She was speared through the heart by the sheer possessiveness she saw. She felt it, like a blanket of fire covering her. He could do that, she bet he could, and the only thing that would burn would be what was inside her, wanting this, wanting him.

He bit. He had powerful fangs that struck hard, and he didn't spare her, as if knowing she'd relish the pain with the pleasure. Her legs locked over his hips as he drove his cock in further. The sting of the serum made her gasp, but he stroked her, kept his hips lifting and falling beneath the lock of her legs, her body rising to his, making pain part of the ecstasy.

Don't ever leave my mind, Kane. Always be my friend. Always be this for me...

Something that was more than friends, more than lovers. A bond shared between two vampires in a world where they could trust very few of their own kind. As young as they were, they already knew that, and she felt it in his mind as if in her own. There were as twined together as their bodies as she locked her arms around his back and shoulders. He held her just as close in his strong arms, thrusting until they were both on that pinnacle together.

Vampires didn't often swim, knowing that body density would make them sink to the bottom, requiring that they fight their way back to the top. But that day at the pond, they had embraced it, knowing hand in hand they could make that journey together.

Now as then, they clasped hearts and hands and made the leap.

§

For awhile they stay coiled by the fire, not saying much, just stroking bare skin, speaking in whispers, where the meaning, not the words, was what mattered, lips touching often.

"How long have you been able to do the thing...with the fire and water?" she asked.

"For these past few months, since I turned twenty-five."

As she stroked his dark hair back from his brow, she saw the shadows in his face. "I can do it to air and earth as well," he said. "I haven't told anyone yet. Though John would have noticed, because he doesn't miss anything. But he hasn't been around."

"You can't blame him for that, Kane."

"I don't," he said simply, and she could hear that he meant it, where earlier she would have heard the resentment that John had noted himself. "But I wanted the two of you to be the first to know, before I tell my parents. Though hell, my mother probably already knows. She knows everything."

"When you've lived a thousand years, it's kind of hard not to know everything."

"Yeah." He rolled them so she was sprawled over his chest, and he played with her hair, an easier smile on his handsome features. "You're such a fierce little thing."

"Don't be patronizing."

"I'm not." He held up both hands in sincerity. "You're strong and mean. I've seen it firsthand. But you're also this. Extraordinary. Beautiful. Breathtaking. When we were facing that Trad, I wanted to kill him for even looking at you like that. But somehow I knew, if the worst had happened, you would have survived. You would have held on until we got you back. Because you're strong as hell. I don't think anything could break you. And that gave me courage."

"Kane," she said, moved. That shadow came back to his gaze as he touched her face.

"When I realized he could overpower me, that he could take you from me, it was the worst feeling ever. I hated feeling helpless, knowing I couldn't protect you myself. But I also realized that what was more important than my pride was protecting you in whatever way I could. Protecting you and John."

Her gaze softened on him. "You did protect me. You kept him talking, you reached out for help."

"Not soon enough. If John hadn't done it first, it might have turned out just as he said. You could have been in that Trad's hands tonight."

"No. I don't believe that. The three of us together, we can figure out anything."

He wrapped her hair around his hand, unwound it. "But it won't be the three of us anymore. We both know it. John's going to go do his think tank. Before long, you'll be back in your corner of the world, and me in mine, all pursuing our lives."

"True. But that doesn't make the connection any less strong. I'm here." Farida laid a hand on his chest. "Inside. The way you're inside me. Even before we marked one another tonight, I think that was true. And John loves you so much. Loves us both."

He pressed his lips together. "He's on his way here now. I told him I wanted to talk to him. Will you stay?"

"Of course." When he showed her his intentions in his mind, she loved having that connection, but she nodded, telling him she agreed. That she believed he was doing the right thing. She was pleased to see the glow of warmth in his gaze as a result.

Rising, he lifted her again. She slid her arms around his shoulders, holding him close. When he bent to put her on his wide couch, she kept him over her an extra moment, sliding her lips along his throat. He ran his hands over her, reluctantly wrapped a fleece blanket around her. When she adjusted so she could fold her slim legs beneath her, she looked up to see him watching her, his gaze coursing over the one shoulder that the fleece wasn't covering.

"Warm enough?"

"Until you warm me further." Her amber eyes glowed, making him bare his fangs in answering promise. He pulled on his jeans, leaving his shirt off and feet bare, a look she appreciated as he leaned over to stoke the fire, his thick hair falling over his shoulder and framing the noble brow and profile of his sharply sculpted face.

"I love you, you know."

He looked toward her, his mouth and eyes serious. "I love you, too, Rida. Always."

"Good." She tossed her hair back, tried a smile. "But don't expect me to say it too often to you. You're a pain in the ass."

"Like you're not?"

John's knock came then, covering her rude answer, though the twitch of his lips told her he'd heard her loud and clear in his mind. "Come on in, John."

When he entered, John found her immediately, of course. His gaze coursed over her hair, in riotous waves around her face, and she saw the subtle flare of his nostrils, taking in the scent of what had been done here. She forced herself not to blush, knowing Kane wouldn't let her live it down. Then she'd just have to kill him.

He shot her an amused look and she stuck her tongue out at him.

"Well, then." John cleared his throat. "About time."

Kane shrugged. "Timing is everything with girls. You told me that when you were fifteen and kissed Darcy Larson on the school bus. Since she didn't punch you, you assumed that made you an expert on sex."

"Well, so did you. For at least a year or two."

"He likes being older and wiser than us," Farida said, her amber eyes twinkling.

John sank into a chair. "Not a matter of like or dislike. Just the truth. Er...so, since I don't see any pools of blood or missing limbs, I assume all the parental units are on simmer instead of full boil?"

"Yeah." Kane straightened, turned and faced him. "But that's not why I called you here, John. You need to take the job."

John glanced at Farida, then back at Kane. As if he felt himself at a disadvantage, he rose, faced him. "If I do that, it's a ten year commitment, at least. Maybe more. Makes it hard to commit to...other things."

"You're not going to be my servant, John." Though the words sounded strained, Kane held John's gaze and put the words out there John seemed reluctant to say. "You're going to be my best friend. A best friend who will accomplish untold miracles with that amazing brain of yours."

John shifted. "Lord Brian and Debra are Master and servant, and she's still able to pursue science."

"Because they're both scientists. They pursue it together. I don't yet know what I'm going to be, but I know I'm never going to be a nuclear physicist, doctor or mathematician. Or a chef, fireman, plumber or Dumbledore."

He grinned, glanced at Farida. "Those were all the different things John told me he was going to be when we were growing up together."

"He told me he was going to be a policeman. Or a Navy SEAL. Though I think that was when he was trying to impress that skank Darcy." Farida gave John an impish look as he rolled his eyes. But then he brought his attention to Kane. "Kane...we don't have to make any decisions now. I mean, yeah, the think tank's important..."

"The think tank is more than important. It's the fucking accomplishment that anyone like you would give your right nut to join. It's incredible, John. Me standing in the way of that, binding you to my side? Who does that serve, except my own selfishness? If there is one thing I've learned from watching Brian and Debra, it's that knowledge can benefit all our races, the world itself. But it's more than that." Kane met his gaze. "This is what you want. More than anything."

A muscle ticked in John's jaw. "We made a deal when you were fifteen that you wouldn't go into my mind without my permission."

"What can I say? Vampires are assholes."

John studied him. "You can be, but not in this. You never have been able to lie to me."

"Careful, human." But Kane tempered it with a wry

smile. "I know this is what you want because I'm not as clueless and self-absorbed as I've been acting. I chose to ignore your heart, and that was wrong of me." As he put his hand on the other man's shoulder, he was gratified to see the struggle in John's face that confirmed what Farida had said. John did love him. A part of him didn't want to leave Kane's side either. Knowing that would help Kane to let him go, even as he wouldn't shy from giving John the same gift, making himself just as vulnerable in this moment.

"You are so much a part of me, John, that I don't remember a time you weren't. We could have shared the womb together. That's why I want you to do this."

John gripped his forearm. "Damn," he muttered. "I wanted to be pissed at you."

"I'm sure I'll give you cause before you take off. I'm pretty consistent that way."

John allowed himself a smile, but then looked between him and Farida. "What about you two?"

"She's another part of me." Kane shifted his gaze to Farida. "She's a light in my heart that won't ever go out. But it's like you and me, John. Our hearts are together, but our paths may need to go elsewhere."

Kane thought of what Lyssa had said about Ingram. "Maybe you'll meet someone along the way and fall in love, want kids. If I third marked you, I'd have denied you the ability to be with her, grow old together. That's the one gift a vampire can't give a human, and I understand it's a particularly powerful one."

John pressed his lips together, and now his eyes got suspiciously bright. "Damn it, Kane..."

Kane shook his head, put his arms around him and pulled him close. After a moment, John's arms wrapped around him, held on. As Kane stroked his neck and narrow shoulders, he thought of John out in the world, not having him by his side. "You promise me one thing, though. You ever need me for anything, even if you're out of range of my mind, you damn well better call me. You have to take care of your ass."

"It's usually only in danger when I'm watching yours." John snuffled a chuckle against his neck, fended off the side punch and returned one of the same. Kane sobered, looking at John's face. His handsome, kind, intelligent face. He found himself at a loss, staring at it.

"Hey, show him the fire and water stuff."

Bless Farida for always knowing how to make a bridge. At John's quizzical look, he made himself smile, despite the heaviness of his heart. Since he was showing another male the gift, he decided to make it far more dramatic.

John jumped back as the fire roared out of the grate at a flick of Kane's hand. Then they were both cursing and stomping on the all too flammable rug, because he'd overdone it, lost control and allowed the flame to make actual contact with the fibers. Farida was giggling on the sofa when they got the fire out, on her side with her feet curled up and exposed by the bottom of the blanket. Kane snaked a hand beneath and she kicked out at him with a yelp when he gave her delectable ass a pinch.

"Jerk." She punched him, landing a nice solid *thunk* on his chest before settling herself back on the couch. Raising her head, she sniffed at him, a miffed queen.

"Show me what you can do with the water," John said, his eyes alight with fascination.

"He did the mall stuff, too," Farida chimed in.

That was easier. Kane poured himself a glass of water, closed his hand around the cup and turned it over onto the side table. As he lifted the cup, John watched when the water was left in place, a perfect mold. Gathering the blanket around her and shifting, Farida touched the water with a fingertip. "Wow," she said, on a breath.

"Do you change the nature of it? What do you do?" John demanded.

"Nothing really. It's like clay. I can feel it, and I just mold it, in my mind."

John muttered a few thoughts to himself, most of it an incoherent string of words that Kane was sure Lord Brian would completely understand. To him, it might as well be ancient Sanskrit. He shot Farida an amused look and found her eyes dancing. He waited until John bent close enough that he nearly had his nose against the cone of water and then doused him in one shot.

"Christ, Kane." John snapped back up, swiping at his face, and snorted when Kane tossed a towel at him. "We should really show that to Lord Brian. Or... wait. Does anyone else know?"

"Just you two. I wanted you to be the first ones to know. I'll tell my mother, don't worry. Relations with the Fae are better than they've ever been. I don't think it will be as big a deal now as it was when the Council found out my mother was half-Fae all those years ago."

"True." Accepting the logic of that, John finished wiping the water off his face. He glanced toward Kane's computer, currently dark. "We don't have to do it now, if you don't want to, but a little later, you two want to see more about what I'll be doing? I can log on to the think tank's private site and show you some of the cool stuff that's happening there."

Up until now, he hadn't even let John talk about it, Kane realized with a shot of guilt. One of the most important decisions of his life. "You bet I do. I want to know all about it, though you know you'll have to dumb it down for us.

"Well that's a given. You're vampires, after all."

"Oh..." Farida was off the couch in a flash and Kane joined her, tumbling John to the carpet as she did her best to pinch and tickle and Kane gave him a mild pummeling.

"Time. Time out. I surrender..." John was laughing when Kane sat back on his heels. Farida stayed sprawled over his second mark, keeping him pinned. Kane looked at the two of them there, together, the blanket barely covering Farida's lovely skin, John's brown-skinned hand resting near the edge of the fleece, his long legs stretched out, Kane still sitting on one of them.

As the man looked up at him, met Kane's eyes, his own narrowed. "I bet they change color when you do the magic."

"They change when I do lots of things. How strongly I feel about something or someone changes them as well."

The smile died from John's face as Kane laid a hand over his thigh, reached down and curled a hand in his shirt. Farida slid out of the way and eased back to the couch, watching them. Since Kane could feel the turmoil of emotions in John as he struggled to deal with what all this meant, he knew John needed something else from him. Maybe they needed it from each other.

"Come here." He was already pulling him to sit up, bring him back to his feet so they could face one another.

Always a command with you, John hedged, with a slight smile that had jagged edges. But he didn't pull away. Kane left his fingers curled in his collar, a fingertip sliding over the small silver cross that John always wore, a gift from his grandfather.

"I want something from you, John. The same thing I wanted from Farida." He leaned in, spoke with his gaze roving over John's face, the sensitive, clever mouth. "I want to be the first man inside of you."

He knew John had played on the edges of it with men, but like Farida, sex had been mostly with women. Though Kane could nurse the idea that the reason might be himself, he knew John was mostly hetero, anyway, which meant Kane might be the only male ever. He liked the idea of that.

"Oh yeah?" John's eyes went more opaque and he licked his lips, an unconscious response. Heat leaped back into Kane's chest, his cock tightening. "Think it's that easy?"

"Yeah, I do." Kane sidled closer, bumped his body against him as his hand slid around his nape, held them eye to eye. "I want you to kneel by the couch, put your head in Farida's lap. I want her to be able to touch you, hold you, while I fuck you. And if you want to put your mouth to good use on her, give her pleasure, that will please me, John. I want to give my serv...you both pleasure."

A muscle flexed in John's jaw. "You almost called me your servant."

"I've thought of you that way a long time."

"I don't mind if you always think of me that way."

Kane stilled as the man put his hand on Kane's hip, dug in hard. "Because I know what it means to a vampire," John said. "When it's meant the right way. Something more than blood or love, something that never goes away. I like the idea of that with you. With both of you."

Kane swallowed. "Then let Farida second mark you, too. So we'll always be able to talk to one another, connect with one another. So nothing and no one can break the bond between the three of us. Even us."

John looked at Farida. At her nod, he brought his attention back to Kane. A pounding, weighted moment passed. Though Kane could have been in his mind to anticipate it, for once he was glad he didn't, because it meant everything to him that John reached for him first. Putting both hands on Kane's shoulders, his grip strong, hard, he yanked them together so he could clash lips, tongue and teeth. The uncontrolled passion of it spilled all over Kane, John's mind opening to him like the earth itself, taking him deep, past mystery, so he could feel and see just how much John had wanted to do this. He scored his lips on Kane's fangs deliberately, bringing him the faint, sweet smell of his servant's blood. John knew how to rouse a vampire. This particular vampire.

Kane took control, breaking the kiss. "Take off your clothes," he ordered low, his eyes blue and green flame. "Do it, now."

John stripped, his eyes never leaving him. He did have a slim, strong build, his mocha-colored skin paler beneath his clothes. His muscles were lean and smooth, his skin firm and warm. Kane wanted to lay claim to every inch. He would tonight. That was what he was being given, what he would take.

John backed up a step, another one. Then he turned toward Farida, meeting her gaze, and sank to his knees as Kane had ordered him to do. She opened the fleece blanket, showing him her naked body, and beckoned him forward. First he laid his head in her lap as Kane had directed, his mouth brushing her thighs.

I can smell you on her. I can smell her as well.

Kane could scent the arousal from all three of them, a heady aphrodisiac weaving them together as he took off his jeans. Lubricant was no more than a desk drawer away. Coming up behind John, he began to rub it on himself as he watched John's mouth tease Farida's thighs. Her amber gaze had gone the color of rich gold as she lifted it to Kane. He saw her breasts quiver, lift as John moved his head to nuzzle them. He moved over one firm nipple, began to suckle it. Her legs parted to let him get closer and John's thighs shifted, his buttocks flexing in subtle invitation.

Putting his hands on John's hips, Kane dropped to one knee behind the other male. "I love tasting her breasts, too," he said on a quiet growl. "Maybe later, we'll both suck her to climax. But right now, I want your head in her lap. I don't want you to do anything but feel her holding you as I push inside you."

John obeyed, a quiver going through him as Farida wound her arms over his shoulders and bent to press a kiss between them. Looking up, she caught Kane's mouth with her own, her fingers gripping his neck, tongue stroking his. Kane made a murmur of desire against her lips, followed by a grunt of pure satisfaction as he found John more than ready for him, pushing out as Kane sunk into his tight channel. He wondered how often John had played with this idea, maybe using toys like Farida did. He'd fantasized about Kane doing this to him, hadn't he? He wanted to see, to find out, but he didn't want to disrespect the pact they'd made.

Fuck, yes, I've fantasized about it. And I want you in here, Kane. Christ, I'd give you the third mark if you want it. Always.

It was a temptation almost too strong to resist, but thinking of his earlier words, Kane knew he would resist it. Maybe he couldn't control bloodlust, but he wouldn't be driven by emotional impulses to the point he denied either of his friends the lives they were meant to live. But a vampire wasn't a selfless creature. As he'd told Farida, he had to take something for his selflessness, and this was the tithe he was demanding. John's tight, blissful ass, which gripped him as he stroked in and out. Through Farida's mind, he knew John had his hard cock pressed against her shins, Kane's thrusting bumping it there in a rhythm that had John grinding against her. She lowered her head over him again, arms tightening over his shoulders, whispering encouragement to him. Kane inserted a hand between them, dug his fingers into John's hair and turned his head back to the juncture between her legs.

"Taste, John. Give her pleasure."

Farida's head dropped back on the edge of the sofa as

John complied immediately. Kane's own cock jumped at the sound of John's mouth teasing, licking and sucking her cunt. Her gaze glazed even as she held Kane's eyes. Her lips parted, incoherent words coming from her, soft gasps and moans that made him harder, thicker, drive deeper into John's ass.

She caught one of John's hands, brought it to her mouth and then she bit. Once a long time ago, John had allowed her to give him the geographical marker, so she'd always know where to find him if she needed him. He'd watched over both of them that way. So giving him the second mark now wouldn't burn as much with that first one already in place. Kane closed his eyes, enjoyed the bliss of it when their three minds twined together, as in sync inside as they now were without.

Fuck...love the way you both feel...

Coming...coming soon...oh God...don't want it to end.

He was sure some of the same involuntary words were rolling through his mind, because there was no rational thought, just pleasure. Yearning, desire and regret, that this moment would have to be enough to hold all of them, no matter how far away they went from each other.

When Farida started to come, Kane changed his angle, reaching beneath John to grip him, stroke. "Now, John. Come."

They came together, the three of them straining and releasing, and now Kane knew it wasn't just him and Farida. All three of them were willing to fall, as long as they fell together.

§

They slept in Kane's bed, twined together until the early dawn hours approached. Sleep would claim him and Farida soon. She was already in that hazy dozing state and Kane was close on her heels. Yet he felt John stroke his hair, touch his shoulder before he left the bed. Through half closed eyes, he watched him bend and press a kiss to Farida's temple. When John checked his phone, he smiled.

Jackie called the safe house, Kane. She's with them

now.

Kane nodded, warmth filling him. Her willingness to trust him was an excellent Christmas gift. He caught John's collar to brush his lips over his cheekbone, his mouth.

When I get up, I want to see what all you're going to be doing. Don't go too far. At least for now.

Count on it.

As John slipped from the room, Kane pulled Farida closer. Putting his head down over hers, he pulled the blanket more securely over them both. He'd received a lot of Christmas gifts tonight. Maybe it really was better to give than receive, though he figured it was pretty circular, all in all. By letting John go, by finally realizing it was more important to express his love for Farida than to hold it out of reach because of his pride, he was pretty sure he'd just received one of the best Christmas gifts he'd ever be given.

The kind that was way too big to fit under a tree.

The Yule Gift

A vignette featuring Daegan's vampire mother, Grace, from the Vampire Queen Series.

Originally posted 12/16/2015

Background: *This vignette tells the story of how Daegan Rei was conceived. Daegan is one of the main characters in Books V and VI of the series,* Vampire Mistress *and* Vampire Trinity. *Grace has never herself appeared in the series, except in reference as Daegan's mother, so this was her first introduction to my readers.*

§

Grace inhaled the night air. It was cold tonight, below freezing. As a vampire, the temperature couldn't harm her, but she still felt the sharp cut of it through her cloak, the bite against her face. It was good to feel something different, though, something...vivid. She'd been tending the sick and dying in the village for so long she'd fallen into a fugue. Time had no more meaning. There was no day or night. The hovels were close together, so she could leave one and duck into another without much harm from the sun at dawn or dusk. The tunnel system they'd put in for her long ago, during her first years here, allowed her to move freely between them even at the height of the day. But working to care for others well past the noon time hours made her weak. So weak.

She needed blood, but there was none to be had. The plague-ridden blood wouldn't harm her--she didn't think--

but she wouldn't draw strength from anyone still in need of it. She'd drunk from one or two poor souls right after they passed the Veil, but the blood didn't seem to provide her any sustenance. Maybe because her heart was weighted down with too much sorrow.

Forty-two years ago she'd come here. She'd only been passing through the area, moving on the outskirts of human dwelling places. This part of Europe was beset by fear and ignorance, people harboring a deep suspicion of strangers. Especially one who could only properly introduce herself at full dark, when most farmers were already turning in for the night. For the past several weeks, she'd confined her human contact to brief forays at the blackest times of night. Stealing into a hovel, she'd taken blood while using her compulsion ability, so that the experience for her human source was a sensuous, dark dream.

But that night forty-two years ago, not far past the dusk hour, she'd detected a child in the forest, and scented her fear. Agnes, collecting herbs on the village's periphery to help her mother, had been distracted by the wonders of nature that called to the young. She'd become lost in the twilight that too quickly turned to full dark, disorienting her. When Grace located her, her intent was to deposit the six-year-old at the dwelling closest to the outer perimeter of the village and vanish back into the night. Two things prevented that. One, Agnes would not relinquish her death grip on Grace's hand until she saw her mother, and two, her mother, who was out desperately looking for Agnes and calling her name, saw the two of them.

That still should have been the end of it. If Agnes's mother had been like most peasant women Grace had encountered, she would have snatched her child away from Grace and shouted at her to begone, making the sign against evil. A beautiful woman with no marks of labor on her face, out with no escort in the night, could be nothing other than a denizen of evil. Yet Mary did not react that way, because Mary was a witch herself.

She recognized what Grace was, but she hadn't reacted with fear or revulsion. The village called Sanctity had a circle of thirteen witches who were its spiritual core. They observed the rituals of the year, raised energy on the full moon, and did all in the power of their hearts and souls to care for their families. The brothers, husbands and fathers in the village accepted what their sisters, wives and daughters were, because love lit the mind with truth, leaving no room for fear or ignorance. The secret of Sanctity was closely guarded, however, because all in the village knew such light was a precious commodity in a world defined by darkness, poverty, fear and disease.

The night she found Agnes, Grace had been invited into Mary's hovel to share the hearth and get warm. Mary fed Agnes, then held her exhausted child in her lap as she fell asleep. "She's such a sensible child, and usually I stay mindful of her whereabouts. But Georg, the blacksmith, had a fever and I've been tending him long hours. I grew careless. A mistake that can so often lead to tragedy." Mary stroked Agnes's soft brown hair off her brow, and her voice wavered. "I owe you a debt that can never be repaid."

Grace shook her head, and tried not to focus on the artery beating in Mary's neck. Snatching blood here and there without waking other family members who shared quarters with her quarry didn't allow her to feed to fullness that often. She was young, by vampire standards, less able to control her blood hungers. She needed to go. However, Mary rose and put Agnes in Grace's arms before Grace could move. The little girl turned against Grace without complaint or distress and Mary smiled a little. "She doesn't trust easily. She senses something in you." Moving to the corner of the hut that served as a kitchen, she found a pewter cup and picked up the knife by a stack of herbs. "As frightened as she was, she didn't panic and leave the plants she'd picked. She knew Georg would need them. She's a good child. An angel."

The lines around Mary's eyes crinkled. "Other times she can be an imp, as stubborn and willful as her father ever was, Goddess grant him peace. But she could be a fallen angel, and I'd love her the same. Maybe more. It's the darkness that challenges and strengthens our love for one another. It's hard to hold a sunbeam, but once it sinks into the dirt and becomes part of a tree, that's when it gains true substance."

She had a mesmerizing voice, the voice of a priestess. Grace's attention sharpened on her like the blade Mary used to cut her own arm. She positioned her wrist over the cup and let the blood flow into it, massaging the area below the cut to keep it coming. "Do you like any flavoring with it?" she asked conversationally. "I have a variety of cooking seasonings I could use."

Grace shook her head. "I did not ask for your blood."

"No. But will you refuse it?" At Grace's silence, Mary nodded. "My Agnes is not the only one who does not trust easily. I expect your journey has been difficult, on your own as you are. Are you old for one of your kind? You feel...younger to me."

"Not too young." She was eighty, and fifty was the demarcation line for fledgling to young adult vampire, though she'd still be fair game to older vampires. She'd managed to stay ahead of them and free to make her own choices. Mostly.

"Hmm." Mary gave her a mother's look, one that said she knew Grace wasn't telling her the whole truth. She hadn't been mothered...ever. Grace would have smiled at it, but it brought back some empty memories. Her mother had been a human whore. Her father had been a vampire indulging in a night of pleasure and a meal of blood he'd wiped from the whore's memory. Grace supposed she should be glad her father had been in the area long enough to hear the woman was pregnant. When he found out the babe was his, he'd stolen Grace away before the afterbirth could be cleaned off her flesh. Before the woman could set her new child to her breast and realize what she'd spawned was going to use infant fangs to seek blood, not milk.

Leo was not father material by any stretch of the imagination, but he'd been a decent sire, protecting her and guiding her in vampire ways until she was fifty-four, at which point he cut her loose, indicating he had his own life to lead.

Mary wrapped a cloth around her wrist and used the knife to chop up some herbs more finely. Grace rocked

Agnes as the child murmured in her sleep and burrowed closer. She was a comforting weight in Grace's arms. But while Mary could tend to Grace like she did her child, that wasn't what Grace was. Grace spoke low, an unmistakable command. "Come here so I can tend your wrist."

Mary glanced up at the tone and met Grace's eyes. Grace didn't blink. Mary needed to realize what she'd invited into her home, what held her child. Setting aside the knife, Mary brought the cup of blood and placed it on the rough table next to Grace. "Unwrap the bandage," Grace directed her. When Mary did, she closed her fingers over her forearm and brought her wrist to her mouth. Pressing her lips and tongue to the cut, she healed and cleaned it at once with the anti-coagulants all vampires possessed.

Mary's fingers twitched, her breath drawing in. Arousal was a natural reaction to a vampire's attention, one of the many abilities they had, but Grace had no designs on her that way. She was grateful for the gift of the blood and didn't want the woman's arm to get infected. The protectiveness she felt toward her, and especially toward the child she'd rescued and now held in her arm, unbalanced her, motivating her to restore a sense of primacy.

When she was done, Mary eased Agnes out of Grace's arms. Grace lifted the cup to her lips as Mary sat in the chair across from her, bending her head over the child to kiss her brow and hum to her. For a time, they sat that way, two women and a sleeping child by the firelight. Grace drank her meal and, for the first time in a while, she experienced a sense of safety.

At length, they began to talk. Conversation wasn't something Grace had done in recent weeks, yet with Mary, the words began to fall like the soft rain that came that night and pattered on the thatched roof. It had a couple leaks, but Mary rose, putting Agnes in her bed and placing pots to catch the water. When she sat back down, the women talked long into the night in low voices. Mary's husband had died some time ago, so she cared for Agnes with the help of others in the village. Over time they talked of what they were, witch and vampire, and Grace wondered aloud that Mary had reacted to her nature so matter-of-factly.

"You are a creature of the night," Mary said practically. "I am a witch, like my mother, my grandmother and my great-grandmother. The power of the elements course through me. In ritual, the Goddess enters my body and I feel the scope of all She is, her and the Great Lord. Why shouldn't there be beings different from us?"

"Your priests would say I am a creature of unholy darkness."

Mary's eyes sparked with bitter humor. "They would say the same of me, wouldn't they? And not just because I'm a witch. For that lot, all you have to be is a woman. Or have a single thought different from their narrow view of the world." Leaning forward, she closed her hand over Grace's. Vampires didn't often allow the spontaneous touch of a human, particularly when that human knew what they were. But she stayed still beneath Mary's close regard. "You wondered that I did not fear you. I am not foolish; I know your kind can be as brutal and ruthless as humans. But that isn't what I read from your nature. It is not what you are that means something to me. It is who you are, and I see your heart is good. You saved a human child from the wood when it would have been a simple matter to most of your kind to leave her to her fate, the way our hunters ignore a fallen baby bird as the inevitable cruelty of nature." A faint smile touched her lips, sadness crossing her face. "Though my Lars would have climbed the tree and put the bird back in the nest. He had a kind heart, too, and did not always assume Nature intends to be cruel, any more than I intended to let my child wander away in the wood tonight."

Her fingers tightened on Grace briefly, then she drew back. "You may stay as long as you wish. Become a part of our world, and see if Sanctity can become your home, if that is what is meant to be."

§

Out of politeness and necessity, she'd told Mary she

would stay just one daylight stretch in Mary's cellar. One day became another, then another. With the unconscionable ignorance and brutality she'd encountered in the human and vampire worlds up to now, leaving such an oasis was difficult.

She'd quickly proven her usefulness. She kept the constant threat of wolves well outside the perimeter of where they tended crops, hunted and gathered. When a band of cutthroats had tried to strong arm them into giving them food they couldn't afford to lose, she'd dealt with that as well. Quietly, viciously and efficiently, the bodies gone before the villagers had to worry about what she'd done or how she'd done it. They'd given her their protection. She would do the same for them.

Now, four decades later, having done myriad things to provide for and care for them, there was not a person in the village who didn't accept her as one of them, or have a mostly amicable relationship with her, though she had remained closest to Agnes, Mary, and the women of the coven. She could have moved on years ago, probably should have, but she'd never had a home, and had quickly discovered it was the outer expression of the soul, something necessary to thrive.

All this time, she'd protected them from anything that threatened them. Unfortunately, she hadn't anticipated an enemy from within their own bodies.

Rumors of the sickness had come with a passing peddler, and hours after his departure, it had arrived, striking Millie's weak son first. While the peddler had said it was worse in the cities, the carnage there a vision from Hell itself, Grace couldn't imagine anything worse than this. Two moons had passed, and during that time they'd lost so many. There had to be something she could do. Something.

Coming back to the here and now, Grace went into the dwelling she most dreaded entering, for fear that the plague would be advancing on the one who mattered so much to her. Agnes's mother had died some years ago, at thirty-nine. Her face had been creased by the elements and her body permanently bent by hard labor, but as her daughter and the protector she'd brought into the village a decade and a half before bent over her, she'd given them the same warm smile in her hazel eyes before she slipped behind the Veil. Grace had held Agnes in those first few heart-rending moments, the woman's hot tears bathing her bodice.

Her daughter was proving more long-lived, because Grace had done all Agnes would allow to ensure it. She'd given Agnes two of the three binding marks a vampire could give a human. While in the vampire world it made Agnes her second-marked servant, this wasn't the vampire world. Grace had explained the marks as a convenient way to help Agnes and her find one another, no matter the circumstances, with the added benefit of being able to speak in one another's minds as needed. Agnes had stepped into her mother's shoes seamlessly, and was the *de facto* leader of their community. With Grace helping as needed to maintain the well-being of the village, being able to communicate so closely was a boon Agnes had accepted.

Agnes had learned a great deal about the vampire world over the years. In the subtle shadows of the heart where forbidden emotions dwelled, Agnes understood what those marks could mean, if other factors weren't involved. Grace had long suspected that summed up why Agnes had balked at the third mark, which would have made her Grace's full servant, binding her mortality to hers.

Grace had respected her decision, though now she wished she'd overridden the woman's will and forced it upon her, no matter how unconscionable that would have been. Because while the second mark had prolonged her life, it hadn't been able to resist the Black Death any more than anyone else. Though for the moment Agnes's case seemed less virulent. It gave Grace hope, but in the face of so much desperation, hope came hand-in-hand with fear.

Please don't let me lose you. Please. She kept such thoughts blocked from Agnes's mind. But because her emotions about it were hard to contain, the block had to be stronger than usual. Which meant she could feel Agnes's life essence, but until she stepped into the hovel and saw her on each visit, she didn't know if the disease had progressed or not.

She ducked into the small shelter with its earth-packed floor and straw and mud walls. The room smelled of the pig snoring in the enclosure in the corner, but Grace had been keeping him and his straw clean, so the scent was like a cozy barn. She hoped the friendly creature gave Agnes some company when she was lucid, since Grace could not help fill the significant silence in Agnes's home during her long hours of tending to others.

She'd been the one to remove the bodies of Agnes's husband and son from this space when they succumbed to the disease. Burning their corpses had been like being stabbed in the chest by a rough stake, over and over. She and Dan had always had an uneasy relationship, probably because he knew his wife was in love with Grace, and had been since Agnes had become a woman. Grace had never taken anything from her that belonged to Dan, however, and Agnes herself had done a fine job helping him understand her impossible love for Grace didn't diminish her love for him.

It didn't hurt that Agnes had fallen head-over-heels in love with Dan at nineteen, and no wonder. Not only was Dan a handsome man, he was brave, hardworking and gave his heart fully to Agnes and his son. He had all the traits of alpha leadership needed to support, respect and stand toe-to-toe with a strong woman like Agnes, and his possessiveness toward his wife was something Grace respected. She felt it toward Agnes herself, after all, and could not fault him for it. If Agnes had ever consented to the third mark, Grace would have been far less accepting of Dan's claim than he was of hers. As possessive as humans thought they were toward their loved ones, it was nothing compared to how vampires could feel about their servants. Well, at least how she assumed they did. Truth, she didn't have a whole lot of experience around other vampires and servants, but she knew the way she felt and figured it wasn't much different.

Grace wondered what it had felt like, being in love the way Agnes and Dan had been. The law outside the village might say Agnes was little more than Dan's property, to be treated as treasure or trash according to his whim, but their village was different. Men and women were partners as well as lovers here, the men in a unique position to see the strength of women exercised fully to mutual benefit.

Agnes was on her pallet. She'd thrown up again, and made a valiant attempt to use the basin at her side, but it had slipped from her fingers and fallen to the floor. Grace swallowed over a spike of fear as she saw the blood. When she laid a cloth over the mess and knelt by the bed, she put her hand on Agnes's head. The woman was burning up. *Damn it.* Her temperature was so spiked, Grace was surprised to find Agnes lucid when she looked at Grace with bright, pain-ridden eyes. She managed a weak smile, so much like her mother's it choked Grace with anguish.

"I've been thinking," she rasped, by way of greeting.

"There's a first time for everything, moppet," Grace said. They'd always teased one another thus. Bending, she brushed a kiss over her lips. She had a cluster of large, blackish blisters on her throat, one of which had burst. Grace was repelled by them, but Agnes herself didn't repel her. It was the sickness that offended and enraged her, not the woman it was attacking. She quelled her reaction to the former though, not wanting Agnes to think it was the latter. Agnes would see nothing in her eyes but care for her, though Grace kept her mind firmly battened down, since it was a riot of worry and anxiety.

"It's Yule tomorrow night," Agnes said. "Did you realize?"

Grace shook her head. She didn't even know what day of the week it was. She'd been so exhausted yesterday, she'd almost stepped into full sunlight. Since then, unless it was the dark of night, like it was now, she'd used the tunnels to get from hut to hut. Over the years, they'd realized the benefit of the system for giving her access to their homes if needed. Since most of the community went to bed early and rose even earlier, it was also a way for her to find her meals quickly in the dawn hours. The women of the circle had taken turns feeding her, so those in the village initially uneasy with her did not have to confront that aspect of her nature.

"The Lord and Lady must be honored," Agnes mumbled. "It will give us answers, help us find our way, make sense of this. Give us a sign of hope. Perhaps a sacrifice can be made. A penance for sins."

Grace gave her a sharp look. Usually the first thing Agnes wanted was an update on everyone in the village, no matter how painful hearing those updates were. She'd also offer whatever suggestions she could, being a skilled herbalist and healer herself. But as the sickness had increased, her mind had been less focused. Since the fever caused delirium, as well as proved acceleration of the disease, Grace tried to quell the cold fear in her belly. Instead, she made her tone as caustically teasing as it always was, to bring Agnes back to earth. "Is this a new side effect? You've been infected by that shite Father Baldwin preaches when you have to suffer a visit from him and pretend to be dutiful peasants without a clever thought in your heads? He'll be delighted."

"No." Agnes grimaced at her, reassuring her with the expression. "But we all carry within us...wrongs, hurts and angers. Regrets."

Agnes's hazel eyes held Grace's. She also had her mother's peculiar way of seeing into a soul as if it were an open room. The unexpected depth of that gaze resurrected the lives Grace had taken, forcing her to push away their untimely intrusion into this moment. She'd made mistakes as a fledgling, exposing herself in places she shouldn't have been and had had to clean up her own messes. She'd been pursued by ignorant humans, forcing her into situations where taking lives was necessary to protect herself and her anonymity. She also had the annual kill. A vampire had to kill and drain at least one human every twelve months, a sacrifice different from their normal blood needs. It was required to stay in a peak mental and physical state. The annual kill had to be a person of worth, to ensure the blood was properly nourishing.

She hadn't given those sacrifices much thought until now, probably because she'd been given no reason to particularly value humans outside this village, but Agnes's unrelenting look made her think of how many of those souls were like these here. Decent, good humans, their lives cut short thanks to her. She'd also killed one of her own kind. She'd made that kill here, when she'd encountered a vampire who was going to cull his annual kill from Sanctity's ranks, and he'd refused to be dissuaded by more reasonable arguments. Yes, she supposed it was hypocritical of her, but these people belonged to her. They weren't fair game for other vampires' needs.

But that was her. What penance would be enough to bring life back to the humans in this village, to their hearts? How did one recover from so much loss? Nearly two-thirds of the village was dead. The last child had died a week ago. Consigning their little bodies to the flames had been the hardest. Seeing Lucille hand over her fourth with nothing but a look of dead, lost hope had been worse than the wailing grief when the mother had lost the first two. Or the helpless desperation in her face when Grace had to pry the third from her shaking fingers. Lucille had died four days ago, and Grace could only think of it as a desolate mercy.

"I'm sorry," Agnes rasped, drawing her out of that dark place. "For the mess on the floor. I couldn't...get up, else I'd have...cleaned up."

"And I would have thrashed you within an inch of your life."

Agnes coughed. "Think we're within an inch now, aren't we?"

"Hush. Let's get you cleaned up," Grace said quietly. "We need to put some food in you." Starvation could sap Agnes's already failing strength.

"Penance is possible," Agnes croaked, back on the same topic again. Grace feared it heralded fever delirium, but she let her ramble as she retrieved clean towels. "Calling down the energy to revitalize us, heal us, quicken our wombs once more. But only by a woman strong enough to bear it for us all. Not by any of us. Only by one who lives in the shadow of night, who feeds on the blood of others."

Her eyes glazed, as if in trance, and Grace's heart hitched. While delirium was a result of high fever, Agnes also had the Sight. Grace just didn't know which held sway at the moment. "You, Grace," Agnes said. "You must do the

Great Rite."

Okay, delirium was in charge. "I don't know how, moppet. I've only ever watched all of you do it. Plus, there's not a man here strong enough to stand with me and call the Lord down into him."

"You've watched us do it for forty-two cycles. I've seen your lips move with the words as you stood in the shadows, your hands lift and fingers spread like bird wings as you imitated my movements..." Agnes reached out and Grace drew close, letting Agnes touch her face with a shaking hand. Grace clasped it as Agnes focused on her. No, this wasn't delirium. Agnes's green and gold eyes were sharp as a hawk's right now.

"So tired and pale, even for you," Agnes murmured. "Yet always so beautiful. The Lord will come for you, Grace. I know He will. Promise me you will do it. You will do the ritual from beginning to end. If nothing happens, then it doesn't. But it is worth a try. The Black Death may take our bodies, but loss is taking our souls. We cannot lose our souls...you have always protected us. You must do this. Please..."

Grace's stomach clutched as Agnes shuddered from the stress, pain suffusing her features. Agony tore through her self-restraint. The pustules sometimes hurt worse as they gathered under the skin, before they even made themselves known. With horror, Grace noticed the other hand Agnes held against her body. The fingers were blackening, the gangrene other victims had displayed before they died.

"Sshh, Agnes." She gathered her close, and Agnes clutched her bodice with her unaffected hand, rough nails cutting through the lacings to Grace's flesh beneath. "Calm down, sweetling. Yes, I will do it. I will do it."

It took some time to settle her again. When the spasm passed, Agnes was weak in her arms. But her fingers tapped against Grace's chin and she looked down to see tears leaking out of the woman's eyes, rolling down her temples to dampen her hair. The chestnut color was streaked with silver, the color of gray clouds lit by moonlight. Agnes's eyes sparked, her twisted mouth getting a hint of the rebellious moue Grace knew and loved.

"See. It's not so hard...to order a vampire around."

She was wrong, Grace realized. She did know what it was to be in love as Dan and Agnes had been. Perhaps as close as a vampire could get to it. She dipped her head and pressed her fangs, very lightly, against the top of Agnes's damaged hand.

"When you get better, moppet, I will take a strap to you like your mother did."

Agnes chuckled, though it was a strangled sound. Grace eased her back to the pallet, registering the soaked and fouled bedding beneath. "I'll get you fed and cleaned up. Then you can walk me through what I'll need to know that I may have forgotten."

"You probably remember it better than I."

"We'll see." She was probably right, but the anticipated task made light flicker in Agnes's eyes, giving her a sense of purpose, at least for the next hour. If she believed Grace would do it, she'd fight to see how it turned out. So maybe for the next forty-eight hours, the Grim Reaper would not visit. Agnes would drive back the symptoms that had taken the rest into the grave. Grace refused to believe anything else. "Food first."

One of the few benefits the second mark seemed to be providing was that Grace's blood helped settle Agnes's stomach enough to consume gruel and small bits of solid food. While the gruel was heating over the fire, Grace lifted Agnes out of the unclean bedding and took her to her mother's rocker, a family heirloom Lars had made for Mary before he died. Sitting down in it, holding Agnes close, Grace was reminded of that first night, when Mary had handed her Agnes as a six-year-old. Her feelings since then had changed from love of the child to love for the woman, but this deluge of feeling was a mix of all of it. It was all the love she'd felt for her, from the beginning to now, in all its changing yet perpetual forms.

In health, Agnes had a fine round backside and generous breasts, but the hardship of this illness, the toll it had taken on the village, had drawn weight from her even before the plague hit. She'd helped Grace until the disease felled her as well. As such, she felt far too insubstantial in

Grace's arms.

The first couple times she'd fed Agnes, Grace had put her blood in a cup to offer it. It was how the witches always offered Grace their blood, at her suggestion. A vampire's nature was to take control, and sexual domination was the sweetest of all seasonings in offered blood. To have her mouth on a bared throat, drinking straight from the vein...just the thought of it could quicken her loins and accelerate her blood lust, making her want to take, to conquer. If she desired the giver uniquely, as she did Agnes, that craving to demand surrender and sexual submission expanded to a throbbing roar in the body and soul. Her fangs would grow sharper and longer, her eyes would glitter with hints of crimson, and her body would ready itself to take full pleasure from her prey, and make them surrender to their own desires.

From the other women, she could take a cup of blood without that feeling overpowering her formidable discipline. They'd chat like women did over a hot cup of tea, only she was sipping their blood. Yet Agnes was different. So many times she'd stared at Agnes's throat and hungered for that mouth-to-skin intimacy, imagining a million ways it could expand into something far different. Tongues tangling, bodies pressed together, her hand sliding between the soft pillows of Agnes's thighs to find the delights of slick flesh.

Grace had her own small dwelling in the village with a roomy cellar room. She'd tried to respect Agnes's privacy, but there were times she couldn't help taking advantage of the second mark connection. Particularly on nights when Agnes and Dan were making love, she'd listen to Agnes's gasps of pleasure, her muffled cry, her lips pressed to Dan's broad shoulder as she climaxed. Often Grace would stroke herself to release while immersed in the woman's mind.

So not just because of Dan, but because of her own feelings about Agnes, she'd never drunk from her throat directly. She rarely took her blood at all and, since the women didn't compare notes on how often they donated to her, assuming she was rotating equally among them, it didn't cause comment. Agnes's silence on the subject, her lack of questions, had acknowledged what they couldn't say. Grace wouldn't open a door that would make things more difficult for Agnes with her husband.

Though Dan likely never realized it, Grace had cared deeply for him. She'd wept over his body and that of Agnes's son, Peter, because Agnes loved them, and they had loved her. Dan took good care of Agnes and knew just how special she was. Grace wished Dan knew that she'd never resented his hold on Agnes. In the vampire world, it wasn't unusual for human servants to have human lovers, though their first loyalty was to their vampire. Agnes's heart was wide enough to include Grace, Dan, her son, and the sisters of her coven. While Grace didn't deny her own possessiveness, she'd learned when one felt like this toward another, those baser, darker cravings sometimes gave way to more enlightened ways of loving.

Nothing about her feelings at this desperate moment was enlightened, though. If anything, those primitive, more savage feelings she'd kept at bay all this time were strengthening in full force. If Dan were alive, she might have snapped at him like a wolf over her mate, interpreting anyone else near Agnes as a threat. And that included Death.

Holding Agnes in her lap, she guided the woman's braid over her shoulder, though she kept her hand wrapped in the rope of it as she nicked her own throat with a knife. Setting it aside, she brought Agnes up higher, directing her lips to the vein. If Grace closed her eyes, she could imagine Agnes's hair loose and flowing, clutched in her hands while her body eagerly strained against Grace's, and not just for the nourishment. She'd rather focus on that than how weak the pull of Agnes's chapped lips was against her neck. She tightened her hold on the braid, on the woman's body, holding her closer. *No. She's mine. You can't have her yet. Please...*

Agnes's hand had fallen on her breast, was massaging limply against it. She was so sick, it was the instinct of an infant, that remembered comfort of kneading a mother's bosom. Hot tears clogged Grace's throat, even as her breast responded the way a mother's wouldn't, the nipple tightening as she thought of holding Agnes's head there, making her suckle her until the point was hard and aroused. Then she'd push her down onto her knees to put her soft, clever mouth to work between Grace's legs.

Why she was having such irrelevant thoughts made no sense, unless it was in defiance of the current reality. Or maybe, all the sexual fantasies she'd harbored were surging forth because the chance they might have to explore them were so close to being lost. She should be ashamed of herself, but with Dan gone, she couldn't help but think that nothing would hold Agnes back from exploring those things with her except Agnes herself. But Grace was too tired to censor herself, and it was far too likely they would never be anything but fantasies. She would take what comforts the moment offered.

I can do this now, talk in your mind for no reason.

Grace started out of her absorption, briefly and absurdly panicked that she'd opened her mind to Agnes. But she didn't see anything in Agnes's mind but a drifting haze of words.

You could always do that, moppet.

No. I did it only when practical before, because otherwise, it was too intimate. Wasn't it?

Grace's eyes closed. She had opened her mind to her. And the answer to Agnes's question was such an unequivocal yes, she couldn't voice it, even in her mind. Fortunately, Agnes was continuing.

Sometimes when you'd look at me, I could feel that heat. It was how Dan would look at me when he was thinking about that. He'd be eating his dinner, but his gaze would catch mine, hold, and I couldn't wait until it was time to go to bed, until we heard Peter's breathing even out. Grace... I so wanted the time to have that with you as well. I...even now, so sick, I ache for you...is that the second mark, that makes me think of such things even when my body just wants free of this disease? I miss my boys, so much... Goddess, I just want to lose myself in you, cry until my heart stops feeling like it's breaking. Until I feel like you're all around me, holding me together, keeping me safe as you always have. Am I being punished for loving you and him both? For not loving him enough to love only him?

Agnes sucked in a breath, her whole body stiffening as the pain invaded again. Standing inside Agnes's mind, it was as if Grace could follow and see all the points in her body where the swollen glands hidden beneath the skin were stabbing her, an attack Grace couldn't stop.

"Cease," Grace murmured, her own throat aching. She rocked her servant--she would no longer think of her any other way--stroked her back, her hip and backside, and returned to her nape, cradling her skull as Agnes's head fell back into her palm, her lips stained with Grace's blood. Grace licked it off, sucked on her mouth gently, then kissed her, soft, easy busses while Agnes's fingers tightened on her breast in dazed reaction, holding onto Grace's succor in the midst of her struggle.

No. A vampire doesn't sit back and let things like this happen. I am not subject to a human's will. I know how to fix this. Lifting her head, Grace cupped the side of Agnes's face in firm fingers, making her look at her. "You will let me third mark you, Agnes. I'm done waiting. You could recover entirely. I will not accept your refusal any longer. Even if it makes you hate me, I won't lose you to this."

Agnes's gaze sparkled, a welcome hint of fire, even if it was also evidence of her stubbornness. "After..." she said, her voice faint. "It's not for me, Grace. The village... I cannot take something I want so much before we try, to offer everything...for hope."

"I don't care. I'm doing it."

Agnes shook her head, pushed at her. "Please, Grace. I know...you can force me, and I could call it that, to make it all right in that moment, but we know it wouldn't be. And the guilt I'd feel if tonight doesn't work...it would kill me...destroy your soul...we have to do it the right way. Please. You have to listen...oh...Goddess..."

The plea became a moan, the pain shuddering through her. Agnes's stomach hitched under Grace's hand, the woman swallowing and eyes going glassy as if she was about to vomit up the blood she'd taken. *Damn it, damn it.* Grace cursed herself and held Agnes, stroking her to soothe the spasm, futilely willing the pain into her own body. *I would bear anything for you, Agnes, but how can I bear losing you....* "Ssshhh, it's all right. Okay, listen to me, moppet. It's okay. I won't push. I won't. I promise." *Though if I lose you, I might not want to keep living.*

Agnes managed to keep the blood down. She had the strongest will Grace had ever encountered, and she showed it now, depleted as she was. Any other person, feeling this sick, having lost the husband and son she loved, might have just given up. Grace could say it was her own will responsible, her refusal to let Agnes give up and let go, but she knew that only went so far. The strongest strand of the tether holding Agnes to life was Agnes herself, specifically her sense of responsibility for the village. Her fingers, despite their lack of strength, had tightened on Grace, and her words underscored Grace's thoughts.

"Promise me...you'll do the Rite. It's important. The only chance we may have. Or rather...the only thing I can think of that might help. And I know you have felt that connection to the Lord and Lady. You can do it. I know you can."

Grace had never claimed to have any special powers beyond the physical powers of a vampire. She'd attributed anything else to the energy the women had woven around their village for so many years. But she couldn't deny that these past few weeks she'd been seeing...things. She'd called it the symptoms of a fatigued mind because exhaustion could eventually affect even a vampire. Yet moving from hut to hut during the nighttime hours, she'd often felt riffles of movement against her clothing, seen gray wisps like tendrils of fog that slipped around the sides of the huts, under doorways, or hovered in the air above the village. Silent, waiting specters.

Spirits of the dead, watching their families continue to suffer, or agents of Death, waiting to claim the next soul? Since she hadn't been sure, she'd been torn between sad grief for the former and hatred for the latter, as misplaced as it might be. Sickness surely had a demonic spirit behind it, because it was incomprehensibly desolate that it was indifferent chance, the deer hit by the hunter's arrow. Yet if it was intended, part of a higher power's plan, that was almost worse than thinking it was beyond anyone's control.

How hard it must be for the women of the coven, those who had touched the true Power of the Lord and Lady with every turn of the moon or phase of the seasons, to see this happen and try to make sense of it. She was losing as many to grief as to plague now. Lucille had died alone in her hovel, her husband and children all gone before her. Dan and Peter had passed within an hour of one another, Dan's grip on his son's hand never slackening. She'd felt the deep, gut wrenching fear of seeing the light die out of Agnes's eyes as she had out of theirs. But Agnes was still fighting. She would fight for the village, if nothing else.

"Grace?" Agnes's voice was thin, anxious, reminding her that she hadn't answered her question. As if Grace could refuse her anything.

"I should have let the wolves eat you as a child. Yes, I promise. Damn the Lord and Lady. I promise you. If you die before you take my third mark, I will be very angry. Forever. You will be the first soul haunted in the afterlife by the living."

Grace realized Agnes's choking sound was a laugh, one that became a horrendous hacking cough. Then Agnes vomited up the blood, which meant Grace wouldn't get any gruel in her. Her body was rejecting sustenance. As Grace held her over the basin, she was in a dark realm beyond tears. She let Agnes finish, wiped her mouth, and held her close once more, the two of them on the floor. Grace's fingers gently supported Agnes's hand where the fingers were turning black. When the woman's body stopped convulsing, she tucked Agnes's head under her chin and willed herself to concentrate on what needed to be done. Grace could only keep moving forward, trying to save the ones whose lives remained in her hand. For Agnes.

A deep breath, and she pulled herself back onto her feet, lifting Agnes and placing her on a folded blanket on the floor until she cleaned the bedding. Then she cleaned up Agnes and put her fevered body back on the pallet. Grace settled her into a fitful sleep with the promise to come back prior to the ritual, so Agnes could give her any final instructions. As Agnes drifted off to sleep, mumbling, Grace trailed her fingers over her hot brow. She wanted to offer her a blessing, but Grace couldn't think of a power that might be listening other than her own aching heart. It would have to be enough.

When she stepped back into the night, it seemed both an eternity and only a blink later. Grace took a breath of harsh cold again, baring her fangs and offering a hiss to the uncaring world. From the heat that swept through her, she was sure her eyes had morphed to crimson irises. She would do the Rite, yes, she would. And maybe she'd demand some answers from Those who had abandoned the women who worshipped them so faithfully.

She was a creature of Darkness. She would not be cowed by beings of Light, particularly those who wouldn't even deign to protect their own.

§

She made her rounds, caring for, feeding and cleaning the others who struggled to live. She also burned three more bodies. A village of one hundred and ten souls was down to thirty-eight.

Her gaze slid from the pyre up to the slice of moon, the rudely twinkling stars, too far away from her concerns to care that their light was inappropriately cheerful. She needed to go to Agnes and then head for the ritual site. The Great Rite was usually conducted at midnight. She still had no clue how she was supposed to accomplish it without a male counterpart, but Agnes seemed to think it was possible. If it wasn't the fever talking.

Grace...

Agnes's voice in her head was barely a whisper. A distressed whisper. Grace was in motion in an instant, covering the quarter mile of ground between the burial fire and the village in less than a few heartbeats. She burst through Agnes's doorway and immediately wished she'd never left her side, no matter who else would have suffered for her neglect.

Agnes was crumpled on the floor. Despite Grace's earlier

efforts, the hated fetid smell of the plague's poison saturated the small space again. Grace knelt beside the woman and turned her in her arms. Agnes's face was drawn so tight, she looked like a skeleton covered by a thin layer of skin. Her breath rattled in her throat. She'd had swellings beneath both arms and they had burst, the fluid staining the armpits of her nightgown like an obscene berry juice.

"Here," Agnes rasped. "My hand. Look."

Grace clasped her wrist and pried the contents out of her closed palm. A walnut. Where on earth had Agnes gotten it in the dead of winter? It must be a dried-up souvenir from the harvest season. But even Grace, with her lack of magical abilities, could feel the power pulsing off of it. It glowed in Agnes's grasp.

Mother of God... Looking around, she saw a mortar and pestle on the table with a complement of dried herbs. Crockery was on the floor where it had been knocked askew by fumbling fingers, Agnes had been out of bed doing this. Grace was torn between wanting to shake the woman until her teeth rattled and wanting to weep.

Don't be mad...had to be done. Crack it and eat the contents before you start the ritual. It will fill you...with our sins. With our regrets, our guilt...our grief and loss of hope. You will offer them all to the Lord, and then see if He will be...merciful. The curve of Agnes's abraded lips, the simmering glow in her hazel eyes, were tinged with mystery. It reminded Grace of another Agnes, the healthy one. The priestess who stood proud and strong during past rituals, a warrior defending her village with the magic they wove around it. Her mother's power shone through her. "If you represent His Lady...for Her, He will always show mercy."

"You're an idiot." Grace was afraid, and that made her brusque. She took the nut from Agnes and shoved it in her apron pocket, then lifted her in her arms. Agnes's head dropped onto her shoulder and she continued mumbling, the words incoherent, inside and out. She'd delivered her message clearly enough, but that missive delivered, her mind tipped off the edge of exhaustion and relinquished consciousness, a mercy for her poor, suffering body.

Grace cleaned her up once more and tucked her back into the cot. She pushed her hands through her own hair, dislodging the blonde strands from the randomly stuck pins. Putting her hand into her pocket, she felt the heat of the walnut. When she ate it, the magic would invade her mind and take from her. She could feel that. But Agnes had dared Death's Door to provide her its power, so she would not shrink from it.

Hell's curses, was there any effort more useless than trying to hold onto control? If anything, the past few weeks had proven it was an illusion of a deluded mind. For this to work, she was going to have trust Agnes, and throw herself on the mercy of gods Grace didn't believe had any mercy to give.

A good trick, when she was so angry she wanted to obliterate the whole worthless legion of them. She paused at the doorway of the hovel and looked back at the unconscious shape on the bed, the far too diminutive curve of Agnes's body. Though it was selfish, Grace wished Agnes was awake so she could speak to her once more. She didn't know what she was doing.

Yes, Agnes was right. She knew the ritual. But *feeling* it enough to raise the energy was an entirely different matter. She had no doubt the spirits were out there. Her problem was with their intent: good, evil, indifferent. She could accept the first two; it was the last one that made her hate them so much. Being indifferent to suffering and loss while having the capacity to change it--could there be a worse sin? In her current circumstances, she didn't think any crime a living soul could commit could be any worse than that.

Hostile and aggressive were not the best emotions to carry into the Great Rite. Putting her hand to her hair again, she realized that wasn't the only thing that needed to change. When the women used ritual to observe the holidays or full moons they were bathed and more well-groomed than at any other time. Hauling bath water in winter was a hard chore, and using precious wood fuel to heat it was a costly indulgence, but the Lord and Lady must be honored. She'd helped them at those times, hauling large buckets of water on a yoke heavier than the largest man in the village could tote. But it had been easy enough for her. In warmer seasons, they simply bathed in the large nearby creek. Unfortunately that was all she had time to do now.

"Talk about penance," she muttered. She built up Agnes's small vented fire with a few pieces of kindling, then stripped off her clothes. She was the only one who'd be up and about around the village, and she intended to move more swiftly than the human eye could follow, regardless. Seizing a cake of the fragrant soap Agnes made, she braced herself for the freezing ordeal to come. Then she darted out the door.

"Fucking holy dog shite," she snarled a moment later as she plunged into the icy water. She was thorough, though, washing herself fully clean, though she didn't stint on her ability to do it as fast as her vampire speed allowed, a dervish of motion that probably looked like a water spout to any watching wildlife. She shot back to the hovel, a pale blur against the snow. Inside, she moved close to the fire, finding a reasonably clean cloth to dry herself and towel her hair. It was past her shoulder blades now, in need of a trim. She usually kept it shoulder-length, but Agnes liked brushing her hair. When Dan and the other men had gone on hunts or harvest trips that took them away overnight, they'd spent many nights sitting by this fire, laughing and talking womanly talk, while Agnes brushed it.

Beautiful.

Grace turned to see Agnes looking at her out of half-closed eyes. "Like a fallen angel," the sick woman said. "Come to tempt me."

Grace managed a smile. Agnes's hand extended from beneath the covers, a trembling bird claw with dark tips at the end of pale fingers. "Come to me," Agnes said. "Please. I know I'm hideous, but..."

"You're not. Never say that." Grace came to her and knelt, taking the hand and putting it on her cheek. Agnes stroked her, hand curving so her knuckles grazed Grace's jaw and moved down to her throat. Grace lifted her chin as

Agnes caressed her. It had been a long time since she'd been touched in the way Agnes was touching her--with sexual awareness, despite her condition. Agnes's gaze slipped down to Grace's naked breasts, cold from the water's touch, the nipples tight points. Agnes made a noise in her throat and touched one curve. It was a jerky, uncertain movement, but Grace cupped the woman's hand and molded it to her breast, giving her the strength to feel its weight and shape.

Agnes sighed, her eyes falling shut, her mouth in a tired half-smile. "I will not take from what belongs to the Lord tonight. But I thought a touch might remind you...that you are Woman. You are the Goddess, Grace. He will desire and want you, because he is Man and the Great Lord. What you do, it will be hard, it will be painful, but if he accepts your sacrifice, you will also find hope and pleasure yourself. You need that. You are as overcome by desolation and loss as any of us. Maybe more so."

She started to cough again, and Grace grabbed one of the cloths she'd been keeping next to the cot. She held Agnes's fragile body until the spasm subsided. If tears fell on the crown of Agnes's head, it was Grace's secret, for when she eased the woman back, Agnes's eyes were still closed, her breathing evening out once again as unconsciousness claimed her.

Grace glanced down and saw that some of the sputum had spattered her chest. She wiped it clean, though a vicious part of her wanted to leave it. She wanted this "Lord" of Agnes's to see it. She didn't want to come to him clean. She wanted to be covered with the sores, vomit and shit of a village of sick and dying men, women and children. She would come to him as Plague, as the Black Death. As a challenger, not as a fucking supplicant. She would toss bitter words of rage at him: "I will offer you this body. You can fuck it until you sicken and die as well, until you suffer as you allow them to suffer. And I will laugh until I break into a thousand bloodied thorns."

She was kneeling by the fire, her head in her hands, her hair curtaining her face. She was weeping openly. Agnes was going to die. Grace could feel it. Either Agnes had known it first and made the magic as a result, or the magic had taken her last reservoirs of strength, but it would not be long now before Grace would feel that second mark connection wink out like a dawn star. It was the least pleasurable of all vampire abilities, knowing when someone's condition was beyond hope. Agnes had said this Rite might be their last hope, though there was no hope for those already dead. If the Lord and Lady could not change Agnes's outcome, Grace had no use for them.

But this was not Their demand. It was Agnes's request. If she wanted to serve Agnes's request honorably, she had to believe it would achieve the results Agnes hoped. How did one convince the mind to believe what it wouldn't? How did she give herself hope, when that reservoir was empty? She'd learned hope and joy from Agnes, from the people of Sanctity.

"Take my robe..."

Was it the agony in Grace's own mind that kept rousing Agnes, when she was obviously so beyond strength she should be nearly comatose? Grace didn't know if that meant she was the tether holding Agnes to life, or the stress pulling her closer to death. But when she raised her head in response to Agnes's whisper, she saw her pointing to the wall, where her ritual cloak hung. It had been Mary's. Over the years, Agnes had added to it. She had a deft hand for needlecraft, so the embroidery on it was breathtaking. The shoulders and back of the cloak were like a tapestry, arcane symbols hidden cleverly amid nimble unicorns, prancing deer and dancing women with long hair. Their hands were clasped so their bodies formed a zigzag pattern across the robe's fabric, the hems and sleeve points of their lovely dresses tapering off into blooming vines. The needlework was as good as anything Grace had seen in fine halls on her many travels.

Agnes lifted her arms, their shaking and the look in her eyes piercing Grace's soul. This was good-bye. It was time to go. Grace went into Agnes's embrace, holding her tight. "Don't you die on me," she said into her ear. "That is a command, moppet. Don't make me come yank you away from the gates of Heaven, because I will do it and spit on the angels at the gates. I agreed to do this, but the price is you give me what I want."

"Anything," Agnes said softly, petting her with drifting hands. "It's okay, Gracie. It's all right. Don't be afraid. It will all be okay."

Miraculously, the words brought Grace strength, and comfort. Raising her head, Grace met her gaze. For all her earlier distress, Agnes's expression now was calm as a lake. "We all know life ends too soon," the witch whispered. "The blessing is when we are given *any* amount of time to love. To truly love another. And yes, if you do this for me, for all of us, I will become your third mark. I would have anyway. But you've agreed to the ritual, so you can't back out now. It would be dishonorable."

Grace saw that mischievous spark she knew so well and adored fiercely, especially at this moment.

"Honor is a male concept, and a mostly useless one," she said tartly. Her eyes were full of tears as she framed Agnes's face. Leaning down, she did what she had never done in their years together. She kissed her as a lover, parting her lips and teasing her with the sexual promise a vampire had in abundance. Even in her condition, Agnes's body stirred to it, likely because it was far better than focusing on the other, far more horrible feelings she was suffering. When Grace lifted her head, she met her eyes as she would if Agnes stood healthy and whole before her.

"My full servant. I'll hold you to that," she said evenly.

"I hold you to the same." Agnes tightened her grip on Grace's wrist. "But heed me, Grace. You don't have to pretend to feel something you don't. Go to Him and Her with an open heart, no matter if it's bleeding and full of rage and sickness. Give Them all of yourself, the way you want me to give all myself to you. Hold nothing back. It's the only way Love truly works."

§

When Grace was dressed in the robe and nothing else, her hair brushed and loose, she departed Agnes's home. Moving to the outskirts of the village, she left it behind. As she moved deeper into the forest, toward the site the witches normally used for their rituals, she saw a lone deer forlornly picking through the snow for a blade of grass or a scrap of foliage. It almost brought her to her knees, the simple evidence of how hard life could be sometimes. She stumbled, a reminder she was dangerously weak. The hunger was dragging her mind back into melancholy, no matter the one precious moment of hope and light Agnes had given her.

One step at a time. She would start the ritual. By going through the motions, the motions might become genuine and closer to what Agnes was asking of her. It was the only way Grace knew how to do it.

Regardless of her godless frame of mind, she admitted the coven's ritual site had a particular energy to it, even when it was silent and still as it was now. Seeing it empty like this was another blow. Eight of the thirteen had died so far, and she already knew they'd lose three more. Agnes and perhaps Gertrude would be the only survivors, since Gertrude was showing some sign of rallying. And Grace wasn't going to lose Agnes. If Agnes could make it through this night, Grace was giving her the third mark, and it *would* call her back from the brink of death. Grace would accept no other possibility. She'd tried once more to get Agnes to agree to it beforehand, using the logic that if the mark healed Agnes entirely, a trained priestess could do the Great Rite, increasing the chance of its effectiveness. Agnes had shook her head.

"It doesn't work that way, Grace. We can't give ourselves something we want before we offer ourselves in all our weakness to the Lord and Lady. We have to be willing to make the sacrifice, to risk all of it."

"Bollocks," Grace muttered. "Human nonsense." If she was a god, she'd want her minions to use all their strengths rather than setting them aside to prove some useless point about their love and devotion. She kicked at a frozen tuft of dead leaves and shuffled through the snow into the center of the clearing. It was ringed with birch, oak and ash trees. The cairn in the middle had been built up over time from stones the women had brought to it, infusing them with particular memories and energy. They'd laid out trails from the rocks, forming spokes to a wheel that surrounded the whole thing. It was far enough from the village and off the commonly traveled paths to decrease the likelihood of discovery by those who would assign the Devil's intent to such a symbol. The witches had also warded it repeatedly so any who strayed too close to it would be compelled toward a different trail.

She drew a breath. Cast the circle, then eat the walnut. She slid the robe off her shoulders. Pausing to fold it over her arm, she stroked the tiny embroidery stitches. It had taken Agnes since her teens to get this far with it, and she still had plans for the bottom hem. Grace would make sure she had the chance to do that. Laying the robe over a low hanging tree branch, she closed her eyes as the cold air enveloped her. Shivering, she stepped out of her shoes, bringing her bare soles in contact with the earth.

Was it her imagination, or did things seem more still here? On a winter night, there wasn't much sound, but usually Grace picked up animal rustlings or leaves quivering from a flitting breeze. Vampire senses could detect the slightest noise, and it seemed to be getting even quieter. She began to walk the circle, drawing down energy in her mind, how the witches said they did it. Whereas she could see the shimmerings of power when they did it, even with her untrained eyes, she saw nothing. Still, she did it three times as they did, imagining the circle as a warded, sacred place, where magic could be raised.

She caught her toe on a rock and stumbled again, dropping to a knee and cutting it on a root protrusion. "Damn it." She sucked back the curse, but it was already out. She was so bad at this.

Can you feel sorrier for yourself? Agnes is facing death, with horrible bulbous things rupturing on her body. You have to walk in a circle and chant and try to call down energy. Poor you. Shut up, stop whining and do it.

"I am sorry, Lord and Lady." She spoke the words woodenly, uncertain, but as they hit the crisp night air, they tingled through her, recalling Agnes's words. *Just be open, even if your heart is bleeding.* "I'm angry, I'm tired,

I'm sad. I don't know if I can do this. But I love my friend. I love all of them. I want to do whatever I can for them. Please...if you're there, please help us. Please...I'm filled with rage and I don't know how to set it aside to call to you, to be worthy, or deserving, or whatever the fuck...whatever I'm supposed to be." She opened her palm and looked at the walnut she'd taken out of the robe.

Yule was usually when the witches celebrated the birth of the Lord, sacrificed at the harvest for the renewal of life, and reborn through the Goddess's womb on this night so he could become her lover in the spring and start the cycle anew. Father to son, son to father, Mother of all, lover to the Great Lord. Their union, the harvest cycle, the cycle of birth, life and death, formed a circle like this one. The Christians celebrated the birth of Jesus, their savior who died for their sins so they could have everlasting life. *Take our sins.* A sin-eater... She couldn't keep track of all the magics and religions that tangled together and crossed, overlapped. It was time to reduce all of it to one act of faith, whatever its intent or outcome.

Her knee was bleeding, staining the snow. It didn't matter. Grace broke open the walnut. The contents looked like a fully formed sweet meat, not all dried up as she'd expected. But it was swollen with magic. When Agnes had first laid hands on it, it probably had been desiccated.

Grace put the walnut in her mouth. She hesitated, not knowing if she should chew or simply swallow, if it would make a difference to the magic, but the pleasant taste inspired her to bite down. Sensation exploded in her mouth. Her throat worked, swallowing it without her command. She felt the magic unfurl and...

She cried out and was flung to the ground, caught in an internal detonation of startling suddenness. Something seized the reins, shoving her flat. She shuddered, her body rolling, convulsing on the hard earth. As the magic spread out within her, excruciating pain took over. Not a physical pain. She wished it was. The tortures of the Inquisition were the playful tickling of a baby's feet compared to this.

There was no greater pain in the world than that inflicted on the heart and soul, and hers were being invaded by an army. Lies, resentment, fear, guilt... Agnes was right. Even the least of the villagers knew sin, sins small and large, regretted, cried over or nastily celebrated. She saw into the hearts and minds of every one of them, unable to turn away from the glare of the light or the sucking weight of the dark. That painful brightness and soulless darkness filled her up to overflowing. These were good people. She could only imagine what it would be like to experience this flood from a village of bad souls.

She couldn't tolerate being held to the ground in such a suffocating way. Summoning all her vampire strength, depleted though it was, she struggled to her feet, stumbled forward and landed against the rock cairn. As she clung to it, waves of feeling crashed against her and through her. She was screaming in agony, pleading for mercy, for forgiveness for them all as well as herself, but she ran out of strength to think or speak. She held onto the rocks as if she'd be utterly lost if she let go against the never ending barrage.

This was for Agnes. For Agnes, she would endure anything. She seized onto that thought, held it in tight fists with the sharp rocks. Her palms were bleeding, as well as her nose. Her legs were no longer holding her. She was also no longer alone.

The wave started to recede, as if pushed back by the new arrival. Lifting her head, she saw Him. Her breath caught in her throat and a denial cowered in her soul, while the rest of her was swept with a bowel-loosening, mouth-parching terror. Even through a blur of tears, she saw his wings were made of fire, stretched out and billowing with orange, yellow and blue flames. He had the head of a stag with a wide rack of antler horns, his head and body more than large enough to support them. He towered over her, at least eight feet tall, naked and terrifyingly endowed, with a cock that seemed as thick and long as her arm jutting up in full erection. He was on the inside of her circle, and his face didn't promise Death, but everlasting torment. He was Hell, the Devil, the punishment for all sins, large and small.

"Sickness must be driven out," he said, his voice thunder. A snake unfurled from his side, with forked tongue and flashing fangs. Then she realized it wasn't a snake, but a whip. A whip encased in flame, with several silver barbed tips. "Are you worthy of being its vanquisher?"

"No." She was shocked she could speak. But she gripped Agnes's memory like a shield. She didn't have the courage to stand before him, but she would not run. No matter that her cowardly soul was shrieking the exact opposite, wanting her to flee like a woodland animal. "But I am the only one who can offer myself to try."

"You lie." His thunderous snarl bludgeoned her bones, made her whimper and duck her head. "You are proud, vampiress. You think you are worthy. You think your hatred and your rage can destroy any enemy."

She dug her fingers into the rock. *Goddamn you, I am a vampire.* She shoved away from the rock, making herself stand on knees threatening to buckle. She couldn't meet his fiery eyes--that was beyond the ability of any living soul-- but she stared up into the flames of his billowing wings. Sparks were showering from them. "If that was true, I wouldn't be here. You are my only hope for Agnes."

She would give anything she had to make this happen. But she wouldn't try to pretend to be something she wasn't. He already knew the answer to His own damn question. If she was worthy of vanquishing sickness, she would have done it by now, right? And she wouldn't need Him, or this.

"You will look at me."

She gritted her teeth, raised her lashes and met those hellish eyes. Crimson flame created a well so deep no one would ever find her. She would never have existed to anyone but her own shriveled soul. All her bravado and anger fled in the face of terror. He moved forward, and the ground shook under his tread. He didn't have feet, but cloven hooves as large as a draft horse's. "You will accept the price."

No. No one could accept that. A place of non-existence where one was fully aware of one's isolation, beyond the help or reach of another living soul...

Agnes. Agnes healthy and well. Able to marry again, have children, be alive...

"Yes." The answer tore itself from her, despite the iron grasp of petrified heart and soul trying to keep her from saying the one word. And just like that, it was done. No going back. But He took even that relief from her.

"If at any point you ask me to stop, then the price is not paid."

"Don't stop, even if I ask you to do so." Her body was shaking as if from plague. She was forced to reach out and grasp the rocks for stability.

"It does not work that way. Your will must prove itself worthy, not mine."

Was it the word worthy that did it? Or weeks of exhaustion and desolation? Nothing should have been able to overcome her soul's fear of what lay before her, but suddenly her head snapped up on her spine and she met that deathly gaze fully. Her heart filled with a rage so hot, it could have come from the forges of Hades itself. The priests said creatures like vampires came from Hell. Right now she agreed with them.

"Fuck all of you." Grace straightened and let go of the rock, though she swayed alarmingly. "They're dying, they're suffering, and you want to play your stupid games. Is this what they get after they die? An eternity with the likes of you? Better for them to be dust, no soul, and this life be it, than have someone who doesn't value their lives or who they are. I hate you. You hear me? I hate you!"

She scooped up a rock from the cairn, receiving a brief impression of a summer hearth and a child's laughter from the memory embedded in it. She hurled it at him. "Why do you do this to them? Why?" The projectile passed through him and disappeared, which just infuriated her more. His whole body turned to flame except the stag's head, the fire roasting her flesh. She picked up another rock. A first kiss, a field filled with wheat... Then another. A mother's passing, a well wish for her afterlife journey from her daughter...

She kept throwing them at the Lord, memories and wishes, hopes and dreams, all disappearing into the fire and tumbling out the other side, useless, forgotten. When she ran out of energy, she collapsed, burying her face in her hands, her shoulders shaking with her sobs. "I hate you." She whispered it, even as a different echo assaulted her inside. *I hate myself, for not being more. Better. Enough to save them.*

She wasn't sure how long it was before she stopped crying and realized everything else had become quiet. She lifted her head. The clearing was silent and cold once more, the forest even more still. She'd failed. She'd done what Agnes had told her, opening her bleeding heart, but Agnes hadn't realized her heart was as poisoned as the sickness gripping her and the village.

Try again. Try. She shook her head, then realized it was Agnes speaking to her. In her rage, she'd opened her mind fully, and her second marked servant had heard her.

"I can't. I failed. He left."

No. He hasn't. They merely wait. Let me help you. Let me walk you through it. Sshhh...

Grace realized her breath was sobbing in her throat in a weird, semi-hysterical way. She tried to slow it down and ground herself, but Agnes's presence in her mind perversely made it harder for her to quell the reaction. *I am here, Gracie. If I was at your side, I'd stroke your hair and hold you, give you comfort. Even vampires need that. It's the one thing you can't do for yourself. You have fought so hard for us, asked for so little. You need someone to love you. It's why you've stayed with us as long as you have.*

Grace closed her eyes. *Time is relative to a vampire. Forty-two years is merely a day. I was thinking of going to Italy for the next fifty. It's sunnier there.*

Of course. Vampires love sunlight.

Impertinent girl. It's for my human servant, so she can recuperate in bright sunshine.

You need to call quarters. You haven't even done that yet. Lazy vampire.

Grace couldn't believe that her mouth tried to stretch into a smile. She was feeling steadier, by some miracle. A miracle named Agnes.

Rude moppet. I was busy dealing with the indigestion that cursed walnut gave me.

Well, that last blood meal you gave me was crap. Fair's

fair.

Grace choked on a chuckle. *Oh, Agnes. What am I going to do with you?*

Agnes's voice mind voice weakened, as if she was running out of enough energy to simply think words at Grace, but her response was spirited. *Get this done and then I'm sure you'll think of things.*

Right, then. Calling quarters. Pushing herself to her feet once more, Grace oriented herself to the circle's compass. She shuffled along the edge of the wheel to the eastern point.

*Spirits of the east, denizens of the winds and the air we breathe, that carry the scents of home and hearth to us...*The scent of Agnes's hair, cleaned with her special soap, the wildflowers she put on her table... *Be with us tonight. Lend us your guidance and aid. So mote it be.*

Agnes's quiet presence in her mind helped her find the words, the feelings. On to the southern point.

Spirits of the south, denizens of fire, children of the sun that grows our food and brings us warmth... The warmth of Agnes's body, hugging her, holding her, pressed up against Grace in the near future so that she could ignite the fires of passion between them... *Bless the witch's craft where the joining of bodies is a sacred addition to its rituals, not a sin...be with us tonight. Lend us your guidance and aid. So mote it be.*

To the west. Where the sun set, a day ending so it could begin again, a task finished, one life gone so another could be reborn. She would not dwell on that. The west was the water. The ocean, streams, rivers and lakes. Icicles that glittered on the trees. Agnes in the creek, her skirt tucked in her belt as she cleaned laundry and pulled fish out of the traps. Lifting pretty creek stones to show Grace, the water dripping down her arm and wetting the front of her bodice. *Spirits of the West, be with us tonight. Lend us your guidance and aid. So mote it be.*

Finally, she stood in the North. The symbol of the earth. She curled her toes into the frozen ground, but even through the cold she could feel it pulsing with life. Agnes was chanting in her head, an ancient ditty about the Earth being the Mother, the source of all. *To Her we shall return*... Grace dropped her head back on her shoulders, breathing deep, letting the chant roll over her. She began to repeat it with Agnes, stronger, louder. The dizziness that gripped her wasn't dizziness. She was swaying, moving in a clockwise rotation.

Be with us tonight, spirits of east, south, west and north. Lend us your guidance and aid. So mote it be.

She stepped into the center, and stood before the rocks again. She was aware of the cloak of air on her bare skin, the heat vibrating through her as she lifted her arms to the sky and grounded her feet in the earth. "Lord and Lady, on this precious Yule night, the birth of hope and renewal, we come to you with heart and soul open. We celebrate your love and creation and submit ourselves to your Will in all things, so mote it be."

Was it Agnes speaking the words and her repeating them? They seemed to be saying them at once. Agnes's voice quieted and once again, Grace realized she wasn't alone in the circle. She couldn't quell the spurt of fear that facing that fiery beast once again brought to her, but when she moved her gaze to the southern end of the circle, she found He had changed. And what she saw inspired an entirely different reaction, emotional and physical.

His wings were no longer made of fire. His feathers were dark as a crow's, the wings drawn in so they flanked his body like a cloak. He was still tall, but not as much as before. Now he was only about a foot taller than Grace. Long black hair, a blue-black contrast against the wings, spilled over his bare broad shoulders. He wore only a short black kilt that stopped at mid-thigh. The sword on which he leaned was stamped with ancient-looking markings, matched by what was tattooed on his shoulders, muscled arms and wrists.

She brought her gaze to his eyes and was captured there. Dark as night, with crimson fire flickering in them. No whites, only fathomless pools. His lips were slim, firm and sensual, like the planes of his face, etched with the finest sculptor's blade. She'd never seen a male so unspeakably beautiful, virile or overwhelming.

Staring at him, she had an unsettling sense of herself as Woman, a sexual being. Every inch of her skin, every part of her, was made to lock with Man's, to create magic and life. Flipping from the terror and rage of moments ago to this sudden, soul-deep arousal was startling. While focusing on calling the quarters had helped center her and change her focus, she had no doubts her primal reaction was entirely due to the Being she was facing now.

Agnes's voice was silent. Either she was as captivated as Grace or her limited energy had depleted once more, taking her back into oblivion. The second mark connection told Grace she was alive, though the thread was far too weak to be reassuring. So it was just Grace and...this, in the clearing.

"Where..." She cleared her throat. "My Lord, where did the other go?"

"That was one of my faces. Your rage called it. Your tears banished it."

His voice still held the rushing roar of flames, and the heat of it bathed her. Grace knelt, her bare knees pressed into the snow and ice. It was melting beneath her, heat filling the ritual circle. She'd felt the Lord at past Great Rites. He was usually called into a chosen male to mate with whoever in the circle was nominated to draw the Goddess down into her. But that had been a mere echo with her standing on the periphery, only observing. She was in His presence and, though she should know what to do, words failed her. So she knelt, her head down, and wished Agnes was awake. *What do I do?*

"You do nothing. You surrender what you are to this ritual. Why do you come alone, vampire? You are no witch."

That voice surrounded her, making her tremble. All her defiance about not groveling, about not begging, was slipping away in the face of this, something she couldn't understand, something that brought all her pain, hopes and fears to the surface, nearly choking her. But in that pain, she found her will and the words. She dug her fingers into the ground. Even beneath the weight of his power, she was still what she was. He'd reminded her himself. Not a witch. A vampire.

"I am all that is able to observe the Yule celebration, my Lord. I do not know how to proceed. Forgive my ignorance." Lifting her head, she met his gaze. Those dark eyes still held the fires of Hell, promising that fate if the wrong step was taken. Maybe even if the right one occurred. Her fear angered her, and she shoved it away, repeating what she'd said to the far more terrifying incarnation of this Being. "Anything. I will give anything to bring them Light and hope again, to save those who remain from death."

"A creature of the dark, offering a sacrifice to bring light." He drove his blade into the ground and left it quivering there. As he moved across the circle toward her, the snow and ice disappeared before his bare feet, revealing earth and brown winter-dormant vegetation. He moved with the grace and power of jagged lightning ripping through the firmament, and she felt the sparks of it ripple beneath her.

"You need blood, vampire. Your deprivation sharpens your senses, prepares you for this ritual the way a human fast does, but you are not like humans. How long since you have let yourself know pleasure? Your carnal appetites are as strong as your need for blood."

That truth and need, something she'd beaten into submission until it was just embers in the base of her spine, flared to life in the face of this Male, with his long, fine limbs, silken hair and dark, knowledgeable eyes. She could taste his flesh beneath her lips and tongue, feel his sex thrusting into her, filling what had been empty for an interminable amount of time--for a vampire. She swayed on her knees.

"Three years." Before then, she'd leave the village for the night once every few weeks. Once she found an easily compelled male or female to feed her, she'd enjoy their body fully before leaving them with their minds wiped and their bodies satiated. Her last had been a woodcutter with brawny hands and energetic cock. She remembered the hard press of his lips against her throat. He'd rolled over on top of her, taking the lead, his fingers curling around her wrists. In the light in his eyes, the set of his mouth, she'd seen the need to conquer was part of his pleasure. It was an innate desire a vampire knew well. She'd allowed it, because she held all the power and he would remember nothing when she was gone. But he'd been particularly generous and he'd lingered in her mind, occasionally recalled when her body ached too much for what she'd denied it since then.

Agnes knew where Grace went on those occasional forays. Always before, she'd said or felt nothing that Grace could detect. But that time, her sadness surfaced, and Grace realized just how much it hurt Agnes every time she did it, adding to a well of melancholy buried deeply inside the woman. She'd merely been able to mask it up until then. Her inability to hide it any longer had told Grace the tug of war between her feelings for Grace and Dan was taking its toll on Agnes.

Grace knew Agnes would never say a thing about it; she'd even say aloud, if asked, that she had no claim on Grace. Yet ever since, Grace hadn't been able to leave the village for that purpose. She'd made do with self-pleasuring in the early morning hours, imagining doing things with Agnes the witch had probably never imagined. Thinking of introducing her to all those decadent delights only made Grace's climaxes fiercer. Even more fierce than what she'd experienced in direct contact with the woodcutter. If ever Agnes was hers, the first thing she'd do would be to tie up that luscious body and feast upon it for several days, taking blood, tasting flesh with mouth and tongue, delving into her warm cunt and bringing her precious servant release in every imaginable way.

"Yes. You want her, so you have denied yourself. It is that way with one who matters. Yet it is a long time to deny yourself."

He was in her mind as if he stood at her side, looking at all those truths with her. As she lifted her head, she saw he'd drawn closer. His hand dropped and Grace drew in a breath as what felt like a heated knife blade slid up the curve of her bare back. But it wasn't pain that unfurled inside her. She gasped at the flood of arousal between her legs, taking her so close to climax she reacted without thought, dropping lower to the ground, curling herself over her knees to contain it. Instinctively, she knew releasing without the Lord's permission would be a mistake.

"Forehead to the ground, vampire. Show the Goddess your obedience, that trait so elusive to your arrogant kind. She comes into a vessel prepared for her, not a fortress locked up to repel invasion. Do you wish to become a vessel?"

"Yes."

"No, you do not. You wish to save your friends."

"I can't be what I don't know how to be." She squeezed her eyes shut as he touched her back again, sending a hard shudder of arousal through her. "I will become anything for them."

"You must become for Her. For you. You must open yourself to everything. The others are irrelevant."

Irrelevant? The word hit her like a mallet, sending the emotions ready to overflow like lava surging up in her breast. Perhaps it was the lack of blood or a million other things that made her this foolish, but the trigger brought her to her feet. She turned on him, fangs bared and a hiss caught in her throat. His hand clamped around it and he brought her back to her knees in a move so swift, it snapped her neck back. His dark eyes had turned to flame and every cell in her body screamed in terror as she saw the precursor to that other face he wielded. Her teeth chattered from the nerves, but she fought through that. "Damn you and Her. They are not....irrelevant. Never."

The flame died back and she remembered he'd said her rage had summoned his other face; her tears this. His grip eased so she sat on her heels, staring up at him. She let the tears fall without brushing them and his gaze followed them along the curve of her face. "You mistake me," he said, his voice an earthquake rumble. "Your fear and your pain blinds you to meaning. Do you want to become a vessel, to discover what prevents you from protecting your Agnes? The villagers?"

A deity would know everyone, but it was still unexpected and hurtful, to hear Agnes's name on his lips. "Yes. Yes, I do."

"No matter the agony? What I said before, about your will being tested, it is the same. You must be able to break through it to see what lies on the other side. Your mind will be broken, and you may be unable to put it back together. You may wander these woods for the remainder of your life, a mindless creature." He touched her face, and fire slid over her skin, her tingling lips. Squatting before her, he met her eye to eye. His dark hair slid forward over his shoulder and fluttered against the base of her throat, the top of her breast.

"If I am mindless, it will not be a long life." Yet the nonchalant words couldn't suppress a cold fear. She could handle pain and a quick death far better than being helpless, waiting for that death and pain to come.

"Is that a yes, vampire?"

"Yes." She faced his unyielding gaze. "Anything. And I will not ask for mercy. Not as long as that is the price for their lives."

"I can promise you nothing. This sacrifice only means something if it is a gift freely given with no expectation of return. You have to let go of all control. It is an impossible thing for your kind."

"Necessary overrides impossible." Mary had said that once or twice when treating the villagers for various ailments. Grace held the echo of her wise, calm voice in her head, and realized it was simple truth, no matter her fear. "I am yours, to do with as you will. I will sacrifice whatever is needed."

He straightened, and he clasped a wooden stake, the point sharp as his sword. Tossing it on the ground before her, he turned away. "You know what to do with that."

No. Agnes was awake again, her voice a faint rasp in Grace's mind. *No. This is wrong. He wouldn't ask that...*

Grace stared at the Lord's broad back as he moved back to his sword and stood there, facing away from her. With his hair still pulled forward, she saw more intricate tattoos on his back. She thought she saw a woman's face etched in them, so wondrously breathtaking, Grace felt as if she could reach out and touch her. Or like She could reach out and touch Grace.

Grace closed her eyes. No promises, no guarantees. She might take her own life and nothing would change. Worthless, pointless, except to the Lord before her. It wasn't enough. But there were times things were so dark the possibility of hope, however slim, was the only pinpoint of light in the wall of an incomprehensible universe. She picked up the stake, ignoring Agnes's cry of distress. She hated the Lord for that alone, for causing Agnes any more pain.

I love you, moppet. There was no point in denying the truth, no matter that vampires weren't supposed to fall in love with humans. She'd basically told the Powers That Be to bugger off; she didn't lose anything from saying the same to vampire kind. Clasping the stake, she lifted her gaze back to the Lord. When he turned to face her, she met his dark eyes. "If this doesn't help her and her village, I pray you suffer every pain imaginable," she said.

She drove the stake into her heart.

§

Agony. Unremitting fire and excruciating pain, beyond description. She screamed until her voice gave out. She felt like a rag doll, being shaken in the fist of a giant, violent child. She wanted to black out, but she couldn't. She was slamming her head against something. A tree trunk, for the bark bit into her flesh on each impact, blood matting her hair to her skull. Then a male hand was there, preventing her from doing it anymore. It was the woodcutter, his eyes alight with desire for her as his other hand cupped her face, holding her. But his fingers were wet with her blood. He disappeared and the pain started to recede like a tide of barbed wire, dragging itself along her flesh, back, backside, thighs and calves, and finally the bottoms of her feet, a ticklish and painful sensation.

Her shoulders hurt, and she realized her hands were tied high above her head, her bare back pressed against the tree's rough bark. Her legs were spread open, ankles bound against the base of the tree. Her toes strained for purchase against the lumpy terrain of tree roots. Someone gripped her hair and pulled her head back. In the midst of all that harrowing discomfort, a warm throat brushed her quivering mouth.

"Drink, vampire. Drink your fill."

She was ravenous, her fangs shooting forth even as he spoke. That tight hand in her hair stirred things in her lower belly, and she was damp with needy lust.

"You need your strength to become a vessel. I'm going to pleasure myself with your pain. A deep down, rare pleasure for a vampire, isn't it? To find someone who can overpower you, who will take what you cannot offer unless he proves worthy of your submission."

She was dead. Wasn't she? She'd driven a stake through her own heart. But she felt alive enough, and this was the Lord, and a reality where nothing was as it seemed. She was given no answers, only that pumping artery. She was blind, she realized, blinking in panic. She saw nothing. Darkness surrounded her, but so did he. He cupped her jaw and gave her a sensual order meant to be obeyed. "Drink."

She bit. His blood was rich, perfect, far more than she'd expected it to be. Full of magic and power, compelling her whole body to strain toward him. His hand dropped to her breast, kneading with casual distraction as she fed. Oh, blessings of the night, to feed. To take her fill. She gulped like a fledgling, as if she thought he'd take it away at any moment. He had other things to occupy him, though. His touch slid between her body and the tree, finding its way into the crevice of her buttocks to tease her rim. His body pressed against her side. And...feathers. His wing was curved around her, an amazing sensation, the feathers stroking her bare skin. Though it was cold in the outside world, inside that wingspan there was heat. The rosy glow of it filled her vision, and she could see again. The Lord with his fiery eyes was pressed up against her, studying her as if he understood everything she was, every dark space, every shortcoming, every sin. Every desire, want and need. Everything her soul was, without apology. No words, no explanation necessary. She was a morass of conflicting sensation: pain, arousal, relief and exhaustion, even as the blood was refueling her, goading her to an energy to tear, devour, want, and take. But she was tied and the bonds he'd used held a vampire easily.

When she glanced down, her mouth still on his throat, she saw there was a rosy glow on her flesh inside the wingspan, as if her skin reflected fire.

"A vessel gives everything, is open to being filled." His knuckles trailed down the side of her breast again. She kept feeding, mannerless, her hunger taking over. She'd had to sit on it for so long. Like her denied sexual needs, it had become a cold, hard, locked chest inside her. Now that it was open, it reached for that other unsated hunger. Or he was drawing it from her, reminding her of the passion that came with the restoration of life.

He buried his fingers in her hair, tightening his grip as she finally came up for a breather. She would have laved his neck with her tongue, clotting the punctures, but as soon as she retracted her fangs, the skin closed, though she licked a single drop of blood that escaped and earned a growl of warning, a reminder that he was the one holding control here, the one who permitted or forbid her every movement, every heartbeat. She dropped her head back and was caught in those dark eyes. So much power. Now that her wits were returning, so too were her nerves. This close to him, her body shook with yearning and awe at once. She wanted to be close, immersed in him. Her soul was opening as well as her body, becoming that vessel he'd predicted. Control was slipping from her, not because of anything he was doing, but because of what He was. She'd been buried in disease and death, and his fire promised cleansing, right down to her heartsick soul.

Knowing she'd likely never again have a chance to stare this close into the face of the Lord, she tried her best to focus past those energy vibrations to absorb his physical features. His face was magnificent, masculine planes and angles, his dark brows and lashes like the silk of his hair. And his long hair drifted over her skin, moving from the whispering wind through the circle. The thick strands bore that same fire-lit heat. He was the center of the Earth. Though she didn't know from where the thought had come, she knew it was true. The Goddess was the Earth, wasn't she? And the Lord and Lady, they were the balance for one another... He was Her center, and She surrounded him, his whole world...

The bonds on her ankles disappeared as he turned her to face the tree. She was a vampire, used to being stronger than everyone around her, so it was a new and unsettling experience to know from nothing more than the touch of his hand and the press of his body that she couldn't match him. When he closed his hand over her wrist, she tested it, she couldn't help it. An infant would have as much effect as her resistance did against him.

"Do you wish to fight me?" The tone of his voice was a challenge and...a taunt. An invitation.

She shook her head, nodded, then bit her lip, her fangs pricking the inside of her mouth. His chuckle sent erotic thrills tingling down her spine. "An honest female. You like the fight. A dominant who will give way only if clearly outmatched. Struggle all you wish, pretty vampire. There is nothing you can do to stop me. And it will arouse me further, so I will use you all the harder. She will only come to us when you are a truly empty vessel, and I want to be inside Her tonight."

He stroked her hip, thumb sliding so close to the juncture of her thighs in front she growled in need. "You dream of that yourself, don't you? Your lovely little Agnes...you think of her fighting you, of running her to ground like prey, in a way you will both enjoy. She knows that will arouse you more. She's dreamed of it herself. She understands your nature and trembles when she thinks of submitting herself fully to it."

Her fangs lengthened once more from the images he was planting. He tightened his hand on her arse, a bruising grip. "You know what I want now, do you not? Fight me, and I will cut you open, let loose all that stands in the way of what we both desire."

She had fought off wolves, vagabonds and the occasional stray vampire. For the villagers she'd felled trees, lifted things beyond their own strength. These last few weeks, she'd deprived herself of sleep and blood. She could handle any of that because she didn't become complacent. She tested her skills constantly, running, fighting invisible foes, imposing endurance tests on herself to stay ready for anything. It was the reality of being a vampire.

Refueled by his blood, she pitted her strength against the bonds holding her arms. This time they broke. Tearing loose from him, she seized a branch, snapped it loose and swung it in one swift, deadly spin. He wasn't there for the blow, his wings propelling him back over the rock cairn and a bonfire that his presence must have kindled. Or it was more of the same illusion and magic that made up this still far-too-real moment. The flames caressed his muscled thighs and the hem of the kilt without burning. For a moment, he appeared a creature wholly of fire again, but when he landed on the other side, he was bronze-skinned, his hair showering sparks.

She charged and he met her, putting her down. She used elbows and knees to thrust free, and was turned and slammed onto the earth, tree roots scraping her skin cruelly. Snarling, she ignored that, pushed up and sprang. He met the tree branch she swung again with his drawn sword, bisecting and knocking it out of her hand hard enough to wrench her wrist. In a move too fast for her to follow, he planted the sword and met her in hand-to-hand combat.

She wanted to shout a battle cry, her nature fully unleashed, wild and unfettered, no longer constrained by despised civilized behavior. Her bloodlust surged, goaded by the violence. Yet the euphoria was swept away by rage once more. The weight on her heart was a millstone she couldn't leave behind. She saw the children and adults she'd had to burn or bury. The hopeless eyes of the witches she'd loved. He could have stopped it. His precious Goddess could have stopped it. Couldn't they? Someone *should* be able to stop it. Was it better to think no one could, that there was no one to blame?

Enough words, enough thought. She wanted to destroy. A restrained wrestling match became a pitched battle. She didn't care that he was a god. She did her best to draw blood, to break bones, to take life as full bloodlust took over. She was only a hundred and twenty years old, but even an older vampire succumbed to that primal directive if provoked enough. She was pushed beyond bearing, the only thing to assuage it the suffering of someone to blame. As she fought him back and forth across the circle, she was caught in a full color montage of horrible nightmares become reality, all packed into the past two moons of loss, grief and sickness. She screamed her hatred at him, and grappled, struck and fought. She exhausted her strength, she bled, she fell and got back up again. Her bones broke and re-fused, but she kept on, fueled by furious adrenaline. She was purging everything inside her, dumping out all the trash in her soul.

He restrained himself--some deep, inaccessible part of her knew he did--but he didn't patronize her. He landed the blows that drew blood, that bruised and broke bones. It only made her angrier and more determined. Her energy started to flag, but she wasn't ready to give in. He tossed her across the fire and she landed hard, rolling and coming to her feet, stumbling. She grabbed the pommel of his planted sword to stop her forward momentum. Sensing him coming over the fire at her fast as a blink, using the propulsion of his wings, she seized the hilt and yanked it from the ground, swinging it in an arc as she spun to confront him.

She saw the brief flash in his vivid gaze, a seasoned warrior realizing he needed to reverse direction a second too late. Her wild swing, propelled by murderous intent, raked the point across his midriff.

The blade burst into flame, as did the hilt under her hands. A blinding light knocked her backward and yanked the world away from her.

§

Time stopped. She was in a rocking chair, holding a child in her arms. He had thick dark hair and solemn eyes almost as black as the Lord's. The babe reached up and touched her bloody mouth with small fingers. She had an ache in her belly, so empty. Yet she held him closer, pressed his face against her cheek, and heard him whisper in the comforting, incoherent language of an infant. She wished she could let Agnes hold him. Her servant needed to hold a baby like this, to help ease the pain of losing Peter. Grace remembered holding Peter when he'd been born, the awe she'd felt at what Dan and Agnes had created.

You grew careless, my love. It has been a long time since a blade has marked your flesh.

Not careless, my Lady. I am giving her what she needs. And then she will give me what I need. You.

Sensual laughter answered that, an arousing, compelling sound. It made the world spin around, then slow. Nothing else seem important but that laughter, and the child in her arms. But female hands were taking the babe from her. As Grace reached after him, the voice belonging to the laughter reassured her. *I will tend him until it is time. My Lord is not yet done with you. He is relentless that way.*

She was back in the circle, the damp, heated earth beneath her feet, the bonfire flickering so close she was in danger of toppling into its grasp, her legs unsteady. She still clutched the hilt of the sword, even though fire was licking up her arm and burning her. She couldn't let go, not until a strong hand pried open her grip. Female fingertips slid over her skin, stopping the burn.

The Great Lord. The Horned God. Lucifer. The fallen angel. She thought of all those names for him as she saw him standing before her, the bonfire behind him. His eyes pinned her in place.

"Not there yet," he said thoughtfully. "A remarkable will. A stubborn one. Turn around, my lady. Stand where you are until I command you otherwise."

As he spoke, she saw a line of energy shimmer from his hand to the ground, becoming the fire-bathed whip again. The look in his eyes sent chills down her body, even as it also tightened it in ways she understood. *I will make your pain my pleasure...*

"Remember what I told you. You must hold out until I say stop. If you ask for mercy or for me to cease, the sacrifice is not pure."

She faced away from him, but some foolish part of her opened her mouth. "Does your stomach hurt?" she asked sweetly, between teeth gritted so they wouldn't chatter. When she looked over her shoulder, he smiled, a dangerous look so full of erotic threat her knees nearly buckled beneath her. In truth she was surprised his flesh had given way at all, since the slab of muscle beneath it looked as resilient as granite. Currently neither showed signs that she'd harmed him. She was relieved about that, though she didn't want to think about why she'd give a damn about his welfare.

"Turn your face from me, vampire."

She obeyed, holding her head up while still shaking. She flinched at the next sensation, but it was his hand, gripping her shoulder. His palm smoothed down her back, a touch that somehow made things worse. She could handle being flayed alive. The emotions he unleashed with tender explorations were far worse. They summoned the rage, an endless tide. Could she ever be this empty vessel he told her she had to be? The hate she had, the anger, seemed limitless.

"Use it to open up and release all that is inside," he said, his voice vibrating through her.

"You and your Lady are useless. You can't even help a single village. Their lives were already hard enough without sickness. You do nothing for them."

"The Wheel is far more complex than that. There are all types of loves in the world, but the Love that explains all is a long journey, often blazed by tears and loss."

"A babe who dies before she gets her first tooth has no journey to take." She closed her hands into fists. "Do your worst. Empty me out through violence and pain, for I can see no other way to accomplish it."

"Very well." There was a sadness in his voice, yet anticipation too, and she knew it was echoed in her own nature. Pain could feed pleasure, could transcend the body and pierce the soul. She'd dreamed of taking Agnes to those kinds of extremes, her cries and tears resulting in orgasms so intense her girl would be too weak to move afterward, for all the right reasons. Grace would care for her, and then do it all over again.

But there was a point past which pain was nothing but pain, a place she would never take Agnes. Penance, retribution, torture, mind-breaking. The first strike told her Lucifer had every intention of taking her into that realm and far beyond.

The agony was horrible beyond description. It was burning, stinging, thudding, a ceaseless poison that whipped through her blood, burying thorns into her very soul. She dropped to one knee, no choice, but she held there, head down, chest bellowing, trying to manage her reaction. The pain held all the concentrated horror of the past several weeks, and it was going to keep coming. The most horrible realization was that he'd only landed one blow. The next one hit her side. She strangled on a sound like what would come from a wounded animal's. She couldn't bear it. But she must.

"Get up." His voice was implacable. "You must stand for each blow. Do you want mercy?"

Fuck, she hated him for asking, because everything in her screamed yes, yes, yes. Tasting her own blood, she stood up. She went back down under the next one. Got up again. After every blow, he asked her if she wanted him to stop, which only made it worse. She speared her tongue with her fangs, making sure she couldn't speak. Yet the pain of it was too much, because it was more than a pain of the body. It what was in that walnut, all the sins and disappointments. It was a deer forlornly looking for grass in frozen ground. It was all the hopelessness of the world, pulled inside and through her, the useless tragedy of it mirrored against those few precious moments of joy and happiness. Yet it was those moments that somehow brought her back to her feet every time, even if only to be knocked down again. She could feel Agnes's hot tears in her heart. Her beloved had her fist against her mouth, trying not to scream in protest on her behalf. She didn't want Agnes to know her pain. But she had no strength to protect her from it.

Love you, Agnes....always have...love you.

I love you, Gracie. Believe...open yourself up...let it all go...

The words planted an image in Grace's mind. Agnes, her slim fingers wrapped around a brown egg, bringing it to the edge of a clay bowl. She sucked in a breath and the egg was cracked, Agnes releasing the unrealized life inside, breaking Grace open at the same moment. She screamed into the night air, her arms somehow lifting despite the pain, her body being racked with it. A fiery energy swept through her, and she tasted her sweat and blood. She felt the poison and the strength both, all of it rising, pulling free, roiling out of the right side of her body, through the heart, which pounded and wept. Useless, pointless...meaningless...

He'd stopped. She was on her knees, weeping as if she'd never stop. "It's too much...no one can bear that. No one can hold that and not wish for all of it to end... Why is there no mercy?"

He knelt beside her, his wing covering her, slowly furling inward so it wrapped around her. She turned toward him painfully, as if she were an ancient crone whose joints and muscles could only move in small increments, but then her face was pressed into his chest as she sobbed and shook. He held her with arms and wings, all that fiery energy that had burned now swirling around her like a hearth fire. He offered no words. Just an incoherent murmuring, a hum of sound. Over his touch she felt that of Another, a female energy. They were both holding her up.

"I'm not empty enough yet," she said brokenly. "I've failed them. I am failing them."

He tipped up her chin and covered her mouth with his. She made a surprised noise, but another form of overwhelming energy swept through her, taking her voice away. The heat was within her as well as without, and she clung to his arms as a very capable tongue and lips caressed and seduced hers. His powerful hands slid down her bare back to grip her buttocks and press her against him, against a male organ impressively engorged. Laying her down beneath him on the ground, he began to taste her skin, starting at her chin and throat, moving to her sternum. The fire mixed with the emotions, lifting her out of that darkness and mire. She couldn't bear the light of hope, but he forced her to feel it, respond to it. She arched up, gasping, as he began to suckle her breasts. Energy was swirling around them, and she lifted quaking fingers, making the fine blue and silver mists swirl over her fingers, a pale green running through it all. The residual pain vibrated through her, the deep relief of its absence giving the pleasure a sharp, silver edge.

"Help me," she whispered. "Please."

Let go, dear child. Just let go. Put down your burden for one moment. It is simple as that. Walk through the fire, the snow and ice, the rock, in nothing but your naked soul. Carry your love in your heart and leave your hands free and empty...

She realized it was Agnes's voice in her head, but it wasn't Agnes. Her girl was channeling the Goddess, speaking into Grace's heart. Pain and pleasure, hope and yearning, twined together around her, binding her to this moment. She cried out as the Lord's mouth went to her thighs and between them, tasting her cunt and finding her slick, her body readying itself for what was to come. His wings spread out, framing the moon rising above. She reached for him. She might not know how to empty her soul, but she knew how to lose herself in this, in the demands of the body.

"I can't change anything. I can't just love them and lose them... I don't know how to accept that. I'm so angry, and hurt, and desolate..."

His mouth teased and tasted, tongue licking her in a way that swept an orgasm over her so quickly she had no way to stop the rush of feeling. She cried out her release, but he wasn't giving her time to settle. As soon as she was coming down off that peak, he was driving her up to another. Feeling swirled in her belly, that pre-climactic tension, but it was building, not diminishing, as she went over the crest of each wave. Her cries were becoming stronger, more helpless.

You have no control. You are ours, and you follow our Will. When the Lord and Lady's Will is accepted, you are

*able to survive. You will find your heart and soul again,
for it resides there.*

Male and Female voices blending. She was going over
another peak, and the ordeal of the past few moments and
the wonder of the current combined, pounding out any
other awareness, the ability to think or do anything but get
swept up in all of it. She opened herself and let go, carried
along in a tide populated by the faces of those she'd lost, as
well as glimpses of Agnes and others drifting on that same
current on this Yule night. She heard singing, chanting,
voices raised in praise and supplication. The eight women
who'd already died, the three more who would die, and
Agnes and Gertrude, wavering but unquenched spirits
outlining the circle, calling out to the Lord and Lady,
believing, having faith, finding hope...

Lucille, Dan, Peter, Millie and her little boy...all the
women and their families. She watched their spirits
materialize, drift around her and away, caught in the Veil, a
gentle net. They turned into wisps of rose-tinted clouds, of
silver smoke and misty fog, journeying to a place far
beyond pain and suffering. The singing and chanting grew
stronger and she was back in her own immediate reality,
finding the Lord poised over her, dark eyes burning into
hers.

He didn't command her to open herself to the Lady.
She'd reached the point she understood that it didn't
happen on command. The Goddess entered because an
open, empty soul was the invitation She'd never resist.
Tears rolled out of Grace's eyes as she felt that power and
strength, the Mother of all Mothers waiting. She felt her
sadness, her joy, her sheer...life. The Lady grieved as well,
for the tragic folly of her children. Knowing she understood
and felt the same pain Grace felt turned tears into sobs.
They cried together and, like Female energy everywhere,
they drew strength from that shared pain and found their
feet once more to persevere, to survive and to love.

Drawing a deep breath, one that went all the way to the
bottom of her soul, Grace invited the Lady in. Invited all of
it to happen.

The power of the Goddess lifted her body up into an

invitation of another kind. Lucifer's gaze gleamed and he thrust deep inside her. The dual possession took away any conscious thought, leaving just sensation. Grace was moaning with a blend of sensations too overwhelming to describe. The energy vibrated through and around her, and she was limp in his grasp. His rhythmic thrusts took her back to climax, but it didn't stop there. She went over peak after peak as her mind fragmented and she let go of her soul. Something built inside her, something hard to describe, a form of release far beyond the other. It was an energy, with power enough to fuel a sun, gathering. It reached through her and outward, and her eyes opened to something she'd never seen before, that she knew she'd never see again, but would never forget.

She couldn't describe it, so she hoped with all the love she had in her heart that Agnes could hear her thoughts, feel them. Something like this had to be shared with the most important soul in her life.

The ecstasy gripping her channeled through the Goddess inside her and the Lord taking them both. She could *feel* the love between the Lord and Lady. It represented and encompassed all loves, the one that fueled and received every experience of love. It was intense, passionate, overwhelming, quiet, ending, safe, unconditional. It answered all questions, though she knew she could never voice the answers. There were no words.

It is. She thought of Father Baldwin's bible. *I AM.* If only those who'd wrote it had been inspired to fill in that missing word. But there were so many, weren't there? I Am Love. Justice. Beginning. End. Healing. Death. Life. All.

And all back to Love again.

"Oh..." It was a long, drawn out syllable and her eyes widened as she saw the Lord's face tighten, felt his body gather the way a man's did, that fulfilling, joyous promise of release. She screamed again as he let go inside her, a rush of fire that brought a new wave of climaxes, so close together and intense she was buffeted by them like a storm. She shared that experience with another female energy, One that bonded and connected to Him as if they'd begun time together.

And perhaps they had.

§

Time had stopped. Not metaphorically; literally. She was sure of it. She also thought she might truly be dead, that initial act with the stake no longer merely a symbolic gesture. Her body had never felt so drained before. Yet something was different, too. This wasn't the exhaustion she'd felt for the past few weeks, the hunger and despair. It was as if the energy in her was concentrated in her core. Creating, making.

Her hand dragged across the ground, following that feeling like a homing beacon. When she found her palm on her abdomen, fingers spread over it, that concentration throbbed under her touch, spreading wonder through her. "Oh my God. Dear Lord and Lady."

The Lord was next to her now, heating her with his proximity like the bonfire, only it warmed her all the way around and within, not just the part that faced him. He picked up Agnes's robe and lifted Grace like a child, wrapping her in it and shifting her into his lap, an entirely unnerving and welcome thing. She heard that Female voice in her mind, vibrating through her body.

You are far more chivalrous than you admit, my love. You do not like to see her shiver in the cold. The winter spirits say you do not appreciate them.

They would say it to my face, except my heat would melt their ice into puddles and evaporate them out of existence.

Far be it from her to interrupt a conversation between deities, but this feeling inside her, so wondrous and amazing, compelled her to do it. "My lord."

It was so difficult for vampires to conceive, she couldn't be sure of it, not until he confirmed it. She saw the curve of his mouth, the flicker in those crimson eyes, and his hand covered hers on her stomach, an odd tenderness in his touch. Well, that wasn't surprising, was it? If what she was feeling was true, it was his babe as well. She felt the warmth of the Lady in her mind, Her own hand upon it, because all were Her children.

It does not often happen, dear child. But you wounded Him, in your struggle to understand. Such remarkable strength, such commitment in the face of personal pain, it deserved a gift of hope. For you and those you love. Care well for His son. It is a gift given only to the very worthy.

A son. Well, this worthy individual suddenly felt terrified and overjoyed at once. Her hand slid through the Lord's feathers. It seemed a miracle to be allowed to do that, to have her limp, trembling fingers fall on the rounded shape of his shoulder, drift down to his warrior-hard biceps. She wet her lips. There were so many things she could say and ask, but she stuck with something simple, ridiculously inane. "Will he have wings...my son?"

Lucifer's lips curved. "No, but he will be a warrior the likes of which no vampire has ever seen. When he fights on behalf of your kind, it will seem like he can fly. He will be a protector, a force for justice."

"Will he know love?" *Like I have found with Agnes?* She was too much of a vampire to say that aloud, but the benefit of congress with a god was he could read her thoughts. Vampire children were so rare, she would never regret this night, but thinking her son might not feel what she'd seen in the Lord and Lady, what she knew she felt for Agnes...

Even if she third marked the woman, Grace would likely outlive her, because a third mark had a lifespan of three hundred years and vampires...didn't die of old age. Though an older vampire might call her resolve the zeal of youth untempered by experience, Grace knew when Agnes died she would never again find anything like that, like this. Having a love of that depth more than once would not be her path. She would love, but never be in love again. Agnes would take most of her heart with her, the only part left devoted to Grace's son. As he grew and became a man, her heart would drift back toward the girl who'd become her whole world. It wasn't approved of in the vampire world, such an attachment to a human, but vampires were isolated from one another. She didn't really care what they thought.

Lucifer's lips curved. "He'll be like that, too. He will set his own path, make his own code. And it will be a formidable one."

She wondered if he'd answer her other question. After what she'd felt between him and the Goddess, she couldn't imagine he'd consider it a foolish female question. He didn't, because he did answer.

"Yes. He will find love, my lady. He will wait centuries, but it will come and, when it does, it will make up for the years of waiting. Your son will be a credit to your own courage and heart. As far as female foolishness," his dark eyes glinted, "I would fear the wrath of She who is my heart if ever I thought such a thing, let alone said it. Look. See an echo of what is to come."

His hand closed over her wrist, slipped to her palm so their fingers twined. As she tipped her head to look into his eyes, the world swam and he drew her through the clouds of time to a different place, as easy as a breath. She stood in a large, open building that had many things she didn't understand: A big metal contraption with an L-shape piece on the front; large crates that looked as if they were made out of thick brown paper; curious fixtures on the ceiling like lanterns, but not, for she saw no flickering flame in their depths, only steady white light. But all those inventions of the future disappeared as she saw the most important thing in the room.

He was tall and handsome. Such a simple, motherly thing to think, her heart swelling with pride and wonder at it. He was a breathtaking echo of his father, though he kept his black hair cut short. He wore strange clothes. Dark, close-fitting trousers and shirt, with a long coat over them. As he moved forward, she saw his intent dark eyes had a hint of his father's crimson to them. She drew in a breath as he produced a flashing blade from the depths of the coat, the silver reflecting off the odd lanterns. Seven men moved out of the shadows, vampires and servants. Several of them were young vampires, she could tell, but two of them were not, and their servants were seasoned fighters, evident by their lack of fear and the concentrated look in their faces.

She put a hand on Lucifer's arm in involuntary

trepidation. "Watch," he murmured.

Her son moved. Or rather, as Lucifer said, he flew like a bird without his feet ever leaving the ground. Swooping, spinning, turning, leaping, the blade an extension of his arm and his elegant fingers. She let out the fearful breath she'd sucked in as he faced his foes. He had the deadly grace of every predator she'd witnessed, animal, human or vampire. As he fought, she saw his father in him again, this fearsome angel who touched her so tenderly and ruthlessly at once. Her son would be unstoppable with an angel's blood in him, yet his heart and soul would also be part angel, untainted by evil. It would be the vampire blood that would give him the edge necessary to survive their cruel, bloody world. Tears inexplicably sprung to her eyes as his lips quirked at something one of his enemies spat at him. He would have her smile, and hints of her facial expressions. Agnes would have recognized that sardonic look in a heartbeat.

The mists closed around him, taking that image away. Instead, now he was but a babe in her arms. His mouth opened against her breast, tiny, needlelike teeth drawing blood from her, sustenance. She would sit by a window in the moonlight and sing to him. Agnes would be there, wouldn't she? *Please Lord and Lady...* She'd be a quiet shadow that moved forward and closed her arms around Grace, their cheeks pressed together as Agnes trailed her work-roughened finger along the little one's face, both of them enchanted by him. Caring for him would help heal Agnes's heart, ease a mother's deep grief.

Lucifer squatted before her, reaching out to touch the tiny forehead. His son grasped his much larger finger. Lucifer's smile took speech from her, everything stilling so she thought the universe itself spun on the tip of this moment. Grace could feel the Goddess looking through her eyes, the Lady as entranced by his expression as Grace herself. It made Grace want to laugh with quiet joy, something she hadn't done in so very long. To imagine the Goddess with weak knees because of her Lord's smile...

The opaque eyes of the Lord of the Underworld lifted to her, his expression warm, responding to his Lady's adulation. "I will give you one more memory to come," he said. "Because the trinity is the most powerful number there is, bringing balance. And because you asked."

She saw her son coming through a metal doorway that parted before him as if by magic. It led into a room comfortably furnished with things that had familiar shapes--chair, table--but unfamiliar fabrics, colors and trappings around them. But she already knew getting caught up in those things would waste the true value of what the Lord was showing her. Her son stripped his coat and the sheathed blade, as well as an impressive array of hidden weapons. After doing that, he moved forward, that room disappearing and giving way to one with mirrored walls, where rose petals were scattered on the floor. The mirrors flickered with the light from a trio of candles placed on a single pedestal in the center of the room.

A sable-haired woman with blue-green eyes was there. She wore a corset, an item Grace recognized, the material an elegant brocade, but it was laced over shockingly snug pants in a slick material and thigh-high boots that were scandalous, but which Grace eyed with female envy after examining the way the outfit complimented her figure. But she didn't dwell on those oddities, either, moving instead to the look in her son's eyes.

He loved this female. Loved her with everything he was. He would die for her, live for her, do anything for her, bear any pain. She recognized it like a mirror in her own heart, the way she felt for Agnes, the way she already felt for her unborn son.

He drew the woman close with one arm. The way he dipped his head down to capture her lips stirred Grace-- how could it not? He would have his father's sensual powers as well, Goddess help the female who tried to resist him. But from the slight curve on this woman's mouth, the light in her eyes, she understood the power his love gave her over him, too. But she cherished it and would use that power only to their mutual benefit. She wouldn't be pushed around, though. Grace approved of that, because that was important to love, too. How many fights had she and Agnes had over the years?

His kiss had taken total, demanding possession of the woman. That feeling of ownership was something a vampire understood. His fangs bared and he scored her throat as her fingers tightened on his arms. Seeing the female's fangs, Grace realized his love would be another vampire.

Then Grace stiffened. She almost called out in warning-- futilely--as another male appeared at his back. But, thinking of the first memory Lucifer had showed her of her son, she realized he would never allow anyone to come up behind him that he didn't trust entirely.

This one was a warrior as well, only thicker, more muscular. Human. A fully marked servant. He was theirs, her son's and his lover's. What she'd initially interpreted as a threat, the man's dangerous restlessness and wounded soul, became something different when his midnight blue eyes rested on the two vampires. All that violence and energy morphed into a protective watchfulness, an absorption in their irresistible energy, and a sense of belonging.

Yes, the male was their human servant, but far more than that. When her son lifted his head, he reached over and captured the man's nape to draw him close. As he took just as demanding a kiss from his mouth, she knew her son would have more than one soulmate. He would have...two.

The mists closed around them, leaving her floating slowly back toward the present. The reality of it hit her once more, exultation and terror. She was going to have a child. She shuddered with joy and anticipation. She saw a brief flash of all of it, birth and infancy, him growing into a boy, learning, smiling at her, becoming more serious as the years went on, as his skills were called to the aid of others. He would serve their kind and serve the angels as well. And she would be his mother.

She opened her eyes, finding herself stretched out on the warm earth by the bonfire. Lucifer was above her once more, his body pressing insistently between her legs. The fire in his gaze saw her, and more than her. He saw Her. They were not yet done using her body as a conduit for their need for One Another.

More than willing to be that intermediary, Grace lifted her arms to him again. The strength of the Goddess flowed through her, to Him, giving Him love and passion as well. He would exhaust her, deplete her, but leave her with a fullness that would carry her through life, that would help her give life to her son, and to the village again. She was empty and full at once, the proper receptacle for bringing together the Lord and Lady's energy--the renewal that would offer them all hope once more.

Agnes had been right. Ritual was vital. No matter how dark the corners of the universe, or how long and deep the reach of those shadows, this restored light. It might only be a flicker in the darkness, but it would fuel strength of purpose, and life and love would continue.

That was the gift the Lord and Lady brought, the gift embedded in every soul.

§

She was alone. Smelling smoke, she opened her eyes to see the fire still crackling, though it no longer leaped high above the cairn. It had diminished in the way a fire would as the wood fuel was consumed. She was wrapped in warm animal skins, soft pelts that still vibrated with the life that had inhabited them, an echo that told her their spirits were safe and at peace somewhere beyond this world. It told her who'd left the gift of them. She sat up, clutching them around her. After the Lord's arduous demands--his desire for His Lady seemed to know no satiation point--she should have been unable to rise, let alone feel strength flowing through her as she did.

Her palm spread over her bare abdomen. A child. Perhaps it was his strength she felt flowing through her now, because she didn't feel weak or depleted at all. She felt...alive and wondrous. She could run, spin and dance through the forest. It was not yet dawn, but when dawn came, she bet the sun would sparkle off the snow, reflecting her mood. She wouldn't be able to see it, but Agnes would. She must.

Agnes. Reality returned with a stab of panic and she

scrambled in her mind to follow that connection, to make sure the life she'd been given had not been an exchange for another, equally as precious to her.

"I'm here."

Grace blinked. Was it a vision? Was she still caught in an alternative reality? Agnes stood on the opposite side of the fire. No boils on her throat, her silver-streaked brown hair down and loose, flowing over her arms. She wore her peasant blouse, long skirt and a cloak over it. She'd washed herself, for Grace smelled her fragrant soap on her. All of that might have convinced Grace it wasn't real, but Agnes showed key signs of their present reality. Her clothes were too loose, her face thin, eyes carrying the shadows of grief and loss. Yet there were other things in her gaze. Hope, pride...and something else as she stared at Grace. Need. It sharpened all of Grace's senses and pierced her with the same craving.

Agnes was alive. And she was going to be well again. The Lord and Lady had given them that gift. It surged through Grace, what all of it meant, and it came to one thing. She wanted Agnes, now. She had a need that would consume her servant. The power of it froze her vocal cords, then she found the one thing Agnes said a vampire always had within easy reach. Arrogance. While the thought amused Grace, she wasn't going to deny it.

"I did as you asked," Grace said, a deliberate edge to her tone. "Now you will do as I demand, won't you, moppet?"

Pure pleasure surged through her at the little shiver that went through Agnes. "Yes," she whispered.

"Take off your clothes. All of them. And stand in place until I look my fill."

The fire was still warm, so Grace knew she wasn't causing Agnes too much discomfort. But as Agnes shed the clothes, easy enough since she wore no garments beneath them, her skin acquired gooseflesh from the touch of the wind, her nipples tightening. Agnes was thin, but her body would become ripe again, and Grace would immerse herself in every luscious curve. She wasn't going to wait on that, however. She looked at the stretch marks Agnes had from bearing Peter, the lower set of her breasts that time and his nourishment as an infant had caused. All of it made her want Agnes even more. She would have thought so anyway, but the coven had taught Grace that all faces of the Goddess were beautiful. Maiden, Mother, Crone. Women carried all three faces in their heart and soul, at every age.

You were wrong, Grace. Agnes's gaze held hers. *It was you holding me to life. I didn't want to admit it. I was afraid that it was dishonoring Dan's memory. But when I was in your mind, and felt hope return to all of us, thanks to you and the Lord and Lady, all I could think about was this. When I could become yours fully, and we could be what we wish to one another. I knew you would help heal my heart, help me understand it isn't wrong to love someone the way I want to love you.* "I couldn't wait," Agnes said aloud, her voice breaking. "They gave me back my strength, healed my body, and I couldn't wait another moment to be with you." *My friend, my love. My heart.*

"My beauty," Grace murmured. She let Agnes feel and see the strong, clean desire that her words provoked. "I will eat you alive if you keep talking like that."

"Promise?" Agnes offered a tremulous smile.

Grace pressed her lips together, her heart wrenching at how close she'd come to losing this female. She reached out a hand. "Come here. Right now."

Agnes moved around the fire. Though her servant was still weak, Grace saw her movements had a priestess's confidence once more. Her hair fluttered over her back, her pale flesh as milky white as the snow on the edges of the circle. When she reached her, Grace gripped her fingers. Agnes let out a little gasp as Grace yanked her beneath the skins and put her on her back so she was stretched out fully on Agnes. No hesitation, no indecision any more. If Agnes hadn't realized Grace was just as naked as herself, she did now, with Grace's body between her spread legs, mons pressed against mons, breasts rubbing with pleasing friction over nipples and curves. Grace wound her arms around her to hold her close and take her mouth in the kiss she'd been wanting for months.

"Grace... Gracie..." Agnes sighed with the pleasure of it, and Grace scored her gently with a fang, moving down to

tease her throat. Agnes's fingers dug into her shoulders, and Grace descended under the furs. *First, I will feast on your cunt the way I've always wanted to do, the way I've dreamed about. And you will cry out your pleasure so the Lord and Lady can hear it...*
She should be taking her time, but she couldn't. Not right now. The first taste was incomparable. She covered Agnes's labia with the heat of her mouth and plunged her tongue in between, curling to collect the cream already gathered there. When she shifted to suck on the swelling clit and its protective hood, she was so hungry she wasn't gentle about it, pulling and nipping, licking and sucking as Agnes's body rolled and lifted, as cries broke from her lips. "Ah, Goddess..."
"Beg for mercy and you shall have none, moppet. I've waited too long." Agnes's body was weak, but her spirit was strong and vibrant, and craved Grace's demands in a way a vampire couldn't resist. Grace flipped her over onto her stomach. Agnes's fingers dug into the furs as Grace rubbed her breasts over the seam of her buttocks, then slid several fingers inside her pussy. As her thumb found Agnes's clit once more to stroke and tease, she bent and sank her fangs into Agnes's backside. Agnes moaned again.
Grace worked her up to a climax in seconds. Agnes's body was starved for the attention, for the need for life and renewal. That yearning bound Grace's heart to her all the more, but she wasn't yet ready to let her go over. It could be that sadistic side to a vampire's nature, wanting to deny and prolong the pleasure, making it an intense, screaming agony. Or it could be merely that, this first time, Grace needed it to be face to face, no ghosts between them. She turned Agnes over once more and lay back upon her. She began to rotate her hips, creating friction clit to clit. Agnes's legs trembled in their spread position.
"Wider, moppet. Spread wide for me." Grace stared down in her face, implacable, needing to see her come apart before she could do the same. Agnes's mouth stretched out in that pre-climax rictus, her hands back on Grace, short nails digging into her.
"Come for me. Go over. Now."

Agnes shuddered, something inside shattering, wrenching a scream from her throat. Tears fountained from her eyes in the middle of the release, and Grace felt the pain overflow with the pleasure, the grief and the need together. She found she could not take without giving. Not from this woman. Curling her arms around Agnes, sheltering her, keeping her from breaking apart, she came down upon her and held her so close their hearts thundered together. Since the position changed the meshing of their bodies, she freed one hand to stroke Agnes to completion.

Agnes hooked her arms over her shoulders, burying her face in Grace's throat, and cried and cried, even as she rocked through the climax that kept pounding through her. Grace was crying as well, pressing those tears into Agnes's hair. Love was here. It had saved them, but the cost of life was so harsh that, without love, it would have been unbearable. It was nigh unbearable sometimes, regardless.

"Sssshh..." She held her as Agnes's orgasm left her with tiny little twitches against Grace's still aroused body. Agnes felt it, lifting her hips against her.

"Let me...I want to hear you release...as well. The way you've wanted to do it. With me...as yours."

Grace drew back, meeting her gaze. Agnes wet her lips, her eyes alive. "I feel it in you, the dark, powerful things you want. And I need a taste of that..."

"You're not at full strength, dearest."

"It doesn't matter. You're my strength. I need to be your vessel now, Grace. I'm so empty." Agnes's lip trembled, but then it firmed and she met Grace's gaze, her mouth quirking in a tender half-smile. "If I can't walk afterward, though, you might have to carry me home."

"I'll carry you wherever you need." Grace studied her face. "I will give you strength, Agnes. Then you can take whatever I dish out, all the things I want to do to you."

That smile became something more feminine and aware, and Agnes's fingers curled into Grace's bare hip. "I will take anything you wish to give me and thank you for it."

Images flashed from Agnes's mind to Grace's, and Grace

had all she could do to bite back a growl. All those times she'd pleasured herself, she'd imagined the things she wanted to do to Agnes were things the witch couldn't even contemplate. She'd been wrong. Agnes might not be as sexually experienced, but the body knew what it craved, and had conjured those images in Agnes's mind. Grace wondered how she'd kept them hidden so deeply from Grace she hadn't even suspected. Well, that was about to end. After the third mark was given, Agnes would never be able to hide a thought or feeling from her again. A soul binding, that was what the third mark was. It opened the servant up beyond the mind, letting the vampire into the heart and down deep into the very depths of the soul.

The expression on Agnes's face said she wanted that soul-deep binding. Which decided Grace on their top priority.

Staying on top of her, keeping Agnes's body beneath her own aroused one, Grace bit her own wrist and put it to Agnes's mouth. "We start with this. Take a few swallows, moppet. And then I'm going to mark you."

Agnes put her lips over the wound and drank, keeping her eyes on Grace's. Grace could feel her worries, her fears, but also her overwhelming need for it to happen. She didn't want her afraid or worried.

Drawing her wrist away, she sealed the wound and shifted further up Agnes's body. She curved her fingers around Agnes's throat, pinning her to the ground as she straddled her, positioning herself where she could do light, circular passes over Agnes's still spasming clit. Agnes bit back a moan. Her nipples were tight points and Grace imagined an evening of doing nothing but tying Agnes's arms behind her in her rocking chair and suckling them until she came from that stimulation, over and over. Grace remembered that period during Agnes's pregnancy when her whole body had been sensitive and aroused constantly. When Dan came back from a day out in the fields, he'd found a wife who barely waited until he was through the door to draw him to their bed, even before giving him his dinner. He hadn't complained.

Would Grace be like that during her own pregnancy?

Agnes's eyes widened, and her fingers spasmed. "Grace."

She'd left her mind open to Agnes. And Agnes, while privy to much of what had happened in this clearing, had missed that significant moment. They would celebrate that together, but not right now. She shook her head, giving Agnes a brusque order. "Later. Right now, you stay quiet. Not a single sound." Her lips curved mercilessly as she started to grind down a little harder on those rotations, then lighter. Agnes had just come, and Grace ached for a release of her own, but she wanted her girl to go with her at the same time.

Agnes's face shone with joy at the news despite Grace's command. Yet as Grace continued to move upon her, Agnes's eyes widened again for different reasons. That slow build brought a surge of desire back through her, growing as Grace let herself draw closer to pinnacle. Her hold on Agnes's throat captivated her, not just physically. Feeling Agnes respond to that collaring touch, that sense of ownership, only heightened Grace's own burning need. "Stay absolutely still," she said hoarsely. "I want you to feel the climax tear through you this time."

Agnes obeyed, quivering harder and harder, biting down on her own lip to the point of drawing blood, just to obey Grace's demand not to move or speak. She would soothe that with her own mouth and tongue. Later. Agnes's self-imposed restraint resulted in an arousal that grew in her mind and body until it overflowed and filled Grace's mind and body as well, joining the turbulent storm that was already there.

As Grace started to fall over that edge, Agnes's lips parted, a pleading look in her eye. Grace shook her head, denying her, making her wait, making it draw out until Agnes was in sensual agony, crying out. Only then did Grace let her go over, crying out her own pleasure. As they moved together as rhythmically as the ocean, she let those waves get higher and higher, holding Agnes with her, spinning in that cataclysmic surf. At the peak of that shared pleasure, she bit Agnes's throat, her fangs piercing her and the third mark flooding her. Agnes surged against her with a scream of pleasure.

Grace had never given anyone the third mark, so the experience was as new to her as to Agnes. Though she'd been told what it was like, words did not come close to it. When she looked at the vastness of the ocean, she couldn't imagine ever understanding the depths of all its mysteries. Yet this was like being immersed in it fully while holding all of it in her cupped hands. She felt Agnes register that connection in a way that was different but the same, that absolute surrender and belonging to another soul. It was something she'd explored and experienced with Dan in some ways, so it wasn't entirely unfamiliar and shocking to her, but the depths of this was beyond human imagination. It was not just desiring or hoping for that connection; it was real, immutable, permanent. Forever belonging fully to another, in every possible way.

Agnes's expression was swept with wonder, for Grace left her shields down so Agnes could see that connection clearly, feel the depths of it fully. As a witch, her honed spiritual senses gave her even more input on that than a normal human would experience. As they slowly came back down, still locked together in mind and soul the way they'd ascended, Grace never wanted to let go or draw back.

The third mark also bound Agnes's mortality to hers, so that if Grace died, Agnes went with her. In return, as long as Grace lived, or until three hundred years had passed, Agnes would be hers, alive and hers, beyond the touch of any human disease. The only thing that could take her from Grace was a stake of metal through the heart. Any who threatened her that way, who even thought of threatening her that way, would die before the thought was complete. Thinking of it, Grace embraced the savagery that lived so close to the surface of a vampire's nature, to protect what was hers with harsh impunity.

Grace at length shifted next to Agnes. They lay quietly for awhile by the fire, Agnes getting her breath back and Grace not thinking of anything, just experiencing the bliss. It was like when time had stopped with the Lord and Lady, and she wondered if that was the lesson. Such divine power was only as far away as the nearest loved one.

Agnes shifted to her side, propping herself on her elbow.

She tugged on the edge of the furs and Grace allowed it, watching her third mark servant study Grace's body, her palm spanning Grace's abdomen, thumb caressing the indentation of her navel. With the second mark, she could hear Agnes's thoughts and deduce her feelings. With the third mark, she felt everything Agnes felt, so when her gaze lifted back to Grace, Grace was hit full impact by the mix of sadness and unspeakable joy Agnes was experiencing.

"He will be ours," Grace told her fiercely. "Yours as much as mine."

When Agnes's eyes filled with tears anew, Grace lifted onto her elbows and captured her mouth with her own, lifting a hand to cradle her face, caress her throat. Unable to resist, she pushed Agnes to her back again. Curling her hands around Agnes's wrists, she held them to either side of her, pinning her as she bit her neck, her shoulder, a scattering of bites that had Agnes murmuring in pleasure and initial little cries of pain. The third mark was not enough. Grace wanted her marked, over and over. She tasted her blood, closed the wounds with her tongue, held her, rocked her. *I will be here for every moment of sadness or joy, moppet. I won't let you be alone with their loss. I'll help you through all of it.*

We'll help each other. Agnes lifted wet eyes to her, but also freed a hand to caress Grace's cheek. The wisdom in the woman's eyes caused something to tremble deep inside of Grace. Grace had not lost a husband or child, but they'd all belonged to her. She'd lost as much of her family as Agnes had, as they all had. They would all help each other.

Grace slid an arm around Agnes's back in profound gratitude, and awe for a two-way comfort that was still unexpected, even after forty-two years of finding the miracle of Sanctity. As she did, though, she was distracted from the intense moment by a different texture on Agnes's skin. It couldn't be scarring, for Agnes hadn't had any of the swellings in that spot. Grace had never marked a servant before, but suddenly she knew what it must be, what it had to be.

Sitting up, she made Agnes turn over, shifting her onto her lap and holding her naked body there, her hand caressing Agnes between the legs split over her knee, her rump raised in the air in a provocative way. "Oh," Agnes said faintly, and Grace saw a flash in her mind that inspired a fang-baring smile and a few answering fantasies of her own. She restrained herself—at least for now—to focus on other things. Mostly.

"We're going to get this fattened up again," Grace said, rubbing one hand over her arse. "Then I'll enjoy strapping and smacking it as much as you deserve. Right now I'm afraid your bones will poke through."

"Evil shrew," Agnes said, trying to twist around. "What are you touching now? It feels...odd. Is it something the sickness left?"

"Not at all. Don't be afraid, moppet. Be still. It's a mark. Your third mark." Grace traced the marking over each of Agnes's shoulder blades. When Agnes realized what they were, she stilled. *Dear Lord and Lady...*

It was the outline of a pair of angel wings. While it was a fitting third mark, Grace still felt a tightening in her gut. One day her Agnes would be an angel, or pass into the angels' arms, and she would be left alone. No. Not alone. She'd have her son. Which would be enough for awhile. When it wasn't, well, she'd become an empty vessel again, let it all go and go back to Agnes's arms. It would be a life well worth living.

As she let the shadows go so anticipation for all of it could fill her, she couldn't resist. She gave Agnes's pretty arse, diminished though it was, a nice pop, and enjoyed the way Agnes squirmed on her lap, her breasts pressing against Grace's leg. "Just wait until I use a belt on it, hmm? Like that one time Dan threatened to take his belt to you for being contrary? He was teasing you, until he realized it excited you. Did he do it?"

"Yes." Agnes's cheeks pinkened. "He did. And we...well, you know."

Actually, Grace didn't know. While it had piqued Dan's interest and goaded his lust, it had done the same to Grace, so much she hadn't lurked in Agnes's mind to hear her thoughts on it or the results. With the third mark, though, she would be able to see through Agnes's eyes like her own.

She still had her mind open to Agnes, so Agnes saw that information, as well as understood Grace hadn't known what had happened between her and Dan that night. She cleared her throat, adjusting in a casual way that drew Grace's eyes back to her bare bottom, the tempting plump lips between them, glistening with her response.

You little tease... But she held that thought, a painful smile in her heart as Agnes gave her the gift of the memory.

"He wasn't sure of it, at first, but I teased him until he bent me over the kitchen table, lifted my skirts and gave me three healthy whacks. It made him hard as kindling, the way I responded, and he took me right there. Then he wrapped both his arms around me, held me so close I couldn't breathe..."

Oh Dan... Sensual memory gave way to loss and Agnes closed her eyes, pressing her face to Grace's leg. Grace bent over her, playfulness dissipating as she turned Agnes and held her in her lap, giving and receiving comfort. Then Agnes's attention shifted, her fingers moving between them to splay over Grace's stomach.

"Oh, Gracie... You're going to have a son."

The ebullience touched her, but a darker thought did as well, one Grace supposed all mothers faced and feared. She would deliver him into the world, give it the gift of his existence, yet the world might take him from her. She might have to relinquish him to death while she still lived, as Agnes had had to do with her son, far too soon. He was no more than a wisp in her womb, yet the thought alone was enough to paralyze her. Grace's arms tightened around Agnes. She would be there for her servant, and would help her deal with the unimaginable loss Grace understood far better now. The Lord and Lady had given them a gift beyond description to help them both.

Daegan. Daegan Rei.

The name appeared in her mind, along with a frisson of power that lifted the hair on her arms. Agnes raised her head, her senses attuned to that energy wave. "Did the Lord and Lady just..."

"I don't know. They must have. But it fits. It will fit. It means Dark Ghost, but he will bring light back to us. We'll love him, Agnes. Together. You, me and the village will raise him. He'll bring us hope and life again."

"A birth that will bring hope to the world. To our little world." Agnes's eyes sparkled with the brilliance of love, life and loss. "There's no better Yule gift than that."

Doms and Sisters

A vignette featuring characters from the Knights of the Board Room Series.

Originally Posted December 2016

Background: *In* Hostile Takeover, *there was a hint that Lucas had a "sisters" fantasy enjoying Cass and Marcie in a shared erotic BDSM encounter (with Ben's participation of course!). Marcie herself had some pretty explicit fantasies in that regard. This vignette explores that fantasy – for real!*

Part One

Marcie opened eyes swollen from crying. She'd done a lot of that tonight. Her voice was hoarse from screaming, sometimes from the pain, sometimes from the orgasms, sometimes from being held on the edge of a climax so powerful that she'd felt like what's-her-name staked out on the cliffs for the Kraken, the waves pounding her, over and over. Her body was still vibrating with them, like the rhythmic sense of movement after spending a day in the surf. She and Ben had done at the beach a couple months ago, swimming and body surfing at the Outer Banks. Eventually, they'd moved past the surf line so she could twine her limbs around him and be held close in his strong arms, her breasts resting against his chest, his distracting mouth on her throat as they rose and fell over the gentler swells.

"What was her name?" Her voice was slurred.

"Hmm, brat?" Her Master leaned over her, pressing

those same tempting lips to her quivering shoulder.

"That Harry Hamlin movie we watched. The girl staked out on the cliffs. What was her name?"

"Andromeda."

"That's it." She winced as he rubbed salve into the welts he'd left on her ass, back and thighs, but they felt better since he'd immersed her in a hot bath. He'd joined her as he always did, holding her in the cradle of his thighs and arms while the soothing salts and soaps did their work on the marks left from the wrapping and tipping of the cane. She'd moved past the embarrassment she'd initially felt when he'd take her so far down this road that she'd lose control of all bodily functions. She was his. He could do whatever he wished to her, because in session or out, she trusted him absolutely. He terrified her, loved her, punished her and drove her to an edge impossible to describe.

She could wryly joke this was just another night for the two of them, but this had been somewhat different. He'd integrated true punishment into it, a clearing of the slate. When she'd risked her life to help save Max's, the former SEAL and K&A limo driver who'd gotten into a sticky situation with some drug dealers, Ben had promised he'd exact his retribution. He didn't disagree with her helping Max; it was just the principle of the thing. If she was going to risk his property, he was taking his pound of flesh to help her remember the consequences of doing so, so that she didn't do it casually.

There'd also been an additional component to his enthusiasm tonight. She'd recently made her career change official, enrolling in the police academy to become one of New Orleans' finest. Considering a normal night on patrol in New Orleans would routinely put her in harm's way, she might find herself suffering his punishment on a weekly basis. She shivered with desire and dread at the thought.

"If Janet had been okay with it, I would have made Max hold you while I administered that last caning," Ben said grimly. "That's the worst punishment I could have devised for him."

"He never would have stood for it. Probably would have

broken your legs, and I like your legs. He doesn't really get this, between you and me."

"I think he gets it enough, but you're right, it would have torn him apart inside. Which would have been my point. But I'm not that kind of sadist."

Speaking of someone not getting something; or rather, someone who wasn't quite at the level she and Ben were at with each other... She suspected this might be the best time to raise the topic, since they were in mellow space right now. "You know, Lucas's birthday is coming up."

"Yeah. He's going to be one year closer to being dead and less a pain in my ass."

"You love him and wouldn't know what to do without him," she corrected. "I was talking to Cass about what he might want for his birthday."

"All right. We'll talk about that. But not right now." He made it an order, softening it with a stroke of her head, and her aching flesh. "Just drift."

He knew her well. She could spend a couple hours floating on the edge of subspace, dozing in and out of consciousness, and she did so now. When she opened her eyes again, she thought an hour had passed. She was alone on the bed, but he'd stayed where he could see her, at his desk across the room. He wore a T-shirt and a ratty pair of jeans so worn and soft they clung to all the good parts of him. And there really weren't any bad parts to Ben O'Callahan. Well, except the parts a woman would want to be bad.

She knew he'd stayed close partly because he took his responsibility as her Dom seriously; the other part was he didn't like even a wall to block his view of her when they had time together. The first time she'd realized that, it had warmed her deeply. Ever since, it had never failed to elicit the same reaction.

She slid from the bed on weak knees. His lids flickered, so she knew he was aware of her movements. Their bedroom was the size of two rooms now, because he'd removed the non-load-bearing wall between it and the adjacent office area. The bedroom part was dominated by the antique canopy bed that was sturdy as a rooted oak tree. A good thing, since its stability was regularly tested. He'd done the caning when she'd been standing and tied spread-eagle against the footboard frame. If the bed didn't weigh a ton, she might have pushed it right into the wall from how she was jerking against the blows.

One of the two Civil-war era wardrobes in the room held an impressive array of toys, including the wood cane he'd used on her. The bed was hung with sheer drapes that smelled like lavender when the ceiling fan gently turned, as it did now.

The office side had two facing desks with their computers and work-related stuff. It also had a large flat screen, a mini-bar with snacks and drinks, and a recliner chair wide enough for her to curl up at his side when he left the bed as he sometimes did in the middle of the night and watched TV. Sometimes he carried her with him, since she'd refuse to let go, her arms wound around him in the bed. After he settled her next to him, her head on his chest and body folded in his lap, she'd listen to the pleasant drone of the TV as she slept and dreamed.

She didn't think he'd be watching much TV tonight. He slept better when he'd worn her out like this. While there were those even inside their world who would never comprehend how taking a pound of flesh from the woman he loved helped exorcise his demons, or how it fulfilled and restored her to help him find that center, he and she did, and that was all that mattered. It wouldn't have worked if she didn't crave every blow, every punishment, as much as she craved his tenderness afterward, all part of the aftercare he gave her on every level—physical, emotional, spiritual. She had her own demons that needed to be exorcised at the end of his lash, cane, hand...whatever he thought would work best. He could make vicious use of kitchen implements and then prepare her a dinner with them equal to what was offered by a five-star restaurant.

The world saw a cocky lawyer, a dangerous shark who would eviscerate his opponents without mercy in business and in defense of his friends, and those things were real and true. As real and true as what lay beneath that.

She assumed they were still in scene protocol, for he'd

not yet spoken the words that released her from it, so she came and knelt by him. As she waited, she studied his bare feet, braced on the wood slat beneath his desk. After about five minutes, he spoke, not looking away from his computer screen. "What is it, brat?"

"I'd like to wear one of your shirts."

"Which one?"

"The one you're wearing now," she said, a tiny smile touching her face as she kept her head bowed. It was a T-shirt she'd bought him at the last Mardi Gras, a trio of brown and gold skeleton musicians playing their saxophones. The shirt was an off-white color that molded to his powerful upper body in a pleasing way. However, she wanted to actually see the pectorals covered in a light mat of gleaming dark hair, the sectioned abs, the ripple of muscle as he moved. She also wanted the smell and heat of his skin against her.

He sighed. "I'm feeling shy. What's your second choice?"

She glanced toward the second wardrobe, where the dress shirt he'd worn for work was hooked on the top of the door next to his silk tie. He'd looped that tie around her throat once or twice tonight, holding her life in his big hands, his green eyes on her face as she experienced the euphoria of that precisely measured breath restriction. "I want to wear that one."

"The one I wore today? That I sweated in during that conference call with Mitchener Electronics?"

"You never sweat. You had them by the balls before they even called."

He grinned, though his eyes remained on his work. "Stroking your Dom's ego. Okay, for that you can wear the shirt."

She rose and went to the wardrobe, rising onto her toes to pull it down. As she slipped it on, she wrapped it around herself, burrowing her nose in it, savoring the feel of it holding her the way he did. She loved his scent, and imagined the fibers still held the heat of his body. Or maybe it was that her flesh still held *his* heat, and the shirt insulated and enhanced it.

"Don't button it."

Looking up, she saw he was watching her, and he'd pushed the laptop halfway closed. The flickering light praised the line of his jaw, his intent green eyes and firm mouth, his thick dark hair, tousled in that artful way a handsome man accomplished so effortlessly. "Come here," he said.

As she returned to him, he shifted around on his chair to bring her between his knees. His gaze passed over the visible curves of her generous breasts, her nipples against the loose fabric of the open shirt, then down to her thighs and the cleft of her sex. He slid his hands over her throat and into her abundance of hair. "God, you're beautiful," he murmured. "End of protocol."

She didn't have to be told twice. She climbed up and squatted on his lap like a frog, her feet braced on either side of his thighs in the roomy office chair. He kept studying her body, touching the new marks he'd put upon her. The wraps across her thighs and stomach were evident in thin red lines. He stopped on a bruise over her hip.

"Who did this?"

She smiled. "How do you do that? Even when you mark me all over, you always know the ones you haven't put there."

"I notice everything about you. I know what's mine." His gaze lingered on the bruise, his fingers treating it with care. "You haven't answered the question."

"That one was all me. I didn't keep my guard up during sparring and Billy landed a lucky blow."

"So Billy is responsible," Ben said with a lazy drawl.

"No, I am. You can't cut up Billy's body and leave it in a swamp. He's a good teacher."

"He's your sparring coach?"

"Yeah." She straightened with pride. "He says he's afraid to let me spar with the other guys. Afraid I'll hurt them and they'll get discouraged."

Ben chuckled, as she'd hoped he would. While he was getting better about her attendance at the police academy, it didn't take much for it to set him off. He was still so not on board with it. He'd had a hard enough time with some of her more risky ventures in corporate investigations. But for now, perhaps responding to her fervent mental wish that they not get into it again tonight, he let it go. Or rather, chose another tactic.

"What do they think about you showing up in the McLaren for class?"

She sniffed at him. "They're totally fine with it. You're not getting that car back."

"It was just a question." He lifted his hands, giving her an innocent look, probably the only thing in life at which he failed consistently, though it always made her laugh. "I merely wondered what the other rookies thought."

"Oh, they pick at me, of course. Gives me a reason to outshoot them in range practice, since Billy won't let me beat on them. When I outshoot them, the ones who are mean-spirited about it pretty much shut up."

Ben shifted, adjusting her so she sat on his lap and straddled him, her feet dangling out under either chair arm as he cupped his hands over her buttocks and held her. "Aren't you worried about getting ripped about being a dirty cop?"

"Not the least. For one thing, you tell me all the time I'm a dirty girl." She dimpled. "I also tell them I have an obscenely wealthy husband, and an even more obscenely wealthy brother-in-law and three adopted uncles."

"I bet they wonder why the hell you want to be a police officer."

"Maybe the ones who're in it for the paycheck and benefits, because it's better than most job opportunities they have. But I think even they have to possess a certain level of calling to stick with it. You're not paid enough for the abuse. So those who've figured out I'm there because I want to be, they get it. They still have to razz me about the car, though. They're cops."

"Yeah." Ben followed the curve of her breast inside the folds of the shirt. His thumb slid over her navel piercing. "You know I do understand how you feel about it, Marcie. Sometimes."

"I know you do. And I know how hard this is for you." Her tone softened. "I'm grateful for every day you're trying to deal with it. If it turns out...if it turns out to be too hard,

I'll figure out something else to do."

His eyes lifted to meet hers, his mouth tightening. "You want this, though."

"There are other ways I can help people. Less dangerous ways."

"Yeah. There are." He didn't say anything, and she felt that familiar sinking feeling, anticipating him listing out those options. Instead, he shook his head. "But there are very few people who want to do what you want to do, who have the integrity and grit to do it the right way and make a career of it. You do. I'm likely to be a bastard about it way too often, but as long as it's what you want, I'm not going to tell you no."

"Not going to pull the 'I'm your Master and I forbid it' card?" She attempted to keep it light, because his words tattooed themselves on her heart and made her want to become inadvisably mushy.

"You and I may be way more 24/7 than everyone else, except maybe Rachel and Jon, and I may come off heavy-handed on things that should be your call..."

"I know how to stand up for myself when you try to bully me."

His lips quirked. "Yes, you do. Don't interrupt me, or I'll smack your very tender ass. I'm clear on what things are your choice, and when I need to be the supportive husband. Even if I'm still working on my learning curve."

"I think you're doing brilliantly." Hoping to leave it on a positive note, she opted for a subject change. "You remember me mentioning Lucas's birthday is coming up?"

"Yeah. I could tell that was on your mind."

"We were thinking..."

He lifted a brow. "We?"

"Cass and I. She wants to do Lucas's sisters fantasy."

That stopped Ben's idle stroking of her breast. His head came up as his fingers stilled. "When did this discussion happen?"

"We were having lunch earlier in the week and she sort of brought it up."

"In what way? Like she's talked herself into it?" The way Ben measured her expression, Marcie knew he'd weigh every word she spoke next, but that was what she wanted. She was pretty sure that Cass was ready, but if Ben was persuaded by what she'd learned from Cass, he could convince Lucas. This wouldn't work unless Cass was in the right mindset, by her Dom's standards of protection and love for her.

"For the longest time, she's said he'd have to settle for it being one of his perverted dreams." She managed a smile. "But as time's gone on and we've all done more with our Masters, and with each other, she's started to be more comfortable with trying new stuff. More than that. I think she's not only ready... she's curious."

"You had some pretty detailed fantasies about Lucas yourself in the same context. At least until you became mine and I drove out all fantasies of any other men but me."

"Of course, Master," she said demurely, and whimpered comically as he pinched her indeed very sore ass.

"Has she told him?"

"No." Marcie shook her head. "She feels like the right thing...the right etiquette, so to speak, is to have you present it to Lucas first."

"Because he might need a little bit of prying to open his mind to the possibility, and that's better coming from another Dom?"

At his steady look, she shrugged. "That, and because she expects he would want to control how it was executed. I know that would work better for her, too, as a sub. She doesn't want to feel like she's taking control of or directing it, if that makes sense.""

"Yeah. It does." Ben pursed his lips. "Okay. I'll talk to him about it."

"You agree with me, that Cass is ready?" Marcie felt a flutter of surprise at his ready agreement, and a little rebound trepidation. What if she'd been too confident? Or Ben trusted her opinion too much? *Don't be an idiot*, she admonished herself.

"I trust your judgment, particularly when it comes to Cass," he said, twining his fingers around a lock of her hair and tugging. "Sounds like she's ready enough to initiate the discussion. And Lucas won't let her get away with it being all third party anyway. He'll talk about it with her first, you know that. So don't start worrying about how it will turn out because you think it'll be your fault for getting this started." He touched her nose reprovingly and she wrinkled it at him. "We leave the final decision to him and her. But if I do this mediation thing, there will be a cost."

"You want me to have *Property of Ben O'Callahan* tattooed on my ass."

His lips quirked. "Not at all. I'm not that much of a Neanderthal."

"Yeah. Actually you are. Did I mention cavemen give me the hots?" She laughed, squirming as he gave her another pinch. "So it's not a tattoo. What is it?"

He paused. "You know how we've been donating to that Catholic mission in Mexico?"

"Father Dominic's place. Father Dom." She dimpled. "I have a very difficult time saying that with a straight face. I'm going to Hell."

"Probably, but not for the reason you think. You aren't allowed to go anywhere I can't go, and I'm fairly certain Heaven has a warrant out to send me straight down if I show up at those Golden Gates."

"I believe that's Pearly Gates, and no, they don't." She softened. "I'm pretty sure God is a woman, and She knows all about you. She won't turn you away. Why did you bring up the Father?"

"Last time we went to check on the operations in Mexico, we played poker with him a couple nights. Man is a card hustler. Doubled his donations that night. Anyhow, I got to talking to him after one of the games, and..."

Leaning forward, Ben kept one arm around her to hold her close as he fished in his desk drawer. "I had him bless this. For you."

It was a St. Jude's medal on a slim chain, something she could wear under her uniform.

"Ben," she said softly, taking it. While she believed him when he said he wouldn't always be able to make this decision easy on her, this gift said he accepted her choice. In his typical way, he'd done something momentous with a small gesture. Also typical for her husband, she was sure he didn't want to make a big deal of it.

"They bless things for a Catholic who's never activated his member card?" she said in a teasing voice, though her throat was tight with unspoken emotion.

"Well, I went to confession and took the sacrament, and lightning didn't bring the church down, so he owed me. Though my confession may have traumatized him for life."

Her gaze flickered up to him, startled. He'd seemed more relaxed this week, and now she wondered if that was the cause. She didn't question it, sensing whatever had motivated him to do this was something he wasn't going to discuss. Instead, she slid her arms around him and held him so close he might have had trouble breathing if he wasn't so strong. She pressed her lips to his temple. "Thank you, Ben. This means so much to me. I love you. More and more every day, and I didn't think I could love you more without my heart exploding."

He cupped her head and brushed his mouth against hers. "Same goes, brat."

Part Two

Ben paused at the half open door to Lucas's office. Their CFO was frowning at his computer screen, an arc of papers fanned out on his desk and the nearby table. A quick glance at the contents showed charts, graphs, and endless rows of numbers. Things Ben understood well enough to be thankful his job was navigating the legal challenges, quagmires and valleys of an operation their size. He'd rather deal with all that than even one set of the numbers on Lucas's screen. But they each had their niche.

Well, okay, Jon might have a wider range. Boy genius could probably step into any one of their shoes. If Ben went MIA, he wouldn't be surprised if Jon suddenly remembered, "Oh, yeah, I do have a law degree. Let me just pull that out of my ass and dust it off."

As Ben grinned mentally at that, he re-thought his assumption. Jon could step into any of their shoes except maybe Matt's. Lucas was the most capable of handling

Matt's job if needed, but Lucas probably didn't want to think about that any more than Ben wanted to think about doing Lucas's job.

Matt was the captain of the K&A ship. They could all take a temporary turn at the wheel when he needed it, like when Savannah had nearly died during childbirth. Matt had taken a month at home for her convalescence and to personally help care for her and their baby, no matter the top-notch nanny they kept on staff. However, when push came to shove, they all admitted without shame and with no little pride that he was *the* captain they most wanted at the helm.

But Ben would trust his life, his heart and soul, to any of their five-man team. And he knew that bond, all the different, complicated layers of it, was the ultimate reason why Cass had come to Marcie, and Marcie had come to him, to talk to Lucas.

Their women...there weren't words to describe what each of their wives meant to them. And yeah, their Doms were all way too protective, but the independence and strength of those women kept that protectiveness from moving over the line into 1950s meets medieval times. As in, stay at home in the kitchen and the bedroom while surrounded by a fortress wall, fifty armed clones of Max, and a moat populated by the unfettered savagery of a...well.

Ben guessed he'd have to own the dragon part of the metaphor. He'd evolved so that civility was a more comfortable fit for him, rather than an uncomfortable coat he'd shaped into Armani style with tremendous effort, but the dragon was there to be called if needed.

But the bond between the men ironically meant they were each other's best choice to help one of them see when he had to let his lady cross that line and not be an asshole about it. They could provide one another the necessary perspective to look past the concerns about her physical wellbeing to see when it was something good for her, something she needed as much as wanted. Life was about way more than staying safe.

Yeah, easy for him to say in this situation with Lucas and Cass. It was still a work in progress for him and Marcie on the whole being-a-cop thing. Her heading out the door each day to rub elbows with the dangerous and unpredictable underbelly of New Orleans was something that initially had had one response from him. That savage side had thrown off the suit to stand naked, blood-stained and roaring under a full moon: *No and hell no.*

The guys had talked him down. They understood, in a way Marcie and the other women never could, no fault to it, how it felt to stand back and let one of their wives step into harm's way. He and Marcie had had some pretty bad fights over it, Marcie's stubbornness and his Irish temper a volatile mix when they weren't in agreement. But those fights had put it all out there, and the subsequent heart-to-heart talks with each of the guys had helped. Which they reinforced daily with their random comments and banter that expressed understanding and the "hey, don't be a prick to her about this", slap-upside-the-head, kind of support.

He'd also talked at length with a friend of their inner circle, Leland Keller, who was on the Baton Rouge police force. Leland's submissive and love of his life, Celeste Lewis, regularly walked the front lines as a crime beat reporter there. She was also one of Marcie's close friends.

Ben would never like it, but he'd finally meant what he'd said to her last night. If it was what she needed to do to be happy and complete, it was part of the whole husband-Master job to support her. He remembered the way Marcie had dimpled and glowed, the first time she'd been introduced as his wife at their wedding. She might not realize it, and he'd never admit it to anyone—though Jon probably already knew, because he knew every damn thing in the universe—but he felt the same damn kick when she or anyone else called him her husband, or even when he thought about it in random moments. It was a damn miracle. He'd never thought he'd be anyone's husband, let alone to the most wonderful woman and submissive he craved above all others.

So he'd learn to be a cop's spouse. As long as that spouse understood if anyone ever did her serious damage or... He couldn't go further than that, because as soon as the image of a uniformed sergeant or captain coming to his door with that somber look entered his head, he shut down. Needless to say, they'd never find that perp. He'd be dead in the most vicious way imaginable, making the work of Dahmer or TV's Dexter look like clean and harmless fun in the Willy Wonka bubble chamber.

He suspected that was why, when she was filling out her paperwork, Marcie had listed two emergency contact names in the event she fell in the line of duty. In typical Marcie fashion, she'd written it frankly:

In case of serious or life threatening injury, contact Ben O'Callahan, husband.

In case I am killed in the line of duty, contact Matt Kensington. He is to be told FIRST, and will inform my husband.

Maybe the wives did understand things better than they gave them credit for.

But he was digressing onto his personal shit. In this case, Ben believed Cass's decision to cross a line was good for Lucas as her Master, as well as Cass's growth as his sub.

Marcie was Ben's perfect match in the Dom/sub area, but if something happened tomorrow where she physically couldn't handle those demands, he'd step and scale back however she needed to find a mutually pleasurable ground. Love was the common denominator that decided everything else. Which was kind of Cass's point in this, right?

Lucas was entirely satisfied with everything and anything Cass could give him. He'd never been the hardcore player that Ben was. But something Ben's perspective gave him that maybe Lucas's didn't was that, as the bond between Dom and sub grew, sometimes that made other levels not only possible but desirable. Trust allowed them the pleasure of exploring new territory, if they both wanted that. Ben knew for sure Lucas had that capacity within him. He'd seen the guy play before he ever met Cass. If Lucas agreed Cass was ready for it, Ben was all about having a front row seat to watch Cass go deeper into that world and learn more about her husband's capabilities as a Dom—and seeing her enjoy the surprise of it.

He rapped on Lucas's door, drawing the man's attention

from that jungle of numbers. "Hey. Looks like you're doing nothing important and have your thumb up your ass as usual. Got five minutes for something not work-related?"

"You know, if my fondest hopes are realized and the legal system is overhauled so we go back to a handshake to honor deals, you will be superfluous," Lucas informed him. "Matt will have to find you work in the mailroom."

"Naw. I'll apply to be your secretary. Easiest gig in this place, if I can put up with the ass pinching and having to wear short skirts to feed your misogyny."

"Uh-huh. I'll tell Beatrice you said that. She's as much responsible for the financial success of this place as I am."

"I'll tell Matt to give her half your salary then." Taking the banter as consent that Lucas had a few minutes, Ben strolled in, moving to take one of the chairs in front of his desk and balance his ankle on his opposite knee. Lucas finished typing whatever he needed to reach a good stopping place and sat back.

"What's up?"

No reason not to get right into it. "Your lady wants to give you something special for your birthday."

Lucas lifted a brow. "Oh? And are you risking her wrath to spoil the surprise? You know she was plotting to kill you just last week.'"

"That was a misunderstanding. Nate wanted to know how much you tip a stripper versus a lap dancer."

"He's barely hit double digits in age," Lucas pointed out.

"He wanted to be prepared. I figured Cass would be thrilled that he wants to see hardworking women properly paid for their work. Let's not get side tracked. You know your sisters fantasy? She wants to give you that."

It was always fun to take Lucas off guard, since it didn't happen a hell of a lot. But the lifted brow immediately drew down to meet the other in a forbidding line, and Lucas's silver eyes steeled. "No. I know her limits, and she's not comfortable with that. If Marcie pressured her in that direction when they were discussing birthday ideas—"

Ben's amusement disappeared. He held up a hand. "Hey. My girl isn't like that, and you know better. Even if she was, Cass's backbone is as rigid as some of those corsets she wore when you first met her. She's not going to let her little sister push her into the wrong kind of session with her Master, even if he wasn't sharp enough to catch her trying to do something she shouldn't in some misguided attempt to please him. And this isn't that, by the way."

Lucas stared at him, but then his penetrating look was replaced by something unexpected. Regret and some frustration—with himself. He shook his head, sitting back. "You're right. That was undeserved to Marcie and Cass."

When Lucas rubbed a hand over his face, Ben recognized just how hard the guy had been working of late. It might be time to get him not only an additional admin, but a couple more accounting managers to take some of his load for this detailed shit. He was a control freak; they all were, which was why sometimes it was necessary to put a bug in Matt's ear to force one of them to let go of the drudge work. He made a note to do that, even if he caught shit from Lucas. Over the past couple years, the guy had gone from dividing most his time between working for K&A and pursuing his amateur cycling, to being a husband to Cass and a guardian for her four younger siblings, three of who were still teenagers and living at home. He'd incorporated those large responsibilities without visibly missing a step, but he'd had to increase the pace. Even while continuing to be a supportive part of their extended family network.

Ben fondly recalled a recent memory of his friend taking Matt and Savannah's daughter for a bike ride, little Angelique facing backwards in her baby seat, tiny head dwarfed by the helmet, her arms outstretched and mouth open, tasting the wind as Lucas pedaled.

He just made handling all those responsibilities look so effortless, sometimes even those closest to him could miss that he was getting winded. Maybe that was part of what had motivated this for Cass, to get him to slow down and change gears. She might also have been driven by what Lucas was explaining now.

"Cass has been mourning Jeremy hard these past few months," Lucas said. "That second-wave grief crap that hits just when you think you're getting past it. I think she feels guilty, like she's somehow been grieving too long, as if somehow me dealing with that is a burden."

Ben shook his head. "She has a generous heart, but that's wrong thinking. Hope you've set her straight."

"Several times, but I've obviously gotten a little hypervigilant if I jumped to such a bullshit assumption about her and Marcie." Lucas's expression sharpened as he connected the dots he'd missed at the outset. It had only taken him two minutes to catch up, so Ben wouldn't fault him on it. "Why are you coming to me about this?"

"Because Cass talked about it with Marcie. She asked her to bring it to me so, if I was convinced, I could convince you this is a shared gift, something she wants as much as she wants to give it to you. Marcie is as aware of Cass's grief as you are, because you two are closest to her. If Cass was doing what you're worried about, Marcie would have caught it just as quickly, and defused it without bringing it to me. Marcie has a radar for bullshit like a bloodhound."

As he well knew. When they were first getting together, she'd seen through every wall he'd thrown up to persuade her he didn't want her, and his insistence that she was misreading his signals. Looking back now, he couldn't believe he'd been such an idiot, denying himself the thing that would save his soul. In fairness, it was because he was sure he would taint hers. But it had worked out because Marcie finally convinced him that she loved and needed him as much as he needed her.

While it would be Lucas's privilege to get to the bottom of all his submissive's thinking on it before anything happened, Ben suspected the same foundation of logic was at work here. If Cass wanted Lucas to have something she'd seemed adamantly against for so long, something had changed for her. Something to make her want it now.

Ben shared that perspective with Lucas. Lucas's countenance became more thoughtful. "So why didn't Marcie come to me directly about this?"

"I think your brain is still caught up in these numbers, so I'm going to sit here for a minute and let you think it through. But here's a hint. This isn't about Nate having a problem with algebra."

Lucas's well-defined jaw eased as he allowed himself a wry smile. "If Marcie had come to me with this, it wouldn't be as my sister-in-law. It's a sub coming to a Dom."

"Amazing. He can be taught. She would never have that kind of conversation with you. She also knew if I believed her, you would believe me, because we evaluate things differently when it's coming from our submissives, versus our wives." Ben shifted, putting the other ankle on the opposite knee. "The other reason she didn't come to you—dumbass—is that your sister fantasy involves my woman. If she initiated a conversation with you about that, I would beat her ass. And not in a way she would enjoy."

"Is that even possible? Cause short of you using a paddle embedded with barbed fishing hooks, I'm not seeing her having a problem with any—"

Ben bared his teeth in a feral grin. "Shut up. What about it? You want to think about it, or you want to put the wheels in motion?"

"I'm still missing a piece here." Lucas folded his arms on the desk and leaned forward. "And that's how you and Marcie feel about it. I expect it wouldn't have reached me if Marcie wasn't comfortable with it, because Cass can read her sister, too. But what about you? You cool with this?"

"You've nursed this fantasy forever about eating both sisters' pussies in the same room at damn near at the same time. Since you're a bitch to buy for because you go out and purchase anything you want before we can do it, this saves me some birthday shopping."

"Yeah. Asshole. Give me a serious answer."

Ben leaned back in the chair, propping his shoe on the edge of Lucas's desk before meeting the other man's eyes. "You're my brother," he said simply. "Marcie and I want to help Cass give you this gift. I trust you with Marcie's wellbeing without reservation. Hell, probably more than I trust myself with her. I hope you know you can trust me with Cass."

"I do." A muscle flexed in Lucas's jaw. "Okay. I'll talk to Cass and get this straight between the two of us. Then I'll let you know."

"Got it." Ben rose. "That Ritz-Carlton suite might be a pretty sweet setting for it. You know Cass loves the terrace overlooking the river and the French Quarter. Me and Marcie could take a suite across the hall and join you guys when you're ready, but give you privacy afterward if you want. Though that king would sleep four easy enough."

"I will not spoon with you, even if you beg," Lucas said.

"I'm crushed. Seriously, let me know. We'll have some planning to do if it's a go. I want details about what you have in mind to do with two beautiful women at your feet for the entire night."

"Sure you have to be there?" Lucas chuckled as Ben shot him an appropriately rude gesture at the door.

"Long fall from that terrace, Bicycle-Boy. Then I'd have two beautiful women at *my* feet for the rest of the night. You know Cass is as practical as you are about money. She wouldn't want to call in the law until we at least got a night's worth out of the suite. And drank all the complimentary champagne."

As the lawyer took his leave, Lucas turned back to his screen, still grinning. Then he sobered. For a few minutes, the columns in front of him were the last thing on his mind as he put together what he wanted to do next. He made a quick adjustment on his shared calendar so Beatrice would know he'd be going out for lunch today.

He needed to have a heart-to-heart with his submissive, and that was something best done on a lunch break, rather than this evening when they'd have the mid-week needs of three teenagers hitting them the moment they hit the door.

But the Ritz-Carlton suite was a decent idea. He shot off a note to the head manager at the hotel, to put the wheels in motion. When he at last started working on the numbers again, his mind had a pleasant side distraction—what he planned to have for lunch.

Part Three

Cass chose to work through noon, but she sent her administrative assistant out to enjoy the late fall weather, since New Orleans didn't have many sunny days that didn't come hand-in-hand with oppressive humidity. Nell had already teased her by shooting her a quick selfie from the overlook of Jackson Square, her hair fluttering in the breeze, the Mississippi behind her. Bitch.

Cass should have heard her visitor approach, but within seconds of setting aside her phone, she was back in a deep analysis of the report on her screen. However, it didn't take too long for a prickling on her nape to tell her she wasn't alone. The exotic, masculine fragrance of her husband's aftershave confirmed it. His fingers tunneled in her hair, an expected caress, but she gasped as he gripped and pulled her head back in one decisive, heart-stopping move that was pure Master, giving her no time to look at him. His lips pressed against her throat as her fingers slid off her keyboard to grip the edge of her desk. She'd slipped off her heels and her toes, clad in thin stockings, curled into the carpet.

He used teeth as he slid his other hand up from her waist to cup her breast and explore. Heat swept through her core, a trembling breath whispering out from between her parted lips. "Did I give you permission to wear this today?" he said.

She shook her head. They didn't really do a lot of the 24/7 stuff, like him telling her what she could wear to work, but she understood why he'd asked. It had been awhile since she'd donned a corset beneath her work clothes. Her nails dug into the wood veneer as he bit her throat harder, tracing her pulsing carotid with his clever tongue. Oh-so-lightly, he brushed her nipple through the thin satin cup of the corset.

"Hmm." Straightening, he moved to her office door, closed and locked it. Leaning against it, he looked at her. *That* kind of look.

He'd stopped by plenty of times to take her to lunch, or to give her a heated but friendly and quick hello kiss, ways to touch base with one another. On a normal day, they were extraordinarily busy, but she did the same with him when she could, their offices only a short distance from each other. She made the time, not because it was the proper, recommended thing to do, some pop-shrink yet very valid advice about prioritizing time for your marriage. They did it because they wanted and needed to see each other as often as it could be managed. Silly as it might sound, when she looked at him, the Christina Perri song about waiting a thousand years for him always rang true. She wasn't anywhere near that age, but the road to get to him had at times seemed endless.

When she'd first seen him in an office environment, he'd been wearing an outfit much like he wore today. Expensive gray suit, silver tie and crisp white dress shirt with the proper length of cuffs edging out from beneath the jacket sleeves. His aftershave combined with his heated male smell had made her imagine an Egyptian prince, never mind the ethnic discrepancy that his streaked blond hair and silver-gray eyes tossed into that analogy. Something about his singular intensity, the steady gaze, the way he moved his lean and powerful body, had made her imagine him walking the halls of an ancient palace. He'd be wearing a silk tunic, and his dark, kohl-rimmed eyes would assess everyone he saw. The way he seemed to be assessing her now, which gave her the desire to do what any concubine in the hallways would do who saw their prince. Kneel, and wait for his attention.

In so many aspects of their lives, they were partners. They shared guardianship of her siblings, and made many decisions related to them. They had arguments, too, like any other husband and wife. Since she was a professional negotiator, he claimed it was almost impossible to win a fight with her. But when he gazed at her with the unsmiling, steady look he had now, there was no question who held the upper hand. When he was like this, she wanted him to have it. But she felt a fluttering too, sensing there was more to this visit than just the pleasurable destruction of her work-related concentration.

"Let me see it," he said softly. "All of it."

Everything in her wanted to obey. With barely any hesitation, she tucked her feet back into her shoes and rose, her fingers already slipping the buttons of her blouse. As she shrugged it off her shoulders, she moved around the desk and unzipped the skirt, letting it pool around her feet.

Since she was decently tall, she'd be able to meet his eyes, but even in heels he still had her by a few inches.

He came to her now, extending his hand palm up. She laid hers in it and used his grip to step out of the circle her skirt had formed.

She wore thigh-high stockings in light pink lace. The corset was white with touches of pink ribbon, but since it was designed to go under clothing, there was little embellishment. Just satin and boning that clung to her curves, nipped in her waist and molded over her hips, the front forming a point over above her mons, the back edged with a ribbon trim over her buttocks.

He moved around her, one hand settling at her waist. His breath was on her bare shoulder blades as he slid his other fingers into the laces tied at the small of her back and twisted, eliciting another gasp from between her moist lips.

"What was our rule about you wearing one of these?" His voice was mild, but the coolness beneath sent a shiver up her spine. She was at work, but he'd timed his arrival well, knowing how likely it was she'd work through lunch and send Nell off without her.

"If I wear one, you put it on me."

"Yes. Why?"

Now he was untying the laces, loosening, adjusting, his fingers awakening need wherever he touched. His thumbs slid over the rise of her backside in the silky panties she wore with the corset.

"Because... the hold of it, you lacing me into it, is a reminder of who holds me." Whenever she needed it, however she needed to be held.

"And?" he queried pleasantly.

She was stumped. "I don't—"

"Because I do this better, sweetheart," he said, pulling the laces taut in one smooth movement.

It constricted the corset's hold more than she could do it, enough to emphasize both his points. Arousal, already simmering, flared hot. And he knew that, too.

He eased her down to her elbows on the desk and nudged at her ankle with one polished dress shoe. Desire and trepidation made her stomach quake. His belt was his preferred tool for reminding her of the rules, and she loved it as much as she sometimes quaked at how effectively he wielded it. But that wasn't what he had in mind.

"Spread your legs and lift that beautiful ass, Cassie. I haven't had my lunch, and I'm in the mood for my favorite meal. What is it?"

Sometimes she stumbled over the word, but today she managed it in a breathless whisper. "My pussy."

"Mm-hm." He slid his thumbs under the delicate straps of her underwear and took them down to her thighs, so she felt the elastic stretch against them. Clasping the cloth between her legs, he rubbed his fingers over the cotton crotch.

"Already getting my lunch heated for me, I see. Here. I think you'll need this. Open up."

He'd rolled his handkerchief into a tight wad he inserted into her mouth, so she could bite down on it. It would muffle the sounds he would undoubtedly wrest from her. Self-control wasn't an option with him. All control was his.

Dropping to one knee behind her, he put his strong hands on her upper thighs and buttocks and settled to it. She'd seen him savor a seven-course meal at a diamond-rated restaurant. He gave the same time and attention to savoring her pussy. Probably more. There was no rush for him when he did this. Oral sex wasn't a bridge to fucking her, though that often happened afterward. He treated her cunt like a multi-city tour. Every inch was a destination, and he didn't rush even one of them.

"Oh...God..." The guttural, reverent moan was absorbed by the handkerchief, but she knew he heard it. Her labia was silken smooth, every nerve ending sensitive to his mouth. Earlier in their relationship, he'd given himself the pleasure of shaving her thoroughly and frequently, but eventually he'd paid for the laser treatment that had left her so nicely silken for his mouth whenever he wanted to take a taste.

He nibbled at her clit and labia, drew endless patterns on them with his tongue, sucked lightly, sucked hard, bit. When he finally thrust into her with his tongue, the indications he was enjoying his meal, the right amount of wet and animal sounds, made her lose her mind. He gripped her buttocks in hard hands, pushing her onto her toes to keep her from the uncontrollable grinding against his mouth and face. Her involuntary response was something he enjoyed at the right moment, but now he obviously wanted her to absorb a barrage of feeling. His jaw had just the right amount of sandpaper feel to drive her pleasure higher.

She was shuddering as he held her on that cusp and kept her there, no matter how much she begged through the handkerchief. Then, when her mind was fragmenting, he rose and loomed over her. Seizing her hair, he yanked her head back, even rougher than before. Her startled noise came out almost against his lips, an inch from hers.

"You want to give me my sisters fantasy," he said. "But you had Marcie ask Ben to talk to me about it. Why? Why not ask me straight out?"

She might be the professional negotiator, but he was no slouch at knowing the exact moment to pose a question and demand its answer, before she had time to raise any defenses.

"I...I didn't know how to ask you. To convince you that...I wanted it. That I wasn't just...being nice."

He chuckled darkly. She found she couldn't meet his piercing hawk's gaze, and so kept her eyes down. He seemed fine with that. When he put her back down on her elbows on the desk, she thought he was going to tease her further. She wasn't expecting what he did next, but he was right. She was already plenty wet and ready for it.

Opening his slacks, he palmed her buttock and slammed his cock into her.

It wrenched a raw cry from her throat, a sound disrupted when he clenched his fist in her hair and pulled her head back again, his other hand holding her fast at the hip, impaling her ruthlessly upon him. "Not entirely the truth," he whispered silkily in her ear. "You know how I react when you lie."

"Not lie." God. The way he'd tightened the corset, his ruthless taking now, was making her breathless.

"Pretty much a lie. Now I'll fuck you in a way that

reminds you that you tell your Master only the truth. Always."

"I always tell..." The attempted defense was lost, because he began to thrust into her, shoving her pelvis against the desk, lifting her heels out of her shoes, keeping his hold on her hair so her every muscle strained and arched; every nerve ending yearned and ached.

The climax rose as fast as a storm wave, and she was screaming into the cloth gag as her clit hit the side of the desk with every shove of his body. His cock was a thick demand filling her up, stretching her, rubbing all the right places inside that made it impossible for her to hold anything back from him. He took her over that dizzying cliff, yet held her as she fell, as he spilled his seed in her.

He took her even farther than she thought possible. But he always did.

When he slowed, she was vibrating like an instrument that didn't want to stop playing. He felt it, continuing to move inside her, keeping her body humming. Eventually, he removed the handkerchief, holding her head back against his shoulder with a gentle hand cupping her jaw. She nuzzled it, putting her mouth against his heated shoulder through the thin dress shirt. She'd leave lipstick on it, but that was okay. Wouldn't be the first or the last time, God bless his dry cleaner.

"Can I—" she whispered.

"No. Not right now, though you're generous to offer." At last easing out of her quivering folds, he bent and picked up her skirt, directing her to hold onto his shoulder as she stepped into it, still wearing her heels. Then he slid the blouse onto her shoulders and began to button it for her, his fingers caressing.

"Tell me, Cassie. Tell me why you went to Marcie instead of to me. You knew I wouldn't do this without talking to you first about it."

When she looked down, flushing, he put his hands on her shoulders. "Look at me, sweetheart."

She did, and his gray eyes, still heated with lust, held other qualities as well. Things that said she would tell him everything, not just because he was that relentless, but because she knew he was right. She needed to say the words to him.

"I need to know this is something you want," he added quietly. "I know that's part of why you talked to Marcie, and I'm glad you already know it's not a birthday present to me if it's not something you want. But to fully believe that you desire this, I need to understand what's changed to make that true."

"Can I..." She spread her fingers out on his chest and gave a helpless little laugh. "Can I look down while I tell you? It's difficult to say when I'm looking into your eyes. You're distracting."

His firm lips curved. "I'll let you get away with it for a moment."

She focused on his tie, the silk of which she'd felt slide between her shoulder blades and the top of her spine when he'd been fucking her.

"There was a time when I thought I would never want to do that kind of fantasy. But things have evolved between you and me...between all of us. There was that place we went with Savannah and Matt in the Caribbean, where it was 24/7 for her and Matt, and most of the others dabbled, going a little further than usual. And when I'm around the other wives, the stories we talk about...they interest me. Sometimes they make me want...more."

He touched her face, and she heard his amusement. "You know we've given serious thought to bugging those female get-togethers. Though we figure that Janet and Dana sweep for recorders ahead of time."

She smiled and curled her fingers in his tie. "Somewhere along the way, I lost my reservations about certain things and, what you've said about that fantasy of yours, it keeps coming back to me as...a turning point of sorts. Not everything I've seen the others do are things I'd want to do, though I like watching them. But knowing you have that fantasy, and thinking about it, I guess I've become...possessive about it. It's a fantasy only I can give you."

His fingers slid down the laced back of the corset to play in the ties in that diverting way of his, encouraging her to continue. She cleared her throat. "It arouses me to think how turned on you'll get, having me and my sister, with you and Ben. Helpless to the two Doms we love...and I trust you to understand the boundaries I wouldn't want to cross."

"Always." His voice was rough, telling her he was pleased with what she was saying—and affected by it, in the right way. "And if ever I missed a line, I'd want you to speak up and tell me immediately. I believe what you're saying to me, but I need to ask. Marcie is so extreme with Ben. Is any part of this because you're worried you need to up your game to keep me interested?"

"No." Her head came up, and for this she had no trouble meeting his eyes. The certainty with which she said it eased the tightness of his mouth. "No," she repeated. Then she bit her lip. "You need to understand all of it, I guess, so you won't worry about anything like that."

"I guess I will," he said after a significant pause.

She winced. "Especially now that I've brought it up. Can't believe I held my own with you on that first negotiation we did."

"Well, we had some professional distance then. If it makes you feel better, you've kicked my ass more than a few times on arguments we've had since. Just not arguments that let me get this close to you."

"Ah, you tipped me off to your advantage. I'll remember that. Keep you at knife point distance if I want to win." She smiled, though, as he brushed a lock of her white-gold hair from her cheek and gave the strand a tug.

"No prevaricating. Spill."

Cass sighed. "I wasn't sure how you'd interpret this. But I guess, maybe because of Dana's influence and Marcie's...we're all exclusive to one of you, in terms of who's our Master, our husband, but from the beginning, there's this feeling that in a key way we also belong to all of you. Sexual, protective, erotic implications. But over time, the desire for it to manifest itself in certain ways has grown stronger."

She realized she was blushing, especially as he merely kept listening, his expression gone fathomless so she wasn't sure what he was thinking. "I've always been the responsible, the steady one," she said abruptly. "I mean, yes, Savannah is reserved, but I'm the conservative, the motherly one. Even though I have my fantasies and desires, I tend not to go after them in as uninhibited a way as Marcie and Dana do. But that doesn't mean I don't feel them. That I don't want to pursue some fantasies that are outside my comfort zone, things I think about and imagine and..."

He cocked his head. "Have you masturbated while thinking about this one?"

"Yes," she said, without missing a beat, and liked seeing pleased surprise go through his gaze.

"Really. Where? How often?"

"A few times. More lately. Sometimes in here, with the door locked. Once, while you were working late and I started thinking about it in that half-awake, half-dreaming way. You came home and found me worked up. You bent and kissed me, put your hand down between my legs, and I climaxed almost instantly."

"I remember," he said, with further wonder. "You told me you were fantasizing about me before I came home and that was why you were so ready."

"It wasn't a lie."

"It just wasn't the whole truth." He tipped up her chin, giving her a long look. "I'll deal with that later. But in the meantime, I need you to remember something."

"What?"

"I love you. More than anything or anyone in the entire world."

"I'm glad," she said, her voice not quite steady. "Every day. Especially now that Cherry is taking trigonometry."

His gray eyes twinkled. "Any other reasons to keep me around other than advanced math homework?"

She moistened her lips. "What you just did is a nice perk."

Leaning down to her, he pressed his temple against hers. With that gesture they could have been in a crowded room, and it would have felt like there was an intimate cocoon around just the two of them.

"So tell me that," he said. "In a way that will keep me

hard the rest of the day."

Cass closed her eyes as his hands, strong and possessive, gripped her waist. He'd closed the distance between them again and she could feel the evidence of his still semi-hard cock against her. She'd just climaxed and yet she wanted him inside her, now, the rest of the work day be damned.

"Don't make your Master wait," he growled against her ear.

When she remembered he meant his question, a spurt of wry humor mixed with the simmering arousal that would not go away.

She could give as good as she got. Sliding her hands up his chest, she tunneled her fingers through the opening of his dress shirt to find his flesh. As she rubbed her abdomen against his cock, her breasts swelled over the corset and provided a tempting view down the two-button opening of her blouse. He obliged her by taking a good long look with his hot silver eyes before he met her gaze.

"I love how you use your mouth between my legs," she murmured. "Love the strength of your hands as you hold my thighs open, as your teeth scrape my cunt and your tongue thrusts inside me like your cock. When I think of that today, I'll feel incomplete until you're inside me again."

His lips firmed as he outlined her parted ones with his thumb. "I'll take care of that, the night you give me my birthday gift."

Her heart stuttered and he brushed his lips over hers, but caught her wrist as she was sliding her palm over his hip, fingers following the rise of his buttock under the thin softness of his slacks. "Don't get ahead of yourself," he told her with mock sternness. "Just because I've agreed to 'let' you give me the fantasy of my wildest dreams doesn't mean you can take advantage of your Master whenever you wish."

She chuckled and he smiled fully, but stroked his hands through her hair and cupped her face. "We'll be staying overnight at the Ritz Carlton," he told her. "Nate, Talia and Cherry are all good with it. Matt and Savannah are going to be their backups if they have any problems at the house.

Ben and Marcie will meet us at the Ritz."

"You already were going to do it," she realized, but he shook his head.

"No. I would have cancelled all of it if I hadn't heard the right answers here." He squeezed her hand as he stepped back. "I'm glad that I did. I'll pick you up here at 2pm, so be sure you can get off work early. You'll be spending your afternoon using the Ritz's spa services, getting the full body treatment."

"Whose birthday is this?" she teased him gently. A different look came into his eyes, the more intense Dom side of him that made her shiver.

"I plan to use my sub hard that night, so I'm going to make sure she's ready for it. And letting me pamper you, that's part of my gift, too. Always. Yesterday, today and tomorrow, you are always enough for me. But hearing you want to take it to this next level, that you're the one craving that..." Grasping her wrist, he took her hand down to the front of his slacks and pushed the heel of her palm against steel.

She swallowed. "Please. Let me..."

"You want to kneel and service your Master, here and now?"

"Yes."

"Good. That's another thought I'll take back to the office with me." He shot her a wicked grin before pulling her to him for a hot kiss that had her knees quivering. Then he eased her back and headed for the door.

"I need one of those remote locking mechanisms like Matt has," she muttered.

Lucas pulled open the door and stopped, sweeping her from head to toe with a thorough glance. Taking out a stick of cinnamon gum, he chewed it thoughtfully as he looked at her. "Ben will know what kind of meal I had for lunch, even with the gum," he said casually. "But then we all do. You know why, Cassie?"

She wet suddenly dry lips. At one time, she'd reacted negatively to being called Cassie, associating it with a time she felt like a helpless child. Yet when he used it, it was almost as effective a trigger to her submissive side as when he locked the silver bracelets on her wrists. The decorative cuffs he'd given her always put her fully in that mode. "Because I belong to them as much as I belong to you?" she said.

He held her gaze. "Almost. Because you belong to me, you also belong to them. An important distinction. You're theirs to love, protect and cherish, always. But anything else is on my say-so." He flashed another wicked, knee-weakening grin, but there was a serious light in his eyes as he added a last note.

"And only what reduces my sub to total, willing surrender. Anything less than that, we don't go down that path, and we pass on it with no regrets. As long as your heart is still mine."

"It will never be otherwise. Even when it stops beating. You didn't say honor," she added, with what she felt was admirable steadiness.

He moved back across the office and cupped the side of her throat. "Women are the heart of honor," he said, with a credible Scottish burr that ran a delightful tingle through her vitals. Leaning in, he kissed her, this time a lingering touch of lips. "So the honor part is a given."

"Ben's been helping you with accents. You sounded just like Liam Neeson's Rob Roy."

"That isn't all he's been helping me with."

"Oh?"

He stepped back, disentangling himself from her grip when she latched onto his shirt to hold onto him, though he retained her hands for one last moment, conveying his own reluctance to let her go.

"Yeah. You'll find out on Friday."

With a wink, he was gone. As always, his timing was impeccable, because she heard him greeting her admin as Nell returned from lunch with a whiff of the Chinese she'd promised to bring Cass. Cass did a quick check of herself in the mirror in her private bathroom to make sure she looked presentable, but nothing could change the soft look of her lips and eyes that made her look bed-tousled and well-loved, even if she had every hair in place. He had that effect on her. She had no doubt he always would. Thank God.

Part Four

Cass curled up on her side on a padded lounge on the terrace of the Ritz-Carlton. She had a spectacular view of the Mississippi River and the French Quarter, all the better because the elevation minimized the less picturesque, more pungent and noisy aspects of the Quarter at street level, and maximized the beauty of the historical skyline. Lucas had taken her here for a weekend on their second anniversary. They'd been tied up with work things around that time so they couldn't leave town for a longer period. Though he'd later taken her to a private island in Canada to spend a secluded weekend together, she had loved this place equally, surrounded by the city she'd grown to love so much since they'd found the plantation house outside New Orleans together.

As promised, Lucas had submitted her to the divine hands and ministrations of the Ritz-Carlton spa services. Her skin glowed and was even softer to the touch than usual. Her hair was piled in an artful twist on her head, because he'd requested it be put up in the secure but feminine style. It was an intriguing request, since she knew he loved playing with her long, thick, white-gold hair. Maybe he wanted the pleasure of taking it down himself.

She wore only her locked silver bracelets and a thin silk robe in a shimmering blue that picked up the color of her eyes. The latter was his gift from a local boutique, the garment laid out on the bed when they arrived, along with several white roses and a small box of her favorite Belgian chocolates.

For the past thirty minutes, he'd instructed her to sit outside with the view, her chocolates, and an excellent wine, while he was inside doing mysterious things. She'd tipped her head back on the sofa, her eyes closed, when she inhaled and knew he'd returned. She put her hand up in time for it to slide along his jaw and tease his hair close to the nape, where the streaked blond strands were darker. While she did that, he bent and kissed her collar bone, sliding the robe off her shoulder. "I'm still wondering how this is your birthday," she said. "I should have at least gone inside to help you do whatever it is you were doing."

"It's my birthday. Your gift is to do what I tell you." Though his tone was husky, his grip shifted to the side of her throat, putting enough pressure there she opened her eyes and met his. She found her Master's gaze upon her, not her husband's. "Right?" he asked, but it wasn't a question.

"Yes," she managed. He nodded and straightened, taking her hand.

"Come with me."

He'd run water in the Jacuzzi tub, and dropped a couple bath beads in it, more of the same spa products that would add to the softness of her skin and the light fragrance the delicate body polish and essential oil massage had left upon it. Unbelting her robe, he slipped it off her shoulders and set it aside, holding her hand and forearm with easy strength to steady her as she stepped into the tub and sat down. "How many of the chocolates did you eat?" he asked.

"Two. I'm trying to save some for later." She smiled. "You're spoiling me."

"That's what I like to hear. And before you ask, yes, Talia is going to text Matt and Savannah with time-stamped proof of home arrival as soon as Cherry's boyfriend drops her off at our place promptly by eleven o'clock. One minute past that, and Matt will dispatch the entire New Orleans police force after that hapless teenage hormone-fest Cherry thinks is Edward from *Twilight* and Peter from *Hunger Games*, all rolled up in one." He touched her face. "You know you can trust Talia to watch after your brother and sister."

She folded her hands on the edge of the tub. "I know. But I'm glad you told me."

"Good." His gaze swept over her. "Turn sideways and bend your knees up. Position yourself over the jets."

The Jacuzzi feature was a straight line of pinhole jets that followed the interior circumference of the tub several inches from the bottom. The water's force didn't reach the "who needs a man" rating, as Marcie would put it with a wide grin. Therefore, Cass wasn't sure what Lucas thought it would accomplish, but she should have known to trust her Dom. At one of their once-a-month wives' dinners, the women had speculated on how much time their men actually spent thinking about and testing different methods of bringing a woman incomparable pleasure, and how they balanced that with their demanding work schedules.

"I'm pretty sure Jon has built some kind of machine so they can step into an alternate dimension where time stops. They have hours upon hours to think of these things before they step right back into the office at the time they left. The closet in Jon's office is probably the portal. Notice how he always keeps it closed?"

That had been Marcie and Dana's theory. Cass wouldn't discount it, but she knew how Lucas managed his time. Never a wasted second, no procrastinating on household chores, his every workout scheduled precisely...

"Maybe they're all aliens," Dana said when Cass pointed it out. *"No men are this focused."*

"If that's the case, let's relocate to their planet," Marcie had said with a saucy grin.

Cass returned to the present moment because she didn't want to waste a second of that precisely scheduled time. And because Lucas was talking to her.

"One arm braced behind you. It tilts your breasts up in that pretty way." He pulled a stool closer and took a seat on it, watching her keenly.

As she angled her hips over the jets, the tiny streams of water rippled over her labia and clit. Ticklish sensations, like...

"Like the tip of my tongue, barely flicking over your cunt. Tasting, teasing. I like those first touches. The way you twitch or squirm, and then your body starts to settle into it, reaching for it. There's that deep place inside a woman that gets quiet, becomes a still point that orients her toward her sexual response. It's a transformation, the shedding of everything but this moment. Move your hips in slow, small circles. Feel the water flutter over you. Your nipples are getting tight, those little buds that make me want to nibble on them."

She dropped her head back on her shoulders. They were damp from the steam rising from the water, helping her understand at least part of why he'd wanted them to put her hair up. But he liked to brush her hair before bedtime, and she thought he might do that tonight, when all else was done. Unless she and Marcie completely wore him out. It was a delicious thought, as much as she enjoyed the way he brushed her hair, his fingers tunneling in behind the brush to stroke her scalp.

Lucas shifted off the stool. He was wearing his dress shirt, the sleeves rolled up, along with a pair of well-fitted slacks. His tie was loosened but not removed. The man didn't know how not to look sexy, but he and all the K&A men knew how to work that executive look for maximum impact. She remembered the first time he'd come home with her, when they barely knew anything about one another. They'd still gravitated toward one another like animals who mated for life after merely one look that told them all they needed to know. He'd taken off his coat and rolled up his sleeves, looking a lot like this as he helped her sister Jessica, now in college, fix her bike.

Her lips parted, tongue moistening them at that relentless little fluttering of water over her sex, at the intent look in his gaze as he watched her. His eyes coursed over her wet throat and breasts, taut nipples, and the position of her body. Her knees were bent up against her torso, backside sliding along the bottom of the tub, creating gentle swirls in the water as she obeyed him and let his tongue—because that was what she was imagining as the water jets—play over her body, causing her to move like a graceful mermaid in the water. Her breasts glistened from the steam as they quivered with the motion.

Removing a blindfold from his pocket, he shook it out. It was black-lined satin with purple laces.

"Come here," he said. Moving to the edge of the tub, she shifted to her knees and rose onto them as he leaned forward. He covered her eyes with the mask and began to lace it in the back.

"Forehead down on the edge of the tub."

She gripped the sides of the tub on either side of her as she did it. The position allowed him to do a thorough job of lacing the mask along the back of her head, over the hair bundled against her skull and nape.

His fingers slid under her face, making sure it was fitted properly over the bridge of her nose and her eyes. He knew she liked the laced mask because it held her securely, like a corset. He'd brought one of her waist cinchers, and had laid it out on the giant king-sized canopy bed of the opulent suite. It was the one that had a blue and white flower pattern across the satiny exterior, with blue ribbon trim for the lacings. Having the mask on made her think about and anticipate when he would put it upon her, shaping and restraining her body for his pleasure.

She knew Ben and Marcie were across the hall, but she'd not yet seen either of them. Right now her only focus, per her Master's orders, was this moment, this bath, any and all the things he was having her experience that shed any connection to the world outside. It was his birthday, but his desire, his fantasy, always seemed to involve immersing her right along with him.

He had her straighten up and stand on her knees with the pressure of his hands, which slid to her throat, his thumbs idly stroking. When he dropped one hand to cup her wet breast, he kneaded it, thumb passing over the nipple so she caught her lip in her teeth on a hum of pleasure.

"Let's ease you back down now." He turned off the jets and helped her to lounge back in the tub, adjusting the bath pillow under her head. "Stay like that and soak."

There was music piped in through speakers in the spacious bathroom, her playlist plugged into the TV with its excellent speaker system. As she lay there, listening to Foreigner's "I Want to Know What Love Is," she was glad she did. She'd been blessed with love in so many ways. Her siblings, Lucas, the other K&A men and their wives, all of whom she considered just as much her family as her siblings. It eased the wounds of other losses. Indifferent and now long-gone parents. Jeremy.

No. Tonight was not going to be about that. It was time, not to let him go, but to let go of the sadness. Although it had happened at the end of his short and tragically self-destructive life, he had found his way. And now he was in a better place. She'd done the very best she could for him. Lucas, Marcie and all of them had helped her understand that. Most days she was starting to believe it.

She heard steps upon the tile. Gooseflesh rippled over her skin at the passage of air in the steam-filled room, but it wasn't from a temperature adjustment. The man who had walked into the bathroom wasn't Lucas.

Dana was blind, and had talked about how she knew each man not only by scent and the way they moved, but by their use of tactile contact, like a wolf pack. Frequent touches, brushing up against each woman in the group during their social gatherings, speaking to her at length and absorbing her responses as if her very voice was imprinting itself upon him, and they were doing the same to her. Dana humorously called it their way of scent-marking. Whether they did it unconsciously or not, Cass thought she was right, because she recognized the men the same way, even though she had her sight and full hearing in a way Dana did not.

Except for what the women called the "initiation," that moment where her Master had committed to her as the submissive he wanted forever, and the other four had reinforced his choice in a quite memorable way, most of the sensuality exchanged didn't cross the lines into blatant sexuality. Well, okay, sometimes it went there in club environments or during arranged private sessions, like when Peter and Ben had shared Dana one night, long before Ben and Marcie became a couple. But the important thing was that the woman's specific Dom was always present, no matter what other member of the team was involved. Which was why it was a little unsettling to Cass, knowing Ben O'Callahan was standing in the bathroom where she was blindfolded and naked, and Lucas wasn't there.

There was a lingering scent of Lucas, though, which made her think that he had watched her at the door until Ben had arrived so silently. It made sense. Even though she was merely blindfolded, her hands and feet unbound, Lucas wouldn't leave her unattended with a key sense like her sight blocked. She could pull the laced blindfold free on her own, but it didn't come off quickly or easily.

He was taking care of her, and the reminder reassured her, as well as clued her in to what was happening. As Ben dropped to a knee by the tub and trailed a light finger over her blindfold, her lips, she tilted her head. His touch set her nerves to tingling. "He's testing me, isn't he?" she asked. "If I get freaked out by nothing more than you being in here and seeing me naked, it tells him I'm likely not up for whatever else is planned tonight."

"Something like that." Ben's hand withdrew and she heard a swirling sound in the water before he rubbed a heated washcloth over her shoulders, down her back, a massaging stroke. "Maybe he also wanted to make sure you and I were good before this happens."

"He thinks we're not good?" She was surprised to hear that. She and Ben had had their conflicts when he and Marcie initially came together, when Ben was working out some serious issues with his past, but that, while never completely in the past, was under control. Somewhere along the line, Cass had become convinced of it herself. And Lucas knew that.

She cocked her head. "No," she decided. "You asked to come in here first. Because *you* aren't sure we're good. Deep down, you think I'm worried you'll turn out like Jeremy. That your self-destructive side will win out in the end and take Marcie down with you."

"I know why Pickard pays you so much." His voice held some wry humor and another quality, easier to define when he spoke again in a more sober tone. "If I ever thought that would happen, I'd cut her loose first."

She shook her head. "Too late for that. You're already part of her. That's what those vows are about. And it goes just as deep for her. If you went down, she'd kill herself to keep you above the water. Or go down with you. But I think you know that. Which is why you've worked so hard to figure it out. She matters enough to you to try and change that part of yourself. Jeremy never did get that far, not until the end, when it was too late and the sickness couldn't be reversed. You're different."

She meant it. To prove it, she found and lifted his other

hand, putting her lips to his palm before pressing her face against it. He was a lawyer, but he had the rough hands of a fighter, probably because he did a lot of workouts at Matt's boxing gym without gloves. "She loves you, and I know why she does. Even though sometimes the two of you scare me to death."

She couldn't see his face, but the energy around her told her that her words had hit a mark, hopefully a good one. His fingertips curled, stroking the wisps of hair on her temple. Then he started using the washcloth again. She lifted her throat as he ran the cloth over it, causing water to trickle onto her breasts. It was a nice sensation, but he didn't follow it, continuing to rub her shoulders and the middle of her back. He had good hands. Amazingly gentle, given what she knew he could do with them, harsh things far beyond Cass's level but what Marcie craved. Which was fine.

She told herself that, though Cass knew she still had some discomfort with it. It was difficult to see marks and bruises on Marcie's skin that made her wince, and know Ben had put them there. But the contented glow in Marcie's eyes, the adoration Ben obviously held for her, couldn't be denied. It was a puzzle she hadn't figured out and maybe never would. Tonight could be wonderful without that understanding, though. She pushed the worry back down and focused on the present.

Setting aside the washcloth, Ben slid his hand down her arm to the wrist, to one of the silver bracelets she wore. The edges were rounded and smooth, making them comfortable to wear. In lieu of a collar, Lucas had given them to her as a sign of her belonging to him. She remembered what he had said. *Because you belong to me, you also belong to them. An important distinction.*

Ben curled a finger under the bracelet, tugging on it. "So that's settled."

She realized he was asking for confirmation, and nodded. "Yes."

"Good. You ready to submit to me, under his direction? If you are, you know how to respond to me."

His tone changed, just that smoothly, and everything in

her oriented to what it meant. It was as effective a paradigm shift as the cuffs on her wrists. He had a harder voice than Lucas in this mode, which made her a little nervous.

"Yes, sir," she said quietly.

"All right, then. Let's get you dried off."

He handed her out of the tub onto a bath mat and dried her himself, thoroughly. Her body responded with swirling tendrils of interest to his attention as he ensured every expanse of skin was dry, the crease beneath her breasts, between thigh and mons, the small of her back. When he was back there, his hand ran familiarly over her backside, a distracting caress, before he dropped a kiss on her collar bone that sent tingles through her neck and side, her nipples. Lucas had left her body awake and humming, and Ben kept that momentum going.

"All right. Your Master wants to get you dressed for him. Put your arms around my neck."

She was going to tell him she could walk out of the bathroom, but realized this was part of turning herself over to their care. Plus, it was no hardship to enjoy a strong man's arms. They all did this so well and effortlessly, lifting a woman off her feet as if they could carry her beyond the end of time.

He was wearing a dress shirt and silky tie, too, no jacket. She loved their clothing preferences for exercising their Dom tendencies. It gave a whole new meaning to the term "power suit."

As Ben set her feet down on the cushioned gold carpet in the bedroom, her Master's hands were upon her once again. She'd enjoyed Ben's touch, but it was a relief to feel Lucas's again, such that she moved into it eagerly.

"I missed you too." Lucas kissed her nose with warm lips. "Was he mean to you? Do I need to kick his ass?"

She shook her head, and Lucas's hands tightened on her. "Then thank him for his care. Properly."

The command caused a little flip and hitch in her stomach. They were keeping her off balance on purpose. She turned in what she thought was Ben's direction. "Thank you, sir."

"She's a gift," Ben said to Lucas. Acknowledging her thanks to her Master, not to her. Marcie called those little touches protocol, and Cass had to admit they were very effective in turning up the heat inside her while gravitating her even more toward submissive behavior that would please her Master, and herself.

Lucas made a noise of assent and brought her to face him again. Putting the waist cincher in place, he began to hook the front, that lovely, gradual process that hinted at how tight the garment would eventually be, the pressure of his fingers leaving a heat trail. When he had it fastened from above her mound to between her breasts, adjusting the crescent underwiring beneath her bosom, he turned her around so her back was to him.

"The laces need to be adjusted so we can enjoy the emphasis on those beautiful tits and gorgeous ass," he said. "But you need something to hold onto, because I'm going to pull it tight. I'm in the mood to be more than a little demanding and selfish."

"My sub can help with that," Ben said. "Reach out in front of you, Cass."

As Cass did, her hands were met by a questing set of slim fingers. Marcie apparently was also blindfolded. She laid her hands over Cass's forearms, slim fingers curling. "I've got you, sis." She sounded like Marcie, but there was a different cadence to her voice, one Cass recognized from her own. Lucas hadn't been the only Dom pleasuring his sub, awakening her body for what might come.

Had they realized it was better to have them blindfolded, particularly her, so she wasn't discomfited and preoccupied by the knowledge that it was her sister in the room? So far, it seemed to be working.

As Cass's fingers tightened on Marcie, she took a steadying breath. Lucas's fantasy had truly begun.

Part Five

Ben shifted into position behind Marcie, putting his hands on her trim waist. He'd chosen a pair of frilly panties for her to wear, where the crotch was provocatively laced in a center line from clitoris to her rear entry. It gave her Master the pleasure of loosening the laces over her cunt to turn it into a crotchless garment, or opening the back when he wanted to fuck her ass, all while keeping all those little frills in place to brush one's testicles and the base of the cock. Reminders of the girly, pretty nature of his feisty sub.

Lucas would enjoy the way those laces created friction over her pussy as he teased her with his mouth outside of them. Or poked his tongue through the crisscrossed ribbons for provocative little touches against flesh. When the right time came and he wanted full access, he'd ask Ben to open the laces. It would reinforce who had primary claim on each woman, as well as heighten those women's arousal, to hear such matter-of-fact directions discussed before them.

For now, though, Ben just enjoyed the hell out of the view. Cass, all that glory of white-gold hair piled up above her slim neck, her beautiful naked breasts held up by the underwiring of the waist cincher. Her cheeks below the snug fit of the dark mask were tinged with color, her lips parted as Lucas drew the garment tighter, emphasizing the mouthwatering curves above and below. Her hands constricted on Marcie's forearms, making the women sway with the effect.

Marcie's delicate back was within tasting distance and he didn't deny himself, sweeping her thick hair aside to kiss her shoulder blades, her collar bone. He set his teeth there, digging in to feel her draw in a breath, one that caught as he cupped her breasts, fingering the already taut, pierced nipples. She tried to keep her sister steady while submitting to her Master, a struggle that caused an arrow of reaction straight down his torso and into his testicles and restive cock.

He hadn't been sure how this would play out for him, since this was Lucas's fantasy, but that wasn't going to be a problem. He was more concerned about Cass. From what she'd said and done in the tub, he knew she did want to do this, but he and Lucas knew she had a few hurdles. She was likely wondering how this would work for her. Would she get too uptight about being near her sister?

Then he saw Cass's head tilt, a gesture that told him she'd registered he was playing with Marcie. As she pressed her lips together and swallowed, her skin flushed a little. Signs of sexual excitement. He thought she was probably imagining how Marcie was being touched, and craving to be touched in the same way. Ben gave Lucas credit for coming up with blindfolding the women as the initial way to move Cass past self-consciousness and negative distraction. And Marcie from getting too caught up in worrying about her sister's state of mind.

When Marcie started to drop her head back on his shoulder in reaction to what he was doing, it confirmed the direction of his thoughts and made him bite back a smile. Though he loved it when she leaned against him, she had other responsibilities right now. He pinched her nipple, tugging on its piercing. "Help your sister. Shameless slut."

Then—because he was a sadist—he made it even more difficult for her to comply. Wetting his fingers, he put them between her buttocks to play along her rim, savoring the shiver of reaction along her lovely back.

Cass expelled another breath and Lucas tied off the laces, smoothing his hands along her hourglass figure. He'd tied her even tighter than usual, a tactic Ben knew was designed to pull her further out of her headspace. It appeared to be working. Gripping her wrists, Lucas brought them up and locked her bracelet cuffs together. Then he had her lace her fingers against the back of her head, which did mouthwatering things to her heavy breasts as her back arched. Ben guided Marcie to do the same. She wasn't wearing her own cuffs tonight. He'd chosen to put her only in the panties and his stainless-steel collar. The band around her slim throat had three forget-me-nots etched in the front and an *Always Yours* inscription on the inside.

Despite the lack of cuffs, he wasn't worried about her hands staying where he put them, laced against the back of her head. She could misbehave, but for the moment she'd be on her best behavior. Mostly.

Lucas slid his arms under Cass's arms from behind and cupped her breasts, fondling the accentuated curves.

"You're beautiful," Lucas told his sub. "You both are. Ben is doing what I'm doing. Two mirror images. He's fondling Marcie's breasts, and probably as hard as I am right now, thinking about how worked up the two of you are getting. Is she wet, Ben?"

Ben spoke in Marcie's ear, knowing he was close enough Cass could hear his command resonate in the delicate shell of her own ear. "Put your fingers in your pussy, brat, and let him have a taste."

Marcie complied under Lucas's avid gaze. Ben wondered if he was giving his eye muscles a workout, trying to capture the reactions of two women in real time. He was no different.

When Marcie drew forth knuckles that glistened, Ben clasped her wrist and guided her hand to Lucas, over Cass's shoulder. Lucas rested his forearm there and took over, sucking Marcie's fingers into his mouth a mere few inches from Cass's cheek. Her pulse was jumping in her throat as if her breath was erratic. Ben brought his now free arm back to circle Marcie's waist as she swayed.

"That meal's just about ready," Lucas said, with pure male approval. "Cass, give Ben a taste of the same so he knows just how damn lucky I am."

It wasn't as instinctual to her as it was to Marcie, to obey Lucas without question or thought in new circumstances. Ben knew Lucas would get her there, though, and it gave him a spurt of Dom's pleasure to watch him leading her in the direction of mindless obedience to enjoy the rewards for making that leap of faith.

Lucas unclasped Cass's wrists from behind her head, holding onto one as he guided the other one down, down. He released her when they reached the juncture of her thighs, his fingertips resting high on the leg as Cass slid her fingers over her labia, then dipped them inside. Her body flexed as the digits were sucked in by the craving need she was feeling. He bit back a reverent oath at the sight.

"Nice and deep," Lucas urged with glinting eyes and a near growl, showing he'd logged Ben's reaction. "You know you like it when I push in deep, all the way."

She caught her bottom lip in her teeth, a sweet effect,

and Lucas made an approving noise. He drew her hand out himself, returning his firm grip to her wrist and helping her bring her wet fingers to Ben's mouth. Ben increased his hold on Marcie, leaning against her back as he reached over, overlapped Lucas's grip and licked Cass's fingers. They were shaking.

"You're right." Ben said casually. "First course is almost ready."

"Bet your ass. C'mere, baby." Once Ben released her wrist, Lucas drew Cass away to the giant bed with its luxurious cream and gold linens that picked up the deep gold embellishments in the dark wood canopy frame. Setting his hands to her waist to lift her up on the high mattress, he eased her down to her back and directed her to stretch her arms over her head before going to work with the straps and ties they'd put in place earlier.

Her knees were bent over the end of the mattress, and Lucas added a matching but thinner set of cuffs to her ankles to make for easier attachment to the straps running from the bottom rail, binding her ankles shoulder width apart. She could brace her heels against the narrow ledge of the black footboard, but she didn't have enough of the width she'd eventually wish for to push herself up into his mouth. She'd have to strain for that, the effort adding to the endorphin rush.

Lucas moved around the bed and pulled ties down from the headboard. He secured her wrists out to either side of her head, leaving her elbows bent. Ben wished he had a freaking camera. Cass tied up like that was a wet dream times ten. She'd give any man with eyes a painful hard-on, and her Master was obviously consumed by the vision of her, running his hands over her spread and tied body. His palm slid over her mound, her hip, up to her shoulder and out along her bound arm. Then across her throat, administering a firm, reminding squeeze there, followed by a brush of fingertips, a more tender touch, along her cheek. She caught two of his fingers between her parted lips, kissing him, licking him, trying to suck him in, and a heated feral look took over his expression.

Lucas's touch glided down her sternum, over the waist

cincher and back to her thigh, purposefully avoiding the seemingly most erogenous zones. Though when done right, every damn inch of a woman's body became an erogenous zone. One of the many things that made a girl the best toy a boy could ever have, if he knew the right way to play with her.

Despite the spurt of humor, Ben knew the look on Lucas's face, because it reflected his own. There was a point where a Master's nature started to kick in hard. It made him want to stretch his sub's endurance to breaking, bring her so close to that climax but hold it out of reach, until she was savage and helpless at once. The pleasure and power of it were indescribable, especially when tangled up with the fierce love he bore for her. If Lucas was like Ben, he'd probably been thinking about this all week, and the women would be no different. They'd hit the hotel lobby already primed for what they each imagined this would be, which was making the intensity level rise all the faster.

At Lucas's nod, Ben brought Marcie to the bed and lifted her onto it next to Cass. He laid her on her back, too, but bent Marcie's left leg over Cass's right knee, helping Lucas wrap the straps over both limbs, thighs and shins, to hold Cass's right and Marcie's left legs together, crossed over one another, knees slightly bent. They each checked the angle and level of restraint to ensure the women were protected from injury if one jerked violently. They'd be mindful of one another at first, though that could change when their Masters started to break everything down. As they fully intended to do.

Fucking, bloody heaven plus a fruit basket. As Ben finished tying Marcie's arms and other leg so she was in the same spread position as Cass, the sight the two of them made, arranged before him and Lucas like this, was incomparable. Two beautiful women, one in a pair of lacy panties and nothing else, the other in a waist cincher printed with tiny flowers. They were garments that emphasized all their cock-hardening feminine attributes. Since both of the women had their knees bent and spread, the position stretched the laces of the panties over Marcie's cunt, pure temptation. Cass's pussy was naked and wet with her honey, already coaxing a man to take a taste.

Lucas saw the direction of his thoughts. "Since you're my guest at this party, seems only polite I should allow you first taste."

Ben shook his head. "Appreciate the courtesy, but your birthday, man. I'll have my turn after you take the lead."

He was as cognizant as Lucas at the shudders that went through their women. In this context, being discussed as if their input had no place in the conversation, was foreplay, and they reacted accordingly. Ben saw that the thin fabric of Marcie's panties were becoming translucent with her own response.

Though they looked sexy as hell, the pretty garments, the bound and helpless position, their long, fair limbs and soft hair, also emphasized their delicacy. While the men gazing at them knew just how incredibly strong their wives were, there was something about seeing them in full submission, and knowing these were their women, that made their normal protective feelings expand to a whole new level, fierce and animal-like.

Ben unbuttoned the cuffs of his shirt, removed his tie and opened the shirt down the front before getting rid of his shoes and socks. He slid onto the bed in his slacks and belt alone. It made him smile a little when he saw Marcie, her wrist crossed and bound with her sister's, had shifted the hand around so she could clasp Cass's fingers and hold on, providing a reassuring support and something indefinable to one another.

There were so many things hard to explain to the mainstream world about Dominance and submission, even if the roots of it were buried in every one. How Cass had arrived at being okay with this, and how it didn't translate into being an incestuous thing with her sister, despite the obvious need they had for contact with one another in this moment, was similarly hard to explain in a politically correct kind of way. But all four of the people in this room got it, so the rest of the world could mind their own damn business.

Seeing the two gorgeous female bodies spread before them made him and Lucas so ready Ben knew he wasn't the only one who'd adjusted his cock a couple times already to try and make room in the rapidly constricting area of their slacks. But when Lucas noted the handclasp between the two women, Ben saw he had the same kind of reaction to it he'd had. Something that went beyond the libido and touched deep on the love they felt for Marcie and Cass, as well as the ties of family, blood or chosen, that held them all together.

But they were guys, after all, so Lucas didn't linger over the sappy stuff too long. He shed his tie and shirt, draping the latter over Cass's face briefly. Her nostrils flared as she inhaled his scent. She tried to make contact with as much of the fabric as she could, by moving her head so it caressed her cheeks and forehead. When Lucas at last lifted it and set it to the side, he didn't take it far, laying it over her outside hand, which clutched the soft fabric immediately. Ben knew she'd be absorbing the body heat Lucas had left in it, another touchstone between Master and sub. He thought of Marcie the other night, asking for the shirt off his back, and then settling on the one he'd worn to work. Yeah, part of it had been her teasing him, wanting him to take off his shirt, but another part had been her seeking that warmth, that cloaking oneself in a Master's scent and body heat. Submissives had their own way of being possessive. Until Marcie, he hadn't appreciated all the variations of it.

"I like to start a full course meal with the appetizer," Lucas said. "But in this case, I might decide to sample from both plates. Too difficult to choose."

He sent Ben a devilish look that said, "I gave you your shot to go first." But it was also a quick check, a "one more time, is this okay?" bro code to touch base. Ben's lips quirked ruefully at the gleam, but he also gave Lucas a nod to go ahead.

Sliding his hands under Marcie's thighs, Lucas tilted her up toward his mouth as much as her bonds would allow. The position meant one of his hands was also holding his own wife's leg, since she and Marcie were bound together there. She licked her lips. Cass had soft, pink-glossed lips, a delicate color that set off her white-gold locks and blue eyes.

Marcie did that little nervous lip licking thing sometimes. Despite some minor feature differences, seeing Cass and Marcie laid out like this, there was no doubt they were sisters. Ben saw it in similar bone structure, how their faces revealed arousal, the way their lips parted. Ben had never given much thought to the sister fantasy, but he was starting to get on board with why Lucas had one, big time.

Still stretched out on the bed long-ways above the women's bound wrists, Ben slid a finger over Cass's pink lips and insinuated it between her teeth. "Get me wet while he's going down on your sister, Cass," he ordered. She complied with a tiny moan. Lucas watched, his head poised over Marcie's cunt but his breath stroking her, if her lovely little shivers were any indication.

"Suck me like you're sucking your Master's cock," Ben said, a tad more sharply. Testing. Cass rallied, pushing past her initial hesitancy to close her lips firmly over his two fingers and comply, throat working and capturing Lucas's attention fully. Ben tossed him a wicked grin. "I get bored up here, I might have to get me some of that."

"You get bored, you're not paying enough attention."

"But the candy shop is the most fun when you can taste and touch."

Lucas grunted in satisfaction. "Tell me about it." He dipped his head and dragged his tongue over Marcie's pussy on the outside of the panties, earning a jerk of her hips and a delicious little gasp, her fingers constricting reflexively on Cass's. Lucas found her clit hood ring through the gauzy cloth and ribbon and tugged on it, hard enough to bring Marcie's hips off the bed.

"Let him hear you, darling," Ben said to her. "Let his sub remember what he can do with that tongue of his. He can do it to any woman, but it's her that will be his main course, the meal he wants for all his life. He tongue-fucked her to climax less than twenty-four hours ago, because he needs pussy like he needs air, but hearing another woman benefitting from it will only make her cream for more of the same."

Bingo. Cass's tongue swiped over her lips, her hips

lifting as if she was channeling what Marcie was feeling. Lucas's gray eyes met Ben's in visceral male approval before he turned his attention back to what he was doing.

"Oh..." The syllable broke from Marcie's throat on a thin, high note as Lucas flicked, teased and tasted, sucking her juices through the cloth. He lifted his head. "I'd like those laces out of my way, Ben."

Ben leaned between the two women, his braced arm against Cass's shoulder as he reached over Marcie's body. He smiled as he felt Lucas's sub turn her head toward him, and her lips touched his skin. Yeah, she was giving herself to the moment. He plucked at the tiny bow at mid-crotch on Marcie's panties and untied it, dipping his finger briefly into her wet pussy to draw out some honey on the tip. Protocol observed, he nodded to Lucas, letting him loosen or pull the laces free at his own rate from there.

As Ben expected, Lucas started simply by loosening them, incorporating the feel of the crisscrossed ribbons into what he was doing. Exploring the sensitive inner labia area, thrusting his tongue into her cunt between ribbon openings, sucking, tugging and nipping at her clit, rubbing his face over her pussy. He was a master at alternating pinpoint sensation with whole area stimulation at the right moments. A woman realized pretty damn fast he didn't need any guidance on an area where most men needed a fucking road map drawn. Which, being men, they too often ignored.

While Lucas was enjoying his "sampling," Ben returned to his own pursuits. He used his wet fingertip on Cass's nipple, circling and dampening the areola. "When Lucas sucks on you here, he'll also taste Marcie's cunt. What do you think of that, Cass? Do you want to please your Master?"

He pinched the nipple and tugged on it, increasing the demand, exploring how much discomfort she could take and stay on the right side of it. Far more than he expected, he saw with a sharp spear of lust. As he pulled harder, her back arched and she came off the bed, throat working.

"Yes," she gasped. "Nothing...I want... more. Oh, God."

The moan that broke from her matched Marcie's,

inadvertent but perfect timing as Lucas did something that had Ben's sub bucking under his mouth, her bent knee flexing over her sister's.

Lucas shifted, replacing mouth with fingers. Pressing them into Marcie to thrust in slow advance and retreat, he moved over and put his mouth on his wife's pussy, his lips glistening with Marcie's response. That was his sub, endlessly responsive at her Master's command. Ben felt a surge of ridiculous pride and laid his other hand on her breast, playing with Marcie's nipple ring, tugging. Her hips went down and lifted, showing her cunt was throbbing with the need to move in a coital rhythm, thanks to Lucas getting her running that hot.

"Un-unh," Ben admonished, with a sharper tug. "Stop moving those hips like you're being fucked. You don't get to do that until there's something in that empty pussy of yours. And I say it's okay. Right?"

"Yes, Master." The plaintiveness of her voice sent a spike of need through his cock. It was probably best she could only guess how fucking hard he was already. She wasn't above misbehaving to goad him further. At this rate, he was going to have to remove the slacks or risk a seam tearing. She'd done that to him once before, and earned a nice punishment for ruining the Hugo Boss ensemble.

At the very first touch of Lucas's mouth, a cry broke from Cass's throat, showing how worked up she was. "That's my baby," Lucas muttered as Cass tried to lift her hips to his mouth to grind. He held her down, lashing her clit with his tongue, making her head whip back and forth. Her guttural cry matched Marcie's as Ben continued to play and flick over their taut nipples, squeezing the two pairs of magnificent breasts at his disposal. Then he shifted so he had a hand cupped under each of their jaws, tilting their heads back at a straining angle, increasing the sense of full ownership of their bodies and responses as Lucas shifted back to eat Marcie's pussy again.

Ben ran his thumbs along their pulses, registering the crashing rhythm, the way each jumped another octave as Lucas went from sampling to devouring. Working his tongue deep in Marcie's cunt, closing his whole mouth over it to seal in heat, he increased the suction on her tender clit. He was thrusting and swirling, because that was what her body was doing. He had his other hand lying on Cass's mound, fingers moving in a deceptively idle stroke, her hips working to increase that friction. Ben bent down to Cass, knowing an intimate whisper in her ear would add to the sensation.

"Work yourself against his hand, Cass. He's barely moving it, because he wants to see how shamelessly his sub will act to prove to her Master how much she needs him."

She renewed her efforts, panting and groaning as Marcie's voice elevated. Lucas was getting her pretty damn close to release, her upper body flushing. Ben could read all the signs himself, so wasn't surprised when Lucas pulled back from that narrow ledge without him having to provide an early warning signal. Relentlessly patient, he turned his attention to his wife again. Marcie was so close, he didn't touch her pussy at all now, only gripping the center bound leg with one hard hand to hold her and Cass steady.

A startled gasp broke from Cass as Lucas gave her exposed labia a series of sharp slaps. It stimulated the nerves in a different way, so when he put his mouth back on her, she reached a new octave in reaction. Lucas nodded to Ben and he moved across the bed to pull the ball gag and handkerchief out of the side drawer of the night table. As Lucas kept going down on Cass's cunt, Ben pushed the handkerchief-wrapped ball gag between her teeth, smiling grimly as she tried to resist him, forgetting herself.

"Yeah, you have some of your sister's rebellious spirit to you. But can't have the other hotel guests thinking we're murdering you. Plus, you know we like to take away all your options, one at a time, until all you have left is trusting us. If you need something, you lift two fingers, darlin'. We'll stop and see if it's something that needs our attention. But don't cry wolf.". He caught the lobe of her ear in his teeth. "I'll be the one punishing you for something like that. I've always wanted to put some hand prints on that uptight but pretty ass."

She made a noise between outrage and frustrated need and he withdrew, grinning. Lucas gave him a wry look, but knew Ben had tossed out the insult to balance out her trepidation about the gag. Now she had other things to think about. Ben had cinched the gag tight, so the straps would mark the sides of her mouth, leave a pair of parallel lines along her cheeks for a short period. It would make Lucas hot all over again to see that. Ben knew for sure it would him.

He'd lost count of how many times taking an inventory of the marks he'd left on Marcie had led to some straightforward animal fucking up against a wall or on their bed, just one more time before he had to remind himself he wasn't a beast, and he needed to care for his beauty, not push her too hard. Because she would meet his needs, no matter what, when or how many times. It was part of the blessing and curse of her, because he had to watch himself to be sure he didn't ask too much. She would give it all and more if she thought that was what he wanted. The unleashed animal side of him did. The man side protected her from letting the other have the upper hand too often.

He might need to gag Marcie eventually, because she could be a screamer, too, but she would be required to use her mouth pretty damn soon, so he'd hold off. Plus, the room was pretty well sound-proofed. The gag had been more to increase Cass's sense of dependence than anything else.

His cock ached at even the brief thought of Marcie using her mouth on him. Lucas must have sensed it. Lifting his head, he met Ben's eyes.

"I'm going to take some more time with Marcie over here," Lucas said casually. "Why don't you remove the ball gag and see if you can't keep my sub's mouth occupied with something else for a little while?"

Ben glanced toward Cass's hand. The fingers twitched, as if she was warring with whether she needed to give the two-finger signal, or if she could handle taking another man's cock where only her Master's had been permitted ever since they'd met. The fingers stilled, though they rested uneasily on the covers. Ben met Lucas's gaze for confirmation, since they often knew their subs better than their subs knew themselves. It was one thing to elevate their excitement with a suggestion; another to have them act on it. He'd threatened to put Marcie face down on a K&A limo and switch her ass with the entire building security force watching, for all the trouble she'd given them at one time when she was trying to connect with him. No way in hell would he ever do that, and he knew deep inside she wouldn't want that, either, but the fantasy of it? Oh yeah. It got her worked up, big time.

Now Cass was facing a crossroad of fantasy and reality, and both Masters would be sure which side she really wanted to be on it before proceeding.

Lucas nodded, though Ben noticed he kept one hand on his wife, not just to stimulate her pussy, but to glide his fingertips along her inner thighs, a sensual stroke that conveyed connection as much as sex. *I'm here. I'm with you.*

He could do his part in that. Because for all that this was pure male fantasy territory, having their subs restrained and at the mercy of all they desired to do for and with them, it didn't work if the journey didn't bring them pleasure. And that thing that all the K&A women understood about their men's unusual relationship with one another—that by belonging to one of them, they belonged to all—also meant every man felt each woman was his to protect, cherish and care for, however much was needed.

Marcie was Ben's soulmate, the woman he'd needed all his life. Yet Savannah, Cass, Dana and Rachel...he loved every one of them. Enjoyed them, was attracted to and turned on by them, could flirt with them and get into a scenario like this without hesitations or concerns about what it said about his and Marcie's relationship. And if ever, God forbid, one of the five men ceased to be, while they'd respect any relationship choices the wife left behind made (after serious and thorough background checks that would even include the guy's last prostate exam), they'd take care of whatever the woman or the submissive side of her would need, in the way the departed Master would expect.

They could each rely on that safety net, a form of life insurance as important as financial security. Yeah, they were Neanderthals, but their inner circle was never a prison. It would always be a sanctuary for the women they loved.

So with all that in his mind, comfortably balanced with the throbbing need in his cock, he loosened the gag and set it aside, using the handkerchief to gently wipe away the saliva that had collected at the corners of Cass's frosted pink lips. Lips that would feel this side of heaven dragging along his dick.

He traced them with his thumb, enjoying the full, cushioned feel. "You've a beautiful mouth, darlin'," he said, the hint of Cajun in the endearment coming easily. "Your Master says I can enjoy it. I know you want to please him. Do you want to please me? Would that please yourself? Have you thought about how it would feel, having my cock there?" He sharpened his tone just enough to run the edge along her submissive nature, to see what response he roused. "You'll answer me as you are right now. Not as her sister, Pickard's negotiator, Lucas's wife or even as my friend. My very dear friend..."

As she lifted her chin, swallowing, he stroked her throat. "You'll answer as his submissive," he said. "As the part of yourself you wanted to embrace even deeper tonight than you have before. Tell me. Who are you right now? One word that covers all of it."

"His," she whispered, with a little tremble through her limbs. Though he missed not seeing the luminous look Ben was sure would be filling her gorgeous blue eyes, he knew the blindfold was key to allowing her to shed all those personas, particularly that of eldest child and Marcie's older sister, and sometimes surrogate mother. He'd test that a little later, break those tethers even further in a manner he and Marcie had discussed, but this was a good first step.

"Good." He dropped his head to kiss her bare shoulder and slid his large hand around her breast again, enjoying the give of the fleshy curve beneath his fingertips. Her nipple was rigid and large, the color of a pomegranate.

When he toyed with it, giving it another tug, a pinch, she drew in a gratifying breath. "You're his. What else are you, right here, right now?"

She licked her lips and he noticed Lucas easing his fingers into her cunt. He had his hand palm up, which would let him rub the fingertips along the top wall of her channel, a technique sure to send erotically-charged tingles deep into her womb, all while Lucas continued to go down on Marcie with apparent singular enthusiasm. Guy was a hell of a multi-tasker.

"Yours," she breathed, and his cock swelled with even more blood, if that was possible. It usually was. Always more room at the inn for that appendage, and not a bit of dizziness to go with it. If Lucas was the multi-tasker, Ben guessed his dick's ability to scare the average woman away was his own superpower. Another good reason for the blindfold.

"Yeah," he growled. "Mine tonight, too, lucky bastard that I am. The two most beautiful women in all of New Orleans." He shifted to his knees over her, letting her feel them by her shoulders, hear the click of his belt and tug of zipper as he freed himself.

Marcie moaned as Lucas did something even more creative, but her hand flexed on Cass's. Amazingly, she showed she was staying in tune with what was going on next to her. With over-the-top sexual experiences, one of two things could happen, though sometimes luck gave you both. Either everything narrowed down to an intense tunnel view, or everything became far more detailed and vivid, so nothing could be missed, even blindfolded.

He might razz Lucas about that later, not doing his job well enough to rob his girl of the ability to think about her sister's wellbeing, but he knew the one thing that would supersede even the biggest sexual temptation in this family was care for and protection of one another.

"Relax your throat," Marcie gasped. "Really relax it. And trust him. Oh...God, how *does* he do that with his mouth?"

Cass managed a strangled half chuckle. "He can make you feel that way for hours...will keep you on that edge forever."

Marcie had a reverent expletive to answer that. Perhaps he should question how well he and Lucas were doing their jobs if girl talk was happening, but Ben was pretty sure the comments only turned Lucas and him on more, even though Lucas didn't lift his head. He'd caught Marcie's clit in his teeth and was compressing it while flicking it with his tongue. She squealed and thrashed, panting, and Cass's grip was the one that tightened this time. Time to put her sister in a similar orbit.

Lucas still had his fingers partially in Cass, so when she was lifting and lowering herself she was creating friction. Ben stripped his belt out of his slacks and ran it under her body and over, cinching it just above her nipples, tight. Curling his fingers in it, he held her in an arched position, almost suspended, letting her feel the pressure of its hold and her helplessness before he lowered her to the bed again. Then he gripped his cock in the other hand.

"Open up, darlin'," he commanded in a husky voice. "And do what your sister suggested. Slow, steady breathing, relax the muscles. It'll go easier on you, though easier isn't always what I care about. I want to feel you struggling to suck on my cock, doing your best while Lucas is finger fucking your sweet, silky-soft cunt. I bet until he got you lasered, he'd rub all sorts of nice baby oil into your mound and the lips, make them even softer. Probably still likes to do that, doesn't he?"

He caressed her throat, her jaw, and she parted her lips as he was crooning to her. He pressed the head of his cock to her lips. She'd felt his size before, but hadn't gotten this up close and personal with it. He registered her jolt of surprise, a flash of alarm, but by then he was pushing inward and feeling the bliss of her quivering tongue weighted down by his girth. A light scrape of teeth, then she tried to open her mouth wider. Yep, she and her sister had a similar generosity of spirit when it came to serving a Dom. They also had similar-sized mouths, bless God. Just tight enough.

He kept his fingers on her throat, stroking, reminding her to follow Marcie's directions. She put effort into it, rousing that simultaneous fierce satisfaction and tenderness he could feel, watching a sub work her ass off to take him. The fingers of her free hand opened and closed, evidence of her concentration.

Marcie wailed, a near climax kind of sound, and Lucas pushed her open wider, getting under her clit hood and the piercing where things were so sensitive, too sensitive to let her come. Ben inhaled the strong scent of his sub's arousal, savoring it, but when Marcie strained against Lucas, Ben put a hand on her, holding Cass in place with the other.

"Be still, brat," he commanded. "Absolutely frozen until you can't bear it and have to beg him to let you move."

Lucas's eyes flamed with pleasure as Marcie obeyed with quivering, twitching reluctance, a petulant mewl on her lips, her fingers clawing the sheets.

"Now that I'm giving him a taste of how my sub pleases me"—Ben bared his teeth—"show me how you please your Master, Cass. Do your best to suck me off, because I might just fuck that pretty mouth of yours until I come."

Part Six

Marcie couldn't believe Ben wanted her to be still. Let him fucking try to stay still under Lucas's mouth, which she was now convinced had been created by demons and blessed by an angelic host, amen. The best heaven and hell had to offer when it came to oral sex.

He overlooked nothing. He used his breath like feathers over her clit and labia, then made soft puffs against her wetness, increasing the acute sensations. He thrust his tongue inside her, leaving swirling patterns on the inside of her channel as he sealed his mouth over her at the perfect moment to suck on her clit, the lips of her sex, all while his hand stroked her thigh, or slid around to cup her buttock. He'd pushed her free leg up to rest her calf on his shoulder, so as he played with her pussy with his mouth, he dipped his thumb into her honey and took it to her rim, pushing his fingers in there. That was when she'd wailed, earning her Master's attention and admonition. Now she did her best to stay still—fucking still—while every nerve ending screamed for movement, to writhe and buck.

She had no reason to doubt her sister's words, but experiencing it and thinking Lucas could draw this out for hours...God. When Marcie was a teenager, she recalled weekend mornings Cass had looked as tranquil and languid as a cat that had been napping in the sunshine for days. And it wasn't just a sex thing. The connection vibes had been so strong between her and Lucas it had made Marcie's heart hurt, because, even then, she'd wanted something like it, fitting her own desires and needs.

She recalled one morning, Cass spreading cream cheese on a bagel for Lucas while he stood behind her, his hands sliding beneath her robe behind the counter where no one could see, but Marcie was good at reading body language. He'd said something in Cass's ear, his voice warm and tender, his eyes full of her, and she'd smiled at him the same way, twisting around to give him a bite of the bagel. The devotion and love were so clear. They were as strongly integrated into all of it, and part of it, as the Domination and submission. It wasn't a separate thing.

She knew Ben had his cock in Cass's mouth. Cass would be feeling a little overwhelmed, but excited along with the trepidation. From the noises and things he'd said, Marcie suspected Ben was using the belt the way he used it on her sometimes while making her service him orally from her back. Her nipples tingled, but so did her buttocks as she thought of other ways he employed it after she serviced him. Then Lucas did something else to obliterate thought of anything but what was happening between her legs.

"Oh God...please..."

"You want to move, Marcie," Lucas said, low. "You want to ask for that?"

"Only...if it pleases you, sir. And my Master."

"Mmm. I think we want to watch you break apart from not being able to move. Get more and more out of control. Maybe a little longer..."

She was quickly passing into that zone all their circle of women had talked about experiencing with the K&A men: the "I'm not going to survive this" feeling. But that was okay, because it was always coupled with another, equally emphatic thought.

Who the hell cares?

§

Cass's mind didn't have any room to form thoughts. Her whole being had become sensation. Lucas's fingers kept up an idle pump inside her, his thumb rubbing over her clit as she worked her jaw and lips to keep pace with Ben's slow and steady thrusts. There was no way he had all of his length in her mouth, because he'd be hitting vital organs if that was the case. As it was, from following Marcie's direction, she'd been able to take him past her gag reflex. He tasted of clean, heated male and his musky pre-come, which had bathed her tongue when she first took him in, a thick, salty taste.

Then he made it worse. Curling his fingers in the belt he had wrapped above her breasts, a contrast to the waist cincher below, he began to use his hold on the strap to lift her in rhythm with his movements and thrust deeper. She choked, experiencing a moment of panic, but was startled when he slapped the tips of her breasts with his free hand, sending shards of pleasure zinging through the points, thanks to the restriction of blood flow from the belt that had made them more sensitized. It helped distract her from her panic, which in turn helped her get a handle on her breathing problem.

She made a noise against his cock as her legs moved restlessly, and he grunted. "You're doing so good, darlin'. Think it's about time I took a taste of your pussy. I'm going to stop moving but my cock's not going anywhere. You try your best to break my focus however you can with your sweet lips and tongue. Else your Master's going to hear you come long and hard from another man's mouth on your cunt and you know he won't like that. Maybe use his own belt on you in an entirely different way."

What? How could Lucas blame her for...oh, hell...

Ben shifted forward, tilting her head with strong fingers under her neck to do as he described, no longer moving his hips in that forward thrust, but keeping his cock rammed deep into her mouth and throat as he stretched over her.

Putting his hands on her thighs to spread them, he pulled her free knee up to her side, making her feel as exposed as possible. "Stay just like that," he muttered, and put his mouth on her cunt.

What else could she do? Oh right, try to suck on him, continue to service him orally, while he destroyed her motor control. At their monthly girl get-togethers, they'd joked that the men swapped techniques, such that they'd all benefitted from Lucas's mad oral skills. Dana had them practically falling on the floor crying with laughter when she imitated Matt's voice and the tone of a K&A meeting perfectly.

"Gentlemen, note Exhibit A. Lucas has provided an anatomically-correct rubber pussy to help us understand the freaky-assed magic he does with his double-jointed tongue." And then...*"Okay, that's all for the morning itinerary. Let's break for the catered lunch. When we come back, Ben will provide us insights on drilling your woman to the wall through her ass."*

Marcie had said the man was incapable of not taking advantage of that area, so Cass could hardly be surprised that, while Ben was so artfully sucking and teasing her cunt, one of his hands dipped, a finger slicked with her juices pushing into her rim, then a second one. Since she and Lucas didn't play there as much, it brought a stretching, burning feel. But that helped her not catapult over the edge of the climax he'd threatened, at least not at first. Then the pain and pleasure started to wind in a tight, unstoppable spiral.

She was licking him frenetically, sucking as much of his cock as she could, but as she started teetering over that edge, she knew she wouldn't be able to stop. "No...please... Oh God..." Her words might be muffled, but the meaning was unmistakable as a hard shudder ran through her body, her pussy rippling against his lips.

Ben took his mouth off her, his hands shifting to grip her thighs, holding them spread and the free one in the air, leg pulled back against his side. So open like that, she should have been able to rein back the orgasm, but she was too far gone. It was surging through her lower body, her breasts flushing, and—

Crack!

She yelped as the belt made solid contact with the tender strip between buttock and upper thighs, sending a stinging puff of air over her exposed sex. Holy fuck, that had hurt. How had Ben, while holding her leg, his cock stuffed in her mouth...

Not Ben. Lucas. Lucas had done it, because he was untying her leg from Marcie's, and she felt the press of the belt he was holding doubled over in one hand. As he did that, Ben withdrew his cock slowly from her mouth. Despite her pain and confusion, she still sucked and lapped eagerly at it as it slid over her tongue and lips, her instincts obeying a deeper compulsion than her rational mind. Once he sat back, Ben pulled her legs up into that spread and bent position, leaving her ass and cunt unshielded against her Master's belt. She gasped as it cracked against her buttocks again, then once more.

"Stop...please. It hurts..."

A familiar knee pushed against her throbbing pussy and Lucas's hand was in her hair, holding tight and using his fist behind her skull to bring her halfway up off the bed against him. He spoke against her lips.

"Who does your climax belong to, Cassie? Who?"

He sounded as stern and unyielding as she'd ever heard him. Though she'd started this by saying she wanted to take things to a deeper level, facing it was terrifying and thrilling. Some part of her knew he had this side to him, but to experience it rather than merely fantasize...

"You answer me now, or you get three more."

"You. It belongs to you." She was shaking uncontrollably, like she was caught in the net of that near miss and it wouldn't let her go. She felt like a tightrope walker standing on one toe on a swaying rope.

"That's right. If I decide to give one of those climaxes to Ben, that permission comes from me, not your cunt. Because it's not your cunt, is it?"

She shook her head, and her voice trembled. "It's yours."

"Good." He gathered her up in one arm, running a hand

down her back, holding her against his chest as she fought inexplicable tears. "It's okay. Just breathe. Calm down, sweetheart." It was only then she realized Ben had unclipped her bracelet cuffs from the straps so Lucas could lift her up like this and cradle her.

When Lucas engaged in sensual punishment, it was almost always his belt, because that had been part of his promise when they met.

"You'll get very familiar with my belt. It will hold you like this. Or I'll use it to slap your pretty butt when you don't trust me. Make you have trouble sitting down in your meetings. You'll also bite down on it when I find you for lunch, take you somewhere semiprivate and fuck you up against the wall."

He'd lived up to all of those things, and she wondered if Ben had used his belt around her upper body because Lucas had told him it was a trigger for her. She wouldn't be surprised how much the K&A men knew about what all their women liked. They probably had their own version of the women's monthly get-togethers, Dana's joke not that far off the mark.

Her mind was torn in two directions, but in a way that left her sitting in the center with no thoughts at all but wanting to be held by Lucas. Even as her body yearned after an orgasm cut far too short. But he was right; it was his. She wanted every climax to belong to him.

§

"You're so close to the edge," Ben murmured, passing his fingers over Marcie's wet sex as she heard Lucas crooning to Cass.

"Is she okay?" she asked, though she strangled on a moan as he fingered her.

"Yeah. Just discovering the pleasure of having her Master tear her down harder than he has before so he can build her back up again. I saw your lips pressing together during those belt strokes. You wanted them, didn't you, greedy girl?"

She shook her head, but then re-thought it, letting a tiny

smile creep over her face. "Maybe from Lucas. He doesn't hit as hard as you."

He snorted. "Better ask Cass about that. She didn't know how much he was holding back until tonight." Ben untied her arm from the bed straps and let her put it down at her side. He rubbed her shoulder, arms and wrist, then her hip and thigh where she'd been tied to Cass, checking circulation and restoring movement to her joints. Then he scooped her up and moved them to the opposite edge of the bed. She expected he was giving Cass and Lucas a private moment, letting Lucas administer a little intermission aftercare. She squirmed impishly on his lap, against the steel bar beneath her ass. "Seems like she took good care of you."

"Jealous?"

"Nope. She puts the wrong kind of moves on my man, I'll toss all her dress heels in the yard and mow over them with the John Deere. She knows it."

She heard the wince in his voice. "You women are mean."

Marcie giggled, but then elbowed him. "Yes," she whispered. "I'm jealous. Not in a bad way, but I don't like anyone taking care of you but me. This is the only exception because all of us..."

"We're family." He nodded. "Same way I'd react if anyone else outside K&A was putting their mouth on your cunt. I'd shove their nose up in it and hold it there until they died of asphyxiation."

"Wow. Boys can be mean, too."

"We're territorial. But I don't worry about that. I've got a kickass sub who would put anyone in the wall who touched her who shouldn't."

"You got that right." Then Marcie sighed and laid her head on his shoulder. "You're sure she's okay?" she asked, low, fretting about the blindfold enough to pluck at it with a restless finger. He clasped her wrist and put her hand back down in her lap.

"Yeah. Positive. I think she wants this, and is ready for it. It won't be the standard for them it is for you and me, but tonight, she's opening up her horizons and going a little deeper and more hardcore." He nuzzled her temple. "How's my girl, other than worrying too much about her sister? You did good, staying still under Lucas's mouth. You mostly held out, though you move more than any woman I know while not moving. You're like an electron. Lucas was charged up for sure, watching you and Cass side by side. I'm proud of you."

It warmed her to hear it, and she put her face into the heated crevice between his shoulder and throat. "Knowing he was going down on both of us..." Marcie shivered. "It was crazy hot."

"Met all those teen fantasies and surpassed them, did he?" There was a growl to Ben's voice that gave her an additional tremor. "Well, good, because now you're going to do the one you thought about the most. Only you'll do it the way Lucas and I want to see it rolled out. If you do it well enough, you might get the belt you're craving before I fuck you. And it won't be Lucas wielding it on your soft ass."

Her pulse leaped, but she reined it back with tremendous effort. She couldn't let go of the worry. "Maybe we should hold off on that until later, when it's just the two of us. I'm not sure Cass..."

"What's rule one in session?" He captured her chin in thumb and forefinger, stilling her. She pressed her lips together, her brow creasing.

"I trust you. I ask permission to tell you any concerns I have and, if you grant me that permission, I tell you. Then it's up to you to decide how or if to act on them."

"You didn't ask permission, but I'll just add that in to your belt punishment. But you've told me your concerns, so now you let go of anything but your Master's desires. I'm ordering you down on your ass, on the floor at the end of the bed."

Closing her eyes under the blindfold, Marcie willed herself to obey the "letting go" part, using the two words that most often helped her do that.

"Yes, sir."

Part Seven

Once he'd moved Marcie there, making sure her back was against the foot board, her knees folded up beneath her, Ben saw Lucas was ready for the next thing they'd discussed. He'd quietly commanded Cass to stretch out again on the bed and bend her knees over the end of the mattress. There was only a short space between her dangling right leg and where Marcie was sitting on the floor, her back to the footboard. The large mirror on the wall across from the foot of the bed gave Ben a view not only of his sub, in back-straight, breasts-thrust-out, submissive-waiting posture, but of what lay between Cass's spread thighs, the ruffled petals of her sex parted and wet, slightly quivering with the nervous movements of her legs. Her breasts were succulent mounds above the trim line of her rib cage, the tips still taut and deep pink, begging to be sucked.

He kept an eye on the women as Lucas completely stripped, then Lucas took over the monitoring as he did the same, folding his clothes over a chair, taking off his watch and laying it on the side table, a noise that had both women tilting their heads like birds in a yard, listening for predators.

Ben slid onto the bed, gripped Cass's wrists above the bracelets and drew her arms over her head once more. "Your sister ever tell you the fantasy she had as a bad, naughty teenager?" he asked. "At least one version of it. She had several."

Cass shook her head. Her upper body was shaking from nerves, too, the right kind, as they drew her into this new territory. Ben folded his knees beneath him, and wrapped her hands around his still erect cock, letting her rest her forearms on his thighs. "That's your anchor point this time, darlin'," he said. "You hold onto that and don't let go until you're told to do so. Trust me, it can take a lot of abuse, so you squeeze as hard as you need to. Want to tell her the fantasy, Lucas?"

"I think it might be more entertaining if Marcie did it, since it's her fantasy."

Ben knew that, of course, but enjoyed watching Marcie get more anxious at the byplay, starting to understand where it was going. "Turn around and stand up on your knees, brat," he ordered.

As she did, Lucas guided her, shifting behind Marcie, holding her shoulders, stroking her hair. When he moved up against her back, Ben saw her register with a jolt that Lucas was naked...and armed with a substantial hard-on. Sliding his hands down, Lucas cupped and fondled Marcie's breasts as she summoned words, though she was a delightful rose color. His submissive was discomfited by this.

He was intrigued by his own response, watching Lucas skillfully rouse Marcie's nipples to aching. They were all good at this stuff, but despite their willingness to share with one another, Ben knew when he had Marcie to himself again, he'd take her even more thoroughly, to re-establish his sole claim on her. He had no doubt that Lucas would do the same. The crazy thing was that it didn't conflict with his earlier thoughts about how he felt about these men or the women they were with. It didn't have to all make sense to be correct and work.

He realized Marcie hadn't yet spoken, and her hedging snapped his Dom's attention right back to the present. "Tell him," Ben commanded.

Marcie cleared her throat. "Um...I would imagine coming into your bedroom."

"Whose bedroom?" Ben said sharply.

"Cass's. Well, Lucas and Cass's."

"You're talking directly your sister. Not to me."

Marcie shifted and Lucas increased his grip on her. "I want to hear it," he said in her ear, a silky purr. "Tell me what the younger sister was imagining when I was claiming her sister, pleasuring her, night after night, behind that thin wall."

Marcie turned even rosier, but she obeyed both Master's directives, now addressing Cass. "Lucas would have you tied up, the way I imagined it when I was listening to you two through the walls. Though you were quiet, the walls *are* sort of thin. I would leave my bed and tip toe to your door, and find it cracked. I tried to slip in without being seen, because I couldn't bear just listening anymore, merely imagining what I was sure he was doing, how he was doing it. I knew because of the tie downs I found tucked in between the mattress and box springs when it was my turn to do laundry."

Cass turned a shade of rose herself, a genetic match that Ben was sure was turning Lucas on as much as it was him. Was there anything as hot as their beautiful ladies being all shy and embarrassed? They were wanton and uninhibited under command, in the throes of arousal, but at the core they were ladies, a hundred percent class. It was a deep pleasure to ruffle them in the right ways.

"But Lucas would catch me." Marcie allowed herself a wry smile, her arms twitching under Lucas's hold. "He wouldn't chase me. He'd just give me that look that tells me I better not run. He had you blindfolded, and so he said nothing and you didn't know I was there until he leaned down and whispered..." She moistened her lips.

"Say it." Lucas tugged on her hair, as he gave the command this time.

"'Your sister has snuck in to watch us,' he'd say. 'I'm going to make her...suck me off while I eat your cunt until you come. Then you'll finish me off.'

"Before Cass can say anything," Marcie continued, "he points to the floor between his feet and the foot of the bed. He's naked, so when he bends over and puts his mouth on you, I know what to do. I get on my knees and take his cock in my mouth."

"And do you know why, in your fantasy, you have Lucas say that to your sister?" Ben asked Marcie. "Other than to make your wanton little pussy cream?"

"Because even in my fantasy, I needed to know it was okay, because I wasn't trying to take what belonged to her. I just wanted to be part of...that feeling. Serving a Master."

"Yes. Well done, baby."

Cass's grip was quivering on Ben's shaft, sending nice ripples up and down it. Lucas eased Marcie back down into the position she'd described, only this time, he put her between Cass's dangling feet, guiding his wife so the soles of her feet rested on Marcie's shoulders, her knees bent and spread wide, keeping her pussy exposed and available to the maximum amount of sensation. Then Lucas nodded to Ben.

"Don't let my girl's fingers cramp, holding that baseball bat of yours so tight."

"Cramping's far more likely to happen when she's holding something with a smaller girth. Like your dick. Ow." Ben winced and chuckled, as he tugged Cass's hair. "Ease up with the claws, defensive kitten."

"That's my girl," Lucas said approvingly, but any words Cass might have mustered vanished as he put his mouth back on the still-swollen tissues between her legs.

Cass's fingers convulsed for a different reason now, her mouth stretching beneath the blindfold in stirred response. Ben settled his hand over hers, guiding her in a slow stroke up and down his length. "Marcie, time to get to work."

She didn't need to be told twice. Shifting up onto her knees, she curled her hand around Lucas's base and put her mouth on him. Lucas made a hungry growl of approval against Cass's pussy, and she moaned, as if all the stimulus, what she could feel and hear, took flight in her imagination. Which was the intent.

Though Ben had a pleasurable view of Cass's magnificent upper body, lifting and twisting against Lucas's ministrations, her breasts wobbling and quivering in sensual display, his eyes stayed trained on the brief, chaste glimpses of his own sub, the movement of her pale shoulder, most everything else hidden behind the block of Lucas's upper body and shoulders. He knew what Lucas was feeling, knew how clever and relentless and sweetly enthusiastic Marcie could be when using her mouth. Sucking, tugging, nipping, licking. She liked to furrow the tip of her tongue into the slit to sip out any juice. Or swirl all the way around the head, then tuck her tongue in the channel beneath the glans and drag it along the circumference in some damnably crazy way sure to have a man clawing for self-control. Yep, there it was, the slight jerk in Lucas's lower body as she did it, then played with the thrumming vein that ran all along his length. He shoved himself more aggressively into her mouth, a tactic Ben knew would also make it harder for Marcie to push him too fast, while stimulating her more with the demand.

While enjoying the talents of Ben's sub, Lucas was also apparently enjoying the hell out of his wife's pussy. Cass's hands squeezed and released Ben's cock in mindless, erratic response, rubbing, digging in, no rhyme or rhythm to it, but that was okay. When Ben came, it was going to be inside his own wife. Fuck, since on a normal day it gave him a hard-on just to say those two words, it was no surprise his existing hard-on made a significant jump in Cass's grip.

But he controlled his response, because he wanted to have enough brain cells left to see Lucas push Cass into full blown orgasm, all while trying to hold out against Marcie's mouth.

Good luck with that, buddy. I know just how difficult it is. But he knew Lucas would do it, because how they'd intended for all this to roll out was a pleasurable fantasy of its own. Of course, there was no reason Lucas couldn't enjoy an orgasm now and an orgasm later. He was a planner, after all.

Another cry broke from Cass, that lovely sound of desperation that came right before a climax swept her away. Having just had the pleasure of eating Cass's pussy, Ben could let his lids drop to half-mast and re-experience it in his mind as he worked her slim fingers up and down his shaft, showing her how to jerk him off. Seeing Cass had brought some pre-come to the top, Ben collected that on his fingers and painted it on her parted, panting lips, pleased when her tongue swiped out to lick it and his fingertips.

Her moans escalated.

Lucas met his gaze, the only cue Ben needed. He slid Cass's hands off his dick but retained his lock on her wrists as he shifted back. In the same synchronized movement, Lucas freed himself from Marcie's mouth with a thumb to the corner of her lips, ensuring she didn't clamp down on him in her fervor to hold on. It told Ben she'd gotten herself into the zone of pure service, his beautiful, perfect sub, and Lucas had recognized it. The quick contorted expression on Lucas's face said she'd almost done her job too well, making him damn near miss his target.

As he straightened, one hand replacing his mouth on Cass's sex, stroking and taking her through the aftershocks, Lucas nodded to Ben. Untying the lacing with swift fingers, Ben removed Cass's blindfold, revealing her Master at last, looming over her.

It ensured she was staring into his face as he began to climax, working his cock, his seed jetting onto her breasts and abdomen, over her mons and the lips of her sex. Grunts broke from his lips at the force of his ejaculation and likely in reaction to the hungry look on his wife's face. Ben noticed Marcie's hands were on Lucas's thighs, her lips nuzzling that terrain as she stayed clear but didn't deny herself contact during his release.

When Ben let go of Cass's hands, she used them to good effect, cupping her breasts and sliding Lucas's seed over them, rubbing it into the areolae, her abdomen and down lower, spreading out that marking. Lucas's eyes stayed trained on her, his mouth firm and eyes gray molten steel. Ben doubted either of them knew he or Marcie were even in the room in this second of time.

Ben slid quietly from the bed, leaving them in that lock, and dropped to one knee at the foot of the bed. Closing his hand on Marcie's biceps, he drew her out from between the other couple. Marcie's lips were parted and slack, telling him her gaze, if he could see it, was likely as hungry and dazed as Cass's. She latched onto Ben's forearm as she rose to her knees, following his lead.

While he led her to the living area, Lucas was stretching out on top of Cass. Her legs lifted and clamped over his hips, a moan emitting from her lips at the full contact between their bodies.

Ben tossed a towel over an easy chair seat cushion before sitting his bare ass down on it, then pushed Marcie to her knees before him. "Finish what your sister started," he said, curling his hand in her hair. But before he let her obey, he cupped her jaw, massaging the muscles. "Sore?"

She nodded, but her lips were already parting in eager

compliance. "Good," he said softly. "That way I know you'll work for it."

Her long lashes fanned her cheeks as she took him in, took him deeper than pretty much any woman ever had, except a high dollar escort he'd blown several thousand dollars on one night in Rio, after he was told her specialty was blowing oversized dicks. Not a thought he wanted to be having here, and one he put away easily. It wouldn't matter to him if Marcie couldn't take a third of his length; he preferred her lips to any others now.

As he removed her blindfold, setting it aside, his good girl kept her head down, focused on her task. Her contented noises made him want to pump into her mouth even more insistently. If he told her to stay in this position all day, she would have no complaints. It soothed and centered her, the acts of pure service, but he was too selfish. He liked to see her get so hot and bothered and keep her there, holding any relief just out of reach long enough she'd get riled up, bare her teeth and unsheathe claws.

But right now, he needed some fucking relief to his own lust to see the next part of their loose plan through. Nothing was written in stone, not in things like this, but there were some possibilities he and Lucas had shared a mutual interest in exploring tonight. Neither had any illusions this was going to be regular thing. Some things were special not only because they were shared with the woman you wanted most, but because they only happened once in a blue moon.

Fuck, she was good at this. No matter what he'd said, he'd kept his hand on her jaw and throat, mindful of her pace so he didn't tax her too much, but his other hand had a whole different agenda, hard on her scalp, pushing her down on him. Deeper. Deeper. Her tongue lashing him, mouth sucking on him, the lovely tears spilling forth from the strain of taking him, her shoulders quivering, breasts against his shins, nipples dragging along his skin, and...

His hand tightened and he held her still, though her mouth continued to work as he pumped into it, head dropping back as his seed spewed into that hot cavern. He came so violently she choked, something she rarely did anymore, but she recovered fast. Swallowing him down even more quickly to catch up, she used both hands to spread the escaped fluid over his shaft and lick it all away, sucking on the velvet skin, teasing him with the edge of her teeth as he shuddered.

"Brat," he muttered with a half-smile, but he tipped up her face, pulling a tissue from a box on the side table and gesturing her forward to wipe her eyes, the corners of her mouth. He tsked gently. "Such a mess you made," he reproved. The soft, amused and aroused light in her brown eyes hit him in the gut as it always did. A deer's eyes were soulful and captured the most primal level of what nature and the world were about. Hers had always reminded him of that, particularly right now. She'd done all he'd asked. They'd stimulated her all the way to the edge, and not let her come. Time to let her go over in one of the ways she liked best. Not the number one way, but that would come later. He'd be fucking her very thoroughly before this night was over. As he'd recognized earlier, he would mark his territory first and last. Lucas would understand. It was a guy thing.

The blindfolds would stay off for this next part, a calculated but deliberate risk, which was why he'd talked about it with Marcie first. He'd been surprised to find she not only understood his thinking, but agreed, even if, now that the moment had come, there was trepidation in her gaze.

He framed her face in one large hand. "Trust your Master," he said quietly.

She gave him her smile that the angels couldn't rival and kissed his rough palm. He shifted her so she was curled in between his feet, allowing her to wrap her arms around one of his legs and rest her head against his knee. It was a position he allowed when he needed her to calm down for a few minutes and center herself for the next thing. He called her brat, but in reality she was such a good girl, a beautiful and willing sub, so much of the time. He fondled her hair as her lips brushed his knee and she pressed her temple against him, waiting quietly for the next thing he'd demand of her, no matter that he could tell from the vibration of her body that she was in near desperate need of release. But she'd learned to ride that edge with him, because nothing satisfied the sadistic Dom side of him like knowing that he'd taken her to that ledge and could command her to stay on it indefinitely.

As he'd said, she was a good girl. Hell, she was a fucking amazing woman.

He turned his gaze to Lucas and his own amazing woman, visible through the wide archway to the bedroom. Though Lucas had stretched out upon Cass and let her hold him, he hadn't given in to her wish that he put his semi-erect cock inside her, not yet. He'd merely reconfirmed their connection, engaging in a few long kisses while her body strained up against his and she mewled in frustration as he held her still and enjoyed her at his leisurely pace. All Doms indulged in a certain amount of sadism, after all.

However, seeing Ben was done, Lucas broke the last kiss and lifted Cass in his arms to bring her to another chair in the living room, on the opposite side of the coffee table with its centerpiece of fresh fuchsia-colored orchids. Cracking a bottle of water, Lucas shared it with his sub, rehydrating, but as he did, he had the fingers of his free hand stroking her sex. There was an ice bucket with the complimentary champagne on the side table next to him, and he dipped into it, coming back with little shards of ice and water droplets to anoint her breasts, making her squirm. She caught her lip in her teeth as he circled a larger piece of ice over her nipple. "Be still," he told her with quiet authority. After a flash of surprise in her blue eyes, she obeyed. Ben saw her fingers curl uncertainly into the arm of the easy chair.

With limited time at home to play unless they arranged for the teens to be away for a night, Lucas and Cass's chances for prolonged play were slimmer than they were for him and Marcie. After the intensity of what they'd just done, some part of Cass's mind might be so conditioned to those limited blocks of time that she'd assumed, if things weren't completely over tonight, they were probably moving into a lower gear, a pleasurable downhill grade where Lucas would allow her to come and then that would morph into some casual lovemaking. Rather than a continuation of the same. Or something even more demanding and intense.

With his succinct command, Lucas told her otherwise. Her gaze was held by his, her breath also held as he ran the ice over both nipples and she responded like a struck tuning fork.

"I'm not done with you," Lucas said. "Not by a long shot, sweetheart. I have you all night long. I'm hungry to taste you again, hear you scream. I want your nails to tear the skin from my back as I take you over that edge where you think if you don't draw blood, you might fall too hard. But I'm not going to give you much choice about that."

When his hips shifted, her eyes widened, telling Ben that his boy had proven to her he wasn't making empty threats. His recuperation time could live up to every word he'd just said. As he lifted his gaze to meet Ben's, Ben received the message without a word spoken. Intermission over.

"Before you get started on that," Ben said casually, "I'll be needing your lady's help. Let me grab some pants." Rising and disentangling himself from Marcie with a stroke of her hair, he went to the corner of the dining room, where they'd tucked away the bag that had carried the straps, gag and any other diversions they thought might come in handy with their ladies tonight. He'd also thrown in a pair of jeans, since the rest of his overnight wear and toiletries were in the suite across the hall.

Pulling the jeans on but leaving the top button undone, he returned to the living room. As he stood over Marcie again, her arms wound back around his leg, her lips on the denim over his knee, and then her teeth. He flicked her shoulder in quick admonishment and she eased back, though her fingers rested on his bare toes, lightly fondling. Little terror. She knew he was ticklish there.

"Arms back," he told her. "Submissive posture, since you can't behave."

She pouted prettily but straightened, arms boxed behind her back so she was straight as a stick, breasts thrust out, knees spread. He saw Cass's eyes follow the movement. Some trepidation had entered her gaze, now that she could see her sister actively engaged in sexual play. But Lucas curled his hand in her hair, tipping her head back with firm force before sliding ice along her throat.

"Was Ben speaking to you?" he asked pleasantly, though his eyes, pinning her in place, were cool.

She shook her head and made a little noise as his grip obviously tightened, pulling her hair harder. "No, sir."

"Then your eyes should stay on me, in case I need something from you." He transferred more ice from the bucket into her palm and guided it down, down until he made her rub it between her legs. She squirmed, but he kept it up, holding her fast. "I want you to caress your whole body with this ice until it melts. Then I'm going to suck the drops off you." His gaze gleamed. "So make sure they fall where you think I'd want my mouth."

"You were saying?" he said, addressing Ben again, though his eyes remained on his sub's attempt to obey him. Watching Cass get into the protocol more deeply brought Ben's cock back to life, too. It wasn't that he'd forgotten how effective a Dom Lucas was; he just hadn't seen it switched up this high in awhile.

"Yeah, my sub has earned herself some punishment. She's going to get to come, but only while I'm strapping her ass with my belt. Figure your sub could be her counterweight while you work her up for your cock again. Win-win."

Cass's fingers hesitated, the ice on her abdomen. Lucas made a noise, sending it moving again. "Higher," he said, with deceptive gentleness. "All over those pretty tits I love to suck. Get the nipples cold so I can make them warm again. Un-unh." Catching her furtive, sidelong glance, he gripped her chin, bringing her face back to him once more.

"Do you know what Ben's sub is doing? Staring at his feet. Who are you in this moment? Are you anyone's sister? You only have one name and identity here. What is it? Do you remember?"

"Yours. Your sub." Cass was getting agitated, Ben could see it. They'd anticipated it, had talked about whether they'd need to bring the blindfold back into the scene to keep this working for her. That remained their fallback position, but that would be Lucas's call. Ben picked up on Marcie's awareness of her sister's distress, but when she shifted, he put his hand on her shoulder, reassuring and stilling her at once. And sending her that unspoken message again.

Trust your Master. And she could trust Lucas in that capacity, just as much. *We've got this. We've got both of you, and we won't let either of you fall down or be hurt.*

He knew she knew that, but it was a good feeling to see her register it and settle back down. That would help Cass as well.

"All mine," Lucas confirmed, tipping up Cass's chin and kissing her slow and long, winding one arm around her. Gripping her wrist with his other hand, he guided her back to the bucket to release the ice before bringing her palm back to his side. He shivered and smiled against her lips as he stoically took the cold and warmed her palm with his own body. The playfulness seemed to calm her, as did that kiss. Ben noticed Marcie sneaking a look, but since he saw the dreamy look on her face, the seemingly universal female response to movie quality kisses, he didn't dissuade her, just wryly grimacing at Lucas. Smooth operator. But it worked because it was genuine, not merely seductive charm. Lucas loved his wife and it showed.

Ben knew the feeling. He'd have taken the same tactic, but it wasn't the right timing for where he and Marcie needed to go. But he fully intended to indulge in some long, drugging kisses later. He never stopped craving her mouth, no matter what they were doing.

"All right, baby," Ben murmured. "On your feet."

He took her arm to steady her, since she was still on deep burn with all the other provocation saturating the room. Guiding her to the sofa, he had her brace her hands on the arm, spread her legs and position her body in a half-folded-over position that canted her hips up the way he wanted.

Lucas lifted Cass and carried her to the sofa, too, stretching her out on her back so her head was near the arm where Marcie's hands were gripping. She could look up at her sister. Marcie mischievously shook her loose hair down into her sister's face. Cass wrinkled her nose and batted at it, her visage relaxing more at her sister's teasing. Ben gathered up Marcie's hair, using one of the hair ties he habitually carried for just that purpose so her lovely locks wouldn't cause her an unwelcome distraction or, in this case, an impediment to her view.

"And you thought you were the only one who was going to get a strapping," Marcie told Cass. "You don't get to have all the fun."

"She will if you keep speaking without permission," Ben advised. Marcie made a face of exaggerated compliance and lifted her hips even higher, a coquettish move as she looked back at him. The position was sure to get him rock hard and drive his Master's instinct to thrash her brazen ass. He knew part of her impertinence was intended to help Cass make the transition to what was to come, but he'd only give her a certain amount of latitude for that. However, being Marcie, she'd push it to the limits. The Always Yours, forget-me-not collar gleamed from the soft lamplight in the living area of the suite, though her hair was further haloed by the gentle illumination provided by the terrace lights outside the French doors.

Lucas had disappeared into the bedroom during their byplay and now reappeared. "Just to get you in the right place," he told Cass, and produced some of Jon's diabolical warming oil.

Part Eight

Oh, holy hell. Marcie understood the half-terrified look on Cass's face all too well. Jon's warming oil should be classified as a controlled substance or dangerous street drug. The oil, when placed on nipples or sex, didn't merely heat and mildly stimulate the flesh, adding to an already erotic encounter. It brought to life nerve endings to full scale arousal, just the opposite side of lose-your-fucking-mind. When it reached its full potency, it was like being stopped at the top of the orgasm train and held there, in throbbing, insane stasis. All the recipient wanted to do was climax, and every touch of your Master's mouth and hands only intensified the condition.

Ben had restrained her last time he used it because he'd kept her in that frame of mind for the maximum amount of time Jon recommended it be used, probably because at that threshold it reduced the submissive to the deepest, darkest realms of an erotic jungle of response.

A weak protest was on Cass's lips, but Lucas knelt beside the couch, putting an almost chaste kiss on her smooth mound.

"I want you to understand what Ben is about to do to Marcie," he said, meeting his wife's gaze. "I think this will help you. And give you pleasure." His brow cocked, his eyes sparking with a hint of mischief. "Plus, using this oil on you is more of my evil yet charmingly boyish fantasy. Will you refuse your Master?"

Despite the teasing, there was a serious tone beneath it Marcie detected, as she was sure Cass did. If she truly didn't want it, Lucas would let it go, because if Cass didn't believe his words or intent, letting him use that oil was like agreeing to let someone roofie your drink to get you past inhibitions you wisely should have.

Marcie recalled Dana telling the women about a conversation she'd had with Jon after Peter had used it on her.

"Conceivably, it could do that," Jon had said when Dana asked him the question so bluntly. *"If your Master has no ethics at all, let alone love for his sub, your will could be overwhelmed when it's applied, because the physical response is so extreme, it would make it difficult to hold onto your objections. You'd just let yourself get swept away. But when it wears off, emotional fallout from going too far under its influence can slam down on the sub like a ton of bricks. That's why it will never be used outside this group unless it's by select, trusted friends, like Leland.*

"If your Master knows you, if he's listening, even when you are fully under its influence, he will know the line past which you are not willing to go, even if he could push you past it with its help. A Master's goal is for your experience

to be what you truly desire on every level, beginning and end. The oil's ideal intent is to provide an eye-opening, adventurous experience the sub is interested in exploring or understanding. It's not to push her into new territory before she's ready to be there, or into a place she never wants to go at all."

As if picking up on that thought process, Lucas held her gaze and added another question, same as what Ben had asked Marcie. "Will you trust your Master? Your husband? The man who loves you and holds your wellbeing over anything else?"

Cass's expression softened and she pressed her lips together. "You forgot one. My best friend. And yes, I do. To all those things. But just for the record, I hate you."

"We all do, when you guys use that stuff," Marcie muttered. "Even when we're screaming and worshipping at your feet because you did use it."

"The joyous mystery that is woman, and the blessing that is Jon's deviant mind. A match made in the dungeon club of Heaven." Ben chuckled, gripping her hips. "Elbows down on the sofa."

As Marcie complied, Ben went back into the bedroom for a moment. Marcie enjoyed the backside view, shirtless and in the worn but intriguingly fitted jeans, then shifted her attention to Lucas, smearing the oil on Cass's sex. Cass arched up at the stimulation of his touch, the initial heat. Setting the bottle aside, he leaned forward and blew on her, which Marcie knew would accelerate the effect. Then Lucas gave his wife another command.

"Reach over your head and grip Marcie's upper arms to help anchor yourself and her."

Marcie's braced forearms on the sofa arm would take care of her own stability for what was about to happen on her side of things, but she understood Lucas wanted to keep Cass's attention on Marcie's face, and the physical reactions she'd feel through her palms.

Marcie leaned down and puffed air in her sister's face. "Check out how badass these guns of mine are getting," she said, flexing her biceps a little under Cass's touch. "I'm going to beat Ben at arm wrestling any day now."

Cass wet her lips and shifted. Her eyes were already glazing a little, telling Marcie the oil was kicking in. But her sister succeeded in offering a typical older sister reply. "Yeah, and you'll be so butch you'll have no body fat. Let him arm wrestle the other guys. Keep the boobs he likes so much. Else he'll be staring at mine and Rachel's. More than he does already."

"God would not have made breasts if he didn't intend men to stare at them," Ben said, returning.

Marcie made a face at her sister, but when she glanced up, she saw Ben was carrying the belt from his slacks, and the gleam in his gaze was unmistakable. Anticipation and fear surged through her vitals, an adrenaline spike.

She knew how to handle that. As her Master circled behind her, Marcie started her deep breathing, relaxing everything from the center outward, which put her in a different headspace. Impulsively, she bent and kissed her sister's forehead. "You are so beautiful," she said. "I'm saying that in a total sister way, but really, you are. When I was a shallow teenager, I used to pray I'd be as beautiful as you, but now...I'm just so proud to have such a beautiful sister."

"You're far prettier..." Cass said. The oil was making her sound breathy, but there was surprise in her countenance at Marcie's words.

"I said beautiful," Marcie corrected. "There's a difference. In and out, and you have it. It's in Lucas's eyes every time he looks at you, because he sees all of it. That's really what I wanted, when I started realizing what beauty meant. You helped bring me to Ben as much as anyone, Cass, because I felt that way with him. Everything I wanted to be, could be, I knew I could make happen with him. He looks at me and thinks I'm beautiful, too."

She realized the men had paused, caught by her words. Even though Cass's mind was the one being swept away, Ben had conditioned Marcie's body and mind to switch to a highly aroused state from the moment he locked a collar on her. While it made her ready to serve her Master upon command, that state was inextricably linked to her emotions, so they were also close to the surface and ready to be called, like now.

Lucas slid his hand down to play his fingers over Cass's clit. Cass lost her focus entirely, her throat working. As she tried to answer Marcie, Marcie shook her head. "Ssh. It's okay. Just feel all the wonderful things they're doing to us. Listen, watch, feel…and get lost in all of it."

Cass moaned, her legs shifting. "Un-unh. Time to deal with those." Lucas moved down and secured the cuffs on her legs to straps he pulled out from two of the wooden sofa feet. One of them he ran up the back of the sofa and over the top, wrapping it under her knee so her leg was propped up on the top cushion, while the other was cinched down by the ankle against the leading edge of the seat cushion, keeping her limbs spread. "Got to keep these apart, no friction to move that oil around," he said. Then he leaned over her and put his mouth on the rise of her breast, his fingertips sliding lightly along the underside of her arm, her rib cage, to her hip.

Cass made an incoherent plea, her nails digging into Marcie's upper arms. Marcie absorbed the pain as Ben's belt licked around her thighs. Her Master curled an arm around her waist, curving his body over her, his straining denim-covered cock against her ass, his bare chest a wall behind her shoulder blades. "Still talking without permission," he said pleasantly.

"Yes, Master. I wanted to help relax her."

"Which was fine, if you'd asked first. But you know that." He gripped her hair in one strong hand and jerked her head to the right, teeth latching onto her shoulder, hard enough Marcie flinched and squirmed, a whimper of pain breaking from her as he held the pressure on the bite and made the effect even more acute. Cass's eyes widened, a reaction to the force and aggression Ben had used.

Oh, sis, you haven't seen the half of it, Marcie thought with desperate, lust-infused humor. Her body spiraled up at it inevitably did, her response building with every demand and strain he put upon her. It was a special magic between them, and Cass was being given a front row seat, though fortunately buffered by Lucas, for her mind was obviously torn between what was going on above her and the wet sounds Lucas was making. He'd moved from teasing her breasts with his lips to suckling one of her nipples. He firmly kneaded the other breast as he did that, pinching the tip. Cass's spread legs quivered and jerked, trying to get some relief from the stimulation and the building effect of the oil.

"Didn't you?" Ben growled. "You knew you were disobeying."

He was good about that, reminding her what his question was, knowing how hard it was for her to concentrate when he took command of her body. "Yes sir," Marcie whispered.

"And why do you do that?"

"I want...to please you. And punishing me pleases you."

He gave a dark chuckle and drew back, rubbing his fingers along the bite impression, a touch as gentle as the bite had been rough. That was another way he unraveled her. "Well, I plan to be pretty damn pleased when I'm done with you, little girl."

She closed her eyes. Thank Goddess. His next words made her smile, though.

"No way in hell you're ever going to beat me in arm wrestling. Even if I have to cheat."

She instinctively lifted her hips as she heard him shift the belt to his other hand. "Pretty slut," he said. "Showing me your wet cunt. Think that will buy you mercy? Think you can lead me around by my cock?"

She shook her head and yelped as he popped the belt against her upper thigh. He'd had it doubled over. "Yes sir. I mean, no sir."

She bit back a feral grin at the intentional mistake, and heard his muffled chuckle. This was going to get serious, pretty fast, but such initial flirting and rebellious playfulness could be part of the foreplay. One of her favorite tactics at home was trying to run from him and doing her very best to stay out of his grasp. The longer she managed it, the more creative and intense the punishment she received. But it was thrilling—and scary—how he always, always caught her. She wouldn't ever want to be the thing Ben O'Callahan was hunting if he intended harm, but when he was determined to capture *her*, it merely sent erotic thrills through her entire body.

Cass's gaze locked with hers, but Marcie knew in a matter of moments she wasn't going to be any more cognizant of anything than Cass would be with the oil at full intensity. She stroked her sister's hair, a small infraction amid the others, and put her hand back on the couch, latching onto the cushion, though she tried not to grip too hard, because locking up her muscles was against the rules. She bit her lip as Ben fed a lubricated thick dildo into her pussy, one with a clit stimulator that began to vibrate at a low hum, sure to keep her hot and worked up, no matter the pain.

"You belong to me," he said in a deep-throated purr. "But you need something in your pussy to keep you focused. "Now, how many strokes have you earned?"

"As many as my Master thinks I should have." Because she was never wise when it came to these things, she added impishly, "Probably a million."

He grunted and slapped the belt against his leg, a sharp pop that made Cass jump, her hands holding onto Marcie. "Marcie...oh..."

Whatever thought or concern Cass was going to utter got caught and died somewhere as Lucas did something with his mouth on Cass's nipple, at the same moment he dropped his hand to feather it over her clit again. "Oh God." She strained up against her bonds as if she'd been hit by an electric charge. The oil itself was overwhelming, but when your Master touched you, adding to that intimacy, it was devastating to all the senses.

Marcie let go of everything but what her Master was about to demand of her. From blissful experience, she knew he was exactly like that oil. In full blown Master mode, he allowed no room to think, feel or experience anything but what he demanded she think, experience...or feel.

Would she ever tire of this anticipation, one part terror, two parts eager anticipation? Yet how would she feel if it truly horrified Cass to glimpse how she and Ben expressed what was between them? Trepidation disrupted the building anticipation in her stomach. If her sister didn't understand, if they'd judged wrong, if they never should have brought this part of it into Lucas's fantasy, the gift Cass had so wanted to give him, that was supposed to be good for them both...

"Ben." She'd whispered it, but his hand curved over her shoulder, strong, solid, reassuring.

"I love you, brat," he murmured.

And she knew it would be okay.

Part Nine

Cass felt like she was in a tropical storm, held only by Lucas's arms. He'd created that storm inside her body. Her cunt was rippling in pre-orgasmic spasms, her nipples achingly tight from that and his mouth. With every pull on them, the feel of his teeth, the constriction of his hands around the curves, she was undulating and bucking as if she was being whipped and spun, lifted and dropped by those winds. But he had her, his hands not just focusing on breasts and pussy, but also caressing her sides and hips, his eyes flicking up to meet hers, giving her an anchor and mediating what was going on above her, keeping it from disrupting her even as she was digesting it.

She knew Ben was a hardcore sadist, but that move, when he'd jerked Marcie's head to the side and bit her, had startled Cass, but not as much as the glittering, dangerous look in his eyes, the suddenly harsh set of his mouth, almost cruel. All the K&A men were powerful. He could break Marcie's neck by drawing on very little of his strength.

But as the oil changed her view of everything to shades of sensual reds, lush greens and the rolling blue of warm, wet seas, something more than the force of his movement captured her attention. Marcie's look of near bliss at the rough treatment, her eyes half-closed and lips parted, fingers digging into the sofa cushion even harder. So hard that her biceps contracted under Cass's hold.

The crack of the belt had made Cass jump, but it hadn't even touched Marcie. Maybe she'd just close her eyes during this part and get lost in Lucas, blacking out anything or anyone else in the room. Some of that happened naturally anyway, she reasoned. The more he swept her along where he wanted her to go, the more the world narrowed down to just him and his demands. But for some reason she couldn't do it. Some primitive, fascinated part of her, connected to the thundering heat between her legs, and the erotic, dense heat saturating the room, made her keep watching. Even as her fascination warred with the voice inside her that said, "This is my sister. I need to protect her, evaluate what's being done to look out for her wellbeing, because she's too young, I'm her big sister, it's my job..."

But that voice was overridden by other voices. *"Who are you in this moment?"* And if she looked at Marcie as a fellow submissive, the wife of the Master punishing her, Cass knew she wasn't looking at a teenager anymore, but a woman. A deeply submissive woman who needed a hardcore Master's touch to find satisfaction.

Ben curled one large hand over Marcie's delicate shoulder, steadying her as he landed the first blow with the doubled-over belt. Marcie's breath left her in a whoosh that reminded Cass of when she'd had the wind knocked out of her as an amateur gymnast. Marcie had fallen off the high beam and landed flat on her back on the mats. Yet though her face tightened as it had then, she licked her lips and shifted, obviously eager to meet the next blow. Cass could hear the faint buzz of a vibrator and knew Ben was countering the effect of the pain, but she couldn't imagine it was enough...unless Marcie was embracing and craving the pain.

"Oh..." Cass dropped her head back deeper into the decorative throw pillow supporting it, exposing her throat as Lucas did that feathering thing again, only this time he stayed there, rubbing between her legs in a steady motion that fanned a flame into an excruciating blaze. He kissed her stomach, brushing his golden-streaked hair over her breasts. Moved down to kiss her thighs, her hip bone.

Crack. Crack. Crack.

Marcie cried out and jerked as if trying to avoid the

blows. Ben took a firm hold on her hair and kept going as she resisted, fighting him, trying to twist out of his grip. Cass's eyes snapped up to them.

"Easy." Lucas moved up her body, dragging his lips over her throat and to the sensitive flesh beneath her ear. "Notice her range. It's as if there's an invisible circle drawn around her, and she's not going outside of it."

As Cass struggled to focus, she realized he was right. Though she could, Marcie wasn't moving out of the reach of where the strap could hit her. Instead, her gyrations allowed the belt to hit her buttocks at multiple angles, as well as her upper thighs, and occasionally—making Cass wince—the tender area between her thighs. Her writhing, and Ben's permitting her the movement, seemed designed to let Marcie spread the effect of the blows so it didn't get too intense in one area.

"It's resistance play, sweetheart," Lucas said softly. "Looks rough, but it's the way tigers play. They're like tigers, the two of them."

Cass drew in another startled breath as, in a move as quick as a pouncing tiger in truth, Ben gripped the back of Marcie's neck and shoved her down so her forehead was against the couch arm, her upper arms pulling out of Cass's grasp. Holding her down, Ben increased the speed of the strikes, hitting her ass, her tender thighs, her back. Cass reached for her hands, still holding the couch, and conflict gripped her as Marcie cried out into the cushions in true pain. Only Lucas's hold on her own body, her struggle to remember he'd never misjudged or led her falsely, kept her from protesting. Yet as Ben at last relaxed his hold on her nape and Marcie lifted her face, Cass saw her expression. Tears from the stress ran down her face, and her mouth was open and gasping for air, but her eyes were filled with as much arousal as Cass's were.

When Ben set the belt aside and dropped to one knee, Cass suspected he'd used those powerful hands to grip Marcie's buttocks, part them and go to work on her rim with tongue and lips, because the strangled, strange cry from her lips sent sensation spearing through Cass's own vitals. It was the sound of undiluted desire, a keening female in heat, caught in pleasurable agony.

She had to have welts on her ass and thighs, but Marcie was still pressing herself deeper into Ben's hands, against his mouth. The whispered "Master" from her lips was as reverent as a prayer to God for His blessings. His mercy.

A feeling Cass understood too well, because seeing the transition from pain to pleasure tore her loose from whatever control she had over her own body. A deep, tearing need filled her lower belly, a convulsion jerking through her. "God...please...Master. Lucas...I can't bear anymore. Please." The oil had reached its full raging potency, where this hanging climax feeling could go on and on and on. Her hips bucked, her head thrashed, and she licked her lips repeatedly. Flailing, she reached up and latched into Marcie's forearms again. But she needed Lucas's touch, his mouth, his cock. It wasn't just the oil. It was all of it; watching Ben and Marcie, all the ways Lucas touched her, and a whole night slam-packed full of stimulation. She needed him inside her. *Now.*

Then the world disappeared in flame, because he bent and put his mouth on her clitoris, sucking on it so very gently. The oil adhered strongly; he knew just how much he could do without removing or lessening its effect. Her whole body jerked, and her nails tore skin from Marcie's forearms, probably enough to draw blood.

"Oh God...sorry..."

Lucas rescued her sister from permanent scarring, grasping Cass's flailing hands and bringing them back down, hooking the two wrist cuffs together and holding the connector. Her fingers curled around his, digging into the top of his hands, only this time that won an approving look.

"Those nails are all mine," he reminded her with a sternness that only made her hotter. "As are you." Bending, he scooped her off the sofa and took her away from Ben and Marcie, striding toward the bedroom. Ten steps, and every one of them jolted through her core, so she was writhing like a captured wild animal when he laid her down on the mattress.

"Now," she demanded. "Fuck me now."

He unlatched the cuffs. He stood above her naked, the

tip of his cock coated with viscous fluid, the organ jutting up against his sectioned stomach muscles. "Beg, love," he said. "Or you get nothing."

"Please. Please, Master. Fuck me...Please...oh God, I can't take anymore." It was too much. She knew how an animal in a trap felt, this overwhelming feeling that was making her want to do crazy, insensible things, but there was no escaping this. She wanted to rear up and fight him, have him put her down on her stomach and fuck her like an animal in truth. Only he could relieve this agonizing need. She reached for him, knowing she shouldn't, but he wanted her, too. His control was at the finish line. She saw it in the fire in his eyes, the hardness of his flexing muscles, the set of his mouth. He'd deny himself no longer, thank every deity there was.

He stretched out upon her, earning a cry of gratitude, followed by a vicious wail as he held her down with his body, pinning his cock against her abdomen and preventing her from adjusting to the right angle to take him into her immediately. She was far beyond any vestige of self-control. As he held her wrists to the bed and went after her breasts again, sucking and playing, she screamed, cried, begged and cursed him, her head thrashing back and forth, heels clamping around his calves.

Then he lifted his upper torso and framed her face in his hands, his chest against her aching breasts, muscled stomach flexing against her weeping, throbbing cunt.

"Lucas," she sobbed.

"You are my fantasy," he said softly, his eyes holding the fierceness of a star's center. "The fantasy I want every day, until the end of time." Tilting up her chin, he circled her throat with his big hand. Miraculously, at the constricting pressure, her restless, vibrating body stilled and centered for one key moment, her eyes locked with him as she responded to that thing between them that defied description, the internal dialogue between Master and sub that could supersede anything, even Jon's crazy oil.

Then, gift of the gods, he thrust into her just the way she needed it. Hard, brutal, filling her up to a painful stretch. It told her how much he'd been affected by all of this. As large and impressive as he normally was, right now he could give even Ben's excessive proportions some competition.

"Mark me, wild cat," he muttered in her ear. "Make me suffer."

Once the friction of the thrusting started to dislodge the oil, the climax would advance, building higher and higher, but in an agonizing, gradual way that summoned long, thin cries from her lips long before she reached that peak. The need and desire did make her savage, so she obeyed like the wild cat he'd called her, digging in and raking her nails up his broad back, over the powerful, rippling muscles, her heels hammering against his taut, thrusting buttocks as he penetrated her deeper and deeper, all the way to the soul and the dark and light places beyond it.

Nails weren't enough. She set her teeth to his shoulder and bit, a guttural sound coming from her throat so beast-like it would have startled her if she'd had any brain cells to recognize how far behind she'd left civilized behavior. Lucas gripped her hair to break that lock and fastened his mouth on hers instead, taking over with a demanding, punishing kiss as he thrust so hard into her body he was shoving them up against the brace of pillows buffering the headboard.

Hammer, hammer, hammer. It fit everything, the way he was taking her, the insistent pounding of her heart and pulse, the need between her legs and in every cell of her body. And that was all before the climax finally broke free.

He had his mouth on hers, so her hoarse screams were swallowed by his breath, his hand dropping to palm her ass and tilt her up, a different deep angle that took her well past the limits of any safety advisory for climaxes to keep the body from shattering and the brain from exploding. He was whispering things to her, things possessive and wonderful, dark and cruel, but all boiling down to the essentials.

Mine. Mine forever.

If someone tried to get between them, to defy the biblical vows they'd said to one another to have and hold forever, it wouldn't be their union torn asunder. Lucas would take apart whoever dared to try and get between them. Piece by piece. If she didn't take them apart first.

It was during that ferocious three-word declaration that he let himself release within her, the heated jet of his seed inside propelling her ever higher, along with his primal groans against the shell of her ear, the tight coil of his hand in her hair, his bruising fingerprints in her buttock.

This was animal passion. No, beyond that. Animals understood and respected the balance of nature and the boundaries that kept them within certain parameters, even between life mates. Only people pushed past that boundary into obsession like this, where their love could shatter every concept of right or wrong and just leave this glowing, vibrant energy beyond reason or thought, forever straddling the line between life and death, limited by neither, even if it destroyed the balance of the universe. Having one another was everything.

When she'd watched it start to manifest between Ben and Marcie only a few moments ago, some part of her recognized it, but it was here, in the arms of her Master and knowing that dark realm was accessible to all of them if the need and bond were strong enough, that she accepted it. And was at peace.

As well as pretty much destroyed and content to be that way. Lucas continued to move inside her, his eyes on hers, his right hand linked with her left. The other palmed her buttock, helping her move on the waves of pleasure still carrying them. The oil could keep her shuddering and contracting upon his length for a good fifteen minutes after climax. Her considerate Master, not averse to feeling the tight glove of her sex clutching his cock, was more than willing to help her ride those aftershocks.

Further visual stimulation prolonged the reaction. Sometime during their lovemaking, the rhythmic sound of strapping and Marcie's sharp cries of reaction had ceased. Cass didn't know what Ben had done afterward, but when he brought Marcie to the bed and stretched her out on her stomach next to Cass and Lucas, a foot of space between them, her fellow submissive was gasping, moaning and pleading, her face suffused with desire and marked with tears. Cass knew her own cheeks had similar evidence, in half-dried tracks.

When Marcie's hand fell near hers, Cass managed to slide her hand under her sister's. Their fingers immediately linked, just as they'd done at the beginning.

"We end as we started," Cass whispered, meeting her sister's lust-infused brown eyes. It might seem weird to anyone else, but so much of this was hard to explain to anyone else anyway. Even as a submissive, before tonight, she might have wondered if they were right, outsiders who thought a fantasy such as what had just played out in this suite was past the line of acceptable behavior. Now she was fiercely, deeply glad she'd made this journey with her sister and her husband, as well as her own. She felt she saw and understood things far better, not just about Ben and Marcie, but about her and Lucas. The wonderful thing about marriage and love was there was no end to the rooms to explore, if both hearts were willing. Always worlds within worlds to find.

Marcie's nails dug into hers. While Cass was drifting into a reflective, mellow, half-aroused but post-coital bliss, she realized her sister still teetered on the pinnacle of near-climax. And Ben...

Her breath drew in, pussy clutching hard on Lucas as she looked at her sister's Master. Ben's visage was suffused with all the pure male hunger that had so overwhelmed Cass, seeing it in Lucas's face. Yet there was an additional dark savagery to it that went along with Ben's sadistic nature, giving it a different, titillating edge. It goaded feminine desire as well as deeper, anxious feelings of self-preservation, the rabbit wondering if she should run or let herself be caught. While Marcie obviously wanted to be irrevocably caught in the jaws of that trap, yearning for the consequences, Cass indulged the thrill by watching from the safe warren of her husband's arms.

Merely the visual of the two of them spiraled things into Cass's lower body, a nice pleasurable echo that had her muscles clutching Lucas's cock again. He responded by pressing in deeper and putting his mouth on her throat, nuzzling and kissing. His long, beautiful body moved under her hand as she slid her palm over his back, the curve of his buttock, her other holding onto Marcie.

Ben was lubing up his giant cock with a tight fist. He'd brought Marcie up on her knees and elbows, cheek to the bed. She seemed to still have the vibrator inside her, because when Ben guided himself into her rear entry, he bumped it up, increasing the subtle buzzing hum. Marcie's mouth went wide, her facial muscles reacting to the stimulation. Ben didn't slam into her the way Lucas had taken Cass, for obvious reasons, but Cass was nevertheless amazed to see inch after inch disappear, Marcie's eyes closing and body shuddering. She undulated in a sinuous dance, her and Ben's movements synchronized like a melded creature of fantasy as he completed the full lock, all the way in to the hilt. Then he dropped over Marcie's body, covering her, impressive back and arm muscles rippling. Marcie's free hand latched onto his thick wrist where it was braced next to her shoulder.

"Hold out for me a little longer," Ben demanded, green eyes sharp and vivid as glass in sunlight. "Squeeze down on me and that vibrator. Make it last."

Cass clutched Marcie's hand, mesmerized as Ben braced himself on her hip and began to move. Lucas added to her voyeuristic response by curving his back enough to grip one of Cass's breasts, tilt it up toward his mouth, and begin to suckle again. The slow thrust and retreat he'd been doing began to be a little more deliberate. He was hardening inside her again and her body responded with a starburst of sensation. When Cass's gaze fluttered to him, startled, Lucas lifted his head to meet her eyes with heated silver ones of his own.

"You're getting me worked up again, sweetheart," he muttered. "Your blue eyes so big, mouth so soft, watching them fucking. Think I'm going to have to let you watch more often."

She lifted her free hand to his face, and he sucked on her fingers when she traced his lips. *I love you so much,* she mouthed. Everything she was feeling was so close to the surface. The bed adjusted with Ben and Marcie's movements beside them, as well as the slow rock of her and Lucas's bodies together. Marcie made that pleading noise again, and her fingers clutched Cass's. Cass noticed she had her mouth on Ben's wrist, in addition to clasping it with her hand. That need, the intimacy, had its reciprocal response from her husband. Ben had slowed his thrusts so he could drop a kiss between her shoulder blades and on her nape, where her stainless steel collar had slipped forward with her hair, baring that vulnerable spot.

He said something Cass couldn't hear, but Marcie tilted her head up to him and their mouths met in a deep kiss, with a hint of the tongues that tangled and stroked. Ben cradled her face so Marcie wouldn't strain her neck. As they kissed, their lips curved in near smiles, as if whatever Ben had said and Marcie had answered had brought them a tender, shared moment of humor that didn't dilute the intensity between them at all. If anything, it made Cass's female heart pound a little harder, the evidence of how it could work together so perfectly, when love guided all of it. Passion, demand, need, tears, laughter.

She and Lucas had that, and now she was even more certain Marcie and Ben did.

Turning her attention back to her own husband, she found him waiting to cup her face and kiss her, just as deeply. Cass wrapped her arms around his shoulders, holding on as he stroked inside her. "Never enough," he whispered in her ear, his voice hoarse in a way she treasured. "I'll never get enough of you, Cassie."

She moaned as his thrusts increased, as she started to rise toward release again.

It was a glorious, deep-water energy that filled the room, that surrounded all of them. Marcie's hand in Cass's, Marcie holding Ben's wrist, Cass with one arm and both legs wrapped tightly around Lucas, his mouth against her ear. All the visual beauty of it: Marcie's blond hair fanned out on the mattress between them, the lovely convex line of her back, Ben's palm on the center of it. Ben looming over Marcie for those last hard thrusts, his green eyes glowing in the semi-darkness of the bedroom. His broad chest, covered with a light mat of gleaming dark hair, expanding and contracting with his breaths, his biceps flexing as he gripped Marcie's hip with his other hand. His dark hair disheveled over his silken black brows, the tautness of his buttock as he pressed in deeper. Her sister overwhelmed by his demands, muffling her raw, pleasured screams into the mattress.

Then there was Cass's own work of art, the one that belonged to her. Lucas's silver gray eyes were the color of woodlands in winter, or those slender slivers of gray through an early sunrise sky. The planes of his face looked like a sculpture as he drew closer to bringing them to climax, the roll of his powerful shoulders and ripple of his stomach muscles against her soft skin all imprinting themselves on her mind in a way she'd take out later and relive again and again. That fine, mouth-watering backside, tight as a drum under her calves, the legs streamlined with cycling muscles rubbing against the inside of her thighs.

His strong, capable hands tightened on her ass, allowing him to plow her deeper. When he did that, all the erotic beauty in the world couldn't take her focus from him. Ben and Marcie disappeared completely. Everything narrowed to his eyes, pinning her to this second in time with him. He demanded she surrender everything to him as he pushed them to the edge. He added to the thrill of it with his rough words.

"Scream with her, sweetheart. Let us hear it. Keep us hard, wanting to fuck the two of you endlessly. Never stopping."

It crashed over her within seconds of when she heard Ben give the command to Marcie to come, as he started to release himself. Lucas was barely a heartbeat behind him. What had been created expanded beyond each couple, the release heightening the pleasure for each of them. It swirled around and bound them in ties with so many connections, Cass knew it was a web that could hold them above the darkest shadows—except when they embraced those shadows without fear, craving what lay within them.

Part Ten

When they finally rested on the shore beyond those powerful waves, the room was silent except for rasping breaths, a thumping undercurrent of pounding hearts and slowing pulses, a quiet whisper or low exchange of words. All of them were loath to break the spell.

Sliding from Cass at last, Lucas moved behind her on the mattress edge side, turning her to spoon up against her body and hold her close.

Ben eased out of Marcie, putting more kisses on her nape and shoulder. He maneuvered her to her side also, her back to Cass, but he adjusted her so she was closer to her sister and Lucas. "I'm going to go run the two of us a bath to tend to her," he said, meeting Lucas's gaze over Cass's head. "Look after her for a few moments?"

Lucas nodded, and a light smile touched Ben's lips as Cass reached out with her Master, drawing a depleted and trembling Marcie into the shelter of their spooned bodies.

As Cass cuddled her sister close, Lucas enveloped them in his long arms. Marcie overlapped both their arms with her hands, as mindlessly trusting of their hold as she'd been when much younger, giving Cass's heart a poignant twist. Ben brushed a lock of hair out of Marcie's face, smoothing it back, and met Cass's gaze. "She's fine," he promised her. "She's just nonverbal afterward. Takes her awhile to come back. She's all good."

"I know," Cass said, and meant it.

Ben's smile stayed, as if he'd heard the emphasis. He stroked Cass's hair from her face, too, trailing a thumb over her lips before he dropped a kiss on Marcie's mouth. To Cass's bemusement, he did the same to her before he left the bed.

As they heard the water start in the Jacuzzi tub, Cass let out a contented sigh, nestling her hips deeper into the cradle of Lucas's. He responded with a nice push of his cock against her ass, and shifted to caress her hip, his knuckles following the curve of her breast accessible under the arm she had stretched over Marcie. She watched him use the benefit of those long arms to do the same to Marcie, playing his clever fingers along her biceps, the curve of her breast, also generously available since her arms were bent for a prayer fold of her hands under her cheek. When he slid his hand down, he kept stroking them, moving between thigh, breast, hip, side, hair... His cock stirred against her ass, amazing Cass but also reminding her of how many mornings he woke her just by adjusting her knee forward and working his thick length inside her at the tight angle, holding her pinned that way. His fingers would work over her clit until the two of them came, so closely locked together, her teeth biting down on his hand to muffle her cries from her siblings in the upstairs bedrooms.

He wouldn't do that now, not while she was holding Marcie so close, and not when they were all so momentarily sated, but it was a lovely thought to anticipate for breakfast. She expected Ben had a similar ritual. All the K&A men were insatiable.

Cass tipped her head up to find Lucas's eyes closed as he fondled both sisters. She kissed his throat. "Enjoying this, are you?" she said, a soft tease. His firm lips curved.

"Abso-fucking-lutely."

Marcie was coming out of her haze, because a quiver ran through her shoulders, as if she'd managed a tired chuckle. Cass laid her cheek on her sister's back and increased her hold around her waist, even as she savored the feel of Lucas's hard body against her, the provocative contact that, despite her exhaustion, could still make her respond. He had so much skill in those capable fingers, so much knowledge of a woman's body; how she liked to be touched before, during and after.

As Lucas stroked Marcie's hip, Ben returned, amusing Cass when he gave Lucas's hand a reproving slap, like a wife keeping her husband away from fresh pie. "Taking advantage of my sub's vulnerable aftercare needs," he grumbled.

"You kissed my wife," Lucas said.

"Couldn't help it. She looks so well-used, lips all pouty and pink." Ben winked at Cass. She narrowed her gaze at him, though it was hard not to chuckle.

"No," Marcie mumbled drowsily. "Not taking advantage. I like it when he touches me. It feels good. All of you... I love all of you."

Ben's teasing became tenderness as he gathered her up in his arms. "Yeah, you're floating, baby. Let's go get cleaned up. Want me to start the tub refilling when I'm done?" He directed that to Lucas.

"Yeah." Lucas nuzzled Cass's shoulder. "A bath will be good. Keep my sub's muscles loose. I might want to put her through another couple workouts before dawn. We haven't taken advantage of that 1800s-styled billiards table in the other room yet. And she's definitely the first thing I'm having for breakfast."

If he meant it, she might need the spa's professional masseuse services again. As well as that bath. He was going to kill her—but again, who cared?

"Don't worry," Ben told Cass in a mock low voice, as he cradled Marcie. "Bicycle-Boy doesn't have that kind of stamina. He won't be bothering you until he's had his second cup of coffee and checked the stock reports."

Lucas had a suitably rude retort for that. Ben headed for the bath with his precious burden, chuckling. Folding his arms over Cass again, Lucas snugged his thighs under hers, to spoon them together even more securely. She thought of how she'd imagined Ben and Marcie as one melded creature during their lovemaking, and she felt that way herself. Lucas's cock pushed into the channel between her thighs and she adjusted so she could hold it there, rubbing pleasantly against her wet cunt. He had more than enough stamina to live up to his threat...or promise. He could make her tremble with desire at just the thought, but for now she couldn't be more content, basking in the intimacy of their pose and feeling his breath against her neck, providing her the sure knowledge that he was awake and tending to her state of mind as closely as Ben did Marcie's.

"So, after this night is over, are you going to be able to handle having only one sister for your sexual needs?" she asked.

He chuckled, a deep, masculine sound. "Always have, always will. But if one of us ends up killing Ben, which you know is very probable, we could convert to a 24/7 D/s household and she could be my sex slave. Help you with chores, bring me my slippers. You'd still have top ranking as head submissive, of course."

"Or I could ruin that new wood chipper we bought,

getting rid of your body. But I will miss you."

He anticipated the thud of her fist against his thigh but let the blow land as her just due before capturing her wrist and lifting it to his mouth to kiss. "You know that's never going to happen anyway. For one thing, Dana would call dibs. She'd want Marcie as her own personal cuddle toy. Who she'd magnanimously share with Peter."

"And would you say 'lucky bastard'?" she asked archly.

"I would. But none of them are luckier than me."

"Good save."

"I thought so." He smiled against her shoulder. "What pleases me is knowing you're being playful, that you have no true worries about that. Not all couples, no matter how close, could have done this without some kind of fall-out to handle."

She thought of that key moment, when he'd told her she was his only true fantasy. She'd known without a doubt how much he'd meant it. He'd won her trust a long time ago and had only consolidated it exponentially ever since. What pleased *her* now was that he'd trusted her enough to believe she was truly ready for this.

When she shared that with him, she earned another tight embrace, one she returned, forming a cocoon of legs, arms and the feelings they'd shared and experienced here tonight. The strength of it sent another vibration through her body. Without him holding her, she might have been shivering the way Marcie had when Ben turned her over to their care.

So many of her concerns about tonight had been handled earlier, Lucas orchestrating things so well to help her leave them on the streets far below. Yet as she recalled holding her sister, the scent of Marcie's hair, those well-toned biceps, and Marcie's jokes about being a badass, Cass also thought about the look in Ben's eyes at the height of their passion, his feelings for Marcie so blatant. And thinking those thoughts, one of those concerns couldn't help but return.

"What happens if he loses her? If we lose her?" she asked quietly.

Ben wasn't alone in his apprehension about Marcie's

decision to become a police officer. Cass couldn't imagine—actually, wasn't sure she could endure—losing another sibling. But unlike Jeremy, Marcie lived every day with vigor and sought out value, wanting to contribute, accomplish, excel. Sometimes her drive to overachieve was overpowering. Cass understood the part she'd played in that, the example she'd provided her. Cass's path to achievement had been driven by the desperate need to support all her siblings, and Marcie had not escaped unscathed from that difficult path. She might not have had to bear as much of the load as Cass, but she'd shared enough of it to carry that need to prove oneself, to overcome the scars left by uncaring parents, into adulthood.

And layered on top of that was Marcie's own overachieving personality. Cass knew her sister would become anything she wanted to be—a cop, a police commissioner, a senator. A female President. Or she'd break herself trying. She had that spark that a person with such strengths and drive had.

Ben helped her keep some of that drive manageable, so it didn't pass into unhealthy areas, and Cass was glad for that. But the point was, no matter what happened, Marcie wasn't Jeremy. Her life would never be wasted. Still... God, how would she handle it, the many times she heard a snippet on the news about an officer-involved shooting, a far too common situation in New Orleans, and...

"Hey." Lucas's tone had her tilting her face up to see his serious eyes, his firm lips. "She'll be fine. Probably end up being New Orleans' Superintendent of Police."

He was so good at following her train of thought. "That's what I hope and believe," Cass responded. "But I worry about it."

She didn't have to say the rest. Lucas loved Marcie, and it was as hard for him as it was for any of the K&A men, accepting the idea that one of "their women" would be embracing such a dangerous job. Peter and Dana had already had several run-ins about the dangerous location of her church. Despite her being blind, she didn't hesitate to challenge local gang members trying to recruit youthful members of her congregation. But Dana had been an Army sergeant before an IED had taken her sight, and Peter was retired National Guard with a couple Middle East tours under his belt, so he had some predisposition to manage his reaction to his wife going into dangerous situations.

But Cass knew Lucas and the other men had equally deep worries about Ben, and Cass shared them. Marcie was her blood, but Ben was the center of her sister's life.

"If the worst happened, we would help him," she told Lucas. "We'd take him in, make him live with one or all of us. Hell, we'd all move into Matt's ranch for as long as it took to get him back on his feet. We'd make him see that life is worth living and has gifts to give, even if he felt like his heart had been taken from him. I wouldn't let him give up, because that's what she'd want me to do. All of us to do, for him and for ourselves."

"Is that so?" He raised a brow, curious at her tone. She gripped his hand, stroking her face, and nodded, pressing her lips to it.

"Death matters so much only because life does. It's what I finally learned from Jeremy, and you helped me see it, with your help and love. You and all our family. His life was so hard, and so much of it was destructive and wasteful. But he made those last days count. You remember the pressed flower the monastery sent me, from the garden he planted and tended? Even if it was only at the end of his life, he made an impression worth remembering. He wasn't just a morality tale. He still had the capacity to inspire hope against all odds. Which means he was a miracle. A small, softly shining, brief miracle. I'm glad he had that. I'm glad Marcie is pursuing her dreams. I'm glad she and Ben love one another so fiercely. The stars wouldn't be anywhere as special if they didn't believe it was worth shining as bright as they can."

He tightened his arms around her. "I love you," he said, with a fervor that warmed her from head to toe.

"I love you." She nuzzled her face into his hand again, then gazed up at the canopy ceiling. It was a lovely wheel of cream-colored pleated folds around a center of satiny rosettes. She focused on that and sharing this quiet moment with her husband, letting the worries fade back into their hearts. Still there, but able to be at rest for tonight.

"So you'd be okay adopting Ben if needed?" When he spoke at last, his teasing tone told her he was taking them back toward their earlier mood. She was more than willing to flow in that direction. Love had taken her down this more serious path, but love could also lead her back to smiles and hope.

"What was that you said? Abso-fucking-lutely. I'm sure he could prove himself useful. If you can have a sex slave, why can't I? And I bet he'd look totally hot, doing our yardwork in nothing but those jeans he wears that can't hide the fact he's hung like a—"

She was already laughing, but it elevated to a shriek as Lucas went after her with tickling fingers and chased her across the bed, initiating a wrestling match that resulted in tangled covers and more kissing, his body stretched out on hers. Her eyes lifted to his, finding them suddenly more serious, and he whispered the command to her that her body was already obeying.

"Spread your legs for me."

He wasn't completely hard, but she understood another full-blown session wasn't his intent. At least not right now. She'd seen that pool table he mentioned, all gleaming wood and crimson felt. She could only imagine what use Ben and he might make of the pool cues, balls and wooden rack. Or they'd stretch her or Marcie out on the table and shoot a game under bent arms and legs. Whoever won points would be allowed to indulge diabolical pleasures with one or both of them.

Lucas slid back into her, re-establishing the connection as he banded his arms around her. He pressed his face into her throat as she held him, inside and out. Closing her eyes, she simply floated in his arms, like angels in the sky. They'd have a bath and then the four of them, clean and sated, would sleep in the giant bed, bodies companionably close together, part of a pack that drew warmth, comfort and pleasure from one another in so many ways.

"Oh." Her eyes opened. "Did—"

"Yes, Matt texted me. Cherry got home safe and sound. Her date went well. At least if Talia's text, 'She says Chad is so totally awesome' means that. Don't worry, Mama Bear."

She smiled. After a few moments, she hummed against his throat, her mind turning elsewhere. "Do you think we could get room service this late?"

"For what we tip the concierge? He'll get restaurant owners out of bed to cook for us if we want. You want pancakes, don't you?"

She wondered when she'd ever stop being surprised how easily he read her mind. She chuckled as he slid from her. As he kissed his way down her body, he left an easy, tempting kiss against her pussy, using his tongue and breath to make her squirm in pleasurable reaction before he slid off the end of the bed and started looking for his slacks. "I'll ask Ben what he and Marcie want. Might as well get a spread to carry us through to the morning."

Part Eleven

When she and Ben emerged from the bath, Lucas had managed a late night delivery of favorite foods Marcie was sure would put a serious twist in the panties of cardiologists and diabetes nutritionists everywhere. They'd indulged in their respective choices and, between the eating and everyone getting a bath, they were on their way to restoring themselves for what she was sure was more pleasure to come. But during the lull period, Marcie had simply enjoyed watching her sister and her husband. She hadn't seen Cass so relaxed, playful and happy in so long. If they hadn't all been mostly naked, she would have been tempted to snap a picture with her camera phone to show Talia, Nate and Cherry. But as Ben had said, even the most innocuous picture couldn't hide that Cass looked exactly as he'd described. Well-used, tousled, her lips swollen and body flushed from continuous attention from her Master. And Lucas's eyes glowed when he looked at her, seeing the same thing Marcie did.

Marcie had enjoyed the same treatment from her own Dom, but then Ben never shut down his libido except when he slept. And he didn't sleep that much, she thought with a grin. Except for now.

They'd eventually drifted back to the bed, and there'd been an amazing, quiet session of lovemaking, each couple in their own world, yet within a couple feet of one another on the spacious mattress. Then, for a while, they all dozed. Even Ben.

When Marcie opened her eyes, she was clasped in Ben's strong arms, the best place to be. She saw it was about two in the morning. A moment later, she realized she'd been awakened by a shift of the terrace lights as Cass moved in front of them, slipping out the door to the outside. She'd donned one of the suite's complimentary fluffy white robes. When she braced her arms on the rail and looked out at the city and the river, her profile was hard to read. Her body language didn't suggest she was discontent, but if she'd left the bed and the warmth of her husband, her mind was probably turning something over.

When Marcie heard Lucas shift, she knew he was already aware that she'd left and was likely going to head out there, but Marcie turned over in Ben's arms and lifted up a little to look over Ben's shoulder at her sister's husband. Ben's eyes opened the moment she moved, so she laid her hand on his muscled biceps as she drew Lucas's attention.

"With both your permissions," she said softly. "I'd like to go to her first. Help with a little 'after' aftercare?"

Lucas's gray eyes warmed and Ben stroked a hand over her back, tugging the ends of her loose hair. "End protocol, brat. We'll be out in a bit. Go be with your sister, if Lucas is okay with it."

Lucas nodded, though his eyes tracked Cass, probably taking in ten levels of what was going on with her that Marcie would need a closer evaluation to pick up. But that was okay. That was his job, after all.

Marcie found another robe, feeling Ben's eyes on her as she wrapped it around herself. She sent him a soft smile before she combed her hair back from her face and padded out to the terrace. Cass was now seated on one of the cushioned patio sofas. She'd turned around and had her arms layered on the back, her legs folded and tucked under her, feet bare as she studied the French Quarter lights. Her hair was loosely tied on her shoulders, the planes of her face soft and yet pensive.

She looked merely thoughtful, not stressed, which was good. Yet with the bare feet and the multi-layered expression, she reminded Marcie of how she'd found her sister one night when Cass was fifteen. Mom had been drugged half out of her mind most of the day, Dad MIA as usual. Cass had been sitting at a window seat in the darkened kitchen at midnight, staring out into the night. Marcie, restless, had come down with the excuse of needing water, but really needing that reassurance that someone was there, watching out for them. They'd all done it in different ways, using Cass as the hub around which their uncertain family wheel turned.

Nate had slept in Cass's bed more often than not, something she was sure he remembered but she'd never tease him about. She'd tease him about plenty of things, now that he thought he was so grown up, but not that. Marcie would come in from a babysitting job, and he'd be sacked out and curled up like a puppy in the comforter while Cass was at her bedroom desk, still typing away at school work or one of the endless administrative jobs she did until she landed the internship with Pickard. That was when things had gotten better, more stable, but it still took Nate quite a while before he could sleep a full night in his room without visual confirmation that Cass wasn't going to disappear sometime in the middle of it, the way Dad did pretty much his entire life, and Mom would do right in front of your eyes with a pill bottle.

Marcie slid onto the sofa beside her, taking the same backward-facing pose, her hip and shoulder companionably against hers. "These are the thickest, softest robes I've felt in my entire life. Are we sure they didn't murder some animal to make these?

"Only a lot of cotton." Cass dipped her head, smiling a little as Marcie brushed her nose against her cheek affectionately. "You used to do that when you were younger."

"I remember."

Cass nodded, her eyes returning to the skyline. "Remember when Lucas and I went to adopt our two cats? I saw a kitten doing that to its mother, and the volunteer told me rubbing faces together is sort of the universal way for the thumb-less to show affection."

"Maybe not just the thumb-less. Sometimes those animal instincts are closer to how we need to express things than the human way. Like tonight?" Marcie gave her the gentle prod, knowing it might be the root of the pensiveness.

"Yes. Maybe."

"Did you enjoy all of it?"

"Yes." Cass gave her a lopsided smile. "Obviously. But during, it's so easy to get lost in it. I surfaced with the typical 'okay, am I going to hell for this' followed by 'should I have encouraged this, with my little sister involved'..."

Before Marcie could say anything, Cass lifted a finger. "The oil, the stimulation, opened me up to deeper instincts and understandings. Instincts as real and true as the protective ones I took on and accepted fully when you were growing up. And I saw it for what it was, between you two, though I still can't describe it. I didn't watch you and Ben at the wedding afterparty, you know. But I guess you, Ben and Lucas have known I've wondered, and it's festered a little bit, the worry, staying unresolved. Thank you for helping me resolve it once and for all tonight."

She met Marcie's gaze. "My *younger* sister is a beautiful, amazing grown woman, able to make her own decisions. This is a part of your soul I don't fully understand, which makes me even less qualified to make the call about it. So...I realized I can enjoy tonight for exactly what it was. An erotic adventure that exemplifies the love and trust we have in our husbands and that they have in us."

"Well, yeah. Duh. But God, that sounds so...corporate. Exemplifies."

Cass chuckled. "I assume you have a better way of saying it?"

Marcie pursed her lips. "How about a really fucking awesome time that makes us grateful we're married to two of the hottest Doms and most amazing men on the planet? Who we should never tell that we feel that way, because they're already in the top 1% of the world's most arrogant males."

"That works, too." Cass sobered, considering her. The robe had slid off Marcie's shoulder, and Cass ran a light fingertip over one of the belt marks on her shoulder blade. "When you and he started that, it was the only time tonight I had a true moment of trepidation, a desire to call things to a halt. I made myself hold my tongue, and hold you, and what I felt from you, saw in your eyes...as I said, I don't understand it entirely, but I don't have to understand it to know it works for you both. That you need to experience it as much as he needs to do it. I perhaps didn't really know that until tonight...or realize I could stop thinking that it was my fault you were like that."

Marcie tried not to flinch at the word choice, but she didn't mask it fast enough. Cass shook her head hastily, laying her hand on her sister's. "No, honey. I'm sorry. That's not what it sounds like. I didn't expect that of myself, that I would..." She stopped and began again. "Let me step back and try to explain it a little better."

"You don't have to—"

"Yes, I do." Cass said it firmly, holding Marcie's gaze. "I am a submissive, far more deeply than I ever realized. Lucas helped me uncover that. Yet I forgot how easy it is for a comfort zone to become a judgment boundary. As long as those around me were in that same comfort zone, like Savannah, I thought I was the height of self-righteous tolerance: 'oh, Dominance and submission are totally healthy and okay' and 'why doesn't the rest of the world understand'? Yet in dealing with what you and Ben have, I have been pushed out of that comfort zone. My thinking that 'it's my fault that you're like that' was resting on the belief that you two take things too far together."

She gripped Marcie's hand. "But tonight I was able to realize what you and Ben have...it's beautiful, wild. Untamed and unleashed at a level that isn't better or worse than what Lucas and I have. Just a different tree in the Garden of Eden. No matter how it was planted or grown, it was meant to be."

When she gave Marcie a searching look, Marcie could see Cass was worrying that her misstep had offended her sister deeply. She could reassure her on that, because Cass had spoken simply and from the heart. She wasn't Pickard's top negotiator because she could bullshit; she was the best because she got to the heart of a problem, whether it was her own or someone else's, laid it out to solve it, and brought everyone back to the table.

She gripped Cass's hand with both of hers. "You are the best sister ever," she said fiercely. "Even if you still won't loan me your shoes."

"You're far too rambunctious. You'd get a wild hair to go do cartwheels in a park, or chase down a pickpocket on Canal Street and scratch the heels to pieces in the sidewalk cracks." Cass nudged her, then became serious again. "I guess some part of me thought you endured a certain level of it because of your love for one another. Then I realized he's your safety net. When he stopped, you didn't want to stop."

Marcie bit her lip. "Yeah. He makes sure I don't get swept away in my head past the point of no return. And I want to say something to you, in the same spirit of what you just said to me. Okay?"

"Okay."

Marcie took a breath. "We grew up in such uncertainty. Cass, you were Wonder Woman, you know that? You and Gal Gadot, you could have been twins. You have nothing to worry about, or regret, and I mean that. It pisses all of us off when you think you're at fault for anything that happened during that time. You not only did the very best you could in the circumstances, you fucking blew away all expectations. All of us bear wounds from growing up with Mom and Dad like that, knowing what it took out of you, out of all of us."

She nudged her sister. "Some of what's in me, the need for pain, it's like an absolution of sorts, a need to purge this build-up of anxiety that comes from knowing exactly what the dark side of the world looks like because we were there. We came so close to tipping right off the edge into the abyss itself, so many times. I don't consider myself any more broken than anyone else and, unlike a lot of people, I've chosen paths in my life that even me out. And that part of me, it meshes with his so perfectly. If there is such a thing as soul mates, we're it." She glanced over her shoulder into the darkened room. "Honestly? I'm not sure I'd survive losing him, now that I have him."

Cass pursed her lips. "So we're not the only ones who've thought about what you mean to each other, and the consequences if..."

Marcie's countenance clouded.

"Yeah. I know the police academy thing is flying in the face of that. But I think that's how we have to live. On that edge, daring it to cut us. We can't live without each other, but we can't live safe. That's no life at all. So we figure it out as we go."

"Okay." Cass slid an arm around her and Marcie returned the favor, so the sisters twined around one another. "If I never said it, I was so glad to have your help while we were growing up. You could be a pain-in-the-ass teenager sometimes, but on the whole you were the best backup I could have had."

"I love you, sis." Marcie pressed her temple to her sister's as they looked out at the skyline. "And I know in a lot of people's minds, this is kind of a freaky, twisted way to spend a family evening together, but honestly, I had a blast. I liked sharing it with you." She gave Cass a quick grin. "It's a one-timer I don't need to do it again, but I'm glad we did it."

"Me too." Cass dropped her voice to a whisper, giving her a conspiratorial wink. "And if you ever tell him, I'll tear all your hair out by the roots, but that Dom of yours is fucking scary. Because he has a way of making a woman go along with anything, no matter how crazy."

"I know. He's awesome. But *whoa* on the scary side of Lucas. Who knew that was hiding under the cool and unassuming accountant persona? Well, okay, I did sense it, but seeing it full blown?" Marcie shivered. "Far better than even my fantasies, and those were scorching hot."

"You've reached your quota of fantasies about my

husband." Cass tugged her hair. "It's bad enough I have to deal with Dana's. The girl has no filter."

"God bless her. You should hear Rachel when she gets going. She's worse. You know we are totally going to get the award for best share at the next monthly get-together."

The two women nestled together in familial companionship, falling into affectionate silence, broken pleasantly when Lucas joined them. They saw with mutual appreciation that he'd eschewed the fluffy robe, instead pulling on a pair of old and faded jeans he'd apparently brought with him.

"You ladies broke the bro code," he complained. "You left Ben and I in the same bed, no barrier between us. Naked. He's trying to spoon with me in his sleep." He gave a mock shudder. "If he sneezed I might have gotten impaled."

"If you weren't so pretty, I wouldn't have thought you were Marcie in my sleep," Ben defended himself, coming out of the shadows almost on his heels. He was also wearing his jeans, in his usual low-slung, top-button open way, doubling the aesthetic pleasure of the two women. On top of that, he was carrying a bottle of wine to pass around.

"He never sleeps that deeply," Marcie said, even knowing Lucas was joking. He was as aware as she was that Ben slept so lightly it was as if he lived in an active war zone. He was getting better about it, but some instincts, just as she'd told Cass, were hard to leave behind. The open warmth in Ben's eyes as they landed on her told her a lot of bad things were getting easier to push off to the side of the road. Or they didn't snap as close to his heels as they once had.

The things she and Cass had talked about were still close enough to the surface she wasn't surprised to see her older sister rise from the sofa, go to Ben and, with only a quick hesitation, put her arms around him. Drawing him down into her embrace, she held him tightly. Marcie didn't know what she said to him, but Ben set aside the wine and glasses to smile and return the gesture. When he put his cheek to hers, a serious expression crossed his face as he answered her. "Always. But I'm glad you feel it for sure now."

Then, breaking the moment, he winked at Lucas. "You'll have to indulge me." Dropping his hands to take a firm two-grip hold of Cass's generous backside through the robe, he lifted her up against his body, giving her a warm kiss before dropping her gently back to her feet.

"That's your final indulgence of the night," Lucas warned. "Give me back my wife before I cut off your dick with pruning shears and Marcie feeds it to the pigeons."

Ben snorted. "You'll wear yourselves out. You don't cut a major branch with pruning shears. You go for a chainsaw."

"I'm sure I can find one."

While he was talking, Marcie had left the couch to select a chocolate out of the fruit basket on the glass table. As she moved around Lucas, she stopped short, feeling a spurt of shock, followed by some wry humor. "Looks like you bedded a tiger, brother-in-law," she observed, reaching out and running a fingertip over his back. Winking at Cass, she leaned forward and put her lips on one of the marks. As Lucas lifted a hand to cup her jaw, he tipped his head back to toss her an amused look. It had enough reproving heat to give her a thrill. She shot a playful look at her sister. "Just to get back at Ben," she said.

"Uh-huh," was Cass's only response, along with a lifted hand in a claw shape. "There's other, softer skin these nails can mark."

Marcie winked but left Lucas, pressing his shoulder fondly before crossing the terrace. "I'll grab the first aid kit so we can touch those up."

"They're fine," Lucas said.

Marcie backpedaled, popping the chocolate in her mouth. When she ran butt-first into Ben, she rubbed her hips playfully against his groin before pivoting and escaping his mock grab.

"Nope, sorry. We subs are very particular about the care of our Masters. Just as overbearing about it as they are about taking care of us."

Cass returned to the terrace couch with a smile. Though she tried to see the marks Marcie had noticed, Lucas captured her hand and drew her down beside him.

Propping his back against the sofa arm, he wrapped his arms around her while she drew her knees up, tucking the robe demurely around her thighs. "Should I say I'm sorry?" she asked. If Marcie had been startled, she was a little worried.

"Only if you want me to get out that oil again and have me do it all over again." He squeezed her. "You were breathtaking, sweetheart."

Marcie returned as Ben took a seat on the other end of the couch, close enough to reach out and grip Cass's toes affectionately before he settled back. She noticed his eyes didn't leave Marcie as her sister used peroxide with sterilized pads to clean the scratches on Lucas's back. Cass suspected her sister was returning those lingering looks just as often over Lucas's shoulder. When she applied the cool antibiotic spray as a finishing touch, Lucas made an appealing little shiver against Cass's back.

Cass would have tended to her husband herself, but he seemed pretty determined to keep her right where she was, her hips in the cradle between his thighs, his arm around her waist.

When Marcie went to put the first aid supplies away, Ben offered Cass a cookie from the plate he'd retrieved from the room service cart. By the time she split it with Lucas and accepted a glass of wine, Marcie had returned. She and Ben adopted a mirror pose on the couch with Lucas and Cass, thanks to Ben resting his back against the opposite sofa arm. As Marcie nestled in front of him, he stretched an arm along the back cushion, letting her rest her head on his biceps. Cass watched him feed Marcie a bite of cookie and brush the crumbs from her lips with his thumb, her hand coming up to circle and caress his wrist.

Though she and Lucas had reached a deeper level tonight, she expected Marcie and Ben were covering some good ground too. The evening was a good breather from the tension they'd been dealing with about Marcie's career choice. As Cass studied them, she thought any session between Dom and sub could turn into that kind of gift, resolving problems and leading to so many other, even more wonderful, things.

"So..." Her younger sister gave her a sparkling look of mischief that immediately made Cass wary. "While I might not get to see the two of you explore new ground in such a firsthand way again, I'm sure you'll bring the deets to the tell-all on girls' night."

"Only if her Master says that's okay," Lucas said in a mock stern tone. "Nosy woman-child."

"Hey, monthly girls' night is a Dom-command-free zone." Marcie sniffed. "Believe me, the chance to be totally honest with one another and commiserate has saved some of your lives, more than once."

Ben's arm tightened around his wife. As he slid his lips along her neck, Cass noticed Marcie's toes curl into the cushion in reaction to the caress. "Behave, brat," he murmured.

"Never," Marcie said, albeit a little breathlessly. It sounded like a promise, though, not a denial. Ben responded to it like one, his firm lips tugging against his own smile. Cass bit back one herself at Lucas's exaggerated sigh.

She settled back even more securely in his arms. For a while, there wasn't much conversation, or much need for it. Marcie and Ben were in their own quiet world, speaking low to one another, exchanging easy kisses and touches, sharing the cookies and Marcie sipping from Ben's champagne.

Lucas slipped his hand into Cass's robe to stroke the curve of her breast as he gazed out at the night. "This is as perfect as it gets," he said quietly. "Until tomorrow, when it will be even more perfect."

Because we're together. He didn't need to say it. She felt it from him, and turned in his arms so she could wrap her own around him, get even closer.

She felt his eyes upon her as he stroked her hair and her back. He wanted her to be totally relaxed, embracing simple enjoyment of this moment and the blissful pleasure they'd experienced so far—and likely would again before dawn's light. As well as at breakfast, in the shower, right before they checked out...

She had no objection to any of that. And, for the

moment, no more worries.

Her gaze slid to Marcie, nestled up to her own husband and Master. Thank God for the bond between sisters. As her own husband pressed his lips to the crown of her head and held her tighter against his strong body, she added one more to her list of life's blessings.

And thank God for wonderful Doms.

The End

###

Afterword

Did you enjoy reading this? Was it a true pleasure to spend time with Joey's characters? If you feel it was, then she asks that you do one simple thing in support of her future work. Please share that experience with at least one other book-reading friend who hasn't read her. Or mention her on a Facebook page, at a book club meeting or online forum, on Twitter, in an Amazon or GoodReads review, or wherever you feel comfortable. You, the pleased reader, are the best marketing strategy an author can have. If you do just one of those things to spread the word about her work, she will be very grateful! And thank you again for taking the journey with her characters.

Ready for More?

Check out Joey's website at storywitch.com where you'll find additional information, free excerpts, buy links and news about current and upcoming releases for all of her books and series.

You can find free vignettes and friends to share them with at the JWH Connection, a Joey W. Hill fan forum created by and operated for fans of Joey W. Hill. Sign up instructions are available at storywitch.com/community.

Finally, be sure to check out the latest newsletter for information on upcoming releases, book signing events, contests, and more. You can view current and past editions and subscribe to receive upcoming editions at storywitch.com/community or click the link under the Community menu.

About the Author

Joey W. Hill writes about vampires, mermaids, boardroom executives, cops, witches, angels, housemaids...pretty much wherever her inspiration takes her. She's penned over forty acclaimed titles and six award-winning series, and been awarded the RT Book Reviews Career Achievement Award for Erotica. But she's especially proud and humbled to have the support and enthusiasm of a wonderful, widely diverse readership.

So why erotic romance? "Writing great erotic romance is all about exploring the true face of who we are – the best and worst - which typically comes out in the most vulnerable moments of sexual intimacy." She has earned a reputation for writing BDSM romance that not only wins her fans of that genre, but readers who would "never" read BDSM romance. She believes that's because strong, compelling characters are the most important part of her books.

"Whatever genre you're writing, if the characters are captivating and sympathetic, the readers are going to want to see what happens to them. That was the defining element of the romances I loved most and which shaped my own writing. Bringing characters together who have numerous emotional obstacles standing in their way, watching them reach a soul-deep understanding of one another through the expression of their darkest sexual needs, and then growing from that understanding into love - that's the kind of story I love to write."

Take the plunge with her, and don't hesitate to let her know what you think of her work, good or bad. She thrives on feedback!

Find more of Joey W. Hill's work by following her on Facebook and Twitter, and check out her website for more books by Joey W. Hill.

Twitter: @JoeyWHill

Facebook: JoeyWHillAuthor

On the Web: www.storywitch.com

Email: storywitch@storywitch.com

Also by Joey W. Hill

Ice Queen
Mirror of My Soul
Mistress of Redemption
Rough Canvas
Branded Sanctuary
Divine Solace
Worth The Wait

Naughty Bits Series

The Lingerie Shop
Training Session
Bound To Please
The Highest Bid

Naughty Wishes Series

Part 1: Body
Part 2: Heart
Part 3: Mind
Part 4: Soul

Vampire Queen Series

Vampire Queen's Servant
Mark of the Vampire Queen
Vampire's Claim
Beloved Vampire
Vampire Mistress
Vampire Trinity
Vampire Instinct
Bound by the Vampire Queen
Taken by a Vampire

The Scientific Method
Nightfall
Elusive Hero
Night's Templar

Non-Series Titles

If Wishes Were Horses
Virtual Reality
Unrestrained
Medusa's Heart

Novellas

Chance of a Lifetime
Choice of Masters
Make Her Dreams Come True
Threads of Faith
Submissive Angel

Short

Snow Angel
Cantrips: Voume #1
Cantrips: Volume #2

www.ingramcontent.com/pod-product-compliance
Lightning Source LLC
Chambersburg PA
CBHW051932020726
47501CB00001B/91